Journey - Book 2: Joseph of Arimathea

by Debbye Graafsma

For every heart
awaiting the
fulfillment of
Abba's Promise.

Journey - Book 2: Joseph of Arimathea
Table of Contents

Part Three

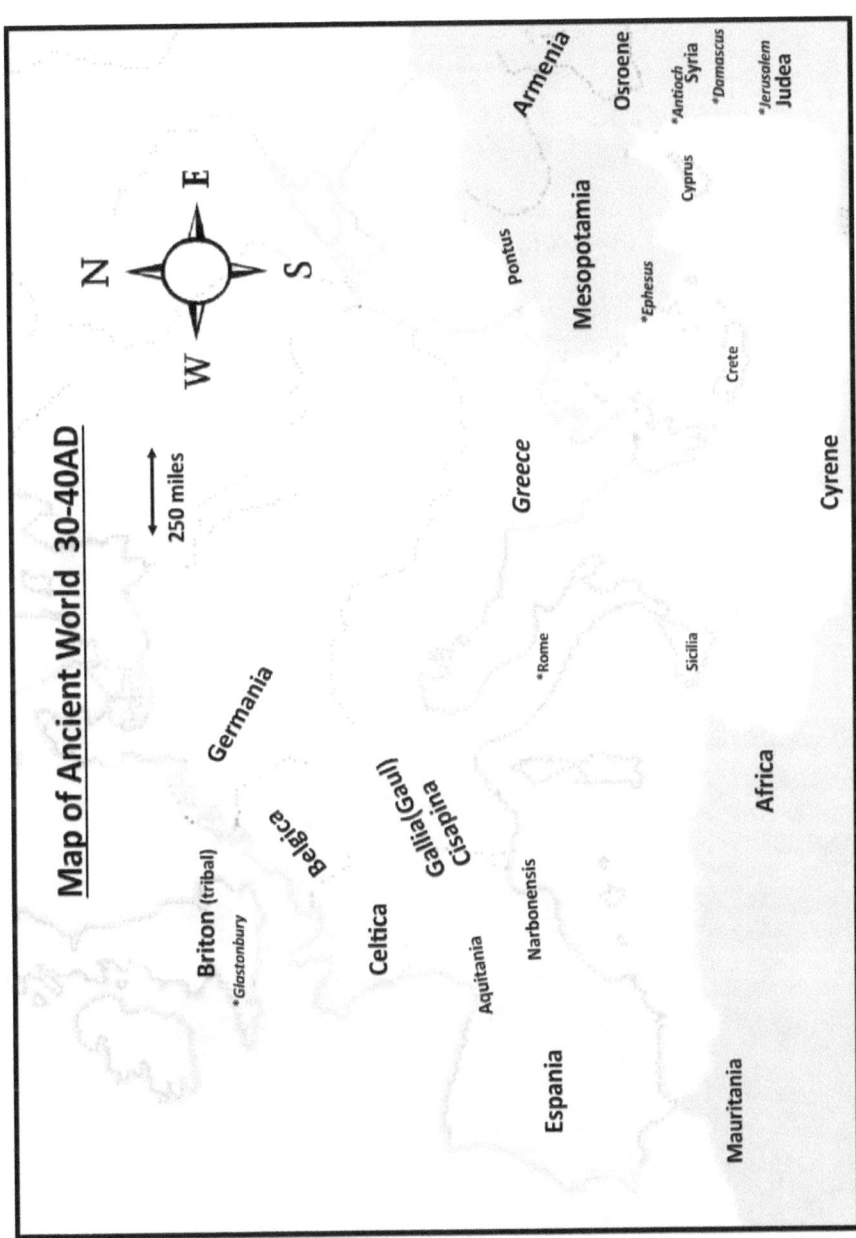

Map of Ancient World 30-40AD

250 miles

N
W - E
S

Briton (tribal)
*Glastonbury

Germania

Belgica

Celtica

Gallia(Gaul)
Cisapina

Narbonensis

Aquitania

Espania

Mauritania

*Rome

Sicilia

Africa

Greece

Crete

Cyrene

Pontus

Mesopotamia

*Ephesus

Cyprus

Armenia

Osroene

*Antioch
Syria
*Damascus

*Jerusalem
Judea

Part One

Prologue

6CE

Trachonitis, near Gamala, in the mountains

Kindling would spark the flames in no time.

Laying more of the smaller, dry twigs he had gathered on the bed of coals from the night before, the man cupped his hands over the fire. Gently blowing on the glowing embers, he worked carefully. Soon, tiny promises of a greater blaze emerged. Gradually, he added larger pieces of wood from the stacked logs nearby. As he worked, he shivered. They would need the warmth today.

Judah looked at the horizon. It would be daybreak soon. That meant the priest would be arriving any moment. Over the recent months, Zadok had become a trusted and proven friend.

In determined silence, he looked toward the tents of his still-sleeping companions. They would need all their energies today. These were the remnants of those who had rallied to his call, leaving everything to join him.

Sadly, without a miracle, today would mark their last stand.

He had hoped.....

He sighed. It was time for action once again.

Today was the first day of the Feast of Lights, or Chanuka. It was a day for remembering the Pious Ones, the Hasidim, who had freed their nation from oppression. It had been two hundred years since Judas and Simon Maccabee won the battle against the Seleucid king, Epiphanes; the tyrant descended from the great Alexander.

The Maccabee brothers had rallied the nation the last time. Seven years of resistance had established eighty years of freedom. Miracles had ushered in that family's rule.

Priests and Kings. Their dynasty had brought peace to Israel.

The Hasidim; the Hasmoneans.

But then......

Only ElShaddai should rule the nation.

His nation. His people.

11

He sighed. He had thought there would be another rescue..... That it would happen again...

Judah's tight smile was a faint one. Celebrating such a feast today would have been..... No it had added an element of comfort to the inevitable events of the day ahead.

The rebellion had not prevailed the way he had anticipated, or planned it would.

Where was ElShaddai in all this, he wondered? Surely their defeat was proof He was removed, disinterested in the affairs of men.

Judah stoked the fire, sending sparks flying upward.

He mused. Now Rome had conquered; Caesar ruled.

Why would any man think himself entitled to rule the world? For that matter, why would anyone choose to rule another? It certainly could not be God's plan for such things to happen.

ElShaddai could not be pleased with a king who had to number his subjects. And this was the second time.....

He had heard from those he knew who were citizens of Rome. Even they resented the tightening of Augustus Caesar's unseen fist. The man had declared himself "Emperor;" an unquestionable authority.

Two hundred years. It had been a long time since the Maccabees. He had hoped... No, he had believed it was time for another revolution. This time, against the new conquerors. Against Rome.

Was this what he had been prepared for? Had this been his destiny?

It was too late to consider such questions now...

No matter today's outcome. In quiet whispers, out of the earshot of the Romans, he could yet hear the crackle of freedom's blaze, still burning strong in the hearts of his countrymen.

The flames had consumed his own heart; from the time he had seen five summer seasons.

As his memories continued to present themselves, Judah stood and stretched to remove the night's stiffness from his knees. Hezekiah, his father, had built many fires like this one; also in the midst of encampment. In the wee hours, sometimes it felt as though they were still sitting together, tending the flames and talking.

"Father, why have we left our home? Why are we camped in the mountains like this?" Judah had asked.

His father had rubbed his son's head as he answered. "The king, Herod, who calls himself 'the Great,' has given us over to the Romans. He has also added to our burdens, because now we must work to pay his new taxes. So, our village of Gamala is organizing this group of freedom fighters to oppose him. It is ElShaddai's desire we live as free men."

"Can we really win against the whole Roman army?" the boy had asked in wonder.

"I don't know, son," Hezekiah had answered grimly. "We may not win; but we will be true to what we believe in our hearts. We will be heard, and we will be remembered."

Judah had seen ten summer seasons by the time the Romans had burned their house down, executed his father, and forced his mother to the streets. Finally, Hezekiah's brother had taken them in, and Judah had grown up in his uncle's home.

As he considered in retrospect, subconsciously, Judah's jawline and neck muscles tensed. Images and situations long stored, hidden in his memory, began to surface from the depths...

The Romans operated with such cruelty.

The soldiers had made sure he and his brothers watched their father die, along with every man who had stood with him in the revolt. Each man had been stripped completely naked and crucified with his wife and children as forced witnesses. To see a family member naked, unless it were small child, was a violation of the Law of Moses.

Wives and daughters had been raped at the will of the soldiers.

Any protesters were taken into slavery to the Empire, forever separated from their families. Judah still remembered sleeping outside, hearing the groans of the dying, huddled with his knees under his chin. It had taken no more than three days. But those days had imprinted him forever. For miles, the roads were lined with hundreds of crosses. Most of those suffering hung for days before life completely ebbed from their bodies.

It was Rome's brutal method of making an example, he surmised. "Maintain the Empire at all costs." Those who spoke of Rome as "merciful" had not seen what he had seen. There had been no mercy.

Remembering now, Judah considered. His father, Hezekiah, had been the instigator in the initial rebellion, so the soldiers had nailed a sign on his cross, just above the man's head. "He who would conquer Rome," it read, in three languages.

Such was the reminder.

Hezekiah had been condemned to death for his crimes.

13

Ten year-old Judah and his brothers remained by Hezekiah's cross until long after their father passed. They heard their father's last words, uttered first to them, and then to ElShaddai in a prayer...

That day, they had made a pact to avenge him.

Their father would not die in vain.

But then, the years passed. And, although there were many conversations filled with rhetoric and anger, sometimes even vigorous planning, his brothers had lived relatively peaceful lives, and even prospered under Roman rule. It seemed Judah was the only one who remembered their promises to each other.

Then had come this past year.

Judah was more than fifty now. His mother had died the year before. With her last breath, she urged him to lay aside the vendetta in his heart. "There are many things more important than revenge," she whispered. "Judah, see to your family. Build your sons."

Her words had troubled him.

He did not understand her. Anger had become his friend.

Stoking the fire, Judah shrugged. She was just a woman, he reasoned. She couldn't possibly understand his passion.

Didn't the rabbis teach that a woman's passion should remain within the home, and a man's belonged in the outside world?

No, it was better his mother hadn't known of his plans; his wife, either.

He added a log to the fire, glancing once again at the sky.

They would fight well today. At least they would be heard.

They would be remembered.

Two of Judah's sons were with him for the battle today; grown men with their own wives and families. They had stayed with him in the mountains, knowing they might die, fiercely holding on to a hope for an independent future for Judea. Several of their childhood friends had joined the ranks, also leaving their homes and families.

These had stayed to fight as well, refusing to return to their homes, even when the tide of the fighting had turned.

Only Judah's oldest son, Simon, had refused to join the cause, choosing to remain behind. The decision had been difficult for his father to accept at the time. But now, Judah was thankful his older sons' widows and grandchildren would have at least one man left in the family.

Judah also considered the fighters from Galilee who had stood with him; so fierce; so ardent in their patriotism. He had come to appreciate these young men, almost as much as he did his own sons.

How many evenings had they sat together in the past many months, imagining what life in Israel would look like should their efforts succeed? How many days had each of them spent away from their wives and children? What would history say about them?

Sadly now, he could see, Israel's politics would not; could not return to the days of the Judges.

Judah sighed, stoking the fire, sending embers flying upward. Now, it would have to be enough to be remembered as the ones who tried to bring freedom from Roman oppression.

It didn't matter what was decided by those who wrote such records, or even if their passion was misunderstood. He was proud of all of them.

Judah's younger sons remained at home with his wife; too young to even lift a sword. He still remembered his two youngest boys following him out to the road when he had left home more than two years ago. Jacob and Eli would be three and five years of age now. What would they be doing today? Helping their mother prepare for the feast?

And their sisters?

Or the smallest son, still nursing?

It seemed a lifetime since he had seen his family. Suddenly, Judah was overwhelmed with a desire to see his wife, Judith.

As the tears rose, he closed his eyes, trying to imagine her sitting next to him; here, now. He remembered the sweet smell of her hair when he would stroke her head; and the softness of her smile.

Perhaps tonight he would sneak home once more, under the cover of darkness.

How he missed her.

A new sound halted his reverie, alerting his instincts.

There were horses on the road. Perhaps Zadok was bringing new recruits. Judah stretched, looking toward the thunder of hoof-beats. It would be good to break bread together on this last day. Standing, he took a look towards the source of the sound, preparing to welcome his friend.

Judah's hopes disintegrated as he glimpsed the first sight of Roman red. The Empire had found their encampment. He shouted an alarm, but it was too late. Roman infantry began emerging from the woods... How long had they been waiting; watching him?

Before his men could rise, they were rousted from their beds by Roman shouts and swords, and then drawn into a circle near the fire he had built. Each man was stripped to his loincloth, his hands shackled in iron, held in front of

15

him. Were they all to be taken captive, rather than killed, Judah wondered? As he watched, a rope was threaded through small iron rings on the shackles, linking the captives together in line. They would be led out of the base camp, perhaps to the torture chambers at the Antonia Fortress, he thought to himself.

"Where are your sons? We know they are here with you. They won't escape." The centurion rasped the words out, as he shackled Judah alone, and attached the rope to his horse's saddle. He drew his dagger held it at Judah's throat.

"Did you really think you would defeat the entire Empire?" he sneered. "Your friend, Zadok, is already on a cross. I didn't know a priest could scream like he did. It won't be long now, Judah. Your little fanatic, "Zealot" movement is dead, cut down, finished. What did you think you would accomplish? Are you crazy? A war with the Empire?" His harsh laugh echoed against the hills. "If we didn't have orders, I'd slice you open right here and feed your entrails to the vultures!" The hand not holding his dagger moved to make a slicing motion through the air.

Judah refused to flinch. Before answering, he gazed across the firelight, finding the faces of his two grown sons. Steadily, he looked at the centurion, knowing the man would not understand his words. "We have been heard," he said loudly, to encourage his troops. "We will be remembered."

"Only for a season," the officer grunted. "Just like all the others; only for a short season." His eyes followed Judah's gaze. "Bring those two here! We have plans for them!"

A little over an hour later, in the village of Gamala, Judah's wife, Judith, was gathering the family around the table for a morning meal. She had been up since daybreak, drawing water, grinding grain, baking bread for the day.

"Meira, help your brothers come to the table," she instructed her oldest daughter. "David, you and Micah go and get some more firewood. The winter chill feels deeper this morning for some reason."

"Yes, mother," David, the oldest boy still living at home, moved towards the front door of the house. Just as he reached for the door, it was kicked open from the outside.

"Mistress Judith! Wife of the rebel, Judah of Gamala, you are under arrest!"

It was the voice of Rome.

Startled and surprised, Judith and her children scrambled, the little ones afraid of the soldiers. They were herded out the front door at point of sword.

Coming through the open door, with her children in tow, Judah's wife was shocked by the image of her husband and oldest sons; beaten, bloodied and half-naked, tied behind a Roman centurion's horse. Instinctively, she ran towards her husband, but was halted by a silent threat from the tip of a Roman sword, wielded by a centurion astride a horse.

Her eyes searched for and caught her husband's gaze. What was he trying to say to her?

"You will go no further, Mistress Judith. These men are condemned criminals, rebels to the Empire. They have instigated revolt against the Empire, and must be executed." As he spoke, the centurion motioned to one of his soldiers. "Get them together where we can control them!" he ordered.

Judith found herself looking at her husband, backed up against the outside wall of her home. Strangely numb, she tore her eyes away, and looked into the eyes of the centurion speaking.

"Mistress Judith, the Empire orders me to show you respect because you are a woman. I have no idea why. Personally I feel no such emotion. As far as I'm concerned, you are a Jewess, and therefore a whore. However, because the Senate commands me to show you mercy, you have one opportunity to clear your name. Such is the mercy and justice of Governor Quinirius." From his saddle mount, he pointed to Judah with his sword. "Are you the wife of the rebel, Judah of Gamala, and the mother of his sons?"

Shaking, aware of the consequence of even one wrong word, Judith stepped away from the wall, into the emerging daylight. "Yes," she answered. "This is my husband. These are my sons, although they are grown men, and have their own families; here in this very village."

The centurion appraised her coldly. He smirked at her. "Did you know of your husband's rebellion against the Empire?"

Judith looked the centurion in the eyes, sensing the dead coldness within him. "No, I was not aware of everything," she answered truthfully. She looked beyond the sword in her face and fixed her eyes on her husband.

Her Judah. His eyes were full of love for her. He was silently pleading. Don't endanger yourself or the children, she could hear him say. Quietly aware, she contemplated.

"I told you, she has had nothing to do with any of this," Judah protested. "Her place is at home with the children; not in battle with me."

The elbow of the foot-soldier next to Judah cut off any words he might have uttered next, bloodying his nose, and knocking him to the ground. A corporate gasp was heard from the rest of the children, who were lined up against the wall with their mother. The littlest sons, Jacob and Eli, ran to hide behind the folds of their mother's dress, knocking Judith off-center.

She clutched them close, looking down for a quick moment, regaining her balance. In the midst of the momentary distraction, she did not see Levia, her seven-year-old daughter. The child broke away from the wall to run towards her father.

"Papa! Papa, what did they do to you?" she cried. Judah opened his arms wide to receive his daughter's hug, but she was stopped midstride, run through by a Roman foot-soldier's sword.

"Stop! All of you!" The reacting solider ordered. Quickly, a detail of three soldiers formed a guarding stance in front of Judah, with the little girl's blood dripping from the center sword. "Who is next? Give me a reason! Come on! Make a move!"

The centurion dismounted and moved towards where Judith was standing, his sword still drawn. He stepped closer to her. In the crisp morning air, she could feel and see his breath. He lowered his voice, threatening.

"Are you an insurgent as well, Mistress?" His eyes raked over her. "Do you know what I am allowed to do to insurgents? Keep your little pigs in line!"

Immobilized, Judah's remaining children froze, now fearing for their very lives as well. Suddenly calm, Judith disentangled herself from her younger sons, and moved farther away from the wall of her home, stepping closer to the centurion. Inwardly, she was trembling and terrified. Outwardly, she was composed and cold.

"Sir," she spoke, drawing herself up into a regal posture. "Why do you assume that my husband's stupidity is a family affair? Why do you murder my smallest daughter who holds no threat, militarily or otherwise? Is she such a menace to so great an Empire? Please, leave us alone. I have had enough of my husband's grandiose ideas and plans. Please leave me as a widow to fend for these small lives he has now made my sole responsibility." Suddenly broken, she looked down. Her voice broke, as she pleaded for her life, and the lives of her children. "We knew nothing of Judah's plans."

"All right then," the centurion responded. He looked at his captain. "Take these two older boys into custody, and leave the youngest children with the woman."

"No!" Judith cried, moving to shield her sons. "Why? I told you we had nothing to do with this."

"Perhaps you think I've not been merciful enough?" The Roman moved close to her face, taunting her, threatening her. He paused, looking around. "By orders of the Emperor, all young men at or approaching military age are to be bound and taken to Rome. We are quelling this rebellion completely. No sons will be left behind to muster their fathers' causes." He looked at Judith, scorning her. "Bid goodbye to your sons, Mistress. You will not see them again." He glanced at David and his brother, Micah. "Gather your things, boys. You have permission to take with you only what you can carry. You will not see this house or this village again. Rome will send you where she pleases, to create settlements for the Empire." He laughed, looking towards Judith. "Why, you might even be sold as slaves."

That day, and for three days following, Judah of Gamala, his two oldest sons, and more than five hundred other men were crucified; executed for their part in carrying out the first organized Zealot revolt against Rome; what would later come to be known as the Jewish-Roman Wars. The road from Jerusalem to Galilee was lined with crosses; the bodies remaining impaled until removal by the families suited the mood of the conquerors.

As those crucified hung, their loved ones scattered flowers at the base of each individual cross, building a memorial of appreciation for each man whom they hoped would be remembered as a national hero.

Judith stayed by Judah's cross as he died. His small sons also stood, watching their father die, vowing to avenge him as soon as they were old enough to do so. His daughters gathered wildflowers to lay at the foot of his cross.

In addition to executions by crucifixion, over the next two years, Rome gathered more than 4,000 young men "approaching military age" (twelve years and older), from the regions of Trachonitis and Galilee, from villages such as Gamala, Capernaum, Bethsaida, and Magdala in the north. In the south, the Zealot movement had extended as far as Nain and Cana. Knowing the extent of the resistance, and to ensure a maintaining of peace, however shaky, Augustus Caesar then sent troops into Judea, annexing the entire region into the Empire.

In so doing, the sons of Herod the Great became puppet kings, paying tribute and gathering taxes for Rome.

And what happened to the 4,000 uprooted and deported young men? After undergoing schooling in Rome, many were sent from Italy to Spain, Briton, Gaul, and even Asia; forced to labor as paid workers in the building of Rome's colonies. Some were exiled to Cyrene, the northern tip of Africa, where they *married and began settlements and trade. Still others were sent to even more distant shores.*

By order of Rome, they could not return to Israel for twenty years.

As a result, Judah's prayer that his band of insurgents and their cause be remembered was answered. No family in Israel had remained unaffected by his death. Nearly every family in the region had lost a son, a brother, a father, or a relative. Or a friend.

No home had escaped the pain of loss... or grief.

In every home, in quiet moments, families spent time wondering; imagining what had happened to their young men.

As the years passed, the Roman government relaxed, settling into a misconception: the revolt had been extinguished.

But they were wrong.

In Gamala, Judah's two smallest sons, Jacob and Eli, grew into manhood. Their oldest brother Simon, shocked into action by the death of his father, experienced a change of heart as well, becoming ignited, enlisting himself as a new leader in his father's cause. As a result, the personal development of young men raised in Galilee would now be accompanied by the patriotic reminder to "Remember Judah of Gamala."

In every village, ranks of young, would-be Zealots, continued to grow. Eventually, the fiercest of these Zealots would rally, to see the political restoration of Israel as ElShaddai's plan, requiring "men of action."

Under the tutelage of Judah of Gamala's son, Simon, many would take vows to further their patriotism, calling themselves the "Sicari;" or the "Dagger-men."

These were those who equated their faith and patriotism with the ability to serve as assassins. Along the coast, these young men became known as the Sons of Kerioth.

When a member of the "Sicari" walked alone, he was called "Iscariot."

Simon the Sicari, or Iscariot, began a movement to be remembered for centuries, due to reasons different from his intentions. His training camps, and call to national identity moved the heart of everyone who heard him. A movement began, preparing for a war destined to change the face of his world.

In every home, in every heart, the embers remaining of Judah's rebellion against the Roman Empire were stirred by memories and ache for lost sons.

And within the heart of every father; every mother; every brother; every sister; an awareness grew. It was an angry whisper which would eventually become a roar. A simmering vehemence that would one day destroy a nation.

Not long after the deportation of the 4,000, a young couple and their children returned home to the little village of Nazareth. They had been living in Egypt for some time, but now knew it was time to be re-united with their families. In fact, neither of the couple had seen their families since they had left to be counted in Caesar Augustus' first census, in 4CE.

Just before the second census, they had fled the country to Egypt, when the life of the young woman's son, had been threatened as a toddler.

But an angel had told them in a dream; now it was time...

In the heart of ElShaddai, preparations to provide His people with comfort had been in the workings for a long time.

From eternity past, in fact.

The Comforter was already walking among them. The Redeemer had come. It was time.

His name was Jesus.

April 3, 33CE

1 ~ Qumran

It began with a low rumble, pulsating the bowels of the earth. As the deep roar surfaced, the room began to shudder in response. Next to him, his half-full, clay cup of water toppled into a water-pot, crashing and dousing him in wetness. Startled awake, the man opened his eyes in inky blackness.

He was terrified. Clutching his cover, he sat up on the mat, leaning against the wall of his compartment.

Surely the inevitable had happened by now. He hoped things had gone according to plan...He would know more in the morning.

Had he really been asleep *that* long, he wondered? Why was it so dark?

He had spent many nights at the settlement. Usually the moon, or at the very least, the stars, would light up the entire settlement. And wasn't there supposed to be a full moon tonight? He glanced in the direction of the small window opening, cut in the wall above his head. Everything was black around him.

Why couldn't he tell where it was? And where had all the stars gone?

As the earth's trembling beneath him subsided, the man became more aware of what was happening outside his small room. A great wind was blowing outside, and for a few moments he wondered whether it might be raining as well. No, he decided it wasn't raining. It must be a sandstorm.

Strange, he thought to himself. *I didn't know sandstorms could happen at night.* He moved onto his all fours, groping towards the direction of the door. After his head collided with the wall several times, he leaned against the door, waiting for the tempest outside to wane.

He had never been in darkness like this before; no light at all, anywhere. He lifted his hand in front of his face, wriggling his fingers.

Nothing. He blinked. No change in the depth of darkness.

Why were there no shadows?

Eventually, the wind began to die down. As the sound faded, rain began.

He wouldn't be able to find a fire in the encampment outside now. Not with the rain.....He decided to wait until morning. Eventually he dozed off again.

Without knowing how much time had passed, the man was startled awake once more. But this time, the agent was human; a man's voice. He thought he recognized the voice. Was it Isaachar, one of the settlement scribes?

As the voice neared, an oil lamp's dim light shone through the window slit above his head. The man was calling. "Hello? Anyone there? Is everyone all right?" The light moved away.

In response, the man heard a small chorus of voices reply from what had to be a short distance away. As he sought to move toward the door, his head rammed the wall once more, restraining him in darkness. He finally managing to move outside.

"Issachar?" he shouted after the lamp light.

The light began to move back into his direction. "I'm here!" came the reply. "Keep talking so I can find you."

"I'm here," the man said, as he stood and stretched. "It's the first door at the corner of this row." He waited until the lamp's light rays became stronger. He moved to open the door of the room. "The rain made everything cleaner. I love the smell of the earth after a rain."

"So do I," Isaachar answered, arriving. He lifted his lamp to get a better view. "Who *are* you?"

"It's just me, Isaachar. I have fulfilled my vow."

"Oh, we didn't know you were coming this week. Why aren't you in the city for Passover?"

"I didn't think anyone would be here honestly," the man replied. "I didn't feel safe in the city any longer. Why are *you* here?"

Isaachar assessed the visitor's demeanor as he spoke. "Overseer Nachum fell and could not travel to the Essene Quarter for the Feast. So, I stayed here to take care of him. Everyone else went to the city."

"Is he all right?"

"Oh, he's fine. I think he just sprained his foot, and can't walk very well."

"It will be good to see him," came the answer. "I need to debrief from my assignment. May I stay?"

Isaachar smiled. "I'm sure it won't be a problem. I know he will be glad to see you. Did you say you came from Jerusalem? Did you happen to see your uncle? He has been in the Quarter for some months now."

"Something like that," the man answered. "Can I ask you something?"

"Anything," Isaachar replied.

"Why are we talking in the middle of the night?"

Momentarily surprised, the scribe's mouth dropped open. "You must have been sleeping! It's *not* night. It's sometime just past midday. The earthquake and the storm came a long time after the darkness fell. It felt like it had been a little over two hours ago when the storm actually began."

He paused. "The Overseer said he's never seen this kind of darkness in the middle of the day before; that these happenings are strange. At first, we thought it was just an eclipse. It began like one, but the last eclipse only lasted about ten minutes, based on the sundial, and just acted like a shadow. This is different. Maybe it's just me, but I think there is something hiding in it. It *feels* like.... It's just.... Well, you know. You're standing here.... It's *thick*, isn't it? Kinda ominous, don't you think?"

The man had fallen silent. Just past midday? Yes, it *was* ominous. And yes, the darkness did seem to carry *something*. Something..... *spiritual?* Quietly, he decided it was more than he wanted to discuss; and certainly much more than Isaachar might grasp at this moment.

Unaware of the visitor's thoughts, the scribe continued. "Would you like me to take you to see Nachum now?"

"That would be good... yes," came the stiff reply. "I'd like to complete my purification as soon as possible."

23

Some three hundred miles to the northeast, a slave-girl named Adina was working a large, drilled pearl into a braid in her mistress's hair. Transforming her mistress's hairstyle had taken most of the afternoon. For over two hours now, she had worked meticulously; weaving strands of golden thread and precious stones into the early queen's tresses, the two young women talked and giggled together as though they were old friends.

Around them, palace servants moved at a hurried pace, completing preparations for the king's birthday celebration that evening.

"I'm having a hard time stringing this pearl, your majesty." Adina spoke, her lips pinched together to prevent the loss of a needle made of bone. "I'm not sure the hole was drilled big enough."

The queen smiled. "I think it will be just fine if we leave one pearl out of the design. After all, Abgar is just happy to have been alive for another year. He won't even notice. And I know I won't see it."

The blunt honesty of her mistress's response surprised Adina. "Has there been any news from my country yet, mistress?" she asked.

Queen Helene's eyes grew bright with excitement. Raising her first finger to her lips, and lowering her voice to a whisper, she turned her head to look the slave-girl in the eyes. "Yes, there is," she whispered. "But I'm saving it for him to hear at the celebration this evening."

"So it's good news, then?"

"It is *better* than good! We can't really talk about it until after tonight, but I think the emissary found a prophet who can help my husband."

Adina was genuinely happy for her mistress. Queen Helene's parents had taken her into their home to be a slave-girl when war had left her a young orphan. Originally, Adina had served as a playmate for their only daughter. Then, as years passed, she became a private attendant for Helene as the young woman had become older. Gentle and quiet, Adina had proven a compatible friend and gracious companion. As a result, the girls were now more like sisters than mistress and slave.

When Adina's husband, Abgar had been crowned king of Osroene, he became a king, whose Arab kingdom was sandwiched between the Roman and Parthian Empires. It was quite a huge responsibility for such a young man. But Abgar needed only one thing to gain credibility in the hearts of his subjects. A wife. To marry somehow provided proof of his intention to establish a stable home, providing a legacy. To marry dispelled fears in his subjects of him being a war monger.

And it hadn't taken long. Abgar's mother had been the one to introduce the young king to Helene. The story of the romance between the two of them had been repeated until it had become the stuff of legend within their small province.

It had been Abgar's decision to build a new palace in Edessa; to move the capital to the newer city. He had wanted to break from the style of leadership those living under his father's rule had experienced. For this reason, and because Abgar's marriage to Helene had occurred only a few years prior, the young couple experienced an unusual amount of support and loyalty from their subjects.

In the past year, however, a shadow had fallen over the seemingly idyllic life of the young rulers. Abgar had begun to experience unpleasant physical symptoms. He woke up in the middle of the night with unexplained nerve pain; his eyes were becoming sensitive to daylight; periodically, his hands and feet would just become numb. Then, when sores began to emerge on his body, the royal physicians sadly provided the fledgling king with a diagnosis of leprosy.

In actuality, it was a death sentence.

From that day forward, Abgar wrapped the affected parts of his body in strips of rags, maintaining distance from everyone he loved. He ate alone, slept alone, essentially living his life in isolation.

His touch could transmit the disease.

Even in the face of such circumstances, he was a kind, strong, and generous ruler.

It had been Adina who had suggested the emissary. One afternoon, in the palace gardens, she had been sitting with a grieving Helene. In the midst of comforting her mistress, the slave-girl remembered the story of a Syrian commander who had travelled to her country of Israel. The man had been healed of leprosy by a prophet who prayed in the name of Adina's God. The man's name was Naaman.

Strangely enough, the young Osroenian queen, Helene, had heard the story of Naaman as well. Having been educated as a child in the history of her nation and those around her, she knew additional elements of the story; the length of the captain's disease, his family's desperation, the impact of his healing in his home country, and so on. *Could* there *still* be a prophet in Israel, she wondered? The story had taken place more than a hundred years ago. Were men like the prophet Elisha a common occurrence in Adina's country?

And then, would Abgar even be open to the idea? She knew her husband tended to become stubborn when he was discouraged. Would her husband even be *willing* to send a fact-finding emissary? He had been so close to simply giving up for so long.

This illness wasn't what she had hoped for.

Her life was becoming far from what she expected. She sighed.

She had desperately wanted children. But now, her husband; the love of her life; would not.... No, *could* not... even touch her.

Thankfully, Abgar responded to her suggestion affirmatively, commissioning a messenger to search out and find a prophet in Israel who would pray for him to Israel's God; to bring healing to his body.

And now, the emissary had returned. Just yesterday, in fact. Thankfully, Abgar had been resting when the caravan arrived at the palace. Her slaves brought the man to the Queen's Court where, filled with joy, he could not wait to tell her the news!

It was *good* news! There *was* still a prophet in Israel! A man named Jesus was travelling through Galilee, Judea, and Palestine, teaching and healing everyone he touched! The emissary had even spoken to a man from Samaria who had been healed of leprosy, along with nine others. And, just like Elisha, the prophet had only spoken a word.

The Samaritan had been healed without even a touch. Apparently, Jesus had told the group to show themselves to a priest. Laws in Israel regarding leprosy were apparently stricter than in Osroene. Always had been.

Thinking about it, Helene suppressed a giggle.

"Your majesty!" Adina reprimanded. "I need to finish this. Please stay still."

"I'm sorry," Helene smiled. She could not wait to see the look on her beloved Abgar's face as he heard the news tonight! And there were other stories of this man! She could hardly wait for the dinner.

What a wonderful birthday gift this would be!

At the soon-to-be eastern end of the Empire, a little over 300 miles past the borders of Gaul; beyond where Celtica met Belgica and Germanica; across the mighty flood-etched river referred to as "The Bristol Channel," a gray-headed man sat at a table. He squinted as he worked by lamp light, tallying columns and rows of numbers. He paused, rolling his head in a circular motion to relieve the tension built-up in his neck and between his shoulder blades.

He glanced at the scales. Almost done.

How long had he been sitting here, he wondered? Weary, he rubbed his eyes, and reached for the water-cup nearby. Extending his legs, he sought to stretch the stiffness from his knees. Unsuccessful, the man stood, noticing the fire needed tending. Yes. He would be working long enough to justify adding a little warmth to the room.

Moving towards the stack of split firewood and dried branches by the door, he opened the small door to look outside. Still cloudy. Strangely, the unexpected, sudden storm promised by the black and ominous clouds above had still not broken. Just then, a blast of unseasonably cold air swept through the entryway.

One of his lead assistants came huffing on its heels.

"Master David! What are you doing standing here with the door open?" he queried, pushing past the older man. "The Goddess could show her anger toward you, and make you sick!"

David patted the younger man's arm as he squeezed by. "Your Goddess has no power over me," he replied. "You know my beliefs, Caedmon."

He paused, observing the youth as clay tablets tumbled out of overloaded arms. "Here, let me help you."

"I know what you have told me," Caedmon said. "But I have also seen the power of the lord of the Underworld at the Tor. And I have to tell you I have felt the energy rise when I walk the circles, just like the Ovates teach." He paused for effect, looking at his overseer. "*And* I know what the Druid priests say about you."

The older man smiled. "Did I ever tell you about the prophet Elijah, of Israel, and the god of the Phoenicians, called 'Baal?' In *one* day, just *one* prophet was able to show the power of *my* God to over a *hundred* such priests," he answered. "The power of this God is so great, that one word from *His* prophet can stop the rain from falling for three years! And just as easily, in just one day…*one day*, that same drought was broken because of one prayer from the same prophet!"

Caedmon sighed. "I have never heard anyone speak with such confidence in a god, like you do. It's disturbing. Your words make me think I will come up in the lot for sacrifice. I am always so afraid."

As always, David's answer was calm and reassuring. He placed his hand on the younger man's shoulder. "A time will come Caedmon, when the *Living* God will help you. You'll see. Just speak to Him. He can hear you."

Caedmon looked uncertainly into the older man's eyes. Did the overseer *really* believe the things he said? Was he truly brave? Or was he just crazy? Outwardly, he shrugged in response.

David moved once again to the stack of firewood against the wall. He added a few smaller pieces of wood to the fire. Picking up a metal poker, he worked the coals and logs into a healthy blaze. As he did so, the mud-brick partition he had created pulled the smoke through a hole in the stone, wattle-and-daub wall of the overseer's hut.

The room fell silent.

Caedmon watched him, not sure what to say. Master David, King Arviragus's steward and overseer, had arrived in the lands of the Dumnoni tribe over twenty years prior. Caedmon had been but a small child, but he remembered. The visit by Tiberius Caesar had stirred the entire country!

Master David had, in effect, been one of many "gifts" from the Caesar. Educated in history, reading, writing, mathematics, languages, engineering, court politics and the ways of war, David had been part of a diplomatic trade between the Dumnoni and the Romans. It seemed the king's younger brother, Caractacus, had two small sons whom Tiberius suggested might enjoy a Roman education.

In exchange, Rome gained trading rights for tin, lead, silver and copper. As an added bonus, the Caesar had sent Master David and a group of young men from varying backgrounds and ethnicities to work in the mines. As far as Caedmon was concerned, Master David had always been in charge of these young men. None of these had received as much education as he, but rather were brokered to work in the mines as slaves; gifts to the king of the Dumnoni. Some were conquered-nation laborers; others carried physical deformities.

These young men would ease the burden of the increased expectations of precious metals from Rome.

Over the years, a majority of these young men had married and added children to the tribe, actually ascribing to Dumnoni culture and practices. Some had sickened and died. Still others had been commissioned by the king to travel to other parts of Briton, conducting trade with additional tribes in Dumnoni metals. Some had even developed trade connections as far away as Eire, Caledonia, and Cymru.

The trade agreement with Rome had occurred a little more than twenty years ago now. Master David was now in his forty-seventh year. Caedmon had long wondered how such a young man as he, could have been forced to leave his homeland? And how had he become fortunate enough to receive a prince's education, *and* a Roman citizenship?

Caedmon had seen merchants from Rome bring gifts to Master David, saying he was paid by the Empire. Such merchants came from Italia every month.

Master David amazed Caedmon. How was it that the man knew so many languages? He was perfectly suited to be an overseer. How had he learned Cyragg, the Celtic language of the Selurians, ancestors of the Dumnoni tribe? He had been fluent in their language when he had arrived.

When he had asked his overseer, David had replied with a smile. "It's really not very different from my own language of Hebrew."

As far as he could tell, the man was able to relate to every merchant and government official who came to their shores! Particularly astounding was his relationship with the owner of the great merchant ships; the Roman *"Nobilus Decurio,"* who was rumored to be one of the wealthiest men in the world.

It was strange, he considered, *how the two men were close to the same age. They seemed to have so much in common. Had they known each other in another setting?*

Perhaps it was just the way Master David and the Decurio lapsed into an ancient language whenever they greeted each other. His overseer had identified it as Hebrew. Caedmon heard the language nowhere else. Sometimes, however, he thought he understood parts of their conversations, so similar were many of their words.

Come to think of it, there were others who had come to Briton speaking in Hebrew as well. Once, when he had been too young to leave his mother's side, he remembered a woman and a boy coming with the Decurio.

The younger man considered. He knew his overseer had married one of the Dumnoni king's cousins some years ago. His marriage to Mistress Eiless had been arranged by King Arviragus himself. Caedmon wondered whether he would have handled an arranged marriage as well as Master David apparently had. As far as the young man could tell, David and Eiless were happy. They spoke kindly to each other, apparently accepting each other completely. What's more, they seemed to actually *love* each other.

Caedmon considered. Had *any* of the men in the mines shown such happiness in their marriage; in the way Master David had? He had heard David say many times His God had blessed them with two sons and three daughters.

Caedmon wished he had learned to read the way he had seen his overseer read. He had wished many times for an education. Sadly, learning such things were reserved for men with money.

Only rich men were allowed to read.

His overseer was not a rich man. And yet, he had seen papyrus scrolls delivered to Master David's family hut.

How had *he* learned to read? And why?

It didn't make sense.

Someday he would have the courage to ask.

Apparently lost in his own thoughts, Master David had been silent for a few moments. The younger man spoke. "The clay tablets give the smelter's counts for the tin, copper, lead and silver melted into bars for today and yesterday, sir. I put the identification marks into the clay tablets the way you showed me."

Without looking up, David continued to absently stoke the fire. "Thank you Caedmon. You're a good man. I'll be finished shortly."

"Is there anything you need, before I go to my home?"

"No, son," he answered. "I think we've done almost all we can today. I'll be along before the Feast Bell."

Nodding, Caedmon exited the overseer's hut. Strange, he thought, how much Master David reminded him of his own father. Turning to return to his parents' house on the mainland, he felt a twinge of compassion for this older man. He smiled to himself. Come to think of it, King Arviragus' steward was just another old man tending his fire, lost in his thoughts.

Inside the hut, David heard the door close. Even though he was near the fire, he shivered. His usual positive demeanor had temporarily become clouded.

Had there *ever* been a land as dreary as Briton, he wondered? True, the temperature had never risen even close to the heat he remembered in his boyhood village of Gamala. There were no deserts here. Yes, Briton experienced a decidedly cooler climate. But there were days when the overseer just missed seeing the sun peek out from behind the clouds. There were days when he missed the dry heat and bright sun.

He missed the sandy beaches in Galilee.

And there was always rain here … so much rain.

Stop, he admonished himself. *The crops always do well. And there is always plenty of water to drink.*

He shivered.

Even *Rome's* climate had been a little warmer than Briton's. His ten years there had been good. He had come to love the city, as well as the men and women who served the Emperor. He and his brother, Micah, had been placed in the same classes.

It was difficult at first. He had missed his mother and his remaining siblings terribly.

The first three years in Rome, he had experienced recurring nightmares, seeing his father and brothers captured. There were nights when he saw his little sister, Levia being sliced open, over and over again, slaughtered by a Roman soldier's sword. He had awakened delirious on more than one occasion; in a full sweat, dreaming he was being stripped and crucified for failing to anticipate the needs of his conquerors. Even now, he occasionally would awaken, terrified, screaming, only to be calmed by Eiless's gentle soothing and comforting words.

Eventually, he had learned how to compartmentalize his memories, gradually excelling in his studies. In fact, when he was twenty, he had drawn the attention of Augustus Caesar himself. He had been allowed to participate in a research journey taken by several of his instructors to the library in Alexandria, Egypt. Returning to Rome from the journey, the Caesar had asked for his opinion on a matter he had studied. Having a naturally analytical mind, David had given a many faceted answer.

After that, David had found himself in the presence of Augustus Caesar. In fact, he found himself in the royal court on a regular basis, even as a student.

It had been nothing more than the favor of ElShaddai, he reasoned.

As a result, by the age of twenty-five, David had been placed in a supervisory position, as a compensated conquered-nation laborer, over many men who were older than he. It had been Augustus who had given him Roman citizenship just before he died.

Over the years, David had learned to identify his life with the Torah's account of Joseph, the son of Jacob. David's mother, Judith, had loved the story as well. "Every person has a moment to make a difference in the world around them," she had taught her children. "Prepare as best you can, and be ready for your opportunity. Like the stars above, your brief turn will come to be remembered." David had taken her advice to heart. Somehow, recalling his mother's words had helped him to deal with his losses over the years. The words had now distilled into his motto for living, even as an exile.

Moving back to his position at the records table, the overseer thought of the last time he had seen his brother, Micah. The two had walked together with Micah's group to the galley ship slated to take them to their life assignment. By Roman law, the two brothers could not be sent as representatives of Rome to the same destination in the Empire.

Sadly, even though David had repeatedly asked, even begged the most trusted of his Roman caregivers, he was never told where his brother had been taken.

He reached for his stylus, then dipped its end into the ink and then to the papyrus. He began once again to tally the total of mined metal bricks the Dumnoni tribe had added to the storehouse this week. Eiless and the children would be waiting for him to end his day soon.

The Sabbath would begin at sundown.

It would be Passover soon. He smiled.

Because of his standing as Arviragus' personal overseer, David was allowed to practice any personal religion of his choice. Seven days of rest and additional feasting would follow the Seder, or Passover Feast this evening.

Their family would celebrate as best they could; just as they did every year.

However, he considered, there was one final responsibility remaining before he could take his days of rest.

He had told Eiless this morning he would meet her at the Feasting Hall when the bell rang this evening. As the king's steward, David would be expected to at least attend the opening ceremonies for tonight's Feast. His responsibilities for the Roman Empire dictated he at least be seen as supportive of the local rulers; for now anyway.

It was inevitable Rome would seek to annex the Isles of Briton into their Empire. Everyone knew it. Only the precious metals still in the mines and the Dumnoni Tribe's sophisticated diplomacy prevented the Tribes of Briton from becoming swallowed up, used for the Roman war machine.

Instinctively, David had been aware of the reason for his education and training, even as a young man. He and his companions had been groomed as tools to take nations. As one of his slave tutors had told him, they were to be "the pointed tip of a great iron wedge, an insatiable eagle, known as *Roma."* Eventually, he sensed all of Briton would be drawn into subservience, just as the nations across the Bristol Channel would be.

For a moment he stopped writing, and deliberated.

This year, the commemoration of the Druid feast of ShroveTide would be celebrated tonight. It was rare for such a feast to coincide with Passover. In fact, David could not remember ever hearing of the two feasts occurring within even a day of each other before......Ever...

So many had arrived at the mining fields today from other tribes. He would have to guard his wife and daughters this evening. These were the moments when he was thankful for his protected standing with Arviragus, and his privileges as a Roman citizen.

"Not one hair on this man's head is to be harmed," Tiberius Caesar had written to Arviragus when David arrived in Briton. "To wound him in any manner will be received as an affront to our Empire and as an action tantamount to war. Much is invested in him. He will serve you well."

The steward glanced once more at the work waiting to be accomplished. If he maintained his focus, he could finish one more stack of tallies before the Feast Bell rang.

He would have to hurry.

The rising tide would cut off the land bridge to the mainland soon; and he had no raft. He certainly didn't want to be trapped on the island for another six hours.

In the large Feasting Hall, King Arviragus, the *Pendragon*, or "Chief of Chiefs and King of Kings," was in the midst of a preparatory meeting. Many representatives from family tribal regions throughout southern Briton had gathered for ShroveTide.

Tonight would be a Druid feast like no other!

There would be meat tonight! Roast pig, mutton, and beef had been turning on great roasting spits since early in the day, cranked by hand. Roasting cooks rotated in shifts every half hour, supervised by the Druid Ovates, Bards, Priests and Wikka. Fruits of the earth and trees were being prepared. Roots had been dug from the ground; scrubbed and boiled. All would be served on great trays, by virgins dressed as nymphs. The feast was a special offering to the Lord of the Dark Underworld, Gwyn-ap-Nudd, and his brother Avallach, the Fisher King, and their mother, the Mother Earth Goddess, Vivien. Many of the village women had been working for two days, crafting honey-sweetened breads flavored wines, and mead.

By comparison, the Celtic peoples who had settled the large island, were considered less civilized than the more progressive citizens of Rome. They had descended from migratory Cymric peoples who, over the years had wandered from a far land, where desert winds whipped with a fury. Cymru, by definition, meant "people of the heart," which held true in the way the developed tribes of the area viewed family and relationships.

To the Celts, it was important to honor tradition, and history, they believed. For this reason, many of the Ovates, Bards, Priests, and Wikka could trace their lineage back to the days of Solomon of Israel.

King Arviragus' meeting was being held in the midst of the Great Feasting Hall's preparations, in an effort to avoid the impending storm. And, because it was a large enough structure to house everyone involved with today's decision-making.

The king had learned early in his reign he would experience more loyalty as a ruler when he was willing to listen, to negotiate, and to invoke change.

For some time, the fertility rights of the ShroveTide Feast, as well as the practices of other feasts, had raised concerns in his heart; particularly in the years since his daughters had been born.

The Druid religion required human sacrifices, dismemberment, and draining of blood, especially of virgins and infants. It was rumored the High Priests, who were honored among the citizenry as having supernatural powers, secretly ate the roasted meat of human sacrifices at ShroveTide.

Each feast day, he sensed the intensity rise in the fears of his people. And, over the years, he had watched hopelessness and grief overtake many of his subjects who experienced the loss of a child due to sacrifice.

What kind of a god would require the death of an innocent?

Or the rape of a virgin?

It was difficult to admit to himself, but Arviragus was disillusioned with the teachings of the Celtic religion. There were days when he found himself harboring anger against each of the four classifications of Druid leaders. He had come to believe what he had heard whispered was true; these leaders wielded the threat of human sacrifice to counter anyone who even questioned their festival celebrations and teachings.

In fact, recently he had wondered why the "selection by divining" of a sacrificial candidate had to be determined in *Secret Rites*. As far as he could tell, those who had expressed most vocal in resistance to the Ovates and Priests seemed the ones most affected by the mysteriously "random" selection.

Random indeed.

Someone always ended up dead.

No longer a threat.

He wondered whether there were other reasons to explain the phenomena surrounding those who brandished threats of spiritual power. Were weather patterns and sudden accidents *really* the expression of the displeasure of the the Mother Earth Goddess, and her sons?

Were the accidents *really* accidents?

He knew from personal experience the effect such threats could have upon a family. Since the manifestation of their early womanly development, his daughters had lived in fear. Come to think of it, his daughters were not the only young women who feared death, dismemberment or the draining of their blood. For this reason, Arviragus and his small group of Counselors gave the Druids a wide berth, seeking to avoid conflict. He no longer asked for druid opinions.

34

But this year his resolves were beginning to strengthen.

This year, he had come to a decision.

From this point forward, he told his wife, Izolde, that morning, ShroveTide, would become a feast time when the Pendragon expressed definite boundaries for the leaders of the Druid religion!

Fragile, she had smiled weakly at him in agreement. He winced as he remembered.

He had trusted them to heal her. And now she was close to death.

He was now convinced they held no real power for good.

As was planned every year, tonight's feast was designed to culminate with the satiation of every human appetite. There was no method of limiting the amount of wine, mead, or beer consumed by the working men at such a time.

Tonight, he knew, many of his people would throw off all restraint.

Any sexual expression was acceptable in Druid worship.

Tonight's feast would be followed by the enactment of fertility rituals. Children conceived at ShroveTide were almost certainly destined for sacrifice. It was the Druid Decree. And, if by some provision of the gods, a child *did* live to adulthood, they were used as sexual tools for the fulfillment of fertility rites. As a result, many, if not all of these young people to become diseased, the majority of whom had slowly died.

Even the Druid healing arts had not been able to help them.

Not even one. In *any* of his fifty years as king.

For these reasons, Arviragus was meeting with tribal leaders to determine just *where* the ensuing orgies would be allowed to take place. This was his first attempt to create a designated place for such activities. Someday, perhaps, the fertility rites of his peoples' religion could be held inside a grove or shelter; perhaps on top of a mountain somewhere.

Not in openly public places.

If the practices *had* to continue, they should be *put* somewhere.

Away. Far, *far* away.

The king's steward, or overseer, David, had described to Arviragus the temples built for the worship of gods in Rome and Alexandria. Many of *those* gods demanded sexual expression as a form of fertility worship also. However, in those settings, sexual expressions were deemed fit more for a private cubicle within a building, rather than in a public expression under the stars.

As his mind trailed, King Arviragus realized he had come to respect the education of his steward. At first, he had resented the young man, feeling manipulated by Rome. And even though his perceptions were correct, he had come to understand; the sense of competition and control being communicated by Rome's Caesar really had nothing to do with the man. To be honest, David's manner and kindly disposition had won the ruler over. David had become a friend in his eyes.

He considered his steward. How did a person respond to the loss of family and homeland without bitterness, he wondered? How might he have responded to experiencing the same treatment from Rome as David had?

Of course, Arviragus realized, David took no credit for his personal successes. He expressed appreciation for those around him who contributed to whatever achievement was in question. He deferred the recognition to others. In watching him operate, one could not help but realize the high levels of his intelligence and wisdom.

Additionally, David acted as though he had a *relationship* with his God.

Never afraid.

In thinking about the fertility rites associated with tonight's Feast of ShroveTide, and others, his was the *only* God his steward described who did *not* demand human sacrifice or sexual expression.

David's God.

According to his overseer, this God was *not* angry.

This God not only *ruled* the elements, but had *created* them … from nothing. In fact, David had shared many of his homeland's history and laws with him in quiet moments. It seemed the Nobilius Decurio had provided him with scrolls of the Torah, and the Prophets, as he called them.

Particularly interesting to the king, was David's description of the temple built to this God. It was fascinating. Such an entity must be powerful indeed to deserve such a large palace.

2 - Darkness

Some three thousand miles to the east, unusual darkness continued in Jerusalem.

In the lower level of the Temple, the High Priest, Joseph Caiaphas, was holding a meeting of the Circle of the Friends of God behind closed doors. The Court of Hewn Stones had been the center of Jewish government decisions for centuries.

Annas, Caiaphas's father-in-law, was reviewing the trial of the man from Galilee just the night before. Although Caiaphas had been appointed to High Priest by the Roman governor several years before, Annas had served as High Priest in a prior term.

In the words of Hillel, "Once a High Priest, always a High Priest."

These days, Annas allowed his son-in-law to oversee most affairs. But today, he was suffering with self-doubt over his recommendation of his son-in-law to Rome. In fact, today he found himself experiencing no small amount of rage.

His angry voice could be heard even through the Court's closed doors.

"You misused this Temple, Joseph! You convened a trial without giving *all* the members of the Sanhedrin notice!"

Joseph sat in his great chair, still gloating over his victory. He shrugged, appraising his fingernails. "It is of no consequence, Annas," he responded, indifferently. "He was a subversive and now he is dealt with. Just like all the others."

"We needed more time," the older man answered, pulling at his cloak, as though to rip it apart. "What have you *done?*"

"Time!" the younger man scoffed. "That's what you always say. Answer me this: what *should* I do; what would *you* do? An Essene Sicari approached *me*, and says he has taken a vow to see Israel restored to power?"

At the mention of Sicari, the older man stopped. "What does that have to do with this man?"

"The Iscariot is, or *was*, one of his leaders." Caiaphas paused for effect, looking around the room for support from his peers. He didn't care much whether "lesser" priests on the Council supported his decisions. In truth, those men carried no real power for change. However, Joseph knew he needed Annas' unquestioning backing in order to continue his present course of political action.

More than anything, he wanted to establish a priestly family's reign of the nation once more. This time it would be *his* family's reign.

He could be king.

Simeon, a priest who was not a participant in Joseph's Circle of the Friends of God, ventured a question. "Sicari? Joseph, are you saying they actually exist?"

Joseph chuckled. "Exist?" he sneered. "They are building in power. They are being trained. *We* are organizing."

"We?" Simeon echoed.

"Yes, *we!*" the priest who-would-be-ruler scoffed. "How do *you* think we will restore the fortunes of our nation? Roman oppression must be thrown off. We must break off this yoke!"

He stood to his feet, his voice rising with passion. Facing Annas, he pounded his fist into the palm of his hand. "This man, this *Jesus*, was the first prophet to rise in Israel who captured the heart of the people! They are ready! Did you hear them calling him "our king?" He had the support of the rabble!"

"But he never spoke about restoring the nation," Simeon countered. "He's a teacher, and a healer. If you saw him as a king, why did you arrest him?"

Caiaphas wheeled around to face the younger priest. "It is a sign of the *peoples' readiness* to rally. He carries *power,* you idiot! He is the first prophet to work miracles since the days of Elijah and Ahab! And he has the loyalty of the *people!* We don't *need* him to re-establish our government. But we *do* need to be able to control the *masses!* We are going to bridle the population's loyalties, and use their belief in God's power. We will steer them to our way of thinking. We will see our plans succeed!"

Simeon was taken back, suddenly seeing his leader with new eyes. Joseph Caiaphas noticed the reaction and took a step towards him, his eyes narrowing. "And why have you intruded on this private meeting, anyway, *Pharisee?*" he snarled. "This is not your place! You overstep yourself!"

Undaunted, Simeon pulled himself to his full height and stepped into Joseph's comfort circle, until his nose was just a few inches from the nose of his adversary. "We are gathering to discuss *your* behaviors, Joseph. My father…"

"Oh yes!" Caiaphas retorted, mocking. "The great Hillel's legacy continues! Go get your great *Abba,* Gamaliel, to help you! Leave the real men to make decisions!"

Not one to be intimidated, Simeon raised his voice, beginning his sentence again. "My *father* is on his way with the rest of the Pharisee contingency from this Council. You Sadducees think you can manipulate men, even God; with your secret meetings and political plotting. *You* are the ones who will destroy the nation! *You* will be the ones to bring the wrath of Rome down upon us."

He raised his finger. "Whether you believe it or not, our God's power is real. Even over death. Your actions tempt God, Joseph! You need to repent before Him!"

Furious, Caiaphas reached toward Simeon with hands ready to choke the younger man, his face red with rage. "Rebel! No wonder God took your sons!"

Instantly livid, Simeon raised his right hand, and began to repeatedly press his fingers into Joseph's chest, in a tapping motion as he shouted his response. "You are an evil serpent! Both of *my* sons are dead because of *your lack of leadership, Sadducee!* God's Judgment is coming on your head!"

As Joseph Caiaphas, the High Priest, moved in to literally take Simeon's life into his own hands, his father-in-law, Annas, moved to step between the two men. "Now boys, there's no need to get into all of that." The senior High Priest moved to push the younger men apart. "Let's not have a brawl between Pharisee and Sadducee."

Looking around the room, Annas realized Simeon's observations had merit. The Council chamber *was* filled with only Sadducees, excepting himself. He looked at his son-in-law. "Why *are* there no Pharisees here, Joseph?"

Joseph looked at him blankly. "*Simeon's* a Pharisee," he answered.

"Yes," came the reply, "and I am the senior High Priest. One word from me and the governor will remove you from your office." He stepped away, moving towards the door. Taking Simeon by the arm, he drew the younger man away. "Come with me, Simeon," he said. "I will go with you to find your Abba, and the *others* who were left out of these proceedings. Perhaps there is more to concern myself with here than I realized."

Annas opened the Great Door to the Court of Hewn Stones, and waited for Simeon to walk in front of him through it. As he did so, Annas followed just behind him. Pausing, to look over his shoulder, the older man added a few last words in his son-in-law's direction.

"Joseph Caiaphas, if I discover you have murdered a true prophet of the Living God, I will be the one conducting an investigation and trial." And although he made the threat with bravura; more for show than any other reason, the reply he received sent a chill down his spine.

Caiaphas smiled coldly at his father-in-law. "Rome doesn't even know who you are, Annas," he said, finally speaking with unmasked candor. "As far as the Roman government is concerned, *I* represent Israel. I've been working to that end for some time. Are you just now realizing? *And,* I am married to your only daughter. Your *Nitza*. Your *blossom*. She adores me. You touch *me*, and you will never see your grand-children again. You know these are true statements."

Although he said nothing, Annas knew in his heart his son-in-law would follow through with every veiled threat he uttered.

So this was the man, revealed, he thought. *Finally! In some ways, it was a relief.*

He had wondered about Joseph's loyalties to the High Court, when Caiaphas had used his influence to discover a plot against the life of Caesar several years prior. Then, as the plot had unfolded, it had become clear the provincial Roman Prefect, Pontius Pilate, had been involved on some level as well.

Suddenly it was clear to him. Joseph had used his knowledge to force Pontius Pilate into action against the prophet; the Galilean man in question.

Yes, there definitely *needed* to be an investigation.

For a few more moments, heavy silence hung in the Court, as the two High Priests, young Sadducee and old Sadducee, appraised their future steps. It was evident to everyone in hearing of the verbal power struggle there would be a battle between the men at some point, but it wouldn't happen yet.

Each man had reached an impasse.

Giving his son-in-law a stern look, the older man shut the door in anger. In truth, there would be no further investigation into Joseph's actions toward the Galilean. At least not today. As usual, Joseph had sabotaged Annas' efforts to maintain integrity in the nation's assembly of leadership, by redirecting the conversation.

As the door closed, every Sadducee on the Sanhedrin Council in the room let out a collective sigh. Joseph looked around the room, appraising them.

"What?" he cried. "Don't tell me you didn't expect a little resistance!"

"We did expect a *little*, Joseph," answered Gad, one of the Council members. "But not from Annas, himself! Not from the senior High Priest!"

"You worry too much, Gad," Caiaphas countered. "At least we know we can continue to meet without fear of an investigation today. It takes him too long to regroup. He's getting older, you know."

A ripple of laughter began to move through the room.

That did it, Joseph thought to himself.

"Malchus!" he called. "Come here, I need you!"

He looked at those in his Circle. "We did it! That insignificant detail is now dealt with. We can get on to the business at hand. What issues were we to discuss today?"

Two priests went to fetch the records. He dispatched another to fetch food. He rubbed his hands together. "I'm so hungry, I could eat an entire loaf of bread!" he exclaimed. "Gad! Go and get us something!"

The would-be king looked down at his shoes. "Oh, look," he said sarcastically, "I have Galilean blood on my sandals! I will have to get Malchus to clean them again."

Without warning, there was an eerie movement in the room. Were the walls shifting, he wondered? Then, a great roar; a bass rumble issued from just below his feet. It seemed to pulsate. Then, a sound, almost a loud, deafening growl filled the room.

What was happening?

Why was everything shaking?

Glancing around the room, Caiaphas saw shadows of the other priests dancing on the wall in the flickering lamplight. Were the lamps in the room glowing brighter, he wondered?

How could that happen with no windows in the room?

Suddenly, and unexpectedly afraid, he felt something brush against his face. A sudden crash caused his head to jerk to one side. The room went black.

As the earth's sub-surface thunder subsided, men in the room began calling out for each other. One groped for the Great Door, and opened it. A dim stream of light began to filter through the doorway. Somewhere a lamp had continued to burn.

Captivated by the light, Caiaphas moved through the crowd of priests, into the hallway. Feeling his way against the stone walls, he came to an opening in the stone, where he could see outside. The wind was whipping by, blowing with greater intensity and strength than he had experienced before. The trees were bending! Some had broken in two. Debris was flying through the streets.

Where had such a destructive tempest come from?

Behind him, several of the Sadducees followed, and were making the same observations.

"Look at the sky!" one said in amazement. "Isn't this the middle of the day?"

Caiaphas looked upward and realized the sky had not only blackened, but the sun had disappeared completely. He couldn't see at all! It was as though he were blind!

He blinked. Still black.

Behind him, a man's voice called, and a lamp's light grew around him as the sound came closer. It was Amihud, one of the priests he had sent on an errand.

"Master Joseph, come quickly! Come quickly!"

He turned, and saw terror on Amihud's dimly illuminated face.

"What's happened?" he asked. "Is there a fire?" He asked because it seemed the most logical conclusion. "Has there been an accident?"

"I'm not sure what to call it, sir," Amihud answered nervously. I just think you need to see what's happening."

Caiaphas followed the man up the steps into the main part of the Temple in silence. He was just about to speak, when the two of them arrived at the entrance to the Second Court, or the Holy Place. At that point, Amihud turned around, looked toward Joseph, and motioned the older man to step into the Second Court.

Caiaphas stopped short upon entering the threshold. What he saw took his breath away.

The large Candlestick had been overturned, as had the Table of Showbread, and smoke had ceased to rise from the Altar of Incense.

A sound of ripping fabric could be heard. What was it? Looking toward the sound, he was transfixed.

There, sitting in the middle of the floor, also observing the phenomenon, was his father-in-law, Annas. He was seated next to Simeon. Gamaliel, who was Simeon's father, sat next to another member of the Sanhedrin Council named Joseph of Arimathea.

As they all watched, the 3-inch thick, many-layered, embroidered Curtain, called "the Veil," began to tear apart. For centuries, the curtain had separated the inner areas of the Temple. The first Veil had been hung, in the days of Moses and the Wilderness Tabernacle.

But now, from its top to its hem, the layers were being shredded in one movement.

As the Veil ripped into two pieces, a Light with no source emanated from the Third Court, or Most Holy Place. In Moses' day, the days of the Wilderness Tabernacle, the source for that Light had been the Ark of the Covenant; the Mercy Seat of God. In Caiaphas' day, the Mercy Seat had been absent for some time.

Rituals and sacrifices had continued, however, without the Power; without the Presence of God; without fire or cloud. And most assuredly, without Light.

As the worship of the nation's leaders had faded over the centuries, so had the supernatural Light which had resonated from the Most Holy Place.

But now it was beginning to increase, like the dawn. As its intensity grew, Caiaphas noticed the light was emanating from the place where the Ark of the Covenant would have been.

Where is the Light coming from, he wondered?

His peers looked at him, questioning in their glances, shock mingled with wonderment. Silence hung in the room.

Joseph of Arimathea spoke first. "This has to be an act of God."

"But *why?* Why today? The day before Passover?" It was Gamaliel, Simeon's father, who broached the subject. "What is happening that has caused this to take place *today?*"

Simeon stood, his body shaking. Slightly bent, as though not able to stand up straight, he pointed his finger at Caiaphas. "It's the judgment of God on us!" He cried. "Caiaphas broke more than 20 laws yesterday! He murdered a true prophet of the Most High!"

"He was no prophet, Simeon!" Caiaphas retorted. "There are *other* explanations for his miracles. Its superstition. Use your head. Everything Jesus did had to come straight from the pit of Gehenna. The whole thing is nothing but a deception."

"Would you argue with the power of our God over Pharoah through Moses, Caiaphas? You cannot argue with how He moved on our behalf in times past." It was Joseph of Arimathea speaking now. "Think about the miracles; the *real* miracles; things you know in your heart to be true."

"Pharisees!" Caiaphas spat out, shouting. "You're all blinded by your desire to see something happen you can't explain! God doesn't do those things anymore! We are the makers of our *own* fortunes!"

The room fell silent once more, as the Light from the Holy of Holies continued to fill the room, dispelling more and more of the darkness.

"Is *that* why you arrested Jesus last night?" Annas asked quietly.

Sighing, Caiaphas pulled off his head-dress, and rubbed a hand through his hair. Suddenly, he was very tired. He sank down on the stone floor.

"Yes," he answered. "And because I'm a Sadducee. Most of the others on the Council agree with me; Sadducees, I mean." Purposefully, he looked at Joseph of Arimathea. "Don't you Pharisees meet privately together, sometimes?" Without saying so, he was letting Joseph know he knew of the daily meeting for prayer, attended by many of the Pharisees, in the home of Judah, another member of the Sanhedrin.

His spies kept him well apprised of the opposing party members' activities.

"Yes, we do meet together," Joseph answered. "But we *don't* pay people to lie under oath, and we *don't* condemn men to be scourged, *and then additionally insist on crucifixion.* We *don't* manipulate Roman *and* Jewish laws to accomplish our purposes."

"Fine! *Fine!*" Caiaphas put his hands in front of his body as though he were blocking a punch. "Look, one of Jesus' followers; one of his twelve leaders, is Judah Iscariot."

Annas was surprised. "You mean Judah of Gamala's grandson? Is his father Simon Iscariot?" he asked.

"Yes, he is Simon Iscariot's son."

The Pharisees looked at each other. This was news indeed. Simon's training camps at Qumran had been rumored to be taking place, but as far as anyone knew, they had only been a rumor. *Until now.* Those who said they knew, contended there would be an uprising against Rome, and the "next time" they would be prepared.

They would regain the nation.

His mouth surprisingly dry, Caiaphas nervously licked his lips. He continued.

"Anyway, on the first day of the week, the crowds had already begun to come into the city for Passover week. That was the day when Jesus came into town riding on the donkey. Apparently, most already knew him, or knew *of* him. Even before he entered the city gate, there was a throng causing a disruption. His men even went in front of him. Some people laid their cloaks on the ground, so the donkey would walk on them. And then, it was as though the crowd shifted all at once. We never did discover who started it; but someone cut off palm branches, and began waving them."

"I remember," Simeon said. "It was as though no one cared about the Romans at all that day. They were calling him 'King of the Jews,' and shouting 'Save us, Son of David!' and 'Hosanna!'"

Caiaphas looked at Simeon, momentarily thankful for a point of agreement with anyone. He continued. "Well, to the Romans, it could have appeared he was getting ready to begin a revolt. I mean, the palm branch is the symbol of our rebellion against them…"

"…. Of the Zealots, and the Sicari, and just about every person who still honors the Law," Annas interrupted, saying the end of the phrase with his son-in-law.

"That day," Caiaphas went on, "the Iscariot came to us here at the Temple, and said he had taken a vow. He had first attached himself to John, the Essene prophet three years ago. You remember, the one Herod beheaded?" He looked for assent in his listeners.

"Then, one day, the Essene was preaching and baptizing. Jesus stepped out of the crowd and asked to be baptized. Judah told me he transferred his vow to

Jesus after John baptized him. John introduced Jesus as being the Lamb of God, the Promised Deliverer; the Messiah."

"Joseph, that doesn't make sense," Simeon replied. "Why would an *assassin* attach himself to the Deliverer? Was he planning to kill the man?"

Joseph Caiaphas looked at Simeon with disdain. "No. He wasn't going to *kill* him. He was going to make sure the Rabbi *survived* and made it to power."

"So why did you arrest him, then?"

"Judah came to *us*. I respected his thinking because of his father, *and* his grand-father, Hezekiah. He said it was the perfect time; that a Second Deliverance for Israel should take place at Passover. He said Jesus was at the height of his popularity; that it would be a good time to move."

Caiaphas paused, not sure if he should share the last part of his story.

"Go on," Annas prodded.

"He also said it didn't look as though Jesus wanted to *use* his power to help us to become free of the Romans. But, *he* thought if Jesus were put in a precarious position of danger, like the threat of death, he might become more radical and more inclined to our way of thinking. He might save himself, and in the process, rescue the nation. Judah thought surely he would use his powers to protect himself. Surely he would rise to supremacy. I agreed with him." His voice trailed off. "I thought once he was in power I could make a move of my own."

"But he *didn't* resist, did he?" Joseph of Arimathea spoke again. "As the Promised Deliverer, He is the Man of Sorrows written about by the prophet Isaias. I'm beginning to believe His kingdom will not have much to do with the governments of man. I think it will have more to do with who is allowed to rule the individual hearts of men."

Caiaphas sighed. "No, he *didn't* resist. Judah just thought a little push would help take matters where they needed to go." He paused, and turned suddenly angry. "And stop making this about your spiritual nonsense!" he snapped at the Arimathean, a Pharisee, in complete agitation.

Gamaliel, the only one who had been silent throughout the entire discourse, spoke. "How else do you explain this Light, if not by spiritual means?" he countered, moving his arm in a sweeping motion to indicate the now bright Light without a source, streaming from the Holy of Holies.

Suddenly, Joseph Caiaphas found it difficult to breathe.

He stormed out of the room back into the darkness. Some things just couldn't be explained; that was all.

Standing in the Light, the sage from Arimathea observed Caiaphas' hasty retreat. His mouth formed a determined line. Someday the man would have to give an account for his choices. Suddenly, a thought flashed across his mind. He moved toward the fallen Candlestick.

"Where are you going, Joseph?" Annas inquired.

Distractedly, the Pharisee answered. "There is something.... something I need to do," he murmured. Picking up an extinguished candle, he moved toward the Altar of Incense and opened it, lighting the candle from its diminishing coals. Looking at his colleagues, he spoke a little more coherently. "I have to run an errand. I don't know when I will return."

As he left the Second Court, or Holy Place, Joseph moved into the Court of Sacrifice, and then to the outer courts, where he found Caiaphas groping his way along, against the wall. But the Pharisee was on a mission, and ignored him.

He was intent on his task.

Making his way to one of the antechambers of the Temple Courts, Joseph perched his candle on a table, and began searching. Successfully locating his items, the Pharisee loaded them into a basket, and made his way to the areas of the Temple Mount open to the outside air. Holding the basket under one arm, he once again held the candle high to light his way.

Why was it so dark outside, Joseph wondered? Where had the sun gone? Surely.... Wasn't it was still the middle of the day?

Had Caiaphas' actions brought about the end of the world? As he considered the implications of that thought, he was spurred onward.

Unconsciously, he glanced eastward. A hint of light could be seen edging out from the.... What was it? A black fog? Why was it not raining? Why wasn't the black turning into cloud as the sunlight rose? Why was it remaining black?

And where was it disseminating to?

"Joseph? Is that you?"

Startled, the Pharisee shook his head, as if to remove a similar fog from his own mind. He turned and looked in the direction of the voice.

"Nicodemus? Oh, it's you." He sighed in relief, as his friend came into sight. "Where's Malchus?"

"I walked part of the way with him, and then came back for the Court's proceedings. I just made it back here when the darkness fell."

The two friends stood silent for a moment, each considering their own thoughts. "When was that?" Joseph asked. "I've been in the inner rooms of the Temple since we parted ways."

46

"About three hours ago," Nicodemus responded. "And then, when the earthquake happened, it was followed by a windstorm."

"The Veil in the Holy Place was torn into two." Joseph said the words factually, logically, as though somehow distanced from it.

"What?" his friend asked. "How? When?"

"It was like watching two great invisible hands rip one side from another; from the top to the bottom."

Shocked at the news of such a thing, Nicodemus reacted, and moved toward the entrance to the Second Court. Just then, he noticed the basket under the Pharisee's arm. "Where are you going?"

"I have to run an errand. Come to think of it, I could use your help if you're willing." He noticed Nicodemus moving toward the entry way. "Go and see. I'll wait. Oh, here, take the candle. You'll need it in there. I think there is enough light rising outside now I won't need it. I'll be right back. Can you be out here in a few minutes when I get back?"

"I can," Nicodemus replied, taking the candle. He turned, shielding the candle, and walked into the Temple.

Joseph watched his friend hurry away. Then, as his eyes adjusted to the increasing light, he made his way through the empty streets to a nearby livery; a rental station for visitors to obtain horses, wagons, and other properties. Here, he discovered a wagon hitched to two donkeys.

Amazing, he thought. How were the streets so empty in a town of more than fifty thousand people? And weren't there more than four hundred thousand in the city during Feast Week?

Throwing his basket into the back of the wagon, he jumped up onto the driver's bench, and flicked the donkeys with the reins.

Approaching the Temple, he saw Nicodemus emerging from the steps. From behind him, the priest could hear the voice of an alarmed Caiaphas screaming from the inner parts of the Temple, reverberating against the stone walls.

"Malchus! *Malchus!* Where are you!? I need you! Come here *right now!!*"

As his friend mounted the wagon, Joseph of Arimathea found himself smiling in strange amusement at the sound of Caiaphas' distress.

But Malchus was not even in the Temple, nor on its mount. He was standing in the middle of the largest mass of people he had ever seen, even larger than the ones he had used for anonymity when he had worked as a spy for Caiaphas. Those crowds had gathered to listen to the Rabbi, Jesus, when he had traveled.

47

Then he realized; this crowd had *also* gathered to see Jesus.

Pharisees, Nicodemus and Judah, had walked with him part of the way from the Temple. Malchus smiled. Both priests had always been so kind to him. It seemed natural to discuss his thoughts with these older men, especially since both priests were members of the Sanhedrin.

Why would anyone murder a man who could heal people, he wondered?

Had it really been just last night when he stood with the Temple guard and priests in Gethsemane? Had his ear really been cut from his head? Had Jesus really restored it, and healed him?

Why would the prophet do such a thing for an *enemy?* The man had looked into his eyes.... no, deeper.... into his very soul.

In his heart, Malchus knew had the situation been reversed, *he* would not have responded in the same way.

This was truly an innocent man.

How could the High Priest pay strangers to fabricate testimony against such a guiltless man?

That morning, in the midst of his household duties, the servant had come upon the image revealed in blood in the wall in Caiaphas' home dungeon. It had suddenly appeared. Overnight. Yesterday the wall had been simply dingy, and blood-stained. But this morning?

This morning was another matter.

It was the face of the man. The face of *this* man.

This Jesus.

Hadn't he told them the rocks would cry out?

Malchus decided he would never be able to understand his employer. Looking back now, he could see so many areas where he had violated his own conscience while in Caiaphas' service. Even during his employment he had known many actions he had been asked to take had been questionable.

Why was it? Somehow, he had believed he was serving God's purposes when he did as Caiaphas bade him. Even when he knew what he was doing was wrong. He had been so passive; silent; afraid to speak honestly.

But not now. Now he could see. Now he understood.

Now, strangely, he felt inwardly stronger.

Caiaphas would never again stand in the place of his *God*.

He was aware now. Now, he could *choose*.

He would never work for Caiaphas again. He would not return to the Temple again. Ever. He would never again fear a man more than he trusted his God.

Master Judah had helped him to discover his inner resolve. As they had parted, the priest had even invited him to the family home.

"You will have no place to go now, Malchus," Judah had told him when they had parted ways. "I have to go back to the Temple Court now. Come to our home this evening. My wife, Hadassah, would feel honored, as would I, to have you join us for a meal; especially for Passover."

He had been almost to the edge of the throng watching at the Place of the Skull when the deep darkness had fallen. It had come so quickly. Without warning, the air around him had become so dark he hadn't been able to move forward, or backward without fear of injury.

Without warning, the atmosphere also became heavy. It was hard to breathe. Malchus simply stopped, sat down, and waited for the blackness to lift. And what was this deep gloom he sensed, he wondered? And were there voices he could hear? No... Yes.... Was it the wind? Was it part of the darkness?

It was as though light had ceased to exist.

Malchus wasn't sure how long he had been waiting when the ground began to tremble. The intensity of the mighty, surging reverberation beneath him was truly frightening. At one point, the man moved to his knees, and placed his forehead to the ground, praying aloud for ElShaddai's mercy to cover him.

It was then the wind began to swirl. A tempest wind blew for a short time. He was sure he would be stripped of his clothes, or at the very least, be killed by a flying object. In the darkness, it would be impossible to find a place to hide. He clutched his cloak a little closer, hugging his knees to his chest.

He decided he would proceed towards the Galilean's cross when the darkness had gone, even if he had to wait all night, he told himself.

He was waiting at the foot of a small hill just outside of Jerusalem, known as the Place of the Skull. It was here several thousand people also waited for the darkness to lift. They had stood for hours, watching the Galilean die between two criminals.

According to Roman custom with every criminal, soldiers had nailed notices to each cross of the three men being executed. The posted signs explained the reason for each man's death according to law. Usually, a simple notice in Aramaic, the trade language of the area, was sufficient.

But the notification above Jesus' head was different. It was written in three languages, as though the persons responsible for his sentencing wanted to make it clear that *this* man; this Jesus had sought to overthrow the Roman government.

Some said it was because Judah Iscariot had been involved in the matter, and the Romans had posted his grandfather's crimes in three languages.

No one knew for sure.

On the other side of the multitude from where Malchus was kneeling, a mother named Mary stood in the middle of the small band of those who had followed Jesus of Nazareth. Her sister, Salome, had continued to hold her hand throughout the hours of darkness. So many things had happened in the past twelve hours. Her heart was numb.

Her first-born son hung dying on the cross in the center of three crosses, not far from where she stood. His younger half-brothers, all four of them, had gone into hiding just after the arrest in Gethsemane. She knew she would not see Joseph, Jacob (whom they had nicknamed "James"), Jude or Simon for several days at least.

The Romans were known for separating and executing entire families of those considered to be rebels.

She considered. They had probably gone into hiding....as had many of Jesus' followers. He had told them this would happen. Why had it not seemed like a real threat to her? Why did it still not seem to be actually happening?

She felt as though she were watching someone else live her life... someone who looked like she did, who had known her...and yet....

She knew it was real.

Why couldn't she *feel*?

The falling of the deep darkness had generated her first sense of grief. Thinking about it now, she realized the catalyst had actually been the words spoken from the center cross. "My God! *My God!* Why have you *abandoned* me?"

Upon hearing her son cry out, she had suddenly become aware of wetness springing from her eyes. His phrase had given words to her own unspeakable experience. That had been some hours ago now, she was sure. Just before the darkness, she had seen person after person approach her son's cross.

She was unsure of their purposes.

She was so dazed, it had not even occurred to her to ask.

She watched the Roman soldiers gambling over his robe. Her eyes focused on the fabric. As she did so, her brain became preoccupied with innumerable thoughts. Images of better days winged their way through her mind, as though being carried away forever on the wind.

She had woven that robe for him on her circular loom. Joseph had given it to her when they lived in Egypt.

How long ago had it been?

He had been a toddler then; just learning to walk.

It was just after they left Bethlehem, where they had lived for two years.

Men had been trying to kill him then as well.

Her husband, Joseph of Nazareth, had been warned in a dream to pack everything up and move out of the country. Then, just two days after their little family crossed the border into Egypt, they heard accounts of Herod the Great (as he called himself), commissioning his army to murder every boy child in Bethlehem.

Had the king really been trying just to kill her baby boy?

On their journey into Egypt, the threesome had stopped overnight at an inn. As they tried to rest that night, the door to their room had proven impossible to close. The following morning, Joseph had offered his carpentry skills. They had ended up staying much longer than one night. The innkeeper had paid them with the loom, in addition to free lodging. It was a round loom, unique to Egypt, enabling Mary to weave a garment without seams, a skill she had come to enjoy immensely.

They had stayed in Egypt for some time, hiding from Herod's son, Archelaus. They had been safe there.

Jesus was anything but safe now, she considered.

Another shout of soldiers' laughter erupted, shaking her from her thoughts. Another roll of the dice; a shout of reaction.

She remembered weaving that garment for him. Always, she wove with linen, without seams. She had used the rare herringbone overlap pattern she had learned from her friend, Mary Magdalene, who had been a fabric merchant. On the open market, the linen cloth she had woven would have sold for many coins.

No wonder they wanted it so badly.

She had given the robe to her son in the spring season marking his thirtieth year. She had given him a special garment during the season of each growth marker for Jewish sons. His third spring, at his first haircut. His fifth spring, when he began to learn to read and write, and study the books of Moses. His twelfth spring, when he began to learn a trade.

And this garment in his thirtieth year. The year when men in her priestly family could receive *semichah*, or ordination to priesthood. Thinking on it now, Mary could trace her own lineage back to the wife of Aaron, the first High Priest.

Very few women in Israel could say they were related to Elisheba, who was remembered as one of the great mothers in the house and lineage of King David.

Mary barely remembered her parents, Joachim and Anne. Both had died before her fifth year. She had been the youngest, a surprise child in their older years. According to Jewish custom, when orphaned, her father's brother had taken responsibility for her care.

The Roman term for his adoption was *paranymphos*, which meant caregiver and protector; coach and bodyguard.

Her Uncle Joseph and his wife, Escha, had taken her into their large estate home in Arimathea. For centuries, the village had been maintained as a community for levitical families; for those who served in the Temple. In fact, her uncle's home was less than a mile from the birthplace of the prophet Samuel. She had loved living with them.

They were the only parents she could remember.

And they had been so good to her. Because of her own considerable experience with loss, Mary's aunt, Escha, had been a wonderful comfort in the wake of her parents' deaths. Mary remembered her as being kind, big and soft. She couldn't remember how many times she had cuddled in her aunt's lap, while being rocked back and forth.

She had felt safe there.

Escha had been the only mother Mary had ever known.

Escha's daughter, Anne, had been named in honor of Mary's mother. Such was the gap in their ages that Mary had only known her cousin for a few years, before she had married and moved away. She had been too young to remember the wedding, or even who she had married.

Her uncle, Joseph, was a natural teacher. He had taught Mary to read and write. She had even been allowed to travel with him to several business destinations when Escha had been alive. The three of them had traveled together many times.

She had especially loved the time they spent in Jerusalem in the family's smaller city home. Uncle Joseph and Aunt Escha spent many hours designing the flower garden in its outside courtyard.

Not one to deprive any child of learning, Joseph saw to it his niece received the education he would have given a son, had he been blessed with one. The history she had learned as a child from her Uncle Joseph still amazed her.

But that was then.

Somehow, she had known a day like this would come.

How had she known?

So many prophecies. *She should have been ready.*

Unbidden, an image of herself holding a baby boy in the Temple, standing next to the old prophet, Simeon, emerged in her mind. As she and her husband, Joseph, had approached the sacrificial court, Simeon had taken the baby boy in his arms. She could still remember his words, and the enthralled look of joy on his face as he spoke, not to her, but to their God in prayer:

"Lord God! You have kept your promise to me! I can die in peace now. I have seen Your salvation with my own eyes. You have been preparing your Plan in plain sight of all of the nations! This is the light! The revelation of your glory for all of the earth!"

Mary remembered the conversation she and her Joseph had shared following their encounter with Simeon; especially the man's words to Mary as they parted. *"This child is destined to cause the falling and rising of many in Israel. His life will be spoken against, and the thoughts of many hearts will be revealed."*

And then had come his final sentence. As he placed the baby back into her arms, he whispered, *"A sword will pierce your own soul too."*

Had he known this day would come?

Had it been a warning?

A weak but familiar voice broke into her thoughts. The man hanging on the central cross was calling out once again.

"I'm so thirsty!" The sound gurgled in his throat has he rasped out the words.

She yearned so greatly to run to him as she had when he was little; to ease his pain; to comfort him. But she dared not. Rome was a merciless conqueror indeed.

Just ahead of her, Mary saw a flicker of spark as the soldiers' fire on the hill was being again stoked into flame. The atmosphere had been so black for the past few hours, even the minimal amount of light the fire provided seemed blinding. In the shadows, she could just discern the image of a sponge with the usual vinegar and wormwood mixture being lifted to the man on point of a spear.

When he tasted it, the condemned man turned his head, refusing it.

How much longer could he continue like this, she pondered? What more had to happen for the prophecies to be completed?

Oh God, help him now, she silently prayed.

"Are you all right, Mary?" It was Magdalene, the "other" Mary, asking. "We've been out here a long time, without water."

"I haven't thought about it, honestly," the mother replied. "I just keep wondering how much longer this will go on."

Salome put her arm around her sister, comforting her. "It can't be much longer now," she replied.

"As soon as there is light, I will find some water-skins for all of us," Zebedee promised. "I noticed vendors in the crowd before the darkness fell."

"That sounds good to me," Mary answered her brother-in-law. "Thank you."

Faintly, she smiled. Salome's Zebedee was so much like her Joseph. The sisters had discussed the similarities between the two men so many times. It was strange how her uncle had chosen Joseph for her, and their father had chosen Zebedee for Salome. Both matches had been successful.

Mary felt fortunate for that.....

But then.... Oh well....

It didn't really matter now.

She remembered the angel's visit, and her uncle's response to the news. They had been in Nazareth, in Galilee, visiting the family of the carpenter who had arranged to marry her. She had been walking in the hills just outside the village, when a man clothed in light brighter than the sun had suddenly appeared in her path.

After telling her not to be afraid, he had told her she would become pregnant with a baby, without having sex with anyone; the baby would be a boy; she should call the baby "Jesus." He had given her other instructions as well. When the angel disappeared, she had immediately raced back into the village to find her uncle.

He had *believed* her. She had been sure he would pack her up and send her away. Or at the least think her insane.

"We will have to take good care of you," he had said. Then, he had looked at her questioningly. "Are you still willing to follow through with the marriage to Joseph of Nazareth?"

She remembered being surprised by the question. Of course, at fifteen, she was of marriageable age. According to custom, her uncle had made the arrangements. He told her afterwards, he had first thought she told him about the angel to give herself a little more time before becoming a wife and mother. For that reason, he did not share with the carpenter regarding the angel's visit.

At least not at that time.

They had returned to the estate in Arimathea. Mary knew he had deliberated a long time before communicating. It was a good match. He hadn't wanted to jeopardize her future. Looking back, she realized he had been giving her time.

It was only fair. The intended groom needed to know! Especially if the girl he had arranged to wed was losing her mind. Then, a few weeks later, her uncle had sent word to Joseph of Nazareth, explaining the problem of his niece's pregnancy, and of her unusual explanation; that she had seen an angel while they were in Galilee, and that the promised baby was divine.

Hadn't that been the hope of every daughter born since the days of Eve?

To carry the "seed of the woman?"

She had wondered if her pregnancy with Jesus was what the ancient prophecy had been referring to. In fact, in light of the past few days, she still wondered.....

Joseph of Arimathea's estate had been somewhat removed from public view, in the mountains of Ephraim. She remembered his quiet support, especially in light of his position on the Sanhedrin Council.

Then, a messenger had arrived at their home. The carpenter in Nazareth had asked for a meeting. As her uncle knew, he wrote, his lineage was similar to Mary's. He *was* open to discussing the possibility to consider accepting Mary's story, *and* that her baby could be the Promised Deliverer. He would reserve making a decision, he said, until he met again – this time with her *and* her uncle. He had priests in his family as well, and was well versed in the Torah. If they didn't mind, he had business in Jerusalem at month's end. Could he come to her uncle's estate?

She had been so relieved at his response.

In truth, at the time, she had secretly speculated her uncle might be testing her to see if she might have a hidden lover somewhere. But he had never treated her that way before. Why would she think he would do so now? She remembered moments when she thought he might call in a physician to drill a hole in her skull to drain out the disease... But he didn't do what she expected.

He had remained kind.

He had been gentle.

He had even cancelled a voyage that year, she remembered.

And then had come the day she and Joseph of Nazareth met. The baby was beginning to show by then. Much older than she was, her potential husband had tried to act as though he didn't notice at first. But after he met with her Uncle Joseph, he sat with her for a long time in the vineyard. Mary remembered sitting with him in awkward silence for some time. She had been afraid to speak. Finally, the carpenter voiced his concerns.

"You think you still want to marry me?" he had asked.

"Really?" She questioned shyly. "I thought my uncle would have asked you the same thing... about *me*."

Joseph had laughed in relief. "Well, to tell you the truth, my original plan was to meet with your uncle and suggest he keep a better eye on you; him being a single father and all. I was going to give him all sorts of advice. You know, how he could have raised you better, and how he should banish you to the City of Hebron until the child is raised, or at least until after the birth. You would be safer in a City of Refuge like that."

"Did you say those things?" Mary was curious and intrigued by his honest demeanor.

Joseph had looked down at the ground. "No," he replied. "No, I didn't say *any* of those things. Although I had even written a few ideas down so I wouldn't forget. I expected him to be much more intimidating than he is."

"Oh, he hears that a lot," Mary smiled. She looked at the man. In her fifteen years of life, she had never met anyone she felt so comfortable with, she thought. She decided to speak candidly. "Why didn't you?" she asked.

"Well," he answered, "like I said, I was prepared to walk away from this arrangement. I've been married before, and I wouldn't want to begin our relationship with a mark against it."

"Thank you," Mary interjected quietly.

"But.... I've been having a lot of dreams lately," he continued. "Last night I had the same dream twice. It was so vivid, that today, after meeting you and your uncle, I can truthfully say I'm not sure it was a dream. It might have been real. Either way...." He lifted his hands in front of himself, palms upward, as if to say he had been convinced by his dream to change his plans.

"Can you tell me what you dreamt?" Mary asked.

"Surely," he responded. "Although you might not believe me. You might even think I'm a little crazy."

Mary had laughed. "Oh, no! I'm familiar with *those* feelings!"

Joseph chuckled to himself. "I'm sure you are, dear girl." Suddenly serious, he looked at her. "I saw an angel. He stood next to my bedside. In my dream, I stood next to him, and he touched me."

"Did he say anything?" Mary asked.

The carpenter nodded. "He did. I memorized it. *'Joseph, son of David; do not be afraid to take Mary as your wife. What has been conceived in her, is born of the Holy Spirit.'"* Turning towards her, Joseph took her hand. "Then he said, *'she will have a son.'"*

She felt her heart jump in response, and found herself quoting the words Gabriel, the archangel, had spoken to her. Amazingly, they were the same words as those coming from Joseph's lips.

"You will call his name Jesus. He will save people from their sins."

Jesus. Her baby was a miracle.

Everything had been a miracle.

Joseph had been a wonderful husband. He had been older when they had married. He had protected her.

In fact, after discussing the situation with her uncle, it had been decided he would return from Jerusalem with her to Nazareth. He would introduce her as his wife. That way, any shame over her pregnancy would fall on him.

"I can handle it better than she can," he had told the sage. She had fallen in love with him, despite the difference in their ages. And he had been such a gifted craftsman with wood! He had lived to see Jesus come into his fourteenth spring season. He had collapsed in the back outdoor courtyard just one year after they had lost Jesus in Jerusalem for three days... And, they had seen the birth of the younger boys together: Joseph (Joses), Jacob ("James"), and Jude.

Her husband's younger brother, Cleophas, had lived as a widower since his wife had died in childbirth several years earlier. In the years that followed her death, Mary and Joseph had helped him in caring for his children.

They had made it a practice to share the family table together.

Then, Joseph had died. The loss had stunned her. She had thought she was prepared, considering the difference in their ages. She thought she had been prepared for loss, because she had been orphaned at an early age.

Somehow, her heart was broken, irreparably it seemed.

Jesus had been due to begin his schooling at the University at that time; due to leave home that spring.

When spring arrived that year, her uncle had offered to take her with him when he took Jesus to begin his schooling. He had made preparations to combine trade with the journey. "You should be there, Mary. He is your firstborn," he told her. "Besides, you need a break. It will be good for you to get away."

She had worried about taking the trip, until Cleophas had offered to allow her younger sons to stay behind with him. He had seen how truly overwhelmed she had become. "A little quiet will help you to grieve more thoroughly," he said. "I remember how difficult it was for me to care for my children when Ruth died. Go. I promise they will be well cared for."

Then, when she had returned to Nazareth, it had felt only natural to follow Jewish tradition and marry the man. After all, as Joseph's brother, Cleophas was the one designated to care for her after Joseph's death, as a paranymphos.

It was just the next logical step, she had reasoned.

But then, they had fallen in love.

Two daughters and two more sons had come when she had married Cleophas, known to his friends inside the Jewish community as "Alphaeus," or even "Clopas." Levi was the oldest, then Simon; with younger sisters, Mary and Keshet.

Someone in the crowd brushed by her. Startled, Mary was drawn back into the present happenings around her. Her older step-daughter, Cleophas' Mary, stood with her now. Over the years, they had become close friends as well as mother and daughter. In fact, their age differences made them more like sisters than step-mother and daughter. In the firelight, the older woman reached out, putting her arm around her.

I could not watch this happening to him, to my son, without these friends, Mary considered. She was grateful for their care and support.

The others in the small group were not part of Jesus's mother's thoughts. Now, only a comparatively tiny band remained of those who had followed Jesus of Nazareth. Clinging tightly to each other, they spoke in whispered conversation as they waited for the uncanny darkness around them to lift.

Suddenly, the man hanging on the central cross let out a loud shout.

"It is finished! Into your hands I commit my spirit!"

Where had he found the strength, or even the air, to create such a cry, many wondered?

No sooner were the words spoken, than the ground beneath them began to heave and growl. Great shifts were being felt in the earth by all those near the hill. There was no question in anyone's mind... One event had served as the catalyst for the other.

The magnitude of the earthquake caused by the man's death-cry, knocked every person to their knees. Then, as the trembling earth began to calm, a few people here and there stood to their feet once again, still unable to see in the surrounding darkness.

"How long has it been dark now, Simon?" Mary, the mother of Jesus, was asking.

"I don't know exactly," Simon replied. He had been a Pharisee, a leper, finally becoming a follower of Jesus. "I feel something. It's as though we are in the middle of a great battle."

"I feel it too," John answered, standing with his father, Zebedee, and his mother, Salome. "How long do you think this blackness will continue?"

As he spoke, a great wind began to blow, causing each person to sink to the ground once again, holding to each other so as not to be propelled away.

A few moments later, the wind began to weaken. As it did, the blackness progressively lifted, as though it were a rolling fog. Then, as light returned to the hill, the swarm of people began to disperse. Many were hitting their chests as though dealing with the loss of a family member; bemoaning the death of this great man, whom they had hoped would restore the fortunes of the nation of Israel.

At the foot of the center cross, an immense mound of fresh flowers and plants had collected. A few had been left by family members of each of the two thieves, and those were arranged under each specific man; but the assortment at the foot of the Galilean's cross was unbelievable! The colors of the blossoms at the top of the pile were obscured now, after several hours, with the blood of the one suffering above. Such had been the level of respect this man had inspired in those who followed him.

As the earth shuddered, dark powers both seen and unseen shifted from their comfortability. Many homes were experiencing shaking as well. Behind private residences in Jerusalem, and on the Mount of Olives, at the east side of Jerusalem, something extraordinary was taking place. Not only was the ground trembling, quaking under the weight and strain of Death's tug-of-war with Life, but burial sites all over Jerusalem were breaking open.

3 ~ Waiting

Sunlight around them was normalizing. There was much to be done before sunset.

Joseph of Arimathea and Nicodemus BenGurion were headed toward the Roman army barracks and Praetorium, both of which shared land with the Fortress of Antonia. In reality, the Fortress was only some seven hundred feet away from the Jewish Temple. But, the presence of a Roman temple within walking distance from the Jewish Temple offended many of the Jews, who refused to even set a foot on the ground, calling it "defiled ground."

Joseph and Nicodemus were headed to the Praetorium, the seat of Roman judicial authority for Jerusalem and the surrounding area. Rather than walk around, taking the long way to the Prefect's Court, the two men opted to cut out the extra time involved, taking the most direct route.

Joseph had been here many times.

His family's business responsibilities required it.

Today's reason to see the Roman Prefect differed from his normal capacity, Joseph considered. He hoped Pontius Pilate would agree to see him, even though he had no official authorization to appear. Besides, his request today was not financial, but personal.

The normal protocol was to present the type of request he had to the Roman governor and then wait for an answer. But there was no time, he realized. He would have to ask Pilate to make an exception in his case.

It was not really a viable option to present his petition to the governor. The man ruled from a distance; several hundred miles north in Syria, and such an answer would take weeks to receive.

Joseph sighed. No. Today's request would require an immediate answer.

Pilate would have to choose.

There would be no time today. He looked at the sky, trying to ascertain the actual time of day. How many hours were really left until eventide, he wondered?

The Law dictated his great-nephew be buried before sundown.

He was hoping Pontius Pilate had remained at the Fortress, and had not yet returned to his family's apartments in Herod's palace. If he had not remained, the journey to Herod's palace would use precious moments he could not recover.

Had they not needed the wagon, he and Nicodemus could have made way from the Jewish Temple to the Fortress by using the underground passageway constructed by Herod the Great some fifty years ago.

As Nicodemus held the donkeys still, Joseph jumped from the wagon, and ran up the steps near the fortress archway entrances. Today, he hoped no guards would be posted.

As he neared the building, he hoped everyone was still at the execution. He could make his way to Pilate's Courtyard more quickly if not delayed by questioning. At the top of the stairs, his expectations were confirmed; no guards. The courtyard stood empty.

Hurrying along the column-lined courtyard, he made his way to the entry of the building he sought. He hoped the Prefect would still be hearing cases. After all, he considered, the execution of three criminals was just one item to be handled in a day to the Romans.

Surely there had been other decisions for Pilate to make today.

Joseph rushed past the granary, as well as several soldier barracks, finally making his way to the Praetorium. It was here he hoped to find Pilate resolving the remaining cases of the day; in the Roman High Court. And, although he had stood before Pilate many times before, his knew his visit today was altogether different.

He hoped he would be well received. Seeing how the day had gone so far, he was unsure what reception he might experience.

Arriving at the Praetorium, he was startled by the unexpected appearance of a guard in full regalia. With eyes lit up in recognition, the man greeted him.

"Master Joseph! I did not think I would see *your* face today!" The guard greeted him in amazement.

Joseph's forced his face muscles into a smile. "Quintus!" he responded, with much more enthusiasm than he felt. "Is the Prefect in session? I would very much like to see him, if he is here."

Surprised by the priest's request for an unscheduled conference, the guard answered. "He was due to be in session all day today. But we were afraid of a mob action after the Galilean was sentenced. So, he has cancelled all cases until after the Jewish Feast. Why?"

Joseph patted the man's arm, and spoke in a conspiratorial tone, taking the man into his confidence. "I have a personal matter of some importance I am seeking his help with." He paused, looking behind the guard, and then into the man's eyes. "Is there a way I could see him, you think?"

Quintus was a seasoned soldier. He had commanded men in battle. He assessed Joseph with an experienced and observant eye. There was great weariness around the man's eyes, and mud along the hem of his robes. Upon inspection, he saw small smudges and animal hair on the chest portion of his inner toga. Whatever was troubling the priest, had certainly left behind signs of distress.

Quintus had spoken to Joseph many times, and had never seen his respected friend in anything other than prime condition. Something terrible must have happened, he decided.

With an affirming grasp of both hands on Joseph's upper arms, the guard spoke kindly. "Let me go and see," he whispered. "Wait here."

"Thank you, Quintus," was all Joseph could say. Somewhat relieved, he watched the man turn in military fashion to walk away. Strangely, he felt hope for the first time since he had heard of Jesus' arrest the night before.

61

But then, if he spoke truth in his heart, however, he felt there was less than a straw's hope of succeeding today. It was not right something so important could be easily blown away forever by another man's whim or mood…

There were never any guarantees, he thought sadly. *Well, at least he was trying to prevent a criminal's burial.*

If Pilate agreed, it would indeed be a miracle.

Just seven hundred feet away, unaware of what was taking place in the courts of the Fortress Antonia, Joseph Caiaphas was making his way once more to the Court of Hewn Stones.

I don't need the rest of them! I will make judgments alone, he told himself. *Why should the day become worthless?*

Things happen.

People die. Every day.

But Governments continue.

As he walked through the portico, he heard a young voice calling after him. "Master Joseph! Caiaphas!"

The High Priest turned to see who was seeking to delay him from his goal. "Oh, it's you, Saul!" he said. "I thought you went home!" At the sight of the younger priest, his voice broke into a wide smile. He liked this boy even if he *had* been raised a Pharisee.

"I did sir," Saul answered respectfully, "but only after I finished the records you asked me to complete this morning. I placed them in the High Court for you."

"That's where I'm headed now," Joseph answered. "Walk with me."

Feeling honored to receive such undivided, individual attention from the High Priest of Israel, Saul quickened his step. He didn't want to waste this important man's time, so he spoke quickly and nervously. "Prince Caiaphas?"

With false humility, Joseph replied. "You don't have to call me that, Saul. I'm just a priest like you. What brings you back to the Temple?"

"I…. I…" the young man stammered.

"Yes?" Joseph was enjoying the young priest's discomfort immensely. He pulled on the front of his own, outer cloak as though to straighten it.

"I wasn't going to do it today," the young man blurted. "I've been waiting. But now…." He paused. "Well, I took the darkness to be a sign from God."

Caiaphas sighed. "You will never get very far if you give in to all that emotional garbage, Saul."

"I want to speak to you about requesting your daughter's hand in marriage." There. It was out. Saul licked his lips. There was no going back now.

Pleased and surprised, the High Priest beamed a smile, then chuckled. "You chose *today* to speak to me about marrying my daughter? Why today, son?"

"Well, it's like I said. The darkness falling let me know I didn't want to lose her. She has been all I can think about for several weeks now. Since I came to your home for the Sabbath meal. I don't want to go into the Passover feeling guilty if my...... mind ....wanders.... where it shouldn't. If I know you consent; that she is mine, then I can .... stop thinking about it."

Joseph Caiaphas stopped in his tracks. He turned in amusement and looked at the redness in Saul's cheeks. Then, with a loud guffaw, he slapped the young priest on the shoulders.

"That isn't how it works, Saul!" he declared. He continued to laugh, as Saul shifted uncomfortably. Finally, he spoke once more.

"My boy," he said, trying to be serious, "You certainly have given me a lot to consider. My little Shira is the joy of my heart, and I want to be certain I have selected the right man for her."

Saul stared at the man in surprise. He hadn't really expected the great Joseph Caiaphas to take him seriously, he realized.

"So I have a chance?" he asked timidly.

Joseph chuckled. "You have more than a chance, dear boy. There's just a little matter of your political motivations. I'm aware Gamaliel has been your instructor since you arrived here from Tarsus. *He* is a Pharisee, and your *father* was a Pharisee. That in itself is not a concern. But you must become aware, the world is changing. And, as leaders, we must change with it if we are to survive. Additionally, Shira has been more educated than most girls her age, and will need a firm hand. She out-thinks even me sometimes." He paused, waiting for Saul to respond.

When the younger man nodded, he continued. "I will not see her widowed because her husband goes off on some wild spiritual pilgrimage. Zeal for the nation must *mean* something. It cannot be based in dream thinking and 'prophecies'."

Saul sighed in relief, giving his future father-in-law a huge smile. "I will not disappoint you, sir," he said. "I will always want to take good care of her. And I have not typically been given to violence. I will be a good husband."

"Oh, I know you will," Joseph said matter-of-factly. "I know you will. You have no choice if you want to succeed." He paused, wanting to drive his point home. "As I said, there are a few matters I want to clear up with you before we proceed."

"Is there a problem with a dowry? My father has pledged to help me." Saul was pressing for his own agenda now. "If that is a concern...."

"No, no, my boy. I have no concerns about that," Caiaphas chuckled once again. "I have no trouble providing a dowry. But, we can discuss terms when you come to the house."

"When may I speak to her?" the young man wanted to know. "I mean, *may* I speak with her?"

"Well, I don't know..." The older man stroked his beard for effect. "Do you have plans for Passover?"

In Qumran, light was returning to the desert settlement. The scribe, Isaachar, sat near a window, copying information from a copper scroll onto papyrus. Another man sat next to him. Periodically Isaachar would comment on the information he was copying, sparking conversation and conjecture.

Nearby, the elderly overseer of the Essene Settlement, an elderly man named Nachum, sat on a bench. His back was against the wall, his foot propped up on pillows in front of him. He was mid-conversation with a Sicari, or Iscariot, who had arrived at the settlement the night before.

"I can't believe I turned this thing by stepping into a hole! I know better than to be in such a hurry!" Nachum leaned forward, trying to loosen a few of the cloth strips wrapping his ankle. "These things are so tight!" He stopped momentarily to appraise the status of the man sitting across from him. Mentally, he recounted the events of the past hour or so.

They had eaten together. So he *couldn't* be hungry.

He had congratulated Judah on the anticipated success of his mission; and upon the completion of his vow.

The candidate should be thrilled; ecstatic; happy. But this man was far from any of those descriptions.

"What's troubling you, Judah?" the overseer asked.

"Perhaps it's just guilt," the Sicari answered. "I'm not sure. I thought I would have a sense of accomplishment about all of this." He looked down at his hands. "Instead, I have this impending sense of doom."

"Did you stay to see how everything played out?" the overseer prodded. "Sometimes, the sense of the unknown can leave that type of fear behind."

"No, I didn't stay," Judah replied. "Everyone scattered, except for a few. One of his other followers, Simon, took out a sword, and cut off the ear of Malchus, one of Caiaphas' servants."

"Had Jesus *asked* to be defended? Was Simon acting as his bodyguard? I mean that *could* be a sign he was planning to step up and take power."

"No, he didn't ask. In fact, he corrected Simon for bringing a weapon at all! He said, 'those who live by the sword will die by the sword.' The problem was, just after he corrected Simon, he looked at me, as though he was talking to me as well. And the funny thing was…" his voice trailed off.

Nachum was no stranger to helping members of the Essene *yahad,* or community, work through differing levels of post-mission guilt. "What was?" he asked.

Judah looked up at him. "He *knew*."

"What do you mean, 'he knew'?"

"It's like he knew what I had done, and what I was planning to do."

"How do you *know* that? Did he have a strange look? Did he treat you differently?" Nachum was curious.

"No," Judah answered. "Before that, when we were eating; he said to everyone at the table, 'the one who betrays me is the one who has his hand in the gravy bowl with me.' And, there had been no way to plan that happening. He looked at me when he said it. He told me to go and do what I was planning to do, and to do it quickly."

Nachum was amazed. "What?"

"I'm telling you he knew." Judah wiped his lips with the back of his hand, as though trying to get rid of an itch. "And he washed my feet." Judah finished. "He told us that we wouldn't be clean unless he washed us. And then he washed my feet."

Silence hung between them for a moment.

"And listen. I tried to do all the right things," Judah continued. "I kept the money for the group since I was better able to defend myself. I tried to support the poor, and protect him from the rabble. That will be something we will have to help him change as a ruler. He is too concerned about the common people. He doesn't seem to care about opposing Rome. He certainly made the priests and scribes angry this week."

"When you were training here," Nachum asked, "did you know an Essene named John? He went out in the desert preaching and baptizing a few years ago."

"What happened?"

"I knew him," Judah answered. "We were here at the same time. He wasn't too concerned about national heritage either. He used to say that when the Presence of the Holy One was restored in the hearts of the people, the national identity would take care of itself. When I first took my vow, I attached myself to follow him. I thought *he* might have been the Promised Deliverer."

Judah looked into Nachum's eyes. "You know they are second cousins, right?"

"Who?"

"Jesus and John the Essene. Their mothers are related to each other."

He paused. "But John's father was a priest. I knew him."

Nachum was amazed.

Judah continued his story. "One day, John was baptizing, preaching at the Jordan River, down by Jericho. He was letting the religious rulers have it, something fierce. Suddenly, he stopped in the middle of a sentence, and pointed to Jesus, who was standing on the shore. He said, 'behold the Lamb of God!' Then he pointed at Jesus, and said, 'he must increase and I must decrease.' That was when I decided to transfer my vow to Jesus. Apparently, he and John had not seen each other since childhood."

"I have a question," Nachum interrupted. "In Capernaum; did this Jesus fellow really raise a little girl from the dead?"

"He raised more than one person from the dead…. *And* he cast demons out of both men and women…"

"Women too? *And* he has the power to create bread?"

Judah nodded. "He fed over 7,000 in a single day. There were 5,000 men in the crowd. All he had were five small barley loaves and two fish."

There was silence as Judah considered his own memory. "And he seems to like children." The Iscariot spoke the last sentence with disdain.

Nachum chuckled. "You say that as though it were against the Law of Moses to like children."

Not able to see the humor in his overseer's statement, Judah ran his hands through his hair, distressed. "I don't know what to do…."

Leaning forward to loosen the strips of bandage on his ankle a little more, the older man decided it was time to dispense comfort. "I think you probably had no other choice, Judah. You did the right thing. What could be more perfect than a national deliverer declaring himself at Passover? Your timing was perfect.

"After all, if, as you say, he wasn't going to just step up and take power on his own, he needed a little push to do so. Some men who hold the power to influence others don't know how to use their ability. Those who *do* use it, and use it well, become like the Maccabees and the Hasmoneans. Those men write history.

"You are a direct descendant from such a man: Judah of Gamala. His son, your father Simon, named you with your grandfather's name. Your destiny was given to you by your fathers before you could speak. You are Sicari; an Iscariot; a trained warrior and assassin. A patriot. One of the first.

"Whether he knew it or not, or admitted it or not, Jesus was blessed to have you for his protector. When he is king, you will be rewarded. He will thank you. You will see. Sometimes, we don't understand these things until they are over.

"As Essenes, we believe in the purity of the Law and the prophets. We are not like the Sadducees, who have allowed the Greek ways to change them. We are not like the Pharisees, who burden men with loads they cannot carry in the name of ElShaddai. We are the sons of light, and we do battle against the sons of darkness every day. Some do it with words. Some do it with shekels. And you, my boy, do it with a knife."

As he finished his last sentence, Nachum shifted his injured foot from the pillows, and placed it on the ground. "Isaachar?" he said, summoning the scribe's attention. "Give me my walking stick, please. Let's get Judah washed of his guilt and fear. He has been out in the world too long."

Isaachar put down his stylus. Standing, he looked at the man he had been working with during his overseer's discussion with Judah. "We will have to finish this later, Moshe," he said. "Can you stay until tomorrow? I'm sure we will be able to finish in the morning."

The man fidgeted with his hands. "I have a vow to complete, sir. May I borrow the copper scroll?"

Nachum and Issachar looked at each other, exchanging glances. Nachum chuckled and then responded. "No, it is our only copy. Besides, it is very valuable. It discloses the position of every treasure buried in Samaria and Judea." He paused, assessing the young man. "Moshe, what is the purpose of your vow?"

Moshe stood up to engage the gaze of the overseer. "To unite our people, and bring freedom from our oppressors, sir. I have made a promise to God."

"Have you training?"

"I have, sir. Not here, but elsewhere."

Nachum patted him on his shoulder. "There is never a panic in heaven, son. If your vow is truly born of God, then his purposes will be fulfilled. If it is truly taken in obedience, you cannot fail."

"Besides, Moshe," Isaachar interjected, "I can only copy and explain to you the parts of the scroll pertaining to the area of the country we have been discussing. We cannot allow you to have the entire scroll."

The man looked at Isaachar. "I understand," he replied, nodding. "I will stay and wait. I will be back to this place in the morning. Thank you."

The overseer smiled. "Let's make it day after tomorrow. It is Passover after all."

Nachum took his walking stick from Isaachar, and spoke once more to Moshe. "We are going to take Judah here, through purification rites. He has completed his vow. Would you like to join us?"

Moshe shook his head. "No, thank you," he answered. "I will wait in my room."

"All right then!" Nachum declared. "Let's go, Isaachar! You lead the way!"

Smiling, Isaachar responded. "Yes sir!" he beamed. He handed the walking stick to Nachum. "Do you need help getting there?"

The overseer waved his hand. "No, no, I'll be fine. It will just take me longer than usual," he replied. "Just take Judah to the baptismal site, and get him some clean clothes for afterwards. He has fulfilled all the requirements for cleansing. I'll meet you there before he is ready to get into the water."

Isaachar and Judah moved to comply with the overseer's instructions. As they stepped into the restored, bright sunlight, Judah squinted. He looked quizzically at the scribe.

"What is it?" Isaachar asked.

"What Nachum said to me helps," the Sicari began. "But I am still troubled. I mean, what about the darkness? And the earthquake? The windstorm? Aren't those indications God is doing *something?* Isn't that what we learn about these things from the Books of Moses and the prophets?"

The scribe fell silent, his brain moving into deep thought. "I don't know, Judah," was his simple answer. "*If* what you did to fulfill your vow was born of God, then these things *could* be signs of His judgment against Rome. If you made a mistake, they could mean something else. It's too soon to say, really. We don't have any news from the city, to know the outcome of your actions." He patted Judah's arm. "We will know more after the Feast." He assessed Judah's eyes. "Stop worrying. You're about to be free from your vow. Either way, the waters of purification will wash it away, and you will be able to move on with your life."

As they moved toward the ritual baths, Judah noticed evidences of the great earthquake. It had nearly destroyed the settlement sixty years prior. Some 30,000 lives had been lost in that shaking. Then, the Hasmonean king, John Hyrcanus, had spent much to restore the ritual baths, as well as the buildings. Herod the Great had added to those investments. In fact, Isaachar and Judah found they had to cease talking in order to find their way down the stairs to the lower level. Walking carefully, they worked their way towards where the baths were located; where the underground spring surfaced to fill each room.

Carefully treading down the stairs, Judah remembered once again how easy it was to injure oneself at Qumran. The stone steps were still split down the middle, with uneven ground between. So far, no one had been able to discover a method to repair them.

Watching his feet, Judah discovered maneuvering was a challenge. He nearly lost his balance several times. Had it not been for Isaachar's strong arm, he would have found himself in the long-term company of the injured overseer, with much more damage than a sprained ankle.

In the village of EnKarem, just a few miles south of Jerusalem, an elderly landowner named Eleazar, sat with his two of his adult children, along with his steward and wife. They had drawn together in the man's home office when the deep darkness fell.

Miriam, his oldest daughter, had lighted lamps to provide illumination. As with everyone else living in the region, the family had been unprepared for the emergency brought about by the deep darkness. For the past three hours, they had huddled together, fearful and in prayer.

"How long has it been like this now, Eleazar?" Miriam's question was directed to her brother, named for his father. He looked across the lamplight to meet her gaze.

"There is no way to tell," he answered. "It feels like at least a couple of hours. How much oil is left in the lamps? If they were full when we lit them, we usually get three hours of light before needing to refill."

Miriam moved to check the levels of oil left in the two lamps she had filled prior to lighting. As she did, the earth's deep, rolling thunder began under her feet. She fell against the wall as she lost her balance.

"Did you feel that?"

Baruch, the senior Eleazar's steward, sat with his arm around his wife, Leah, comforting her. "What is happening?" she queried, looking up at her husband's face.

"Probably just sudden storm," he whispered to her.

"Oh, it's much more than that," the older Eleazar spoke.

"You heard that too?" Baruch was surprised.

"I'm not *that* old," came the reply.

"So what do *you* think is happening?" the steward inquired.

The old man paused before answering. As the silence mounted, all attention in the room gradually focused in his direction, anticipating an answer.

"Well," he began, "we made a group decision to stay here during Passover, instead of going into the city. And why did we do that?"

Leah answered. "The chief priests came looking for Miriam and Eleazar in Bethany, so they could arrest them when they arrested Jesus."

"That's right," Eleazar responded. "They both have agreed not to leave the house unless they go by their Latin names; Martha and Lazarus. Mary was away for enough time they didn't come looking for her."

"You would think Caiaphas would have given thanks for the power of God when Jesus raised Lazarus from the grave," Martha stated. "What kind of man wants to kill a man who *helps* people?"

The room fell quiet once more.

"But that doesn't answer my question," said Leah. "What is going on? Why is the earth shaking? Why has it been so dark outside for so long? I mean, I've never felt darkness like I felt when it fell on us outside. Isn't anyone else afraid right now?"

Her husband stroked her hair. "I'm afraid too, Sweetheart," he told her.

The older Eleazar spoke once more. "We all know what Jesus told us when we ate together at Miriam's home in Bethany. When Mary broke the alabaster box of spikenard; do you remember what he said to Judah the Sicari?"

Martha and Lazarus spoke in unison, without rehearsal. "Don't criticize her. She has anointed my body beforehand for burial."

He continued. "I would say; in light of the miracles he performed, and the stories surrounding his birth; the prophecies; and the power over Mary's demons… most of all, his ability to raise Eleazar from the dead. I would say the earth is trembling because Jesus is dead."

"Why do you think this blackness came?" Baruch asked.

Lazarus answered. "When I died last year, I didn't stop being aware, even when my soul left my body. As my body completely failed, I became aware of another realm; an unseen realm; a spiritual place. Suddenly, I was in a huge room, waiting with a huge crowd of others whom I knew somehow were believers in ElShaddai, our God. They were also in my same condition; their bodies had also ceased to function.

"Well, there was discussion among all of those who were there. It's funny, but people looked like they do here. Somehow I knew who each person was, and they seemed to know me too. Anyway, everyone was talking about the Promised Deliverer. There were questions asked about when he would come to rescue us from the holds of Death and Hell. I also sensed we wouldn't able to leave, or really rest, until the Deliverer came. So it was an important theme in everyone's mind.

"Then, Jesus stood outside my tomb in Bethany; *here*. He called my name. And, a bright light filled the place where we all were; *there*. The prophet Ezekiel was standing near where I was, and you should have seen his face when he heard Jesus' voice. He shouted out, 'That's Him! He's the one who I talked to by the river!' Then, a man who stood next to me shouted, 'That is the voice I heard tell me to build the great Ark!' Several others shouted their recognition of his voice as well.

"Then, the bright light narrowed and I realized I was standing in its light all alone. Adam, the first man, looked at me and said, "Remember to obey his words!"

I felt myself being lifted up from the crowd, and suddenly I was back inside this body; still inside my shroud wrappings. I flew like lightning to the door of that tomb. It was impossible to walk. Jesus' calling of my name actually carried me!

Then, while I was standing there, I heard Jesus tell Miriam and Mary, 'Loosen his shroud, and help him get free.'"

He paused, looking at Leah. "Don't be afraid. If this darkness does have something to do with Jesus, we will know it. And, I have no idea what he is going to do, but I do know it will be bigger, better, and brighter than any of us are even able to imagine!"

Inside the Fortress Antonia, built by Herod the Great, named for his friend Marc Antony, the centurion and Praetorian Guard named Quintus approached his superior, the Prefect of Judea.

It had been a long day, with several hours still left to go. In fact, it had been a long night *and* day. Quintus knew Pontius Pilate had been roused before dawn to come to the Fortress from his home. Caiaphas, the Jewish High Priest, demanded the poor man make a judgment about some Galilean.

Walking past the Prefect's personal scribe, he nodded. As he approached the *bema*, or Judgment Seat, Quintus noticed that Pilate's wife, Claudia Procula, was sitting near him. At her feet, their five-year-old son, Pilo, played with a small white dog.

The couple had come from Rome during the reign of Augustus Caesar, Claudia's grandfather. The marriage had been arranged as part of a peaceful takeover of Pontus, a province far north of Italia. Pilate was the son of the king of Pontus, so it made sense any arranged marriage would have been made with someone related to the Caesar.

But then, the couple had fallen in love. It was fortunate, the centurion considered, when so many peacekeeping unions were ironically hostile these days.

The soldier sighed. It must be a fruit of entitlement, he concluded.

Quintus remembered the day Pilo was born. It had been his duty to guard Pilate's wife that day. She had spent most of the day in Herod's gardens, just off the verandah of the couple's small apartment. She had also sent for a slave to give her a massage.

Then the labor pains had begun.

The baby had been a tiny boy. They named him Pilo, meaning "pillar," because they hoped the name would cause his withered foot to grow straight and strong.

Considering the couple today, Quintus realized. Today was certainly unusual, in many ways. On normal days, when Claudia Procula was with him, Pilate was jovial and entertaining. But not so today.

Today, the couple sat quietly, speaking in hushed tones, taking comfort in watching their son play.

"I just couldn't go back over there," Pontius was saying as Quintus approached. "I know Herod tried him last night, and will want to talk about it, and laugh about it. I'm just not in the mood. What would you think about a quiet dinner here in my chambers?"

"That would be wonderful!" his wife replied. "It's been so busy lately. I do miss you these days."

Pilate grabbed his her hand, and raised it to his lips. He looked in her eyes. "I don't think I could get through this without you, Claudia. I did get your messages. I already knew about your nightmares. What I *didn't* know was that they had to do with Jesus."

"You did your best, Pontius," was all she could say.

He looked at her, his heart low. "Caiaphas uses his knowledge of the incident with your grandfather against me. He threatened to inform the Senate if I refuse to comply when he wants something done. It wouldn't matter who was acting as Caesar, I'm sure the facts would be misunderstood; especially if *that* man is telling the story. Even if your father is now emperor, I just don't want to take the risk."

"But my Grandfather understood. He liked you," Claudia replied. "He allowed us to marry, didn't he? And father would never believe an accusation against you." She could see her husband was guilt-ridden already. There was no point in compounding his already evident sorrow with her own.

Watching them, the seasoned soldier smiled.

She really loves him, Quintus considered. He hesitated. Surely the Prefect would not want to be disturbed now. He stood silently in the Court, visible to Pilate, but not close enough to intrude on the conversation.

At that point, the ruler called for a slave. "I need another towel, and another bowl of water," he said. "I need to wash my hands."

Claudia took her husband's hand, and held it, rubbing the top gently with her other hand. "There's nothing to do about it now, dear," she said quietly. "We have come through difficulties before this."

His troubled eyes found hers. "I think I might be losing my mind, Claudia," he confided. "Ask the scribe. He saw it too. When they brought Jesus in for his trial, I could have sworn the eagles on top of the standard bearers bent over in a bow of respect."

She looked to the wooden poles he referenced. Atop each one was a bronze eagle with wings outstretched. "The bronze ones?" she asked, not sure if she should believe him.

"The very ones. Tell me, am I a crazy person? I've never thought of myself that way, but perhaps I am."

His wife shook her head. "No, I don't think so. Perhaps it was stress. Perhaps it really took place. I don't know. If it *did* happen, then it would tell us something more about Jesus, and the nature of his identity. Don't you think so?"

Determining to push the question out of his mind, her husband shrugged and decided to redirect the conversation.

Pilate leaned over to his son. "Pilo, come and sit on my lap for a moment?"

In response, the five-year-old bounced up, bringing his small, white dog with him. The Prefect laughed momentarily, to see the poor animal nearly choking in his son's desperate grip.

"Here, Tata!" he grunted. "Hold my doggy too!"

Rescuing the pup, Pontius pulled his son up onto his knee.

Claudia Procula looked up, and noticed Quintus standing nearby. "Do you remember the letter I wrote about our son, Quintus?" she asked. "You delivered it for me. Remember?"

Quintus knew this was the cue he had been waiting for to enter the conversation. He stepped forward with a closed right fist salute over the left of his chest. "Yes my lady," he answered. "I do remember."

"Did the woman ever respond?" Claudia wanted to know.

"I don't know about that, my lady," Quintus replied. "What I do know is that the letter was copied and widely circulated in our entire area. If she did not respond, many others did. I'm sure many were helped."

Claudia smiled a weak smile. "If only he were here to help Pontius today," she said.

"I'm fine!" Pilate looked up. He had been massaging his small son's little feet, seemingly inspecting them for injury. He ruffled the hair on his son's head. "Aren't we, Pilo? We are having a good day off."

"Yes sir!" came the reply. "Look, Tata! I can run the entire length of the room in one breath. And I can fly like a bird!" With that, the child bounded from his father's lap, extended his arms from his sides, and ran from the *bema* to the door, making "eagle" noises.

All three adults found themselves smiling.

How good it would be to be young and carefree once more, each one thought.

Pilate turned his attention to the waiting guard. "What do you need, Quintus?"

The guard responded. "Sir, the *Nobilus Decurio* is here on a matter he says is of some importance."

Surprised, Pilate looked at Quintus intently. "We didn't have an appointment, did we? Did I forget?"

"No sir. He came unannounced."

The ruler was immediately concerned. "He is a Roman official! Is he here in that capacity?" He looked at Quintus for more information. "Has there been more trouble? What does he want?"

"He didn't tell me, sir. But I don't think he would be here, especially today, if it wasn't necessary. Also, from what I can tell, the trouble might be his own."

Pilate thought for a moment. "Thank you, Quintus. You're right. Joseph always has a good reason. He isn't like some of the others. Show him in, and then stay with us."

Quintus gave a chest salute, and turned to bring Joseph of Arimathea, the *Nobilus Decurio,* into the Court.

As the guard walked away, the Prefect turned his head, and spoke quietly to one of the slaves standing against the wall behind him. "Imani? I need another bowl of clean water and a towel."

A young, dark-skinned slave stepped forward. He opened his mouth as though to remind his owner of the fact he had just washed his hands moments before. But before he could speak, Claudia Procula motioned, intercepting his motives with a warning gesture and a head shake. She motioned for the slave to be quiet and do as he had been bidden. Imani nodded to her in response. Observing his master, he backed out of the room, toward the doorway behind the Bema.

"Yes. Right away, sire," he replied.

Her concern rising, Claudia glanced at her husband. Head down, he was staring at his hands again, his right hand once again repeatedly rubbing his palm. She reached for his hands, halting his action. "My love?" she said quietly.

With troubled, watery eyes, he looked at her, dazed. "I can't get it off, Claudia. I can't believe what I did."

She took his hands into her own. "You *touched* him, didn't you?" she asked.

He nodded. "We were talking about Truth. Things became so clear when he was speaking to me. I remember knowing in my heart that he had no intention of leading a revolution. He was a rabbi; a teacher. And.... he was something else."

Pilate rubbed his hands over his face. "I touched his shoulder. I wanted to reassure him; to comfort him." He sighed. "I am supposed to be a man with power... yet, and I feel so powerless."

He looked at his wife once more. "I certainly have proved to be today."

"Nonsense," she replied.

The sound of a door closing at the far end of the Praetorium, followed by hard leather heels on the marble floor tiles echoed through the room. Alerted, Pontius and Claudia prepared themselves for Quintus' return.

Procula observed her husband. She had heard of this happening to other rulers, in other provinces. Had this particular execution been the one to push him over the edge? Would they still be able to salvage something of a happy life together? Would he still have the ability to conduct business as Rome's provincial ruler?

Stirred from her worries, she watched her husband rise from the Judgment Seat. He stepped down to the main floor to greet the priest walking towards him, Noticeably, he brightened; stepping forward in greeting with his hand extended. Under the pressure to maintain his image, the recognizable Pontius Pilate temporarily emerged once more.

In a traditional Roman greeting reserved only for members of Caesar's family, Senators and Ambassadors, the Prefect addressed the *Nobilus Decurio,* or "Illustrious Counsel." The man was known as the friend of kings, and obtainer of treasurable metals; tin in particular.

In fact, it was rumored Joseph's family had learned the secrets to creating bronze from the ancient Phoenicians, long before the days of the Greeks, long before the Great Alexander.

Without Tin, there could be no bronze. Every army needed it. Every home needed it. Every coin maker needed it.

And Tin was only found one place on earth willing to trade: in undisclosed mines partly owned by this man; Joseph of Arimathea, his friend. It was rumored that he was in partnership with primitive tribes....

Somewhere ......

Near a place called Land's End.

No wonder it was a secret.

Before speaking, Pilate assessed the man; his gait, his stance. Like Quintus, he appraised the mud on Joseph's robes, and the stress lines around his eyes.

What had *happened* to him?

This was a man who was welcome in any ruler's throne-room in the civilized world! His merchant ships were the largest and fastest; in demand from Syria and Greece to Germania, the empire of the Franks, and even Rome itself.

"Welcome, Joseph! My friend!" Pilate hugged him. "I hope you are well."

Joseph responded warmly, returning the hug. "I have had better days I think," he commented.

Pontius looked over at his wife. "I think we probably have some matter to discuss, my love. Can I ask you to take Pilo to the gardens for a few moments?"

Seeking to hide her personal fears, maintaining an outward sense of decorum, Claudia Procula nodded. Standing, she motioned for Imani to help her. The three made a quick exit to the outside.

76

Pilate turned once more to speak with Joseph of Arimathea. Quintus had taken a post not far away, near the closest column. "How can I help you? Would you like some wine?"

Joseph shook his head to decline. He took a deep breath. "I have a family responsibility I need your help with, Pontius," he answered. "As you know, the Galilean prophet, Jesus, was crucified today."

"Yes," Pilate could feel his emotions rise in his throat. He swallowed hard to push them back. Why would the Decurio bring up the very case he was troubled about? He felt the heat on his face. He took a deep breath.

Back. Not now, he thought.

"It is part of Jewish Law a man be buried before sundown on the day he dies."

"Yes," Pilate said again. "And to facilitate that I have asked the soldiers to break the legs of the men executed so they will die more quickly. Is that your concern? Are you here as a priest?"

"Not exactly." Joseph paused. Now he understood the fear a member of the general population felt when addressing a ruler who had the power to refuse a desperate request. Suddenly, he wasn't sure he could continue.

Pilate sensed his friend's hesitation. "Joseph, we have known each other a long time. You were the one who brought me the message about the prophet, Jesus, being able to heal our son's foot." His voice broke. "And now he runs.... Everywhere."

He paused until he had gained control of his emotions once more. "Please. Just speak. It is obvious something is troubling you."

Joseph sighed. "Well, this man's mother is my oldest brother's daughter. Both of her parents died before her fifth spring. So, since her father's death, she has lived in my home in Arimathea. My wife, Escha died a few years ago, and I am the only father she can remember having...."

Unconsciously, the ruler drew in a sharp breath. This was an unexpected disclosure. "Oh," he said numbly, moving up to the nearest chair, which happened to be the Judgment Seat.

"Oh no..." He looked at Joseph, his emotion surfacing once more. "I *did* try to release him. I'm so sorry."

Pilate was sure the powerful man standing before him had come to inform him a message was being sent to Rome; that he would be placed on a list for exile to a more remote part of the Empire.

Had he really executed a close relative of the Nobilus Decurio? How had he not known? What had he been thinking?

How appropriate he was sitting in a Judgment Seat. Judgment would certainly be coming down upon his head.

In his deep weariness, Joseph found himself moving toward the Prefect. He took the seat where Procula had been just moments before. "I wanted to help him too, Pontius, but Caiaphas held both Sanhedrin Judgment Councils without the input of the Pharisees. He broke many of our laws in order to get what he wanted." The priest sighed.

"I am familiar with his methods," came Pilate's weary reply. "More than familiar." His voice drifted into hopeless silence.

The quiet hung heavily for a few moments. Finally, Joseph broke the silence. "I came because my niece, Mary, has suffered so much loss in her life. And, even though Jesus was *crucified* as a criminal, I was hoping to could prevent a criminal's *burial.*"

"What do you need me to do for you, Joseph?"

"If possible, I would beg you for permission to take his body from the hill. I would like to bury him as a family member according to the laws of Moses. I would use my own garden tomb here in Jerusalem. I will bear the expense myself."

Pilate was genuinely surprised. "*Is that all?*" he wanted to know. "That's nothing. What else?"

Joseph looked at his friend. "That's it," he said simply. "All I need is your word."

Pilate was amazed at the humility in the man.

He looked at Quintus. "I will do better than that. Go to the barracks and fetch Antonio Longinus, and the other centurion from Capernaum. Joseph will need a guard to accomplish this. We will not allow Joseph Caiaphas to interfere with *these* plans."

After Quintus had left, Pontius looked at Joseph. "Do you know Caiaphas had the gall to actually send a complaint party over here this afternoon, just before the darkness?"

Joseph looked at him in disbelief. "What was his complaint?"

Pilate felt an unexplainable snicker. "He wanted me to change the terminology on the sign over Jesus' head. He wanted it to read, 'He *said* he was king of the Jews,' instead of just 'King of the Jews.' I mean, the man is dying. When does the Sadducee stop?"

"Did you change it to please him?" Joseph wanted to know.

Pilate smiled and waved his hand as though sweeping something distasteful away from himself. "I sent the message back. It said, 'what I have written, I have written!' I haven't heard from him since."

After the stress and tension of the day, both men found themselves chuckling together, although neither one could explain why. As they spoke together, Joseph looked down at the floor. He glimpsed a small rolled papyrus which had apparently been dropped during a case hearing earlier in the day. He reached down and brought it up, handing it to the Prefect.

"This was on the floor, Pontius," he said. "It might be important."

"Oh, it is," the ruler responded. "But not in the way you might think. It is a copy of a letter my wife wrote a year or so ago. She wanted a record for herself, so she wrote the letter twice. She brought it with her this morning. I'm sure to encourage me.

"You might remember. A woman in Jerusalem was ill, a family member to someone we knew. Claudia wrote to her, telling her about Pilo. She wanted to make certain the woman knew Jesus could heal her."

"I do remember! That was a wonderful day," Joseph replied.

"Here," Pilate offered. "Let me read it out loud to you. We were discussing it when Quintus came in to tell us of your arrival."

Pilate unrolled the scroll, and began to read the Aramaic letters his wife had so carefully copied.

From Claudia Procula, grand-daughter of Augustus Caesar, daughter of Tiberius Caesar, wife to Pontius Pilate, Prefect of Judea. Greetings.

My son, Pilo, is so beautiful; so bright in his smile that even the slaves look up when he passes. He was born with a withered foot. But soon, he learned to walk with a very little crutch. Pontius was divided between his difficulty in having a son who could not be a soldier, and his pride that he had an heir to his name. I would have died of loneliness in Jerusalem had it not been for our son. Withered though his foot was, he was brave. Then a strange sickness fell upon us that summer. Its malice gathered with the heat. It wasted the children with an apathy like Death itself. It numbed my boy. He thinned, whitened, and fell. I turned desperately in every way to try to get to Jesus. But the crowd crushed against me, and tided us further and further away from him. I sobbed in my despair, and I knew I could not get to Jesus to ask him to heal Pilo. But then, someone helped me get through the crowd. Jesus touched him. From Jesus' touch, sprang Pilo into my arms. Pilo, erect and firm, without any sickness in him. And there was more. He was no longer dragging a withered foot. My Pilo leaped, walked, danced, all sound. His feet were as lovely as his face. Pilo, my son, made whole.

"Thank you, Pontius," Joseph said quietly, when the Prefect had finished reading. "I *am* encouraged."

"I am as well," Pilate answered, also remembering. "Just a little."

Just across the Fortress' Inner Piazza, two centurions were discussing the events of the day. The first, Antonio Longinus, had served Rome on the hill, commanding the company of soldiers responsible for crucifixion detail. The second, Justus Flavius, had been temporarily assigned to Jerusalem with most of the militia from Capernaum in Galilee, in the north.

The Imperial Legate, Lucius Flaccus, presently served as the Province's Roman governor. As so, he ruled the province from Syria. He had sent express orders that a revolt be prevented at all costs. To accomplish this, he had centralized all troops to the Jewish capital during the Passover Feast week.

The two centurions had left several of their men at their relative assignments, and were on a dinner break.

Longinus was finishing his meal, when a knock sounded on the door.

Justus rose to answer it. "Go ahead and eat, Antonio," he said. "I'll get it."

When he opened the door, Justus was greeted by Quintus, Pilate's Praetorian commander, dressed in the regalia of the Roman court. "For the Commander," the messenger said, handing Justus a sealed scroll.

"Yes," Justus answered, not remembering the message would be for Longinus. He took out his hand and took the sealed scroll.

The man put his fist to his chest and saluted, then walked away. Closing the door, Justus looked at Antonio. "It's a message from Pilate, I think," he said.

"Go ahead and read it," came the reply.

Justus opened the message and read. "We have both been summoned to come to Pilate's Court."

"Why?"

"It doesn't say."

"Let's go then. Let me just clean up a little."

When they arrived, Quintus took the two officers immediately to the Judgment Seat. Pilate looked up from a scroll he was reading. He rolled it up and gave it to the scribe who stood by him.

"Yes, that is what I wanted to say. Make sure you include the extra details I gave you. And seal it."

"It will be done, sire," the scribe responded.

Pontius Pilate looked at the men before him. "So, Longinus, I'm sorry to call for you. I know you've had a long day." He looked at Justus. "Who is this?"

Justus gave a chest salute. "My name is Justus Flavius, sire. I serve Rome in the Capernaum Garrison. My men and I were commissioned to provide reinforcements for the Passover detail."

"This has been a nasty business," Pilate commented. "At least it will be over tomorrow. Hopefully the next week will provide days of rest for all of us." He looked around the room, and raised his hand to indicate a man in muddied Jewish priest's robes standing on the main floor, just to the left side of the bema, where he sat.

"Longinus, this is Joseph of Arimathea. He is the *Nobilus Decurio* of Rome. He is a wealthy man; well-respected in this city and elsewhere. He is a friend to me, and I expect you to treat him as you would treat me. He has asked for the body of Jesus, the Galilean. He will be taking care of the burial requirements, according to the laws of his religion. Help him as you would help me; especially in getting the body down."

Longinus and Flavius looked at Joseph. "We will see to it, my lord," Antonio answered.

Joseph smiled at them. "Thank you," he said. "I also have a wagon to transport the body, so I'll meet you at the bottom of the steps outside."

"Oh, there's more," Pilate said, interrupting their exit. "I also called you here because we have a small complication. Caiaphas has yet again managed to put a fly in my ointment. He has 'requested' I set a detail 'watch' at the tomb for the next three days. He says he wants to prevent the body from being stolen by the man's followers."

He paused. "I sent a reply just now, which I think will satisfy him, at least until his next crisis. Joseph tells me he has a hewn stone which will roll over the tomb opening to close it. I want you to seal the tomb with mortar, and then mark it all the way around with this cylinder."

He handed a carved cylindrical stone to Longinus. "This is the Sacred Roman Eagle signet. When you seal the tomb, press this image into the mortar all around, making sure to leave no place where the mortar is unmarked. I don't want any chance of another incident causing a disturbance. Set a twenty-four hour watch with six shifts. No one is to leave the tomb watch until I send a messenger from this court that you are released from your assignment. I'm sure it will be more than two days.

"If there is an emergency, make sure you send word. Food will be brought to you. Again, do not leave the tomb without a watch until I release you in writing. And be prepared. If Caiaphas responds to this the way I think he will, I'm sure there will also be a guard assigned by the Temple as well. Should this happen, try to avoid any conflict. Do you understand my orders?"

The men nodded in response.

The Prefect paused. When he spoke again, his voice had lost a little of its edge. "Also, gentlemen, all of these preparations must be completed before the sun sinks below the horizon. That means you don't have much time." He looked at each of them. "Thank you. That's all. You may go."

He moved over to stand once again next to Joseph. "If you need anything else at all, my friend, send me a message at Herod's Palace. I will be taking my family home after this."

"I am so grateful, Pontius." Joseph's eyes were moist as he gripped his friend's hand tightly. "I owe you so much. Thank you."

His eyes clear for the first time in many months, Pilate returned his friend's steady gaze. "No, my brother," he replied. "It is *I* who am in *your* debt. You will never know what you have done for me today. Thank *you*."

At the foot of the outside steps, Nicodemus drew the wagon and donkeys to a halt. During Joseph's meeting with Pilate, he had run an errand of his own. Now, he was returning from his own home in Jerusalem. Pulling up, he noticed Joseph coming down the steps to meet him.

"What did he say, Joseph?" Nicodemus asked, as his friend boarded the wagon.

"He gave me the body," Joseph answered. "And you won't believe what Caiaphas has done now. Where did you go?"

"I drew some water for cleansing his body," Nicodemus told him. "And, I have myrrh and aloes to anoint his wounds and prepare him for burial, here in the wagon."

"It will take a huge amount," Joseph said, with a sad sigh. "How much did you bring?"

"About a hundred pounds," came the reply.

"That might be enough," Joseph answered. "We need to wait for the soldiers. I hope they hurry. Nightfall will be here before we know it."

4 - Judgments

"The Place of the Skull," or *Golgotha,* was the established site for Roman execution by crucifixion in Jerusalem, hence the main reason for the name. Secondly, the location was an unusually shaped hill formation just outside the city. From a distance, its peak looked like a human head devoid of skin.

Strategically, just above the "forehead" of its natural rock formation, a flat grassy area jutted out, creating a three sided platform with one side capable of being accessed from below. Many were sure the Romans had chosen it as a killing site because it was easy to access, and easy to defend.

It wasn't as though anyone would try to rescue a prisoner, really.

Not from the Empire.

But Rome took no chances. Especially in Galilee, Palestine and Judea. Golgotha was a perfect stage for the exhibition of Roman power over the masses. No one could miss the outline of a cross against the sky for more than a mile.

A little farther than a stone's throw away was Mt. Moriah, where Abraham, the Jewish patriarch, had offered his son, Isaac, back to his God. In fact, as light returned to the area, Moriah's summit became the first visible margin of the line between earth and sky.

As the darkness retreated, and the light invading once more, most of the thousands gathered in the valley to observe the execution returned to their homes. The ground was littered with telltale signs of the trampling it had experienced; a forgotten toy, a half-eaten loaf of bread, apple cores and date pits. The vendors of breads, roasted/skewered meats, fruits, wineskins, and water-skins had left long ago. The majority had left in haste, having been trapped for three hours in the intense blackness. Everyone was now feeling time-compressed and pressured with perceived responsibilities.

What was the time of day?

There was so much to be done....

After all, a major holiday would begin at sundown: The Passover Feast. The yearly celebration of the birth of the nation of Israel would be celebrated in every Jewish home just after dark. Even under Roman possession, the population celebrated. And because they were no longer allowed their outdoor parades and ceremonies, every private commemoration had become more elaborate.

Women hurried to the marketplace to gather final supplies. Merchants and shop-keepers returned to their booths, once more setting out their wares.

Watching everything taking place around her, Mary Magdalene was lost in thought. Unaware, she murmured her considerations aloud.

"It's strange," she said. "They wrote 'King of the Jews,' above him, and yet they reserve crucifixion for poor people. What does that *mean*?"

"What? Did you say something, Mary?" Zebedee, the fisherman, asked.

Startled, Magdalene looked at him. "What?"

"You said something."

"Oh, sorry. I didn't realize I was speaking out loud," she said. "I was thinking, 'they wrote King of the Jews above him, and yet they reserve crucifixion for poor people.' What does that mean?"

John, Zebedee's son, answered. "Isn't it a silent signal of what they think of our nation, as a people? Even our *king* deserves a cruel death?"

Mary looked at him. "I know that's what *they* mean. But what does it mean for *us* as his *followers*? Surely this can't be all there is!"

No one had an answer.

"I don't know." It was Simon, the former leper who spoke now. "He had such power. What now? I understand what you're saying Mary. These are about to be dark days, I think."

"Who is that?" John was pointing toward the top of Golgotha. A company of soldiers could be seen ascending the hill to the execution site. Leading the foot-soldiers, were two centurions on horseback. At the end of the military procession came a wagon, with…. Two priests?

Two Pharisees?

Instinctively, the small cluster began to make its way towards the dirt road leading to Golgotha's hilltop. As they neared the wagon, it was the older Mary who voiced recognition first.

"Uncle? Uncle Joseph?" she cried. "What are you doing here?"

"Mary!" his face brightened, and he jumped from the wagon. "We have permission to take Jesus' body down."

Stunned, she stared at him. "Wh…wh…*how?*"

He smiled at her consternation, as he pulled supplies from the wagon. "Well, Pontius Pilate sent a detail to help us get him in the ground before sunset. Nicodemus brought aloe and oils. And I have brought linen from the Temple Storeroom."

"Really?" she asked, somewhat dumbfounded. She had been convinced she would never be allowed to touch her son again.

Her Uncle Joseph was addressing John, Zebedee, and Simon. "Can you help us get these supplies to the cross?"

Glad to be able to do something, the men began carrying the baskets of aloe, and stone jars of olive oil to the execution site. Joseph carried the basket of linen he had loaded into the wagon less than an hour ago. As they made their way to the center cross, the women in the company followed.

Looking ahead, Magdalene noticed the soldiers had moved ladders to rest against the back of each of the three *ptibulum,* or crossbeams. One soldier was climbing the rungs to reach the legs of the man crucified on the first cross. He felt behind the man's knees for a pulse.

"Commander Longinus?" he called. "This man is still alive. Do you want us to break his legs now?"

Longinus walked to the foot of the first cross. He spoke quietly to the soldier. "Septimus!" He called up to the foot-soldier. "We are under orders from Pontius Pilate himself. The people here are grieving the death of these men. We are to conduct ourselves as though the Prefect himself were here. Now, keep your voice down on this one, Septimus. That's an order."

Chagrined, Septimus looked around, suddenly aware the effect his actions might have on those standing near the wagon.

"Yes, sir," he replied. "Sorry sir."

Longinus motioned to another soldier to come where he was standing. "Help Septimus break this man's legs. We need to get all three of these prisoners in the ground before nightfall, to prevent more resentment toward the Empire."

He paused, and then whispered. "And for the confidence of each family with their God. It helps them hate us less."

The other commander, Justus Flavius, walked to the third cross, and assigned two of his men to do the same with the man on that cross. Roman soldiers had learned the process of *crurifragium,* or "hastening death in crucifixion," during the first month after enlistment.

Silence on the hill was momentarily interrupted by the reverberation of cracking and breaking bones, as spears were placed behind the knees of each victim, and legs were twisted into multiple pieces. As the minimal support provided by each mans' legs fragmented, lungs collapsed; thus hastening death. As upper weight increased, the victims sank, giving a final exhale. Sinking was always accompanied by an almost imperceptible moan of death.

Today was no exception.

After making certain each of the two men was really dead, the soldiers worked to remove the bodies from the crosses of execution; cutting the palm ropes. Then, the process continued, either by leveraging nails from the wrists and feet, or just pulling the body free by pushing the nails through the holes produced during impaling. There was no dictated method. Each army regular assigned to an execution detail was expected to find the most efficient and speedy method possible on their own.

To lower the bodies, a sling more than forty feet long was used. Two men, one on either side of the body, stood on ladders. Working as a team, they placed the center of the sling at the center of the man's chest. As the arms were freed from the cross, great care was taken to thread the sling under the man's arms and over the crossbeam, where another two men were ready to receive the sling's ends. Then, the feet were loosened from the foot-plate. This was accomplished by removing one long spike, which had been hammered through the arches close to the twisted ankles. As the corpses descended, the men on the ground shifted attention from the arms to the feet, lifting the dead body slowly. Finally, the sling-supported corpses were then lowered to the ground.

After the dead bodies of the two men on either side of the center cross were brought to earth, the soldiers gave them a quick wash, threw salt on top of them, and quickly wrapped each man in muslin. The shroud-covered bodies were then thrown over a horse, and transported to one of the criminal burial chambers owned by the city.

Crucifixion was normally reserved for capital offenses, such as treason or murder. It was a form of execution known to be exceptionally gruesome and traumatic. Not permitted on the hilltop, criminals' families were notified by Roman military messenger the next day. That is, unless the family had been able to stand and observe the crucifixion from the valley below.

As these burial preparations were taking place, Antonio Longinus turned his attention to the center cross. He climbed the ladder, and used two fingers to assess the Galilean's heartbeats by pressing hard behind the knees.

There was no pulse.

Strange, he thought. *Was the man already dead? How was that possible? Was his body already stiffening? He had been on a cross less than eight hours!*

But then, the centurion considered, had he ever heard of *any* man being both scourged *and* crucified? Until today, the centurion had believed it was against Roman law to dispense two forms of lethal punishment upon the same person.

Why was this man different, he wondered? Longinus looked around at the sad and wretched group of mourners waiting on the hill.

If this man were a member of my own family, he thought, *it would be heartbreaking to hear a death moan.*

He called another soldier out of formation. "Bring me your spear."

The infantryman did as he was bidden. Upon receiving the man's weapon, the senior officer did something he had done for men under his command on the battlefield, who had experienced a lethal wound, but were still breathing.

Standing on the ladder on the right side of the cross, Longinus aimed the spear towards the center of Jesus' chest. He pulled back, and then extended his arm with full strength, aiming for the heart.

He had to be sure of death.

Immediately, Antonio Longinus' face and chest were bathed in a mixture of blood and water streaming from the hole created by the spear's plunge. A strong spray shot from between the dead man's second and third ribs.

Suddenly, a series of images flashed in sequence across the man's mind; memories of his experiences in regard to the victim; his silent conclusions during assignments for Rome when he had observed Jesus in Jerusalem.

The deep darkness.

The earthquake.

In unexpected amazement, the centurion looked at those around him. "Surely," he told them all, not caring who heard, "this man was the Son of *God.*"

At the foot of the center cross, Joseph of Arimathea and Nicodemus BenGurion stretched out a length of white herringbone linen. This was to become the *tachrichim,* or burial shroud, for the body.

Joseph motioned for his niece, Mary, to come closer to him and join them. From the corner of his eye, he had watched her sway a few times in the last few minutes.

He was concerned she might faint.

With her uncle's steadying arm around her, Mary turned her head into his shoulder. She had no desire to observe as Jesus' naked body was lowered by the soldiers. Unbidden, a tidal wave of intense emotion began to well up from somewhere deep within her.

A soldier bumped into her in the process of lowering the body.

"Sorry," he mumbled. Brusquely moving past her, the men positioned her son's feet a few inches above the end of the linen cloth.

Jewish law dictated the body of a man requiring burial preparation could only be cleansed by men. If the body were female, then women were to do the cleansing. Simon, John, Zebedee and Nicodemus took up rags and water-pots brought from the wagon. After adding the myrrh supplied by Nicodemus to the water, they began a hurried form of the required traditional ritual cleansing of Jesus' body. Nicodemus began recitation of the *Tehillim;* selections from the Prophets and Psalms, lending a sense of comfort to the process, as they worked together to dab debris from Jesus' back, front, and extremities.

Zebedee and John encountered difficulty re-positioning Jesus' arms. The goal was to place his hands in a position to shield the most private parts of the body. Father and son worked for some time to cleanse the innumerable wounds and bruises from each arm, cleaning out the wrist punctures, and applying aloe to help the skin to hold together well enough for burial. Because of the amount of blood loss and physical trauma, Jesus' bodily frame was already in advanced rigor mortis. Shoulders were hunched and frozen from lung collapse.

So, in order to move the arms into a posture that would withstand being enshrouded, the two men had to exert combined pressure on each shoulder, leveraging each shoulder joint until its rigor mortis worked free. As each limb became movable, a loud snap was heard.

The sound echoed in the silence, seeming louder on the hill. And, although she thought she had been prepared for the sudden sound, Mary emitted a loud and startled cry in response to the first pop.

For a few moments, Joseph of Arimathea held his niece, allowing her to process her emotions. Short quiet sobs punctuated the quiet.

On the ground, Simon the Pharisee used a small stick and olive oil to cleanse the man's toenails, then hands and fingernails. From there, he moved to use the oil to cleanse Jesus' ears and hair.

Why didn't they have more time?

Surely this man deserved better.

The amount of bruising from the Roman *flagrum,* or whip, was unbelievable. He couldn't believe what he saw. Had anyone else ever suffered as much as this? Small indentions of the tiny lead balls attached to some ends were clearly visible. And.....

"Oh my," the former leper exclaimed.

"What is it, Simon?" Zebedee asked, now working intently with the other men. They were using the one hundred pounds of aloe Nicodemus had brought. It was working well to piece the skin's surface back together. Roman scourging, or whipping, did such damage to a human body.

Many men had died from the beating alone.

Simon looked up at Joseph of Arimathea. "When I first looked at this from a distance, I thought it was just a crown of smaller thorns they placed around his forehead. Look at this...." His voice trailed. "I'm not sure we can get it off. It's a helmet!"

Joseph momentarily let go of his niece, and moved to help Simon. "What is it?"

"Whoever wove this put a lot of work into it. Look! They used new branches from the longest thorn bushes; *Lyciodes* and *Ziziphus*. There are several other varieties here I don't remember, but here are some *Crataegus*. I can deal with the shorter ones, but the longer ones were pushed down into his skull. It's like they combined two different sections together. And now, with the stiffening of his body, I'm not sure we can loosen any of them."

"Here," Jesus' mother offered. "Can I help?" She looked at her uncle. Her eyes were swollen from weeping and deep emotion. "I don't think Abba would mind if I helped *a little*, do you?"

Joseph nodded. "What are you thinking, Mary? A little oil on each thorn, perhaps?"

Feeling glad that she was finally able to do something practical, the grieving mother nodded. "Exactly," she responded.

Joseph handed her a small flask of olive oil, which she poured over the lethal helmet covering her son's head. The woven vines made of two, four, five, and six-inch thorns were interwoven. As the oil poured down over the longest thorns, it provided a coating which separated each thorn from the blood and serum secreted around each puncture wound. Mary wiggled each of the piercing thorns carefully, working to pull those proving more stubborn with extra care so they didn't break off. As she did, she placed every thorn encrusted with blood together next to her son's body.

In the process, her hands became punctured, and began to bleed as well.

As she worked, the woman's thoughts went to the teachings of her culture. After all, she gathered, the Law stated the life of a man was in his blood. So, according to the *Tanakh*, or oral law, anything in close proximity to Jesus' body containing his blood, would need to be placed in the shroud with him. Items like the thorn helmet would be placed in the tomb as well.

When Mary had finished her task, the helmet, or crown of thorns, had been completely removed from her son's head, with bloodied thorns separated from unbloodied.

"Salome?" she called. In response, both Magdalene and Salome came to her side. "Do either of you have a comb with you?"

Salome looked at Mary Magdalene. "I'm sorry, I don't," she replied.

The younger Mary brightened. "I do!" she answered. "I didn't even know why I put it in my pouch yesterday. But I do now!" From a small bag hanging on her belt, she pulled a small boxwood comb, carved with two sides; one for detangling, one for cleaning away lice.

Taking the comb, Jesus' mother smiled. "Thank you, Magdalene! Can you girls hand me the flask of oil so I can comb oil into his hair?" Eager to help, Salome did so. The older Mary wept, as she worked to remove the debris of torture, ridicule and death. Her sister and friend watched, falling silent, as unconscious tears began to flow freely.

Joseph took the crown, inspecting it gingerly. "No one could have come in contact with this thing and not have been injured themselves. I would like to see the hands of the men who wove this. What kind of cruel mind thinks of this kind of thing?" he wanted to know.

Joseph reached up and pulled off the box he wore on his head, strapped between his eyes. It was the phylactery the law required him to wear. It was small, and made of silver with a tiny scroll inside. His great-nephew had quoted its contents many times. "Hear O Israel, the Lord your God is one God. You shall love the Lord your God will all of your heart, soul, mind and strength." He replaced the thorny crown with the phylactery, and gently placed Jesus' head back down onto the linen.

Seeing his actions, his niece reached to her own neck, removing a necklace given to her by her son several years prior. It was simple, tied on a leather cord. Mary lovingly placed it just below her son's neck; a small, flat, silver square engraved with just one word, "Abba."

"May our Abba help you now," she murmured quietly.

Magdalene found herself in deep thought. Until now, she had been sitting silently, observing the quick haste with which her friends were going through the preparation rituals. More would need to be done later, she considered. They would still need to prepare the frankincense, and lavender, and other spices after the Feast.

'She has anointed my body for burial,' Jesus had said. Had it only been a few days ago? He had known this would happen to him, she reflected. Why had he still come to Jerusalem?

Crucifixion was a horrific way to die, she decided.

Her thoughts were interrupted by hoof-beats. Looking up, she noticed the centurion and soldiers responsible for burying the other two men were returning. As they approached, she thought she might have recognized the centurion. Then, a sense of shame washed over her. He was probably one of the many men she had known..... *before.*

Before the day of her freedom.

Before.....

Now what would she do, she wondered? She supposed she could always go back to EnKarem. She sighed, and tried to focus on the task at hand.

"Mary?" a man's voice called, "is that you?"

Steeling herself, preparing to be leered at, she turned to face the centurion. In years past, before Jesus' entrance into her life, she had lived a wild life. Only once or twice since the changes in her life had taken place had she found herself in the predicament she was anticipating now.

But the face she encountered was not at all who she expected. "Justus Flavius!" she exclaimed, in sudden recognition of Capernaum's military commander.

Everyone in the small group stopped working and looked up upon hearing Mary's declaration. Zebedee jumped up and moved over to the centurion. The two men grasped arms, hugging like brothers. "Justus!" he greeted his friend with surprised enthusiasm. "I thought your responsibilities kept you in Capernaum."

The centurion answered. "Normally, but my company was ordered to report to Fortress Antonia here in Jerusalem this week. We were warned of a potential revolution."

Joseph and Nicodemus looked at each other, and then at Zebedee. "How do *you* know this man, Zebedee?" Joseph inquired.

The older man smiled. "This is the centurion I told you about from Capernaum. He is probably the main reason we were able to complete the synagogue in our little town."

Simon the leper interjected, explaining. "When I was the leader of the synagogue, I knew him as well. His wife was kind to mine."

"His servant, Adelphos, was raised from near death by Jesus," John, Zebedee's son, added. "And my mother is good friends with his wife, Julia."

"Julia helped me also," Magdalene added. "In fact, I stayed in their home for a time."

The centurion nodded. "That is all very true." His gaze went to the face of the man lying on the shroud's surface. "Jesus healed Aldelphos with just a word. He didn't even have to touch him."

Nicodemus was amazed. "How is it that of all commanders in the city today, *you* would be assigned to help us bury him?" He asked in wonder. "How did that happen?"

No one else had considered this.

"I don't know." Justus was astounded as well. He looked at his colleague, Longinus. "Antonio," he said. "This assignment will be remembered as your command. My men and I are here only as supporting troops. What do you need me to do?"

Antonio assessed his new friend. He had already decided he liked Justus Flavius. He was convinced they would have been close friends had they both been commissioned to the identical city.

"Who among you knows where the Nobilus Decurio lives?" Longinus referred to Joseph by his Roman title, to remind his soldiers of the man's position with Rome. He did this to prevent anyone forgetting Pontius Pilate's orders.

"I do," Zebedee answered.

"Then you come with me," Antonio ordered. He looked at Justus. "I will leave you with these people, and all but two of the soldiers. I am going to procure the supplies needed to seal the tomb, and I will meet you there."

He looked at Joseph of Arimathea. "Am I correct, sir, in assuming the tomb is located at your home?"

Joseph nodded in affirmation. "Yes. If you should arrive before we do, go through the gate to the back. The tomb is somewhat hidden. It has been carved out of rock in the hill. There is a rather large garden there; past the mill stone, and the well; closer to the winepress. You will see the square hole-opening when you get closer to it."

"Do you have a stone door, or covering?" Longinus wanted to know.

"Yes, there is a round stone, also carved to fit. We can roll it into place after the body is in place."

Wasn't it uncanny, Joseph thought, *that I felt so strongly to check the stone's whereabouts just yesterday morning?*

"Thank you, Antonio," said Commander Flavius, looking his friend in the eyes. "We will be there as soon as possible."

His communication concluded, Commander Longinus turned to go. "You. You. Come with me." He chose two soldiers from the company, and left for the marketplace.

Nicodemus assessed the position of the sun, and looked at Justus. "Are we almost done?" he asked. "We have to be. His body has to be in the ground before the sun sinks below the horizon. It is required by our laws."

Joseph replied, while looking at the sky as well. "What is still needed?"

Simon, the former leper, put his hands on his hips as he thought aloud. "We need to put coins on the eyes, and go through the flowers there at the bottom of his cross to find the ones needing to be put into the ground with him. We need someone to place the face napkin, the *sudarium*. Then we can wrap him up."

"From what I can tell, we have perhaps an hour; a little more, a little less," Joseph said, still looking toward the western sky.

Salome broke in. "Speaking of the marketplace, we will need food this evening," she said. "Uncle Joseph, has anyone made meal preparations for the Passover Feast at your home?"

Stirred from his observations, the priest looked at his older niece. "I have a housekeeper, but I gave her today off to make preparations for her own family. The house has been cleansed of leaven, and I have herbs and oil. We will need more bread and wine…. And meat…"

Salome went into action. "Mary," she said.

At the sound of her voice, three women answered. "Yes?"

Salome laughed. She pointed at her sister. "Not you," she said.

Then, she pointed at Cleophas' daughter, also named Mary. "Can you come with me? We are going to the market. If you don't mind, Magdalene, I think my sister needs you to stay."

"I agree," Mary Magdalene answered, reaching out to stroke her friend's arm. Then she stood, in order to open the purse on her belt once again. "Here," she said, putting silver coins into Salome's hand. "Let me help with the meat purchase."

"There was a merchant who was roasting lambs early this morning in the marketplace. I think he was taking orders. He might have made extra," Justus told them. He motioned to one of the soldiers. "Septimus! Go with them. You are to help carry, and to protect."

Septimus stepped forward, and gave a closed right fist chest salute. "As you say, sir."

"We will meet you at the house," Salome communicated. She looked at Septimus. "Do you know how to begin a fire with a flint, or a firestone?" she asked.

Septimus gave a respectful nod. "Yes my lady," he answered. "I have a bow drill and firestone in my pack. Right here." He patted a pouch hanging across his chest.

Salome let out a sigh of relief. "Oh good," she said. "That is a skill I still haven't mastered."

Removing his entire purse from own his belt, Joseph put it into Salome's hands. "Get whatever you need," he told her. "I trust you. Make this as good as we can at this late hour."

Her mouth open in amazement, Salome responded. "But Magdalene already gave me *silver*! How much food do you think we're going to need, Joseph? There are only a few of us."

"Don't forget the soldiers," the Pharisee answered with a smile. "And, if I know the Prefect, and I do, these men will be with us for more than a few days."

Justus looked at Joseph. "Pilate said he would send food for the men," he reminded the priest.

"Roman food? Garrison food? Not for guests in my home," Joseph replied. "In any event.... Go now. Thank you, Salome. We'll meet you there."

As Salome, Mary of Cleophas, and Septimus went down the hill toward the marketplace, those remaining at the foot of the cross began placing all the bloodied flowers around Jesus' body.

"So many!" Joseph was astounded. "There are more than three hundred blossoms here, just with the chrysanthemums!" The priest picked up several and put them around Jesus' head.

Simon began handing flowers to Joseph and John, who in turn placed the flowers on the shroud. "I hope they will all fit," John commented.

"They *have* to fit," Nicodemus murmured. "*All* of a man's life-blood must be buried with him. Especially a *king's blood*."

Magdalene glanced at the priest. *So he saw Jesus as a king as well.*

She watched him for a moment. He was searching through some coins in the palm of his right hand. "What do you need Nicodemus?" she asked.

"I am looking for a couple of *leptons*," he answered, referring to the copper pennies of the Empire. "They are about the right size to cover his eyes, I think." He paused. "Here we go." He pulled two coins from his palm, and placed the rest of the money back into his purse. Gently, Nicodemus placed a leptons on each eye. The coins were marked with the identification marks of Rome; one with Tiberius Caesar's name, and the other with Pilate's name. One had been minted two years prior, and the second more recently, during the past year.

Jesus' mother, Mary, stood back to take a last look at her son. So many plants and bouquets of flowers had received the crucified man's blood.

It is the burial of a king, she thought.

There were hundreds of blooms surrounding her son's body: Pink Rock-Roses, Chamomiles, Tumble Thistle Flowers, and Pistachio fruits to name the few she recognized. And the chrysanthemums; there were so many!

Close to his feet, the needle-like Black Hawthorns she had pulled from his head were laid together in a heap. Next to these was the reed placed in his hand by the soldiers, with the small ropes made of twisted palm fibers. These ropes had tied him to the crossbeam.

John, Zebedee's son, placed the *sudarium* over his friend's face.

After folding the sides of the shroud upwards, the other end of the long sheet was folded over Jesus' head. The shroud was then made to match ends at his feet. In tandem, the men walked down the body from head to foot, working to wrap the body as tightly as possible.

Nicodemus noted the linen shroud was adhering to the body pretty well; held in place by all of the aloe.

"Are we ready to lift him to the wagon?" Joseph asked, looking around at Nicodemus, Simon, and John. "We need one more."

"I can help." Justus Flavius stepped to the side with an empty spot. "Ready?" he asked. "On three. One, two, three." The men lifted the body, and worked their way to the wagon as a team. There, they placed Jesus in its back.

Climbing up onto the driver's bench, Joseph gathered the reins, and looked at Mary, his niece. "Why don't you and Magdalene ride up here with me?" he suggested. "Nicodemus, you and the others can ride in the back of the wagon."

"That's a really good idea," Simon answered.

The three men jumped up to sit on the open end of the wagon. "Someone really should steady the body too." John commented, moving to the front of the wagon.

As they prepared for the ride to Joseph's home in Jerusalem, Justus remounted his stallion, giving orders to his men. "If you used your tools, gather them back into your *loculus*, or satchel. We are heading to the home of the Nobilus Decurio. I will lead the procession, followed by the wagon. March in formation behind the wagon. The Prefect's orders are that we are to perform our duties as though this was his own family."

As Justus Flavius walked his stallion down the path worn in the hill, Joseph clicked the wagon reins, and the donkeys responded. It was an unusual sight indeed. Two members of the Sanhedrin Council drove a wagon through the streets of Jerusalem, carrying the enshrouded body of a Jewish crucified "criminal." Lending even more uniqueness to the situation was the presence of a Roman army Commander in full regalia leading the procession, and seventeen Roman soldiers who marched behind the wagon in full uniform.

Those on the streets of the city, enroute to Joseph's home, without exception, stared in surprise and confusion; captivated by what they were witnessing.

Only Roman citizens were allowed such treatment.

Who had the man been?

And why were priests of the Sanhedrin involved?

Why was a company of Roman soldiers and a centurion flanking the wagon?

Had the man been a *king?*

And if he was, what kingdom would have the support of both the Sanhedrin *and* Rome?

Yes, strange things were continuing to happen today.... all day.

These would become the questions in the minds of everyone in Jerusalem; and the subjects of dinner conversation in every home.

Antonio Longinus and his men were waiting in the garden when the wagon procession arrived at Joseph's home.

Septimus was working outside, with a drill bow and fireboard to begin a cooking fire. Inside the house, Salome and Mary of Cleophas worked to prepare a last-minute Seder; holiday meal. The trip to the marketplace had been productive.

The afternoon's darkness had delayed business dealings in most of Jerusalem. This was the last day for a decent shopping trip anywhere in Judea, Salome thought. Unless a Jewish person was poverty-stricken and simply *had* to work, the law would not allow anyone to work in the market for the next seven days.

Those who *weren't* Jewish could work anytime they chose.

As she had shopped her way through the market, Salome realized she had no idea what might have been previously prepared for the Feast. There was no way to know what Uncle Joseph's housekeeper might have done beforehand. The older niece had decided to purchase all the ingredients needed, as well as baked honey cakes, and nut breads made with *matzah* flour.

As she inspected the storeroom and outdoor kitchen, Salome discovered that her sister, Mary, had also transported several items needed for the traditional meal from Galilee when she had arrived earlier in the week. It would be good for her to stay here tonight, she considered. For both their sakes.

"Little Mary?" Salome called, using the nickname that helped them all to distinguish between two women in the family with the same name. "I need to get started on the unleavened bread right away. We will have a lot of people to feed tonight."

Mary of Cleophas was sorting through the basket of supplies. "Did we buy horseradish?"

Salome was measuring flour into a large wooden bowl. "Check the corner, under the shelf over there," she answered. "And I saw some plants we can use for the bitter herbs in there as well, I think. I did purchase green lettuce leaves at the market."

Mary investigated, and found some parsley, and other items she needed. "I'll wash and clean these for the *karpas*."

The two women worked together to create the Seder Meal celebrating the Deliverance of the children of Israel from slavery in Egypt. After cleaning the parsley, and placing it on a platter, Mary chopped horseradish with lettuce leaves for more *karpas*. She then began working on a vegetable dish of celery, parsley and new potatoes.

After rolling out the flatbreads, Salome pierced each one multiple times, readying them for the fire. She then began pitting and chopping dates; mixing in raisins, nuts, cinnamon, sweet wine and honey; adding chopped apples. This dish was *charoset*. Its stickiness represented the mortar used between bricks in Egypt. She was mixing it in a clay pot, and would take it to the outdoor fire-pit to heat it through, until it was the right thickness.

There had been no fresh eggs available in the marketplace. However, Joseph had purchased a basket of brown eggs the day before. Picking up the basket and another clay pot, Mary spoke to Salome. "I'm taking these outside to boil them for the meal."

"Thank you, Mary. Can you ask Septimus to come and get the lambs?"

"But, aren't they already cooked *through?*" Little Mary protested, confused.

The merchant taking orders for roasted lambs in the marketplace had been closing his booth when they had arrived. Because of the falling darkness, several of his orders had not been picked up. He been so relieved to have purchasers come to his booth, he had given them two roasted lambs for the price of one.

Salome smiled. "I know that, silly," she answered. "Don't you think it would be nice to heat them through so we can eat warm food?"

"Sure," little Mary answered. "Great idea. I'll ask him to come inside."

Just fifteen minutes later, both lambs were being turned by Septimus on a spit over the fire. Next to the spit, three metal stands were placed in the fire to provide a cooking platform. On top of these stands, three clay pots simmering with dishes for the Seder meal.

On the eastern side of the city, Joseph Caiaphas stood with his father-in-law, Annas, in the Temple's Outer Court. The conversation was private, and therefore needed to take place in an area where they could not be overheard.

Events today had taken an unusual turn. As a Sadducee, Annas, like Caiaphas, was a skeptic of the supernatural. He didn't believe there was a spiritual realm. It was his view, there was no after-life, nor angels or demons. Whatever happened in this life was the be-all-end-all of man's existence. He had heard the stories, as had every Jewish child.

But these were only oral traditions as far as he was concerned.

What mattered was the *Law*. The Torah was written down after all.

He did believe in Moses *and* the Commandments. But logically, those Laws had only been provided to give the nation its identity. Now, apart from the health laws helping people live longer, he could see no reason for any of them.

Yes, the Law should be honored, but only inside the Temple. A man was free to choose every other day of the week.

Hadn't that been the lesson learned from Adam, the first man, he rationalized?

No, God didn't do miracles anymore.

That age had passed.

Any thinking person could see....It was up to man now.

That was why sacrifices were needed. Especially today's sacrifice.

But today....

Annas was troubled.

The yearly Passover sacrifice had never been delayed before, going back as far as he could remember, not even in the oral accounts so revered by the Pharisees.

It was true, he considered. *Today was different.*

The yearly Passover sacrifice for sin had been delayed on this day, due to the afternoon's darkness.

Usually, following Rome's release of one prisoner, and whatever subsequent executions by crucifixion would take place, the entire city gathered at the Temple for the announcement of the Passover sacrifice's completion. As a result, the nation could live without fear of God's judgment for another year.

Today was usually a festival day. The day before Passover. Businesses usually made more coins on this day than any other day of the year. He knew it was certainly true of the Temple. Why, didn't they even raise flocks in Bethlehem just to be sold for sacrifices?

Yes, today was different indeed.

Usually, when the Passover began on a Friday, the customary hour for the Passover sacrifice was the eighth hour. No one knew why. It had just always been done that way.

Annas knew the Pharisees taught the people the number eight had a meaning. Resurrection, they said; the gift of a person's new life because of sacrifice; the returning of God's purpose and plan in an individual's life.

But then, the Pharisees saw spiritual significance in *everything*.

No, he deliberated, something was wrong with how this day had gone. It hadn't been just darkness overtaking them all. It had been the quality of the darkness; the deep *black*. Then there had been the earthquake; the Veil's tearing, the windstorm....

This year, no crowd had gathered for the sacrifice. There had been no way to see through the black cloud settled on the ground.

However, many of the scheduled levitical musicians had gathered in the Temple's rehearsal room earlier that morning. Before everything had happened. Sequestering away, they had practiced their trumpet announcements and musical accompaniments for the day's festival sacrifice.

Still, many of the pious Jews in the city had brought sacrificial gifts that morning as well. There were some, it seemed, who had not attended the execution of the Galilean.

Then, plunged into the darkness, everyone in the city simply stayed put where they were for the most part. Strange, Annas considered. Even during the plague of darkness over Egypt, in the original Passover, the nation of Israel had had light. But the Egyptians had been in darkness like this.

However, Israel had not *had* light for the sacrifice today. As the darkness lifted, Annas and Caiaphas brought resolve and purpose to the small group of priests remaining in the Temple during the earthquake.

The Sacrificial Lamb still had to be offered.

It was their duty.

Before God.

Caiaphas had given orders to the Temple's priests, spurring them into action. One had gone to gather the lamb chosen for the yearly sacrifice. Two others had gone to tend the fire on the Brazen Altar, stirring it to flame. Three others went to check the cups, bowls and knives. The earthquake most certainly had disturbed any of the tedious preparations made earlier.

Annas was still in his woolen robes used for the lamb's killing, and the catching of blood. This year, he had opted to do the slaying himself, due to a lack of manpower.

He needed to change back into his linen garments in order to complete the sprinkling still remaining to be accomplished. He looked around. This would need to be quick. The priests were gathering into formation to transfer the blood to the altar.

He noticed, Caiaphas, his son-in-law, heading his way. Inwardly, he groaned. *How could one man carry so much drama inside of himself? And stir it up wherever he went?* he wondered.

What was it Caiaphas needed? He pulled off his cloak to signify his impatience. "What do you want, Joseph? I am not finished here." He looked at the younger man, reproaching him. "You're supposed to help with this, you know. It is your office."

"I know, father," Caiaphas responded, unexpectedly using a term of endearment. "I'm sorry for my words before. I have been so disturbed by this Galilean affair. Please forgive me."

"Oh, it's all right, my boy," the older man responded. "We can have that discussion later. Is that all you need?"

"No," Caiaphas answered. "I have just received a dispatch from Pontius Pilate. It came by courier just now."

"Oh?" Annas' eyebrows went up.

"He released the Galilean's body to one of our own, it seems; Joseph of Arimathea. The man is being buried in a tomb of Joseph's choosing here in Jerusalem. He is to be given a proper burial, the Prefect says, seeing that the man's mother is *Arimathea's niece!*"

"And Joseph's position with Rome as Nobilus Decurio now troubles you?" Annas was amused, watching one of his son-in-law's schemes begin to unravel. It was interesting to observe the man's hidden panic.

"No, it's not that," Caiaphas answered. "Pilate has placed a Roman guard, and two Roman centurions on duty at Joseph's home, to seal and guard the tomb." He paused. "Not only that. They wrapped the body on Golgotha; under guard. His mother was allowed to help clean the body!"

"I imagine it would have taken a lot of them. His skin looked like chopped meat pieces," the senior priest noted.

"No," Caiaphas was frustrated. "You're not hearing me. Arimathea broke the law. He allowed a woman to help cleanse a man's body."

"Her *son's* body," Annas reminded him.

Caiaphas rubbed the back of his neck under his head-dress. "And there was a processional. Through the center of the city. The man didn't even go around as is customary. He took the dead body through town as though the Galilean were a king."

"The Romans *did* recognize Jesus with that title," Annas reminded him.

"I'm going to arrest him." Joseph stated flatly. "He conducted an act of treason against Israel, and I'm going to have him arrested."

"We are under Roman occupation, Caiaphas," the older man stated. "He is a Roman official. You don't really have the authority to do that."

"I don't care, Annas," he cried, his voice rising. "Arimathea will have to choose where he stands. He cannot be with Rome, *and* stand with his countrymen at the same time. I have to do something to shake him back into reality."

Annas sighed. "Be careful," he warned. "He has diplomatic connections... everywhere."

"Oh," came the snarled reply. "*He* will be the one who needs to be careful. I'm tired of all of the subversion in the High Court. It's time to clear the clutter from the corners!" He turned to go, then decided to add another comment to the conversation. "And *I'm* going to post a *Temple* guard at that tomb as well. I will not allow the Arimathean to pay off the Roman guards when the body is stolen. No one is going to steal this revolution from me. I am still a prince, after all."

With that he turned to go, flicking his outer cloak with a regal air. He pointed at a Temple guard. "You!" he commanded. "Get a company of twelve together, and come with me! I will give you instructions on the way!"

As Caiaphas stormed away, Annas hurried into an antechamber in the Outer Court. He exchanged his woolen tunic for a linen one, and exited within moments. He nodded to a temple Levite standing near the Brazen Altar. "You can burn it all now," he instructed.

Walking just past the Brazen Altar, he inspected the line of priests extending into the Most Holy Place. Yes, each one was holding two cups, one silver and one gold. Good.

Annas inspected the blood bowl on the Brazen Altar. Yes, it was full of drained lamb's blood. He lifted the blood bowl with both hands, and poured as much blood as would fit into the silver cup of the first priest in line. In exchange, the priest handed him an empty golden cup.

Following this method, the blood of the lamb was transferred from priest to priest, with blood and silver being exchanged for gold, all the way from the Brazen Altar into the Inner Court; finally ending in the Holy of Holies.

Only a few hours prior, the Veil between the two Courts had been mysteriously destroyed.

How was it possible?

He had no explanation.

Upon entering the now unified Inner Courts, Annas noted the light without source had continued to brighten. Was it coming from the altar, he wondered?

What was causing it?

He had no clue.

Observing, as the cup exchange arrived at the final priest in line, Annas reached for the last cup, and sprinkled its contents on the empty altar.

The altar without a Mercy Seat; the Ark of the Covenant.

Had the light intensified when he did this, he noted?

Or was it all just in his head?

Exiting the Court, he indicated to the court musicians they should continue the reciting of the Hallel, and playing musical accompaniments.

At least for a little while longer.

Annas sat down in the Outer Court, next to the Brazen Altar, and closed his eyes.

If only for a moment, he needed the peace.

In a garden, not far from the Temple mount, Joseph of Arimathea stood in front of a stone basin behind his Jerusalem home. Next to him, stone rain barrels full of water lined the outdoor walls of a plastered storage shed. His chest bare, he was scrubbing his hands, arms, face and chest. Standing next to him was Mary, his niece; along with her dear friend, Magdalene.

Nicodemus BenGurion had gone to his own home a few moments before. Simon the Pharisee, the former leper, had left at the same time. He had headed to the home of his parents, Judah and Hadassah, also dear friends of Joseph. Judah also served with him as a member of the Sanhedrin, Joseph considered.

Had he even seen Judah today, he wondered? He couldn't remember.

He hoped his friend was all right.

The sound of a chisel brought his mind to the present. Uneven edges of mortar were being chipped away in order to leave a smooth seal.

The man's body they had enshrouded at Golgotha and brought through the streets of Jerusalem was now laid to rest inside the tomb.

"You girls should go inside and clean up," he told the women standing with him. "There's nothing more we can do now."

He looked at the sky. "The sun will be setting any moment, and these men will begin their assigned watch duties. Zebedee and John will need to clean up as well." He paused. "Besides, we will need to light the lamps at sundown for the Seder."

The two women looked at each other. A bath of any kind sounded wonderful, they reasoned. As though reading their minds, Joseph spoke. "There is a room for personal cleansing inside, with a basin like this one and drawn water beside it. And, if you look in one of storerooms, some of your Aunt Escha's garments are still folded on a shelf. They might be a little large for you, but you are welcome to anything you find."

"Thank you, Uncle," Mary answered, touching his shoulder. "For *everything* you have done for me... for *us*.... for *him* today."

Surprised, Joseph continued to scrub his arms. "I did whatever I did to honor my God first, Mary; *and* because I love you...*and* Jesus."

"Ok, so thank you," Mary repeated, kissing his cheek. Moving away, she pulled on Magdalene to come with her. The two women walked into the house.

Some twenty feet from where Joseph was washing up, a company of foot-soldiers stood with the two Roman centurions. Two of the men were working together to seal a huge, round piece of limestone over the rectangular opening into the small cave. As one man spread thick mortar over the seam between the rock and the cave wall, the other followed his trowel. Then, he pressed the cylindrical stone signet provided by Pilate deeply into the thick mortar. As he did so, a continual image of the Roman eagle was imprinted all around the stone.

Such was Roman security. Should anything disturb the large limestone's position in any way, the breaking of Rome's Sacred Eagle Seal was a crime punishable by death.

So saying, the job had to be done well.

After the women had retreated into the house, the Jewish men stripped down to their undergarments, and began the process of ritual cleansing. After all, each of them had touched a dead person today.

They were unclean until evening.

And no one could eat a Passover Feast if they were unclean.

Suddenly remembering something, Joseph spoke to Antonio Longinus. "Commander," he said, "Can I ask you a favor?"

Longinus stood. "Anything, sir," he replied.

Joseph smiled at him. "Well, the wagon we used to transport the body was borrowed from the city livery just as the darkness lifted. Do you think someone in your company could return it for me?"

"Yes, sir," came the reply. Longinus motioned to two of his men, who went immediately into action.

"Let me get you some coins to pay them with," the priest ventured. With that, he stepped inside to gather his purse from Salome. He was back in a few moments, counting money into the soldier's hand.

Curious, and aware this might be his only chance to ask, Justus Flavius spoke on behalf of his men. "Master Joseph?"

"You don't have to address me that way, Justus," came the reply. "Just Joseph is fine."

Justus cleared his throat. But this was the Nobilus Decurio. In any Roman setting, the man would be sitting next to those who certainly outranked a lowly centurion. "We were wondering?"

Joseph's eyebrows went up, and he smiled in a quick flash of amusement. "Yes?"

"How long did it take to carve your tomb from the rock? It certainly isn't just a cave."

Joseph nodded. "You're right. It is a hewn cave. And to be honest, I don't know how long it took. I hired a team of stone masons just before one of my business trips. When I returned it was finished. They did a good job too. I was pleased. Did you get to see the carved levels for ossuaries in the floor? And they hauled all the stone away as well. I can give you the man's name if you like."

"No," Justus answered. "I wasn't asking for that reason. None of us would be able to afford a tomb such as this on a soldier's salary. We were just trying to determine if the cave was natural or man-made."

"A little of both, I suppose," Joseph replied. "I wouldn't have thought of doing it at all, had I not been to the mines. The men who work for me there, dig rooms from rock every day."

"I hadn't considered that," Justus commented.

"Anyway, when my wife, Escha, and I purchased the house, we wanted to add to its value, and make it a little more self-sufficient. We added the winepress, and the millstones. We designed the garden as a team. She loved flowers.

"One day when we were working out here, I noticed a small opening in the stone wall there. I thought it might be sandstone, but then, when I worked my way inside with a lamp and a chisel, I saw limestone."

"Will this be your family's burial place, sir?" one of the soldiers asked.

Joseph looked at him and smiled. "No, my wife's body is sealed in the family tomb at the estate in Arimathea; along with my mother, father and brother. Escha and I just wanted to add to the house's value.

Escha also thought Mary might like to have it someday."

As end-of-day shadows lengthened, the family and friends of Joseph of Arimathea gathered into his Jerusalem home. The smell of holiday foods was aromatic, filling not only the house but garden as well,

"Do you think they might share?" Septimus inquired, looking at Antonio Longinus. "I've been turning that spit non-stop for the past hour. It's like I can taste it."

Justus Flavius replied. "The Prefect said we will be receiving food from the garrison." At this comment, every man in the garden involuntarily groaned.

Both commanders laughed.

"Garrison food in Jerusalem is better than what *we* got in the field," Longinus told them.

"That makes it all so much better," complained Ursus, one of the soldiers, in sarcastic reply.

Longinus patted the man on the back. "You'll be fine, son. Just be glad you're not on a battlefield somewhere."

As he was speaking, the Nobilus Decurio of Rome, friend of kings and emperors; Joseph of Arimathea, came out of the back door of his home. With him was Zebedee. In their arms were clay plates and cups. They began distributing the dishes to the soldiers on duty.

"What's this?" Justus asked.

"Well, we've been watching Septimus turn the spit," Zebedee told them with a wry grin. "He looked like he might swoon from weakness."

Joseph commented. "I didn't want to have to call for a physician. He kept looking at those lambs like a man falling in love."

Zebedee chuckled. "I was concerned he might drool a little on them."

One of the other soldiers joined in the banter as he took his plate. "Septimus always gets attached to his meat. Not me. I'll take mine crispy!"

"Hey, Seven," jibed another. "When you gonna look that way at a woman?" The men whistled, and one slapped Septimus on the shoulder.

"Hey!" Septimus replied, a hint of a smile etching its way across his chiseled face. "I've known a few…"

John and Salome came out of the house next, with Cleophas' daughter. They were carrying pots of water, and amporas of wine. As the three began filling glasses, those from the house began to filter outside as well, carrying their own plates and cups.

It was Joseph who addressed the soldiers. "We want to invite you to share our holiday meal with us," he said. "We have plenty of food, as you can see, and nothing can be left over. Our laws regarding Passover say we must eat or burn all the leftovers."

A collective "aah" went up from the soldiering detail.

Commander Flavius moved over to stand by Joseph. "I think we have enough stomachs here to help with that problem, Joseph," he said.

Everyone in the garden courtyard laughed.

Joseph put his arm around the centurion in an attitude of camaraderie. "You are all welcome in my home. Let me say a blessing, and then we can begin." Around the courtyard, his family and friends closed their eyes in respect of their God.

Out of respect for Joseph, the Romans closed their eyes as well.

"Blessed are You, the Eternal, our God, the King of the world, who has sanctified us by your commands, and ordained we should eat the Passover."

Opening his eyes, he addressed the group of soldiers once more. "If you will forgive us, because of our law, we must eat separately, and walk through the remembrance of our oppression from another conqueror, centuries ago. If you like, I will explain the reasons for our Passover meal as we eat. If you have any questions, please ask!"

Then, he clapped his hands. "Let's eat!"

At that command, the soldiers reacted as though they were children being let out of school. Near pandemonium broke out as each of the men sprang from their seated position. No one in Joseph's circle minded. In fact, it felt good to serve.

No one was terribly hungry anyway.

It was almost two hours later when Joseph Caiaphas, and a company of Temple guards arrived at Joseph's home in Jerusalem. The traditional meal was completed, and many of the Roman soldiers had been amazed at the accounts of Israel's Deliverance from Egypt.

They were beginning to feast on sweet wine and honey cakes when John noticed the first sign of torches and the clang of spears. He nodded toward the firelights approaching.

"I think we are in for company," he told everyone.

Caiaphas, the High Priest, entered the garden without announcing himself, or knocking. Upon seeing the number of persons gathered together, and the unlikely mixture of cultures, he was momentarily halted.

He had not been aware Joseph had so many family connections in the city. *Where had all these people come from?*

"Hello, Caiaphas!" Joseph of Arimathea ventured a greeting, as he took a piece of bread from the open basket in front of the table. "I should think you would be with your own family tonight."

Gathering himself, Caiaphas masked his vulnerabilities once more. He snarled a response. "I would be if I didn't have so many matters to take care of."

"Why are you here?" Joseph asked calmly. He broke the bread into two pieces and offered half to the High Priest. "Would you like something to eat?"

"No! I don't want anything to eat!" the priest cried, pushing the man's hand away. He glanced around the courtyard. "I don't eat with uncircumcised Gentiles!"

"Just thought you might be hungry," Joseph answered, biting into the bread and chewing thoughtfully.

Caiaphas nodded to a Temple guard. The armed regular pulled a coil of palm cord from his belt, and moved towards the Nobilus Decurio of Rome.

"You are under arrest, Joseph," Caiaphas spoke with pomposity. "You have broken our laws, and you consorted with the Roman Prefect without my expressed permission. Both are punishable by stoning."

"Can he *do* that?" Zebedee asked, without thinking.

Caiaphas wheeled around to see who had asked such an irreverent and apparently stupid question. "Well, I *am* doing it!"

With that retort, the angry priest motioned to two of his men. "You two come with me. We will put this traitor where he belongs." He looked at the remaining ten men in his company. "The rest of you remain here. Keep an eye on the Romans. Who knows what plots have been schemed against the patriots of Judea? Especially now that this traitor's identity has been exposed. It is *your* job to make sure they don't tamper with the tomb *or* the body."

A ripple of laughter made its way through the soldiers of Rome.

Incensed, Caiaphas gaped at them, not believing he could be mocked in his position.

It was Commander Longinus who stood up. "I'm sorry, sir," he began apologetically. "Our men were given a stone signet; the Sacred Eagle Seal of Rome. Pontius Pilate gave it to us with orders this afternoon. We used it to seal the tomb. To break that seal is a crime punishable by death. No one will be bothering this grave."

Not convinced, Caiaphas looked once again at his men and reiterated his command. "You heard me," he said. "Keep your eyes open."

Having said that, he noted Joseph of Arimathea's hands were now tied behind his back. He looked at his men. "Let's go!" Flourishing his great robe once more, Caiaphas led the way down the path toward the gate.

Joseph sighed. Somehow he had half-expected this reaction when news of his burial of Jesus had reached the Sadducees. He had hoped for at least a little sleep before the questioning began.

As he exited the courtyard, the Arimathean stopped. He looked around with genuine affection. "Goodbye, my friends," he said. When he neared his niece, he paused. He was not sure when, or even if, he would be allowed to return. His eyes filled with momentary moisture.

"Mary, this house and everything in it is yours. If you have any questions, there is a scribe who is a lawyer in the city named Jannaus. He has been the manager of my affairs for some time now. John, take good care of her; that is what the Master wanted."

In shocked silence, the group in the garden courtyard watched four men exit the gate in front of Joseph's home. A few moments passed before anyone could speak. When a voice was heard, it was once again the voice of Zebedee, this time addressing the Temple guards.

"That's two arrests of innocent men in four days. I think something must be coming apart inside Prince Joseph's head."

An awkward silence hung in the air.

Well, Salome thought to herself, *a change of direction would be a good idea.*

"Have you men eaten?" she asked the Temple guards out loud. "Let me get you something to eat."

Listening to the conversations taking place around him, John, the son of Zebedee, fell silent. He began to consider the events of the day, trying to make sense of it all. How had things come to this place?

In a fleeting thought, he wondered whether he would be able to see the stars tonight. Perhaps he could go for a walk. There had to be some way to escape the intensity in the atmosphere around him.

The city was so much busier than the family home in Galilee.

He needed a place to think. A little quiet.

Suddenly, he wanted to find Simon Peter, and his brother.... And the others. Were they all together?

Had anyone else been arrested? What would happen now, he wondered?

Getting up, he stepped away from the crowd, and walked towards the gate. As lights from the garden faded away, John looked up at the sky.

Suddenly, he was reminded of words the prophet Joel had written long ago.

"I will show wonders in the heavens and in the earth, blood, and fire, and pillars of smoke. The sun shall be turned into darkness, and the moon into blood, before the great and terrible day of the Lord will come."

Well, as far as he knew, he thought, only *some* of those things had happened today.... So the "great and terrible day" might not happen right away. What did it mean, he wondered? Why had he remembered that particular prophecy? It must have been the line about the "sun being turned to darkness."

Well, if for no other reason, the darkness certainly *had* been part of the day, he reasoned.

John had expected Jesus to bring in a new era. He had followed him; believed him. How had he healed people? Why had he come, if not to free the nation? If he hadn't been the Promised Deliverer, who had he been?

It would take time to understand.

He had thought he understood.

He would have to get his head around this.

He wondered whether his parents were ready to leave Joseph's home, to walk to their own family's business home in Jerusalem. They rarely were all in Jerusalem together. Usually, it was John's responsibility to come to the city on business, trading salted fish from the Sea of Galilee for money, or for goods.

Usually John stayed in the business home alone, or with his brother, James, if they had travelled to the city together.

Turning around to walk back towards Joseph's home, he glanced up at the heavens. The stars seemed to be hidden. Was there a moon? He had thought there was supposed to be a full moon that night. Where was it? Searching the sky, he gasped involuntarily, and then held his breath.

How had this happened, and why today?

What could it possibly mean?

Had it ever happened before in the history of man, he wondered?

The moon was blood red.

5 – Passover

As the two Temple guards hurled Joseph of Arimathea into his cell in the basement of Caiaphas' palace, the High Priest went to find his family. He was arriving a *little* past sunset, he knew. But he *had* been attending to Temple business, after all.

She would just have to understand.

As Joseph entered the courtyard cooking area behind his palace, his wife, Nitza, jumped up to greet him with a smile. "Joseph!" she cried. "I was beginning to worry!"

Placing his arms around her, he gave her a gentle kiss. "I'm sorry I'm late, my blossom," he said. "The yearly sacrifice was delayed because of the darkness. And then the earthquake…." His voice trailed off as he caught sight of the young priest, Saul, sitting near the well a few feet away.

"Saul! I'm so glad you could make it!"

The young man stood up. "I'm honored to be here, sir," he stammered, his cheeks turning red.

Caiaphas chuckled and whispered into his wife's ear. "He wants to discuss a possible marriage to our little Shira."

Delighted, Nitza giggled, and glanced at their fifteen year-old daughter, who was watching her parents' unheard communication with no small amount of curiosity.

Joseph pulled away from his wife, and spoke out loud. "Saul is a priest from Tarsus. He is currently mentored by Gamaliel."

"Oh," said Nitza. She looked at Saul. "You are a Pharisee, then?" she looked at her husband quizzically. She had never known him to approve of a Pharisee, much less consider allowing one into the family. He was too politically motivated for that, she considered. Hadn't he said many times Pharisees were "too spiritually minded to be of any earthly purpose?"

"I am a son of a Pharisee," Saul spoke clearly in response, as they all walked into the house together. "I only know what I have been taught. My mentor, Sage Gamaliel, is also a Pharisee."

Caiaphas moved over to the young man, and spoke invitingly. "Well, I'm hoping to be more of an influence on this bright, young man's life in the near future. A balance of views can only help him to excel."

Saul looked at Caiaphas with surprised admiration. "You do? Thank you, sir."

Caiaphas looked at him with seeming appraisal. "Of course I do, my boy. For example, if you were married, and you would allow *me* to mentor you, you would be eligible to be considered for the Great Council, the Sanhedrin. After all, we Sadducees are small in number these days."

Saul flushed. This was more of an honor than he would have expected from the High Priest.

Caiaphas continued with an affected sigh. "I have long thought that it would be the plan of God to bring more unity to our ranks in the Sanhedrin. There is far too much division at the moment; what with Sadducees fighting against Pharisees. We argue way too much, don't you think?"

"I have wondered why there is so much time spent in heated discussion," the younger priest offered.

"It's just ridiculous," Caiaphas answered. "We would get much farther if we spent time in prayer."

Saul was surprised to hear these words from a Sadducee. His father, the synagogue ruler in Tarsus, as well as his present mentor, Gamaliel, had each confided separately to Saul. In their eyes, Joseph Caiaphas was far from being a spiritual man; he was manipulative and shallow; he deceived many in order to achieve whatever agenda he had on hand at the moment.

Strange, Saul thought. *That isn't the man I am speaking to.*

He wasn't acting as he had been described.

Perhaps the two older men had misunderstood his new friend.

Yes, they had been mistaken. They had both made errors in judgment.

He would prove them wrong. Neither of them really knew Caiaphas.

Yes, he had decided. As of this moment, he had chosen a new mentor. He would now align himself with the High Priest. And, hopefully, his future father-in-law.

Without thinking, he glanced at Shira, Joseph and Nitza's fifteen year-old daughter. He found her eyes fixed on him. As their eyes locked, Shira smiled, giving Saul courage he might have a chance to gain possession of his prize.

"Uh, sir?" he began. "I wondered whether I might be able to ask you something this evening."

Joseph Caiaphas watched the silent exchange between his daughter and the young priest in amusement. Chuckling, he patted Saul's forearm. "All in good time, son. Not tonight. This is a holiday feast." He looked at his wife.

"Would you tell the servants we are ready, please?"

Nitza walked to the door leading to the outside, where she had a quick conversation through the door. Upon rejoining the group she announced, "They are prepared for us."

Caiaphas rubbed his hands together. "All right then! Let's go outside where we can eat under the stars!"

In the lower dungeon of Caiaphas' palace, dim light filtered in from above. The square room had two carved openings, where prisoners could be tied with hands and feet spread apart, for physical chastisement. The ceiling had a perfectly round circle, roughly two and a half feet in diameter, chiseled from its center. Surrounding the walls above was an observation gallery. From its vantage point, methods of torture could be instructed, questions could be asked, and judgments could be declared.

Directly above the middle of the carved circle, fastened into the beam of the upper level's ceiling, was a great iron ring, from which hung a huge wooden pulley. A long rope was threaded around it. This had been the means by which Joseph had been lowered into the darker cell the night before. For prisoners, it was the only way in.

He rubbed the fresh rawness under his arms. The rope had not been knotted quite well enough when tied around him, he remembered. About three feet from the bottom, the knot had broken loose.

He had hit the floor hard, and had both heard and felt a hard snap in his foot.

Now, Joseph was sure his ankle was broken. *I'm not as young as I used to be,* he thought.

Why had he not considered the purpose of Caiaphas' lower dungeon before now? How many men had been condemned or experienced torture in these cells? How many had died in this room? As far as he could tell, there were more cells surrounding the one where he had been placed.

How long did the High Priest intend to keep him here?

Suddenly, the very real possibility he might learn the answers to his questions first-hand presented itself in his mind.

He shuddered.

The large cell had been used for food and wine storage until several years prior, when Caiaphas had commissioned the present changes made. The High

Priest had kept the work a secret, disclosing the private prison only after a Jewish man had stolen coins from the Temple treasury. As far as Joseph knew, the man had been beaten with rods, and then released.

He had not considered the possibility of further implications until now.

Thinking about it now, he remembered a conversation he had overheard between Caiaphas and Annas many months prior. "The people need to know we are serious about the Law," the High Priest had told his father-in-law, Annas. He refused to make apologies for hiding unauthorized imprisonments from his father-in-law. He had shrugged. "It must be done. These cells will be reserved for heretics, dissidents, adulterers, and those who evade the Temple taxes."

"Caiaphas," the older man had warned, "You must be careful. I was given explicit instructions during *my* time in office. I know you were given similar instructions. Don't do anything to invite the Caesar's wrath. We don't need more of Rome's iron fist to be lowered against us."

Caiaphas had scoffed at his warning. "You have to know how to deal with these people, father," he said. "We don't need the Romans to administer our Law. We should be able to handle these things ourselves."

The Sage considered the attitudes of the Temple Guards who had imprisoned him. They had been shaken by his arrest, he could tell. Unsure what to do, or how to treat a member of the Sanhedrin being placed in a private prison cell, they had asked him how they could make him more comfortable. And, although Joseph had not asked, the two men had provided the poor man with an oil lamp, a water pot, a cup, a privy pot, a scroll, and bedding for the night. One guard had even apologized for having to follow orders as he had locked the upper level door.

Both were so deeply conflicted, they had carried on a conversation in front of him. After all, they reasoned, why would anyone dare to arrest the Nobilus Decurio of Rome? Or *any* member of the High Council for that matter? Wouldn't these actions of the High Priest bring a greater threat of Rome's vengeance down on all of their heads?

What could this great man have possibly done?

When they had asked him for answers, Joseph had responded as simply and truthfully as possible. "I chose to bury my niece's son."

Not comprehending, they had shrugged, and walked away, wishing him a good night's rest.

Apparently, *everyone* was afraid of Joseph Caiaphas.

Joseph was not sure whether he would see Caiaphas again tonight. Come to think of it, he hoped the man *didn't* come to gloat this evening. It had been a really long day. And, truth be told, if he were to come, Joseph was sure the High Priest would deprive him of many, if not all, of the small comforts he had been provided by the guards. He decided he would take in his surroundings before reading from the scroll and trying to get some sleep.

He had been sitting on a stone block, with his back against the wall. The block had been carved from the wall long ago. Its original purpose had been to keep grain bags from absorbing moisture in the cool space. Now, it was used as a bench, or a sleeping platform.

Leaning back against the wall, Joseph had been resting his injured ankle; elevating it on the cool stone. Joseph was thankful he had some sort of a place to sleep. No mice, or other creatures would be able to climb up to bother him in his sleep.

Wincing, he stood up and hobbled over to the small table just a few feet away. He picked up the water-pot, and poured liquid into the small, clay cup. Then, he picked up the scroll and made his way back to his stone bed ever so slowly. Returning to the table, he picked up the small oil lamp and his bedding.

It wasn't until he turned to toss the coverings to the stone slab that he saw it. One of the two blankets fell short of its goal, and Joseph bent over to retrieve it. In the process, he turned his head sideways.

What he saw took his breathe away.

In the blood spatters and smudges on the wall, an image had emerged. Was it just the shadows, he wondered? Perhaps his mind was playing tricks on him. He lifted up the lamp to be sure.

There, as though painted with a sponge, was the image of his niece's dead son.

Immobilized, Joseph stared at the image. How did it *get* there? Was this some cruel joke of Caiaphas'? If it hadn't been manufactured by man, what did it mean?

Pontius Pilate slept fitfully that night. When he did sleep, his dreams were invaded by images of his son, Pilo. In his first dream, his son was hanging on a cross, with vultures pulling away pieces of his little body, bit by bit. There was blood everywhere, and the small boy was screaming his father's Latin nickname, "Tata! Where are you! Tata!"

Startled awake, the Prefect ran his hands over his face. With the edge of his covering, he wiped the sweat from his face, neck and forehead. He wiped his clammy hands dry once more.

Laying back down, he tried to get back to sleep.

After long moments of listening to his wife's deep and rhythmic breathing, he began to drift off once more.

Immediately, he was dreaming again.

This time, he saw himself standing on a high hill, covered with snow. Clouds obscured his view. Behind him, a giant golden eagle suddenly swooped down from the sky. As it flew past him, its wings fully spread, an enormous, glistening, black cobra sprang up from the valley below. In its ascent, it spread its hood, stopping to look into Pontius' eyes. He expected it to strike him with lethal poison. Writhing back and forth in its approach, the cobra's face drew closer and closer, until he could feel its hot breath on his face. Its eyes were cold stone gray, with fiery red centers glowing with an evil light.

Looking down at his own feet, Pontius found he could not move. He was frozen in place. Even though he tried with all of his strength to run, his feet would not budge. Then, he saw piles of grain rising where his toes had been.

Pontius looked at his hands. To his horror and surprise, they began to melt. But the liquid dripping from where they had been, was not wax or water. It was blood. As the blood from his hands began to touch the grain at his feet, the grain began to separate.

Without warning, the wheat burst into flame.

Panicked, the man grasped for the eagle, desperate to be rescued. But instead, the giant cobra opened its great mouth to consume the eagle in one swallow. After consuming the bird, the snake's belly began to glow like a furnace. Taking a deep breath, the cobra opened its mouth and blew out a steady stream of fire down on Pontius.

Promptly, his entire body began to burn.

Unable to breathe, he could feel the heat rising to his face. Pontius began to scream. Looking up, he saw a terrifying sight. The glow inside the cobra had enlarged, causing the snake's belly to swell, growing larger and larger. Unexpectedly, there was an immense explosion. Pilate felt the very mountain quake under his feet. As the ground split into pieces under him, the great golden eagle appeared once more, in midair, where the serpent had been. Extending its talons, the bird picked the man up as he was falling, carrying him up higher into the clouds.

Stirring after *this* dream, Pontius sat up. He was too tired to get up just yet, he decided. Punching his head cushion, he closed his eyes, not sure if he really wanted to go back to sleep. It would be wonderful to rest without dreaming, he thought, even if just for a little while.

As he closed his eyes, an image of his son's withered foot superimposed itself over his entire sphere of sight. Then, he saw himself running, but continually falling down. A black, unseen cloud of screams and growling sounds was creeping after him. Each time it touched a part of his body, he could feel it, as though he were on fire once more. As he pulled himself to his feet, he noticed both of his feet were withered. No wonder he was falling down.

Coming awake in a full sweat, Pontius rose from the bed he shared with Claudia Procula, his wife. She had had difficulty sleeping of late, and he didn't want to wake her since she was finally resting soundly.

He walked to the open window. Closing his eyes, he took a deep breath.

The darkness that afternoon had been disconcerting enough, he reflected. Not wanting to think about it, he had written it off to a sudden storm. Compartmentalizing, he had tried to focus his thoughts on time spent with Claudia and Pilo.

Had the dreams come from his personal conflict over the death of the Jesus the Galilean? Was he afraid of retribution from his actions today? What had the middle dream meant?

He wasn't sure what to do.

As the Prefect opened his eyes, his attention was drawn to the sky. Where was the moon tonight, he wondered?

And then, he saw it, and drew in a quick breath.

The moon was dark red.

Pilate moved into the main living area of the family apartments. He lit a lamp, and decided he could not experience another dream. He would use this time to catch up on dispatches needing to be sent to Rome. For more than two hours, he worked.

Then, it was time to do the report he had been putting off.

How could he tell his superiors he had sanctioned the crucifixion of a family member of the Nobilus Decurio? He wrote an introduction, and then launched into a short explanation of the current situation in Judea. At the end of his report, he wrote:

"Now when he was crucified darkness came over all the world,
the sun was altogether hidden, and the sky appeared dark while
it was yet day, so that the stars were seen, though still they had

their luster obscured. Wherefore, I suppose your Excellency is
not unaware that in all the world they lighted their lamps from
the sixth hour until evening. And the moon, which was like
blood, did not shine all night long, although it was at the full. –
Pontius Pilate, 33 AD

Upon finishing the dispatches, he wrote a final, private letter to his friend and father-in-law, the Emperor Tiberius. He knew the Caesar was miserable without his only daughter.

Tiberius' widowed mother, Livinia, had married the ruthless Augustus, son of Julius Caesar, when Tiberius had been just a boy. When he had become old enough, he trained and was commissioned as a general in the Roman army. Then, after proving himself successful as a strategic conqueror, Tiberius had been adopted and groomed by Augustus for the throne.

Then, when Tiberius was renowned by the Roman senate for his military successes, Augustus had offered him the opportunity to be voted to the throne by the Roman Senate.

Flattered, the married Tiberius had agreed.

But then, the second shoe was dropped. In order to become the next Caesar, Augustus forced Tiberius to divorce his wife and soul-mate, Vipsania. The cost of the throne was a happy marriage. Claudia, the daughter, had been wrenched by the will of the Senate from the arms of her loving mother. In Augustus' mind, Julia's marriage to Tiberius was the only method to insure his own daughter would remain in the ruling family.

A miserable Tiberius, filled with hatred for his new wife, took the throne. His daughter, Claudia, had been forced to live in the palace; torn from her childhood home. Pontius had spoken many times with his wife of her feelings of abandonment; of her anger with her adopted grandfather; of her fears.

He smiled, as he considered how practical and hands-on his wife had become during her years in Rome. As she matured into womanhood, she developed values of a seasoned woman much older than her years.

While her friends made entire days of gossiping at a nearby spa, or searching out new ways to imbed beads and pearls into their hairstyles, Claudia had found joy when her hands were working the soil in her small garden. Delicate in frame, but not in her physical aptitude, she was known for absenting herself from the royal court, returning hours later with a basketful of wild grapes or berries.

Her father, Tiberius, had once confided to Pontius his concern she might go out walking one day and fall irretrievably into a deep hole. Sadly, he said, each time he had assigned her a bodyguard, she had given the man the slip, preferably spending her time alone.

Pilate knew Tiberius would want to know what had been happening. More importantly, he wanted to tell his father-in-law about Jesus. Aware of the stormy turmoil surrounding the Caesar, Pontius found himself writing to console and comfort his favorite father figure.

He wanted to give Tiberius hope; even in the middle of a difficult situation. When finished, the Prefect read through his letter, making sure his words conveyed his true meaning. In truth, the letter was so profound in its timing the Emperor Tiberius wrote back a month later:

Would that an emperor could follow a god, but since I have been made a god by the Senate, I cannot. Were I not an emperor, I would declare him divine.

Pilate found sleep was still eluding him. Moving to a small cabinet, he removed a wooden easel, and a few small camel's hair brushes. Drawing out three clay cups, he filled each one with drawn water. In a small basket were small stone containers, each one containing a color of pigment. These he put in order on the table. Lastly, he removed a small towel and a thin, rectangular, wooden board.

Although he loved to paint, Pontius made it his practice only to do so when he came upon a worthy subject. He never really had painted just for the fun of it, he considered.

Well, now he had a subject worth remembering.

He closed his eyes. Suddenly his mind was filled with the face of the man who had healed his son's feet. The fear he had been avoiding all day suddenly emerged.

Would Jesus take away Pilo's ability to walk to punish him for the sentence of crucifixion? When a healer died, did his deeds cease to exist? The priests of the Roman and Greek gods believed they did.

Silently, he took up the widest brush. Dipping it into one of the cups of water, he dabbed the excess away, and then began creating a background layer of color for the portrait he would eventually keep in his possession.

Perhaps, he thought, committing the images to a visible form, would pull them from his tormented mind.

In Qumran, Judah the Sicari placed his oil lamp on the table near his sleeping pallet. It had been a good evening, he decided. He was finally feeling some relief.

The Passover Feast's meal had been simple. Several others had been present; those who came to the Essene settlement the night before, just as Judah had. They had all worked together to roast the lamb, shape and bake the bread, and so on. The meal had taken place in the large eating room.

Judah met a few of those who were in the settlement over the holiday. One family with five children had been in transit to Jerusalem for the Feast, and their wagon had broken down. The husband had tried unsuccessfully to fix it. They trudged in on Thursday, looking for help, but everyone capable of travel or repair work had gone to Jerusalem. Watching them interact, Judah was reminded of his own family life back in Gamala.

Since his Uncle Eli was in Jerusalem until tomorrow evening, he had not been able to connect with any of his family members on a personal level in a very long time.

The cleansing baptism had been a powerful experience, Judah considered. He had disrobed, and stood in the cool waters. As Nachum and Isaachar had read the psalms and prophets, he felt his heart return to the simplicity of living before his God.

Perhaps it had been the fulfilling of the vow which had robbed him of his ability to hold to this peace, he decided. Hadn't this been what he felt in his heart when he had asked his Uncle Eli's blessing to attach himself to John?

Tonight, as his head had gone under the waters, he had felt a strange sensation of peace wash over his inner soul.

Now back in his room, he took off his sandals, and knelt on the floor. It was the first time he had felt like praying in what seemed like a lifetime! His heart was back in his chest again!

He hadn't felt this way since his father had been alive!

Before the Romans had crucified *him* as a subversive.

He remembered his first day in the settlement. Judah and his mother had come to Qumran, basically because Eli, his father's brother, lived here. According to the Law, Simon's death had made it now Eli's responsibility to care for Naomi and her son.

The Qumran settlement was where the nationalism movement had seen its birth. Judah spent many hours here as a boy, learning the Law and the Prophets, but particularly studying the history of his nation. Named for his grandfather, the heroic Judah of Gamala, his father and his uncle had raised him with somewhat of an Essene belief system.

God's hand was always in play in the affairs of men, Judah understood. In fact, it was a man's responsibility to live his life according to the Law and the Prophets, receiving only those things written down as coming directly from God; rather than the oral traditions and additional conclusions from the Law like the Pharisees.

A person's life was planned out for him by God, and there was no ability to choose one's direction or to make life choices. At least, this was what he had been taught.

However, the Essenes did believe God was still speaking. He used anything and everything to make his direction and plan known. Circumstances, situations, and relationships were included in His communication with man. He was a God who used revelation. A person could have a vision, such as Isaiah; or a dream, such as Joseph. This inspired interpretation would then have the same validity in the person's life as the written Law.

But, where the Pharisees would find a way to make a personal experience fit with the Law, by argument, debate, or theological explanation, the Essenes did not. A person's revelatory experiences and the written law had to agree, or the revelatory experience came into question.

Essenes were respected throughout Judea as being prophetic instruments of God.

Judah's grandfather, Judah, and his father, Simon, were revered among the Essenes for the fresh revelation they had brought to bear upon the Jewish population. The identity of the nation *could* not, *must* not be lost as it had been in the days of the Babylonians. Any influence from those who didn't believe in the Law and the Prophets had to be resisted. The purity of Jewish distinctiveness had to be maintained and defended.

There could be no compromises.

Men such as Joshua, Gideon, Ehud, King David and Judah Maccabee were revered, studied and respected. Women such as Keshet, Abigail, Esther, Ruth and Hannah were role models to be copied. Like the Pharisees, children of the Essenes knew these role models as heroes and the founders of their national history.

The nation could not be separated from its spiritual identity.

Rome would have to learn, that was all.

Essenes believed the conflict between good and evil would continue in the afterlife. Those who pleased God in this earthly life would have a greater chance of spiritual survival in the afterlife, than those who disregarded their need for God's personal direction. Becoming pleasing to God, the Essenes taught, was about passively yielding to God's fore-ordained design.

In fact, where the Temple leaders in Jerusalem looked to the moon's cycles for indications of feast days and sacrifices, those in the desert of Qumran looked only to the sun.

"We are the children of light."

If Judah had heard it once, he had heard it a thousand times in his lifetime.

When his mother had died, his uncle Eli had truly taken him under his wing. The Essene community became his home. It was here he met his childhood friend, John.

John had apparently been a miracle child, given by God to his parents, Zacharias and Elizabeth, in their advanced old age. The angelic prophecy had foretold John to be a prophet in his adult life. So, upon the death of his parents, as a ten-year old boy, John had joined the Qumran settlement.

He and Judah were near enough in age they had become good friends.

As they had grown together into manhood, John's inclination to follow the footsteps of the prophet Elijah had emerged. Judah's desire to follow the more militant path towards nationalism had also emerged.

When Judah had taken his vow, it had seemed only natural to attach himself to John.

Smiling, Judah realized the sense of foreboding he had been experiencing on his arrival late last night had lifted after the purification rituals. This was what he had felt like all the time when he had lived here!

Perhaps he should wait a season before taking another vow.

Fleetingly, he wondered what was happening in Jerusalem right now. By now, Jesus would have convinced Caiaphas of his place in the nation's history. The two men would have had a chance to discuss the re-establishing of the nation of Israel. The Sanhedrin would be weighing in to make sure the right steps would be taken.

Yes, he knew.

It was happening right now.

Judah was sure Jesus would be declared the face of the national revolution. There had been no other way he could think of to get the two men together where a discussion could take place.

Rome would not suspect an arrest of this sort, he deliberated.

He had even violated his Essene training of not recognizing any man as his master but God. He had even carried the purse, which meant he had carried the "graven" images of men who ruled over others on his belt at all times.

Should he have greeted Jesus in Gethsemane with "Hello, Master?"

It didn't matter now. He had gone through purification.

He had completed his vow before God.

And, he was not really an Essene, he reasoned. He was Sicari; a rare member of the new sect. Their type had not been seen before. Not like this. Judah felt they were going to be even more passionate to restore the nation than the Zealots. The Zealots were, as a whole, ready to fight for the nation's survival, but turned somewhat squeamish when it came to suicide missions.

"I was born for this," Judah told himself. "I am Sicari. Judah the Iscariot."

When Jesus retook the throne of Israel, not too many days from now, Judah hoped he would be recognized and remembered as leader of the Sicari.

Judah had loved being one of Jesus' leaders. He had discovered the reality of the unseen realm. He had seen Jesus heal the deaf, open blind eyes, mend crippled limbs, cure leprosy; and multiply bread and fish to feed thousands.

More than anything, it amazed Judah how the prophet had handled conflict between his leaders. They had all been so different; the twelve. And every one of them had sensed Jesus would be king. As a result, they all vied for future position; for the teacher's approval.

Judah wondered what they were all doing today.

He decided he would travel to Jerusalem as soon as the sun began to set; the end of the Sabbath. He would be walking all night, he knew, but it would be worth it to be part of the celebrations with his friends, the other eleven men who would certainly be leaders in the re-established kingdom.

God never intended such power to go to waste.

It was later than they had planned to stay. But then, no one really wanted to leave Jesus' mother, Mary, and Magdalene in Joseph's home alone; especially with twenty-two Romans, and ten Temple Guards sleeping just yards away in the garden.

It had been half-way through dinner, when two of the foot-soldiers had recognized the Magdalene. Members of the contingency from Capernaum, they conferred quietly together. After a few moments, one found the courage to speak up.

Standing up to walk over to her, the young man waited directly in front of her. He greeted Mary with an obvious effort at good manners. Salome was sitting close enough not only to observe, but to hear as well.

"Mary?" he inquired, somewhat cautiously. "Mary from Magdala? What are *you* doing here?"

Startled to hear a man's voice refer to her with the name describing her in a former life, Mary looked up self-consciously. Looking at the man's face, she felt badly she wasn't placing him. Then she remembered.

"Titus!" she said with relief. She had met him the day before she met Jesus. The Greek foot soldier had been ordered to escort Atticus, her companion, back to Capernaum's garrison from Caesarea Philippi. He had always treated her with kindness. "It's been a long time!"

"Yes, it has," replied the man somewhat shyly. "How have you been?"

"Did the commander tell you what has happened in my life?" she asked.

"No," Titus answered, looking over at Justus Flavius. "But, to be truthful, I haven't asked him about you."

"Oh," Mary said. "Well, there is a lot to tell you. The past three years have been unbelievable. I look at who I was back then, and wonder how all the changes have taken place. I would have to say Jesus was the reason."

"But the commander *did* tell me about Jesus," Titus told her. "I was assigned to crowd control by the garrison commander in Capernaum several times. I remember hearing him teach. He was phenomenal. Then, my brother, who is a physician, was visited by one of his patients. He had treated the man for years, and suddenly the disease disappeared. Jesus had healed him."

"I didn't know you had a brother," Mary said, surprised.

"Oh, I thought I told you. I do have a brother. Our family is from Antioch in Syria. Luke is older than I am, but he came to Jerusalem when I was commissioned into the Roman army. He decided to stay. He began following Jesus around the countryside. He would tell me about the teachings, and his miracles. I must say my entire life is different now than it used to be."

Mary spoke simply, her voice choking somewhat. "Jesus changed my life completely as well. I will never be the same."

Titus looked at her quizzically. "Was your relationship with him... like your relationships with Atticus and some of the *other men* in Capernaum?" He ventured.

Surprised, Mary looked at him in shock. "What?" she sputtered. "Oh.... No! It was nothing like that. I had some things happen in my childhood that... well, set me up to make the choices I did. Like when you and I were together. I had demons inside me, Titus. They talked to me all the time. There were seven of them. And I had nightmares almost every night.

"I'm sure Atticus told you about the scars on my body the day we were in the baths together, so you know I used to cut myself. Jesus set me free from horrible torment, and now.... now..... *everything* is different."

She had been looking down at the ground while she was speaking, unaware of the soldier's reaction to her words. Upon speaking her last word, she looked up, half-expecting him to have walked away, or at the very least, be eyeing her as though she were half-crazy.

But Titus' response was different than she anticipated. He was smiling.

"I'm so glad to hear it, Mary," he said.

"What do you mean?" she asked. The look in his eye intrigued her.

"Over the past three years, I had many opportunities to observe Jesus, *and* his leaders. I don't believe he was a subversive, or even had a *desire* to become a king. After listening to him teach, and watching him do miracles, I think he was something greater; something more."

"I know that as well, Titus," she responded. "I don't understand all that happened today."

"Neither do I," he said. "Something must have gone terribly wrong. Even the Roman gods don't operate this way. I've had a few dreams of my own lately, telling me to walk away from the Greek and Roman way of thinking. I think there must be a better path."

"I believe in one God, now too," Mary answered. "Since Jesus died today, I don't know what to believe. I think he might have been a sign of someone greater who is still to come, or, at the very least, he was a prophet."

"Well, I'm glad to see you again," Titus finished. "I just wondered why you were here. Perhaps we will have a chance to talk more soon. I will be here guarding the tomb with the others, until we are relieved from duty by Pilate's order." Then he turned and walked back to the other side of the garden, to join the guard assigned to the tomb.

Hearing the conversation, Salome had been surprised to realize Magdalene actually had been friends with a Roman soldier. Now, thinking about it; she had been aware of Mary's reputation before joining the circle of those who followed Jesus.

It must be difficult for her, she considered.

It was another hour before Zebedee and John stood up, making a move to leave Joseph's home. After burning the leftover Seder meal in the fire, they had made sure the guards were aware of the location of the well, and had enough oil for their torches. Then, coming inside, it became a group effort to clear away the food preparations and wash the dishes. Cleophas' step-daughter, "little" Mary, decided to leave with Zebedee, Salome and John. The foursome took a small oil lamp, and began walking toward the fisherman's family business home on the other side of Jerusalem.

They walked several hundred yards together, and arrived at an intersection. Zebedee handed the small oil lamp to his son, John. "Tell James good night for us," he said. "And let the rest know we are here in the city."

John nodded. He put his arm around his mother and gave her a hug, kissing her on the forehead. "Good night, mother," he said. "Thank you for all you did today."

"I was glad I could help," was Salome's answer. "It felt good to be able to do something. And I knew Mary and Magdalene couldn't help to prepare the food because they had touched his body today. They were ceremonially unclean."

"It was a wonderful meal, wife," Zebedee encouraged her. "Let's go to the office apartment."

Parting ways, John headed toward the home where his brother, James, and the rest of Jesus' leaders had been hiding since the night of the arrest. The homeowner was a Roman business owner, an architect named Ampliatus. He had become a follower of Jesus over the past year, and opened his home several times when the group had been in the city. His teenage son, John Marcus, had tagged along on many of the team's journeys over the past couple of years.

Coincidentally, his wife Maria was an aunt to his father, Zebedee, although the families had never spent much time together.

Arriving at Ampliatus' home, John noticed lamp lights burning on the rooftop. Mounting the outside steps, he went up to the shielded arbor to see who was still awake.

"Hi, John," his brother, James spoke in greeting. "How was your Seder meal?"

"It was really good," John answered. "We ate with the two Roman guard companies, and one Temple guard company. His body is in Joseph of Arimathea's garden tomb, sealed with the Sacred Great Eagle Seal of Rome.

"We heard he went to Pilate and asked for permission for the body," someone else added.

"Tell us about the day," another man requested. "None of us can sleep."

"Did you see the moon?" someone interjected.

"Come and sit with us," said a fourth. "All through the meal tonight, I kept remembering how he fed us last night."

"How was *your* Seder meal?" John wanted to know.

"Maria is a wonderful cook." "It was great." "Unbelievable." A chorus of answers were heard in reply.

Joining the men with whom he had travelled for the past three years, John took a cushion, and joined in the conversation. Counting himself, there were ten present in all. Two of the twelve were missing.

One was in the street outside, stumbling towards the lights on the rooftop. He was alone and frightened. He had thought he knew his path, but now was unsure of his steps forward. He had not feasted. He had watched the day's events unaccompanied and troubled. He had wept bitterly all day, sitting alone in a cave just outside the city.

Angrily, he had torn his clothing, wishing to rip his actions and words from his being.

When would he learn to stand his ground, he asked himself, beating his hand into his fist? Looking at the lights up on the rooftop, he stopped. He had intended to make his way into the house, and explain to his wife where he had been all day. But standing in the street, he realized he wasn't ready to see anyone he knew just yet. So, he trudged on by, passing Ampliatus' home.

Back into the darkness.

The second was also unaware of many of the day's events. Concerned for him, each of the others wondered where he had gone after they had all fled from the Garden.

Had he been arrested as well?

Was he dead too?

They were unaware of Judah's vow, and its intended purpose.

The betrayer was on his way from Qumran.

As everyone departed from Joseph of Arimathea's home, Mary and the Magdalene retreated into the house from the courtyard. They would not be spending time in the garden again they decided, until the soldiers were gone. In the master bedroom, the two friends prepared themselves for sleep.

For each woman, it seemed they fell asleep as soon as coverlets were pulled into place.

April 4, 33 CE (Passover)
6 – Interval

In Edessa, King Abgar of Osroene pressed his royal seal into the melted wax, sealing the scroll he had just completed. Even small tasks like correspondence were proving to take too much of his energy these days.

Seeking to relieve the tension he felt from working on the letter, he rotated his shoulders and sighed. The pain in his eyes was increasing these days. Had he always been so sensitive to the light? He couldn't remember.

The disease had come upon him so slowly.

How much worse could it become, he wondered?

The birthday celebration his wife, Helene, had organized on his behalf the night before, had been one of the high points in his life. He knew she had been trying to lift his spirits, and in truth, she had succeeded.

The young queen had given orders. All his favorite foods were prepared. There had been music, dancers, jugglers and acrobats. There had even been *pollo*, his favorite daily cold drink, made with lemons and honey.

He closed his eyes, trying to taste the *baklava*, and other pastries which had been served. He had eaten until he stuffed himself.

Suddenly, a wave of despair overtook him.

He wanted to be alone now, he realized. What if Helene had sensed this would be his last birthday?

The king motioned for his personal slave to close the shutters, to diminish the bright sunlight streaming through the windows. "I want to sleep now, Hakim. There is no need for you to stay with me." He handed the man the scroll. "Give this to the queen, please, and tell her to dispatch the emissary to return to Israel; today if possible."

Hakim nodded and took the document. "At once, my lord. Do you want to dismiss those who are waiting to see you in the throne room?"

Abgar appraised the slave as he replied. "No. Feed them. Entertain them, and ask them to wait. Say I am sorry, but I have been detained with another matter. Wake me in an hour."

The slave saluted his master with his right hand closed to a fist, tapping the left of his chest twice. "As you say, it shall be done." And then he was gone.

129

As his eyes relaxed, the young ruler sank down into the pillows. If he could sleep for just an hour, he might regain his strength. Could he dare to even hope for healing? It would take at least six weeks for a caravan to reach Israel. Then the envoy would have to *find* the prophet, and convince him to travel to Edessa. That would be another six weeks. The man would have to agree to come to him.

He was too weak to travel anywhere now.

Abgar hoped he would live long enough to at least *meet* the man.

Well, it was too far away to consider even putting out any hope just yet.

The royal physicians had delivered grave news just this morning. His body was apparently beginning to enter the final stages of the disease. The disfigurement of his facial muscles was now becoming a concern in the minds of his ministers.

How long before someone tried to oust him, he wondered?

He would not discuss his fears with the queen.

His Helene. How he missed her.

Punching down his head cushion, he tried to find a comfortable position.

He sighed. He had had such hopes for his little kingdom. He would never know now, he reasoned. Surely the three gods had conspired against him. He had always wondered about the beliefs of his fathers. *Shamayim*, the lord of the heavens, ruled as the supreme deity over everything. Since the days of his earliest memories, he remembered his mother's strict adherence to the worship of this god. In fact, whenever his mother had seen an eagle, or a lightning bolt, she had touched her forehead, then her chest, and said his name.

Upon occasion, Abgar had heard the astrologers and diviners refer to the same god as the *Baalshamen*, on the days when sacrifices were offered. He had never understood why, if the Baalshamen was so benevolent, as these wise men taught, why were fertility sacrifices to the moon god, *Ablibol*, and the sun god, *Malakbel*, still necessary?

It didn't make sense to him, he realized. No matter what the people offered, and no matter how faithfully they sacrificed, the great scorching winds still came. The droughts still happened. Babies still died.

Last night, the Royal Diviners' presentation of offerings to the gods for his birthday had troubled him. He wished he could discuss it with Helene.

But then, he didn't want to add to her stresses, he decided.

He knew she was dealing with fears of her own just now.

Seeking to ignore the painful spasms in his shoulders, Abgar tried to focus on the wording of the letter he had just constructed. How would the prophet respond?

"From Abgar to Jesus, the Good Physician who has appeared in the country of Jerusalem, greeting:

I have heard of you, and the healings; that you make no medicines, and use no roots. I am told that you open the eyes of the blind, and make the lame man walk again. I am told you cleanse lepers, and make the deaf able to hear. That by your word you raise the dead to life again, and have power over lunatic demons.

"Learning the wonders you have done, it has been born within me that you must either have come down from heaven, or be a son of God. I pray you will come to my house and heal me.

"I am a leper, and I am a king. I possess but one small province, but it is beautiful, and large enough for us both to live in peace."

In another palace, some three hundred miles south, a woman gazed at the ceiling from her bed. She wasn't used to rising late. Usually, she stirred when Pontius would get out of bed just before sunrise.

Each morning, her husband's man-servant awakened him just prior to dawn, bringing in two enormous, steaming, glass cups full of *mulsum*, the couple's favorite mixture of boiled wine and honey. Each oversized breakfast cup was called a *scyphus*. Each side had a round finger-handle, with thumb rests on the rim above the handles. When it was cold outside, Claudia loved to put her hands around the outside of the cup, warming the palms of her hands on both of its sides.

On spring days, she tried to sleep as long as possible, allowing the steward to put her mug on a nearby table to cool. Then, while Pontius dressed for the day, she would sit up in bed, drinking the warm drink.

Then she and Pontius would greet each other, talking a little, beginning the day.

But this morning was different.

Apparently, her husband's man-servant had not come to their room this morning. There were no steaming mugs of anything.... Anywhere in the apartment. The other side of the bed was empty. Her husband was not there.

Strangely, this end of the palace was quiet. More quiet than usual.

Standing up, Claudia wrapped herself in a sheet from the bed, and moved into the other rooms of the family apartment.

Where could he be?

A few moments later, she stood in the gardens, at the foot of a great stone chaise. From her vantage point, she could see several of the servants peeking through the windows, watching her.

In front of her, sound asleep and snoring loudly, was Pontius Pilate, her husband.

He must have been awake most of the night, she reasoned.

Smiling and shaking her head, she tiptoed away to find their son, and then acquire her first morning scyphus of mulsum.

She would not be able to face the day without it, she decided.

It was still somewhat early when a Roman military wagon appeared at the gate at Joseph of Arimathea's home in Jerusalem. The two centurions leading the tomb watch, Justus Flavius and Antonio Longinus had divided the watches into four; with each watch comprising six hours, to be completed by groups of five.

The group taking the fourth watch had been relieved at the first hour (6am), by the men responsible for the first watch. Now, in the middle of the fourth hour (10am), Justus Flavius noted the fourth watch had found a quiet corner in the garden to sleep for a few hours.

The guards from the Jewish Temple had divided themselves into groups of three, also rotating the watch every six hours.

The arrival of the food wagon from the Jerusalem garrison was met with an enthusiastic shout of greeting, and subsequent boisterous conversation. Justus Flavius was amazed his men weren't waking.

They must really have needed the sleep after yesterday's events, he surmised.

Inside the house, Magdalene was startled awake by the loud exchanges taking place just outside her shuttered window. Looking around the room, she saw the older Mary dozing in what appeared to be an uncomfortable position.

"Her neck will feel a pinch when she wakes, if she stays asleep like that," Magdalene considered. Quietly, she moved to where her friend was sleeping, and helped to shift the woman's position. Then, she covered the older woman up, hoping it might help her to sleep a little longer.

Dressing quickly, Magdalene went to the courtyard to see what the excitement had been.

"Good morning, Mary," Titus called.

"Good morning," she replied. "Did you sleep well?"

Chuckling, the foot-soldier replied. "Does anyone sleep well in all of this armor? No, I think not."

"Sorry, Titus," she said. "What's all the excitement?"

"Oh, it's just the food wagon from the garrison. I can't imagine any of the men being hungry after all the grub last night. I know I won't be able to eat much today."

Mary laughed. "That's good to know. I didn't eat much, but I'm still not too hungry."

Several of the men were unloading baskets from the wagon, creating a designated central space for foodstuffs to be stored and made available to the men.

As she observed the movements of the soldiers, she was unaware of a man approaching from the gate on foot. She did not see him until he spoke to her. The sound of his voice caused her to visibly jump.

"Excuse me," he said.

Mary put her hand to her chest, and took a sudden inward gasp. "Oh!" she cried.

"I'm sorry," he offered. "I thought you had seen me. I didn't mean to frighten you."

"It's quite all right," she answered. "How can I help you?"

"Are you Magdalene?" he asked. "Salome and Zebedee sent me here to find my wife."

Mary noticed that Titus had silently stepped a little closer to her, as though protecting her. His hand was on the hilt of his sword. She smiled.

"You are Cleophas, aren't you?" she asked. "I don't think we've met. I'm Mary from Bethany, and I lived for a time in Magdala; some call me Magdalene."

"My wife has mentioned you. It's good to finally meet you, Mary," he said. "Is my wife here? Is she all right?"

Mary nodded. "She is still resting this morning. Everyone was here until late last night. Then the watch was set up at the tomb over there. The light from the soldiers' torches lit the entire back of the house. So, it lit the chamber where

133

we slept as well. Pontius Pilate ordered a round the clock watch on Jesus' tomb until further notice." She paused.

"So he is buried here, in this garden?" Cleophas asked. "Why did they put a watch on the tomb?"

It was Titus who provided the answer to these questions. "It seems there are some issues between the High Priest and the Prefect. After Pilate posted the Roman watch, the Jewish High Priest, Caiaphas, posted an additional one with his own men, just to be sure the body wouldn't be stolen. He said false claims of resurrection might be circulated by his followers. His body is buried there."

He indicated with a head nod the location of the tomb a few yards away.

"Your wife's uncle, the Nobilus Decurio, requested his body from Pilate, and it was given to him. He dressed and buried the body."

Cleophas was shocked. "Joseph did? I will have to thank him." He looked at Mary. "Did Mary sleep at all?"

Magdalene responded kindly. "I'm sorry, I don't really know," she answered. "I fell asleep the moment I lay down. Hopefully she did as well. She had a hard day yesterday. She told me you were in Syria on business. When did you get back?"

"Just this morning," came the answer. "I had a client there who needed wood carvings added to a room. It is impossible to do the carving and installation without exact measurements. So, I regret that I must travel so often. My son, Simon, and I rode all night when the message reached us. I feel so badly I wasn't here."

"Why don't you go in and wake her?" she offered. "I know she will be so glad to see you."

"Are you sure?" he asked. "We missed seeing a client at another village on the way back, so we will have to leave again at dawn tomorrow. It was bad enough we missed the feast. I just had to get here."

"Cleophas, it's fine. Go on in," she assured him. "I know it will help her."

"Thank you, Mary." He looked at the soldier. "Titus." He turned and walked quietly into the house.

It was time to comfort his wife in the loss of her son.

Across the city, Zebedee and Salome were sitting with their sons and nephews in their own family office courtyard. Looking around, Salome realized how deeply connected she felt to the people sitting here. She looked at her younger son, James. What would *she* feel had she been in her sister's position?

It had been kind of their uncle to invite them to his home. She couldn't believe he had been arrested.

How could it have happened?

Why would the High Priest *imprison* him for wanting to take care of a *family* member?

She had always believed her Uncle Joseph to be untouchable due to his position with Rome.

She looked up at the arbor Zebedee had built and planted with grapevines so many years ago. "We will want some shade when we are in the city for the feasts, or when one of the boys is here on business," he had told her. He had been so right, she considered. They had spent many happy hours in this courtyard.

They had planted the grapevines to fill in the arbor when the boys had been small. She remembered that year well. That had been the year of Governor Quinirius' second census; the year of the uprising. Zebedee's younger brother, Joses, had been one of the thousands of young men rounded up and taken to Rome. She had been at home the day his first letter had come from Cyprus. He had found a young Jewish woman in his exile, from a reputable family, and had married her.

Zebedee had been so relieved to know he was alive.

Why did Rome have to divide families, she wondered?

Her Uncle Joseph's home was situated closer to the Temple than Zebedee's office apartment. While her uncles' was located in the upper-class residential district, their commercial office for the family fishing trade was in the business district of Jerusalem. The front of their house had a small receiving court, where customers could purchase fresh, salted and dried fish. Just inside the front door was another receiving room, where group clients could discuss contracts and trade. In the back of the building were several additional rooms. These rooms, Zebedee and Salome had chosen to utilize as living areas.

The courtyard with its stone water well, where everyone was seated now, had been built as an outdoor enclosure with tall rock walls. In earlier years, the couple had planted hibiscus bushes, fig trees, and other smaller, flowering plants in the corners. The color of the blooms brightened up the sandstone shades and plaster walls.

Against the wall, Salome had dug a twelve-inch wide length of soil for a vegetable garden. Every year, she planted cucumber vines, onions, garlic and herbs. There was nothing like cooking with fresh ingredients, she considered. Even away from home.

Next to the well was one lone date tree.

Molded into one side of the courtyard's walls, was an outdoor fire-pit, with a roasting rack and clay oven.

Usually, it was a wonderful place to retreat from the world, she considered. But not this week.

She looked once more around the family circle gathered here. She sat next to Zebedee on a stone bench. Their sons, James and John, were seated across from her. They had grown into such fine, strong men. She felt fortunate to still be married to her first husband, and to have sons living at home.

Not many women from Galilee could say such a thing.

Mary's sons, from her first marriage to Joseph of Nazareth were sitting on the floor nearby. She and Joseph had had three additional boys after Jesus was born: Little Joseph, Jacob (called "James"), and Judah.

The boys had chosen to stay in the office apartment during the feast, for fear of being rounded up by those who had arrested their half-brother, Jesus. She was thankful Cleophas' youngest daughter, Keshet, had been willing to stay and help prepare the food to feed them all. She could not have left her sister, Mary, alone during any of the day's events, she considered.

It was strange, she thought. They had both named their sons with names beginning with the same letter. Since Joseph and Mary's son, "James," was younger than her and Zebedee's son James, the family referred to Zebedee and Salome's son as "Big James," and Joseph and Mary's son as "Little James." Always focused on fairness and justice, he would become known later in his life, as "James the Just."

Zebedee's son would be known as "James the Greater."

When Joseph died, Cleophas had become Mary's second husband. His oldest son, Levi, had not been seen for a couple of days. Simon, his second son, had arrived from Syria with his father a few hours before. His sisters, "Little Mary" and Keshet were in the middle of a quietly whispered conversation in the corner under the fig tree.

Salome looked at her husband. "Was Cleophas going to bring Mary back here?" she asked.

He reached for her hand. "I don't know. He was very concerned she be cared for."

Simon spoke. "What happened? When we left for Syria a month ago, Jesus was in Perea, doing miracles, and making food multiply from nothing. How did he end up being crucified?"

Those in the circle looked at one another. Who wanted to tell the story, they wondered? Would anyone be able to get through the story without breaking down?

Finally, it was Zebedee's oldest son, John, who spoke first. As he continued, others in the circle interjected their experiences as well, until everyone was involved in helping Simon feel once again a part of the group.

"When Pain is shared; Pain is divided."

No one remembered where the statement originated, but at this moment, Salome considered, they each understood it to be true.

Joseph Caiaphas had been so thrilled with the events of the night before, he had asked the young priest, Saul, to return that morning. Would the young man be interested in attending Sabbath synagogue classes with his family on Passover morning?

Caiaphas walked with Saul on the way back to the palace.

As they approached the gate, the High Priest motioned for Saul to slow down their gait a little. "So, Saul," he began, "what is it you wanted to discuss with me?"

Saul had anticipated speaking with Shira's father at some point today. He felt more prepared today than he had yesterday. Perhaps it had been the deep darkness, or the death of the Galilean. Honestly, it could have been any number of things taking place the day before. It didn't matter.

The guilt he felt over a conversation shared the night before had certainly played into things, he determined.

The prior evening, his mentor, Gamaliel the Pharisee, had stopped by the room where Saul lived. It was his custom to invite Saul to his own family home for the Passover Feast each year. Saul had attended every year for more than twenty years.

"A lot happened today," his mentor said. "I wanted to let you know. As usual, Passover Shabbat will begin at our home at sundown. You are welcome to come early, and spend time with Simeon and the rest of the family."

Saul had flushed and felt immediately uncomfortable. Haltingly, he let Gamaliel know he had been invited to the High Priest's home for dinner.

The older man's eyebrows had gone up. "Are you still considering marrying his daughter, Shira?" he inquired.

"Yes," Saul answered, a little embarrassed. "I can't get her out of my mind."

"You are smitten, my boy," his mentor noted with a wry smile. "Just remember, Caiaphas is not a Pharisee. He does not believe he has to adhere to anything outside of the books of Moses, and only they should be obeyed when a person is inside the Temple. He does not believe there is a spiritual realm. He believes in saving the national identity, but not the spiritual identity."

Curious, Saul had pursued the matter. "What do you mean, sir?"

Gamaliel had answered straightforwardly. "For one thing, he secretly likes the Romans, even though he pretends he hates them. He descends from aristocrats, and yearns for the luxuries of unquestioned authority. He is all about power. Once you marry into his family, you will become just like him. Your concerns will become political, rather than centering around spiritual life and personal development."

His words had replayed in Saul's mind throughout the entire dinner the night before. Fears of losing his grip on spiritual truths he had been taught since childhood robbed him of his sleep. At one point, in the middle of the night, he had risen to look out the window of his room.

The sight of the blood-red moon had prevented him from sleeping at all for the rest of the night. The remainder of the night, he had rehearsed what he would say to prove to Joseph Caiaphas he was a trustworthy candidate to marry Shira, his daughter.

How long did the betrothal need to be in the High Priest's mind? How much would come with her for housekeeping, and how much would he need to plan to purchase? The young man tried to work these and other questions which presented themselves, until long after the sun rose.

Now, he was having the conversation he had hoped for. The High Priest was speaking.

"Whom were you named for, Saul?" the man asked.

"My father named me for King Saul, sir. Like his family, mine is also from the tribe of Benjamin."

"Hmm," replied Caiaphas, looking intently at the young man. "One of the lost tribes. How far can your father trace your lineage?"

"Back to Moses, sir. He taught me the Law and the Prophets himself. He is the synagogue ruler in Tarsus."

"How did your family come to Tarsus?" Joseph asked.

"My father made the decision to remove us from the town of Gascalis just after the first Roman census by Governor Quinirius. He became further concerned for the safety of our family after news of King Herod's massacre of the infants in Bethlehem during the second census."

"So how did you come to Jerusalem?"

Saul smiled. "By boat." Seeing his host was not amused, he coughed and gave a more serious answer. "Uh, I was sent to the Hillel Boys' School when I was eight, sir."

Caiaphas nodded. Gamaliel's family school for boys was world renowned for developing young men for positions of leadership in their adulthood. The ten-year school was separated from the Temple's University in Jerusalem, which drew sons of wealthy Jewish families from all of the civilized world. Gamaliel's family directed the theology wing of that school as well. Without exception, all priests in the Sanhedrin had graduated from that school with their *semichah*, or ordination.

Caiaphas was aware Saul had attended the Temple's University as well.

Looking at the young man, the High Priest sensed an inner neediness in the young man. This sense of abandonment, he realized, meant Saul would be a prime candidate for recruitment into his own following. He decided to pursue this opportunity, and see whether the young priest could be swayed from his teachings.

"Have you seen much of your family?"

Saul's looked down at the ground. "I see them if they come to Jerusalem for the feasts. I have had the opportunity to travel home twice in the past twenty-years."

"Did a family adopt you when you were sent here?" the High Priest.

Saul looked directly into the High Priest's eyes. "I have been a part of Gamaliel's family these twenty-two years, sir."

Joseph returned his gaze. "Saul, I will be honest with you. I like you. I really do. I think you have a bright mind, and a willing heart. I sense you are forwardly motivated, and would take good care of my daughter."

Saul blushed. "Thank you, sir."

Caiaphas raised a finger. "*However.....* However, I have concerns about the training you have received from the Hillel School. To be sure, there is no finer school in this end of the civilized world, for teaching reading, history and mathematics. You probably understand the history of the world much better than I do."

"I'm not sure that's true," Saul began.

"No, no, now," Caiaphas continued. "That being said, I have concerns about your future. The inflexibilities of our political position as a nation have cost us over and over again as a people. And, while I agree we must honor the Law and the Prophets, we must also learn to work with these people, or our nation will die."

"But sir," the younger priest interjected, "I thought you were working with the nationalists at Qumran."

Caiaphas was surprised. "You have unexpected depth, young man," he exclaimed. "How do you know this?"

"I have just made it my business to listen and learn all I can, sir," came the reply. "Whenever I have noticed you taking interest in something, I have tried to follow your example, in order to understand. I am sure you have good reasons for everything you do."

Caiaphas assessed him. He was silent for a moment or two, and then he nodded. "I understand you are a Roman citizen, as well as a Jewish priest?"

Saul nodded. "Yes, sir."

"That is a valuable asset to be in possession of in the cause."

"Sir?"

"I can see how God has put all the right pieces together for you to become a nationalist hero."

Saul beamed with appreciation of the positive attention. "Thank you, sir."

"All right then, Saul," Caiaphas answered. "I will give you an answer."

"Yes, sir?"

"I realize you already have received your ordination, or *semichah,* but you are still studying under a mentor. If you will transfer your mentorship to myself, and consider the party of the Sadducees as your loyalty, I will consider you as a suitor to my Shira."

Delighted, Saul answered. "Thank you, sir! Is there anything else you require?"

Caiaphas paused. "We can discuss the business end of things later, son. Let's go in and eat. Say nothing for now. I will let you know when you may approach her. As far as I'm concerned, you are betrothed. We can mark today as the beginning of the year."

Saul could not stop himself from smiling.

He was elated.

This was turning out to be a pretty good day after all.

Late in the afternoon, Ampialitus and Maria sat with the circle of guests who had arrived one at a time late Thursday evening. At first, Rhoda, one of the house slaves, had not known exactly what to do when followers of Jesus began coming to the door like refugees.

Ampialitus arrived home in the middle of the night on Thursday. He had been surprised to find all of the guest rooms and living areas filled with sleeping visitors. Where had they all come from, he wondered?

Had Maria invited them *all*?

Tiptoeing through the house, he made his way to the bedchamber he shared with his wife. He was startled to find her sitting up in the bed, searching through a scroll of the prophet Isaiah, by lamplight.

"Why are you still up?" he queried, entering the room.

"I just had to look up something Jesus' mother said to me today," she answered distractedly.

"Why right now? Aren't you tired?" he wanted to know.

She had looked up at him. "Do you *know* what has happened tonight?"

"No," he answered. "I rushed to get to Jerusalem so I wouldn't be traveling on the Sabbath tomorrow. I didn't want to be caught in the crowds for the execution and then the sacrifices tomorrow."

"How did your meeting go?" she asked. "Did they like your designs?"

Ampliatus smiled. "They did. I have been asked to oversee the construction. I have to return to Antioch next month to begin."

Maria beamed at her husband. "I knew they would." Her husband was an architect. A very good architect, she considered. He had designed many of the government buildings, and columned town squares in the Roman-styled cities springing up all over the region.

Remembering her prior thought, she commented. "They arrested Jesus tonight."

Ampliatus had stared at her. "They did what? Who did? Why?"

Maria put up her hands in surrender. "Caiaphas took Temple Guards to the Garden of Gethsemane where he was praying. It seems Judah Iscariot made a deal to broker him to the High Priest. He was taken to Caiaphas' palace to be held over for trial."

Ampliatus sank down onto the bed next to her.

He was silent for some time. "Oh," was all he could say.

"I can't find the section she was talking about." Maria had rolled up the scroll, and tossed it to the floor. She looked at her husband. "I'm so glad you're home. I'm so tired. Are you ready to get some sleep?"

Ampliatus had pulled off his sandals, allowing Rhoda to wash his feet. "Yes, very ready," he had said. "It was a long day."

They had talked long into the night, finally drifting off.

Now lost in silent reminiscing, Maria ignored the conversations taking place around her. It was all too much to think about just now, she decided.

Thankful to have her husband home after such a long period, Maria put her arms through her husband's, and rested her head on his shoulder.

She would focus on the family.

She regarded their teenage son, John Marcus, sitting next to her. He had been out late yesterday, she considered. He had left that afternoon to try to find Jesus. He had been the first one to come through the door with news of Jesus' arrest.

She had been worried last night, trying to wait up for him. Her friends, Elsbeth and Tahlia, had stayed up with her.

So much had happened the past few days. She was ready for sleep now, too. She looked around the rooftop courtyard. Philip, with his wife, Tahlia, and four daughters; Andrew and Eleanor with their eight children; one of the twelve who was a single man, Simon. A proclaimed patriot, he had followed Jesus from the sect of the Zealots. Come to think of it, most of these had come to the house as refugees on Thursday around midnight.

Although.....not everyone was a refugee, she reasoned.

The last time they had all been together had been when Jesus was in Jerusalem a few months back. Ampliatus invited Philip, Andrew, and Simon Peter to bring their families for Passover; to come a little early for the week's festivities on Monday. That way the families could spend some time together for the feast.

Looking around the rooftop, she noted Elsbeth and the children were here, but no one had seen her Simon since Thursday night after the supper with Jesus.

Maria had expressed concern that he might have been arrested.

He had completely missed the Passover.

Nor did anyone seem to know where Thomas was. Phillip had told Ampliatus of a conversation he had experienced with the man. It seemed Jesus had told all of them he would be crucified in Jerusalem.

If God had shown Jesus such a thing, why would he come to the city anyway, she wondered? At the time, Phillip had assumed the prophet was just showing a pessimistic side.

Thomas had replied with loyalty. "Let's go with him so we can die as well."

But now? Where had Thomas gone? Was he still in the city?

Nathaniel was also missing. Were they all together, she wondered?

In the master bedchamber of Joseph of Arimathea's Jerusalem home, Cleophas sat on the edge of the bed, stroking his wife's hair. The tears had stilled for now. The grief seemed to come in waves. Both of them had been shaken by the execution.

Even though her boy had *known*.

It was hard to understand.

"Do you want to go with me in the morning, Mary?" Cleophas asked. "I can rent a wagon, or even a couple of horses. Simon would be glad to stay behind."

Mary rolled over onto her back so she could look at him. "I don't think I'm ready to go anywhere, my love," she answered. "I've been very tired the last couple of days. I could stay here and just get some sleep. We have to go back to Galilee sometime."

"Are you sure?" he wanted to know.

"I think so," she nodded. She reached up and grabbed his hand.

Cleophas laid back down, spooning in behind her. He put his arms around her, and whispered into her ear. "I can always cancel tomorrow's appointment, if you want me to," he offered. "If you need me, I can stay. Do you want to go over to Zebedee and Salome's? I'm not sure I like the idea of you being alone."

"I know, Cleophas," his wife responded. "I do want to go over there; but I don't. I don't really want to go to Salome's. It's strange. I just feel numb all over. I don't think I'm ready to go anywhere. It's fine, really. I think Magdalene will stay with me."

There was silence for a few moments.

"Besides," she added. "We really need the money right now to repair the roof."

"Oh, yes," sighed Cleophas. "There is that. The roof. All right. Simon and I will leave in the morning."

In Briton, King Arviragus had been resting all day. The Seleurian ruler, by many referred to as the "Black Bull," had not felt like himself for two days now.

Strange, he thought. Hadn't he struggled with the same physical symptoms as these last year, immediately following the Feast of Shrovetide? And hadn't he felt like this more and more frequently in the last two years?

The continual, painful pounding of an invisible hammer had resonated within his head from the time he had awakened that morning. He had eaten too much again, probably, he reasoned at first.

Or perhaps swallowed too much mead. He purposely never drank that much alcohol, he considered. It must be a hangover. That was all.

The delicacies served had been beyond anyone's ability to decline.

His stomach hurt, and all through the night, it had seemed impossible to return to his bed from the privy pot.

No, this was not drunkenness, nor its morning aftermath, he decided. The lethargy was less than it had been on prior occasions. The confusion was not as intense. His mind was clear, but not as clear as on his better days.

He had felt for some time some sort of sabotage or conspiracy had been plotted against him. He had reacted with these same symptoms after the *Day of Brighid* festivals, during *Imholc,* the February Fire Festival.

Why hadn't these symptoms appeared at other times, he wondered?

Why did he feel this way only after the Druid leaders had prepared his foods? Was this the same illness affecting his wife, he wondered?

Laying on his bed, he decided to begin a quiet investigation. He would send for David, his overseer.

Had others been ill today as well? Had one of the meats been undercooked? Had one of the raw dishes become too warm, perhaps?

He remembered the stories of those who had lived centuries ago. His people had at one time eaten fish, but not now. So many had fallen sick, they had ceased their consumption of seafood.

Now, only those who could afford an oven built of stone were able to cook fish properly. Instead, his people had become shepherds of sheep and goats. They raised, herded and ate cattle. They drank cow's milk, and made cheeses. And, more than anything, they loved pork. The drippings from the fatty meat seasoned many of the dishes they ate.

Perhaps it had been the pork, he considered.

His overseer wouldn't eat pork, or even touch a pig, for that matter.

In fact, he had observed David at the feast. The man had not eaten the ShroveTide foods. Nor had he been present after the first few moments.

He had explained the Feast day of his own religion, and had asked for permission to commemorate it. The king had heartily given his approval. "After all," he had told the man, "if I wasn't king, I'm not sure even I would attend the ShroveTide Feast. Besides, you have been putting in extra time. You need the time off."

Truthfully, Arviragus had not expected him to stay. He extended David the privilege of choosing to avoid the Druid feast days. Why should he be forced to attend their feasts, the king considered? The man did not worship their gods, nor did he live according to their customs.

He was a Roman representative, and had brought great increase to their profits, and organization to their settlements. The man deserved much more than he asked for. Arviragus respected him.

Were he not a king, he might have pursued David for a friendship.

And he had never seen anyone so consistently healthy.

The king decided to make David his overseer *and* his investigator.

David could be trusted.

And, at this very moment, King Arviragus was not sure he could trust anyone else completely.

In the basement of Joseph Caiaphas' palace, a tired and sore prisoner with a broken ankle was nursing fresh cuts and bruises. He had now been beaten with rods by one of the guards assigned by Caiaphas. He looked around the cell for a cloth and some water.

Nothing.

The temporary comforts provided by the guards the night before had been confiscated as soon as the High Priest had come to his cell. Just after the midday Sabbath meal, the man had come to the observation gallery with Saul, the young Pharisee from Tarsus.

"You are going to be executed, Joseph," the High Priest had gloated from his perch. "You are a traitor, and a subversive."

Saul had expressed surprise. "This man, sir? What did he do?"

Caiaphas gave him a warning glare. "Be careful, Saul. This man is not who he appears to be. He is not *just* a member of our Sanhedrin. No, he is much more important than *that*."

"Sir?"

"He is the *Nobilus Decurio* of Rome! He is a friend to rulers and kings. Because he feels he is so far above us, he does not think the Law we all live by relates to him. No Saul, *he* is an exception. And he is dangerous.

"He went behind my back, and requested the body of the criminal, Jesus. You remember, the man who called himself the King of the Jews. He even gave the man a royal burial, as well as a procession through the center of the city. In fact, Pontius Pilate provided him with Roman escort."

He looked at Saul. "What do you think we should do with him? It seems he has had a secret friendship with the Roman Prefect. It is quite possible he has been conspiring against us."

"I don't know, sir. What has the Council decided?" the young man inquired.

"Bah!" the High Priest scoffed. "We don't need the Council. Eventually we will, yes, but understand this, Saul. Any threat against the national identity of Judea must be defended. Our way of life must be preserved. Men like this are at the bottom of every conspiracy designed to destroy us."

"What does that mean, sir?" Saul asked.

"It means, my boy," came the reply, "that we must destroy *them* before they destroy *us*."

The two men had left the observation area, laughing and talking.

Coughing, shivering and in great pain, Joseph of Arimathea huddled into the corner of the stone ledge. Weary beyond words, he wondered why sleep eluded him. Pulling his knees up in front of himself, he leaned against the wall etched with an image in blood.

At the end of his resources, he finally dozed off.

He was sure Joseph Caiaphas would see to it he was executed when the sun rose again.

It was after midnight when Simon Peter plodded his way back to the home of Ampliatus and Maria; where his wife and children were staying. As he approached the front door, he hoped it would be unlocked. Quietly, he turned the handle, and entered.

Making his way slowly through the house, he looked for the room he remembered being assigned to Elsbeth and himself just days prior. Almost without noise, the man entered the room.

Aware of his need for a bath, Simon Peter stayed in his clothing. He lay down at the foot of Elsbeth's sleeping pallet, and fell fast asleep.

April 5, 33 CE

7 – Transition

It was still at least an hour until dawn.

In the business district of Jerusalem, Salome was up, working by lamplight; pulling foodstuffs from her apartment store-room. Cleophas and his son, Simon, were gathering the items needed for their journey. Walking to the outside, she gathered two water-skins, and filled them with water from the family well.

She had been up early, wrapping cooked meat and rice in grape leaves. Such treats had always been her own family's favorite finger foods. They were also an easy method of using up little bits of leftovers. Then, packing a satchel with small barley loaves, dried meats, and fruit, she readied the supplies by the door. Cleophas and Simon approached a few moments later.

"We will be back in three days' time," Cleophas whispered. "If Mary should need me before then, or if something happens, I will pay for the courier. Don't wait. I'm still not sure I should go. But she insisted I keep this commitment. Something about fixing the roof." He looked at Salome in the eyes. "You know I've always said family must come before business."

"Don't worry, Cleophas. We will take care of her," Salome assured him. "I know my sister. She needs the sleep. And she's right; that roof does need repair. I've seen it."

The two of them laughed.

"I suppose," Cleophas answered. "And, the more normal we keep things, the better she will feel."

The two men loaded their shoulders with a satchel of papyrus building plans, a food satchel, water-skins, and sleeping pallets. They headed out the small house's front court into the street, beginning their journey to the city of Emmaus-Nicopolis some eighteen miles to the west.

It was named for the famous hot mineral springs which drew masses from all over the region.

The stars would light their way for the next hour or so. Then, the mounting sun would provide the light they needed. It was a full day's journey. Leaving this early in the morning would enable the two men to find food and lodging in town before nightfall.

As they exited the city, Cleophas noticed others on the road with them.

Why were so many traveling today, and this early too, he considered?

Then he remembered.

It was the Day of First Fruits.

These were those citizens of Jerusalem who followed the High Priest, Joseph Caiaphas, in the convictions of the Sadducees. Today was the first day of the week after Passover, marking yet another festival day in the week.

Today, before the sun rose, hundreds of people were heading toward the Valley of Rephaim, on the western side of the city. Each person, or group, carried a sickle and a basket. They were heading to the ripened barley fields, where each one would harvest (or glean) an *omer,* or sheaf, of barley. After binding each sheaf, these would be taken to the Temple for an ingathering; a wave offering of the First Fruits to God.

In times past, the entire city had harvested the offerings on the same day. But, after the exile years, two differing viewpoints had emerged on the timing of such an offering. Those who followed the Pharisees had already harvested their offering before the Passover, while those who followed the Sadducees were harvesting today.

Cleophas considered. His own ancestors had followed the teaching of the Pharisees, and had all gathered their sheaves on Friday. But, no matter *when* they had been harvested, all the sheaves would be gathered into the Temple this morning.

In the center of Jerusalem, inside the hand-hewn cave of limestone owned by Joseph of Arimathea, something unexpected was happening.

Just before the first hour (6am), an earthquake began. It was not as long, nor as intense as the pronounced shaking which had occurred Friday afternoon. This disturbance was a quick shift in the plates of the earth. However, the convulsive burst of violence attached to it was intense enough to wake every sleeping person for ten miles in every direction.

Simultaneously, in Joseph of Arimathea's elaborate garden courtyard, a dazzling light, brighter than the midday sun, or even a supernova, sent ever increasing flashes of brilliance bursting through every open orifice.

The Light burst through window openings, cracks in and around doorways, disclosing places where plaster and mortar needed repair.

Suddenly, there were no shadows.

Startled awake, both Mary, and the Magdalene jumped out of their beds in sudden concern. Hurriedly dressing, they ran to investigate.

Inside Joseph's limestone tomb, the cavern was filled with the same brilliant light and energy. In fact, it emanated from the burial chamber in the back of the cave.

Its intensity was so great, it confounded every law of physics.

During what is known as an "event horizon" occurrence, radioactive emissions streamed in every direction, finding their source in the body of the man body wrapped in linen.

As it did so, the human form lifted from the stone several inches and the linen was stretched taut.

The power surge lasted for more than three minutes. In that time, every occurring presence of *laminin*, the microscopic protein cells required to hold the human frame together, ceased to exist. This began a process known as "weakened dematerialization." Every electron within the confines of the linen's frame was freed from its orbit. The protons and neutrons making up each atom's center were unbound as well.

As a result; pure, bright, blue-white light overcame each of the physical elements, electrical energy was released, accompanied by a yet-to-be-discovered form of radiation.

The Creator had redefined His creation.

Matter had turned into energy.

The body disappeared, and its linen sheet dropped back to the stone, freed of its contents.

The entire event had taken only four minutes.

Coming from the back door of Joseph's home into the courtyard, Mary Magdalene and Mary, the mother of Jesus, made their way to the garden tomb.

Was the world coming to an end, they wondered?

Then, they realized. Each of them had asked the same question on Friday.

149

Entering the clearing in front of Joseph's tomb, they stopped in astonishment. The great flat stone, had been rolled away from the door. Who had broken the mortar seal?

Around them, on the ground, looking as though they were dead, were five Roman soldiers. Where had the others gone?

However unusual, these were not the things drawing their attention. Sitting on top of the stone, to the right of the open doorway, was a young man. He was clothed in a blazing, white garment. He shone with a piercingly bright light. It emanated from him and enveloped him. It moved as he moved.

And yet, they observed, he was real.

The young man looked at them, as though they had been expected.

He smiled. "He is not here," he announced. "He is risen -- just like he said."

"What did you say?" the older Mary asked him.

"Come and see." The young man indicated the open doorway to the tomb. "Go in, and see the place where he was laid."

Not exactly sure what they should do next, the two women looked at each other. They would have to pass by this glowing figure in order to go through the door.

The older Mary took the lead. She had seen an angel before, she considered. Taking Magdalene's hand, she led them through the doorway.

Was he authentic? Magdalene watched the young man, to see what he would do. He seemed safe. He seemed real. In fact, he appeared to be enjoying himself.

Smiling, he watched silently as they passed.

Entering the cave, the two women were greeted by two more young men in glowing, bright-white garments. Both were standing where Jesus' body had been placed the day before the Feast.

Was it brighter in here, the older Mary wondered? Where was the Light coming from?

Who *were* these men, Magdalene questioned? They carried Light and Substance. They carried the same atmosphere she had encountered on the night of her deliverance… with Jesus.

Were these *angels*, then?

She couldn't stand up in this atmosphere, she realized. She fell to her knees. So did the older Mary.

The angel standing at the head-plate spoke, looking directly at Magdalene. "He is not here," he said clearly. "He has risen. Look here. This is the place where he was."

The second angel, standing at the foot-plate, looked at the older Mary and smiled. "Go and tell the learners -- and Simon Peter --- He is going before you to Galilee," he said.

What? The women looked at each other, and walked out of the tomb. Upon their exit, they were greeted by Salome, Elsbeth, and three other women. Each was carrying a bag spices.

"What are you doing here?" Magdalene asked.

"We came to anoint the body," Salome answered. "We've decided we will unwrap him if we have to."

"It's not here." The older Mary spoke with a new conviction.

"What's not here?" Salome asked.

"The body; it's not here." Mary looked from face to face as she repeated her words.

"Did you see the angel?" Magdalene asked. "He was sitting right here."

"No, we didn't see an angel." Joanna looked at her strangely. "But we did see Temple guards running down the road as we were coming. One of them said something about going to make a report."

"To Pilate?"

"I don't think so. They said something about giving account to Caiaphas." Abigail answered.

The older Mary looked at Salome. "The angel said we should tell the twelve the Master is alive, and will be waiting for us in Galilee."

Salome's face broke into a smile. "Are you sure?" she asked.

Smiling as well, Mary glanced back toward the open door. "Pretty sure!" she answered.

The group of women left together, talking and sharing. It would be wonderful to share this news with John, and James, and Andrew.... They couldn't wait to see their faces.

What did it all mean?

But Mary Magdalene couldn't find the strength to leave the garden area. Old emotions began to surface.

If he wasn't *here,* where was he?

She looked back through the tomb door.

Yes, the two angels were still standing there. She just wanted to be sure.

Her thoughts began to race.

Her eyes filled with tears. The pent up fears of the past few days began to rise in a torrent of emotion.

She began to weep; the sense of abandonment overwhelming her once again. What would she do – *without Him to ask for answers?*

"Why are you weeping?" The angel at the head plate asked, his voice coming through the open doorway.

She turned, and walked back into the tomb.

"Because they have taken my Master away. I don't know where he is," she answered.

How would she learn to live her life, she wondered? Who would teach her the things she was still missing? Who could she ask?

Would anyone else understand her heart?

Perhaps she just needed to find a place to finish having a good cry, she thought. She wiped her eyes and nose with her sleeve. Looking down, she turned, and almost ran into someone.

Oh, she thought. *Joseph's gardener is here to tend the grounds. I will have to go somewhere else to be alone.*

"Why are you weeping?" the gardener asked.

There it was; the same question. Magdalene decided to get some answers. There *had* to be an answer. She would find strength somewhere inside herself to handle this. She took a deep breath.

"Sir," she said, her voice choked with emotion, her eyes filled with tears. "You are the gardener. If you have taken his body somewhere, please tell me where it is...." Her voice broke, and she began to weep harder. Sobs were beginning now. She had to get the words out. "I .... will...come and take... his... body... away."

There was a short stretch of silence. She didn't know what else to say.

Where could they have laid the body?

The Gardener spoke, gently; kindly, quietly.

"Mary!"

From the deep caverns of her soul, her being resonated with recognition and response. She fell to her knees, and took hold of his feet, weeping. "Oh, Master!" she cried with relief. "Jesus!"

He knelt down and lifted her to her feet. "I haven't yet ascended to the Mercy Seat, Mary. Don't cling to me yet." He paused. "Go and tell my friends that I am ascending -- to my Father; and your Father -- to my God; and your God."

She stood up. She lifted her head to look at him, and realized he was shining. It was the same light she had seen surrounding the angels; but it was brighter, stronger, somehow, coming from Jesus.

She took a deep breath, and smiled at him.

He was glistening white.

"I will," she replied, her heart suddenly becoming unencumbered; glowing.

Perhaps she could still catch up with the others.

A few moments passed.

The older Mary, Salome, and the others, were still walking across the city. In actuality, they were not too far ahead of her. The small group was just preparing to walk through Joseph's entry gate and turn onto the main road.

Suddenly, a man dressed in white stood six feet in front of them.

"Good morning, friends!" he called in greeting.

Stunned, the women looked up. No one had seen this man walking down the road.... Where had he come from?

"It – it's *Jesus!*"

The older Mary stood in shock for a moment. Then, all at once, she ran to him, and dropped to her knees, grasping his feet. Was he real? Was it really true?

The other women gathered around him as well. Each one found themselves wanting to confirm with their hands what their eyes told them.

Smiling he said, "Go and tell my friends I am alive, and I will meet them in Galilee."

The women ran elatedly to deliver the message.

But their words, initially, had not been well received.

At first, the men had not believed them. "Silly females!" a few said. "Women are always just too emotional! They've been seeing things."

But then, Simon Peter and Zebedee's son, John, decided to confirm the story. John had gone into the tomb first.

He was convinced, and had told them also.

Poor Simon Peter, Mary considered. He had been sure it couldn't be true: even when his wife, Elsbeth, told him her experience!

Then, he had looked into the tomb's doorway and observed the wrappings laying crumpled together in a heap. The handkerchief, or *sudarium*, John had placed over Jesus' face on Friday afternoon, was over to the side, still folded, just as it had been when laid on Jesus' face.

Some sort of image had been transferred to the linen.

In wonder, Simon touched it. Was it the face of his Friend? It *couldn't* be. Where was the body, he wondered?

He gathered the linen wrappings to his chest, and buried his face in them in despair, weeping bitterly once more.

In the basement cell in Joseph Caiaphas' palace, Joseph of Arimathea was huddled in a ball, trying to stay warm, laying on the cold stone slab. Without water, without cover, without care.

Above him, on the wall, was the image etched in blood of Jesus, which had inexplicably appeared just after Jesus' trial.

He had been sleeping fitfully. Each time he tried to move, he woke.

Every part of his body hurt. The bruises from his beating had begun to surface. Raw wounds from the restraining ropes were oozing. Black and blue, his ankle throbbed mercilessly, swollen to three times its normal size.

Invading his efforts to rest, suddenly, the cell filled with a bright light. Joseph blinked, unsure whether he was awake or dreaming. His pain had rendered him into a fog, a stupor-like incapacity that seemed to resist reasonable thought. He had heard of such things from those who had endured torture in the past.

Was it happening to him? Had his mind broken? Was he going mad?

For a moment, he felt as though he were flying. At the same time, someone was washing him from head to toe, but without pain causing a reaction. He felt ointment being rubbed into his wounds; again, without a bodily reaction.

He never wanted to wake again.

He was finally warm.

He felt someone sponge his face and kiss his cheek. A man's voice said, "Joseph, don't be afraid. Open your eyes and look at me."

When he opened his eyes, Joseph saw the face of his great-nephew, Jesus. He was dressed in glowing white.

Looking at what he feared was a phantom, Joseph abruptly found it difficult to breathe.

Had he died as well? Was this an apparition?

Could it be an effort of Satan to deceive him, he wondered?

Well, he thought, *when I say the Commandments, the devil has to flee, because he can't endure the Word of God.*

So, the priest began to quote the Ten Commandments. As he began, the man in white stayed with him, reciting the commandments out loud also.

He must be from God, Joseph concluded.

"Sir, are you the Rabbi Elijah? Or an angel?"

"No, Joseph, I am not Elijah. And I am certainly not an angel. I am Jesus. I am the one whose body you asked Pilate for permission to bury. You placed me in clean linen, and John covered my face with a sudarium. You laid me in your hewn cave and rolled the great carved stone over the door."

Joseph found himself still a little doubtful the man with him was really Jesus. "Can you showed me the place where I laid you?" he requested.

Immediately, the two of them were standing inside the tomb at the priest's Jerusalem home. Joseph looked, and saw the linen sheet in a crumpled heap, with the face cover still folded the way John had folded it on Friday.

"Jesus?" he whispered.

In response, Jesus took his great-uncle by the hand. Suddenly, they were inside Joseph's master bedchamber in the estate at Arimathea. Without warning, Joseph found himself under blankets on his own bed.

His body no longer hurt.

His ankle had ceased its throbbing.

Jesus reached down and pulled the covers up, as though Joseph were a young child. He kissed his cheek and then spoke.

"Peace on you, Joseph," Jesus said. "Wait here until forty days are over. I am going to my brothers in Galilee."

Suddenly warm, the Pharisee fell into a deep sleep.

What a wonderful dream!

It was late in the day when the Jewish, exiled steward, David, arrived in the throne-room of King Arviragus. The king had sent for him that morning, requesting his attendance at the end of his day. David had been surprised by the king's summons, but was used to being called upon for the king's odd tasks here and there.

But nothing had prepared him for the confidential information the Briton ruler would share with him.

"My king," David greeted him. "I'm sorry it took me so long to answer your summons. I had extra inventory duties, and one of the miners fell sick. I took him home and settled him with some herbs and teas."

Arviragus was surprised. "You didn't take him to the Druid priest?" he asked. "They have always treated the sick in our tribe."

"No, I didn't sir," David replied honestly. "Would you rather have me do so?"

The king waved his hand as though to brush away an insect. "No, no, David," he answered. "He has probably received better treatment. I was just surprised, that's all."

David decided it was a safe time to speak his mind. "I have noticed more of our men die at their hands than live. And those who live are those who didn't seem that ill to me to begin with."

Arviragus nodded in agreement. "I have noted the same things," he said. "How is the miner doing?"

"He should be fine in a couple of days, if he takes the herbs I have given him, and eats the soup I showed his wife how to make. Truthfully, I believe he has just worked himself into exhaustion."

"That seems to happen to our workers on a regular basis, don't you think?" the king inquired.

"Yes sir," David replied with a smile. "Have you given any thought to my suggestion to close the mines one day a week so the workers can rest?"

"I have, David," the king answered. "And we will have to discuss that one day soon. I summoned you here to ask you to put yourself in danger."

The steward was intrigued. "In danger?" he asked. "What do you mean?"

Arviragus shifted his position, motioning for the man to come closer. He whispered his words furtively. "I think someone is trying to poison me, and my wife. I have noticed the sickness comes just after ShroveTide each year. Each time it is a little worse than the time before. I know whatever it is, the poison must be accumulating inside my body. And, I know there is no way to reverse it.

"So my death is coming sooner than planned.

"I have learned from one of our purchasing visitors about a poison called arsenic. It seems one of the rulers in Gaul had an idea that he could turn lead and iron into gold. The poor man tried and tried, and failed. When his failure became known to the ruler, the alchemist was forced to eat the powder he had developed because it wasn't gold. Eventually, the man died, and the ruler realized his servant had developed a poison that would kill gradually, without a trace.

"The only ones who have access to that kind of information would be the Druids. But one of the miners must be stealing our metals, or even mining secretly, to obtain the materials they need to produce it.

"I want you to find out who is making the poison, and who is supplying them. I also want anyone involved, male or female, brought to me alive."

He paused. "Are you willing to do this for me?"

David appraised the ruler, returning the Arivargus' gaze with steady, clear eyes.

"Yes, sir," he answered. "I will begin working on this matter first thing in the morning."

When Jesus had uttered his final cry on Friday, the earth had quaked, trembling as Father God's eternal design was being restored to Created Order. On Friday, burial sites all over the area had broken open in response to the shaking. And today, on the Day of FirstFruits, the physical bodies of those responding to the Lamb of Heaven, were also being raised. Unrealized, they had been inside the opened graves since Friday; now they were alive once more.

For a five-mile radius around Jerusalem, men and women were rising up, and walking out of their graves. With no clothes available, each of the resurrected held the only thing they could, a burial shroud, wrapped around the body. Instinctively, without conferring, most of the "reborn" headed towards Jerusalem.

On the way into the city, those reaping barley for the First-Fruits offering were amazed to see these individuals; some were known and some were not.

One such family occurrence was the resurrection of a woman named Hannah. Her son, Shachar, was reaping barley when his mother approached him.

"Shachar?" she asked. "Is that my son?"

Surprised, the young man turned around. He had not heard his mother's voice in three years! Surely he was mistaken! But then he saw her, wrapped in burial muslin, walking barefoot.

"Mother?" he asked, his voice hoarse, in disbelief.

"Yes, it's me," she answered.

"How did you get here?"

"I walked."

"No, I mean; how did you come to be here? Haven't you been dead for three years?" he wanted to know.

"I am.... I mean, I was," she replied. "There is so much to tell you." She looked around. "Can we go home? Is your father alive?"

"He is. In fact, he is reaping in another field. Would you like to see him?"

"Oh, I would! So much!" Hannah exclaimed. "Even if it is just for a little while!" As they walked together, she continued. "I am only here for a time. But there is so much to tell you. I want to share it totally with you both; together."

All in all, over three hundred bodies resurrected that early morning. Reunions such as this took place all over Jerusalem and the surrounding area. Many, just like Hannah and her family, took place in the barley fields.

One man said he spoke with the prophet, Jeremiah, for more than an hour. Another spoke of seeking the prophet, Isaiah. Still another family reported being roused from sleep by a woman knocking on their front door. She had lived in their home before the captivity, and wanted to know if she had family still living there!

The sheer volume of resurrected persons walking into the city of Jerusalem caused no small stirring among the population.

At Herod's palace, in the Prefect's private apartments, Claudia Procula was playing with her son, Pilo. Sitting on the floor, legs apart, toe to toe, the pair rolled a ball between them. Pilo had just thrown the ball. As his mother caught it in midair, he laughed.

Just then, Candace, Claudia's personal maid entered the room. "My lady?" she asked breathlessly. "Is this a good time to give you news?"

Noting her maid's excitement, the Prefect's wife stopped the game. "What is it?"

"The man, Jesus, has risen from the dead!"

The announcement hung in the air between them.

"What did you say?" Procula wasn't sure she had heard properly.

"The Galilean is alive!" Candace's face was flushed.

"Are you sure? Where did you hear such a thing?"

"My lady, the wife of King Herod's steward told me personally," the maid answered.

"Joanna? How does she know this? What happened?"

Candace flurried to her mistress, and sat down on the floor next to her. "Apparently, Mistress Joanna went to his tomb this morning, with several other women who were part of his company. They had planned to open the tomb and anoint his body for burial."

Procula's mouth dropped open. "They were willing to break the Roman seal?"

"They didn't know about it, I don't think," Candace answered. "Anyway, when they got there, Mistress Magdalene had seen an angel. And then, he appeared to them in the road."

"The angel?"

"No, silly," Candace responded. "Jesus. Jesus appeared to them. He still had holes in his wrists and his feet. But he spoke to them, and they touched him."

"Go and send for Longinus, the centurion at the tomb. I want news of this firsthand," Claudia commanded. "Then come back here to stay with Pilo. I will see this sight for myself."

It was almost an hour later, when Longinus and several soldiers arrived at Joseph's garden tomb with the Prefect's wife. Greeting Jesus' mother, Mary, a stunned and thankful Procula wept inside the hewn cave.

So he *had* been Divine.

Her husband would want to know.

Surely, she considered, Jesus would allow a small boy like Pilo to retain the healing he had received. Even if his father had been the one to sentence him to crucifixion.

In Qumran, Isaachar and Moshe worked to copy the final portions of the copper scroll pertaining to Moshe's vow.

"So, let me understand," Moshe spoke quietly. "You are saying my vessels are buried in Samaria?"

"That is what the scroll says," Isaachar told him. "You might be able to decipher the meaning of the descriptions written here."

"Thank you," Moshe said. "Is that all you can help me with? Don't you know the meaning of the clues written here?"

Isaachar shook his head. "No, I'm sorry, I don't. It is part of my job here at the settlement to help those in the Temple to untangle these descriptions."

"How did you come by these instructions, anyway?" Moshe wanted to know. "How do you know they are real?"

"Well, our country had been attacked many times. Over the years, we have learned there are only two ways to hide valuables: in the caves, or burying them in a field. Many times, when someone has riches they cannot take with them; or they need to leave the country because they are forced into exile; they come to us. They donate it to the cause. When they disclose the nature of their treasure, where it is buried, and how to find it, we add its description and location to the Copper Scroll."

"And how do I know you people haven't secretly gone and dug up everything?" Moshe demanded.

Isaachar chuckled. "We are Essenes. We despise worldly goods. In fact, when the Romans annexed Judea, they didn't even worry about us. They left us alone. We are trusted; even by our enemies."

Moshe nodded. "Thank you, Isaachar. If I find what I am looking for, you will be the first to know."

On the Mount of Olives, just across the Kidron Valley, was a public city Garden, called Gethsemane. There, a weary man leaned against an olive tree, and closed his eyes. He had been hiding there for some time; since running from the tomb at Joseph of Arimathea's home.

He had thought his weeping was finished. But now, the brokenness of his soul re-emerged once more. He knew Elsbeth would be looking for him. But he wasn't ready to go back just yet, even though he had not been able to tolerate another person's company for more than thirty minutes at a time in the past three days.

They had come for the Feast, intending to take a vacation of sorts. But, in truth, Elsbeth had spent the majority of the time they had set aside alone. The days had been meant to be festival-centered and family focused.

He had abandoned her.

It was yet another reason to be ashamed.

She was probably worried about him, he realized.

He was worried about *himself.*

He had done nothing but weep for three days. He hadn't been able to face his friends. He was sure his denials of even knowing Jesus had become fodder for rejection and exclusion.

How could he have *lied?*

He had made promises to Jesus; pledges of allegiance he had been so confident in. He had broken every one.

How had Jesus known he would? He could still hear the rooster crowing in his head. When he closed his eyes, the look of compassion in the Master's face haunted him.

How could he feel compassion for me, when he knew I had just denied even knowing him, he thought? *I wish I had never been born.*

Suddenly, a voice startled and surprised him. "You don't want to let your mind go there, Peter."

Who? What? Where did the voice come from? Was his mind fabricating things now? Simon was sure he had come to Gethsemane alone. He hadn't *heard* any approaching footsteps.

I'm going crazy, he thought. *I am absolutely losing my mind. This is proof of it. I'm hearing voices.*

"Not *voices,* Peter. Just my voice."

Opening his eyes, the man looked around the small garden and grove of olive trees. And there, leaning against another olive tree, not far from where he sat, was a man dressed in white. He looked strangely familiar, Simon thought.

But Simon knew his eyes were swollen. He wasn't sure he was seeing *anything* very clearly. He was especially unsure of his personal sanity.

The man in white stood up and walked over to him. He sat down next to the fretful man. He put his hand on Simon's shoulder.

At his touch, Simon felt as though a bolt of lightning moved through his entire being, rearranging his mind and his soul. The man spoke to him.

"Peter, my friend," he said. "You're entirely too dejected about this."

Without warning, Simon Peter became aware of the identity of the man.

For a few moments of silence, he looked into the eyes of Jesus, whom he had denied knowing just days before. Then, once more, waves of emotion welled up within him.

"Oh, Master!" he cried, putting his head in his hands. "I failed you! I thought I was stronger. I'm such a failure, and I can't get it back. They wounded you. They killed you. And now you are dead."

Jesus chuckled. "I'm not dead, Peter."

Simon was sure he was losing his mind. "I'm seeing things," he said out loud to the apparition. "I saw you die. There is no way anyone could have survived what you went through."

Jesus took the bewildered man by his shoulders and shook him just a little. "Peter. *Simon Peter!* Look at me!"

The disciple lifted his head once more, and looked into the same compassionate eyes he had seen in the court of the High Priest's palace on Thursday night.

"How could you ever forgive me, Lord?" Simon Peter's broken question was expressed with a hoarse voice.

"I *am* forgiveness, Peter. There are so many things I want to tell you. And so many things I have prepared for you. I will be with you for just a little longer. So, don't be afraid, my friend. You will be a fisher of *people!* Now, go and comfort your wife. She was convinced when she saw me, and she's been concerned about your reaction to the news ever since. Don't cause her pain, or to fear. I will meet all of you in Galilee."

Then he was gone. He just vanished.

Simon Peter looked around Gethsemane's garden.

Where had he gone?

Had Jesus just appeared to him? He felt his clothes, and pinched his hand to make certain he was really awake. Yes, he was standing in Gethsemane, in somewhat of a right mind.

But then it hit him. Jesus had appeared to him!!

Jesus was alive! Suddenly, Simon's fear was gone!

He turned and headed towards Ampliatus' home.

In the corner of an outside courtyard in the business district of Jerusalem, a young man was contemplating his future. He had taken a silent vow three days prior, at a dinner shared with twelve other men, and his half-brother, Jesus.

If his older brother could go without drinking wine, he could do it too, he had decided. And what had Jesus meant by saying, "…until I drink of it with you when my Father's kingdom comes?"

Growing up, he had thought his older brother was crazy. His whole life he had thought so. After all, James was the first *legitimate* son.

He was the *real* first-born.

Everyone knew it. Jesus had been a mistake. As he thought about it, he knew his own father, Joseph, had covered it well.

But Jesus was a mistake just the same.

Someone had told him Jesus was born already destined to die because he had been born illegitimate. Bad blood, and all that…Why had there been such stories around him? If they weren't true, why had their mother allowed them to continue? And why was there such complete support for Jesus' work, when James had worked harder than anyone else since their father's death?

He wasn't sure that even Cleophas understood.

And, if Jesus *had* been the Promised Deliverer, something had certainly gone wrong? What did it matter?

He was dead now.

Now what?

James huddled in the corner of his Uncle Zebedee's office courtyard.

Something about all of this was terribly off-track.

He just had to think. What would his mother's life look like now? He had made it through the last three years; through the humiliation of his brother's irrational teachings; through the rejection of his friends because of a half-brother.

Who *had* Jesus' father been anyway?

In spite of his unexpected anger, James felt a pang in his heart. His mother had never lied to him. She had told him about the angel telling her she would be pregnant. She had told him about the choir in the heavens, and about his father's dreams.

But what if they had conspired to lie to him, just to make things look better? Then there were the statements and gossip he had heard from his friends' mothers back in Nazareth.

On the other hand, he considered; what about James' personal experiences with Jesus himself?

As a boy, he had always been talking about his father, like the man was something special. But if he had made it all up, how had the miracles happened? How had people been healed of leprosy, or raised from the dead?

James considered. He wondered what *he* would have done if he had realized he didn't know who or where his father was. Come to think of it, James supposed he might have created an infallible hero as well.

But why couldn't Jesus just have accepted his life, and quietly followed Joseph's example?

"Do you remember saying things like that to me when we were growing up together, James?" A man's voice broke through James' battle with his negative thoughts.

Opening his eyes, James looked up. His eyes looked around the courtyard. Who had said that, he wondered?

"*I* said that, brother." James followed the direction of the voice. And saw a man dressed in white sitting at the stone table just to his left. In the morning shadows, he wouldn't have seen him.

Was it *Jesus?* No, it couldn't be!

James blinked and shook his head. He was seeing things!

He looked again. The man was still there!

He stood up, and made his way to the portico, where the serving table stood. Yes, it *was* his half-brother.

"Come and have breakfast, James! I have fresh bread here. It's still warm!" He paused, and then added. "I know how tired you are!"

Dazed, James sat down across from his supposed nemesis; his half-brother. What was going on?

Jesus smiled at him. "The Son of Man is *alive!* I have so much to tell you! So much is about to happen!" A hearty laugh erupted from the resurrected man's throat. His eyes shone as he looked at James in the same way he had when they had played together in their childhood.

After all, they weren't that far apart in age.

"Let's talk, James," he said. "I want to help you."

For the next two hours, James spent time alone with Jesus. He found himself beginning to understand. Jesus had always been who he had claimed to be from the start. As they broke bread together, he discovered a deep joy and purpose.

He also discovered the ability to grasp truth for the first time in his life. Many of his questions were answered, and those not connecting with an answer, he discovered a willingness to wait for understanding.

Most of all, James found himself regretting the many rivalries and unkind words he had allowed his mind and heart to accommodate against this man; his half-brother?

After all, why would anyone seek to compete with God?

Especially, God come in human form.

Forgiveness and Reconciliation felt really good, he decided.

In the early morning light, several bread and fruit vendors were setting up booths in the Jerusalem marketplace. There would be very few vendors today, since the priests only allowed those who *had a desperate need* to work during a Feast Week.

Judah the Sicari made his way to the fruit vendor, and then to the bread vendor.

"Greetings!" he said.

"Good morning," came the answer from Salah, a fruit merchant. He was just beginning to set up his booth in the marketplace. "You're up early this morning, sir."

"Just coming into town," Judah replied. "Is there any news the past few days?"

"Yes, much has happened in the past few days," Salah answered. "Which fruits do you want, sir? I'll pull them from the baskets in the wagon for you."

"Do you have any apples, or figs?" Judah asked. "Any large events take place yesterday or the day before?"

Walking over to his wagon, Salah pulled out two apples, a small cake of figs, and a cluster of raisins. "I'm not sure what you might have heard, sir. The festival gatherings on Friday were not much different than a regular year. The Prefect released a prisoner, and then the executions of the condemned prisoners took place. Come to think of it, though, there was a larger crowd in the valley this year than in other years."

"Oh?" Judah replied. "Why do you think that was?"

"Well, I heard someone say it was because the Galilean was crucified. You know, the prophet Jesus, who was healing people and teaching the past few years? It seems one of his own men turned him in."

Salah returned from the wagon to his vendor booth. "Will these do, sir?"

Judah nodded, numbly. "He was *crucified?*" he asked in shocked surprise.

"Mm-hmm." Salah replied. "The Prefect had him scourged, but then he was crucified as well. I had always thought combining those was against the law." He looked at Judah. "Why would they break their own laws?"

Without looking up, he kept talking. "It was the strangest thing too. There was a darkness like I've never seen. It was so deep, I could feel it. It lasted for hours; too long to be an eclipse. Then there was an earthquake. I've never been in an earthquake before, have you?"

The Sicari shook his head. "What do I owe you?" he asked, shaken.

"Ten leptons for all of it," Salah answered.

Judah pulled the pennies out of his purse. "Does anyone have water-skins close by?" he wanted to know.

Salah indicated the vendor a few booths down. "I think he might have fresh bread as well," he added.

"Thank you." Stunned, Judah tucked the fruit into his satchel, and moved to the indicated vendor's booth.

Had Jesus really been crucified, he speculated?

How was that even possible? Had he misread the signs? What about the vow he had taken? If Jesus had been executed, then Judah had failed miserably.... again.

After purchasing a fresh water-skin and two small loaves of bread, Judah decided to look for his Uncle Eli in the Essene Quarter of the city. He was just knocking on his uncle's door, when a bright explosion of light took place somewhere behind him in the city.

The earth pulsated so fiercely, he was knocked to the ground. As he fell, his head hit the door. At that point, Eli, the scribe overseer of Qumran, son of Judah of Gamala, and brother to Simon Iscariot, opened the door.

"Judah! My boy!" he exclaimed in joyful surprise. "What brings you to Jerusalem?"

Judah clambered slowly to his feet, rubbing his head. The night-time journey had wearied him, and he was finding it difficult to concentrate. Reaching down, his Uncle Eli helped him into the house.

"I... I'm not sure now," Judah answered. He looked at his uncle. "I have to know what happened to Jesus the Galilean. Is it true he was executed?"

Eli looked evenly at his nephew. "Yes, on Friday," he said simply. "I saw you just before the meal he had with you and the others here in the Quarter on Thursday night. You must know that Ezra, the Overseer here in the Quarter, and I had come to believe that Jesus was the Promised Deliverer"

"Had come to believe? *Was?*" Judah echoed. "So it's true then."

Eli patted his nephew on the shoulder. "You didn't know, Judah. You did your best. Some things just don't work out. You will do better next time."

Next time?

Judah was lost in his own thoughts. He looked at his uncle with a sense of anger. "He lied to me, Uncle."

"Who did?" Eli asked. "Jesus?"

"No," came the answer. "The High Priest. Caiaphas."

Judah had just settled into a chair, but with this last statement, he stood up. "I'll be back in a little while."

"Where are you going? You just got here!" Eli was surprised.

"To settle a score." With that Judah was gone.

A few moments later, an angry Judah arrived at the Temple. It was the morning of the First-Fruits Offerings, so he knew the priests would be on duty at this early hour. Walking into the courtyard, he looked for the High Priest.

A young man approached him, and asked, "Can I help you sir? Do you have your barley sheaf with you?"

"Uh, no," Judah replied. "I need to see Joseph Caiaphas right away."

"He's very busy today, sir," came the answer. "This is the day of the First-Fruits Offering."

"Please tell him that Judah Iscariot wants to see him."

The young man's eyebrows went up. "Excuse me," he said.

A few moments later, the same young man returned, and motioned for Judah to follow him. They walked in silence down the steps to the Court of Hewn Stones.

Only a very small number of men outside the priesthood had been privileged to enter this hallowed place, Judah considered. He had been here twice.

As they entered the door, Joseph Caiaphas stepped down from the platform on which his chair stood. There were several others in the room as well, but Judah could not place them. He knew they were members of the Sanhedrin, and probably Sadduceean adherents.

"Judah!" cried the High Priest. "It is so good to see you! Are you here for a job? The national cause needs a man with your skills!"

Judah moved away from the High Priest as he approached. He had taken the purse from his belt while he had been waiting. "You lied to me!" he cried. "You promised me! You said if I would give Jesus over to you, you would guarantee the birthing of a new Israel! I thought it would be like Joseph of old in Egypt! We would see the birthing of a nation once again!"

Caiaphas cut him off mid-sentence. "I did *not* make you any promises, Judah! I told you that you were a part of something larger than yourself; that you would make a difference! And you have!"

"You lied to me..." Judah repeated. "Here, take the money back. I don't want it, and I don't want anything to do with any of you or your plans." He looked around the room. "You are evil men. All of you."

With his last statement, he hurled the bag of coins at Caiaphas' head. The High Priest thwarted the blow, sending the purse back in Judah's direction. As the man's hand hit the bag, it broke open. Coins flew in all directions, spraying the room.

"That means nothing to us!" the High Priest spat out, snarling back at Judah. "It's too late for changes now. Besides, you knew exactly what you were doing. You came to us. Remember?" He turned to the young priest who had conveyed Judah in. "Saul, would you show the Sicari out of this hallowed room? His kind is not wanted here."

"Yes, sir!" Saul replied. He pulled Judah's arm, and ushered him back through the door, and out into the court.

Shocked and dismayed, Judah stumbled away from the Temple. He wasn't sure what he had hoped for. In his heart, he realized he had wanted to hear a different response. He had wanted to hear it had all been a terrible mistake.

But the mistake had been his own.

How could he have even begun to believe it would be all right, or he could please God in doing such a thing?

He had betrayed his best Friend for a bag of silver.

Thirty pieces of silver.

It had all seemed so righteous. So logical.

Oh…..

Now he could see it had been political.

Had he always been so money hungry, he wondered?

He stumbled from the Temple, and wandered the streets until he found a dark corner where no one would invade his space.

He had to think. He needed to do something.

He needed …..

Sinking to the ground, he leaned against the outside plastered walls of an unidentified building. Pulling an apple and bread out of his satchel, he began to eat. He hadn't realized how hungry he had become.

He took a drink from his water-skin.

He would not return to his Uncle Eli's, he decided. He had been told since childhood there were no choices in his destiny. He had been born and bred to become a Sicari. He had been told it was a place of honor. He had been convinced bringing about the death of another man was doing an act of service to God.

Service to God? He shuddered now, thinking about it.

He had been wrong.

So wrong……

Had *everything* he had been taught been wrong?

As he bit into the fruit, he heard a voice. "Not *everything* was wrong, Judah. The teachings of the Books of Moses and the Prophets were handled well."

Who was speaking? Judah looked around the small alleyway.

It was then he felt a hand on his shoulder. At first touch, he felt a shockwave move through his being. *How had the person come behind him,* he wondered?

Suddenly, his emotions overtook him.

"I can't believe what I did," he said out loud, his voice choking. "My whole life has been a mistake."

The Man in white sat down next to him. "Judah."

Startled, he looked in the direction of the voice. He was face to face with Jesus, the man he had sold to the Sadducees. Words failed. Surely this was a ghost. He needed sleep. That was it. Seeking to clear his mind, he shook his head, and blinked hard several times.

"Did you mean what you said?" Jesus asked.

"Wh — when?" Judah asked.

"Did you mean what you said in Gethsemane?"

The bite of apple in his throat caught half-way down.

168

Judah's mind went blank. So much had happened, he couldn't remember anything before Qumran's baptism.

"Who did you say you are?" he sputtered. Recognition failed him.

Jesus touched the man's shoulder once more. "Judah," he said again. "Judah Iscariot. I *chose* you. You are one of the twelve."

Judah was surprised. *How could this be Jesus? Jesus was dead.*

"I'm not dead, Judah," Jesus said. "Look at me."

The betrayer turned his head. "I thought I chose you," he answered.

"So that brings me back to my first question. Did you mean what you said?"

Coughing, Judah prayed inwardly. *God help me.* Outwardly, he sputtered, "What did I say? I don't remember."

Jesus smiled at him. "You called me 'Master.' Did you mean that?"

Suddenly, Judah's mind cleared. "I did mean it. Now, more than ever. But I thought you were going to set up your kingdom."

"I am."

"But you can't if you're dead."

"I'm not dead. I'm very much alive." Jesus put out his hand. "Here. Touch me. See? The wounds in my wrists are real."

Judah stared at the hole in Jesus' wrist. It was a gaping hole, large enough he could see the ground below through the opening between the bones. His eyes widened, as he realized this man *was* Jesus, and he was serious.

It must be a dream, he determined.

"It's not a dream," Jesus said. "It's me. And I'm here."

"Why didn't you take power?" Judah wanted to know.

From somewhere deep within himself, Judah felt a deep wave of emotion rising. It was regret. It was conviction. It was embarrassment.

But mostly, it was anger.

"How will you go about setting it up now?" he continued. "When will you take power from the Romans?"

"You have been with me for three years. Do you remember me saying the Kingdom of Heaven does not involve the same kind of throne or government as those political organizations here on earth? It is a more essential battle; it carries an *eternal* significance."

"Then what good is it?" Judah asked. "How does that kind of Kingdom have any power *now,* in *my* life; in changing the direction of the lives of men?"

"Is control and intimidation the only kind of power you think matters, Judah? Where do you think true power comes from?" Jesus asked "Abba Father is the only True Source of real power."

Judah could feel his confusion beginning to return. "But this isn't what I was taught. It doesn't make sense to me. If what you are saying is true, it should make logical sense."

"That's why I'm *here*, Judah." The words were spoken gently, with great compassion. The Master let the words sink in for a moment. "I want you *with* me."

Judah wasn't sure what to say. Inside his head, the traditions and imprinting of his childhood were providing tremendous arguments, protesting loudly. Had *anyone* ever come back after a crucifixion? Surely he was dreaming, or worse..... He sat, conflicted for several moments, and then spoke with a degree of resolve he wasn't sure he actually felt.

"If I believe in you and this new kind of Kingdom, then my vow means nothing," Judah protested. "If you *are* really alive, and you have no plans to re-establish the throne of *David*, then my entire life means nothing. Protecting the Promised Deliverer is what I was trained to do since my boyhood. To finish what my grandfather started. I was named for him; Judah of Gamala. To restore the nation of Israel. How do I change all that? How can I yield to something so opposite from everything I know?"

As he spoke, his anger hardened into resistance.

The resurrected Man in white did not say anything in return. He looked at Judah sadly, and patted him on his shoulder. "I understand," he said.

Cleophas and his son, Simon, were about halfway to their destination. They had been travelling for almost three hours, and Cleophas was beginning to feel somewhat weary. Part of his being wished he had slept a little longer before beginning their journey. In truth, he *had* been stressed about disappointing his client in Emmaus-Nicopolis. One day would not have made that much difference, he realized now. The best he could do at this point, however, was to follow-through, finish the task, and return home as soon as possible.

He looked up at the sky. Cleophas estimated the time to be around the third hour (9am). They were making good time. At this rate, they could perhaps conduct their meeting and make it home either late tonight or early tomorrow.

"Why don't we stop and have a little something to eat together?" he suggested.

Simon had been silent for close to an hour. "That would be wonderful," he answered.

The two men left the road, and walked through a patch of soft grass to rest. They found an appealing spot under a rather large fig tree. Because of its low lying branches, the space under the tree was well-shaded.

Pulling off his head covering, Cleophas laid it down on the ground. He then sat down on the spread-out cloth, with his back against the tree. In this way, his cloak and toga were shielded from the sandy soil, and he had a makeshift table on which to place his food. Simon followed suit.

Both men began looking through the foods Salome had packed for them some three hours ago. She had sent stuffed grape leaves, skewered cooked meat strips, dates, and a few other items. Their water-skins were still almost half-full, so there was no need to find a well.

As they ate, Simon began to share some of the thoughts he had considered during the previous hours. They emerged as questions.

"Do you think there is a connection between all of the things that happened this week?" he asked.

"What things?" Cleophas wanted to make sure he was answering the right question.

"You know, Abba," Simon said. "The darkness, the earthquake, the way Jesus was scourged *and* executed. I know we weren't there, but Joseph and James were telling me about it."

Cleophas answered quietly. "I don't know for sure," he said. "I do remember how Mary and my brother met, and I know some of the things she has told me."

"Like what?" Simon wanted to know.

As they ate breakfast, father and son discussed the miraculous events surrounding Jesus' birth, and life as a boy.

Just as they were finishing their respite, another traveler approached the tree where they were resting. He was on horseback.

"Excuse me," he said. "Is this the road to Qiriat-Yearim?"

"Yes, it is!" Simon replied. "But I think you passed it if you are travelling from Jerusalem."

"Oh," the man answered. "I must have galloped right past it."

Cleophas stood up to speak with the man. "You have business there?"

The traveler sighed. "I came to Jerusalem for the feast last week. Then I had intended to then come to see my father, who is dying. I wanted to take him to see the healer; the man named Jesus."

Simon was surprised. "Jesus is dead. They crucified him on Friday."

"I know," the man replied. "I was in Jerusalem. I saw it happen. But didn't you hear?"

"Hear what?" Cleophas asked.

"His grave was found empty this morning. The Temple Guard are saying his body was stolen by his followers. But the Roman guards say a great angel broke the seal and rolled the stone away. People in that neighborhood said there was a great flash, followed by something like an earthquake around the tomb's area this morning. I spoke with a woman who said she saw a light brighter than anything she had ever seen before coming from the inside of the cave."

Simon and Cleophas looked at each other. How had they missed something like this? It must have happened just after they left the city.

The traveler continued speaking. "You say Qiriat-Yearim is back down this road?"

"Yes," said Cleophas. "Just a couple stadia."

"Thank you!" the man shouted over his shoulder, riding away.

In amazement, father and son stared after him. "Do you think we should head back to Jerusalem, father?" Simon asked.

Still watching the fading rider, Cleophas answered. "I don't know what we could do to help if we were there. And if it *is* true, I'm sure there will be far too much activity for us to be *needed* in any way."

He reached down for his head-covering and shook off the dust. Putting it back in place on his head, he readied himself to continue the journey.

Stepping back onto the road, Simon noticed another man travelling alone just ahead of them. Speeding up, he paced himself until he was walking stride for stride with the man. "Excuse me, sir," he said. "Have you heard any news from Jerusalem?"

The traveler turned and looked at him. "Regarding?"

"About the body of the Galilean, Jesus, being stolen? That his tomb was empty this morning?"

"I *do* know about that," the man replied. "What have *you* heard?"

Cleophas caught up with the two men. "Not much," he panted. "Only what we have been told."

"But don't you understand how everything that has happened this week is a fulfillment of the Law and the Prophets?"

"So it does fit together!" Simon exclaimed. "It *is* connected!"

The man smiled. "Yes, more than you know," he replied. "Here, let me explain what I know. Feel free to interrupt me if you have a question."

At a private residence in the center of the City, another cave had been fashioned into a family burial site. It had been used for generations. According to custom, when a person died, the body was cleansed, treated with spices, wrapped in linen and laid inside the cave. After a period of time, when decomposition had completed, the person's bones were collected and placed inside a stone box, called an ossuary.

Inside the cave in question, were many such ossuaries, with carved stone tablets providing the name and date of each individual's death, attached to the outsides. In addition to the stacks of stone boxes, two adult bodies, wrapped in linen were awaiting decomposition. Both were men. Both had been priests, and had served at the Temple. Both had died of the same illness which had swept through the city a year before.

On Friday, as the ground shook, the stone in front of the family burial crypt had split in half, breaking apart. Today, just after the second earthquake, anyone inside the grotto would have heard an astonishing conversation.

"Charinus? Are you awake?"

"I'm here. Can you move?"

"Trying. My elbows are a little stiff."

There was silence for a few moments, as each man tried to free himself from the linen trappings around his own body.

"Leucius? Are you out yet?"

"I just sat up. You?"

"Can you help me?"

A few moments later, the two brothers stood, naked, in their family's burial cave. Sunlight shone into the cave, through the opening caused by the cave's stone splitting into two.

"Should we go inside the house?"

Leucius picked up his brother's linen wrapping and threw it at him. "I think we ought to wrap up first," he said. "Don't you?"

Laughing, his brother took the linen. "What a good idea!" he said. "I'm thirsty. Let's go."

When Simeon the Pharisee, the son of Gamaliel, arrived home that afternoon, he was greeted by two of his sons; once dead; now alive. His wife was still sitting on the floor, wide-eyed, convinced she was hallucinating.

That day, more than three hundred bodies walked out of their graves, suddenly coming alive, covering their naked bodies with the cloth shrouds in which they had been buried.

Homes all over the city opened their doors to be greeted by unexpected visitors.

And in each case, the account of the journey was identical.

How this could happen, many wondered?

Did it have anything to do with the death of the Galilean on the hill?

It would certainly be the subject of conversation for many weeks; and there was one thing of which everyone in Jerusalem was convinced;

From this point forward, nothing would ever be the same.

8 - Aftershock

Joseph Caiaphas sat inside the Court of Hewn Stones. He was alone, and somewhat confused. In his right hand, he rotated several of Judah Iscariot's returned silver coins.

What was happening, he wondered? He could feel the control slipping from his fingers.

The Temple Guards had appeared some time ago, with news of seeing angels and a bright light; of an earthquake breaking the ground, splitting the Sacred Eagle Seal of Rome; of the carved, round limestone being rolled away from the tomb's door by a glowing man in white with massive golden wings.

He had no idea *what* Pilate's Roman detail had experienced. Worse, there was no way to prevent what *those* men would leak to the public. He could imagine the aftermath.

Why would anyone believe such things, he wondered? *There is no such thing as the resurrection of a dead person. And angels are only figments of imagination, dreamed up by weak minds.*

But how could all of these men; men he had put into positions of authority himself.... How could all of these men have seen the same things?

There *had* to be an explanation.

He looked up as the great door to the Council Room opened. Gamaliel and his son, Simeon were entering, along with Caiaphas' father-in-law, Annas. Two other priests were walking behind them. He thought he might recognize them, but couldn't quite place where. Behind them stood his new protégé, Saul.

Annas was the first one to speak. "Joseph, you remember Simeon's two sons, Charinus and Leucinius?"

Caiaphas' jaw dropped open. He looked at the two men. *Were* they who his father-in-law was saying they were? He found it impossible to say anything in response.

All he could do was nod.

Annas continued. "Since we have an ultimate disparity between what we Sadducees believe, and what the Pharisees hold to, we are going to hold a test of sorts. Simeon and Gamaliel are convinced these men are who they present themselves to be. But... they are Pharisees.

"Now, Gamaliel and Simeon have both convinced me they are innocent of any conspiracy, and I believe them. So, if these men can tell us the same story, without having conferred, we will see whether they can convince the Saduccees."

With that, he took Leucinius by the arm, and walked with him towards the door.

"What do you want *me* to do, father?" Caiaphas finally asked.

Without looking back, his father-in-law spoke. "Stay here, and make sure these two men don't speak to each other to create a story. I am going to gather as many of the Council as I can find to conduct separate interviews with each of them."

When Annas returned, he had gathered a mixture of both Pharisees and Saduccees; all were part of the 71 men who made up the Sanhedrin, or Great Council. First, Leucinius was brought before the Council, and then Charinius.

Each man was subjected to a grueling interrogation.

Throughout each interview, Saul watched and listened, seeking to discern the differences between his two mentors, past and present: Gamaliel and Joseph Caiaphas.

The questions were numerous, but necessary, if one was to prove or disprove such a story.

What is your name? Where were you born? What is your mother's name? Who were your brothers and sisters? What was the order of their birth? What was your favorite food as a child? Who was your mentor in Temple School? Were you ever married? What was your wife's name? What were the names of your children? How old would they be now?

And then they moved to the more pertinent questions.

How long ago did you die? What caused your death? What were your last words? Where did you go when you died? What happened after your death?

Why are you here? What caused you to come back to life?

In both cases, the answers to the first set of questions were answered without hesitation, and all were answered correctly. The answers to the second set of questions varied, based upon each man's personal experience. In both experiences, the answers were correct.

But answers to the last two questions drew the most attention from the members of the Council in attendance. Here is a compilation of the accounts:

"We sat together with all of our fathers in the deep obscurity of darkness, when suddenly, a Golden Heat and Royal Light shone on all of us. Immediately, the Father of the whole race of men spoke, saying,

'This Light is the beginning of Everlasting Light.' In response, the prophet Isaiah cried out and said, *'this is the Light of the Father, from the Son of God, as I prophesied when I lived on the earth.'*

"Then, the prophet Simeon, who, in his old age, lived in the Temple, spoke, and said to all of us: *'Give glory to the Lord Jesus Christ, the Son of God. I received him into my arms in the Temple when he was born a child. When I was moved by the Holy Spirit, I made confession and said that now my eyes had seen his salvation, which he had prepared for all the people; He is the Light to the Gentiles and the glory of Israel.'*

"Then a man named John spoke, who said: *'I am John, a voice and a prophet of the most high, who sent me to prepare His way; to give knowledge of his salvation to His people. And when I saw Him, I said, 'Behold the Lamb of God, who takes away the sins of the world.' I baptized him in the Jordan River and saw the Holy Spirit descending upon him. I heard a voice speaking saying 'This is my Beloved Son, and I am pleased with Him.''*

"Then Adam spoke, who was the first man created. He spoke to his son, Seth, and admonished him to tell everyone what had been prophesied in his day; that after 5,952 years had passed, the most beloved Son of God would again open the doorway to the Tree of Life and the mercy of God.

"Then Satan, the prince and chief of death spoke to Hell: *'Make yourself ready to receive Jesus, who boasts that he is the son of God.'* And Death spoke: *"Hell cannot receive him, because I have no power in him. He has come to reclaim those who believe and are dead."* And Hell answered: *'You have told me he is here to take away dead men from me. But where does his power come from, that he can do such a thing?'*

"Then King David spoke and said, *'Did I not foretell? And He has broken gates of brass and smitten bars of iron asunder? Open up your gates that the King of Glory may come in!'*

"And as the Bright Light of the Son of God approached the gates of Hell, Death and its wicked ministers were shaken with fear. They cried out *'We are overcome!"* Then, the King of Glory, in all of his majesty, trampled on Death and laid hold on Satan the prince. He delivered him unto the power of Hell.

"He drew Adam to himself, and into His own Brightness.

"Then Death and Hell reproached Satan, the prince, and said, *'Look at what you have done! You promised us great spoils when Jesus was crucified. Like a fool, you did not know what you were doing. You have been the holder of the keys of Hell! When you hung him on the cross, you caused us to lose those keys! We gained them by the tree of transgression and the losing of paradise!*

"But you; you are the author of Death and the head of all Pride. Because of you, the Innocent and Righteous One has been brought into our realm. Because of you, we are now going to lose the hold we have had on the guilty, ungodly, and unrighteous of the whole world until now.'

"Then Jesus turned, and stretched out his hand to all of us, and said: 'Come to me, all of you; My saints who bear My image and My likeness. You are the ones the devil and Death condemned by the tree; but now they are condemned.' And all the saints gathered under the hand of the Lord. And the Lord took the right hand of Adam and went up, leading them all out of Hell, and all the saints followed him.

"As they went, David the king cried aloud and sang: "Sing unto the Lord a new song, for He has done marvelous things. His right hand has brought salvation. The Lord has made known his saving life before the face of all the nations.'

"And then we awoke in our physical bodies, and came to the home of our father, Simeon, and then to the home of our grandfather, Gamaliel."

For some time, after questions ceased, there was silence in the Court of Hewn Stones. No one knew what to say. Both stories matched exactly. Everyone knew there had not been time or opportunity for these men to fabricate such answers.

Additionally, all those who had served on the Council with these two men recognized them, and discovered their personal relationships to be intact and authentic.

Every Sadducee in the room was reconsidering his beliefs regarding life after death and the spiritual realm. Every Pharisee in the room was delighted to have his personal beliefs confirmed.

Confused, young Saul of Tarsus battled within his own being. Into which set of beliefs he should place his loyalties?

It was mid-afternoon when Joseph Caiaphas decided to head towards his palace. While sitting in silence in the Court, with his new protégé, Saul, he looked at the bowl of fruit on the table, and realized how hungry he really was.

"You ready for some food, Saul?" he asked.

Saul's face brightened. "Yes sir!" he answered.

"Let's go home!" the High Priest exclaimed. "It's been a long day."

As they walked through the streets of Jerusalem, Saul found himself with so many questions presenting themselves, he felt he would burst.

"What did you think of the testimony of Simeon's sons, sir?" he asked.

"I'm not sure, Saul," Caiaphas answered. "To be truthful, I'm about to choke on all of the superstitious dribble I've heard today."

Saul was surprised. "You don't believe it, then?"

Caiaphas snorted. "I'm not sure I know *what* to think just yet." He paused. "I haven't spoken to any of the *Roman* guards yet. I did pay the Temple Guards to protect our interests."

"*Our* interests?" Saul echoed, questioningly.

"Yes," came the answer. "Imagine how difficult it would be for us, as leaders, to manage the people's spiritual experiences if everyone began to believe this story of Jesus being resurrected. Imagine what would happen to the relative security we experience, if someone whom Rome had condemned as a criminal were actually to come back from the dead. Their heavy hand would come down on us even more so than it is now. There is a reason why the Governor has appointed the Sadducees as the leaders of the High Council. I believe they are aware of the superstitious nature of the Pharisees, and don't want things to get out of hand."

"But what if it's *real?*" the younger priest wanted to know. "Wouldn't you want to be on the side of ElShaddai, and the Law and the Prophets?"

Caiaphas chuckled. "You are more naïve than I thought, Saul! Right now, you are idealistic, and think you have figured out and know how things work. This is the weakness of every man in his youth. Give me some time to show you how reality shows itself. There are things we must do as leaders in order to protect and preserve the way we want to live as a nation. That is our true legacy. Not all this mystical thinking. Sometimes, it is wiser to ignore such things."

Saul fell quiet. In his heart, he felt a conflict; a clashing between what he had been taught by his mother, father, and Gamaliel; a warning against what he was learning from Caiaphas and the other Sadducees; a concern with something which had been showing itself in his dreams and quiet moments.

But now, his new mentor was telling him he should ignore such things.

And to be truthful, he reasoned, *hadn't his own inner voice of concern been fading of late?* He hadn't really thought about it until now. Perhaps it *was* just the voice of his childhood, and he didn't *need* it now that he had the *High Priest* as his mentor.

Yes, this was better, he determined.

He had definitely outgrown Gamaliel.

As they walked into the front doors of his palace, Joseph Caiaphas spoke to the servant who opened the door. "Please let my wife know I am home, and that we are hungry." Then he winked at Saul. "What do you say we see how our prisoner is doing?"

"I had forgotten all about him," the younger priest answered. "Did anyone give him water today?"

"Don't worry so much, son. If no one has, he will be more willing to comply with our demands. This is the kind of thing I'm talking about. You are going to have to learn to be a little less soft-hearted."

As they approached the area of the palace where the prison cells were located, the High Priest motioned to the guard at the door. "Good afternoon, Jehu," he said. "How is our traitor today?"

The man smiled. "He's been rather quiet today, sir. He didn't touch his food."

"Did you check on him? Is he breathing?" Joseph wanted to know.

"No, I didn't even unlock the door, sir," came the answer. "I wanted to follow your orders and leave him alone with his thoughts."

"Good man, good man," Caiaphas responded.

The guard pulled a key ring from his belt, and handed the keys to the High Priest. Joseph unlocked the door leading to the stairwell, and opening it, motioned for Saul to go in in front of him.

As the two men moved down the stone steps, their eyes adjusted to the dim light. Saul noticed there were no amenities for the Sanhedrin member who had been confined here. Except for a privy pot.

He looked around the cell. "Which cell is he in, sir?"

Joseph looked at him, surprised. "This one. He was lowered through the stone hole in the ceiling three nights ago. Why?"

Saul moved to look in the other cells also down in the basement level. "He doesn't appear to be here. Do you think someone came and took him?"

Joseph Caiaphas was instantly angry. "Jehu!" he shouted. "Where is the prisoner?"

A flustered Jehu appeared at the top of the stairs. "I don't know, sir. I was here all night, and have been here all day. I have not even dozed off. *No one* has come to see him. *No one* has gone through the door. When I checked on him last

180

night, he was in the cell. Right there, on the stone slab." He pointed to the stone ledge where the prisoner had slept without a cover the night before.

Saul looked to the slab, and thought he noticed something on the wall above it. He tilted his head, and suddenly, there, etched in the blood stains on the wall, was an image of the Galilean prophet, named Jesus.

How did that happen, he wondered? *And what did it mean?*

He shook his head. No, his mind was just playing tricks on him. It had been a long night, and today had been a long day, he decided.

Considering, he glanced once more at the image.

What was it the High Priest had confided? The Galilean had made the statement on the day of the impromptu procession last week? "If I tell these people to be silent, the very rocks will cry out." Is this what he had been referring to? And if it was, how had the man known?

Caiaphas and Jehu were searching through the cells, as well as the entire basement level of the palace, looking for Joseph of Arimathea. But, he was nowhere to be found. All of the locked doors from the night before were still secured, just as they had been. None of the iron bars were loose. Everything was just as it had been.

Where could he have gone?

And more importantly, how did he get out?

Caiaphas looked at Jehu with suspicion. "How much did he pay you to let him out?" he snarled in an accusatory tone.

Jehu stuttered. "I—I—didn't..." he began. "I did my job. I was awake all night, sir. And besides, he said something about his ankle being broken. He wouldn't have made it very far if I had let him out." He paused, licking his lips. "But I didn't. I swear before God, sir, and by the Temple!"

"I don't know what to believe, man," the High Priest retorted. "I do know this; you aren't going out of this cell, until I find him."

With that, Joseph motioned to Saul. The two priests made their way up the stairs, leaving a bewildered Jehu standing in the middle of the stone cell.

"I'll be back to question you." Caiaphas spoke to the guard, threatening. "I want you to consider telling me the truth."

With that he slammed the door shut and locked it, hanging the key ring on his own belt.

"I'm hungry," he said, looking at Saul. "Let's have lunch; then we can figure something out. He can't have gone very far."

Judah Iscariot stood at the gate to Ampliatus and Maria's home in the center of Jerusalem. He knocked again.

They probably won't answer, he thought. He couldn't blame them. After waiting a moment or two, he turned to go. He had taken a couple of steps away, when the door opened. Judah found himself face-to-face with Maria.

Surprised to see him, Maria ventured a greeting. "Hello, Judah!" she said with more brightness than she felt. "I'm sorry it took me so long. We are all up on the roof. There's a great breeze up there today. You want to come up and join us?"

Judah appraised her manner. "I don't have to, if you think it might make people uncomfortable. Is John here, or James?"

Maria shook her head. "No, they are at Zebedee's office home today, with their family."

"Is Simon Peter here?"

Maria once again shook her head. "He was here earlier, and he slept for a few hours. But Mary Magdalene came with John, and told us she had seen Jesus alive. Everyone here was concerned for her sanity. So, Simon went with John so they could see for themselves. He hasn't been back here since."

"Oh," Judah answered.

Maria watched him. He seemed troubled to her. "Why don't you come up and wait for them to return, Judah? You look tired. Are you hungry?"

Judah's eyes brimmed suddenly. Angry at himself for being weak, he blinked the tears away, shaking his head.

"That's all right," he said.

"Come on in," she coaxed. "We have plenty of room, and plenty of food." She stepped forward and pulled on his arm, drawing him into their home. She indicated a couch of pillows on the floor in the corner, and said, "Why don't you rest here for a little while? I'll get you some water."

"Oh, it's okay," Judah protested. "I'm not really hungry or thirsty." Somewhat unwillingly, he moved towards the couch Maria had shown him, and fell into it.

Maria moved away, intending to return to the gathering on the roof. As she walked away, Judah fell fast asleep.

At an inn in Emmaus-Nicopolis, three men were sitting down to eat an evening meal. They had travelled a long way in just a few hours, and not just in physical miles.

Cleophas and Simon had spent the afternoon with the new friend they had met on the road. The three had traveled together the last miles of the journey. The man was quite knowledgeable on the subjects of the Law and the Prophets, and had offered suggestions as answers to Simon's questions about the torture and execution of his step-brother, Jesus.

And then, there was the news of a possible resurrection.

Cleophas admitted, he didn't know what to think. Simon was suddenly awash in possibilities; imagining supernaturally assisted uprisings against Rome; complete with Abraham, Elijah and Moses coming down out of the clouds to pass judgment on the earth.

Addressing his words to Simon, the man asked. "So.... do you think this Jesus might have been the Promised Deliverer?"

"I hadn't really considered that possibility," the young man answered. "I mean, he was my *step-brother*. How many times do you really try to get along with a step-brother? He was Mary's son, and even my Uncle Joseph told us Jesus wasn't his son."

"What do you know about his birth?" the man asked.

"Well, it's what I've been told, but I wasn't there. I'd like to think it's all true, but I'm not sure. Supposedly, an angel appeared to Mary, and told her Jesus would be the Promised Deliverer; she was pregnant without ever having sex; that her cousin, Elizabeth was also miraculously pregnant with a son who became John the Baptizer from Qumran. Uncle Joseph said that they went to Bethlehem for Governor Quinirius' first census, and he was born there, in a cave that was part of an inn like this one."

"Did he say anything special about the night Jesus was born?" the man asked.

"He did tell me that there was a bright star that situated itself over the places where they stayed, for over two years after the birth," Cleophas told him. "He said there was a huge company of angels who appeared to the Temple Sacrifice Shepherds at Bethlehem the night of his birth. Those angels told the shepherds where to find them."

"Anything else?"

Cleophas continued. "That those shepherds came where Joseph and Mary were staying, and wanted to worship the baby."

"Worship him," the man echoed. "You're sure he said that?"

"Yes," came the reply.

There was a pause. "I can tell you what I understand to be true about the coming of the Promised Deliverer from the Law and the Prophets, if you like," he offered.

"Oh," Simon interjected. "There is one more thing. The star disappeared two years later. A company of court advisors from a king's court somewhere in the East came to their house in Bethlehem with gifts for Jesus. There were about fifty of them. The rumor was that King Herod slaughtered the infants two years old and younger just after that, because those mages asked where Jesus was. They told Herod all of their astrologers and magicians had been reading the signs in the sky; that Jesus had been born to be the King of the Jews."

The new friend looked at Cleophas with interest. "What do you think about that, Cleophas?" he asked.

"Truthfully, sir, I don't know. His mother was pregnant with him when my brother married her. I have tried to make it my practice not to have an opinion on such matters."

"But you *do* know what you believe…. Don't you?" The stranger wanted to know.

Cleophas shrugged. "I suppose. Sometimes. Well, mostly. I think I must avoid having conflicts; especially with family members."

The man chuckled. "Well, I know it can be confusing. Let me see if I can help you understand."

For the next few hours, the man explained what he said *he* believed had been spoken by the prophets about the Promised Deliverer; where he would be born, how he would die, what his purpose in coming was; and so much more.

He reminded them the Deliverer was to be born from "the seed of the woman," which would mean the woman would have to be a virgin, like the prophet Isaiah had foretold.

Strangely, he spoke just like Cleophas' brother, Joseph, had described the angel's instruction in his dreams so long ago.

Now, it was evening. They had shared more than seven hours together. They had been in Emmaus-Nicopolis for several hours. Cleophas realized his client meeting would be delayed until tomorrow; again. He hoped the man in question would still be willing to consider his estimate.

But somehow it didn't matter. Today's conversation had piqued his interest, like nothing had in a long, long time. Somehow, his soul was being fed and nurtured by this man's dialogue.

Something inside had been roused; awakened.

He could sense they would need to part ways soon. Surely this educated man had somewhere else he had to be. No one made a trip like this alone, unless they offered services very much in demand. This man's time was worth something, he realized.

Intentionally focusing his mind on the present moment, he pulled out of his reverie. Their traveling companion was reaching for one of the flat loaves of unleavened bread on the eating space in front of them.

Simon was the first one to realize.

The stranger broke the loaf in half, and then in half again, placing a piece in front of each of them. Then, he lifted the wine carafe to pour three glasses of new wine.

Fascinated, Simon couldn't take his eyes off their companion. What was it, making this ordinary conversation so stimulating, he wondered?

There was a short pause.

In the silence, Cleophas took a sip of his wine, and bit into the bread. He wondered where this man worked. Was he a business owner? How had he come to understand the Law and the Prophets so well?

The day's conversation had made everything he had ever been taught somehow make sense again.

Their new companion reached across the table, and took hold of Cleophas' hand. He waited until the wood carver looked up and met his eyes.

"Remember me," he said, with a thoughtful pause.

Suddenly, he vanished into thin air.

Completely gone.

With mouths hanging open, the father and son looked at each other in awed recognition.

The man walking with them all day had been the resurrected Jesus!

"Why didn't I identify him sooner?" Cleophas asked out loud. "Look! He didn't touch his bread, or his wine!"

Hungry, Simon picked up his bread, and bit into it. He picked up his cup and took a long drink. "I always enjoyed eating with him. I don't know why I didn't recognize him either. No one breaks bread like Jesus does," he said to his father with a grin. "I can't wait to see what he's going to do next."

Cleophas jumped to his feet, and began repacking their satchels. "We have to tell the others we have seen him, Simon!" he declared. "Let's go."

"What about your client meeting?" his son wanted to know.

"It will be fine," his father answered. "I just know I have to do this. They have to know."

In the Court of Hewn Stones, in the lower level of the Temple, Joseph Caiaphas had shifted into high intensity. Amihud, Saul, Annas, Gamaliel, and Nicodemus had been gathered together in a hurry.

"We need to get to the bottom of this," he fumed. "Now!"

Nicodemus smiled. "What if the stories *are* true, Joseph?"

The High Priest wheeled to face him. "There is no way these stories are true, Nicodemus. There has to be a conspiracy in the wind. Too many things are happening all at once!"

"But what if...." Gamaliel paused. "What if Jesus actually was, *or is*, who he said he was; the Son of God? What if he *was, or is,* the Promised Deliverer, and all of these are signs to confirm such a thing?"

"I will not get into a debate over this with you, old friend," Joseph Caiaphas answered. "At this point, I really need some answers, and I can't afford to give in to superstition. You may, if you will, since you are a Pharisee, explain it all off to some mystical experience. I need just a little more proof than that."

"Very well, then," the Pharisee responded. "Where do you suggest we begin?"

The High Priest began a fiery rattling of strategies and instructions.

"Saul," he ordered, with pointed finger, "find out where the followers of this Jesus are hiding. I want to know if they stole his body. I don't care what you have to do to find out the truth."

"Amihud," he continued, "go to King Herod's palace, and ask to speak to Pontius Pilate. Ask him what the soldiers from his guard detail have reported regarding the body of Jesus. Find out what really happened at the tomb this morning."

Both men nodded, and left immediately.

As soon as the door was closed, Annas ventured a question. "All right, Joseph, you have our attention. What is so important that we are all gathered here?"

Joseph spoke in a conspiratorial tone. "I arrested Joseph of Arimathea on Friday night. I put him into the private prison in my basement."

Annas was surprised. "I thought we discussed this. I told you not to do it."

Nicodemus noticed a redness beginning to grow on the sides of Annas' neck. Surely the older man was angry with his son-in-law.

"I know you did. And I didn't listen, and did it anyway. I am still convinced the man is a traitor. There is no way he can serve as Nobilus Decurio of Rome, and maintain a loyalty to Judea."

"What happened, Joseph?" Nicodemus asked.

"Well, last night, he was in the large cell. I checked on him before I went to bed. After the First Fruits Offerings were gathered in this morning, I went home. Saul was with me. The door to the cell stairway was locked. The guard was still outside. He said he had been awake all night, and no one had come in or out.

"But Joseph was nowhere to be found.

"I sent a Temple guard to his home here in the city. He is not there." He looked at Nicodemus. "I sent the same man to the home of your friend, Judah, as well. I wanted to make sure neither of you were hiding him." The Judah of whom Caiaphas spoke was the close friend of both Gamaliel and Nicodemus. He also owned a large home in the city. Many of the Pharisees met at his home for prayer on a regular basis.

Nicodemus was that priest's closest friend.

"I see," Nicodemus answered. "Why would you think either of us would hide him?"

"I don't want to get into it," Joseph waved his hand. "I just need your help to find him. Where do you think he could be?"

Gamaliel spoke quietly. "In light of the fact that my own grandsons were here this morning, and were raised from the dead since yesterday, *and* many of the same kind of stories are being told by those coming to the Temple today….." he paused. "I would say it's possible something unexpected and miraculous has happened."

"Well," the High Priest responded, "I want the four of us to take a trip to Arimathea. If he escaped, and he is not in the city, he has to be there. If we leave early in the morning, we can travel there, do our investigation, and be back tomorrow evening."

"What makes you think he would go there?" Annas asked.

"I don't know. Honestly, I don't think he could have gotten that far. After all, he had a broken ankle." Caiaphas answered.

"How did that happen?" Gamaliel asked.

"I don't know!" Caiaphas retorted. "He must have fallen or something. That doesn't matter really. I just think we need to locate him. Are you willing to go with me?"

Each man nodded; each had his own reason for agreement.

Annas wanted to settle the dispute between his son-in-law and a humble man who held power but never wielded it;

Caiaphas wanted to find the man and execute him;

Gamaliel and Nicodemus wanted to protect their friend, Joseph of Arimathea, from more accusations, evil plans and threats of danger.

It was mid-to-late afternoon when the young priest, Saul, knocked on the door of Zebedee's small office in the business district of Jerusalem. He had begun searching for Jesus' followers at Joseph of Arimathea's Jerusalem home. After all, he reasoned, the tomb was there. Loyal followers might be found there as well.

He had pretended to be a supporter of the Galilean, looking for the grieving. Apparently, several of the Roman soldiers had also been deceived by this Jesus. They told Saul to look for John the son of Zebedee. He had been a visitor to the tomb after the bright light had appeared. Since he was there, Saul decided to ask them what they had seen firsthand.

It was too fantastic to be believed, he told himself. Someone had to be lying. He found his inner dialogue continuing, with one thought within his mind gaining strength: *What would Caiaphas say about this?*

Now, he was waiting. An older man opened the door. "Can I help you?" he asked, noticing Saul's Temple attire.

"Yes, sir," Saul began. He looked the man in the eyes. "My name is Saul, and I am a priest at the Temple mount. I was wondering if I could find some of the men who traveled with Jesus the Galilean."

"Why?" the man wanted to know. "Are they in trouble?"

"Oh, no sir, nothing like that," the young priest replied. "I just heard that some strange things happened around Jesus' death, and wanted to know what was true and what was rumor." He paused. "And you are...."

"Zebedee," the older man answered. "You are welcome to come in, but the only ones here at the moment are myself and my wife, Salome. We were too tired to join the others. They are at the home of another friend, not far from here."

"Do you think they would mind if I dropped by?" Saul was putting great effort into coming across as nonchalant.

Zebedee was not blind to his efforts. Being a man who dealt in directness, he decided to voice his observations.

"Saul, is it?" he asked.

Saul nodded.

"I realize Joseph Caiaphas must have you scurrying around on many errands. As a father with sons about your age, let me encourage you in something."

Intrigued, Saul responded. "Yes?"

"Just don't get drawn in by the wrong influences. Anything causing you to focus on yourself, bringing hardness and numbness like a stone, will eventually destroy you. Jesus' message was about keeping our hearts open and obedient to God. Just don't forget what is really important in your life."

Taken by surprise at Zebedee's frankness, Saul was instantly offended. "Where is this friend's house?" he asked coldly.

The fisherman smiled and gave him directions. Ampliatus and Maria's home was only a few minutes' walk away. "You should find enough people there to get the true story. I hope you find what you are looking for, Saul. Have a great afternoon."

With that, Zebedee closed the door, and went back to the courtyard to sit once more with Salome.

When Saul reached the home of Ampliatus, he could hear discussion coming from the rooftop. He could tell a large group of people was in conversation. He contemplated Zebedee's words during his walk from one house to the other.

They had struck a nerve. Emboldened by his anger, he walked up the outdoor steps built on the side of the house to the rooftop.

Ascending the stairway, he spoke a greeting, "Hello?"

When he reached the top, he was greeted by the sight of a large circle of people of varying ages. Because he had called up in his approach, every face was turned toward the top of the steps where he stood.

Surprised to see a man in Temple priest's attire on his rooftop, Ampliatus rose from his seat and came to stand near Saul. "How can we help you, sir?" he asked.

Startled, Saul unwittingly blurted questions. "*You're* not Jewish! Who are you? Whose house is this?"

Taken back, the Roman architect reacted. "Excuse me? Who are you? What do you want?"

Saul realized his mistake. "Forgive me. I was just surprised to see all of you here together in one place."

"All of *us*?" the homeowner rejoined. "My name is Ampliatus, and I am a Roman citizen. This is my home, and these are my friends. Why are you here?"

189

"I'm sorry for the intrusion, sir," the young priest ventured. "My name is Saul, and I am a priest at the Temple. There have been several rumors floating around the city today about Jesus the Galilean, and his death. I have been asked to find out what his followers have experienced today. The leaders I serve are concerned in finding out the truth, rather than relying on stories or hearsay."

"Why did you come *here?*" Ampliatus asked.

"Well," Saul tried to be affable. "I first went to the marketplace, and someone who was purchasing fish told me about a man named Zebedee. They directed me to his office home in the business district. He is the one who told me how to get here."

A young man stepped forward. "Hi Saul," he said. "I'm John. This is my brother, James. Zebedee is our father. What is it you want to know? Would you like to come and sit down?"

"I am supposed to find out if any of you stole his body."

The statement was met by shocked silence. For several moments the followers of Jesus sat in stunned silence. Then, a ripple of laughter began. Finally, John spoke.

"Mary Magdalene came to my father's office this morning. She stayed with Jesus' mother at the home of Joseph of Arimathea last night. Joseph is Jesus' great-uncle. He parented our Aunt Mary after she was orphaned when her parents died. He also arranged her wedding. Her sister, Salome, is our mother."

Saul had been following the family connection. "So, you are saying that Jesus is your *cousin?*" he asked.

"*Is?*" Ampliatus interjected. "So *you* think he is alive as well?"

"I meant '*was,*'" Saul replied, flustered. "Anyway, tell me about your experiences." He moved to sit down, joining the circle.

Unseen by anyone, Judah Iscariot had arrived at the top of the steps. Quietly, he moved to a corner of the rooftop, where he could hear and observe what was happening in front of him.

"Where would you like us to begin?" James asked.

Saul blinked. "I have no idea," he said. "I guess you should begin with whatever you think is important."

The group exchanged glances. Who would explain? Who could tell the story? Finally, another young man spoke up.

"Hi Saul," he said. "My name is Levi. My father is Cleophas. My own mother died in childbirth years ago. He took Mary as his wife when his brother, Joseph of Nazareth, died. My brother, Simon and I, and our sisters here have been part of the household for our entire lives.

190

"Let me give you some background, to help you understand how any of this happened in the first place...."

For the next hour or so, Levi shared the account of Jesus' life, with intermittent additions from others in the gathering. When it came to the day of Jesus' arrest, an unexpected voice was heard from the top of the stairwell.

"He washed our feet. I didn't want him to wash mine." A strangely different Simon Peter walked across the rooftop to sit next to Elsbeth, his wife. He kissed her cheek. "I told him I would follow him anywhere, and I was strong enough to withstand anything to protect him. And yet, within 6 hours I had denied I had ever met him. But he knew it was going to happen. He told me before the rooster crowed in the marketplace that morning, I would deny even knowing him three times. And sure enough, no soon were the third set of denial words out of my mouth, but I heard a rooster."

"Simon!" Elsbeth greeted him. "When did you get back?"

"Just now," he said, looking into her eyes, with a quick touch to her face.

"I sold him to Caiaphas," Judah Iscariot's tired voice spoke from the hidden corner where he had been sitting. "He asked me if I meant what I said to him in the garden."

"When did *you* get here, Judah?" Ampliatus wanted to know.

"Oh, I let him in earlier today," Maria told her husband. "He came to the door, looking for several of the twelve. I invited him in to wait, and he fell asleep."

Simon Peter was looking at Judah quizzically. "What do you mean, he asked you? When would he have asked you?"

The Iscariot met his eyes. "He came and sat by me in the street this morning. Just before I came here. He said the kingdom he wanted to set up is not physical or political. He didn't make sense to me. We had a discussion."

Simon Peter's eyes grew wide. "I saw him too!" he exclaimed. "Alive!! He came and sat by *me*. After John and I ran to the tomb; I couldn't face what I felt. I had failed him, and felt tremendous guilt and shame. But when we met together, that all lifted from me." He looked at his wife. "I don't think I will ever be the same man again."

Mary Magdalene spoke up. "When I saw him in Joseph's garden early this morning, he said to tell all of you that he was alive, and would be going to Galilee before you. I think he wants us all to meet him there."

Saul couldn't believe what he was hearing. He looked at Judah Iscariot. "You took money from Caiaphas?"

"I did," Judah answered. "I was sure if Jesus were able to speak with Caiaphas, they would come up with a plan to set up the throne of Israel once more. We Sicari have been training for years in the desert at Qumran. We all feel we must at least try to take a stand for our national identity. I thought Jesus was the Promised Deliverer, so I tried to give things a little push."

"You certainly messed *that* up, Judah," Jesus' half-brother, James, interjected. "Didn't it occur to you they might want him *dead*? Didn't you hear him tell us that he was going to be executed in Jerusalem?"

"I have realized it *since* then, but I didn't at the time," Judah spoke defensively. "I was raised to be Essene. We are taught to believe our lives happen without choices. I had to follow every opportunity presented me."

Saul looked at Judah. "What *did* you say to him in the garden?" he asked. "I wasn't there."

"I called him 'Master.' I did mean it, but I meant it in the way I thought he was going to be crowned as king. I thought God was speaking to me, because Caiaphas wanted to pay me in silver shekels, just as Jacob's sons sold their brother, Joseph, to the Amalekites."

Saul looked at him. "Thirty pieces of silver? The cost to redeem a first-born son?"

Sighing, Judah shrugged. "Exactly."

Simon Peter spoke up. "I thought that way too, Judah," he admitted, his voice breaking. "I even drew my sword in the garden and cut off a man's ear. But no longer. I know something has changed inside of me. I don't have the words to express it all yet, but I think they will come in time."

These people really believe this man rose from the dead. They are sincere, a surprised Saul determined.

Having reached his decision, the young priest stood. "Well, thank you for your time. I need to get back to the Temple." He looked around the rooftop. "I appreciate your help. Thank you for sharing with me."

Ampliatus walked down the outdoor stairwell with the young man. "I'm glad we could help you, Saul," he said. "Come back anytime."

As Saul walked down the street, he contemplated the gathering of people he had just met. If they had stolen Jesus' body, why would they have shared their personal stories of change so freely? Surely he would have sensed it, had they been trying to hide something. And to have so many with similar stories?

Caiaphas would not be happy about this, he knew. His mentor would require a more ordinary explanation.

A few moments after Saul left, Judah Iscariot also rose. He had observed the group of Jesus' followers for a while now. There was a quiet sense of acceptance and inexplicable confidence working its way through how these people saw their lives, he determined.

He would never be able to believe like they did. Thinking logically, he wasn't even sure now it had really *been* Jesus he had spoken with earlier that day. Perhaps it had been an apparition, brought about by a lack of sleep and stress.

He was leaving, and would not return. He had decided.
He no longer belonged here.

A few hours after sunset that evening, everyone drew together for dinner with Ampliatus and Maria. Salome, Elsbeth, and both Marys were working to put together the meal. Earlier in the day, Ampliatus suggested they move the conversation downstairs into the main part of the house, or at least to the ground level courtyard, where the gathering would be more privatized.

"After all," he observed, "I'm not really sure what young Saul's motives really were. If he should assemble a group to come and arrest us, I would like it to be necessary for someone to at least need to knock on my front door."

In the middle of the meal, an excited Cleophas and Simon arrived. After greeting his wife, Mary, Cleophas addressed the group. "We saw Jesus. He came and joined us on our journey to Emmaus-Nicopolis. We walked with him and talked with him for seven hours, and we didn't recognize him until he broke bread and poured wine for our dinner at the inn."

Everyone wanted to hear their story. Again and again. Everyone wanted to hear Simon Peter's story, again and again. Everyone wanted to hear Magdalene's story, again and again. As they spoke, the women were comparing notes on their experiences that morning.

What had happened?

Was it real?

Was it true?

Dinner was winding down, and everyone was feeling a sense of comfort after the meal. Compliments to the cooks were heard repeatedly. Was there more baklava? Was there any honey wine left, or beer?

As she inspected the outdoor courtyard, Maria assessed the outdoor kitchen area. She definitely would need to go to the market in the morning, she considered. It was good some of the merchants set up their booths after the second day of the Passover week.

Cleaning and scrutinizing the stone countertop where the evening's food had been prepared, she noticed the light coming from the interior of the house was shining more brightly than usual. Turning around she was amazed at what she saw.

Jesus was standing in the middle of the main room of her home, dressed in white! He was standing with his arms extended, to enable everyone to see the wound holes in his wrists. And somehow, the wound in his side was visible also. Maria was transfixed.

He looked toward the window. "Don't be afraid," he said. "Peace to each of you."

There was an immediate sense of awed amazement, accompanied by pandemonium. "Jesus! It is really you?" "Where have you been?" "How did you come back to life?" Each of these were questions distinguishable in the midst of joyous chaos.

"Here. Look at my wounds," he told them. "Don't be afraid. Touch me. I'm real. I'm Jesus. I'm the one who was crucified. I'm alive again. A ghost doesn't have flesh and bones like I do. Here. See for yourself."

Maria hurried into the house.

Jesus sat down with them, and everyone eventually followed suit. As the group settled, attention remained focused on the resurrected man.

He motioned for those standing to be seated, and then he said, "Do you have anything left to eat?"

Salome and Maria hurriedly moved to find a plate, a cup, and food. *Of course he's hungry,* Salome considered. *He's a man, and has been very busy traveling all day.*

Salome brought Jesus a plate of food; broiled fish and a piece of honeycomb. Maria poured him some water.

As he ate, Jesus answered questions, putting their minds at ease. They were not to worry about the Jews, or the Sadducees. He was going to go to Galilee, and wanted them to follow him there. He would be with them a little longer, he said.

"I am going to send you out, in the same way Abba Father sent me out," he told them.

Then, he inhaled deeply, and breathed on them. "Receive the Holy Spirit," he said. A light breeze blew through the room. As each one sensed it, an inner rush of Peace and God's Approval settled hearts and minds.

As he vanished, one more phrase was heard, "Prepare to go to Galilee. I will meet you there."

9 – Awakenings
April 6, 33CE

Just after sunrise on Monday, five men walked together on the road heading east from Jerusalem to Arimathea. They were dressed in normal, everyday attire, rather than their normal priestly garments. Each one felt it would be unwise to draw attention to five Temple priests traveling together, especially since the road to Arimathea was on the way to the *Via Maris*, or Sea-Road, international trade route. Since Joseph of Arimathea's estate was situated on a high hill plateau in the hill country of Ephraim, it rarely received visitors, unless those visiting were intentional about doing so.

"I don't want anyone knowing we are coming," Caiaphas told them beforehand. "It's better if we are dressed as normally as possible, so we don't arouse suspicion."

The distance to Joseph's estate was just a little over two miles from Jerusalem, but the gradual increase in elevation caused the passage to take a little longer than if they had been travelling on level ground.

For most of the time, the four trekked in silence behind an angry Caiaphas. Nicodemus and Gamaliel walked together, with Simeon walking with Saul. The two younger men had grown up together, and although Simeon was much older than Saul, their relationship was like that of close brothers.

An hour later, the group reached the entrance of Joseph's estate.

Nicodemus, as a close friend, had been to Joseph's home many times in the past. He walked between the entrance pillars, to the front doors of the plaster covered stone-and-mortar house.

"Joseph?" he called. "Joseph, are you here?"

Silence responded.

Nicodemus turned to his companions. "He doesn't seem to be here."

Caiaphas snorted. "It will take more than that to prove he's not here," he retorted.

Just then, a young woman came to the front door, opening it. "I'm sorry," she whispered loudly. "He is sleeping. It's too early to wake him. Are you gentlemen expected?"

"Not exactly, Raziela," Nicodemus ventured. "We came to see Joseph. When did he get home?"

The housekeeper smiled. "Welcome, Nicodemus," she answered. "He wasn't supposed to be here. I thought he was staying in the city for the rest of the Feast Week. It was the funniest thing too. Whenever I clean for him, I lock the doors when I leave. He had left his keys behind when he was here a couple of weeks ago. I had expected him to come to my home to get his keys when he came back."

"Then how did he get inside?" Simeon asked.

Raziela shrugged. "I don't know, unless he had another set I wasn't aware of."

"What happened?" Caiaphas asked.

She looked at the High Priest. "Well, when I got here this morning, all the doors and shutters were still locked, and the house was secure, just as I had left it. No supplies were disturbed in the storeroom. But when I went through to check on things, I found Master Joseph asleep in his bed; but the doors were still locked as they had been."

She looked back to Nicodemus. "Do you think he *might* have had another set of keys in Jerusalem?" She paused. "And there was one other thing."

"What's that?" he asked.

"Well, he must have gone directly to bed without taking off his clothes or even his shoes. There was no laundry needing to be done. The only change in the entire house, was Master Joseph in his bed. He didn't even use the privy pot."

"Those are things I can't explain," the sage answered. "Do you have any idea when we might be able to see him?"

Still whispering, Raziela responded. "I'm not sure how long he has been asleep, or when he arrived, so that I can't answer. I do know he will want to see you when he awakens."

Even though Caiaphas demanded Raziela rouse her employer from his sleep, the housekeeper refused to comply. "This is his home, and I work for him. He has instructed me not to wake him unless there is an emergency."

Caiaphas had become angry. "This is an emergency, woman."

Smiling in response, Raziela lowered her voice, looking the High Priest with a steady, even gaze. "I will tell you what I tell my children, sir. Unless someone is bleeding or dead, the rules apply to you, and I will not change them.

"Now, please have a seat in the courtyard, and I will bring you something to drink while you wait for him to wake up."

At that point, the men realized there would be no arguing with this woman. She might as well have been armed with swords, spears, and dressed in full armor. In resignation, they sat down to wait.

It was over two hours later, when a groggy Joseph of Arimathea emerged from his bedchamber. Rubbing his head, he walked into the courtyard area where Caiaphas, Gamaliel, Nicodemus, Simeon and Saul had been waiting since their arrival. Unaware, he stumbled to the well, and drew out water. He took a drink, and then splashed water on his face. As he reached for a towel, he looked up, saw his visitors, and froze in place.

"Well, hello!" he said, greeting them.

Nicodemus stood up and came over to stand beside his friend. "Good morning, Joseph! Did you sleep well?"

Somewhat dazed, Joseph looked around. "I—I think so," he answered. "Where *are* we?"

"What?" his friend replied. "We are in *your home* in Arimathea."

"No," Joseph answered. "This has to be a dream. I am not in pain, and I am standing on my ankle, which I know for a fact is broken. If I were awake, I would be in Caiaphas' palace dungeon, praying for Death to come."

Hearing his words, Gamaliel and Nicodemus looked at Caiaphas in shocked surprise.

"What did you *do* to him?" Gamaliel demanded. "Torture is in contradiction of our laws; *especially* against another priest; especially *this* man."

Caiaphas unthinkingly flinched. "He-- He is friends with Pontius Pilate. He is a traitor."

Gamaliel was incensed. "Of *course* he is, Caiaphas! He is the *Nobilus Decurio* of Rome! His *mines* and Rome's *need* for them keep us at peace for now. His *friendship*, as you call it, is probably one of the main reasons why we are still even *allowed* to *have* a Temple!"

The grandson of the Great Hillel continued. "Who have you *become*, that you can arrest men without the Council's consent? Or have a man executed because he embarrasses you, or believes differently than you do?"

Caiaphas was silent for the first time, confronted with the truth of his actions. He had no response to give.

At least for the moment.

Nicodemus appraised his friend. "Joseph, you are at your own estate in Arimathea. Do you remember how you got here? Or when?"

Joseph nodded. "I guess it wasn't a dream after all," he said. "The last thing I remember, I was laying on the stone slab in Caiaphas' prison cell. My ankle was broken, and I had raw rope burns under my arms. I tried to go to sleep, but it was too cold to rest. Then, Jesus came to me. He washed me. I didn't believe it was him, so I asked him to show me where I had buried him. Suddenly we were standing inside my garden tomb, and the Roman seal on the door was broken. Then, he carried me here, and placed me in my bed. I was suddenly warm, and no longer hurting; no longer cold. Then I fell asleep. This morning I woke up, and all of you were here."

"Jesus?" Simeon interjected. "As in, Jesus the Galilean? The man executed on Friday?"

Joseph looked at Gamaliel's son. "Yes, that's the man. His mother is my niece."

Simeon's eyebrows went up in surprise. That explanation was amazing, he considered. It certainly made Joseph's actions over the past few days understandable. He decided to share his own news with Joseph.

"Did you know Jesus also appeared to my dead sons yesterday, while their souls were in the nether-regions of Sheol? They told us he came where they were. He took the first man, Adam, by the hand, and led all of those who believed in him out of the hands of Hell and Death. My boys are alive, Joseph! They came to our home! Caiaphas has seen them, and *touched* them! Each of the men here have seen them!"

Nicodemus and Joseph exchanged glances in speechless amazement.

Joseph thought he should explain his actions. "He told me to wait here for forty days, and then it would become clear to me what I am to do. He is not ordinary. Something about my life is changing, because of him. He is so much greater than I had ever considered. I'm not sure what is happening, but I know I must do as he asks."

That night, at the business office apartment for Zebedee and Salome's family fishing business, friends joined Zebedee's family for dinner. In fact, a rather large group gathered in the enclosed courtyard. Salome was counting the cups needed to serve warm wine and *baklava*. She had also made *bourekas* for dessert.

In addition to Zebedee and Salome; their sons, James and John; their daughters, Tirzah and Tehila; Cleophas and Mary, Mary's sons; James, Joseph, and Judah; Cleophas' sons and daughters; Levi and Simon, Mary and Keshet; Simon Zealotes; Mary the Magdalene; Thomas, his wife, Kelila, and four children; and Judah the Sicari.

The conversations centered on reviewing the accounts of Jesus' appearances to various groups of people over the past few days. At the present, Mary Magdalene was describing the moment when Jesus had called her by name just after his resurrection.

"You are making this up, aren't you?" Thomas asked, looking around the room.

The Magdalene was surprised. "No, Thomas," she answered. "I'm telling the truth. Jesus really is alive."

Thomas looked at her with no small degree of condescension. "Oh come on, Mary!" he said. "You can't possibly actually think you have seen a dead man resurrected."

"I can, and I do!" she replied, somewhat indignantly.

"Well, it's not logical!" he declared, dismissing any view other than his own. "I *know* he is dead. I saw him die on Friday. So, I'm sure, if he *is* alive, he won't mind proving it to me. I will need to put my fingers in the holes in his wrists, and in his feet. I will need to put my hand in his side to verify his identity."

"Simon Peter saw him. So did Judah the Sicari."

"So *they* say. I don't believe them either."

In the corner of the room, a commotion began, with expressions of surprise and amazement. An excitement ripple began, gathering momentum as it moved forward. Curious, Thomas looked towards the corner of the courtyard. He noticed light emerging where there normally was shadow.

How was it possible the corner had more light than the rest of the room? Weren't corners normally darker, he wondered? Unconsciously, he rose from his seat, and went to investigate.

Stepping away from under the arbor, Thomas couldn't believe what he saw. Jesus was sitting with Mary's son, James. He was dressed in white. The two men seemed to be in the middle of a profound conversation.

Thomas couldn't help himself. He sat down next to them.

Was this really Jesus, he wondered?

Fascinated, he was drawn into the conversation taking place. James was speaking.

"There are so many things I said during our childhood," he was saying. "Now, I wish I could go back and change things. I keep wondering what I missed because of my attitudes."

Jesus chuckled. "I understand. Just remember, James. Everything we experienced will be used for good in Abba's design to *prepare* all of you. And to prepare you for the future I want you to follow in building the *Ecclesia.*"

"I keep hearing you say these things, Jesus," came the answer. "I'm not sure I am the right choice. I wasn't part of the twelve."

Jesus patted his half-brother's knee. "Don't worry about that. All of you are going to be very busy." He turned his head and looked at Thomas. "So Thomas, would you like to put your fingers in the wrist wounds now? I don't want you to have any doubts. And the wound in my side is still open as well, if you want to check for my identity."

Shocked, Thomas' jaw dropped open. His eyes widened. "How did you know I said that before?"

Silence was the response. The Master smiled as he assessed his fearful disciple. "Well, Thomas?"

Almost automatically, Thomas dropped to his knees, and grabbed Jesus' feet. "Oh, my Lord!" he cried. "I do believe! You are now my God!"

Smiling, Jesus reached down to help the man to his feet. "Thomas, you believe now, because you have seen and felt." He looked around the room to each of them. "But there is greater joy to be found when a person believes even when they have *not yet* seen."

For forty days after his Resurrection, Jesus walked and talked with his followers in Galilee. He met with those in the fishing villages around Lake Gennesaret, just as before. He taught about the Kingdom, and prepared them for the days ahead. He trained them, taking time with each of them individually. He shared truths to help them, prepare them, to develop them.

"Is this when you will be restoring the nation of Israel to power?" one of them asked one day.

"It is not for you to know the exact timings and seasons Abba Father has designed, or the day He has set for his purposes to be seen," Jesus told them.

"Only the Father knows his plan. He will share His plan when it is the right time."

Towards the end of the forty days, Jesus led more than five hundred of them all back to Jerusalem, to a place just outside the village of Bethany. They sat down on the grass, to listen to him teach.

It was like the days …. Before.

A hope it would be like this forever permeated everyone there.

But then, at the end of the teaching, Jesus gave them instructions. "I want you to go back to the city and wait. I will be sending Abba's Promise to you; the Holy Spirit. He will fill you with power to live the life I am calling you to live. He will help you to hear my voice. He will give you the strength to speak truth about your experiences in the Kingdom.

"I want you to go into all parts of the world. Tell everyone the Good News that I love them and want to give them Life. Tell everyone. Heal the sick. Raise the dead. Cast out demons. Make disciples in all the nations. When you do, baptize them in the name of the Father, the Son, and the Holy Spirit.

"When people believe, you will see these evidences: they will speak with new tongues, they will cast out demons, their lives will be protected for my purposes to be fulfilled; they will lay hands on the sick and they will recover."

They stood, watching, as Jesus rose from the ground. Around them, also rising, were those whose bodies had resurrected on the day of Jesus' resurrection: the day when the grip of Death was overturned. He was still speaking to them, saying good-bye, in a hovering position, as those now alive again; more than three hundred of them; continued to be lifted up higher and higher. The group became a heavenly host, and then became like a cloud.

As they were watching the phenomenon, Jesus spoke once again.

"Wait for the Promise. He will come with power. You will receive this power. You will be able to express what has happened so people will understand; first in Jerusalem, and Judea, and Samaria, and then the entire world."

Rising, he looked upward. Then, he disappeared into the clouds of those waiting above them. For long moments, everyone stood, looking up, waiting for something else to happen.

"Why are you standing here looking up into the sky?"

A man's voice took them by surprise.

Two young men in brilliant, blazing white stood where Jesus had been standing. "This same Jesus; the one you just saw being taken up into heaven, will come back; *in the very same way He left*."

He had ascended; like he had told them he would.

And He would come back again.

Eagerly, they all returned to Jerusalem. Some returned to the Temple, and some to the Great Room in the Essene Quarter. Jesus had asked them to wait.

Just southeast of the city, outside the Dung Gate, the Valley of Hinnom opened into a large, open place known as *Hakeldama.* Designated as public land, the soil of the area was dark red in color, and in great demand with the pottery merchants of the area.

In this field, all remnants of sacrifices not consumed by the fires on the Brazen Altar were burned until completely consumed; turned to ashes. For this reason, no one had ever built on this land.

The spiritual significance of the area was clear to everyone who worshipped at the Temple. One could not follow ElShaddai with an obedient heart without realizing the need for personal inner sacrifice; or without understanding the necessity for yieldedness to the Unseen Altar's Fire to cleanse the heart like He had with the prophet Isaiah.

One could not maintain spiritual integrity while allowing sin to remain in their heart. It had to be removed. Just as the city of Jerusalem had a Dung Gate, those who served ElShaddai also needed a place to confess and discard sin's remnants. Thus receiving cleansing. Thus discovering freedom.

It was to the field of Hakeldama the Sicari fled. He stood at the Dung Gate, just outside the city, overlooking the Valley of Hinnom. He stood on a narrow, level terrace, under the low hanging branches of a sycamore tree.

My life means nothing, he told himself. *It's too late for me. I have made too many mistakes now to change. This is not the kingdom I wanted.*

With the lies of his imprinting screaming in his mind; with his heart believing there could be no hope; with tears streaming down his face, his chest tight with fear; Judah tightened the noose around his own neck, closed his eyes, and stepped out from the terrace's edge. As he did, the knot he had tied earlier pulled apart, but not before breaking his neck and severing blood flow. The knot's breakdown released Judah's body to drop into the valley below. As his frame hit the red earth below, it broke apart, spilling life-blood and gore in all directions.

As the sun sank below the horizon that evening, Joseph of Arimathea sat at his *scriptoria*, or desk, in the large receiving room of his estate home. Rizela had filled and lighted the room's lamps before she left for the evening. As he sipped a warm cup of herbed and honeyed wine, he opened the first of the two codices he had purchased in Rome during his last business trip.

The first codex; the one he was reading now, was smaller and thinner than the one waiting to be read. It had taken the priest a long time to adjust to the new method of publication; turning the square-shaped skins to read on both sides, rather than unroll one continuous page stretched between two elaborate rollers.

Knowing his love for study, Joseph's steward, Janaus, had suggested he consider purchasing a codex or two. "They are easier to store than scrolls" he told his employer. "I believe they will be the next form of information storage as the world moves forward."

He had been intrigued. During his last stop in Rome, Joseph visited his literary supplier, and chose two codexes (books) translated into *koine* Greek: the writings of the prophets Jeremiah and Isaiah.

"We will see, Janaus. We will see." He spoke aloud, beginning to read.

For tonight's reading, he had chosen the accounts of the prophet Jeremiah. Since his release from Caiaphas' prison a little over a month prior, he had felt drawn to read these particular prophetic accounts. He had sensed an inner nudging from the Spirit of God to draw out truths for his own life's application from Jeremiah's story. Over the past few days, the nudging had become stronger and stronger, until he had no doubt he would miss something Abba wanted to tell him if he procrastinated in any way.

Now, he was amazed at what he was discovering. Within the first few paragraphs, Jeremiah's relationship with Abba struck a chord in his heart.

The LORD gave me this message:
"I knew you before I formed you in your mother's womb.
Before you were born I set you apart
and appointed you as my prophet to the nations."
"O Sovereign LORD," I said, "I can't speak for you! I'm too young!"
The LORD replied, "Don't say, 'I'm too young,' for you must go wherever
I send you and say whatever I tell you. And don't be afraid of the people,
for I will be with you and will protect you. I, the LORD, have spoken!"
Then the LORD reached out and touched my mouth and said,
"Look, I have put my words in your mouth!
Today I appoint you to stand up against nations and kingdoms.

Some you must uproot and tear down, destroy and overthrow.
Others you must build up and plant."

Halted, he could read no further. Unbidden, tears came to Joseph's eyes. *Why would these words affect him in such a way,* he wondered?

Perhaps it was all of the unsettling events of the past two months? Was he just that fragile? Were his emotions so close to the surface because of weakness?

Contemplating the words he had read, he readied himself for sleep.

Pulling the covers up to his ears, Joseph fell fast asleep. As he did, he began to dream.

He was standing on top of a white cliff, in bright sun, overlooking a sandy beach. Visible in the distance, over the sea, was the edge of another continent, one which he knew was remotely attached to his homeland. Then, a shadow began to fall. Looking up to find its source, he saw an immense, black moon rise from the far land. It rose to block out the sun. He turned and saw the shadow had taken shape, becoming a solid image filling the entire land where he stood. For as far away as he could see, the moon had blocked out the sun's rays.

Suddenly, he was no longer on the cliff, but standing in a strange sailboat, with two canopied areas on its stern.

Then a woman appeared. Dressed in white, at first, he assumed she was working to restore the sun's light. But then, her face drew close to him, and he felt icy fingers around his neck. It became hard to breathe. Her eyes grew black and then turned to glowing red. Her lips grew green, then black, as did her teeth and the inside of her mouth.

Joseph looked down at his hands, and realized he was carrying his walking stick in his right hand. Still struggling to breathe in his dream, he took the staff with both hands, and drove it down into the ground where he stood.

Immediately, the atmosphere exploded into bright light.

Then, he stood alone inside a mining cavern. He could see veins of silver and copper running through the stone, along with tin. He looked once more at his hands, and saw a codex, and a crown.

The Voice he recognized, and had known oh so well, spoke.

"They are gold and diamonds, Joseph. Mine them well."

Upon waking, Joseph contemplated the meaning of the images he had witnessed in his dream. What did they mean, he wondered?

Instinctively, he sensed they were important messages from his God. "What do they mean, Lord?" he asked.

He had recognized the cliffs as being part of Briton, the land where the Dumnonia were ruled by King Arviragus and Izolde, his queen. But what did rest of the symbols mean?

Being a Pharisee, the priest was wise enough to understand the parabolic nature of dream language. Taking a clay codex, Joseph marked the significant points of his night vision so he would not forget its teaching when its time presented itself.

In the valley of Shechem, between Mount Ebal and Mount Gerizim in the nation of Samaria, two men were seated near a campfire, reading instructions from a rolled papyrus. Beside them stood a donkey, loaded with supplies for excavation and transient outdoor living.

Moshe's brother had always been good at puzzles. He had concentrated his attention on the translation of the Essene copper scroll for the past few weeks, and had come to a conclusion after much thought and deliberation.

They would begin digging here.

Shechem had been historically important since the pre-slavery days of the patriarch, Jacob, and his family. When the liberated children of Israel had settled, the original Tabernacle of Moses had been constructed on Mount Gerizim. When Solomon's Temple was built, the site had been abandoned by many as a sacred site in Israel. For the Samaritans, however, the Mount continued to be held as sacred. The loyal had continued the offering of sacrifices on Mount Gerizim, even without the presence of the Ark of the Covenant.

Then, had come the days of Persian and Macedonian occupations, when conquerors destroyed the Tabernacle, and constructed temples to false gods on the same site. Through it all, the Samaritans continued to hold the site as ElShaddai's first choice as the center of worship in the nation.

According to the Essene's copper scroll, golden vessels used in the original Moses' Tabernacle had, at some point been buried near the original worship site.

Moshe was convinced they would find the vessels very soon.

Seven days later, a Mighty Wind blew through the Great Room where more than one hundred and twenty waited. It was a Feast Day, designed to remind them of the day ElJireh brought water from the rock in the desert.

It was a day to connect with the Living God.

It was a day to remember Jesus. What was it He had told them?

"I am going away to prepare a place for you. I and the Father are one. I will send you another Comforter, and He will teach you all things. He is the Spirit of Truth."

Suddenly, the shutters of the Great Room blew open. A strong east wind began to blow in the windows. Accompanying the wind was a rushing sound.

Was it wind? Was it water? Thunder?

Here and there, hands were raised, as people were giving praise and glory to God. Some groups were more expressive. Some groups were not.

The wind grew stronger. Over the heads of those in the room, Light began to glimmer. Tiny sparks of Light hung in middle space, growing and intensifying as the corporate worship continued. Finally, iridescent flame hovered just above each person's head.

Even the children present were experiencing this amazing phenomenon.

Each one realized, with the Wind, a brand new sense of intimacy and relationship had come.

It was like Jesus was actually with them again.

They could sense His Presence.

Nicodemus found himself remembering Jesus' words, and receiving unsullied understanding: "The Spirit of God is like the wind. You can see what He is doing, but you cannot contain Him, or see Him."

As the Wind penetrated their space, each person was breathing in; receiving fresh Life from the supernatural manifestation of their Master's pledge.

As each person breathed in of the Wind of the Spirit; their breathing out was filled with new language. Everyone was suddenly speaking a language they had not known before.

The language of angels. The language of Heaven.

One by one, people stood, unexpectedly desiring to experience movement outside of the Great Room. In the street outside, the wind had been localized to just the Essene Quarter.

People stopped to discover what was making the sound they were hearing. All through Jerusalem, dedicated believers in ElShaddai, the Living God, had gathered for the feast from every corner of the empire. Now each one was hearing the story of Jesus in their own language.

For a long time, those from the Great Upper Room moved about the city, continuing to speak in this new Expression of God's Grace.

"Aren't the people who are speaking to us, mostly from Galilee?" someone asked. "How did they learn my language?"

"How is this happening?" someone else questioned. "This man has never been to my country!"

Someone else said, "These people are just drunk on new wine!"

In the middle of the excitement, Simon Peter stood up. He drew the rest of the twelve around him, and began to address the crowd.

"Brothers and sisters!" he shouted. "These people are not drunk! It's only nine in the morning!! No one has been awake that long!"

The crowd laughed with him. He continued.

"This is the promise that was spoken by the prophet, Joel: 'I will pour out my Spirit on all flesh; and your sons and your daughters shall prophesy. Your young men will see visions; and your old men shall dream dreams. On my servants and my handmaidens, I will pour out My Spirit.'"

As Simon Peter shared, anointed and filled with the Promised Comforter, the Holy Spirit, more than three thousand people decided to believe in Jesus, and who He said he was.

In one day!

Looking back, John realized the Holy Spirit had been poured out like Living Water; to satisfy the hunger and thirst of everyone who would believe in Jesus.

It was a spiritual explanation of the picture of the Moses' miracle; just as water had come from the Rock when it was struck, so the Living Water had poured out from the Spiritual Rock who had been struck down, Jesus.

On the day set to remember the sending of Abba's Law to seal the Old Covenant, Jesus had sent his Holy Spirit to seal the New Covenant.

208

Part Two

10 - Connections

Autumn, 33CE

His friends would be arriving soon.

Uri BenYaniv leaned back against the stone wall of his house and closed his eyes. Why was every move such an effort these days? Why did every shift seem to pull his joints apart with pain? He sighed. It felt like an eternity since Rimona had left him here, to wait for them. In truth, he knew it hadn't been more than an hour. He checked the tabletop. Yes, she had laid out his belongings for the workday. She was a good friend; a true neighbor.

"Simeon and the boys will be right over, Uri," she told him. "Just finish your breakfast."

Uri sipped the warm wine, munching on the dates and olives she had placed in front of him. Looking through his open door, the beggar gave the sky an appraisal.

It would be another hot one today, he mused. He would need to ask to be placed in a spot where the sunlight would put him in shadow the whole day. He smiled, remembering his younger years. There had been days back then when he had asked to be placed where the sun would shine hot and bright. Such a placement evoked more pity in the street passers-by. He had done well in those days. People had stopped to speak; some even becoming friends.

But times had changed. Over the years, he had become a known fixture; an anticipated hindrance in the path of those walking into the Temple. These days, he knew he was blessed when those making pilgrimage into the city ever remembered to throw a few coins into his cup on their way to worship.

He had stopped looking at faces years ago.

The work of begging had been easier then. His parents had been alive. Yaniv, his father, had died first. Then, in the years following, his mother, Jasmina, had cared for him with such gentleness. He missed her. His parents had been his only friends. Back then, someone had been there to help massage his joints, to help him straighten his fingers, to cook his meals.

Had there ever been a time when this incessant physical pain had not been his constant companion? Or a time he had been able to stand on his crippled feet, or move his left arm?

Involuntarily, he shook his head.

He couldn't remember such a time.

As time, and his age, had advanced, Uri grew accustomed to living alone; isolated; insulated from the world by his condition. After all, he thought, who would want to be friends with a cripple? His neighbors only took care of him, he believed, mostly out of duty.

When was the last time anyone other than they had expressed the desire to sit together to just share a moment with him?

Well, he told himself, why would anyone? After all, he was a sinner; born a sinner. The priests had made that clear to him. He was bearing the penalty for his past generations. He was "a son of iniquity;" a sign of God's judgment. He sighed. Those words had come from the priests; the men closest to God.

They must know God better than he did.

Did God's use of his life to pay the penalty for past family sins mean that his own life had no value? Over the years, he had come to believe so.

Silently, Uri wished he hadn't been chosen to be the one to pay. There were days he wished he had never been born.

Why had his life been singled out to suffer?

It was an old and well-worn thought-path; one he found himself travelling almost every morning, as he waited for transport to his designated workspace. He shook his head as though to clear his mind.

He was weary of such thoughts.

Such feelings never accomplished anything. How desperately he needed a good day; and not just financially, he realized. What was it then? It was something deeper; something he had never before formed into words.

He was needy and waiting. That much he could describe; desperate for a life change. How long could he continue this way?

For as long as Uri could remember, he had lived in this house. Born with balls of flesh for feet, and joints that drew into contorted positions, the beggar had been a cripple since the day he was born.

Was it a blessing or a hindrance to possess a normal intelligence in his situation? He longed for human company. He sighed to himself.... At least most others who were like him were blind, or mentally impaired. Those were spared the frustration of looking at empty walls....

Oh well, he said to himself in resignation. *It doesn't matter.*

Intentionally, he turned his attention towards the open door. Birds were gathering. It appeared Rimona had scattered crumbs for them before she had departed to her home.

She had done that to lift his spirits, he realized.

What must it be like to have a wife to love you, he wondered?

It had been a good day when Simeon and Rimona had moved next door. The family had travelled to Jerusalem for the Feast Days; just this year in fact, and suddenly decided to stay. They had travelled from Cyrene, Rome's colony on the northern tip of Africa.

Before meeting Simeon, Uri had seen, but never developed relationship with anyone with skin darker than his own. Oh, there were Samaritans who occasionally threw him coins in the marketplace. There were Nubians and Ethiopians living in Jerusalem's population. Sitting in his begging station, he had had the opportunity to learn much about the customs and practices of families from nations other than his own.

But none of the people he had observed over the years, were as darkly skinned as Simeon. His friend's hair, and that of his sons, was as black as the night; coarse in nature; different from his own. It reminded Uri of the thick, fluffy wool on a sheep's back. Rimona had quietly confided one day that due to the type of hair on his head, Simeon was regularly required to comb coconut oils through his hair to keep his scalp clean.

He had come to the idea one day while watching the Temple shepherds in Bethlehem as they were travelling to Jerusalem. The men were readying their flocks for the upcoming summer.

"What are you doing?" Simeon asked one man, as the shepherd lifted a small flask of olive oil and poured the entire contents over one ewe's head.

The man looked at Simeon and then begun to rub the oil into the skin of the sheep's face, head and ears. "This will protect her skin from irritants, and those little bugs that burrow down under the wool. She has no claws. She cannot scratch herself."

"I never thought about that," Simeon replied.

The shepherd continued. "The oil heals the skin, and also works as a preventative. Not only that, but when I do this, I've found I can more easily comb the wool when she is sheared later this year.

Simeon noticed the shepherd holding a small cup under the sheep's head. It was working to catch the runoff oil. As he watched, the oil the shepherd poured had collected in the cup over the sheep's back. He worked to massage it into the skin under the wool.

Simeon later told Rimona he had walked away thinking; comparing himself to the ewe being cared for by the shepherd. "The song King David wrote kept coming back to me," he told her. "I don't remember the whole thing, just a few lines, and the melody. He had sung to her, 'the Lord is my Shepherd, I shall not want…. You anoint my head with oil; my cup runs over.'"

Simeon had used oil to comb his hair from that point forward, telling Rimona that when he did, he was reminded to let God remove the irritants he experienced in his days.

The life lesson had helped Uri deal with his own difficulties.

Uri considered Simeon. He was a man to be respected to be sure. His ancestors had been travelling to Jerusalem for the Feast Days since the days of Ptolemy, some four hundred years prior.

In fact, the practices of Jews living in Cyrene had, by necessity, changed over the decades. The cultures were completely different from those native to Jerusalem. So great was the contrast, the Cyrenian Jews living in Jerusalem had been provided with their very own, very unique synagogue in the city. Uri had attended with Simeon and his family a few times, and found the services vastly dissimilar from the central religious sects' practices on the Temple Mount.

They were more celebrative, it seemed.

Happier somehow ...

"How is my friend?" a deep bass voice suddenly rumbled. Although he had been expecting Simeon, Uri physically started. In response, Simeon let out a deep throated laugh. His bright white teeth glistened in contract to his skin, as he walked towards the beggar. He gave the cripple's shoulders a quick rub as he spoke.

"Are we ready for the day, my brother?" he asked.

Uri smiled. "I think so, Simeon."

As he spoke, two young men entered the tiny house. Uri recognized them. "Good morning, Rufus." He greeted the oldest.

"Morning, Uri! How's the old man this morning?"

"Good," the beggar responded. "I'm good. Your mother left me some wonderful food here. Did she feed you?"

The younger son, Alexander, spoke up at that moment, feasting on a piece of fruit. "Are you kidding? The woman could stock the entire marketplace with what she cooks," he laughed. "Where's your satchel and cup?"

Uri grinned good-naturedly. "My bag and cup are here beside me." He paused, and looked at Rufus. "And who you callin' *old*, son?"

Rufus looked around the room in jest. "Why no one *here*, GrayBeard."

Simeon and his sons worked together for the next few minutes. As a team, they lifted Uri and placed him in the back of Simeon's open wagon. They would drive him to his assigned begging station, just outside the Temple. They would spread his large woven mat in front of the Gate, and seat him with his water-skin and food satchel. Then, Simeon and his sons would join their friends for prayer in the Temple Portico before they headed to their places of employment for the day.

It was considered Uri's lawful employment to sit at his station each day. The Jewish city officials had assigned him his place. Further, if a beggar could have rank and status in Jerusalem, Uri was at the top of the list among those to be considered. After all, he had been a beggar since birth.

Everyone in the city knew him. Everyone knew his story. As a child, his parents had taken turns sitting with him each day, teaching him to ask for alms. When he became an adult, he solicited alone; dependent upon his family and friends to help him in his quest for daily survival.

It wasn't as though the priests and rulers were uninvolved or disinterested, he realized. They regularly checked in with him, asking how he was doing. They even made sure he was supplied with the obligatory sacrificial animal when necessary. Sometimes, he even felt important when he sat in his station. In fact, because he was stationed next to the most popular entrance to the Temple mount, many of the scribes even made an open show of putting coins in his cup.

He considered himself blessed; more than many he knew; more than most.

But none of those people had become his friends.

How his heart ached for relationship....

Simeon urged the mule forward into the flow of humanity on the busy street. He assessed the position of the sun's shadow on the sundial.

Good, he thought. *We have time.*

He looked at Rufus, seated next to him. "Do you have the clay tablet with the list?" he asked.

213

Rufus reached into the folds of his over-wrap, pulling out a small wooden box, filled with firm clay, about the size of his hand. Words were scratched into the clay. Looking at the words, the young man reached once again into his over-wrap, and produced a stylus, made of reeds. "Yes, I have it right here," he smiled. "Is there anything else we need to add?"

Simeon thought for a moment or two. "I don't think so," he replied. "Hold on to the tablet. We'll go to the market after Temple prayer."

A little over an hour later, the three men stood in the marketplace, next to a vinedresser's stand. Simeon was bargaining with the man for the best price. When possible, it was the custom when a grower was selling fruit in bulk, for those making the purchase, to also be required to do the harvesting, ensuring that the product purchased was exactly what was desired.

"These are the best red grapes in the region!" the merchant declared.

"I'm sure they are," Simeon replied. "What price will you give me if I buy every grape you have?"

The man was surprised, and somewhat taken back. "You want my entire harvest?" he asked in disbelief. "Do you know how many grapes we are discussing here?

"Well, not me, but my employer. We need this specific grape for the fabric he is dyeing tomorrow. I am supposed to fill the wagon today with red fruit."

The man frowned. "Who is your employer? There is only one Dyeing House in the city, and I know the owner well."

Not one to be intimidated, Simeon's teeth flashed in a disarming smile. His deep laugh resonated. "You know Lucius? Well then, I have come to the right place. He is getting ready an order of red silk, and another of purple for priests' robes tomorrow. We found the berries to give us the blue hues yesterday." He paused, looking at the sun's shadow. "How much for your entire harvest? And then, can you show me where to purchase pomegranates?"

"Surely!" The man beamed, realizing he had suddenly made all of his money for the week with just one customer. "To be done so early in the day is a great blessing!" he said. "Thank you. Now, let me show you the way to the vineyard."

On the way out of the marketplace, Simeon noticed a roadside stand with large baskets full of pomegranates. He purchased enough to fill a third of the wagon-bed. "Come boys," he urged. "Let's get going. We want to bring Lucius a wagon full of good fruit before nightfall."

As they traveled, the merchant on his mule, riding next to the wagon, held a conversation with Simeon's son, Alexander.

"How far is it to your vineyard?" the young man wanted to know.

"It's not far," the old man answered. "Just a few miles. I wish I had known Lucius wanted the grapes. I would have delivered them."

He paused, and looked at the father. "What is your name?"

"Simeon," came the reply. "This is my first season working for Lucius. My family came for one of the Feasts a little less than a year ago, and just couldn't bear to leave. There's something about this city that gets into your bones."

"Where are you from?"

"We came by ship from Africa, along with several from our city, who wanted to eventually experience the Passover in Jerusalem. My older brother, Thaddeus Adai moved here years ago, with his wife. We stayed with them, so they could explain some of the differences in our cultures."

"You mean to say this last Passover Feast was your first experience in Jerusalem?" the merchant asked.

"Yes," Simeon answered. "The one when the darkness overtook the earth."

They all fell silent for a few moments, as each considered the things which had taken place in the city just a few months prior. It was the vineyard owner who broke the silence.

"Simeon?" he queried. "Are *you* the one?"

Surprised, the hulk of an African looked him in the eye. "The one?"

"Yes, the one who carried it... for *him*." The words were said simply, but they hung in the air, waiting to be recognized.

Simeon looked ahead to the road they were travelling. This wasn't the first time he had been asked the question. His jaw tensed. Who was this man, and why did he want to know? Was he one of the Sadducees from the Temple sect? When would they realize he had not had a choice that day? That he had been forced at the point of a Roman sword? When would they stop following him around?

He flicked the rein straps leading the mule. Appraising, he looked sideways at the old man. He didn't *look* like one of them.

Still, Simeon had learned the hard way he had to be careful these days.

How he longed for this season to pass! Had it really been a good idea to keep his family in Jerusalem?

"Simeon?"

The African sighed. "Why do you want to know?"

"I wasn't there, but I was told a strong and muscular man from Cyrene helped him. I was glad someone did....Simeon, he helped me. I was a beggar on the streets in Jerusalem. I had lost everything."

215

The old merchant paused, appraising the younger man. Was he listening? Would he understand? It didn't matter. He decided he would finish his story anyway.

"I've made so many mistakes. When my wife died on the birth-chair with our youngest daughter, I began to drink the wine I made. Eventually, I forgot most everything, except where the alcohol was stored. We lost everything. All I lived for was gone. I hurt others. I damaged my children. I ended up on the streets in Jerusalem.

"One day, some children found me on the street, and took me to their family's home. It was through them I met Jesus. The first time I heard him speak, I knew I had found the answers I had been searching for."

Simeon's defensive posture dismantled. "My brother, Thaddeus, and his wife, Kahina, travelled with him for more than two years. The day we arrived here, I heard him speak at the Temple's Portico. I continued to follow him, until the day he died," he explained, looking at Eleazar. "His words always shook me... I know what you mean."

The older merchant smiled at him. "So you are the African, from Cyrene?"

Simeon shrugged. "Yes, I suppose I am. Forgive me for my first response. At first I thought you were one of the Temple sect. They have been following me, asking questions."

"You'll be safe with me," the old man told him. "My home at EnKarem is far enough away to force them to find a good reason to come the long distance. Besides, several of the Temple Pharisees have chosen to follow him secretly. They are also friends of mine."

"What is your name?" Simeon asked.

"Eleazar," came the answer, "although I do have a son who carries my name as well. My son and two daughters are staying with me for a time. It's nice to have them home once again, even if it won't be forever. My steward, Baruch, and his wife also live with me, as well as a few of his followers who stayed in the city much the same way you and your family have. They are working with me right now, to get through the season.

"If there is anything I have learned over the years, I would say it would be that no situations like this happen by accident. There is a reason why we are meeting today. I know they will... *we* will all want to spend time talking with you tonight."

"I have to get the fruit to Lucius before nightfall," Simeon told him. "I cannot stay. I also have a friend for whom I provide transportation. I will have to pick him up before nightfall as well."

Eleazar laughed. "You might be surprised who shows up for the evening meal at my home, son. Your employer, Lucius, has been coming to see us in the evenings of late. He and Miriam, my oldest daughter, have discovered they have plans to make and matters to discuss these days."

Simeon didn't know what to say.

Silently, he prayed. *Spirit of God, please show me what to do in this situation. Teach me what I need to say and not say.*

"I'll speak with Lucius, and see what I can do, Eleazar," he replied. "If I can come, I will bring my wife and sons with me."

"That would be exactly what I would hope for, my boy," Eleazar responded. "I would love to hear your story about the day he died."

Simeon smiled. "My *story?*" he echoed. "I'm not sure I have a story to tell."

Eleazar patted his arm. "Every person's story is important. Try to come. It will be a help to you, I promise."

Silent, Simeon nodded.

Somehow, he sensed he had just stepped into a wider world than he had ever known.

Jesus had told them to baptize.

So here they were, standing in the Jordan River, just north of Jericho.

There had been more than fifty to be immersed in water today; making a physical testimonial; an outward statement of an inward change.

Peter and John stood in the water, receiving those wanting to step into a public commitment of their convictions about Jesus' identity. Those baptized were signifying, by walking into the waters of baptism, they wished to bury their former life, leaving their past in the water.

As each person came up from the waters, it was a symbol of the person's choice to walk in a new way. They were resurrected; living a new life.

That they had been born again.

After the majority of those baptized had left, three additional converts to the Ecclesia, or Community of Jesus Christ, arrived at the riverbank. Greeting them, Simon Peter called out.

John stepped into the river. "You ready?" he called.

"I'm ready," came an answer from the first man.

"Me too!" spoke another.

"And me!" said the third.

Coming back into the river, Simon Peter smiled. He took his place next to John. "There is a statement to help you define what you are doing today. Do you mind if I lead you through it?"

"I welcome it," answer the first man.

"Please give me your name."

"My name is Nicodemus BenGurion. I am a Pharisee, serving on the Sanhedrin council."

Then, as Simon Peter led him, Nicodemus repeated a few sentences, which would, over the following centuries, become known as the Apostles' Creed.

"I believe in God the Father, Almighty,

Creator of Heaven and earth,

And in Jesus Christ, His only begotten Son, our Lord.

He is my God, and it is my choice to follow Him."

Then, Nicodemus crossed his arms over his chest, and pinched his nose closed with one hand. Helping him keep his balance, Simon Peter leaned him backwards, to help him go completely under the water.

As he did so, Simon Peter spoke, "I baptize you in the name of the Father, the Son and the Holy Spirit."

As Nicodemus went under the water; the same electrifying power which had surged through Jesus' body at the time of resurrection; the same dynamic strength of creation… That same spiritual energy tangibly coursed through his entire being. As the priest emerged from the waters, his hands involuntarily shot up in to the air in exclamatory praise.

"I feel Your Presence!" Nicodemus cried. "I worship you, my God!"

Subsequently, following the same pattern, the two other men confessed their belief and confidence in Jesus as their God, and role model of how to live. During each baptism, the same manifestation of the Holy Spirit's power was evident and tangibly sensed. At the end of each immersion, a personal, intentional worship erupted from human hearts and lips.

It was an awesome experience for each of the three new disciples.

They had followed Jesus' instructions, and become baptized as the Master's disciples.

In response, the Holy Spirit of the Living God met each of them there.

The two men?

Gamaliel BenSimon BenHillel, and his son, Simeon BenGamaliel.

In the Roman port city of Ostia, some fifty miles southwest of Rome, a merchant and passenger vessel was loading, setting sail for trade in Espania, Belgica and Briton. The Dumnoni Prince, Eubulus Beli, and his young wife, Anne, were boarding the ship any moment, readying to travel to see his family. They had travelled from their home in Rome with their children the day before, spending the night at a local inn. At the moment, the family was on a walk, in the midst of conversation.

"I've been wondering if your father might be in Briton while we are there," Eubulus commented. "How long has it been since we have seen him?"

Anne considered. "It's been at least two years," she replied. "He did send letters for me with the latest dispatch from Pontius Pilate a month ago."

"Is he still serving in the Sanhedrin?" her husband asked.

"He is," she said, "but he last wrote he is needing to be more cautious these days. Since Jesus' resurrection, there are those in the Sadducean sector who want to remove his influence completely. To remove him. His position with Rome has put him in an awkward position since they annexed Judea."

Eubulus smiled. "We know that position well, don't we?" he said, giving her a squeeze. "I have had such a hard time living in exile. It was kind of the emperor to give us permission to travel. Are you looking forward to getting away?"

"Oh, yes," she answered.

Stopping their oldest son from jumping into a puddle, Anne called the boy by name. "Eubulus Joseph! Didn't I tell you this morning there are no wells on board a ship? You have to try to stay clean today!"

"Eubie *always* gets dirty, Mama!" protested their daughter, Gwynnelle, who was only four. She was pulling on her mother's gown. *"I'm clean! Look!"*

Laughing, her mother picked her up. "Me too, Gwynn!" she declared. She looked at her husband. "I want you to know I left my finer outfits in Rome. I don't want to repeat what happened the year we married."

Her husband laughed. "Did we even open your baggage on that trip? I still remember my mother worrying, rummaging through her clothing to find you something you could wear."

"Something good did happen," she recalled with a giggle. "I learned how to remove that nasty black mud from clothing!"

Eubulus hugged her. "You do just fine, my love. All of my family loves you. Just as they have always loved your father."

"I miss him," she noted.

"Me too," he agreed. They were silent for a moment.

"Have you heard how your mother is doing?" she asked.

"No recent news," he told her. "All I know is my father thought someone was trying to poison them both. That was the dispatch from David, his steward. But we will have a chance to find out when we get there. I hope she doesn't die before."

"Is the villa ready?" Anne asked him.

Beli nodded. "The Caesar has given me a letter giving us permission to live in it during our stay. He sent dispatches to my father, requesting it to be prepared for us, since its been sitting empty these ten years. We can always hire servants, or buy a slave."

Before Anne could reply, a voice interrupted them.

Tatius, Eubulus' personal slave, called from the docks. "Prince Beli! Princess Anne! They are ready for us!"

Putting their daughter down on the ground once more, Anne spoke excitedly to the children. "Are you ready to go on an adventure? We are going to see your grandparents!"

Silently, she prayed she would also be allowed to see her own father, the Nobilus Decurio of Rome, very soon.

In the realm of the Dumnoni tribe, an investigation was underway. In the weeks following their last meeting, David, the king's steward, had begun looking into the concerns Arviragus expressed that afternoon.

In the steward's hut, David was training Caedmon how to keep inventory records. For the past few months, he had been increasing the young man's education. The young man was reading quite well now, and could add and subtract. Today, he was learning to balance the accounts.

Now, in addition to marking down exports, Caedmon was responsible for making sure the miners had the tools they needed, and that those tools were ready for use each day. It had become his job to sharpen antler rakes and iron pickaxes, scrape iron shovels and iron hatchets, sharpen knives, clean copper sieves, as well as make sure all baskets and buckets were sturdy and usable. At the moment, the day's tools were leaning up against the walls, and hanging from hooks in the ceiling; waiting for the morning's arrival.

"Look, Caedmon, when the numbers aren't the same in this box," David was saying, "it means the counts don't match. See, this column has to add up to the same thing this row does. Reaching the same number in this box is what we call 'balancing' the accounts. In Greek, the correct number in this box is called *logos.*"

"Logos," David repeated. Then he thought for a moment, then asked a question. "What if it doesn't balance, Master David?" he asked. "What does it mean?"

"It means that either someone is stealing, or you have made a mistake somewhere. That's why you want to make sure you get enough sleep, and take walks every day. It is important you have enough water and protein to eat during the day. Your brain needs these things to work properly." The steward watched to make sure Caedmon understood his words.

"I get it!" Caedmon said excitedly. "That's why you are always able to remember the details! Is that how you are so focused?"

David laughed. "Perhaps. The teachings of my God have protected me, Caedmon. There are ways to take care of the vessel, called your body, he has given you. Your body carries the real you around while you walk this earth. It is important you steward it well to stay strong."

"I want to learn more," Caedmon said. "Will you teach me?"

"Absolutely," David replied. "It is really my job to do so. I need to replace myself." He paused. "Now, about the other matter. What have you discovered?"

Caedmon took a sip of water before answering. "As you know, I have been attending classes at the Academy. I am learning much. When you first suggested it, I was confused at first, because in my heart, I want to learn about your God, and the teachings you live by. So, when you asked me to do this, at first I thought you were trying to find a way to tell me I was no longer needed as your assistant."

"Oh," David responded. "It's nothing like that. It has an important reason, but I'm not free to tell you what it is."

"Well," Caedmon told him. "I was thinking about this, and correct me if I'm wrong, but I think that means you must be doing something secret for King Arviragus. And, thank you, by the way, for paying my tuition."

David smiled. "The king is paying it, and you are very welcome. No harm can come from learning. And you and I will work to maintain your values as you study."

Caedmon repeated his question. "You *are* doing something for the king, aren't you? Aren't *we*?"

"You know I can't answer you, even if it's true, don't you?" his overseer asked with a light laugh. He was surprised at the young man's level of perception.

Caedmon lowered his voice. "Along those lines, I do think I am gaining the trust of a couple of the teachers. I have been invited to share a meal after classes tomorrow with Maedoc. He is the Chief Bard, and assigned to be my mentor."

"Are you able to guard yourself from the spiritual nature of what is being taught?" David asked.

"I'm not sure I know how to guard my heart," came the answer. "But I am being careful about what I allow myself to believe. They are teaching us how to write in our language, and how to make words rhyme. Maedoc is a master poet, and he is teaching us music as well. I am really enjoying that. We are also learning geography and how to read the stars."

"That's good. That's good," David replied. "You will be able to use those lessons in your everyday life later. Would you do me a favor? Tomorrow, when you are with this man, ask him if they teach alchemy in the courses of learning at the Academy. Alchemy is the mostly the art of mixing science and magic to discover ways to make more powerful weapons. So, when you bring it up, Maedoc will assume you are interested in specializing your training in that direction. Just act interested, and ask the questions that present themselves. Observe everything, and try to memorize what you see. I specifically need to know about the abandoned lead mines. Don't mention it to him, but listen carefully."

"Yes, sir," Caedmon said. "Oh, I did want to tell you what I discovered in the mine yesterday."

David's interest was piqued. His eyebrows went up, as his assistant continued.

"I created a ruse of inspecting the mines yesterday after classes. I told them it was on your behalf. I checked the areas where we are currently digging. The levels of mining had been touched after the tools were retired yesterday. All of the counts are also the same as our records; the tin, the copper, and the silver.

"Then I checked the deeper mines, and a few of the ones we have abandoned. Someone *has* been digging for lead and iron. There are also signs of digging in a couple new areas for tin. When I thought about it, I remembered the old man up in the Mendip Mines who still operates a private mine. They could have always purchased lead from him."

"Hmm..." David replied, thinking. "We are the only tribe in Briton to have the rights to mine tin. I wonder if they have been trading tin for metals without the king's knowledge."

"It's possible," Caedmon answered. "Because I hadn't been to the older mines before yesterday, I had no measuring point to use to begin. But I took careful measurements yesterday, and will continue to go back to do so."

"When you do, mix up your inspection times, in case someone discovers what you're doing. That will protect you. Look for clues like clothing, or food remnants. They might help us discover who is involved."

In Jerusalem, in the home of Ampliatus and Maria, some fourteen hundred miles to the east, a fifteen-year-old young man was clutching his left hand in a cloth. Tears were spilling down his face.

"Hurry, please!" he cried. "Abba, help me!"

Ampliatus began removing the makeshift bandage the boy had placed around his hand. "What did you *do*, Mark?"

Through sobs, the boy gasped out and answer. "I fell... in the... street.... The boys were.... playing with....a ball... The soldier... just ....rode on through..."

Shocked, his father assessed the damage to his son's hand. The top of the left thumb was completely torn away. It would need a physician's needle if it were to heal.

"The horse crushed it?" he asked.

The boy nodded, tears streaming. Silently, he looked at his father.

"Can ....you.... fix it?" he asked.

Ampliatus didn't answer. "I cannot. But it will heal, son," was all he could say. "It won't be the same as it was, but you will get used to it. We need to find a physician to clean it up though."

"Luke, the physician, is staying at Zebedee's office home with John." The voice was Maria's. She had just returned from the marketplace. Shocked, she stood in the doorway, her arms filled with baskets of vegetables and baked goods. "What happened?"

Moving towards the door, his arm around their son, Ampliatus answered. "I'm taking him there. You want to come?"

Maria moved to the side, and put the baskets down. "Absolutely!" she answered. *"Look at all this blood! What happened?"*

"A horse crushed his hand in the street," the hurried answer came. "He has lost his thumb." He looked at his son. "Keep a lot of pressure on it, John Marcus," he instructed.

"I'll be there a little after you," she told her husband. "Go on ahead."

The two men made their way to the business district of the city.

In Zebedee's Jerusalem business office, a meeting was taking place. James and John (sons of Zebedee), Luke, Simon Peter and Andrew, Thomas, Joseph of Arimathea and Mary, the Magdalene and James the Less (Jesus' half-brother) were in the midst of discussing a letter delivered to Joseph earlier in the day, along with a group of men travelling in a caravan. The travelers were dressed in the travel attire of a royal court.

It seemed an emissary from the nation of Osroene to the north had arrived in Jerusalem with a letter from the king of Edessa. The letter was addressed to Jesus.

The caravan had originally stopped in Nazareth, and been directed to Capernaum. In Capernaum, they met Zebedee, who directed them to Jerusalem. Arriving in Jerusalem, the men were told Jesus had been executed some months prior. However, his mother and great-uncle were still in the city.

So, after asking directions, the caravan had come to Arimathea. They had made known their requests to Joseph. After reading the letter, Joseph had sent word to the leaders of the followers of Jesus in Jerusalem. "Please meet me at Zebedee's office at midday. We have some decisions to make."

Joseph read the letter out loud.

> "From Abgar to Jesus, the Good Physician who has appeared in the country of Jerusalem, greeting: "I have heard of you, and the healing; that you make no medicines, and use no roots. I am told that you open the eyes of the blind, and make the lame man walk again. I am told you cleanse lepers, and make the deaf able to hear. That by your word you raise the dead to life again, and have power over lunatic demons.
>
> Learning the wonders you have done, it has been born within me that you must either have come down from heaven, or be a son of God. I pray you will come to my house and heal me.
>
> "I am a leper, and I am a king. I possess but one small province, but it is beautiful, and large enough for us both to live in peace."

When he finished, silence filled the room.

"What do we do?" Magdalene asked. "Jesus isn't here, at least not in physical form."

"We will need to send someone," Simon Peter ventured. "But who?"

"The Ecclesia is becoming a huge group to manage," John ventured. "How many thousand now?"

"At least five thousand here in the city," James the Less answered. "And more in the villages. We are getting to the point where we will need to add more structure soon."

He looked around the room. "Magdalene's right. Who can we send?"

"We haven't had to think this way before," Andrew spoke up. "Edessa is three hundred miles north. Jesus said we would be going into all the world. This could be the beginning."

"You think he would receive anyone other than Jesus?" asked John. "He is a king."

"He is a man who needs healing," Joseph interjected.

"Who in our group has travelled that far north?"

"Oh, sir," spoke Abgar's emissary, "whoever you send will not need to worry. We will provide protection, and everything he needs. We will even provide a bodyguard to travel home again."

"Cleophas travels to Antioch on a regular basis," Mary spoke up. "But he is working in Emmaus-Nicopolis until next week."

Just then, Ampliatus knocked on the door. "Is anyone there?" he called. "We have a small emergency here."

John opened the door, and immediately saw the blood dripping from John Marcus's left hand. "Luke," he called over his shoulder. "I think this one's for you!"

The meeting paused as Luke went into surgeon mode; cleansing, and trimming. All the while, John Marcus clamped his jaw down on a long, flat board, gritting through the pain. James and John held his arm down and still to make the physician's task easier.

"I'm sorry, John," Luke said, using the boy's Latin name. "This is a real mess. I'm going to have to cut through the bone, or I won't be able to close the flesh over it."

As he was speaking, Maria stepped through the open door. In her hands, she held cup of warm wine. "Can we take a moment, Luke? I have made him some warm medicine for pain."

"What's in it?" the physician asked.

"Wine, arnica, some ground poppy seeds, feverfew, and couple other herbs," she answered.

Luke turned and looked at her. "Wonderful! I would have made the same mixture!"

He paused while John Marcus took a sip.

"Drink it all, son," his mother prodded. "Please."

Luke spoke up. "Maria, do you have any more warm wine?"

"Yes, a little."

"Pour it on the wound, would you?" he asked. "Let's make sure we get rid of anything I didn't see."

The warmth of the heated wine served as something of an analgesic to the wound. A few moments later, John Marcus fell into a fitful sleep.

"All right, here we go," Luke spoke to James and John. "Hold his arm again."

Luke drew a small hand saw from his bag, and held it over the lamp on the table to cleanse it. After fanning it to make it cooler, he pulled the flesh away from the bone and began to saw the bone to a smooth end.

"Do you need help, Luke?" Ampliatus asked.

"Not yet," the physician answered. "I will need you to hold the flesh together so I can stitch it shut in a moment though." He looked at Simon Peter. "Would you pour water over this to rinse it out?"

"Sure," Simon Peter answered. He picked up the nearest water-pot, and poured a steady stream of clear water over the wound, until the bleeding was cleansed away.

Luke picked up a bone needle and flax thread from his bag, and stitched the wound closed with small stitches. Toward the end of his efforts, John Marcus began to stir. As he began to come back to consciousness, his mother once more gave him a cup of the warm, medicated wine.

As soon as the wound was stitched, Luke brought out a stone box filled with ointment made from Gilead balm and covered the stitches. He then tore linen strips for bandages and wrapped the boy's hand from his fingers to his forearm.

When he was finished treating John Marcus's hand, he held it in his hands and prayed. "Abba Father, I lay my hands on John Marcus's hand. You are the Great Physician. I have done what I can do. Please help this injury to heal, and protect him from infection. Holy Spirit, I ask you to give this boy rest and peace. Please help him recover from this injury. Thank you, Lord. In Jesus' name, Amen."

A chorus of voices echoed his last word. "Amen."

"Settle him down to sleep for a while," Luke instructed, looking at John Marcus's parents. He will wake up with it throbbing for several days. He might not sleep well. Get some peppermint oil in the market for his headaches. And, give him the same pain mixture you gave him here, at least three times a day.

"It would be a good idea to perhaps read to him to keep his mind distracted. Have him drink a lot of water, and change the dressing every day for the first week, and then every other day until it is a red seam in the skin. I will come by your house in a couple of weeks, to take out the stitches. He should lie still and not get the wound wet for all of that time."

Luke moved outside to wash his hands, and Ampliatus followed him. "How much do I owe you, Luke?" the architect asked.

The physician looked at him in the eye. "I would love to come to your home for dinner, and perhaps bring my brother, Titus, with me sometime."

"We would do that anyway, Luke. I want to pay you," the architect insisted.

Luke shrugged. "My needs are met. And, you and I are brothers in the Lord, Ampliatus. Just do whatever you sense the Spirit of God telling you to do."

Inside the office, James, Mary's son, was reframing the former conversation. "Who has been with us from the beginning, or close to it anyway? Who would be able to respond the way we know Jesus would respond?"

"We have all felt the leading of the Holy Spirit to recognize your leadership, James. So, I think this decision is one you will ultimately have to make." John said, patting his friend's shoulder. "I don't know who to choose. How about someone from the seventy? There are many of those men still in Jerusalem; some who are not as busy in the day-to-day shepherding as we have all become."

"What's happening?" Ampliatus inquired. "Unless I am intruding into something and shouldn't ask."

"Nothing like that," James answered. "I welcome your help, Ampliatus. Here is the issue: the king of Edessa, in Osroene, is a leper. He wrote a letter to Jesus, asking him to come and heal him. But it just arrived. We were wondering who we could send to pray for him."

Thomas spoke up. "I have an idea. Do we have anything that belonged to Jesus, we could send to the king? That might give him a sort of connection to help him believe."

Everyone looked at Jesus' mother, Mary. "I don't have anything of his," she said. Then she remembered. "No! Wait! What about the linens we wrapped him in when we buried him?"

Simon Peter's mouth dropped open. "They were stained with something when I held them. They *were* the last thing that touched him."

Humbly, Mary spoke up once more. "I would really like to hold on to the face cloth, though, if you don't mind. At least for a little while. I still sense such comfort when I look at it."

"I have an idea," Ampliatus spoke up. "Does anyone remember Thaddeus Adai from Cyrene?"

James, John's brother, responded. "Isn't he the brother of Simeon from Cyrene?"

"He *is*," Magdalene offered. "Simeon works for Lucius, who purchased my father's weaving house."

Ampliatus chuckled. "I think he might be a candidate for going to Edessa. He speaks their language and knows their customs."

"I agree with you, Ampliatus," John said. "He and his wife, Kahina, followed Jesus with us since the second year. He was sent out with us. And Simeon's sons, Rufus and Alexander, have been strong in helping in the Ecclesia here."

"Does Kahina know the language used in Edessa as well?" Magdalene asked.

"If not, she can always speak in Aramaic," Simon Peter responded. "Surely someone in his court has done trading and speaks it. I know Adai is well versed and well-studied. And, I'm sure they have had to make allowances for foreign visitors at some point."

James the Less considered for a moment and then looked at Simon Peter. "What if we sent Thaddeus Adai and Kahina with Jesus' burial linens to Edessa? He has Mari who he has trained, and those two men work together well. We will have to send a small team."

"Holy Spirit," John prayed, "what do you want us to do? Is this a plan you want us to follow? Is Adai the right man to ask?"

And so they prayed together. At the end of prayer, both in the languages of men and angels, everyone sensed an unseen Seal of approval on the plan to ask Thaddeus Adai and Kahina to consider traveling to Osroene.

In the outdoor courtyard of Joseph Caiaphas' palace, Saul and Shira sat together on a stone bench. The firelight created a cozy glow which reflected off the walls.

"I want to always take good care of you, Shira," the young priest told her. "I think I have loved you from the moment we met."

Shyly, she giggled. "I have felt that way too."

Feeling a little braver, he touched her hand. "Thank you."

"For what?" she asked, surprised.

"For saying 'yes,'" he told her. "I know that your father had some hurdles to jump over because I am a Pharisee."

"Oh, Saul," she soothed. "I don't really care about that. Once we have our own home, I will believe whatever you tell me to believe. That's what I do to keep my Abba happy. So, it's what I will do with you."

Saul paused. Her answer troubled him somewhat. Did he really *want* to marry someone who didn't really know her *own* beliefs? Did he want a wife who would agree with him, just for the sake of agreement; to avoid conflict?

Didn't he really want a girl who knew her own mind; who would love him as deeply and fiercely as he wanted to care for her? Wouldn't that be a better arrangement?

No, he was happy with this arrangement, he decided. He pushed his concerns to the waiting corners of his mind once more, and flashed his most brilliant smile.

"You're right," he agreed. "It will be different when we have our own home. And I purchased it today. I wondered whether you might like to go with me to choose furnishings tomorrow."

Shira clapped her hands. "Ooh! Where are we going?"

Saul smiled. "I have found a wonderful wood carver who is willing to build what we need. He has drawings we can choose from."

She grabbed his hands. "I'm so happy!"

"As soon as our home is furnished, we can make plans for our wedding." He looked into her eyes, opened wide in innocent trust. "I love you Shira."

Her cheeks blushing, she responded. "I promise to love you too, Saul. I will try to be a good wife."

Cleophas stood just outside the Dung Gate of Jerusalem. The gate was the main entrance into the older parts of the city. The poorest and neediest of the city's inhabitants lived here. It had been in this area of the city where Jesus had taught most often. It was here, he had healed so many.

The wood carver wasn't exactly sure why he had come by this gate early today, except for the fact he had recently learned the formerly public "Potter's Field," had recently been purchased by the Sanhedrin. One of the pottery merchants had mentioned it to him during the daily distribution of food. The man was concerned because he could no longer harvest clay from the earth for free, but now had to pay a price. Would Cleophas pray for him? He had barely been getting by, but now was afraid he would not be able to purchase the clay *and* pay his taxes.

"If I have to pay, then my pots will cost more, and I will have less people to purchase what I make," he said.

They had prayed for a miracle.

Thinking of it now, Cleophas remembered someone else telling him about the field. He had been discouraged to learn the rumor was true. Caiaphas and the Sadducees had used the silver coins returned by Judah the Sicari to make the purchase.

Cleophas looked down. The drop from the ledge where he stood was a little disconcerting.

The field looked so far away from where he stood.

It had been from the very ledge on which he stood, Judah had taken his own life. What would drive a man to do such a thing?

There was something disturbing about the way all these events had tied together, he considered.

Today, he was meeting with a young couple who were supposed to become married in a few months. The groom was a priest at the Temple. He had purchased a small home in this part of the city, and was going to need furnishings.

Could Cleophas do the job?

The wood-worker smiled. He had committed himself to take the contract. The young priest seemed upwardly mobile. He definitely knew what he wanted. Cleophas told him he would be able to begin when his project in Emmaus-Nicopolis came to an end next week.

Cleophas was looking forward to this meeting.

Saul and Shira made such a sweet young couple, he considered.

In Capernaum, adjacent to Simon Peter's home, workmen were constructing a large room to eventually be joined to the family's home. Zebedee was overseeing the construction, with help from Jairus BarJacob and several of his rabbinical students.

Jairus was a Pharisee, and ruler of the local synagogue. His daughter, Amita, had been raised from the dead during Jesus' ministry in Galilee. As a result, Jairus had become a follower of Jesus.

For some time now, they had been meeting in the synagogue for prayer each day. But now, the gatherings were becoming too large. Simon Peter had suggested beginning a sort of training school to help those who wanted to learn more; perhaps modeling it after the pattern Jesus had utilized in teaching the twelve, and then in training the seventy. The idea had been well received, and construction had begun almost immediately.

During the forty days after Jesus' resurrection, his instructions to his followers had been more concise, more focused than they had been before the Resurrection. Since their understanding had become engaged, they each had found a greater realization of His plan. He had been developing them into the leaders he had seen them to be before each one had been conceived.

Now he had ascended, and the Holy Spirit had been poured out, a sense of anticipation as well as mission filled each one of them.

These were good days to be alive.

Considering these things, Elsbeth looked out the window, watching the stone walls being constructed. What was it Simon Peter, her husband, had observed yesterday, as he helped with the process?

"This Ecclesia; this new entity the Spirit of God is building," he had told her, "is a living *organism*. It is a house made up of *living* stones. We each are significant; with each one fulfilling his or her own place in the Kingdom. I cannot do what you are called to do, and you cannot do what I am called to do. Abba Father's favor and acceptance is the mortar that will hold us all together."

Elsbeth smiled, and went back to chopping celery for the dish she was putting together.

I am a woman, and I have a calling! And, God is holding me together with His favor! He accepts me!

So, the dignity the Master had bestowed upon the softer gender when he walked in Galilee, was being continued. She had seen such a change in her husband in the past few months, she realized. He had become less impulsive; his harsh temper was disappearing. He had been more affectionate. He had certainly become more patient with the children.

231

He prayed and wept quite often, since the day Jesus had spoken with him and instructed him, "feed my sheep."

Were these changes the result of what had happened to all of them on Pentecost? She hoped so.

A well of gratitude began to rise from deep within her soul. She found herself humming, and then, unbidden, words poured out in a melody she had never heard before. Happy droplets formed in her eyes, as she expressed worship to her God. Before long, she was repeating the lines she sang, and a hymn of thanksgiving had taken form.

Was this how King David had felt when the Holy Spirit had given him songs of praise, she wondered? She felt as though she had been privileged to participate with an unseen choir.

Were they *here … with* her?

In Briton, the Dumnoni Tribe was beginning to prepare for ShroveTide once more. The only happy tribe members seemed to be the Druids. This was their season to take the stage. And take the stage they did. Beginning two months prior to the feast, the Ovates would work their way through the local villages, searching for young virgins whose families might sell them for sacrifice. The trouble was, if no family offered a virgin, the Ovates' choice just might show up missing; forcibly taken.

It was a custom referred to as "trick us or treat us."

So many children had lost their lives during the Druid Feasts over the years, Caedmon silently wondered how the Dumnoni Tribe had survived at all.

David had been working with Caedmon in the overseer's hut. They had been working on the young man's accounting skills. He was showing himself to be a quick learner.

At the moment, they were taking a break. Caedmon asked him to listen to a musical piece he had been assigned to compose for his final exams.

As David listened to him play, practicing with his whole heart, he had sensed a need to provide the boy with a copy of the psalms, just for fun. As a result, David and Eiless had spent thousands of hours recopying many of the steward's favorite Psalms onto a parchment scroll for the boy. Not only would it encourage him, teaching him spiritually, but it would also give him a place to begin should he want to write worshipful musical compositions as his gift developed.

Caedmon had been recognized as a Bard of the Copper Branch. Bards of this designation carried a handcrafted, copper branch, fitted with copper bells. This indicated Caedmon was a beginner, but still no one to be trifled with.

Caedmon was progressing well in the Druid Academy. In the first months, Maedoc had assigned him a hollowed-out, gourd-shaped instrument, with a set of strings stretched across the hole. It was called a lute. The boy had surprised even himself. He had begun to find ways to rhyme his words, and now enjoyed being able to sing his lines as he stroked the lute.

"It's very hard to get used to," he told David. "When I carry the branch, and they ring, everyone looks at me, because they think I might have something to say....."

When the investigation had begun, David had been concerned the endeavor might confuse Caedmon, and sully his ability to think things through. But thankfully, unlike the majority of the students in the Druid Academy, the young man had not been affected by the seeming mental fog which overtook all those involved in the Druid program.

When David asked him why he was able to remain singly focused, Caedmon smiled wryly and answered with a quiet statement. "My little sister was captured by the Druids when my parents refused to sell her. She was offered in sacrifice when she was only eight years old."

David had been shocked to know how deeply Druid influences had wounded this young man.

Caedmon had all the makings of a strong, masculine leader.

But only time would tell.

In the Essene Quarter of the city of Jerusalem, the fledging Jerusalem Ecclesia was thriving. Since the Day of the Great Wind, many changes had taken place. More than six thousand people had chosen to follow Jesus, subsequently experiencing the waters of baptism.

Just before His ascension, Jesus had instructed all his followers to wait for the Promise of the Holy Spirit's coming to be fulfilled. He told them they would need the Spirit before trying to walk out their lives as committed disciples. As a result, all of those choosing to follow Jesus waited in prayer for a personal outpouring of the Holy Spirit.

In every case, Jesus' promised Holy Spirit baptism was confirmed with the demonstration of the language of angels.

Whenever those who believed chose to obey, they experienced a response from Heaven's side. So many people, of all ages and ethnicities, had become part of this new phenomenon, called the Ecclesia! There was no competition between the classes, or the ethnicities. Those who had very little were treated the same as those who had an abundance.

In fact, an overflowing sense of excitement and anticipation over what was happening in the city accompanied each day in the community. The surrounding areas around Jerusalem had also become part of what Abba Father was doing.

Each day, fresh awareness of Abba Father's purposes served as a catalyst for openness and trust to develop in the relationships in the Ecclesia. As people open heartedly shared with one another, meeting from house to house, praying for each other, laying hands on the sick, teaching and worshipping together; miracles took place. Blind eyes could see, deaf ears were opened, cripples found strength to walk, deformities were transformed, memories were healed, bondages were released, and lives were made new.

It was the most amazing time to be alive.

11 – Miracles

Spring, 34CE

In the city of Edessa, in Osroene, Thaddeus Adai and his wife, Kahina, stood in the court of King Abgar. The caravan from Jerusalem had arrived just hours before. Upon learning their identities, the King's Guards at the city gates, had been quickly ushered into the palace.

They were still in travel clothes, and unwashed. Kahina was sure she could smell her own body's odor. Her back ached from weeks spent on the back of a camel. Her water-skin had been squeezed dry just an hour prior to reaching Edessa's city gates.

Now, they were waiting.

Kahina had never been inside a palace before. She held to her husband's arm, unconsciously insecure in such lavish surroundings. With large eyes, she looked around the room at the marble columns; the tiled mosaic floors.

Her husband patted her hand resting on his arm. He bent down to whisper in her ear. "No fear, my love," he said. "We are here to pray for a very sick man, and to tell him about Jesus. That is all."

She smiled in response. "I've never been in a room this big," she answered. "All of Jerusalem's market could fit into this room!"

"I am amazed as well," he responded. "I keep reminding myself to pray. I don't know what the Holy Spirit is about to do, but I feel we will be leading an ecclesia of some sort. Don't you?"

Her mind regaining focus, Kahina suppressed an unexpected giggle. "I love the way you keep helping my perspective, Thad. Thank you."

"You help mine all the time," he commented. "We are a team."

As they were whispering, Hakim, the king's personal attendant approached the group from one of the doors surrounding the great room.

"Excuse me," he said, coming up from behind them. "Are you the group from Jerusalem?"

Startled, Adai turned around when he heard the voice. "Yes, we are!" he answered with a smile. "I'm sorry we were delayed. Your emissary fell sick in Palmyra. We left him with his companions in the care of a physician there who was of our country. He gave us his young camel boy to guide us the rest of the journey. He is with…."

Suddenly excited, Hashma interrupted Adai midsentence. "Where is Jesus? Is he with you?"

Adai looked him in the eyes, and shook his head. "Not in the way you mean," he answered.

Visibly disappointed, the servant ventured another question. "Did he send someone?"

"We were all sent," Adai answered simply.

Assessing the man speaking to him, Hakim took charge. "You will come with me to the king," he ordered. "The rest of you will wait here."

Thaddeus Adai looked at his wife and company. He directed his statement to one of the men in the group. "Mari, when they ask, please remember the groupings we all talked about. And, if they ask, let them know our dietary restrictions. Can I have the satchel please?"

Mari smiled, and pulled the crossover strap from over his shoulder. "Here, Thad. You want me to go with you?"

Adai looked at Hakim. "May I bring others to pray as well?" he asked.

Hakim answered. "Yes, a few, but come quickly. We only have moments left."

Suddenly, the group came to an understanding. The palace was in mourning, anticipating the manifestation of an unseen intruder.

Death had come to call.

Adai motioned for Kahina and Mari to accompany him. He nodded at Hakim. In reply, Hakim nodded, backing toward the door through which he had come into the court.

"Come now," he beckoned. "There is no time."

Those in the group remaining in the courtroom began to pray.

In silence, the trio hurried to keep up with the fast-moving attendant. They moved through the door and down a small hallway, into another large chamber. Blinking, Thaddeus Adai and his companions waited inside the threshold as their eyes adjusted to the difference in the light inside the room.

It was as though night had come in the middle of the day.

The oversized windows were tightly shuttered. No lamps were lit.

Adai wondered how Hakim was able to care for the king in such a dark room. Where *was* the king, he wondered? Then, as his eyesight normalized, he could see a large lump in the bed in the center of the room.

Hakim was speaking now. In low tones, he addressed the king. "My king?" he spoke. "Are you awake? You have visitors."

No answer came.

Concern could be heard in the servant's voice. "King Abgar? Are you still with us, my lord?" He poked the man's ribs, attempting to wake him.

Adai moved towards the bed. "Is he alive?" he asked.

Intent on his purpose, Hakim did not look up. "I never know," he replied. "He has come close to death this past week several times, only to revive, and take liquids and breads."

Thaddeus Adai motioned to Kahina and Mari. He began to pray out loud, in the language of angels, referred to by Jesus' followers as "tongues," or "in the Spirit."

As the words he did not understand left his mouth, his mind prayed in his own language. *"Holy Spirit, we yield to you. Lord Jesus, there is no entity or possession higher than you. You are the King of all kings. Show us how to pray."*

Kahina began to walk through the room, praying in the language of angels. Praying aloud in the same manner, Mari pulled a small stone bottle from the pouch on his belt. Pulling the cork stopper from the bottle, he poured a small amount of oil on his hands. He then placed his hands on the forehead of the young king, who had still not moved, nor uttered a sound.

Mari spoke clearly in the language of the Seleucians. "King Abgar, we anoint you with oil in the name of Jesus Christ, the God of Creation come in human form. Be healed of your leprosy."

As the three followers of Jesus continued to pray, small changes showed themselves in the visible realm. After a few moments, the body under the covers began to stir. Abgar moved, rolling over onto his back. As he did so, he groaned.

He felt so weak. But how long had he been sleeping this time? What was the language being spoken in his bedchamber?

As awareness returned, the leper reached up, and pulled down the covers which had been covering his face.

Stunned, Hakim let out some sort of expletive in his own language and ran from the room. His voice could be heard calling someone's name as it faded away to another part of the palace.

Around him, the prayers continued. Abgar felt a weight on his eyes. Strange, he hadn't felt anything in that area of his face for a long, long time. His eyes had become blurry, then blind. Finally, he hadn't been able to close his eyes for months. Hakim changed a damp rag dressing over his eyes every morning and evening.

What was happening? He could feel *something* happening inside his head; as though there were movement even though he was lying still.

Come to think of it; he hadn't had the strength to move his arms for weeks. Had he really moved the covers from his own face?

Still in verbal, indistinguishable prayer, Kahina had gently placed her thumbs over the dressings on the young king's eyes. Her hands lingered there for some time, as she followed the inner leading she sensed regarding what she should pray.

For some moments she had recognized the Holy Spirit was displacing unseen darkness in the room. He was also displacing darkness *within* the man for whom they were praying.

When she perceived her prayer assignment for the king's eyes was fulfilled, she lifted her hands. As she did, a wrapped and leprous hand reached up to slide the dressing away. Transfixed, she stared into the eyes of the king of Edessa. She had never seen so much damage in and around a person's eyes.

Was what she observed an improvement from the state his eyes had been in before the disease?

She had never considered how tormented a person with leprosy must be.

"Who *are* you?" a whispered croak emitted from the man's throat.

"Jesus sent us to you," she answered with a smile. "He is healing you … right now."

It had been at least a year since he had been able to close his eyes. He hadn't felt the urge to blink for almost two years. But now, something was happening. Was the pain returning? It felt as though it were returning; still, to feel pain might be a comfort at this point.

He had felt nothing at all for so long.

But he was afraid of the pain.

I am healing you.

Whose voice had spoken? Had a person come into the room?

Don't be afraid. Rest now.

Abgar wasn't sure just how his eyelids closed that first time. He did remember feeling a warm and gentle hand touch his eyes, tenderly closing them. But when he asked others about it later, no one remembered touching him.

Several hours later, the young king awoke from the most restful sleep he had enjoyed in many, many months.

During those hours, Hakim had been busy.

For many days, the servant had been in a death vigil. His friend, the king, had been unable to move or speak above a whisper for some time now. Three times each day, Hakim would feel for a pulse beat on Abgar's neck, and listen for breath by putting his ear close to the man's face. He had fed the king in tiny mouthfuls to keep him alive.

So many accounts of Jesus' miracles had made their way through Syria, and into Osroene, the personal attendant had memorized many. He had shared them with the king, as he washed and dressed him.

"One of these days, you will be added to his long list of healings," Hakim had told him. Later, when the servant thought about it, he realized he had come to believe in Jesus during the long months of waiting.

However, that very morning, the court physicians had told Queen Helene and her attendants to make preparations for the King Abgar's funeral. All hope of his healing had been abandoned as he grew nearer and nearer to death.

For the past year, Queen Helene had assumed his ruling duties, serving as Queen Regent. Although an apt monarch in her own right, Helene refused the full title, insisting she was serving the people until her husband could once again ascend to the throne. The crown's advisors had helped her to make arrangements for Abgar's memorial service, and his burial ceremony.

The tomb had been commissioned almost three years ago, and finished for almost six months now. Helene had buried her heart's attention for her husband into designing an extension to the Royal Garden, to surround and provide a pathway to the building. She had used hundreds of Damascus roses, in various shades and hues. She had also planted perennials to provide scent and color all year long. Adina had suggested also adding benches and a fountain, which had also been accomplished. Last week, the stone masons had added torch pillars on top of which were bowls for burning fuel oil.

It was later that day when Hakim explained his actions to Thaddeus Adai and Kahina.

"It has been a long time since King Abgar has even *moved* without me repositioning his body. I felt something in the atmosphere change when you all began to pray." He paused, looking around. "Where is your friend? Weren't there three of you?"

Adai nodded. "Yes, sir," he answered. "His name is Mari. He wanted to stay in the king's chamber and continue to pray while he sleeps. He is trustworthy."

"I understand," Hakim replied. "Do you need to go back there as well?"

"We will in a little while," Adai answered. "Before that, I'd like to know where the rest of my people are. They have all been traveling for months, and I want to make sure they are cared for."

"Well then, sire," Hakim spoke respectfully. "Let me put your heart at ease. When I left you, I went in search of palace servants who know your language; Hebrew, or at least Aramaic. I counted seven or eight of you; two women and five men. Is that a proper count?"

Amazed at his observational skills, Adai nodded. "Seven. Eight with the camel boy."

Hakim continued. "These servants have been assigned to serve as personal interpreters for each person in your company. They will also help your people with cultural issues, such as customs, food preparation, court protocol, and so on. I know I speak on King Abgar's behalf when I say it is our hope that in return your people will teach us about Jesus."

"That is our purpose in coming," Adai answered.

Nodding assent, the servant went on. "Since you are here at our invitation, it is our custom to assume responsibility to care for you for as long as you are with us. We have a building on the palace grounds designated for ambassadors and dignitaries and their parties. It has been empty for more than a year now, so it was closed. It is not ready for guests. We have dispatched a group to clean it, and set it up for your stay. I apologize, but until it is ready, you and your people will have to stay in the main palace."

"I apologize we didn't send word ahead of our arrival," Adai offered. "I've not done this before."

"Sir," Hakim countered, "you had no one to send." He paused. "Please have no concerns. This is something which happens all the time in palace life. We simply want to make sure you are well cared for."

"Speaking of which," he added, "your ladies were taken to the queen's apartments. They are being bathed and fed, and given a place to rest. They will receive facials and massages according to our traditions to care for their beauty and delicate nature.

"The men have been taken to the royal bath-house, where they will be given food. They will be bathed, massaged and then given rest in guest rooms here in the palace. A meal with Queen Helene and the Royal Council is being planned for this evening."

"There is no need to entertain us," Adai assured him. "We have no expectations. We just want to help."

For the first time in the discussion, Hakim spoke with distinct frankness. "No, sir. It is not a meal where you will be entertained. This is a necessary meeting, required by Queen Helene. She has many questions, as do the members of the Council. She has heard of the Ecclesia in Jerusalem, and desires to be prepared for what your presence in our country will mean for our people."

"Oh," Adai replied, thinking. "I see."

Seeing his lapse, Hakim made a suggestion. "Sir, I would like to make a proposal."

"Sounds good. But before you do, can I ask you a question?"

"Absolutely!"

"What is your *name?*"

The question hung in the air for a few moments. Then, the bizarre humor of the situation hit them.

Smiling, the servant answered. "My full name is Hakim Nurasyl al-Yerkeen. Everyone calls me Hakim. I am King Abgar's personal attendant and administrator." He extended his open right hand in friendship. "And you are?"

"I am Thaddeus Adai BenTimor, from Cyrene of Africa. Everyone calls me Thad, or Adai." As he spoke, Adai grasped Hakim's right forearm with this right hand, and the two men established their late introductions.

"You are from Africa. But you are Jewish?" Hakim asked.

"Yes. My father's family was displaced from the northern parts of Israel during the Babylon captivity centuries ago. There are many Jews in Cyrene. Over the years, our customs have become somewhat different than those in Jerusalem."

"So, who sent you?"

"The leaders of the Ecclesia in Jerusalem. One of the twelve, named Thomas, was my personal teacher."

"How did he know to send *you?*"

Thaddeus shrugged. "I'm not sure exactly. I know they prayed together, and sensed the Holy Spirit wanted them to ask my wife and me. We prayed and sensed we were to come. Is that what you mean?"

"No. How did they know you would fit with King Abgar so well?"

Seeing Adai's confusion, Hakim explained. "We call him, 'King Abgar the Black.' His grandmother was from your continent. All of his brothers were born with brown skin like mine. But he has very dark brown skin, almost black, like yours."

Hakim shook his head in amazement. "So you are saying this is *God's* doing? That Jesus has the power to do things like this?" He smiled, and shook his head. "I already had decided to follow Jesus, but this confirms my choice."

"What does?"

"His power to do things like this."

Thaddeus smiled brightly. "This is nothing, Hakim. Just wait."

"You look like him when you smile," the servant noted. "Your teeth are so white against your skin."

Adai laughed. "I would like us to be friends, Hakim."

"As would I, sir. I will try to serve you well, so long as it does not compromise my master, the king."

The slave rubbed his hands together, palm to palm as though to warm them. "Shall we go and fetch your companion from the king's chamber, and feed you both as well? I am sure you will want to be rested for the meeting with Queen Helene."

"That is a splendid idea!" Adai responded with enthusiasm. "I didn't realize how hungry I really am until just this moment."

Two hours later, a summons came to the royal bathing rooms. A palace slave entered the steamy rooms calling, "Where are the men from Jerusalem?" As he walked through the rooms repeating the question, Thaddeus Adai and Mari looked at each other in surprise.

"We are here!" Adai called out. "Just enjoying the waters."

Breathless, the servant rushed to the side of the cooling pool where the men were just finishing. "Sirs," he panted, "I'm sorry to disturb you. The king wants to see you right away."

"Is something wrong? Is he all right?" Adai asked in sudden concern.

The slave flashed an excited smile. "He is sitting up! He is talking! He was dying this morning, and now he is asking for soup!" He motioned with his hands, and looked around for two of the palace's larger towel-wraps to give them. "Hurry! You must come!"

"Do we have time to dress?" Adai asked kiddingly, as he took the towel-wrap, and secured it around his lower torso, then draping his upper body, in Greek fashion.

"No, sir," insisted the slave, shaking his head. "He was very clear. You are to come right now! And in this kingdom, his word is law."

Laughing, Mari shook the water from his head, and brushed his hair back from his face with his hands.

"Well, then," he declared, patting the servant on the back, "let's go!"

And so it was that Thaddeus Adai and Mari Al-Grigor entered the King of Edessa's bedchamber in bare feet and towel-wraps, directly from the bath-house. It was to become a story laughed about among the servants for many days to come.

Upon entering the room, Adai was more than surprised with what he encountered. The formerly dark and dismal room was now much lighter. Lit with lamps, it was evident there had been a definite improvement in the king's health. The shutters were still closed tightly, with heavy draperies covering them, but now, they could at least see and recognize faces of those persons in the room.

Several men were standing next to the bed. A heated conversation was taking place. Apparently, it had been escalating for some time.

"You must extinguish these lamps, sire," one of the men was declaring, somewhat emphatically. "You must rest your eyes. We don't know how long this sudden burst of energy will last."

"No!" a somewhat hoarse voice was heard in reply. "If anything is tiring, Ikban, it is this conflict. I will say it again, because I am convinced you are not listening to me. Jesus sent the men from Jerusalem to heal me. The God of Jesus has power. They prayed for me, and I am getting stronger by the minute."

The slave who had been sent to bring Adai and Mari from the royal baths, spoke up. "We are here, your Majesty," he announced. "Here are the men from Jerusalem."

Those standing around the bed parted, and a path opened between the king and his summoned visitors.

With all eyes upon them, Adai had never been more aware of being appraised. He could quietly sense not all of it was done in approval. Looking from face to face of the men in the circle, he made a few assessments of his own.

These must be the king's physicians and advisors, he decided.

Without warning, uproarious laughter erupted from the king's bed. Because it was unexpected, everyone in the room began to laugh as well, in various forms and intensities. As the ripple swelled, more stresses were relieved, and the laughs became harder. In waves, it continued. Each time it would wane, one man or another would find himself needing to express an uncontrollable chuckle. And then it would cycle once more.

Adai laughed so hard, he had to hold his insides.

Moments later, the sounds lessened. The king spoke, while still continuing to laugh. "Hakim," he asked, brushing happy tears from his eyes, "is there a particular reason why these men were forced to come to me from the bathing pools?"

Hakim drew the palace slave responsible into the king's view. "This is Adnan, Master. He came to us this week from Mesopotamia. He was purchased as a house slave. He is young, and untrained. Forgive me, sire. The fault is mine. All other slaves were otherwise occupied, and I was overseeing a few details during the time you were asleep. I asked Adnan to remain in your chamber and meet your needs. I also told him that when you speak, it requires instant obedience; and that your word is law. To defy you is to invite execution."

Abgar smiled at the young slave. "So I have become a hard man, have I?" he asked. "Adnan, I admire your diligence. While everything Hakim told you is true, it will prove difficult to raise you to Hakim's level as a trusted slave if you react in fear in your tasks. You are going to do very well here in Edessa. And please know that I am sure you will do better in the future. Welcome to my household." He nodded to Hakim. "Have the hallway guard show Adnan where the kitchen is. I'm sure they need help and will be thankful for his help."

He turned his attention to Adai and Mari. "My new friends, I apologize. If you would like to finish bathing, and dress, I understand. I want you to be comfortable when we speak together."

Adai had been assessing the younger man silently. He noted the bright eyes, and the improvement in the king's overall state. But additionally, his awareness was drawn to something else. Something deeper than leprosy; a yearning in the man for dignity, for true value beyond treasures, for a sense of divine purpose.

Holy Spirit, help me. To heal these things in this man will require more prayer and teaching; and more..... He will need to have an open heart.

Unbidden, the Voice responded.

I have been preparing him. Do not look at the surroundings, or the difficulties. Focus on the man.

Adai took a deep breath before responding. "Your Majesty," he responded, "we are here at your disposal, to see the fulfillment of your request to Jesus. Truthfully, Mari and I were finished bathing, and were ready to dress when Adnan came with your summons. I must say, I'm not sure I have *ever* attended a meeting in a towel-wrap before; but I am most comfortable. I wish my own clothing were this freeing."

At his comment, a second ripple of laughter made its way through the room.

"What would *you* like at this moment, your Majesty?" Adai inquired.

The king smiled a bright smile. When he spoke, Adai noted his voice was stronger, and had deepened. The king motioned for a slave to bring him water. He took a sip, and began to answer.

"Thaddeus Adai, there are many things I want at this moment. I am feeling better than I have in two years' time, and yet I am tired now. I had thought I would never sit up in my bed like this again. I want to stay awake and speak with you, but I think we will be having many hours together if you are willing to stay here in my country. There is a dinner tonight my wife, Queen Helene has commanded for the Council and your company. She has been carrying the load of ruling our kingdom for the past year or more. She is unaware of the miracles taking place inside my body. So, I plan to surprise her this evening. I haven't been able to even touch her for a long, long time; more than two years. I sent for you to speak with you regarding how to proceed wisely, now that I am feeling better. In my mind I want to climb Mount Aragats. Yet, something new inside of me urges me to sleep.

"Does he speak inside your heart, Adai? Who is this Jesus? I want to speak with you, but I must be rested if I am to surprise my soul-mate this evening. Do you hear the battle raging inside me?" He paused, and took another drink of water. "I want to sleep now. I thought I would have more strength, but it is gone."

Adai and Mari looked at each other. There would be no need for persuasive words here. This man was open and honest before God. Without fear, he spoke his agenda.

He was ready.

Adai thought before he spoke. "Your Majesty," he began, "when you awaken from your nap, we will come as soon as you are ready to speak with us. Before we leave to dress, we would like to give you a gift we brought with us. It is a gift from the followers of Jesus in Jerusalem. He was unable to come to you, because he was crucified. However, after three days, he was raised from the dead. And, after walking and talking with those of us who are his followers for forty days, He was taken up into heaven, into a cloud of witnesses."

Seeing the king was riveted by his explanation, Adai moved towards the satchel Mari had left on the cushions in the corner during their earlier prayer time. As he spoke, he opened the bag, and pulled out the linen burial sheet in which Jesus had been buried.

"Your letter arrived some weeks after his going up. Since he wasn't here to respond to your request, his great-uncle, his mother, and other members of his earthly family, wanted you to have this. It was the last thing to touch his physical body before he died."

Adai unfolded the sheet, and laid it over the king bed. He had not noticed the staining on the fabric before.

Abgar reverently ran his hand over the stains. "What are these stains?" he asked. "Are they his blood?"

Adai nodded. "We think they might be."

"Was he beaten?"

Adai nodded. "Badly beaten."

The king looked at his new friends. A defined sense of gentleness showed itself around his eyes. "We must talk. I want to know the whole story."

With that, the young man slid back down into his bed, putting his head on his pillow. He pulled the shroud up to his neck with his covers, and fell fast asleep.

Adai had been so fascinated by Abgar's responses, he had not noticed the room emptying. As slaves moved to extinguish the lamps, he suddenly realized he and Mari were standing alone once more in the room of a sleeping king.

"We are standing in the middle of a miracle, Mari," he said.

"Yes, we are Thad," came the answer.

As they turned to enter the hallway they were met by Hakim, who insisted they be assigned personal slaves to ready them for what now might essentially be turned into a celebration feast.

"You must begin again," he insisted. "And you must have a massage and a short nap. I have a feeling it will be a late night tonight."

Hakim proved to be a very intuitive man that night. It was almost daybreak when the Jerusalem party were escorted to their rooms. The King and Queen had been full of questions. They wanted to hear and understand the story of Jesus.

It had been a touching moment indeed when Abgar walked into the Feasting Hall under his own power. Kahina described it in the days to follow as being one of the most powerful experiences she had ever witnessed. Stunned, Helene had not known whether to jump up and greet her husband, or wait for him to join her at the table. All sense of protocol was completely disseminated in the purity of the entire court's thrill at seeing the man; their king; who had been at Death's door just hours prior. Walking, talking and sitting up.

He was still recovering, still healing. As days continued, further progress was seen every morning.

Such a thing had never happened before in Osroene. Not for as long as anyone in the entire kingdom could remember! The king immediately commanded Thaddeus and Kahina be provided with everything they might need to see the message and power of Jesus and his Holy Spirit become known.

After conferring together, King Abgar, Queen Helene, Thaddeus Adai, Kahina, and Mari prayed and felt directed by the Holy Spirit to construct a building where those in Edessa who chose to become followers of Jesus, forming an Ecclesia, could meet together to worship and to pray.

As the weeks went by, the burial sheet from Jesus' tomb was folded in such a way to show the pattern of the staining from a point just off center. It had been the King's decision to do so. He commanded a box be constructed to protect the sheet. When Thad asked him why he had done such a thing, his answer was simple.

"When I was sick, and it touched me, I felt the power of God bring healing to my body. One day, when it covered me, I wanted to see what the stains were, and I laid it out flat on the floor of my chamber. It holds the complete image of Jesus, the One who rescued me. I have folded it to show His face when people look at it. It is not a play-thing, or even an element to satisfy man's curiosities.

"It was used by God to build my trust in him because I am weak. He has made me strong. It is important to build the faith of my people. I want them to see him.

"To see Jesus, and become whole."

Autumn, 34CE

Over the past few months, Simon Peter and John had travelled the road between Galilee and Jerusalem many times. In fact, as the Ecclesia continued to grow in both Jerusalem and Capernaum, they had discovered a need to help with larger and larger groups of people; not only in Jerusalem but also in Capernaum.

Just this week, two other fishing villages in the north had requested leaders from the two main teaching centers. Could someone come and explain the ministry of the Holy Spirit to them? Could someone come and teach what Jesus had taught? Could someone help the villages to set up a food distribution plan for the poor? Could someone come and pray for the sick?

And then, there was the most common question. Do people who need to be healed have to come to Jerusalem or Capernaum to be prayed for? Were miracles happening only in Jerusalem and Capernaum?

The needs were great. Simon Peter, James, John, and the Jerusalem Ecclesia leaders conferred together. Presently, Simon Peter and John were dividing their time equally between Jerusalem and Capernaum. A week here, a week there.

In Jerusalem, Cleophas' son Levi, had begun making notes on papyrus of his experiences while traveling with Jesus. As a former tax-collector, he knew the value of keeping records. He wanted to write his memories down. He could sense there would come a day when he would be asked to give his entire account of the Master's life on earth.

He wanted to be ready. Prepared.

Andrew, Simon Peter's brother, worked to organize the distribution of food and clothing to widows, orphans and those in need in the area. Those who did not have a home stayed in the Essene Quarter. With Eli's support, they were able to open for day-to-day teaching and fellowship gatherings, meeting in the Great Upper Room.

The overall attitude among those in the Jerusalem Community, was something everyone could sense was designed by God Himself. Each person was aware they were living in a supernaturally-powered environment. Without selfishness, some members voluntarily sold their belongings, and contributed the monies into a common fund. Food distribution was funded in this way, as were many other needs. In fact, many in the city who had become followers of Jesus had sold their properties and goods, and brought those proceeds to the leaders of the Jerusalem Ecclesia.

And, while Simon Peter's work seemed to draw public attention, Andrew's work behind the scenes was phenomenally effective in helping people on an individual basis.

Physical healings and miracles were becoming commonplace.

The entire culture of Jerusalem was changing. In fact, civil support was so great in favor of the changes happening around them; any rare person who might stand in opposition to the movement were now afraid to say anything at all.

One afternoon in Capernaum, Zebedee and Salome were in the midst of conversation with Elsbeth, as workmen finished up the smoothing of the large doorway between the main room of Simon Peter and Elsbeth's home and the large gathering room. They had opted not to close the room off with a door. The Community had been growing so quickly lately, they were convinced any meetings they held would definitely overflow due to lack of room.

It had now become impossible to meet for prayer and teaching at the local synagogue. Although Jairus, the appointed synagogue ruler, was a follower of the Master, he had encountered an obstacle in his ability to use synagogue assets to support his friends.

Justus Flavius, the centurion from the local Roman Garrison, had secretly given money to Simon Peter and Zebedee to fund the completion of the Ecclesia building project.

"Hire workmen to finish it," he instructed. "My men and I will keep watch. If opposition arises against the common peace, it is fully within my power to subdue it."

Gratefully, the leaders of the Community of Jesus in Capernaum had complied. They needed a place to gather in the cooler months. As a general rule, the temperature never went below forty degrees, but it was difficult to hold a meeting outside when the wind whipped in from the Sea of Galilee.

Just this morning, a surprise visitor had arrived. He was older than any of the young men who had walked with Jesus as part of the twelve. No one had been sure of his identity when he first arrived. Arriving at the synagogue in Capernaum, he asked for the home of Mikhael benAron.

Jairus had not been familiar with the name, so he had sent the man to Zebedee. After searching through the village, the traveler had found Zebedee at Simon Peter's home.

"How can I help you, sir?" Zebedee asked.

"Well, I'm not sure. I'm trying to find my family."

"Oh?" the fisherman's eyebrows went up. "Are you from Capernaum?"

"No," the man replied. "I was raised in Bethsaida. I went there first, but the people there sent me here to Capernaum."

He looked around at the building project taking place. "Are you expanding your business?" he asked.

Zebedee laughed. "No, we need the room for prayer and study."

"Are you a rabbi?"

"Not exactly," the fisherman replied. "Although my parents were Levites."

The man's eyes widened in surprise. "Really?" he exclaimed. "Mine were as well. The synagogue ruler sent me here to find someone who might know where they live now."

Zebedee eyed the traveler with interest. "What is your family name?" he inquired.

"My father was Mikhael benAron," he replied, looking at the ground. "I am called Joses."

For a few moments, the shock of the man's disclosure evaded Zebedee's comprehension. Then, the truth began to sink in. He reached out and grabbed the man's upper arms. He looked him in the eyes, studying, looking for clues of recognition.

"Joses?" he asked. "Where have you *been?*"

Joses wasn't exactly sure why the older man had responded to his story in this way. Startled, he answered, "I was taken from my home at ten, and then sent to Rome. From there I was sent to Cyprus."

"Are you well? Don't you know who I am?"

Joses shook his head. He had no idea who he was speaking to.

"I'm Zebedee! Your older brother!"

"Zee?" he asked incredulously. "Are you really my brother?"

"What do you remember?" the fisherman asked.

"I remember Abba and Mami being herded into the courtyard by the soldiers. They took Abba away. Then they put me in a wagon. I was allowed to take a bag with me, and I took the phylactery you gave me when I first learned to read. I still wear it, see?"

He reached inside his cloak to pull up the tiny scroll container. "I wore it around my neck to hide it."

In wonder, Zebedee reached to touch the gift he had given his little brother some thirty years prior.

"Do Abba and Mami still live?" he asked carefully.

Zebedee shook his head, still looking at the phylactery. "No, because our Abba was a Levite, and from Galilee, they assumed he had been part of Judah of Gamala's rebellion. He was crucified the week you were taken."

Joses' eyes filled with tears. "And Mami?"

Zebedee's gaze met his brother's. "She fell sick with a wasting sickness about fifteen years ago. I stayed in Bethsaida alone after she died until I just couldn't bear it any longer."

"The family?" Joses looked around for a place to sit down.

"The only one still living is Maria. She lives in Jerusalem with her husband."

"Is he a priest there?" the returning brother wanted to know.

"No," Zebedee laughed. "She's married to a Roman architect. His name is Ampliatus. They have a son named John Marcus."

Joses laughed. "Greek *and* Hebrew," he commented. "How old is he?"

"He just passed his fifteenth Passover," came the answer. "I need to go to Jerusalem tomorrow for business. I will take you to meet them." Zebedee paused. "I heard you married. Is it true she is Jewish?"

Joses' eyes saddened. "She *was*, that is true. Her father is a synagogue ruler on the island where I lived. They took me in when I arrived there. I guess I fell in love over time. She died over the winter this past year. That's why I wanted to come to see my family here." He glanced at Zebedee. "Did *you* marry?"

The older brother nodded. "I'm sorry for your loss, Joses," he answered. "But what am I thinking? Come inside and meet everyone! Then we will get you fed and settled. Are you tired?"

Joses nodded. "Very. But food sounds good.... and water."

Zebedee slapped his newly found brother on the back. "Or a little wine perhaps?" He raised his voice, and shouted into the house.

"Salome! Come and see who ElShaddai has brought back to us!"

In Briton, King Arviragus was beginning a secret meeting in his private palace. He was seated with his bodyguard, his advisors, David his steward, and David's assistant, Caedmon. These were the only men the ruler felt were trustworthy.

They had each proven themselves to him time and time again.

The king's son, Prince Beli, had arrived with his family not even two weeks prior. They couldn't have come in better timing! Arviragus was sure he would have fallen into an abyss of despair had his two young grandchildren not brought light and laughter into his grieving hours.

His love; His queen, Izolde, had died just ten days prior. Beli had helped as Arviragas and David had made her ready for the Celtic funeral pyre. It was important to the king to take charge of the task himself, instead of allowing the Druid priests and ovates to prepare her.

"How could I allow her murderers to prepare her for the after-life?" he asked his steward. "I mean, I want her to come back as a person I can give love to. Or even as an animal I can adopt as a pet."

David had remained silent, heeding his powerful friend as he expressed his pain and confusion. This was not the time, he reasoned, to present his own beliefs. It was simply time to be present with the man.... and listen.

Since the king's discovery of the poisoning taking place some months ago, the king had added to David's duties as steward. Caedmon was now managing the affairs of the mines more and more, as David had become more of a confidante and counselor to the ruler. One of the duties Arviragus had shifted into the former mine overseer's charge was that of preparing the king's foods, as well as other members of the royal household.

As a result, David immediately requested the king fast for three days from all foods except water. At the end of the fast, he had created a mixture of crushed myrrh and coriander, mixing the powdered herbs with a strong tea. Arviragus still drank a cup of this tonic three times each day.

Additionally, Arviragus found he felt better when he abstained from the fermented beverages which had become his staple, such as beer, wine and mead. His health was continuing to improve, much to the silent annoyance of the Druid leaders.

David considered Arviragus, as they waited for communication from a courier returning from the mines. The man believed his wife's life would be judged after death as to whether she had been a contributor to, or a taker from, society. Arviragus had confided to David his hope Izolde's soul was now dressed in a white gown, with a golden crown, golden belt and jeweled adornments, before being assigned to her new earthly form.

He found his focus settling on the small silver urn on the floor beside the king.

"I will always have her with me," the king expressed. He carried the urn still, everywhere he went.

David considered the funeral practices of the Dumnoni tribe; so completely different from his own culture. In Israel, it was believed the human body had been hand-fashioned by the Creator, in His own image. So, to honor the works of ElShaddai, the body of a dead person was washed and treated with aloe, then wrapped in a long cloth called a *tachrichim*, bound and sealed in a tomb before sundown.

Among the Dumnoni, a corpse was also wrapped in a shroud called an *eslene*; then placed on a pyre. Animal sacrifices were made to the gods. The remains of those animals were then placed on top of the body, along with jars of oil. Those who could afford jars of honey to be added to the pyre did so.

Usually, a person's favorite items in their earthly life were also included for burning. King Arviragus had declined the customary slaying of his queen's slaves and handmaidens. Customarily, those bodies were also included on the pyre of a Dumnoni ruler, but the grieving Arviragus had rescinded the custom when it came to Izolde's passing.

"I have had enough of Death," he told his steward.

After preparation, Izolde's pyre had been set at the top of the Tor, where her people paid their respects for seven days. A bowl had been placed on her chest, for those who desired to provide monies or food for her usage in the next life.

On the seventh night, the candlelit funeral procession created a glowing environment. Arviragus had been irritated by the priests' chants and dirges. He had been angered by their artificial show of concern, whispering into her now deaf ears, instructing her spirit where and when to journey to the afterlife.

David had watched the king during the funeral. The man had waited until the fire was embers before leaving for his home alone. The ashes had been placed in the silver urn the next morning. Arviragus would not allow his servants to scatter the ashes, or to bury the urn just yet.

How long will he hold on to her, David wondered?

It was strange, David considered, how the Celtic people believed they could carry a dead loved one with them, and yet still believed they would come back in another form; as a bird, or a butterfly, or even recycled into the frame of another human being.

He remembered well the day Queen Izolde died. When he entered the king's home that day, he remembered, David had not seen her for some time. No amount of news could have prepared him for the drastic downward turn in her appearance. All over her body, small bumps had appeared, looking almost wart-like in appearance. The skin between her eyebrows and cheekbones had become almost black in color. She had lost so much weight, she looked more like a skeleton than a woman. And her skin had become almost orange in color; in shades of dark yellow as an undertone.

Arviragus had told him she had been delirious for more than a week.

It had been a horrible way to die, he decided.

He had included the account, as well as his own opinion of how the Queen's death had come about, in his monthly report to Rome. It was David's hope Tiberius Caesar would send a comforting message to encourage the grieving king.

His reverie was broken by the footsteps of the courier returning from the mines. In his hand, he carried the results of measurements taken in the older mines.

The man had no idea of the importance of his message.

After surveying the information, King Arviragus looked around the small group.

"This confirms our fears," he told them. "It's time to take action."

In Jerusalem, changes were taking place. It happened one night just after the evening meal. Zebedee's James remembered because it had taken place on the first day of the week. An elderly man knocked on the door of Ampliatus and Maria's home in Jerusalem.

"Is James the Less here?" he inquired when Maria asked him how she could help him. Seating him in the downstairs community room, she went upstairs to the rooftop courtyard to find James.

"James?" she called. "There is a man here to see you."

Surprised, Zebedee's James made his way downstairs. Coming down the stone steps, he looked questioningly at Maria. In response, she shrugged, then whispered. "It's an older gentlemen. He didn't tell me what he needs."

For some time, James had been living in their home. Unmarried, he had several times considered staying in his parents' office apartment, alone. Each time, he had been urged to continue his stay by his hosts. He then had offered to pay a monthly amount to help cover their expenses, but Ampliatus would not hear of it.

"When I have to travel on business, I am so thankful you are here, James. It helps to know Maria and John Marcus are in good hands. And, John Marcus is learning so much about spiritual things from you. He is a different boy these days."

The elderly man downstairs was in a crisis indeed. His name was Amos. He had moved to Jerusalem from Galilee. Like James' uncle, Joses, the man's son had been ripped from his home at the age of twelve, and deported to Rome just after the second census. His parents had received letters periodically, and knew he had been assigned to the Caesar's court in Rome.

But then, Tiberius had chosen a new chief advisor, named Sejanus. Sejanus had gained the emperor's complete trust, and became the administrator of the entire Empire. Weary, Tiberius had retreated to a villa on the island of Capri. With the emperor absent, Sejanus wielded control, seduced women, dosed out poisons, and reigned terror on the conquered people groups living inside Rome, the capital city.

In the year 19, by order of "Tiberius," all Jews inside the city limits of Rome were exiled to other lands. In this deportation, some 3,000 Jewish men were sent to the island of Sardinia, which was owned by Carthage. There, under a treaty with Rome, the Carthaginians trained these men, and compelled them into the Roman military machine.

Amos' son had been included in that deportation as well.

Then, in the year 21, Tiberius returned to Rome. Due to warnings from his family members, he had become suspicious of his administrator. After investigation, Caesar had ordered the man summarily executed, by dragging his body through the streets.

With Sejanus' reign of terror ended, Tiberius began a systematic reversing of the man's edicts, the first of which was to allow the Jews back into the city.

"I cannot allow my people to believe Sejanus did these things in my name with my permission," Tiberius told his advisors.

This was where the man's story became truly heart-wrenching.

James listened carefully as he poured out his deepest fears.

Amos had not heard from his son since the Caesar's reversal, some twelve or thirteen years prior. He did not know whether his son had been killed in Rome during the deportation; or died in internment on Carthage's Sardinia; or been commissioned to a military post after training; or had returned to Rome.

Or, perhaps, his letters had simply not been received.

To further complicate the matter, the man's wife had just died, and his own health was not good. Would James pray for him to be healed? Would he be willing to ask among the many new arrivals in the Ecclesia regarding the boy?

Although now, "the boy" would be in his forties.

As he listened, James found himself wondering whether there might be many others in the Ecclesia with the same difficulties as this gentleman. How many stories were there like this man's?

That evening, he prayed with Amos for healing and for comfort. He had taken record of his name and where he lived in the city. He had promised to initiate what help he could. The bereaved father had left encouraged.

But James had not slept.

Images of young men, uprooted and abandoned, forced to decide the values of manhood without their fathers, haunted him. By morning, he had made a decision.

He would speak with his Uncle Joses. He had experienced exile. James hoped his uncle could provide insight into the mental states of men who had experienced such things.

Over the next few days, the leaders in Jerusalem fasted and prayed. Was this a family-borne sense of sympathy, or was the Holy Spirit leading James to travel to Sardinia?

Two weeks later, James, and one of the seventy, Achaicus, boarded a ship bound for the western shore of Italy, eventually coming to the small island of Sardinia.

In Jerusalem, the daily morning sacrifice was consistently drawing large crowds to the Temple. Each morning and evening, more than two thousand men and women made their way to the Temple Mount in Jerusalem, to offer prayers and sacrifice.

The priests and rabbis had taught the population to offer prayers in two forms; adoration and intercession. But truthfully, most prayers offered this early in the morning came in the forms of weeping and supplication.

In the past twenty years, the population had become so highly taxed many had stopped even asking God for help. Additionally, the state of the economy had caused such great financial distress, the poverty-level need for wages required additional work hours.

This took a toll on every family in the city.

In the past few months, many people in Jerusalem had noticed an increasing number in those attending morning sacrifice and prayers. And, for some reason, the overall atmosphere in the Temple courts had been more positive, especially among those who attended in the afternoons. It was becoming more and more commonplace to encounter clusters of people in the outer courts, and in King Solomon's Portico, expressing verbal gratitude and adoration. These same groups could also often be observed in united prayer, asking God to bring change and solution to various situations.

It was a cultural change leaving many in Jerusalem wondering.

Such a thing had not been seen since the days of Ezra and Nehemiah.

It was close to three in the afternoon.

This week, Simon Peter and John were serving the Jerusalem Ecclesia. They had been in meetings through the morning, with James the Greater, who was Jesus' half-brother, and other members of the twelve.

Today, Simon Peter and John were meeting with several of the city's widows, whose sons had grown up without father-figures. There were more and more widows these days, John noted. Due to the many executions carried out by Rome in the last thirty or so years, it was sometimes difficult to find an unmarried male relative to care for a widow or her children. Was there a way the Ecclesia leaders could help, these women wondered? Did they have to follow Jesus in order to receive care? Simon Peter carried a satchel filled with fruit and vegetables to give to the women. As he walked, his mind was filled with prayer.

These days, he had learned to try *not* to anticipate what those in need would ask for.

"Holy Spirit, please give us wisdom," he whispered under his breath.

Even though they tried to come to the Temple, the crowd this particular morning was heavier for some reason, he considered. Preoccupied with his concerns, he hadn't really been paying attention to what was happening around him. He had just continued moving forward with the crowd. But now, he noticed John had stopped and was speaking to someone.

They were almost to the Inner Gate; a more ornate entrance which led to the Court of Women.

Simon Peter looked over at John, and realized he was speaking with a beggar. He had seen the man before, many times.

Hadn't he been sitting here every day? Why had they not stopped to speak to him before this?

He walked back to join John's conversation.

The man was speaking. "I was born lame. This is my designated place to beg, and it is the only way I can earn money to feed myself. Could you give me some alms, please? I would be thankful for anything."

Uri BenLevi looked at the men. The taller of the two spoke to him.

Simon Peter felt an urging to fix his gaze on the man.

"Look at us!" he commanded.

Uri looked expectantly at both of them. How much would they put into his cup, he wondered?

As Uri returned Simon Peter's focus, the "Big Fisherman," as many had begun to call him, spoke once more.

"I don't have money to give you," he said confidently.

Oh, well, Uri thought. But then, he still felt hopeful. What was different about these two men?

He didn't have much time to consider what was happening around him, or to think of a response. Simon Peter continued speaking,

"But what I do have I *will* give you. This is done because it is what Jesus of Nazareth would do. Rise up and *walk!"*

Then, in one great grasp, Simon Peter wrapped his right hand around Uri's forearm, and pulled him to his feet.

No one had ever done this to him before. Uri was concerned for a moment the man might be insane. Who.... But then..... A strange warming began in the middle of his back, a tingling sense with heat attached. Like fire, it moved quickly from his spine, shooting down into each of his legs. It climbed upward to his neck and took away the formerly constant pain in his shoulders and head.

The sensation was accompanied by a loud cracking sound. With each pop, the beggar's back straightened from its formerly hunched position.

Uri looked down. What he saw was unbelievable!

The stubbed balls where his feet had been were extending! As they did so, he found himself coming up, up... until he was eye-level with the tall man speaking to him. He looked at his stubs once more.

Were they disappearing? As he watched, a foot grew from the place where the stub had been, on his right foot, and then on his left. Gasping in a deep breath, he let out a startled response.

"H...h..how? Wh....wh....at?"

"This is *God's* doing!" John told him, with an encouraging smack on the back.

Simon Peter instructed him. "Give him praise, man! Take a walk on your new feet!"

In shock and awe, Uri looked at them. Surely it was a dream! But he could remember being carried to the Temple's Inner Gate that morning! He had been there all day!

With a dazed smile, he took a step, and then another. He could actually *feel* his feet! Without knowing, he realized what they were! Speeding up his steps, the beggar began to run. He danced back to Simon Peter and John, and then excitedly sprinted away again. Looking down at his feet, he checked the bottoms, just to be sure they were real.

He laughed with glee! He could walk....he could move.... For the very first time!

At the top of his voice, Uri began to shout his thanks to God. He cried aloud until he ran out of breath. Then he took a deep breath, and began again. He ran up to the surprised groups of people in the Temple Courts, to tell them the news.

He shook one man by the arm. "You remember me, don't you?" he cried. "I am the beggar who has been assigned to sit at the Beautiful Temple Gate since I was 4 years old! You know me! I am Uri! Look at my new feet! Jesus did this for me!"

He ran to another group. "Look what Jesus did! I have feet! I can walk! Look!" He jumped up and down.

As Uri moved through the courts, a stirring took place. Everyone knew Jesus had died. Many believed he had resurrected. Some said he had proven to be the Promised Messiah; God come in human form. Some believed he had ascended up into the sky.

And all were aware of the gatherings of those who followed him; of the food distribution; of the sharing and prayer taking place in the Essene Quarter.

Who had touched this man? Everyone knew Uri. He had been a fixture at the Temple Inner Gate for more than thirty years. A visual search began for whoever had touched Uri; where had been the source of the healing?

Then, unexpectedly, from Solomon's Portico, a man's voice rang out.

Peter had taken a stand in the center of the Colonnade.

"People of Israel, why are you surprised at this? Why look so closely at us. We did nothing through our own power or godliness! God has made this man walk! The God of Abraham, Isaac, and Jacob, the God of our fathers, glorified His Servant Jesus. You condemned him, and denied him to Pontius Pilate, even though the Prefect was determined to let Him go. But you denied the Holy and Just One; the Son of God, and asked for a murderer to be freed in his place. You killed the Prince of life. But God raised him from the dead. We all know this to be true.

Because of His name, through believing and trusting in Him, has made this man strong, and given him the ability to walk. We all know this man; this beggar. It is the ability to believe in Jesus Christ, given by His Holy Spirit, which has produced this perfect soundness in this man's body and mind. It has happened in front of all of us. We are all witnesses."

Annas and Joseph Caiaphas had been somewhat quiet since Jesus' resurrection.

In truth, Caiaphas had been in silent deliberation, miserably trying to explain what he was experiencing. On one side, he was struggling to make sense of the realities taking place around him. On the opposing side, the screams of the skeptical and cynical worldview he had come to believe was necessary to survive was making itself heard.

It was bad enough the new group of fanatics had grown so quickly, he considered. *But now, they were drawing in more and more of those who came to the Temple regularly.*

The whole thing had gotten way out of control.

His spies had kept him informed of what had been happening in Galilee. He had even lost a few of them to the Jesus sect's way of thinking. They had supposedly seen Jesus, and heard him teach; *after* the man had been executed.

Had the man Jesus *really* come back to life?

It couldn't be.

If these things were real, and not some hoax, then he would have to rethink everything about his life. The whole idea was just too overwhelming.

"Prince Caiaphas!" Amihud, one of the Sadducees, burst through the Great Door.

"What do you want?" the High Priest snapped.

"You have to see this! Come quickly!"

Sighing, Caiaphas rose to his feet. "What is it now?" he groaned. As the two Sadducees walked together, conversation continued.

"Remember what happened on the Pentecost Feast Day?" Amihud asked. "Well, he's at it again."

"Who?"

"That fisherman from Capernaum... Simon whatever. Uri BenLevi, the beggar whose station was at the Inner Temple Gate; well, he's walking!"

"Uri?" Caiaphas questioned. "How is that possible? He has no feet!"

"Well, he has them now," Amihud replied grimly. "He is dancing around, shouting his praise to God. He says he is completely healed."

Incensed, the High Priest followed the lesser priest out to Solomon's Porch on the Temple Mount. But before they arrived at their destination, they found it impossible to proceed. More than five thousand people had gathered together, pressing together towards the speaker in question. Some yards ahead, and somehow elevated, the man from Galilee was waxing eloquent once more.

Caiaphas moved closer to hear what he was saying.

"Brothers, I know you didn't know what you were doing, and neither did your rulers. But the things God told us would happen through all of His prophets since time began have happened! They told us the Promised Deliverer, the Christ, would suffer. This is fulfilled.

"Step away from those who made these choices! Come to God and be changed. Let His love erase your sins! Then refreshing times from the Presence of the Lord will be poured out on you!

"Remember what Moses said: 'The Lord God will raise up a Prophet like me from among you. You need to listen to him in everything;

take in everything He says. Everyone who will not listen to Him will be completely destroyed.'

"This is true. All the prophets, from Samuel onward told us these days would come. And you are the children of the prophets, and the destined receivers of the covenant God make with Abraham. He said, "in your seed all of the earth will be blessed.'

"God has resurrected His servant, Jesus. And now, He has sent Him to bless you. He has come to turn each of you away from your tendencies to sin."

Simon Peter stopped speaking, and looked around him. Without warning, two rough hands forcibly grabbed his forearms from behind. Turning his head, his eyes met those of the Captain of the Temple Guard. Another guard had restrained John. Yet another had taken hold of Uri BenLevi.

Joseph Caiaphas forced his way through to the steps where Simon Peter had been standing. He addressed the crowd.

"These men are teaching heresy!" he screamed. "They are under arrest, and will stand trial before the Council in the morning! Anyone who follows this Jesus Sect will suffer the same fate they do! You have been warned."

With great bluster, the High Priest maneuvered his cloak so that it showed its uniquely purple, silken lining. It was obvious he was seeking to intimidate the crowd. Despite Joseph Caiaphas' efforts, more than five thousand people became part of the Ecclesia that afternoon.

After confirming the two men had been secured in the prison cell in the lower part of his palace, a fuming High Priest went upstairs to the outdoor courtyard. Angrily, he sat down next to his wife, Nitza, on a stone bench.

"Is something troubling you, Joseph?" she asked, after observing him in silence for a few moments.

"It's nothing really," he answered.

She glanced over at him. He had pulled off his head-covering, and was rubbing his head nervously. "That's not true, my love," she countered. "You answered just a little too quickly."

He looked at her strangely. How had he not noticed how perceptive she could be? He paused, looking down at the ground.

"It's this Jesus Sect," he started.

"Oh, yes," Nitza answered, her voice free of emotion. "I've heard about them."

"How could you miss them?" her husband groaned. "It's like they're taking over." He ran his hand over his head.

Nitza stood up and moved to stand behind her husband. She began massaging his shoulders, trying to work out the tension she knew he must be feeling. "Don't worry, Joseph," she soothed. "Things will be all right."

Joseph lifted his head, and leaned back against his wife. "I will give you an hour to stop doing that," he told her. "Thank you."

It had been a long time since his wife had seen a vulnerable side of the High Priest. Surprised, she remained silent, and continued working the stress out of her husband's neck and upper back.

The next morning, yet another meeting of Sadducees took place in the Council of Hewn Stones. Annas, Caiaphas, Saul, and many of those trusted by them had been called to privately join together. As the group of priests, elders and temple scribes sat in judgment, Simon Peter and John stood, with hands bound in front of them, waiting to be questioned. Uri, the former beggar stood with them. The three had not been fed, nor had they been given water since the day before.

Finally, Annas decided to begin the questioning. He stood and raised his right forefinger to point at the two fishermen, and the beggar.

"Who gave you the authority, or even the permission to do what you have done?"

Silently, the three men prayed. After a few moments, Simon Peter looked up and began to give a response.

"Rulers of the people, and elders of Israel; here is our answer. If we are being judged because we did a good deed, in helping a crippled beggar, then let it be known that we did not do this on our own. We were only able to do what we did through the power of Jesus, the Christ. He is the One whom you crucified. But God raised him from the dead. It is by His power, and His power alone this man stands here before you whole.

"King David spoke of Jesus; He is the Stone who was rejected, and has now become the primary keystone. There is no salvation in any name other than Jesus. There is no other name under heaven with the power to rescue men and women."

Watching Simon Peter's bold response, Caiaphas motioned for the guards to remove the men on trial from the council room. When the door was closed, he spoke clearly.

"These men have not studied the Law as we have! These are not scribes! These are fishermen! Did this style of thinking come from Jesus?"

Amihud spoke up. "They did sound a lot like the Galilean. I heard him tell stories once when you sent us out to trap him in his words."

"What are we going to do?" Annas spoke up. "This is a miracle. It has happened. We can't deny it; we all have known Uri since his childhood. There are no tricks here. Everyone in Jerusalem can see it."

There was silence for a few moments.

No one had a suggestion.

Then, one of Annas' sons, Alexander, spoke in a conspiratorial manner. "I have an idea. Why don't we call them back in, and severely threaten them. If they continue to speak in the name of this Jesus, we will have them killed."

"Excellent suggestion!" Joseph Caiaphas slapped his brother-in-law on the back. "Yes! Let's do that!" He motioned for the guards to once again admit the beggar and two fishermen into the court.

After the doors were closed once more, Caiaphas stood and raised his voice in judgment.

"We have decided to be merciful to you. You will receive one opportunity to show yourself loyal to the God of Israel. We will let you go, if you promise to us all in the presence of God; you will no longer speak or teach in the name of this Jesus of Nazareth. You are not to speak of him as being raised from the dead, or to refer to his teachings when he was alive and you were following him."

The reply was unexpected.

Simon Peter smiled, scanning each man in the room. "What do you think it is better for us to do? Should we obey God or men? Should we listen to you, more than we listen to God? We can only talk about the things we have seen and heard."

Furious, Caiaphas shouted. "We will *kill* you! *Kill* you! Do you understand?"

John smiled at him now. "Yes, sir. We understand."

The Captain of the Guard moved forward to cut through the palm ropes binding the wrists of the three men.

Contemplating, the High Priest watched them go.

There really is no way to punish them, he realized. The people were convinced Uri's healing had come from God. The man had been stationed at the Temple's Beautiful Gate for more than thirty years. If they made examples of Simon Peter and John, they would be subjected to a rioting mob.

He looked at the men in the room. "We are going to have to move very carefully, if we are going to defeat this sect. We need a plan."

That evening, Ampliatus and Maria opened their home to the leaders of the Jerusalem Ecclesia. As they prayed together, they gave thanks for the speedy release, and asked for wisdom to walk through the days ahead.

"Help us to be bold in the face of their threats, Lord Jesus," they prayed.

As a response from the unseen realm, the architect's entire house and its foundation began to shake. But there was no earthquake happening outside the home. Then, as on Pentecost, the Presence of the Holy Spirit filled the room.

Every person present could tangibly sense a personal infilling of joy and empowerment. They were resolved.

Everyone, everywhere needed to know Jesus had resurrected.

They would not, *could not,* keep quiet.

A few days later, the twelve met together for three days of prayer and fasting. What was it the Master had said? ".... to Judea, to Samaria, even to the most remote parts of the world." As they prayed, each considered a map of the known civilized world. On the evening of the third day, they met corporately once more, and found, surprisingly, yet another evidence of the Holy Spirit's direction.

Each member of the twelve disclosed a people group which had emerged as a personal priority; similar to the urging Zebedee's James had received regarding Sardinia. They each could sense the desperation for Truth in the hearts of those they were drawn to; who needed to hear the Good News of Jesus.

Philip, the administrator of the group, kept record as each man shared. At the end of the evening, the map looked as though a circle had been drawn, with arrows emerging from Jerusalem as the center.

In amazement, the group looked at each other. How was it the Holy Spirit continued to bring them to discovery each day? There was no spot on the map not addressed.

Jesus was still leading them! They were still hearing him!

In excited anticipation, they wondered. What would happen next?

12 – Divine Networks

Spring, 35CE

In the early part of the day, Simon Peter sat on the rooftop of his family home in Capernaum. He had taught classes to leadership students the entire day before in the large room attached to his home. It was good to be back in Galilee for a season. He had missed his wife and children.

Over the winter, he had spent time in several places in Judea and Galilee. Additionally, he had helped with decision making and teaching responsibilities in the Jerusalem Ecclesia. He had also traveled to Samaria, visiting the believers in Jesus there.

This morning, he was contemplating how greatly the world had changed for all of them in the past two years.

Just after the Day of the Great Wind on Pentecost, several of the twelve had journeyed to other lands, reaching those of their countrymen who had either moved or been dispersed to other nations. Surprisingly, one of the first to make a missionary journey was Nathaniel. He and another follower of Jesus had set out to India. But, when Nathaniel's traveling companion died, the disciple had returned home alone. That was fourteen months ago.

Not one to be easily discouraged, Nathaniel chose another missionary with whom to travel. He and boyhood friend, Philip, also one of the twelve, decided to journey through Syria, Phygia and Greece with the news of Jesus' life and resurrection.

They had returned just two weeks ago.

From there, his mind went to the situation in Samaria.

When passing through the region a week prior, Simon Peter had been surprised to learn of a new "messianic" sect building in the area of Mount Gerizim.

It seemed a man named Moshe was claiming to be the promised Deliverer. When Peter had asked those in the small community of believers about the rumors, he was told that there were some in Samaria who had not believed in Jesus as the Deliverer, because he had not presented himself with the vessels used in the original Tabernacle of Moses.

Apparently, Moshe was claiming to be the prophet Moses come back from the grave, ready to bring the children of Israel to freedom from the political oppression of Rome. Additionally, now, secret military training was taking place in the remote mountain villages and at Qumran.

Simon Peter sighed.

When would people understand Jesus' Kingdom to come was unseen? That it was eternal, and spiritual in nature? That the freedom Abba Father offered was the liberation of the inner man; not necessarily the outer man?

The weary leader looked out over the Sea of Tiberius, or Lake Gennesaret, appreciating the view. His thoughts were reminiscent. Suddenly, he was reminded of a night storm on that sea, when he had walked on the water, trying to get to Jesus. The Master had been walking across the sea, and Simon wanted to make sure it was really the Master.

I wish I could go back and do that again, he thought to himself. *If I could, I would do it differently now.* He had learned so much in the past couple of years. About himself; about others.

This morning, Simon Peter had asked Nathaniel and Philip to come to a meeting he was having with his brother, Andrew, and Matthias.

He considered Matthias. The man had been chosen from the seventy to take the place of Judah the Sicari with the twelve. He was passionate about serving and had helped many to discover new Life in Jesus.

Andrew had hinted several times in the past few weeks about wanting to go into Mesopotamia, to bring Jesus' life and power to the people living in Anatolia and Turkey. His wife, Eleanor, was very capable. Four of their eight children were still at home. Andrew had accepted proposals for two of his remaining daughters. That would leave his youngest sons to travel with them.

Simon Peter knew his brother still wanted to request prayer and advice regarding choosing traveling companions to serve on his team.

Peter had asked Andrew to bring Matthias this morning because Matthias had also expressed a desire to travel north with the Good News of Jesus.

For some time, those who served in leadership in the Jerusalem Ecclesia had been sensing an inner nudge from the Holy Spirit. There was a need to send someone to begin the work of planting an Ecclesia in the Syrian city of Damascus. When it had first been discussed, Matthias had stepped forward, requesting to be sent out. For some reason, Ananias, whom Matthias knew as another disciple in the seventy, kept coming to mind when he thought of reaching the people in Damascus.

And then, there was the need for a leader to be sent to help the new followers of Jesus in Antioch in Syria. The group had grown exponentially in the past few months.

It would be good to hear the input of these men who knew what it meant to travel, reaching other cultures. James, Jesus half-brother, had asked Peter to work through the plans for the new Ecclesia leaders presenting themselves.

Most importantly, traveling partners would need to be chosen. Jesus had always sent his teams out in sets of two, rather than alone. Long ago, the twelve had decided they would follow that same pattern.

As a matter of coincidence, Simon, the former Zealot, had also mentioned a desire to travel north. Simon Zealotes was amazing, Peter considered. Just after the Holy Spirit's outpouring two years ago, he also had made an expedition. He had traveled into Mauretania, in northern Africa, where he and another disciple from the seventy saw many miracles take place. Many of the inhabitants there had come to believe, choosing to become followers of Jesus.

His traveling companion had died before returning to Jerusalem.

Upon his return, the unmarried Simon Zealotes had travelled with Judah, Zebedee's grandson, to Edessa in Osroene, to experience what had been happening there. He and Judah had returned with thrilling news of Thaddeus Adai, Kahina and Mari's work in a thriving Ecclesia, poised to draw an entire nation from the domain of darkness in the light of Christ.

It would be good to discuss these things; to pray with these men, he considered. *What was the Holy Spirit preparing them all for?*

His mind then went to the local synagogue. It was becoming too crowded for Capernaum Ecclesia gatherings these days. And, as the Ecclesia had grown, the number of students flocking to Jairus for training for the priesthood had decreased more and more.

Several months prior, just after the healing of the beggar in Jerusalem, and Simon Peter and John's imprisonment, three additional students had been sent to Capernaum. Apparently, Annas had sent them from Jerusalem to be trained by Jairus, the priest serving as current synagogue ruler. He had been glad to receive them at first.

Extra income from teaching was always helpful.

However, over the past six weeks, it had become evident the young men in question were sons of Sadducean priests at the Temple. And, while all three students were under twenty, Jairus was finding it more and more difficult to instruct them.

In truth, he wondered whether Caiaphas had sent them to stir up trouble; sparking opposition to the offending but popular Jesus sect.

Recently, these three had begun to ask pointed questions regarding Jairus' methods and views regarding the priesthood. Their attitudes were now affecting even the most motivated of his students.

Why was it necessary to give help to someone who didn't donate money to the synagogue?

Wouldn't it be better to let those who were dying just die; not giving away the food needed by those who could work?

Why did Jairus believe there was a spiritual realm; weren't his personal experiences just signs of madness?

And since there really was no such thing as an after-life; was it possible his daughter, Amita, had really been sleeping, and not dead?

Hadn't Jesus even said she was sleeping?

Hadn't her resurrection been something he had fabricated in his own mind?

Hadn't he brainwashed her and given her the story she told?

In the beginning, other students in the synagogue had laughed at their skeptical questions. Such doubt in the face of factual events everyone had seen and experienced was ludicrous.

In the beginning, their Sadducean views and questions had rankled and disturbed a peaceful environment. Many of Jairus' most loyal and motivated students almost came to blows with the three Sadducean young men.

But now, over the past few months, their attitudes appeared to have flavored the entire cohort.

In a small home in Jerusalem, a newly married Shira BenCaiaphas, stood in the outdoor courtyard of her home. She and Saul and only been married for two months, she realized, but it felt as though they had always been together. Just yesterday they had discussed the timing of having children.

According to her father, Saul had come a long way in the past year. She had been surprised when the young Pharisee's request for her hand had been approved by him. But then, as the months had progressed, she had watched her betrothed become more and more attached to Caiaphas.

It was strange, she considered, how very much alike the two men seemed to be. She had not noticed the similarities before their betrothal. In fact, just recently, she had wondered whether Saul's relationship with her father might have affected him more than he realized. Just this morning, she had seen firsthand how passionate her new husband's thoughts were concerning maintaining the purity of the priesthood, and of the nation.

"I had always thought the Law had to be completely kept, in every place, by everyone," Saul had told her. "Your father has shown me that in order to see our nation survive, we will have to work to make allowances with the Romans."

"What do you mean?" Shira had asked.

"Well, I am coming to understand," Saul explained, "there are times when we are supposed to agree with our enemies, and even those like the Greeks and Romans, for the long-term overall good. And, there are times when in order to ensure a more lasting peace, we must purge our own."

Something in the young bride's heart felt a twinge, hearing her new husband repeating the rhetoric she had heard from her father's mouth many times in her childhood. She felt her heart sink into her feet.

"Like the Sicari?" she asked hollowly. "Killing in God's name?"

"Exactly like that!" Saul had responded. "It is like a physician cutting out an infection."

"Oh," had been her only response.

Set upon performing an errand of some kind, her husband had apparently not noticed her reserve in his direction. He had kissed her cheek, and walked out the door, his mind occupied with whatever tasks her father had assigned him that day.

"See you tonight, my love," he said, leaving.

She decided she would finish her morning chores, and go to visit her mother for the day. As she worked, her mind went into overtime.

The changes in her beloved had taken place so gradually, she hadn't noticed many of them until today. Without warning, she felt so confused; almost as though she were standing in a clearing fog. How silly she had been to believe him!

Joseph Caiaphas has done it again, she thought grimly. *Only this time he had involved his own child!*

Until this very moment, she had thought her father had allowed the marriage to Saul in order to groom him for the Sanhedrin Council. But now, based upon the statements coming from Saul, she realized her husband was being set up as a pawn in her father's vicious battle for power.

Couldn't Saul see he was being used?

To be fair, Caiaphas' ruse had worked on her as well. She had believed her father when he told her he wanted her to become a great mother in Israel. It had been difficult, but she had worked to take down her guardedness; her emotional walls of protection. She had begun to believe he had finally accepted her as his little girl, bestowing his blessing on her.

But now, as she considered things more objectively at this moment, he didn't appear to have actually changed......

Were Caiaphas' sudden expressions of approval just part of some new upheaval he was planning?

She had been wise to hide her daily activities, as her mother had instructed. A sudden pang of fear ran across her chest.

What if her father *knew?* What would he do to her? She was deeply afraid of his anger.

And what would Saul do? She had seen his angry looks more and more lately. He was becoming more and more like her father.....

What if *he* found out?

Trust Me. The Voice spoke into her thoughts, cutting through her haziness. Waves of inexplicable peace washed through her.

She realized she had been holding her breath.

What about the miracles happening in the families of friends she had known since her childhood? So many who had been unable to find work, and had gone hungry; without money for food. But they had found help in the Essene Quarter of the city.

It had been the wood-worker, Cleophas, who first told her about the Jerusalem Ecclesia, the community of Jesus' followers.

Hadn't her friend, Kerina, seen her baby healed from blindness when Simon Peter, the "Big Fisherman," prayed for him just two weeks ago? And the pile of crutches and walking sticks piled just outside the Great Upper Room in the courtyard was beginning to look like someone was planning a neighborhood bonfire!

Nothing could talk her out of what she was experiencing.

She had never felt this way before.

It had begun on a day several months prior, with a visit to the Ecclesia with another friend, Libi. Libi had been born completely unable to hear. The two girls had known each other since childhood, and both were now married. Libi and her husband lived in the same part of the city as Saul and Shira, so the girls usually spent time "talking" during the morning at the neighborhood well.

During childhood, Libi and Shira had developed a method of talking with their hands. It was on such a morning Libi had asked Shira to come with her to the main street in the center of the city. She had been told the Big Fisherman would be heading to the Temple for prayer at a certain time, and wanted to be there, just to see if he would touch her and heal her hearing.

Skeptically, Shira had accompanied her. She knew now she had only gone out of loyalty to her friend. But then, as Simon Peter walked by with John, heading to the Temple, his shadow had passed over the two of them as they sat on the side of the street. Shira's eyes had been on the men walking by, and she hadn't noticed what was happening with Libi.

Suddenly, Libi shot to her feet, and placed her hands over her ears.

"Ohhh! Awgh!" she cried, looking at Shira in intense pain.

Shira turned to look up at her friend. "What happened?" she said, and signed using Libi's "talk" language.

Libi "spoke" back with her hands. "My ears hurt! Is it always noisy like this?"

Stunned, Shira looked around. The street wasn't really noisy today, she considered. But to someone who had always lived in complete silence, she realized, it would be overwhelming!

She walked her friend home, and stayed with her for a few hours that afternoon. They worked together to identify sounds; Shira would never have considered a person needing to undergo development after a healing had taken place. But on that day, she began to understand how the process of healing was working in Libi. It had also helped her to understand the gradual manner in which change took place in the visible realm; not only in her own life, but also in the lives of others.

Since that day, Libi had learned to imitate speech, and to speak properly. She was learning to use her voice.

Everyone who knew her had been amazed.

When asked how they had healed her, Simon Peter and John and answered Jesus had done the healing. Their answer had intrigued Shira. She had been raised in the High Priest's home, and references had been continually made to the Scriptures; but she had never seen God do anything like this! Even though the stories of such miracles filled the history of her people!

Questions were once again being asked in Jerusalem.

Was God really involved in the lives of His people? Or did He just watch from a distance, as she had always been taught?

Shira had attended prayer gatherings several times in the past few weeks as well. There was nothing subversive about the people who called themselves followers of the Galilean. There was such power present when they met together... like nothing she had ever encountered before.

She glanced out the window. The shadows were shortening. There wasn't much time left.

The meeting was at midday.

She would have to hurry if she were to get to her mother's home in time and still make it to the prayer gathering at the Temple. She hoped her mother was still wanting to go with her.

She began to pray in the language of angels. In his teaching from the Scriptures just the day before, John had said "the Holy Spirit will pray for us, through us, even when we don't know how or what to pray."

It hadn't been long ago, she considered, when several of the twelve had been arrested by the Sadducees and placed in Caiaphas' dungeon. But then, that same evening, an angel appeared in the prison, and opened its cell doors, allowing them to walk free. As they parted, the angel told them, "Go, and tell the entire story of this new Life.

"Stand in the Temple and proclaim the truth!"

And so they were. It seemed the Sadducees were afraid to touch them for the time being.

Spring evenings were becoming consistently warmer. It was Joseph of Arimathea's favorite time of year. The nights were cool now, but did not require an outer cloak. The morning chill now lingered until the early afternoons.

During this time of year, Joseph made it a habit to sit by an outside fire, in quiet conversation with friends who came to visit, or in contemplation and prayer. Most nights, he watched the flames until the moon was high in the sky, and he could see at least two or three stars in the sky to retire.

Tonight would be no different, he decided.

Cleophas and Mary had been staying in the Jerusalem house for the past year or so. All of their blended family were now grown, many with children of their own. And, although they did travel between Capernaum and Jerusalem periodically, Joseph could tell his niece had been more tired lately.

He wanted to take good care of her; to make sure her future was as secure as he could. If he were completely honest with himself, he wasn't sure just how much longer Caiaphas would tolerate his presence in Jerusalem. Each time he entered the Court of Hewn Stones these days, he sensed such tension in the room. He and Gamaliel, Nicodemus, Simeon, and Judah had begun meeting for prayer each day once again in Judah's home. It was because of his friends' insistence, he had made the decision not to go into the Temple alone again.

He didn't want to give the High Priest an opportunity.

Joseph had been staying on the estate in Arimathea for the past few weeks. Over the past few months, he had been traveling to Jerusalem to meet with Janaus, his steward, on a regular basis. Over time, they had rearranged a large portion of Joseph's assets, making provisions for the Jerusalem Ecclesia, and for the support of many in the priest's family, in a sort of trust, should something unexpected happen.

He and Janaus had discussed the sale of his estate in Arimathea, and the designation of which of his holdings should pass to Mary and Cleophas. He had also made designations for the Capernaum Ecclesia.

Thinking about it tonight, Joseph could see those had been the simple issues. It had taken some time to disentangle and simplify Joseph's shipping business. Considering the great upheavals occurring in his life, Joseph knew he would not experience life as it had been in the past ever again.

Should he disassemble his trade businesses, or sell them?

He could sense something unknown was about to happen. How much time did he have left, he wondered?

But the steward had been more optimistic regarding Joseph's future. Janaus suggested allowing Joseph's businesses to continue as it had been for the time being. After all, he told Joseph, the overseers and managers in place had been running things effectively enough on their own. Why not allow business to proceed until a change absolutely became a necessity? Couldn't they wait to restructure for easier operation and make the change of hands when a need presented itself?

After lengthy deliberations, Joseph instructed Janaus to transfer most of his remaining resources in Jerusalem into the hands of a former freedman, Felix, who based his offices in Italy. Felix was Joseph's personal *argentinius*, or banker. Felix's offices were based in Pompeii, a little over 200 miles south of Rome. Lucius Iucundus, Felix's assistant, was presently representing Joseph as an agent in almost all of his dealings. The priest had decided long ago to trust Felix's sense of stability in economic matters. He was a Gentile, but he was honest. After all, Joseph considered, Felix was known as the wisest and most intuitive financier in all of Italy, Malta, Cyprus and even southern Gaul.

Additionally, the priest considered it a great benefit for Felix to have his offices in Pompeii. He preferred putting into port there, rather than Rome. The smaller city allowed him at least an illusion of anonymity. It was crucial to avoid being drawn into the volatile circles fueling Roman politics in the capital.

He decided to keep the apartments he owned in Cyrene, in the event he could not live in Jerusalem, but needed a home. For obvious reasons, he would maintain his small home in Pompeii for the time being.

It was becoming more and more obvious he might need to flee the country; or, at the very least, someone he cared for might be forced to flee.....

Joseph stoked the fire, watching sparks fly upward.

There had to have been a reason why Jesus had rescued him from Caiaphas' dungeon, he considered. *Had* there been a reason, besides Joseph's desire to take care of Mary? He had always felt his life was destined for something. And, when it had come time to utilize his friendship with Pontius Pilate and offer his tomb, he had thought he had perhaps fulfilled his life's purpose.

If he had accomplished his task, why the rescue? He had already believed. He had been baptized. To save his life would indicate there was more purpose to his existence. And yet, since that day, he had lost all sense of purpose and drive.

It seemed as though all he was doing was waiting.

And *waiting* ...

Why?

Had Jesus saved him from execution *then,* to allow a murder plot *now?*

No. That was not his nature; nor the nature of his God.

Reeling in his thoughts, he set his focus on the fire, and began to pray in the language of angels.

The Voice spoke. *Not everyone is ready yet.*

Startled, Joseph looked around. Had he actually *heard* the Voice, or had it been his own thoughts? How had he not become used to this?

Then he heard it again.

Preparation is necessary, and cannot be rushed.

No, it *was* the voice of the Holy Spirit. He had been becoming better lately at being able to distinguish the Spirit's Voice from his own private thoughts ... and from other influences.

I will need each of you. All of you.

He pondered the phrases spoken. What did He mean?

After a time, he realized he was feeling a chill. The fire had decreased in intensity, the embers glowing slightly when the breeze brushed against them.

It was strange, the priest considered, how much brighter the stars above were becoming as the night's darkest hours approached. Perhaps they were illustrations of the days to come. He stood and stretched.

Tomorrow would be an eventful day. He would need a good night's sleep tonight.

It was mid-morning the next day, when Cleophas and Mary arrived at Joseph's Arimathea estate. Cleophas and Joseph worked to finish outdoor tasks, while Mary worked with Raziela to prepare the meal and guest rooms for those who would be staying overnight.

"Master Joseph told me to prepare one room for four, two rooms for three, and two rooms for two, in addition to his room and your room with Master Cleophas. If I count properly, that is every room in the house!" She stopped to hold Mary's gaze. "Did he tell *you* who was coming, Mary?" the housekeeper asked, as they made up beds together.

"Well, I know my sister and her husband are coming," Mary answered, counting on her fingers. "They are from Capernaum, and their son, John, will be with them. Perhaps Uncle Joseph is planning for the three of them to share. If not, that would be two of the rooms."

"He said we will need to put three beds in four rooms, and two in another, two in yours, and then of course, prepare his room," Raziela replied.

"And he didn't tell *you* who was coming?" Mary chuckled. "I would have thought you would have been given a list."

"No," Raziela smiled. "No list here." She fluffed a small cushion as she spoke. "He did say I should prepare some toys for a small child."

Mary was surprised. "Oh? Then I have absolutely no idea."

Falling into private thoughts, the two women continued working in silence for the next few moments. Floor cushions were placed, lamps were filled. Fresh water was drawn and placed where needed, and clean bathing linens layed out in to each room.

When sleep accommodation preparations were completed, the two women began preparing the meats delivered the day before for roasting. As anticipated, Zebedee and Salome brought salted, smoked fish and greens with them. She smiled. Her sister never showed up empty handed.

As the housekeeper unwrapped and seasoned the meats delivered from the marketplace in town, Mary rummaged for other items which could be shared as part of the meal. She noticed that apparently, Raziela had either baked or purchased bread the day before. There were sealed jars of stuffed olives in vinegar, and a few, fresh cheeses wrapped in linen.

She need not have worried. There would be plenty of food.

Just after midday, Salome and Zebedee arrived from Capernaum with John. After greetings were exchanged, the two sisters began unpacking food items Salome had brought.

"Oh my!" Riziela exclaimed, as she pulled out parcels, one after another, from the large satchels Zebedee carried inside.

"I made stuffed grape leaves, and some baklava and honey cakes. There are a few other things. It doesn't matter where or when Uncle Joseph uses them, Raziela. I just wanted to feed his sweet tooth."

"Oh, I'm sure we will put them to good use," Mary declared. "Has he told you what's going on?"

Salome shrugged. "All I know is he asked John and Zebedee to come to help him with a baptism. I'm not sure why we can't use the Jordan River, or even who all will be involved. Simon Peter was invited, but was unable to come. Come to think of it, Uncle Joseph was a little vague about that. I didn't think anything of it at the time, but now that you mention it…"

Salome's voice dropped in mid-sentence, as the sound of horse hooves made their way up the lane leading from the estate's gates to the house. Making their way to the door, the three women were surprised to be greeted by the sight of Roman military bright red with brass regalia. Two men on horseback led an impressive procession. Riding next to a centurion commander they didn't recognize, was another Roman official who was equally unrecognized by them. Behind the two men, six bearers carried a large, canopied *lectica,* or "litter." The curtains were pulled back to allow air-flow. Inside, an outstandingly beautiful women, impeccably groomed, could be seen with a small boy. Behind the litter, three well-dressed slaves walked; two women and a young man. These were followed by two foot soldiers in full dress uniform, marching in unison. Finally, a well-dressed man followed on horseback, commanding a stallion with rather large saddle-bags behind the saddle.

Mary and Salome went outside to greet the new guests, while Raziela hurried to gather water cups and a water pot to serve those arriving who might be thirsty.

Outside, in the garden's courtyard, Joseph greeted his guests.

Pontius Pilate was the first to dismount. With a huge smile, he stepped toward Joseph, grasping his forearm in friendship.

"My friend!" he declared. "Thank you for opening your home to my family!"

"I am the one who is honored, Your Excellency!" Joseph replied, stepping into his office of Nobilius Decurio.

Pontius stepped back, and took the priest by the arms, looking at him face to face. "Now, Joseph," he chided. "Let's have none of that. We are in *your* home tonight. It's just Joseph and Pontius tonight. I simply want to rejoice with my new family, without referring to privilege or title this evening."

Joseph was surprised, but tried not to show it. "Absolutely," he answered. He motioned to the remainder of Pontius Pilate's traveling party. "And this, of course, is your wife?"

"This is my Claudia. I don't know if you remember her." He moved toward his wife, who was standing next to the lectica, helping Pilo to the ground. She motioned to her bearers to move the litter to an out-of-the-way corner of the garden, and released them to sit by the well. She turned her head at the sound of her husband's voice and smiled.

"And this is our Pilo," he continued, picking up their son.

Joseph smiled a wry smile. "I do remember our first meeting, Madam. The last time we saw each other, we were having a very difficult day. I much prefer the circumstances today."

Her gentle voice carried calm confidence. "As do I." Claudia Procula extended her hand to Joseph, palm downward.

Joseph took her hand and touched it to his lips in a courtly greeting. "Welcome to my home, My Lady," he said. "Is there anything I can do to make you more comfortable?"

Procula smiled. "Thank you, noble Joseph. It is we who are honored to be accepted here." She took a cup of water from the tray offered by Riziela. "Thank you."

"May my bearers rest here in the garden?" she asked. "We stopped to rest several times in the journey, but I know they are tired. They have walked for more than seven hours today."

Joseph motioned to Riziela. "Wherever they would like to rest here in the shade is fine," he answered. "The weather will be clear and comfortable out here this evening, and they will be secure. We will provide linens for their comfort."

He indicated the slaves walking behind the lectica. "We have prepared inside lodging for your ladies. Would you like Riziela to show you to where you will be staying?"

"That would be wonderful," Claudia Procula answered. She motioned to the slaves to step forward. "This is Candace, my maid. And this is Yasmina, our son's nurse. This young slave is Imani, who serves my husband as servant and scribe."

Pilate looked around the courtyard. "Where are your own slaves, my friend? Every home in the Empire has at least ten! You certainly have been able to afford them!"

Joseph looked at his Roman friend and smiled. "I have no slaves, Pontius. Although some of our countrymen do own slaves, it is not my belief that God desires any person to become the property of another."

"But you have servants," the Procurator countered, somewhat confused.

Joseph chuckled. "Yes I do, perhaps because of my own laziness, or even my age. But I try to see to it my servants are well paid."

"I see," was all Pilate could bring himself to say in response. The concept of a person serving for pay, and voluntarily at that, had never occurred to him before. In fact, his own sense of personal liberty was new to him. Many things were these days, he realized.

At that point, Mary and Salome stepped in to help take Claudia and her maids to their rooms. As introductions had been made, Joseph noticed Quintus, the centurion, had dismounted, and taken the reins to his own horse and the Procurator's. The well-dressed man riding in the rear of the company had also dismounted, and was holding his horse's reins, as he spoke with the two foot-soldiers. He moved towards the centurion.

Joseph was sure Pontius would introduce them at some point.

"Quintus," he said, "the horses can be stabled with the wagon in the shed over there. There is feed, and plenty of straw for the horses. There are several empty stalls. The horses can be left with the servant I have in charge there. He will make sure they are brushed down and cared for. His name is Justin."

Quintus motioned to the soldiers to join the conversation between Joseph, Pontius and himself. He put his hand on the shoulder of the first soldier. "This is Apelles, who has recently made the decision to follow Christ's teachings. This soldier is Titus, who also wants to be baptized. His brother, Luke, is a physician, and he has come with them as well."

Joseph stretched his arm out to indicate John and Zebedee standing nearby. "This is Zebedee and his son John. Zebedee is married to my niece, Salome. John was one of the twelve who traveled with Jesus when he was here on earth."

Pilate looked at John with new interest. "What was that like, John?"

"Amazing," John answered. "Absolutely amazing."

"Our son, Pilo, was born with a crippled foot, and Jesus healed him," Pontius offered. "I would love to talk with you some time."

278

"I would like that!" John replied. "I didn't know about your son. It must have been a difficult thing to go through. Well, he certainly is running well now. I was watching him a few moments ago. I wish I had his energy."

Pilate chuckled. "Me too! I don't know how Claudia and Yasmina keep up with him." He paused, thinking, and then looked at Joseph. "How many people are going to be baptized this evening?"

Joseph looked around the garden. "Let's see," he answered. "You and your wife, Quintus, Titus and Luke, and any others from your party who want to be baptized. I thought we could hold the baptism inside in the bathing room of the house. So, after dinner, it will be easy to have a time of worship together, and then hold the baptism. Following then, it will be a simple matter to help everyone find their place of rest for the night."

"I would prefer to have Pilo with Claudia and myself overnight," Pilate requested. "Is that possible?"

"That is the plan," Joseph replied. "We placed the two women, Candace and... "

"Yasmina," Pilate interjected.

"Yasmina," Joseph repeated. "We put them in the room next to you. Imani has been put with Quintus, and the two soldiers. I have put Luke in my own room."

That evening, after dinner, John and Joseph shared their memories of Jesus' life on earth, and spoke of His identity as God come in human form. Then, a song was sung by everyone. Not many new songs had been written yet in the fledgling Ecclesia, the planting of the Lord; so the song was from the *Tehillim*, or Jewish hymnbook, within the book of Psalms.

As Jesus had instructed, they remembered his last words on the night he was betrayed. They shared bread and wine together, and considered his wounding, as well as the power of his Resurrection.

Then, when the announcement was made baptisms would begin in the bathing pool, every member of Pontius and Procula's visiting party participated. Even Claudia's bearers wanted to be baptized as followers of Jesus.

The decision to follow Jesus' teaching surprising all of them, was the declaration of little Pilo.

"I want to follow Jesus!" he announced. "I want to be baptized too!"

"Are you sure he understands what he is doing?" Claudia asked John, feeling cautious; afraid she might be allowing her son to take the Blood and Body of Jesus too lightly.

John chuckled, and comforted her. "The Master told us to let the little ones come to Him," he answered. "I think Pilo, in his simplicity, has more of the situation settled in his heart and mind, than many of us, as adults."

And so the child was baptized. Erupting from the water, his voice broke out in the language of angels.

Claudia looked at her husband. "That settles it for me," was all she could say, as tears of joy streamed down her cheeks.

As John, Zebedee and Joseph led each one into the waters, he or she was asked to make a public declaration.

"I believe in God the Father, Almighty. He is the Maker of heaven and earth. I believe in Jesus Christ, His Son, come in human form, to help us understand and know the Father. It is my desire to live my life according to the Spirit of God, and the teachings of Jesus. I am his disciple."

As they rose from the symbolic watery grave, into resurrected life, both Pontius and Claudia prayed for the empowerment Jesus had promised his disciples. They both spoke spontaneously in the language of angels.

During the two-day visit following the baptisms, Pilate and Procula spent hours receiving invaluable instruction from three men and two women who had walked with Jesus personally, learning and observing his life on earth day to day. Many questions were answered, and practical lessons were taught.

Luke, the physician, had begun constructing a letter to a beloved uncle, explaining his choice to walk away from the plethora of Greek and Roman gods, to follow a single God, who had come in touchable form as Jesus. He spent many hours listening to Mary, Joseph and Salome share their accounts of Jesus' time on earth.

It was his hope his Uncle Theophilus would read the letter, and choose new Life in Jesus as well.

Quintus, Titus and Apelles discovered a brotherhood deeper than their military training could ever provide. Procula's bearers, and the family's personal attendants discovered a sense of belonging they had not known before.

On the afternoon of the second day, Joseph offered to give Pontius a tour of his estate. Declining a bodyguard, the ruler took a rare, private walk with his close friend. Moving out of earshot, Pilate began to unload his soul to the only man in the Empire he felt he could fully trust.

"Joseph," he began, "something is about to take place."

The priest glanced sideways at his friend. "What do you mean?"

"The Syrian governor has been recalled, which means another is about to be appointed. Tiberius Caesar, my father-in-law, is ruling from Capri, and not doing well."

"Is he ill?"

"Well, yes, but not so that anyone would know just yet. The illness is within himself."

"I don't understand," Joseph ventured.

Pilate sighed. "He has had a horrible life. He is Claudia's natural father. Augustus was determined Tiberius would succeed him as Caesar, so he forced Tiberius to divorce the wife he loved, Vispania, to marry a woman in the royal line named Julia. Julia is Augustus' natural daughter. As a result, Claudia was torn from her mother as a small girl."

"That must have been traumatic for her," the priest offered.

Pilate smiled grimly. "Very," he answered.

There was quietness, as each man considered the ramifications of what had been said. Finally, the Procurator spoke once more.

"Julia is a cruel woman, and the marriage didn't last long. As soon as Tiberius was made emperor, he limited her powers, but the damage to my wife was already done.

"Anyway, over the past few years, he has become angry and difficult to deal with. He has also developed perverse sexual appetites. Now, he feels pain and weakness within his body. If what I have observed in the experience of other men who have chosen the same lifestyle, it will be no more than two years before he dies; probably less.

"That being said, the political climate in Rome is becoming extremely dangerous, especially in regard to the followers of Jesus. Apparently, communication regarding the arrest and imprisonment of leaders of the Jerusalem Ecclesia was presented in the Senate. The movement is presently officially classified as a "sect" with no military danger to the Empire. However...." His voice trailed off.

Joseph waited for a moment, giving his friend a chance to gain his thoughts. "However?...." He prodded.

"The only reason for the present official view is due to correspondence between Tiberius and myself regarding Jesus; first several years ago, regarding his healing of his grandson, Pilo. Then, I wrote him several letters regarding Jesus' miracles and teachings while Jesus was alive. Finally, he had full disclosure regarding Claudia's dreams, and Jesus' crucifixion and resurrection."

"I was unaware you were such a correspondent, your Excellency," Joseph said, amazed at the man's proficient communication.

"Stop it now, Joseph," Pontius chuckled. He immediately became serious again, and continued.

"The truth of Jesus' life and resurrection has reached into some remote areas of the Empire. The inner freedom being discovered by those who follow his teachings, was presented in the Senate as revolutionary; capable of sparking rebellion across the Empire.

"There is only one thing preventing a banishment of the sect; an investigation and execution against the movement being instigated. And that would be the mandate made by Tiberius in a joint session of the Roman government. He forbade the Roman generals to bring any form of judgment or force against the movement, as it appeared to be promoting peace and good citizenship within the Empire."

"So, has he chosen to follow Jesus?" Joseph asked.

"I don't know," Pilate answered. "Anything is possible. You need to know, however: any mandate made by a reigning Caesar can only remain in place until the reigning ruler dies. Succeeding rulers have the option to reverse it, should they desire to do so."

"Who do you think will succeed him?"

"There are no good choices. The most dangerous and most likely, in my own mind, would be Gaius; the son of Claudia's second cousin, Agrippina. He is dangerous because he has something deeply wrong mentally. I believe this is what has made him so extremely mean.

"To be fair, he is extremely intelligent, and creative, but he seems to use those skills to come up with new concepts of torture and cruelty. Added to that, he was bullied in the military because of his limp, and stubbed foot. They call him 'Caligula.' He hates the nickname, but it has stuck."

Joseph was speechless at how well his friend could perceive the happenings surrounding him. How difficult it must be to be a Roman ruler, he thought. He pulled his thoughts back into focus. Pontius was speaking once more.

"I suppose I am trying to warn you. It is a matter of time before something shifts in the political situation toward the Ecclesias of Jesus. I can help you if the Jewish leaders here in Jerusalem step out-of-bounds, but I anticipate something will shift in my own situation as well at some point in the near future.

"You see, Judea and her provinces are part of a four-region military defense on this end of the Empire, protecting Rome from those in the east who might rise up against us. I am not sure how much longer they will want to station me here."

"I can see why you felt so strongly you needed to be baptized at this time," Joseph offered.

"Yes, before the political tide changes. I am not worried for myself, but I do feel I must protect Claudia and our son. As it is, someone in Herod Antipas' palace is continually sending reports to my enemies in Rome on my activities. It was a risk to come here, even now."

"Then, what was your official story for your journey here?" Joseph asked.

"We announced that it was imperative to have our son's feet assessed, since many know he was born with clubbed feet. We said we were going to take a short vacation trip to the villages here in the Hills of Ephraim. So, from here, we will be going to the hot mineral springs in the village.. All of us can use a soaking and massage, anyway," Pilate answered. "It was a gift from God when Luke wanted to attend with his brother."

"How did that happen, exactly?" the priest wanted to know.

"I don't know," came the answer. "Quintus put it together. So, now we are travelling with our own personal physician."

"I'm amazed."

"As am I."

Spring, 36AD

A few months later, as Pilate predicted, a new governor was put in place in Syria. He was considered a knight by the Empire, because his father had served as Augustus Caesar's personal steward.

As such, the present Caesar, Tiberius, considered him a brother; so much so the two men had purchased vacation villas on the island of Capri, less than two miles from each other. As a friend of the Caesar, he had more influence with the ruler than his predecessors. Having served three times as a consul in the Roman Senate, he was no stranger to the political arena. His opinions had been sought after as wise considerations in the capital of the Empire.

He was ambitious for his children, and was purposely setting a foundation for his sons to build upon. In fact, in future years, his son would be crowned Caesar.

The man's name was Lucius Vitellius.

In Samaria, a crowd of just over three thousand had gathered. Just below the summit of Mount Gerizim, Moshe and his brother, Aharon stood together, communicating their intentions to revive the nation of Israel.

Word had circulated throughout the area. The prophet Moses had returned to the children of Israel! A man named Moshe was the reincarnation of the first deliverer, and even his brother, Aharon the priest, was with him.

Excitement was building in Samaria! Many had believed in Jesus in the region, but this – this could be a double blessing! And, it appeared Moshe was willing to *prove* his identity by showing where the original vessels used in the Tabernacle in the wilderness had been hidden. He would produce them in the presence of witnesses. Everyone was being urged to attend. The more who came, the better.

But, if a person did choose to come, they were advised to bring a weapon.

Everyone knew there would soon be a need to defend the nation.

The gathering lasted all afternoon. There were stirring speeches, prayers, and protests. Close to the end of the day, Moshe stepped to the dais, and asked for the trust of his followers. He would produce the vessels, he said, but it was too dangerous to do so today. The items were solid gold, after all, he said, and carried the power of God.

Everyone involved would need protection.

He promised. When he felt it was safe to produce them, he would show everyone where they were hidden. For the moment, they needed to build an army. When the time was right, they would carry the vessels into war, and would be assured a victory, because they worshipped the one true God.

The people continued to gather for days, and the crowd grew from three thousand to ten thousand.

After three weeks, Pontius Pilate dispatched a thousand Roman troops to dispel the rebels. Equestrian officers and heavily-armed Roman infantry took the leaders as prisoners, along with Moshe and Aharon. Several thousand were slaughtered at the foot of the Mount Gerizim.

The rest were allowed to flee to their homes.

"We will show them mercy," Pilate told his wife. "Only the ringleaders need die. And I will not crucify them. They will be beheaded."

When news of the incident reached Lucius Vitellius, it came from a Samaritan contingency. Thinking the accusations might be an indication Pilate had lost his sense of balance, and therefore his usefulness to the Empire, Vitellius sent his military deputy, Marcellus, to Samaria and Jerusalem from Syria.

Marcellus' mission was to investigate; to interview those involved in the incident. *Had* there been excessive violence and unneeded force involved?

The investigation took several months to complete. After Marcellus made a full report to the governor, the governor sent the findings to Rome.

Through his network of military connections, Quintus kept Pontius Pilate aware of the schemes being set against him. It was becoming obvious to everyone under the Prefect's care, the ten-year season of serving Rome in Judea was coming to a close.

"It is a matter of time, my love," the ruler told his wife. "Where would you like to see me be assigned next?"

"Somewhere where Pilo can grow without fear of the Emperor's interference," Claudia Procula answered.

The couple prayed together. "Holy Spirit, please lead us. Show us the next step. Please prepare us, and prepare those we will be responsible to serve to receive us with Your favor."

In Appolonia, a small, coastal fishing village on the Mediterranean Sea, some eighty miles from Jerusalem, a clandestine meeting was taking place in the home of Mennahem, a Jewish ship-builder. His mother, Nurit, had died some month's prior. She had been sister to Joseph Caiaphas. Since her death, Mennahem had fallen on hard financial times.

"I'm telling you," he told Amihud, the priest, "it is difficult to be a Jewish shipbuilder in a Roman port city."

"Well, I think we may have something you might be interested in," the Sadducee replied. "How quickly could you build something to hold a large crowd?"

"For what purpose?" Mannahem wanted to know.

"It's a secret," came the reply. "Just know the ship is commissioned by the High Priest, your Uncle, Joseph Caiaphas, and your grandfather, Annas."

"What are its dimensions?"

Amihud gave Mennahem the measurements of a ship, almost twice the size of a normal Galilean fishing boat. He rolled out a papyrus with a rough drawing inscribed in charcoal.

The shipbuilder raised his eyebrows. "This is an ambitious undertaking," he observed. "Any special instructions?"

"Yes, we have several," came the reply. "But first, I am to secure an oath from you of complete silence and secrecy on the entire project. And, I am to assure you of extra payment should this plan succeed."

"What do I tell my workers?"

"You won't need to tell them anything, except you have a new eccentric client, who is engaging in a new trade venture. The crucial details, your Uncle says, are to be attended to by yourself alone."

"What are the details?" Mennahem asked.

"The ship is to have no sail, and no navigation tools. It is to have no rudder, or method in which to be steered. It is to have no anchor, or oars."

"Why would anyone want such a ship? It is a death-trap!"

Amihud touched his forefinger to his lips. "To ask such a question could cost you your life. You do not need to know." He paused, and then added. "Oh, it is to have no seating; no benches or storage at all."

Stunned by the intimidating inferences suggested by the ship's design, and the conspiratorial tone he was hearing, Mennahem hesitated to agree to the project. But, in light of his financial desperation, and the dangerous turn his communication had just taken, he felt he had no choice.

"How much will you pay for such a ship?"

Amihud named an exorbitant amount; more than a year's wage. Mennahem swallowed hard, and nodded, extending his hand for a covenant agreement.

Amihud laughed and heartily shook the man's hand. "Then we are agreed! Joseph Caiaphas and Annas were both sure you would be in agreement."

In Jerusalem, Cleophas and his wife worked together in the courtyard garden of Joseph's former home. For about an hour, they had been transplanting herb and vegetable plants into the ground, from trays of seedlings Mary had begun inside more than a month ago.

"Are these the last of them?" Cleophas asked her.

"What?" she answered, somewhat distracted.

"Are these the last?" he repeated. "Is this the last tray?"

"Oh," she replied. "Yes. Sorry. I was thinking about what it will be like to see everyone at home again."

"Do you still want to go, Mary?"

His wife stopped working, and sat back. She sighed. "It will be nice to see our old friends. We've been in Jerusalem quite a while now. I know you've been back since Jesus went away, but ...."

"What is it?"

"But I know I will really miss watching miracles happen every day, and our serving place here in the Ecclesia." Mary sat back on her heels, considering. "I have come to love our life here. I think I will miss most the time I spend with the young wives and mothers. Sometimes, I feel as though Abba has blessed me with an entirely new family to raise."

Cleophas assessed her. Her hair had grayed over the past year. As the work in Jerusalem had increased, he had experienced growing concerns for her health. She had experienced so much loss in her lifetime. If she really wanted to stay in the city, he considered, he could go back to their village of Nazareth and sell the property. Or, better yet, they could give the home to the children. It was a small problem.

Would it be better to go or stay, he wondered?

"We don't have to go back to Nazareth, wife," he reminded her. "We can always stay here. Besides, my business does better here." He paused. "And, if you sense purpose *here*...."

Her face brightened. "Oh, I do Cleophas!"

"Well, then," he answered. "Perhaps we should put off our trip for a season. My only concern here is your health. You cannot keep pushing yourself the way you have been. You need to rest."

"I will," she promised.

"When?" he countered.

"Just as soon as these little babies are all in the ground," she replied, digging into the earth with renewed energy.

"If these few are the last, I will draw water to help them take root." Cleophas stood, dusted off his hands and robe, and moved towards the well.

"Thank you, Cleophas."

Mary instinctively began to hum. When the last plant was seated into its growing place for the season, she picked up the tools and trays, and moved to the stone basin with them. "Husband," she said, "Can you help me get water to clean these?"

Cleophas didn't answer.

"Sweetheart," Mary repeated. "Did you hear me?"

After laying the items in the basin, she turned to see why he had become so silent. His back was to her, and he was leaning over the side of the well.

Oh, he didn't hear me, she thought.

Moving over to his side, she leaned into the well with him. "What do you see down there, Husband?" she asked.

There was no answer.

Suddenly aware, Mary went into emergency mode. She pulled her husband away from the well. He slumped onto the ground.

She listened to his chest, and felt for a pulse beat. There was nothing.

"No! Not now!" she cried. Unbidden, tears rose in her eyes, and then fell upon the man she loved. She held him close, rocking back and forth. She stroked his white hair.

"What will I do without you?" she whimpered.

For more than an hour, Mary held Cleophas close, talking to him, saying goodbye. When she noticed the sun approaching the noon hour, she stood. She drew water from the well, and washed her face, arms and hands.

Then, she went to find a neighbor who could help her notify the family. Cleophas would need to be buried before sundown.

13 – Full Term

Late Summer, 36CE

They stood in front of the bema in Pilate's courtroom; an emissary from the Roman Senate, with two bodyguards. The relatively young emissary, Valerius Gratus, handed the Procurator a sealed scroll rolled on brass sticks. On the outside, a red wax seal with Rome's Great Eagle and the name Tiberius Caesar held the edges from opening before the proper time.

Quintus watched as Pontius broke open the seal, and prepared to read the letter. It had been hand delivered. This meant the Emperor required an immediate response in an action. Observing, the centurion realized he had noted changes in his commander since the baptism at the estate home of the Nobilius Decurio. The man had been kinder, gentler somehow. He was still a strong leader, but he seemed … what ? Was he less driven? Was he calmer?

He certainly laughed more.

Come to think of it, Quintus realized, many of the same changes had been taking place within his own character! What a difference the Holy Spirit brought to a person!

How had he ever lived his life without Him?

Pilate was speaking to the emissary. "Your name is Valerius Gratus," he mused. "Are you related to my predecessor by the same name, perhaps?"

The emissary smiled. "That would be my father, sir. He sends you his greetings."

"Is he well?"

"Yes sir," came the answer. "My mother also sends greetings to your wife, as does the Caesar." As he mentioned Tiberius, the emissary gave a chest salute and nodded his head in deference to Pilate.

The Procurator smiled, unrolling the small scroll. He glanced at Quintus, and began to read aloud.

> *"To my beloved son, Pontius Pilate, Procurator of Judea; From Tiberius Caesar, emperor of Rome and all of her provinces; Greetings.*
>
> *"I have learned of the difficulties presented you from the Samaritans, and have heard from the Senate their wish to reassign you. I regret my inability to prevent the politics set against you. I have made my wishes known to those I trust. I have sent you such an emissary.*

"I want more than anything to see your face, and the faces of my daughter and grandson. My health is failing. Make haste to come home to me."

Pontius lapsed into contemplation as he re-rolled the message. He looked at Valerius. "He has sent me such an emissary?" he asked. "What exactly does that mean, young man?"

The younger Gratus nodded. "My father has become your father-in-law's confidant since he left this office. There are those who are set against Tiberius. For myself; it is my wish to live free from the schemes of those who no longer live for the Empire."

Pilate was surprised at the young man's outspokenness. "And exactly whose scheming are you referring to?" he asked, shifting his position on the Judgment Seat, readying himself to test the emissary's loyalty and potential to be trusted.

The emissary faltered, momentarily showing apprehension of Pilate's potential responses to his words. "I…" he paused.

"Yes?" prodded Pilate, smiling slightly.

Regaining his internal fortitude, Valerius made a decision to speak his mind.

After all, he reasoned. *I have nothing left to lose.*

He no longer held to any illusions of power. His life had become empty of meaning.

"Sir, I have nothing left to lose. I fulfilled my military commitments a year ago. I served a tour of duty in northern Gaul. We endured great hardships, as our battles took place in the Alps, and winter arrived early. When I returned home, I discovered my properties had been stolen by a corrupt official; a friend of Caligula, Tiberius Caesar's grandson. Additionally, in my absence, the same man raped and murdered my young wife."

At this point, Valerius' voice broke. Pushing through his momentary lapse of emotion, he continued. "He also….. strangled my baby boy."

Incensed at the brutality this innocent man had experienced, Pilate interjected a question. "Did you seek justice? Did you tell this to a magistrate?"

Valerius nodded.

"What did they do?"

Valerius shrugged, and his composure failed once more.

"Nothing, sir," he said. "They *defended* him. When I appealed, I was called to Caligula's residence."

"What did Caligula do?"

The emissary looked at Pilate, assessing him. "Sir, I know I endanger myself by speaking in this way. If I lose my life, I give it freely. The man Caligula dissolves pearls in vinegar and drinks them. He has his food covered with gold leaf before eating it.

"He calls his horse his 'counselor.' He drapes the animal in pearls and covers the horse's food in gold leaf as well. Anyone, male or female whom he favors, is required to have sex with him, including his siblings. His home is part brothel...." His voice trailed off.

"'What did he do?' He laughed, and told me to 'go home to my Tata and learn what it means to be a man.'"

There was silence in the court, as Pilate considered the man's words.

"*Did* you go home to your father?" he asked quietly.

"I did, sir," he replied. "So you can see why I have no illusions."

Pilate nodded. "I can."

Silence returned to the court.

"Who chose you for this journey, Valerius?" he asked.

"My father and Tiberius, the Emperor."

"What has changed in the Emperor's life of late?" he wanted to know.

Valerius paused before answering. "I would tell you that your letters have served to cause much of the changes seen in him."

"*My* letters?"

"Regarding Jesus, the Galilean. One of the reasons he wants you to come home is to explain the sect and its beliefs. Since you were the one who sentenced the man, and you, more than anyone, would have known he was actually dead. You more than many would be able to give answers to the Caesar regarding his resurrection from the dead."

"I see," Pilate answered. He glanced once more at Quintus. He re-directed the conversation. "And you chose your own bodyguards, son?"

Valerius noticed the redirection, and accommodated it in diplomatic fashion. "Yes sir," he replied. "Both of these men served with me in the Alps in northern Gaul. They have each had experiences similar to my own, and will be my life-long friends."

Pilate stood. "Well, your appointment marks the end of my day today. Quintus, please see to it these men are provided with appropriate lodging here in Jerusalem, preferably here within Fortress Antonia."

He looked at Valerius. "Go with Quintus. He is my own trusted bodyguard. When you are settled into your lodgings, prepare to come to my family apartments this evening at Herod's palace for dinner. I will send a carriage for you at sundown."

Quintus stepped forward to walk with the three messengers. From his stance near the bema, Pilate watched them leave. As soon as the doors to the colonnade had closed, the Procurator motioned to Imani, who stood by the wall near the Judgment Seat. "Let's go, Imani. I want to share this news with Claudia Procula. She will want as much time as possible to shop and pack for the journey home. It appears we have all been reassigned."

"Yes, sir," Imani replied. "Are you all right, sir?"

"Strangely enough, I am," the ruler answered. "I remember telling Joseph it was going to happen when we were all at his home some time ago. I think God has been preparing us for what is ahead. Don't you?"

Imani smiled as they walked together. "I do, sir. The Holy Spirit has been speaking to my own heart for several weeks now."

"Amazing," was all Pontius could bring himself to reply.

Two days later, two catalyst events occurred which began a downward spiral of conflict, from which there would be no retreat or surrender from either side.

The first event was a defined recognition, a sudden awareness of a permanent change in the culture which had emerged slowly and gradually since the Resurrection of Jesus. A majority of Pharisee priests serving on the Sanhedrin and within the Temple had chosen to follow the teachings of Jesus, becoming supporters of the Jerusalem Ecclesia.

Those who made this choice, as a rule, experienced a change in the central orbit of their lives. Instead of self, power, or political gain feeding their personal identities, believers found themselves discovering and appreciating the value of relationships; with God and with other people.

As a result, the culture of the High Court had changed significantly over the past few months. The alteration was unacceptable to Annas, Caiaphas, and to the other Sadducees involved in the court. Their enjoyment in debate and controversy was no longer appeased.

In contrast, those priests who had chosen to become part of the Jerusalem Ecclesia, provided a sort of mutual support system, strengthening the session attendance.

So, the first event was the complete shift in the atmosphere and environment of the Jewish governing body in the Temple. Frustrations were building. Resentments were nurtured.

The second event was more of an opportunity for the eruption of conflict, than it was an unusual occurrence. In a season when many were hungry and went without, it seemed inevitable such a situation would occur during food distribution.

It happened at midday in the Essene Quarter. Nicodemus BenGurion and several young men were helping with crowd control during the daily distribution of food. There were so many poor inside the city's walls these days. And, Nicodemus realized, he was finding himself overseeing the daily collections and disbursements more and more these days.

Knowing of his support of the Ecclesia, being a member of the Sanhedrin, several merchants had begun donating day old foods, such as breads and over-ripe fruit. It had become customary over the past year to cook several large pots of stew, or soup, and serve bread as it was available. Those in need would bring their own bowls and utensils. After a person was served, the food could be consumed within the community in the Essene Quarter, or it could be taken home and eaten in private.

Over the past few weeks, a small group of older widows, most of whom were related to the Sadducean priests, had been sitting together when it came time for the meal. Due to their cumulative age, it was more difficult to get them through the serving lines, and seated, without stirring up some form of impatient expressions from those still needing to be fed.

For three days in a row, the older, Sadducean widows were rudely shoved to the back of the serving line by a group of rough, younger men. The young men in question always seemed to be together, and always seemed to be looking for a fight. Nicodemus made several appeals to them for their cooperation in caring for the women and children first, but he was ignored. On each of the days in question, by the time the women were able to reach the front of the line, there was very little if any food remaining. One day there was nothing left.

On the fourth day, three Sadducean priests from the Temple presented themselves to Nicodemus during the meal distribution. They were angry and accusing.

"If you are going to *compete* with the *Temple's care* for the poor," they demanded, "you will have to do better than this. These poor widows are being overlooked. Why are you showing partiality? Why do the widows who believe in Jesus' Resurrection get to go first?"

As a member of the Sanhedrin, Nicodemus responded calmly and candidly, seeking to disarm them. "Gentlemen," he soothed, "we are new at this. Please know we will handle it. It is simply a matter of becoming more structured and organized."

That evening, those members of the twelve not away on missionary journeys, involved in other areas of evangelizing, or serving, met together. After praying, and asking for the Holy Spirit's direction, they chose seven men from the seventy who had travelled with the Master the last year of his ministry. In choosing, they needed men who had good people skills, possessed a good work ethic, solid character, and most importantly, were yielded to the Holy Spirit's process of reshaping, renewing, restoring and anointing.

These seven men were chosen to serve in taking care of the practical needs of the fledgling Jerusalem Ecclesia. Because of his administrative skills, the group chose Philip from the twelve to become their leader; to communicate with those leading the Ecclesia. The others were Nicholas, Parmenas, Timon, Nicanor, Prochorus, and Stephen.

"This is the best solution we can think of," Nicodemus told them all. "The twelve must have time to prepare teachings, to pray, and minister to the sick. There are so many among us now who never heard the Master's words. Everything they will be teaching us all, will require more and more time.

"Added to this," he continued, "is the fact most of them have families. To take these men from their wives and children destroys Abba Father's original plan and design. These seven men have travelled with Jesus, and were sent out by the Master as part of the seventy. I'm sure we will need more leaders as time progresses."

There were several additional men who volunteered to help the seven "deacons" as they came to be known: from the Greek word *diakonus,* meaning "one who serves practically as a leader, caring for others." Always moving among these men, supporting, working with them, was yet another man; Joses, Zebedee's younger brother.

It was only a matter of time before he was given the nickname, Barnabas, meaning "the son of encouragement."

It was during this time Joses decided to sell the lands he held in Cyprus. Realizing he had found his life's purpose, he decided to accept the name Barnabas as his own. It described the lifestyle he wanted to identify himself with.

He donated all of his monetary profits from the sale to the Jerusalem Ecclesia.

Spring, 37 AD

It was a dark and cloudy night in Jerusalem. The impending rain had ushered cooler breezes than usual in the mountaintop city. In the shadows, a man in dark clothing furtively made his way from an inn just inside the city walls, to the Temple. As he approached the stone steps leading to the Temple Mount, a Sadducean priest emerged from the entry gate.

To anyone watching, it was apparent the two men were keeping an established appointment. They met midway and made a quick exchange. Then, as quickly as the darkly clothed man appeared, he vanished; making his way a little more slowly through the city streets, back towards the inn.

On the northeastern edge of the Island of Capri, the *Palazzo a Mare*, or "Sea Palace" of the Imperial Emperor rose in majestic splendor above the cliffs. The last and largest of twelve villas commissioned to be built by Tiberius, the palace was only accessible by a guarded, private road from the largest village on the island. Attached to the largest village on the island, was the *Marina Piccolo*, a most secure harbor and storage facility for sailing vessels. It was in this marina, a royal vessel's galley crew were raising oars, as the crew put out an anchor. On deck, Pilo could be seen with his nursemaid, Yasmina, at the rail. The boy was jumping up and down and pointing to other ships in the small harbor.

"Look at that one!" he cried. "Why don't they have sails like ours?"

"That ship must have a different purpose than ours," Yasmina answered. "Some ships are made for war. Some are made for trading. Our ship was made to transport and protect members of the royal family."

"Are we royal, 'Mina?" Pilo asked.

"You are, young master," she answered. "I am your servant."

"You are like a mommy," he declared, throwing his arms around her neck. "And I love you."

The nursemaid hugged him tight. "Thank you. I love you too," she answered softly.

"I hope you live with us forever and ever," the boy told her.

"Me too!" she told him. "Why don't we go see what Candace and your *Mammam* (Mommy) are doing?

"Let's go!"

As the two were making ready to return to their cabins, a Roman messenger on horseback reined his horse to a stop on the shore. He tied his animal to the stanchion and walked down the causeway to hail the crew, and requested permission to come aboard.

"Can we watch him, 'Mina?" Pilo asked.

"Sure," the nursemaid answered.

The first mate helped the messenger aboard. As the young man straightened his clothing, he asked, "You have a message for someone on board?"

"Yes," the man answered. "Pontius Pilate."

"Come this way."

As the two men made their way to Pontius and Claudia's cabin, Yasmina and Pilo fell in step behind them. The boy was both curious and fascinated.

"You know what 'Mina?" he asked.

"What Pilo?" she answered.

"When I grow up, I want to live on a ship just like this!"

"Don't you think you might get tired of not running in the grass?" she asked.

"I want to be just like the captain on this ship!" he reiterated. With that, he lengthened his steps, and tried to add weight to his steps by stomping. "Look!" he declared. "I have the see-zee legs!"

At that point, the two men walking in front of Pilo began to chuckle involuntarily. The first mate turned around, and in a very official tone, as though he were inspecting the boy, said, "Yes, you do Master Pilo! You will make a great sea Captain one day!"

The boy responded by giving the man a chest salute and a head nod, which drew more chuckles.

At that point, the door of the cabin in front of them opened. Pontius Pilate stood, observing the scene with a smile.

"Pilo!" he greeted his son by name. "Are you having a grand time again?"

"Tata!" the boy responded. "I am a fine sea Captain!"

Pontius laughed. "Yes, you are!" He shifted his attention to the messenger. "You have something for me?"

"Yes, General," he answered. "I have come to escort you and your family to the Imperial Palace. We have been expecting you."

"Thank you," he replied. "We will be ready to disembark in a few moments."

Ten minutes later, a rather large party made its way up the mountain by wagons. When they arrived at the palace, they were greeted by the older Valerius Gratus, the Secondary Imperial Guard, and a small army of household slaves.

Close to thirty people had come from Judea by way of the royal ship: Pontius Pilate, Claudia Procula and Pilo, personal attendants, bodyguards, bearers, as well as the family's private guard. In addition, the younger Valerius Gratus, Tiberius' original emissary, and his bodyguards.

"They are going to be very busy when we get there," Claudia confided to Candace.

"What is going to happen to us, Mistress?" the slave asked. "Will we be arrested?"

Claudia Procula smiled. "I don't think so. My father has asked to see me before he dies."

The slave persisted. "What will happen to us when he dies?"

"I don't know, dear," came the reply. "But I know the Holy Spirit will lead us."

"Yes mistress," Candace answered, with an encouraged smile. "Thank you."

In Jerusalem, it began.

It was just Morning Prayer one Sabbath.

As members of the Jerusalem Ecclesia gathered to sing together in Solomon's Portico, a line of those requesting prayer for physical healing began to form, howbeit spontaneously. Two men serving on the leadership team of the Seven Deacons were available to help. Philip and Stephen began praying for those in line, with immediate results. Miracles began taking place. Blind eyes received sight, deaf ears were opened, and crooked limbs were put into right order.

Many that day said it reminded them of the day of the Great Wind of the Spirit; Pentecost. Miracles had been happening on a regular basis in all of the area Ecclesia communities, but this event sparked fresh faith in Christ among the general population, as well as a surge of new converts.

In the midst of the crowd, Stephen began to answer questions from several of those who had received healing, or had recently converted. His answers were well received, and within a short time, he was teaching anyone who wanted to learn, how to recognize, hear and listen to the Holy Spirit of the Living God.

On the outskirts of the large crowd, several skeptical Sadducees watched, along with Joseph Caiaphas, and lawyers who served the Temple.

"They have violated our laws, doing this on the Sabbath," he fumed. "And they desecrate this holy ground with their witchcraft. There is no possible way their power has come from God."

Amihud nodded, and spoke conspiratorially in a low voice. "It is only a matter of time, sir."

The High Priest agreed. "Yes. You're right," he answered grimly. "Let's go into the Court."

For the next month, the same pattern continued.

Then, one day, Stephen was in the midst of answering questions and teaching, when a large group of men who sympathized with the Sadducees joined themselves to the group in Solomon's portico.

As a group, they had the shared experience of having been released from slavery, and attended a synagogue specializing in helping those freed from servitude. Individually, each one had travelled to Jerusalem from Africa, Egypt, parts of Asia, and the region of Cilicia, just above the island of Cyprus.

On this particular day, several of the freed-men began asking questions of Stephen, coached by the Greek Jews and Sadducees. Seeking to trip Stephen up, and cause controversy, they made carefully fabricated inquiries. Every question required involved answers and explanations of complicated Jewish theology. The politically based sabotage ended with silence in the circles of the hecklers. In each conversation, Stephen answered with grace and wisdom supplied by the Spirit of the Living God. Observers and antagonists alike were amazed, and left anticipating what might happen the next day.

For several days, the pattern continued, with miracles still occurring when prayer was offered. Each day the crowd grew, to watch with interest what was happening. Then, in the midst of Stephen's teaching, a heckler shouted out an accusation against his character.

"I've heard this man make curses against Moses. He teaches people not to believe in our God."

Several other comments were shouted from others planted in the crowd. In response, one of the Temple lawyers present, nodded to soldiers of the Temple guard on duty. Two men in uniform stepped into the crowd, and took Stephen into custody, binding his hands in front of him with palm ropes.

"Let it be known we have arrested this man for cursing Moses, and speaking against ElShaddai, our God," shouted the Captain of the Temple Guard.

The crowd turned their attention to Joseph Caiaphas, who announced, "We will hold a trial right now! We have enough members of the High Court present!" He looked through the crowd. "Leaders and Elders of Israel! Come into the High Court and let us judge this man according to our own laws! If he is found guilty, he will be stoned to death!"

Priests from both parties of the Sanhedrin; Pharisees and Sadducees made their way through the crowd. Those who supported the Jerusalem Ecclesia were concerned. They followed the dramatic entourage to the Court of Hewn Stones, where the trial would take place.

Joseph of Arimathea and Gamaliel were in quiet conversation as they walked with Nicodemus and several other Pharisees to the high court. The Romans had forbidden stoning as punishment. All judgments, by law, had to be confirmed by the local Procurator. But no man had been appointed yet, and Pontius Pilate had been summoned to the Emperor.

What was Caiaphas going to attempt to do?

Those in the crowd who were part of the Jerusalem Ecclesia, began to rally together, to mobilize. "Go and gather our supporters," they whispered to each other. "Find the members of the twelve who are in Jerusalem. Tell them to come. Tell those who can't come to pray." As a result, believers scattered throughout the city to summon all who would, who *could*, speak on Stephen's behalf.

In the marketplace, a woman stopped to make an announcement about the ongoing trial. It just happened to be a shopping day for Miriam, and her brother, Eleazar. Stunned, they made their way to the Temple Mount.

Also in the marketplace that day were Joseph of Arimathea's nieces, Mary and Salome. The two sisters had ventured out to find a vendor selling fruit.

Since Cleophas' burial, Mary had been staying with Zebedee and Salome in Capernaum. The sea air was good for Mary, Salome considered. But this past week, word had come from the Jerusalem Ecclesia, requesting help in the Essene Quarter. So, the threesome had travelled to Jerusalem. Surprised at the news, the two women made their way to the Temple as well.

In the Essene Quarter, preparations were being made for the daily distribution of food. When news of the trial was heard, everyone who was able made their way to the Temple Mount, including Shira BenCaiaphas and her friend, Libi. Also making their way from the Quarter, were Mary Magdalene, and a woman who had recently been hired by Eleazar to help Miriam at EnKarem, named Marcella. They walked with "Little Mary," Cleophas' daughter. She had been working with Luke, giving medical care to those in need.

As the trial began inside the High Court, hundreds were making their way to the Temple Mount. Some were supportive of the views of the Sadducees, some were supportive of the beliefs of the Ecclesia. Still others were fed up; angry at the circumstances of opposition and oppression. These were ready to take control with force.

Men and women from all stations in the culture; from Zealot to merchant had been roused to weigh in on the issue.

In the courtroom, tensions were running high. Joseph Caiaphas had taken his customary place as High Priest, or *nasi (prince)*, and the remaining Sanhedrin members took their seats to hear the case. Stephen and the men guarding him stood, facing the priests, in the front of the room.

"Where are the witnesses against this man?" Caiaphas made the traditional call.

Nicodemus stood next to his friend, Judah. Judah's son, Simon, had been healed of leprosy in the third year of Jesus' ministry on earth. As a result, his entire family had chosen to become followers of the Master.

"I wonder why Stephen is receiving the *proper* treatment?" he whispered to Nicodemus. "Caiaphas made no such efforts when Jesus' life was at stake."

"I have no earthly idea," his friend responded. "And, to be honest, I'm not exactly sure what his final agenda is here."

The two men exchanged glances.

Just inside the closed Great Door, ready to do Joseph Caiaphas' bidding, stood Saul.

It was good, he considered. *These heretics will soon be brought to justice.*

A man none of the Pharisees supporting the Ecclesia, recognized had taken the stand.

"What is your complaint against this man?" one of the lawyers asked.

"This man is always speaking against the Holy Temple, and against the Law of Moses. He has said men should follow Jesus the Galilean rather than the teachings of Moses."

"I see," said the lawyer, looking at Caiaphas, who nodded. He raised his voice. "Are there any other witnesses?"

Another man stepped forward, also a stranger to those in the Ecclesia. "I heard him say this Jesus of Nazareth will destroy the Temple; that He will change the customs and traditions of Moses and the Elders."

The lawyer indicated testimony had ended.

As High Priest, Joseph Caiaphas stood, and raised his hand in dramatic form, addressing the man on trial. "Stephen BarJacob, you now are given the opportunity to speak, and prove these allegations false. Have you said these things? Are their statements against you factual?"

Joseph of Arimathea looked around the room. How was the lamplight in the room brightening when it had no windows?

He looked at Stephen. The man's face was shining! A light was emanating from his body! Was he imagining such a thing?

Suddenly, the priest realized the room had gone quiet. Everyone on the high council had also noticed.

The man's face was bright. "He looks like an angel!" one of the Pharisees commented quietly.

I wonder what Stephen is seeing, Joseph of Arimathea considered?

After seeing ElShaddai, Moses' face had shone so brightly, he had needed to wear a veil......

Stephen straightened his shoulders.

"Brothers and Fathers, listen to me," he began. "ElShaddai, our God, called our father Abraham from Mesopotamia, to settle in a land he did not know. Our God brought him here to the land where you now live. He received no inheritance here, but he did receive a promise, that his descendants would suffer as slaves for 400 years, but would emerge from slavery and would settle here, and worship Him here.

"He gave Abraham the covenant of circumcision, which was kept by Isaac and Jacob and the twelve patriarchs.

"As young men the patriarchs were jealous of their brother, Joseph, and sold him into slavery in Egypt. But God gave him favor with Pharoah, and he was raised to a high place of authority over the land. And our people were free, and allowed to live and multiply. And we greatly increased.

"But another ruler rose, who did not remember Joseph. This man enslaved our people for 400 years. He commanded our women to kill their newborn children.

"But then, Moses was born, hidden by his parents for three months, and through a miracle was adopted by Pharoah's daughter. She raised him as her own son. He was educated and raised to a place of power. Then, when he was forty years old, he killed an Egyptian who was mistreating one of his people. He ran to Midian. There he married and had two sons.

"Forty years later, Moses met ElShaddai in the flame of a burning bush. Our God appointed him to go back to Egypt and bring our people out of slavery with miraculous signs and wonders; through the Red Sea; through the wilderness for forty years.

"Moses himself told the children of Israel ElShaddai would raise up a Prophet greater than himself from among our own people.

"But our people refused to listen to Moses. They rejected ElShaddai and wanted to return to Egypt. They worshipped other gods; Molech and Rephan, giving those idols credit for their freedom. So ElShaddai turned from them and allowed them to serve the stars of heaven as their gods.

"When they still refused to listen, they were taken into exile to Babylon.

"In the wilderness, they carried the Tabernacle of Moses with them. Later, David found favor with ElShaddai, and planned for a permanent Temple, which was built by Solomon.

"But ElShaddai doesn't live in temples made by human hands. He Himself has told us the entire earth is his footstool, and all of Heaven his possession!

"Like our ancestors, you are a stubborn people. In your hearts you are pagan, just like they were! You are deaf to the Truth! Are you planning to resist the Holy Spirit forever, like they did? Name one true prophet they did not persecute! They even killed the ones who spoke of the Promised Deliverer!

"He is the man you betrayed and murdered! You deliberately disobeyed ElShaddai, even though He provided Life, with the witness of angels! What will you do?"

Those who had rallied the mob against Stephen burst into fury. They began shouting over him to each other. A few made attempts to attack the man, but were warded off by the Temple guards.

Joseph of Arimathea and Nicodemus kept their eyes on Stephen. His face grew even brighter than before, and his gaze turned upward.

"I sense the Holy Spirit in this room, Nicodemus," Joseph observed.

"As do I," the other priest responded. "He is full of the Holy Spirit!"

"Look at him! What is he seeing?" Joseph asked his friend. "I would like to see that…"

Nicodemus nodded, as Stephen's voice rose above the din filling the room.

"Look! All of you! I see the heavens opened! Jesus, the Son of man is standing in the place of honor at EdShaddai's side!"

Caiaphas put his hands over his ears, as did many of the Sadducees. "I can't listen to any more!" he screamed. "The man has condemned himself!"

Then, as though they had each been pitched from catapults, the entire group rushed towards Stephen. They continued shouting, forcibly dragging him outside, back to the Temple Mount.

To the waiting crowd, the incensed members of the Sanhedrin then proclaimed, "He has condemned himself! He is to be stoned!"

Pulling him by his clothes and hair, the mob of Sadducee priests half-dragged, half-carried the still bound man to the Dung Gate, where they threw him off the ledge used by Judah the Sicari to commit suicide. From the ledge, the priests began to pick up large rocks, throwing them down with force upon Stephen's body, as their ancestors had to other prophets and messengers sent by ElShaddai.

As the first of the large projectiles hit him, Stephen sought to right himself. With blood streaming from his nose, he cried, "My God! Please do not lay this at their charge! Forgive them!"

Several other large rocks were hurled at the condemned man, finding their marks repeatedly. Those who loved him were forced to watch his torture in inner agony. Blood began to come from his mouth and ears, as he doubled over, letting out an involuntary groan.

His body was becoming misshapen, as his bones and fortitude shattered. The cracking sounds of his physical frame reverberated in the valley around all of them.

Stephen stumbled and fell, no longer able to stand. Then, as one large rock bounced off his already broken body, he spoke more softly, but still loud enough to be heard. "Lord Jesus! Into your hands I commit my spirit!"

Within moments, he was dead.

Shocked, observers were stilled to shaken silence. Suddenly afraid, most made their way to leave; avoiding a chance of becoming the Sadducees' next target.

Just inside the City Gate, the young priest, Saul, stood watching with a smug smile. The participating members of the Sanhedrin had left their rich cloaks with him, as they carried out their dirty work.

So, he thought, *this is what it feels like to have power.*

It felt good, he decided. This was the only way to make sure the rules were really followed.

When the executioners were satisfied their evil deed was finished, they turned and walked as one back into the Court of Hewn Stones. It appeared they were going to have a meeting. Those who had not participated from the high council remained outside.

In shock from the gruesome violence they had just witnessed, members of the Jerusalem Ecclesia were slow moving at first.

Joseph of Arimathea looked to his Pharisee priesthood brothers standing near him. "What just happened here? What have we seen?" he asked. "Did we just witness an execution, or a cold-blooded murder?"

No one answered. Shocked, they all held the same answer to his question.

"What do we do, Joseph?" Mary Magdalene asked.

The priest put his arm around her. "We bury him," he answered. As the words left his mouth, he was hit with instant concern for Mary. She was still recovering from her second husband's death.

Joseph glanced at his nieces. Both were making their way to the pile of rocks covering the young man's dead body. Philip, Stephen's closest friend, was already at work, seeking to uncover his body for burial. Eleazar and Miriam had knelt near the rock-pile covering the man's battered frame.

Silently, the three began to remove rocks, throwing them into a newly created pile a few feet away.

"They must have been preparing for this beforehand!" Miriam declared. "They laid aside an arsenal! I've never seen so many large stones of the same size in one place!"

As rocks were removed, and the young leader's robes came into view, blood spatter began to show itself on the rocks being separated from the victim. Philip and Eleazar, Mary and Salome put the bloodied stones in a different pile from the others first removed.

They would need to be buried with his body.

Nicodemus and Gamaliel came close to Miriam. Nicodemus held a linen sheet from the Temple storeroom. Behind them, Simeon, Gamaliel's son, carried a silver bowl with a rag for cleansing the body's wounds.

Close by, Shira and Libi observed in shock and deep concern. Shira had heard stories of her father's rage and political brutality, but she had always thought them to be exaggerations. Now, she wondered whether the stories she had heard had perhaps not been detailed enough.

But even more troubling for the High Priest's daughter, was the image of her new husband's smug sneer during the entire event. He had thoroughly enjoyed himself, she determined.

He had shown himself to be a different man than she had believed him to be today. She had been praying for him to become a follower of Jesus, like his first mentor, Gamaliel. But now, she had deep concerns.

She wouldn't have believed it if she hadn't seen it with her own eyes.

Now a man was dead.

Stephen, her friend, was dead.

She brushed the tears from her cheeks. He had always been so kind to her, and willing to help her with her questions. Over the past few months, she had come to understand her life's purpose. She had discovered her life was valued and significant.

She smiled wryly, remembering Stephen's words. "No one can ever take those things from you, Shira. They are part of the inner life journey Jesus has provided each of us in his Holy Spirit."

As she was contemplating, several men she had never seen before joined themselves to the group gathered around Stephen.

"Can someone tell me about this Jesus the man they stoned was talking about?" one of them asked.

Joseph of Arimathea looked up from his task of helping to prepare Stephen's body for burial. "I can," he answered. "Jesus was my niece's son." He nodded towards Mary, a few feet away.

Two of the men nodded and nudged each other. "Then this is the man we need to talk to," the taller one commented.

As they were speaking, Nicodemus, Gamaliel, and his son, Simeon, left to bring back a horse and wagon.

The shorter man looked around. "Are there any more of Jesus' disciples here?" he asked. "I'd like to hear what made all of you decide Jesus was the man to follow. I mean, there are so many men who have claimed to be the one ElShaddai was sending. What made *him* so different from the others?"

There was something about the tone of the men speaking to Joseph that didn't feel quite right to anyone in the group, but no one said anything.

"I can tell you what convinced me," Shira spoke up. "No one else claiming to be the Deliverer has come back from the dead."

"And my deaf ears were opened," Libi contributed, "*after* he rose from the dead; and *after* he went up into heaven. In fact, this man; the man they murdered here today was the man who prayed for me to be healed."

"Jesus raised me from the dead, after I had been dead three days," Eleazar offered.

"He taught us how to live in relationship with ElShaddai," a man named Maximus told them. "I didn't believe his teachings at first; I was so full of tradition. I thought I knew God, but I didn't. He changed my life. Now I know God. His name is Jesus."

As the group was sharing, more members from the Jerusalem Ecclesia had joined those who were sharing. As the Community gathered, more unidentified men circled behind them.

Unexpectedly, the High Priest, Joseph Caiaphas, shouted from the Dung Gate, over those gathered in the "Field of Blood," around Stephen's body.

"Gather them now," he shouted.

Immediately, the mob of hired men moved through the surprised followers of Jesus, the Jerusalem Ecclesia. They tied each person's hands in front of his or her body.

"You are all under arrest," Caiaphas announced. "For heresy, and for cursing the Laws of Moses. You will await our pleasure in the prison cells in my palace."

"Gentlemen," he instructed. "Take them away."

A murmur of questions and comments rose from the group of over seventy who had been rounded up. As Caiaphas, Saul, and a small group of Sadducees observed, they were lead away, through the streets of Jerusalem to the palace of the High Priest.

Shira said nothing.

Surely my father will see me, she reasoned.

Surely she and her friends would be released. To comfort her friend, Libi, she began to hum a lullaby which Nitza, her mother, had sung to her as a small child.

The song had a greater effect than she imagined, or had intended. Those in the group who knew the song began to either hum or sing with her. When the lullaby was finished, another person began a psalm. Upon arrival at the High Priest's prison, the group continued to sing as they were locked in cells.

The mercenaries were confused. What exactly had caused the High Priest to believe these people so dangerous? Were they being punished for *singing?*

How were the women a threat, they wondered.

Really, a few privately asked?

It was late at night when a distraught Saul knocked on the door of his in-laws' home. As Caiaphas had not been home for dinner that evening, Nitza had retired early. Saul's interminable knocking finally roused Micah, one of the older house slaves. The man answered the door with a lit lamp in hand.

"Master Saul!" he greeted the young priest. "Is everything all right?"

"Hello, Micah," Saul answered. "Can I come in? Is Shira here?"

The older man was surprised. "No, sir," he answered. "Isn't she at home?"

The young priest pushed by the man. "Are you protecting her?"

"N-n-no sir," Micah stuttered. "I am telling you the truth."

A sleepy voice was heard from another room. "Micah, who is it?"

"It's Master Saul, Mistress," he called out in response.

A few moments later, Nitza appeared in the doorway from her bedchamber. "Saul!" she greeted him. "What's wrong?"

"I arrived home from the Temple just after sundown, and Shira wasn't home. I thought perhaps she was at the market, so I waited. Then our bedtime came and went, and she still wasn't home. I thought she might be at a friend's home, so I knocked on the doors of our closest friends. She isn't with any of them."

Nitza was alarmed. "Come in, dear boy," she said. "I've been here all day and I haven't seen her. Have you eaten anything?" She looked at Micah. "Let's light some lamps, and help Saul get something to eat."

As they walked into the large meeting room of the home, Nitza asked a few questions. "Did you have a fight recently?" she asked.

Saul looked at her blankly. "No," he answered.

"Has she been upset about anything lately?"

"Nothing I can think of. In fact, we have been talking about starting our family in the past few weeks," he answered.

"So you're sure she's happy, and wouldn't have run away."

Saul looked at her blankly. "I thought she was happy. I've been happy. She is a good wife. But, I guess I don't know how she feels, honestly," he answered. "I just tell her what I think, and she does it. She's a very obedient wife."

Nitza clicked her tongue. "I see," she said.

Micah placed a plate of bread, nuts and fruit in front of Saul. On the table he placed a bowl of feta cheese, and another of olives. He poured the young man a cup of wine, and poured another for his owner.

They were just beginning to walk through Shira's last communications with her husband, when the front door opened.

"Is that you, Caiaphas?" Nitza called.

"It is!" the High Priest answered. "What are you doing up?"

"Saul is here, Joseph. He says he can't find Shira."

"What did you say?" the High Priest walked into the main room, and sat down on the couch next to his son-in-law. "Did you have a fight, son?"

Saul looked at Caiaphas. "No, sir. I have looked everywhere. I have checked with our friends. As far as I know, she was with her friend, Libi, at some time today, but I don't know where the girl lives."

"Oh Saul," Nitza soothed. "Why didn't you tell me that before? They have been friends since childhood. I do know where her parents live, but I'm not sure where her husband's home is." She looked to her Joseph.

Caiaphas smiled. "Don't worry, Saul. She is a good girl. I guarantee you she went to Libi's house, and fell asleep. I'm sure she will be back first thing in the morning, apologizing all over herself for not getting home on time to feed you."

Relieved to have a possible explanation, Saul visibly relaxed. "I love her so much. I don't know what I'd do if something happened to her. I kept seeing her lying in a ditch somewhere, dead."

He didn't notice Caiaphas' warning glance in his direction. But Micah did.

Nitza put her arm around him. "It's all right, Saul," she soothed. "Do you want to stay here tonight so you won't be alone?" Without waiting for an answer, she looked once more at Micah. "Please gather linens and blankets for Master Saul, and fix him a bed."

"Yes, Mistress," came the answer. "I'll come back to get him when his room is ready.

Saul didn't argue. Suddenly, he was exhausted. It had been a long day.

In Capri, two retired Roman generals, Pontius Pilate and the older Valerius Gratus were comparing their tours of duty in Judea. They had taken seats on the outdoor veranda patio, overlooking the Bay of Neapolis, each with an early morning scyphus of warm mulsum. A momentary lull in conversation had rendered a pause. Quintus stood nearby at Pilate's request.

Finally, Pontius decided to bring up the inevitable.

"Valerius?" he began.

"What is it, my friend?"

"When did he die?"

"How did you know?"

"In years past, he would have greeted her by coming down to the ship."

Valerius paused. "He knew it was coming. He wrote the message two days before he passed. He breathed his last in the chair you are seated in, taking in this view. It was the sixteenth of last month."

Pontius looked at him. "How is it both of our Caesars have died in the ides of March? Is it a bad omen?"

"I thought you didn't believe in such things," Valerius countered.

Pilate looked at the man quizzically. "Where did you get such an idea?" The caution in his voice was unmistakeable.

Valerius laughed. "Come now, Pontius! Let us speak with honesty!" he declared. "The Emperor trusted me. You can trust me as well. I am as interested in the sect you have joined, as Claudia's father was!"

Pontius glanced at Quintus.

Valerius followed his gaze, assessing the look exchanged between the two men. "I am no spy for Rome," he said. Then, he lowered his voice to a whisper. "Although Tiberius and I became sure there were spies reporting to someone in the Senate during the Emperor's last days. Someone on the household staff. And Agrippina, your wife's aunt was here a few months ago. She might be behind it. Apparently, her children are lining up to be named next to rule. Things have become very ugly in Rome."

"Ugli-*er*, you mean," Pilate spoke in a normal tone, dropping his guard.

Valerius sensed the change, and spoke again, softly and with greater intensity. "It was Tiberius' wish to protect you. I have remained here for that purpose. It is a matter of urgency for your very life, that we handle this situation wisely. One false move will cost you everything."

"Why is that?" Pilate wanted to know.

"Mistress Claudia's responses to the new Caesar will determine whether you live or die."

"That decision has been made already?" Pilate asked. "Which of Agrippina's children have ascended?"

"I'm sorry, Pontius. From the way you asked about his death, I thought you knew." Valerius took another sip of mulsum. "After a short period of intrigue, my sources tell me the Mad Dog, Caligula, is our new Emperor."

Pilate was stunned. His mulsum caught in his throat, he coughed. "Oh, no," was all he could say. Suddenly aware, he saw his own predicament, and anticipated the last act of love his father-in-law had provided for his daughter, Claudia.

"I think I understand now, Valerius," he said. "We are going to need your help. What is my next course of action?"

"Well," Valerius offered, "as we begin, let me advise you to break this news to your wife. Then, we must prepare. It is a matter of time until Caligula decides to exert his power to control this small island. I anticipate that will happen in the next few weeks. It will take time for him to discover that you travelled here, rather than to the capital."

"I see," answered the Procurator. "Is there more?"

"Much more."

As he listened, Pilate learned of an elaborate plan. It seemed Tiberius and the older Valerius Gratus had made intricate provisions for Pilate and Procula to arrive in Capri, rather than to travel to Rome. False impressions had been acted out in front of those suspected as spies, in order to create false trails and expectations. In that way, Claudia and Pilo would be prevented from the dangers and politics of the capital.

In the event of an unexpected outcome, such as Tiberius' death before his family's arrival, the Caesar's message to come "to me" indicated his intention for Pontius to come where the ruler was presently living. Additionally, travelling to a remote location, rather than directly to Rome, provided a buffer for the tiny family from the whims and emotional impulses of whoever might take possession of the throne, before they knew the man would be the insanely cruel Caligula.

The climate was much too dangerous for anyone to get too close to the new Caesar; not if they wished to keep living.

Over the next two hours, Valerius divulged a plan; one that would ensure a reassignment rather than a wrongful execution; one which would place Pilate's family in a place where their lifestyle could continue to some degree, and yet, keep them out of the Emperor's reach.

Yes, much thought had gone into this plan.

After a fruitful meeting, Pontius excused himself. He fully expected his wife to respond to the news of her father's death with great emotion. Why did grieving a loss like this always dredge up a person's own sense of failure and regret?

She would need comfort this evening.

Come to think of it, he reasoned, he wasn't against a little comfort coming his way either.

"Help me, Jesus, please," he prayed as he walked through the immense seaside villa to their assigned apartments.

As he entered their rooms, he considered the fact that these days could very well be the last hours he would spend with his wife – in this lifetime.

"How did your meeting go, *amasio?*" she asked, in the midst of unpacking and organizing.

Pontius came behind her and slipped his arms around her waist. "I love it when you call me that....your lover," he whispered in her ear. He gave her ear a nibble.

She giggled, and turned to face him, kissing him gently. "I love you Pontius," she confided.

Pulling back, he took her hands in his. "Well, that's convenient! I love you, too! Since we have a mutual agreement, how shall we proceed?"

Claudia appraised him. "What is it? What's happened?"

Pilate pulled her to the settee. "How is it you always see right through me? Let's sit down a moment."

Alarmed, she started. "Is Pilo all right? Did he fall to his death? Is he hurt? Where is he?"

"No......No, my love," he answered. "Our son is fine, and safe with Yasmina." He stroked her hand. "For the past two hours, I have been in a detailed debriefing with the older Valerius Gratus."

"Father's confidant?"

"Yes. That is the man," her husband replied. "I sense a peace about trusting him. He and your father have gone to great lengths to protect us."

Claudia fell silent. Pontius waited.

"My Tata is dead, isn't he?" she asked carefully.

"Yes," he answered. "He died in this house less than a month ago."

"Why do we need protection?"

"Well, Valerius feels is it a matter of time before a dispatch is received from Rome, requesting I attend a Senate investigation into the Samaritan problem. Or, it is possible we could be reassigned. The worst possibility is that I will be executed by the new Caesar because he has believed the descriptions of my rule in Judea from the Samaritans."

Beginning to pace, he shrugged. "Or we could be simply exiled. In any case, either a dispatch from the new Caesar will arrive in the next few weeks, or we will be recalled to Rome for my trial and execution."

He looked at her. "We could always pray they lose interest, and try to communicate through the lighthouses on the Bay."

Claudia Procula considered his words.

"They have chosen?"

"Valerius said he came to the throne through intrigue."

"Who came to the throne, Pontius?"

He paused, and said the next phrase carefully. "Caligula is now the Caesar."

He waited, watching her, to make sure his words had been understood.

The color drained from her face.

"Oh," she replied numbly. She looked into his eyes. "What are we going to do? He is family, but he is insane! He could kill all of us, just because we are a threat to his own lineage of succession!" Tears began to well up. Her hand went to her mouth. "Oh, poor Pilo!"

He took her hand. "Claudia, Jesus did not heal our son just to see him killed. He has greater purpose than that for all of us. Think about our steps so far. Abba Father has gone before us. We are in safe hands. All I know is that we will pray, and step through the doors the Holy Spirit provides."

Claudia nodded, and then was overcome by her fears and grief. She threw her arms around her husband's neck and held him close. As she did, the emotions she had stockpiled for months began to release themselves.

He held her for long moments, until the torrent subsided. He stroked her hair, and rubbed her back.

"Sha, sha – now. Shh-hh," he whispered. "There now, my love. I will do all I can to keep us safe, and insure the life of our son." He repeated the phrases until he was sure she had calmed.

"I love you, Pontius. I'm so glad Grandfather Augustus put us together." She took the sudarium he offered and blew her nose. "Thank you for loving me."

"I do love you," he said. "You are Abba Father's gift to me. You are teaching me how He loves us every day. Thank *you* for loving *me*. Let's stick close to each other during this time. Valerius did say we should only trust our own staff while we are here, and himself and his son."

"Can I ask for a slave to come to our apartments to give me a massage?" she asked.

He smiled. "I have an idea," he answered. "Why don't we send for two slaves, and each receive one? Our attendants can stand guard."

The next morning, just two hours before dawn, the mounted mercenaries arrived at the prison gates in the palace of the High Priest. After spending the night without water, covering, or food, the group of sleepy prisoners were herded out into the streets, tied together, hands in front, in double file.

When every captive was in place, the leaders took the front ends of the palm fiber ropes and tied them to saddles on the two lead horses in the lines.

Outside the lines, men carried buckets of water. They offered each prisoner a drink, making their way from the beginning of the lines to their ends.

Expressions of "thank you" were heard as the buckets were emptied.

When the man serving Shira's side of the line came to her, she decided to speak up. As she took her cup of water, she asked,

"Can I get something to eat, please?"

The mercenary sneered, and mocked her. "Can I get something to eat?" His voice returned to its normal tone. "Are you kidding me? You are an exile, a heretic. You are not deserving of food!"

Shira pulled herself up, straightening her toga wrap as best she could. "Do you have any idea who I am?" she demanded. "You all are going to be in such trouble!"

"I don't *care* who you are," the man replied. "I've already been paid. Your life is of no consequence. You will do what we tell you, or you will die."

"But I am…"

Her voice was silenced by a sudden blow to the side of her face. She fell to the ground. The woman in line in front of her was pulled back as well, the chain reaction ending with the lead horse taking a back step onto the foot of the first man in the line.

"My foot is broken!" the man screamed.

The man responsible for striking Shira laughed, and pointed to her, as she struggled to stand. "It's her fault!" he laughed, pointing. "Don't blame me!"

In the front of the line, the mercenaries' commander cleared his throat and raised his voice.

"Hear me!" he cried. "All of you have been condemned to death by the High Priest! You are rebels and heretics! If you do what we tell you, you will live! If you argue, ask questions, speak to each other, or move out of line, you will die by the knife, and be left by the side of the road. Does everyone understand?" He didn't wait for an answer.

He looked at his men. "Are you ready?" he asked. "Mount up!"

Almost in unison, the men took their places in their saddles.

Once more he shouted, making a forward directive motion with his hand. "Let's go!"

The group began to move. Over seventy persons, tied together in two lines, were flanked on all sides by mercenaries on horseback.

Where are they taking us, many wondered?

Were they going to be sold?

And who else was involved in the plan against them?

A few hours later, Nitza was in deep conversation with a vendor in the Jerusalem marketplace. She had been stirred from sleep by loud voices coming from the prison below the living quarters of her home.

Who had her husband imprisoned, she wondered? Why had there been a large number of horses, and unidentified military men at the entrance of the prison in the middle of the night? Then, she had observed as prisoners had been tied together and driven like chattel down the street.

This morning, she had been to several merchant booths, with no success in discovering any information of value. All she knew was that a large crowd had gathered at the Temple for prayer in the morning the day before, and a man had been stoned by the Sanhedrin.

Nothing about Shira.

Until *this* merchant...... He was more than happy to discuss the happenings he had witnessed, she realized.

"Yes, it is strange," he continued. "I've lived in Jerusalem all my life, and I don't think I've ever seen a High Priest as angry as this one was yesterday. The man, Stephen BarJacob, who was known for doing miracles, with the other one; Philip..... Well, they took Stephen and arrested him yesterday."

"Arrested him," Nitza repeated. "Was there a Roman presence there to sanction it?"

"No," the man answered. "Not that I *seen*.... But they took him into the High Court for a while. While they was in there, a whole lot of people started comin' to the Temple, like they was going to have a meetin' or somethin'. Then, when they come out again, they was draggin' him. They threw him off the ledge at the Dung Gate, and threw rocks at his head til he died."

"Who was leading this?" Nitza wanted to know. "I mean, surely it wasn't approved of by the Sanhedrin."

The merchant looked at her as though she had lost her mind. "Lady," he said in amazement, "are you plum crazy? The High Priest was the one screaming at the top of his voice to kill him."

"You must be mistaken," she protested. "Surely you are just repeating a rumor!"

"Nope." His tone was certain. "I saw it with these here eyes, myself. Ain't no mistaken who the crazy man was. It were Joseph Caiaphas hisself." As he spoke, he tapped his temple to indicate his eyes.

"Oh," she replied. Suddenly, there was a lump in her throat. "Is that all you saw?"

The man stopped for a moment, assessing her. "Eer ya' sure you's okay? Ya' seem a little upset to me."

Nitza breathed deeply and forced a smile. "No sir," she answered. "I'm fine. Please tell me what you saw."

The merchant scratched his head. "Well, after the man was dead; and I mean covered with rocks-n-stones, Caiaphas took the men who done the stoning back inside. Then, them folks that come here during the trial... them started gettin' him ready to bury, ya' know. It was like they was his family or sumpin.'

"Then, this big mob o' men started coming 'round. It didn't look like they was up to any good, and I started getting' worried. Then, the High Priest come back out, and started yellin' about how all of them was heretics and was bein' put in prison.

"They tied 'em up and took 'em away. That's all I know."

Nitza was stunned. *Had her husband lost his mind? Had her father been privy to the plan?*

Suddenly, she felt moved to action. "Thank you," she said, as she moved away. "I think I know where to look next."

An hour later, Nitza discovered Eli, the overseer, in the Essene Quarter. He had been helping prepare for the daily distribution of food. As soon as he saw her, his face brightened.

"Mistress Nitza!" he exclaimed. "Welcome! How are you?"

"I've been better, Eli," she answered. "My daughter has disappeared. Have you seen her?"

Eli thought for a moment. "Mistress Shira?" he asked. "Well I did see her here yesterday. She and her friend Libi were helping us prepare for food distribution, when a messenger came from the Temple with word for all of us."

"What was the word, Eli?" she inquired.

Eli looked at her, appraising her. He knew the wife of the High Priest had attended several meetings with her daughter, but was unsure how much information could be trusted to the woman.

Her voice grew in intensity. "What was the word, Eli? Please. Her husband hasn't seen her since she left home yesterday morning."

The old overseer looked at her. Something in her eyes appeared genuinely afraid. "Are you a believer, Mistress?"

"Excuse me?" she asked.

"Are you a believer? A follower of Jesus? Are you part of this Ecclesia?"

Nitza stammered. "I... I haven't decided yet. I have no offense with you people, if that's what you mean."

Eli sighed. "I suppose that is good enough. She and Libi went to the Temple to join those who felt they might sway the court in Stephen's defense."

"Is Shira part of this Community?" her mother asked.

Eli nodded. "Yes. She has been baptized, and attends studies every day. In fact, several of her friends have experienced healings.... She has brought many to Jesus. I think she brought you to a few meetings, if I recall rightly."

"Yes, she has," Nitza answered. "And I think I believe, but I have a lot to lose.... It is not an easy decision."

Eli patted her shoulder. "It is a difficult decision for anyone who truly desires to become Jesus' disciple. Each of us must count the cost."

Nitza decided to steer the conversation back to her original purpose. "Did you see her after she left here to go to the Temple?" she asked.

Eli said, "Come and sit down Mistress." He led her over to a bench not far from where they had been standing. "If Shira and Libi were with the disciples who went to the Temple, and they were in the Potter's Field when the disciples were rounded up, she most certainly was taken to the prison in your own home last night. You said she has not been home?"

The pieces of the puzzle began to come together in Nitza's mind. "Oh, Shira," she whispered. Startled, she looked at Eli.

"Where were they taken?"

"What?"

"The prisoners. There were men on horses in the middle of the night who cleaned out the prison cells. Where were they taken?"

Eli looked at her blankly. "You know more than I do at this point." He told her. "I sense you may need to go somewhere else to find the answer to that question. May ElShaddai go with you."

The frightened mother nodded numbly. She turned, and hardly aware of her steps, made her way back home, where she hoped to find her son-in-law.

14 – Birthpangs

It was almost midday by the time Nitza found Saul. The process had been one of trying to pin down a moving target. She had been unsuccessful finding him at her own home, or at the small house he and Shira owned. Finally, she made her way to the Temple. There, she found him, busying himself with an organizing task, cataloging the current inventory of sacrifice animals available for purchase. As Saul had requested, Caiaphas had purposely given his son-in-law a task he could do at his own pace, working alone.

Quietly, Nitza made her way through the outer areas of the Temple. Leaving the Court of the Gentiles, she walked through the Court of Women, and stood by the gate closest to the Brazen Altar. As a female, she was not permitted to progress further. There, she waited for a priest, or a Levite to stop in their duties.

After some moments, a Levite stopped by her side.

"Mistress?" he said. "I have passed by you four times, and you are still standing here. Is there something you need?"

Nitza smiled at him. "I am Nitza, wife of Joseph Caiaphas. I am looking for our son-in-law, Saul of Tarsus. Have you seen him?"

The Levite smiled, and his eyes brightened. "I *do* know where he is!" he answered. "And I can take you to him. Would you like to come with me?"

Nitza nodded. "Please," she answered. "What is your name?"

"Azariah," he told her, motioning with his hand toward an area of the Temple behind her. "He is in the storerooms, this way."

As soon as he saw her, Saul stopped what he was doing, and walked where she was standing.

"Mother Nitza," he whispered. "Did you find her? What has happened?"

Nitza shook her head. "No, not yet. But I have an idea where she might be." She nodded at Azariah, and watched him leave. She took Saul's hands, pulling him away from the door. She whispered, "What do you know about Joseph's dealings with the followers of Jesus?"

Saul wasn't sure how to answer. "What do you mean?" he asked carefully.

"Shira has been secretly going to the Ecclesia meetings in the Essene Quarter. She has been baptized, was part of the crowd taken away after that man's stoning yesterday."

The color drained from the young man's face. "Are you sure? How do you know?"

Nitza shook her head. "Don't do that, Saul. I am Annas' daughter, and Caiaphas' wife. I have learned how to survive in this city. I know people, and they are my friends. Believe me when I tell you she has been taken captive."

Suddenly aware, Saul asked a question betraying the amount of his involvement with the High Priest's plans.

"Did the men come to move them yet?"

Stunned, Nitza looked at him. "You are part of this too?" she asked. "How far into the Sanhedrin does this plot go?"

Her son-in-law repeated his question, shaking her. "Did the mercenaries come to take them yet?"

Tears streaming down her face, Shira's mother nodded, searching his eyes. "Two hours before dawn, in the middle of the night, men came with horses, and took them all away."

Saul sprang into action. "Say nothing to anyone, especially your husband."

"What are you going to do?" she demanded in alarm.

He looked her in the eyes. "I am taking a horse from the stables, and I am going after her; to bring her back."

She was startled by his reaction. It was unexpected. "You know where she is?"

"I only have an *idea*," he responded, as he quickly moved to put his tools away. "There are only three routes they could have taken, and I think I can find her if I leave now. But I only have a window of time. If they left that long ago, I will have to hurry to catch them."

In EnKarem, the Sanhedrin Pharisee named Judah, and his wife, Hadassah, were comforting the older Eleazar upon the disappearance of his children, and Marcella. The couple was returning from a three-day journey to the Capernaum Ecclesia. They had been followers of Jesus since the days of his earthly ministry.

"I haven't seen any of them since yesterday morning," the concerned father was saying. "Eleazar and Miriam went to the marketplace, and our Mary went with Marcella to the Essene Quarter. None of them came home last night. I know they are all adults now, but this isn't normal."

The older Eleazar was wringing his hands as he spoke.

Hadassah looked at the older man. "Are you here alone? Do you want to stay with us until we find them?" she offered.

Judah was silent, deep in thought. He listened to the conversation.

"No, I'll be fine, Hadassah," the old merchant replied. "Thank you, but my steward and his wife also live with us. I lived here alone before they all came back home. No, Baruch is here. I'll be fine."

"You're sure?" she pressed.

"Yes, very," he answered. He looked at Judah. "You haven't said much, Judah. What do you know?"

Judah looked up, and met Eleazar's gaze. "I'm not sure these things are connected. And I haven't shared this with Hadassah yet. In truth, I was hoping what I had been hearing was only rumor."

Startled, Hadassah sat down on a nearby chair. "I have a feeling I'm not going to like this," she said.

"No, you're not," her husband replied grimly. "Eleazar, are you all right? I think you should sit down as well."

Numbly, the older man sat down close to Hadassah. "What do you know?" he asked shakily.

Judah looked at each of them. "Before we left, I heard Amihud and another Sadducee talking about a plan the High Priest had been putting together. The plan was to sabotage a prayer gathering. Caiaphas originally wanted to find a way to stop the Jerusalem Ecclesia from filling the Temple Courts. He is a Sadducee, and doesn't believe in miracles or the Holy Spirit.

"That being said, Amihud was telling this man how the plan was to work, and his part in it. He didn't know I was listening."

"What did he say, Judah?" his wife wanted to know.

"That they were going to stone someone, and then round up whoever came to the Temple and take them away."

Eleazar spoke hoarsely. "Take them away?" he echoed. He looked at Judah. "What does that mean?"

"I don't know," the priest answered. "As soon as we get home, I will go to the Temple and get some answers."

It was late afternoon when Joseph Caiaphas returned home. As soon as he walked through the door, he saw Nitza sitting on a stool next to the door. Her eyes were swollen from weeping, her hair disheveled; her sandals were covered with mud, and her hands were bleeding from beating them against the stone walls.

The sight of her shocked her husband. Immediately, he went to her side, and then to his knees. "What happened, Nitza?" he asked with concern. "Is it Shira? Where is she?"

But in one day, his all-believing, blindly-trusting Nitza had disappeared. The woman sitting on the stool felt like an empty shell. All of the illusions she had held onto regarding her life and her marriage had been stripped away.

She looked up at her husband in disbelief.

"How could you?" she asked. "How could you imprison all those people? How could you stone a man to death?"

Surprised by her candid disclosures, he shrugged. "I was doing my job," he answered. "Guarding the purity of the Law of Moses. Protecting the sanctity of the Temple." He looked at her expectantly, hoping his words would make him a hero in her eyes once again. Inside, his mind was swirling with scenarios he could describe to her. He had to make his actions acceptable.

"Do you even know who you told them to take away, Joseph?" she cried. "Are you even aware of the families you destroyed today? Your hired brutes tore people away from their homes, this morning! Those people will never be the same!"

Her husband responded with an unconscious sneer. "They are heretics, with no respect for our God, or for the Law. They are part of a sect destroying the very fiber of our city. They are criminals, Nitza," he said, coldly defensive.

She was shocked at the thickness of callous indifference she sensed coming from him. She wondered how many more lies had been hidden from her before today's discovery….. She decided to give voice to her thoughts.

"Who *are* you?" she demanded. "You *look* like my husband, but you don't sound like him, or act like him. Why are you so defensive, Joseph?"

Instantly angry, Joseph raised his voice. "And why are you so nosey about my duties! It's none of your business, Woman! Know your place! These matters do not concern you!"

Nitza jumped up to her feet. "None of my concern? *None of my concern!!* Shira was one of them, Caiaphas!" she shouted hysterically. "How *dare* you defend this!"

He stood up as well, raising his forefinger and pointing it in her face.

"How dare *I?*" he shouted. "How dare I *what?* Do my job?"

He paused, as her words finally hit their mark. "What do you mean, 'Shira was one of them'?"

320

"She was baptized as a follower of Jesus. She has been working during the days in the Essene Quarter. She was in the Potter's Field after the stoning." Nitza told him factually.

This time, it was Caiaphas who needed to sit down. He pulled off his headdress, and ran his hand through his hair. "How is this even possible?" he asked. "Didn't anyone check identities?"

"Was there someone you asked to do such a thing?" she inquired, skeptically.

"No," he admitted, looking at her. "I had no idea, my Blossom. You have to believe me..."

"Don't you *ever* call me that again, Joseph!" she replied, coolly. "And I don't *have* to believe *anything* you tell me! Ever again!"

Joseph had never seen Nitza so angry. In truth, it scared him.

"So what are you going to do?" she asked. "To what lengths are you willing to go to retrieve our daughter? Did you know she spent the night last night in *your prison?"*

"No," he answered. "I had no idea."

"Do you know who *else* you had carried away in your zeal?" she demanded.

"Who?"

"Joseph of Arimathea. The Nobilius Decurio."

At the sound of Joseph's name, Caiaphas visibly shook.

"Oh," was all he could say.

"So? What are you going to do?" she asked. "How will you retrieve our child?"

"There's nothing I *can* do," he answered. "Monies have changed hands. Arrangements were made. Besides, they are too far away now stop anything from happening."

"So that is it, then?" she said angrily. "Well, at least her *husband* is more of a man than *you* are."

"Saul? Why? What did he do?" the priest demanded.

"This morning, he left on horseback to bring her back."

"It won't matter to them," Caiaphas told her hopelessly. "They will probably kill both of them."

On the main road to the coast, a young priest kicked his horse's flanks to gain a little more speed. But the animal did not respond.

"I'm sorry," Saul said to the horse. "Please don't quit on me now. I only have a little time left."

The horse snorted.

Saul appraised his surroundings. Surely there had to be a livery close by where he could trade this animal for a fresh horse. The animal he had been galloping on since Jerusalem had been a good choice. She was an Arabian, and built for distance travel, but he could tell she was becoming weary.

"I'd be tired, too, girl," Saul said, as he patted the horse on the neck.

Looking up, he noticed a lone house in the middle of a wheat field. He reined his beast towards it. Approaching, he noticed two horses in the pasture.

"Is anyone here?" he called. "I need help! Anyone!"

A man stuck his head out the window. "What do you want?" he asked. "We are eating our dinner here."

"I'm sorry, sir," Saul began. "My name is Saul, and I serve as a priest at the Temple in Jerusalem. I am on a mission of some importance, and my horse is tired. Would you consider allowing me to trade my horse for one of yours? I promise I will return your horse tomorrow about this same time."

The man smiled at him. "Well, that's a new one, I must say," he answered. "A priest needing a horse." He let out a short laugh. "If you take the stallion, you will get better results. The mare is kind of stubborn."

Saul looked the man in the eye. "Isn't that always the way it is?" he asked.

The man laughed again. "Saul, you say," he repeated. "See that you do bring my horse back tomorrow, or I will keep your Arabian for plowing."

"Yes sir!" Saul answered. "Thank you!"

"Do you need help?" the man wanted to know.

"No, I'll just transfer my saddles and reins, if you don't mind. I am in a real hurry."

"Must be, young man. You have yourself a good afternoon."

Saul made his transfer, and was back on the road with a fresh horse in record time. For a few minutes, the young priest warmed him up to a gallop, and then went back to a trot.

"ElShaddai," he prayed, "please let this be the right road. Help me find her!"

In his head, he was trying to ascertain how long it might be until he found what he was looking for. "They will walk about three or four miles in an hour with that large group. They have been walking since before the first hour (5am), so they are probably close to 40 miles down the road by now. I have been traveling about thirteen or fourteen miles each hour. I have been on the road since just after noon, and should be as far as they are by now."

Then, fear spoke in his heart.

What if you are on the wrong road? it taunted him. *You will never see her again.*

Just a few minutes later, he glimpsed a group of men on horseback. These had to be them, he reasoned. He clicked his tongue, and kicked his horse's flanks. In response, the horse sped from a trot to a canter.

The two men flanking the group, turned in their saddles to investigate the source of approaching hoof beats. At the sight of Saul, they turned their horses around to face him, guarding the group from his approach.

Drawing nearer, he pulled his horse to a stop, and then dismounted.

"My name is Saul, and I am an assistant to Joseph Caiaphas, the High Priest. A mistake has taken place, and I need your help to make it right."

The men did not dismount, but they did respond. "Was someone captured who shouldn't have been?" the larger one asked.

"Yes, sir," Saul replied. "May I speak with her?"

The two men smirked, and looked at each other. "Oh, *her*! Of course, it would be a woman."

They gave a signal for the procession to stop.

"Take a look," the smaller one instructed.

Saul began looking through the lines. With at least thirty-five sets of two, he didn't have far to go before he saw the back of Shira's favorite head-wrap. As he drew nearer to her, his heart sped.

"Shira?" he said softly. "Is that you?"

At the sound of his voice, she turned her head and found his face with her eyes. "Saul?" she cried. "What are you doing here?"

"I've come to rescue you. To take you home where you belong," he answered.

"Oh, I love you Saul," she answered almost automatically. But then, she began to think. "What about everyone else?" she asked. "Are you going to rescue them as well?"

Saul looked around to assess the group. "These?" he replied. "No, Shira. These people are followers of Jesus. They are subversives; heretics. They are condemned as traitors to our God."

"Oh," she said in reply.

"I suppose I *could* rescue them," Saul continued, "if they were willing to recant their statements about Jesus the Galilean. You remember he was crucified as a criminal."

Shira straightened her shoulders and looked her husband in the eye. *"I* am a follower of Jesus," she told him. *"I* was baptized."

Saul laughed at her. "No, no, wife. You're not like these others. You got caught up in something you didn't understand. It had to have been different with you, Shira. I know you. You're not that smart. You were deceived. They tricked you, and you didn't know what you were doing. And yesterday? Yesterday, you were just in the wrong place at the wrong time. But now you must realize how much trouble this has put you in, not only with your parents, and with me, but with ElShaddai himself. You know you need to walk away."

"Walk away?" she echoed. "What do you mean?"

"Shira," he spoke more directly. "I want you to denounce this Jesus, *and* your baptism, and come back home with me."

She smiled at him. "Oh Saul, I'd love to come home with you. I love you. I really do," she said kindly, her eyes filling up with tears. "But I can't. I won't."

Stunned, he looked at her in amazement. He hadn't expected this response. Why was she refusing to obey him? He took her by the shoulders and shook her.

"No, Shira. You can't do this. Don't you understand what's at stake here? Your father gave *you* to *me*. The Tanakh even teaches us that you are my property; like my horse, or my house.....You belong to *me*. So, you have to do what I say. Always. So, I order you to renounce this Jesus and come home. You know what the Law teaches about a woman's duty to her husband."

Her heart sinking, her hope struggling, Shira began to weep even harder. She nodded. "I do. But I cannot renounce my trust in Jesus. He died so that I could live."

Incredulous, Saul looked around to the other prisoners for support. "You understand what I am saying, don't you?" he demanded. "Surely this is wrong. She *belongs* to *me*."

"But I belong to *Jesus* first," his wife answered. "He planned me, and called me to Himself before the foundation of the earth."

Saul reached for his dagger, which was strapped to his leg under his toga. The mercenary guarding Shira watched him carefully.

"Sir," the soldier warned. "Put your weapon away. Don't do that. We have instructions. Any of these may walk home if they renounce their deception. The High Priest was very strict. Without a full recanting she is condemned, and we cannot release her."

Saul looked at the mercenary who spoke. "I think he will understand in this case. This woman is his only daughter, his youngest child." He moved to cut the ropes, looking at Shira. "I can cut you free right now, and we can take a horse ride home. Just say the words. Please."

The mercenaries watched. Surely the girl would choose her life with the priest over death. For a few moments, silence hung in the atmosphere.

Saul watched her carefully. He was sure she would recant.

Then Shira spoke. Inside, she felt more clarity of thought than she had experienced in a long, long time.

Meeting his eyes with a clear gaze, she said, "Saul, I *cannot* renounce my beliefs. I believe Jesus is the Promised Deliverer. No, he is more than just that; he is ElShaddai, our God; come in human form, to show us the right way to relate to him. He lives in me, Saul! I have been reborn! I have never been so free or so alive! I know my life has a purpose now, and I know I am significant to God. That means more to me than anything! I don't have to earn approval anymore.

"Do you have any idea how good it feels to be free from that feeling of disapproval that was always just two inches above my head?" She met his gaze, her eyes filled with tears. "No, I cannot and *will not*. Please forgive me."

The young priest was stunned.

She had never told him "no" before. He had been sure he could command her, change her mind. Dazed, he put his dagger back into its scabbard.

"Then you know what this means, don't you?" he told her, anger mounting inside of him. "I will never see you again. We will never have children, and you will never see your parents again. These people, these *'disciples'*," he spat out the word, "have stolen our lives from us. From this day forward you are dead to me. *Dead*, do you hear? It is easier for me to think of you as dead, than living somewhere, headed to Hades."

Shira began to weep again. "Saul. *Please,* Saul. There is room for you in the Community of Jesus too."

His anger turning to rage, he sneered back at her. "Woman, you are dead to me, and I can't hear you," he told her. As a final expression, he pushed her away. She fell to the ground, her head colliding with the earth. Crying, she remained there, watching him.

For his part, Saul flourished his outer cloak, and turned away from her. He looked at the mercenaries. "I thank you men for your service. I must be getting back to the Temple."

With that, he nodded his head as though giving a silent salute to the hired men, and walked back to his horse. He mounted the saddle, reined the horse around, and kicked the horse into a gallop. The sooner he could put this behind him, he reasoned, the easier his life would become.

If he rode hard, he could be back in Jerusalem before midnight.

Weeping, Shira watched his exit from her seated position on the ground. It occurred to her just how like Caiaphas he had become in words and expression. She and Libi exchanged a silent glance. Her friend's eyes were filled with tears too. She made a hand sign to tell Shira she was sorry things had happened the way they had.

Shira smiled weakly in response, and made a hand sign in response.

The woman behind her in line reached up to rub her back. "You held to your beliefs, Shira. You did well. Don't worry. Abba Father has a plan, and you are in the middle of it."

Shira looked up to see who was speaking to her, and gazed into the eyes of Mary, Jesus' mother. The woman had tears running down her face. "Thank you, Mary," she replied, as she struggled to stand on her feet.

The man walking in line in front of Libi leaned down to help Shira to her feet. As he did, he whispered in her ear. "Jesus told us we know we are in His will when we are persecuted and bullied for our trust in him. He knows how you feel. Don't give up."

The leader of the mercenaries shouted from the front. "Mount up, men! It will be late when we get to the stopping place at this rate."

In Capri, a Senatorial Emissary was waiting to be ushered into the room where Pontius Pilate sat with his wife, Claudia Procula.

"My lord," Quintus began, "An emissary from the Roman Senate has arrived with a message for you."

"Please, admit him, Quintus."

Quintus gave a chest salute to the ruler, and turned to fetch the emissary. When he returned with the man, Pilate did not recognize him. He had hoped when the messenger came, it might be someone he knew.

He sighed.

"And you are?" he asked.

The emissary nodded in respect. "I am Gaius Maximus. I have been sent by Caligula Caesar with this message for you." As he spoke, he handed Pilate a small scroll, rolled on two brass sticks, sealed with a red wax seal shaped like the Roman Eagle, which read, "Caligula Caesar."

There was silence as Pilate read the scroll. When he finished, he rerolled it, and looked at the courier who had brought it to him.

"Did Caesar say anything else?" he inquired.

"He did, sir," the emissary answered. "He said I should greet Claudia Procula, his beloved cousin."

Claudia smiled at him. "Thank you, kind Gaius," she responded. "Do you have news of my family?"

"I do, my lady," Gaius said. "You know your father's grandson is now Caesar, after a slight period of intrigue."

Claudia laughed lightly. "I wouldn't imagine it happening any other way, would you?"

He chuckled. "My lady is most perceptive."

She looked at Pontius. "Have we been summoned to Rome?"

Her husband looked to Quintus. "Please take this man to the barracks, where he can eat, bathe and rest." He looked back to the emissary. "When you have rested, and we have an answer, I will send for you, to give my response."

Gaius gave a chest salute. "My lord, Emperor Caligula said you may take up to two weeks to respond."

Pilate was surprised, but did not allow it to show. "Thank you Gaius," he said. "Please make yourself comfortable in this house."

After the man left the room, the ruler looked at Quintus. "Have him shadowed," he said quietly, "by someone we trust."

Pilate reached over to take his wife's hand. He could sense she was afraid, and needed comfort.

"Absolutely," the centurion replied, with a salute.

"Before you go," Pontius stalled him, "I want you to know what this dispatch says."

The general turned his attention to the small scroll. After unrolling it once more, he read through the letter again; this time out loud.

> *"From Caligula Caesar, Emperor of the Empire, Conqueror of all lands between the seas, declared god by the Senate of Rome. To Pontius Pilate, Procurator and Prefect of Judea, husband of Claudia Procula, my beloved cousin.*
>
> *"It is my desire to transfer you to a less volatile location than Judea, preferably a greater distance from the battlefield than Palestine. Having failed so miserably in your assigned task of subduing the Jews into subservient loyalty to me, I am removing you as their ruler.*

"Were you not married to my cousin, I would summarily execute you. However, it is the divine Caligula's desire to be merciful.

"I have sent Gaius, my most loyal friend, as my emissary. He knows my thoughts on this matter of your destiny. He has in his possession, maps and information.

"It is my divine will you choose one of the two assignments. What you choose is of no consequence to me. Both of these battalions of our armies are distant enough from my person I will never be required to see you again. It is my command you choose one of these two locations; either of which will become your new permanent home.

"So long as you do not fail, you may maintain your privilege and rank. Make requests to the Senate for your needs through Gaius. Slaves will be provided you. As I am a magnanimous ruler, it is my desire to provide you with a new life.

"Try not to be a burden where I send you, or incite an uprising against Rome. Should you decide to take your life, I would be overjoyed. You will live as long as I never have need to hear your name again. Goodbye."

Silence hung in the room, creating a sort of heaviness.

Pontius Pilate looked at Quintus. "Fetch Valerius for me, Quintus, and return with him."

"Yes, sir," the soldier answered. He turned immediately to go. Abruptly, he stopped at the door, and looked back over his shoulder. "Uh….Sir," he asked, "the older or the younger?"

"The older. I need a father's input at this juncture," came the reply. "We will be in our family's private chambers."

Suddenly, Pontius understood why Tiberius had summoned him to Capri.

"Thank you for protection," he whispered. Inside, he felt a sense of joy. They would be able to raise Pilo away from the influences of the Roman Royal Court.

Almost 80 miles northwest of Jerusalem, the Mediterranean Sea presented itself with a wide, sandy, beach. Between the open beach and the Via Maris, the coastal trade route, stretched a wide, undeveloped, rocky plain.

As the morning's early light increased, one was gradually able to distinguish the shadows from the presence of a large group of people huddled together on this plain. Apparently, they were accompanied by a unit of armed mercenaries.

At the moment, however, the horses were tethered to a temporary rope corral, constructed among the trees. Away from the trees, the remaining coals of a watch fire were beginning the end of their burning.

Philip recognized the area. From what he could tell, they were just south of Appolonia. Why had they been brought *here*, he wondered?

All was quiet.

As they had during each rest stop over the past nineteen hours, the armed men had circled the prisoners, still bound, into a core group, and camped around them. The prisoners had been given water, but no food, and no opportunity to relieve themselves.

Shira was convinced the mercenaries wouldn't have stopped at all, had the horses been able to travel continually. Her feet were raw from walking. Blisters formed in the first few hours had burst, and now were bleeding. After all, she had not worn traveling shoes to go to the Ecclesia that morning, she reasoned. It was too late now to make changes.

Perhaps being so concerned about her appearance was not practical.

She considered those around her, most of whom had fallen asleep, utilizing another person to lean against. How long had they been here, she wondered? And exactly where were they?

The bedraggled group of prisoners had slept intermittently, if at all. Completely prevented from speech or interaction, those rounded up following Stephen's murder still had no idea who was in their party, their station, or their story.

There was no status here.

In the middle of the circle, being careful not to disturb the man tied to him too greatly, Joseph of Arimathea shifted his legs to get rid of the cramps in his thighs.

Getting older is not for the faint of heart, he told himself. Straightening his back, he rolled his head from side to side to loosen the tightness in his shoulders.

The approaching daylight would allow some observation.

He looked around the small encampment.

They had arrived under darkness several hours ago.

He had known Caiaphas had been plotting against the Jerusalem Ecclesia for some time, but today's events had surprised him. What was the purpose of this show of force? What was the man trying to accomplish? He had expected some sort of attack or denouncement of himself, but not against innocent people of the city, or the High Priest's own daughter!

Would they all be killed under the renegade Caiaphas' apparent new vigilante law? It was evident now. He was taking advantage of the gap between Roman Procurators to follow his own agenda. The man had lost touch with ElShaddai's nature and His heart for His people. That much was clearly evident.

Joseph sighed.

It was still hard to tell who had been kidnapped as part of their party. No conversation had been permitted, even now.

He looked at the guards. What were they waiting for, he wondered? It was strange. All day, the mercenaries had refused to stop. They had beaten anyone who spoke or expressed a need of any kind. *They* had eaten while resting their horses, but had *not* fed their captives.

For a moment, the priest felt he could identify with the experience of Joseph, son of Jacob; who had been sold into slavery by his brothers, centuries ago.

Why were they being given a time to rest? Why now?

Surely, if they were all to be drowned, there would be no reason to wait for daylight, if that was what they were truly doing.

In his heart, he knew he would never see Jerusalem again.

As he was stirring, he noticed four of the mercenaries making their way down the hill to the beach. He couldn't make out what their purpose might have been.

A few moments later, eight men came up the hill from the beach.

That's strange, Joseph thought. Perhaps he had just missed seeing the first four go down the hill when the entourage arrived here.

The men he observed made their way to the watch fire, where the mercenary leader was seated, enjoying a warm drink. Joseph watched them exchange greetings, and sit with the man for a few moments.

So, he speculated, the second four had *not* been part of the original group in Jerusalem.

But they *did* know each other.

Who were they all working for, he wondered?

When dawn's light filled the sky, the mercenary leader rose from his position by the fire. He clapped his hands together, summoning the soldiers in his unit together. He held a short meeting, apparently giving instructions of some kind.

It was frustrating not to be able to hear what he was saying, Joseph thought.

A few moments later the mercenaries began making their way over to the circle of prisoners. Rousing them with kicks and yells, the hired men bullied the weary followers of Jesus to their feet.

"Come on!" the leader shouted. "You are all going to your new home! If you can get there alive!"

At that comment, cynical laughter broke out among the soldiers.

With those words, the two lines of captives began to trudge, pulled this time by two sets of three mercenaries; with three pulling at the front of each line.

It took all of Joseph's focus to make his way down the somewhat steep incline to the beach without falling. He was aware, as he walked; one fall would cause everyone else tied to him on either side to fall as well.

That would end badly, he concluded.

When his feet finally reached the sand, he was able to look forward and understand their destination. Just off the beach, in the blue edge-waters of the Mediterranean, were two empty ships; one larger than another. As he moved forward, Joseph realized. The people in both lines were being cut free and loaded into the larger boat.

It was a strange vessel, he noticed. It was close to 35 feet long, and by estimation, around 15 feet wide. The sides were scooped outward in the middle, and inward once more at the railing. The center of the vessel was constructed with a long, wooden rib which rose above the railing at the bow and the stern. The rib was plain, but curved on each end, presumably to help in tying it to its moorings. On closer inspection, Joseph noticed it could reasonably called a "little ship." But it had no sails, no places for oars, and no rudder. There were no places to sit, or even paddles inside. Where had they found such a vessel, he considered?

He was stunned as the answer presented itself.

It would have been designed for this purpose. And for this purpose alone.

When all the captives were seated in the large boat, four of the mercenaries moved to the bow of the ship. There, they worked together to knot a thick hemp rope around the curved top of the bow's center rib.

Then, holding the ropes, the four boarded the smaller boat. Then, they tied the other end of the rope to an iron ring protruding from the railing of the smaller boat. Taking their places on the four benches inside the smaller boat, they picked up oars and began to row away from the mainland.

In so doing, the smaller boat had become a pilot-boat. Rowing in unison, the men in the pilot-boat pulled the larger ship out to sea. When the mercenaries were certain the larger boat had been discovered by the dangerously strong, circular currents in the Mediterranean, they untied the rope from the iron ring, and dropped it into the water. The currents received the vessel onto the surface of the Sea. When it became evident the ship of refugees was on its way out to sea, they turned their own boat around and rowed back to the shore.

Their mission was completed.

None of the mercenaries cared what would happen to those forced into the ship. None of those who funded the persecution cared either.

It had been the Sadducees' fondest wish to rid themselves of as many followers of Jesus as possible that day. And if they could not get rid of them, perhaps word of what they had done would be whispered in the secret corners. Perhaps it would scare them into leaving Jerusalem for good.

Then, they reasoned, life in Jerusalem could go back to the condition it had been before.

Such is the belief of every persecutor.

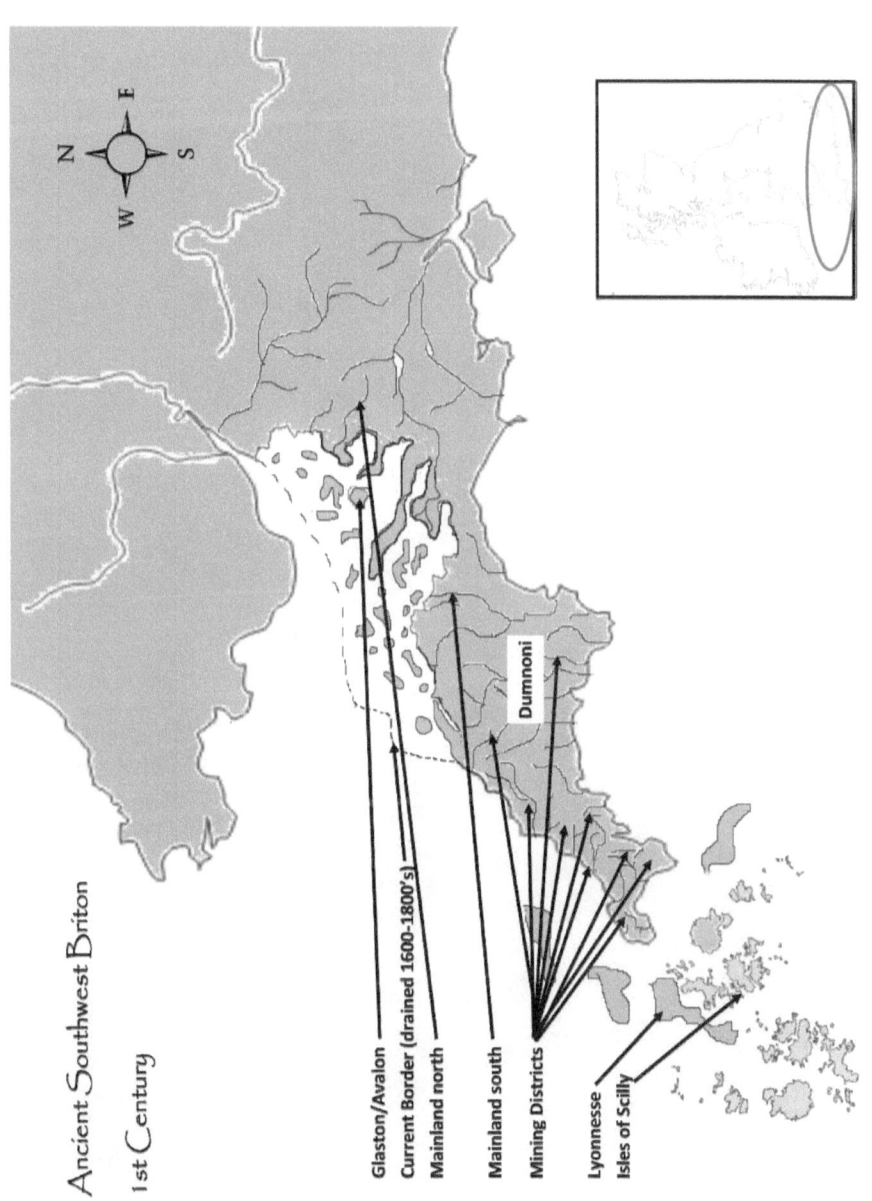

Ancient Southwest Briton

1st Century

Glaston/Avalon
Current Border (drained 1600-1800's)
Mainland north

Mainland south
Mining Districts

Lyonnesse
Isles of Scilly

Dumnoni

Part Three

15 - Bridge Journeys
Spring, 37AD

Saul talked to himself during most of the horse ride back to Jerusalem. The more he thought about Shira's words, and pictured her with her hands tied in front of her like a common criminal, the deeper his anger became.

"I worked hard to get her," he muttered, "and she is *mine!* No one has the right to steal her from me. And that's what they have done! They all deserve to die!"

By the time he reached the city, his hurt and anger had turned into rage. Like a kettle full of boiling water, his thoughts churned, burning up energy.

There had to be someone to blame.

And yes, something had to be done to stop the conversions of the faithful in Jerusalem into followers of Jesus. If ElShaddai wasn't going to stop this destructive belief from ruining the nation of Judea, then Saul decided he would become a tool to express God's will.

After all, didn't God expect people to step in and do their part?

He would be the tool. He contemplated his life's pathway to this; his believed destiny.

It had been the plan of ElShaddai, he had changed his allegiance from Gamaliel to Caiaphas. Although he still believed in the resurrection and the after-life, he saw strong value in the political leanings of the Sadducees. And, he reasoned, even if a person believed in something; if it wasn't practically possible to see happen, or it was more mystical than tangible; then, it *had* to be deception.

Some things a person just had to push through. Think about it hard enough; work hard enough; and a person could make their own miracles!

If a leader was going to be effective, and have influence, after all, he would need to know how to sway people.

And, no one did that better than Caiaphas, Saul reasoned.

It was evening when Saul arrived in Jerusalem. Instead of going straight home, he stopped to his father-in-law's home. He really should let them know what had happened with their daughter.

Upon his arrival, Nitza opened the door. She had not yet decided to go to bed.

"Good evening, Saul," she greeted him. "How can I help you?"

"Well, Mother Nitza," he answered. "I just wanted to come by and let you know what I discovered, and the outcome of my journey. I'm sorry I left so quickly this morning."

"Oh, I understand," she replied. "Caiaphas is always needing to change something in our lives because of his duties. I'm used to that, believe me."

She looked over her shoulder, and called for her husband. "Joseph? Joseph, Saul is here and has news about our Shira." She looked at Saul. "How long were you on the road today?" she asked.

"Oh," I'd say a good twelve to fourteen hours," he replied.

Her eyebrows went up. "That's a long time in a saddle!" she exclaimed. "Aren't you tired?" Over her shoulder she called again. "Joseph Caiaphas!"

"Yes, it is a long time," Saul answered.

"How long since you ate something?" she wanted to know.

Saul paused. "You know, I don't think I've thought about food all day. I guess I've had other things on my mind."

Nitza took him by the shoulders and steered him to the nearest bench and table. She gave him a little nudge. Startled, Saul landed on the bench, surprised.

"What?" he started.

"You are going to sit right here, and tell me everything that happened today. And I am going to fix you something to eat," she told him. A third time she looked over her shoulder and yelled. "Joseph, I swear, if you don't get down here, I'm going to burn your best sandals!"

Surprised to see the level of assertiveness expressed by the High Priest's wife, Saul said nothing. It was evident something had changed in her attitude towards her husband. Did it have something to do with Shira's disappearance, he wondered?

A few moments later, Joseph Caiaphas entered the room. "You don't have to be so impatient, Nitza!" he reprimanded. "I was in the outdoor *latrinum,* or toilet!"

He noticed Saul sitting nearby. "Are you making some food?" he asked.

"I am," she replied.

"Are you making enough for three?" he inquired.

Without looking, she continued working. "I wasn't planning on it," she answered grimly.

"Nitza... *Blossom*...." he began.

336

She turned to look at him. "I told you never to call me that again!" she snapped.

Caiaphas looked at Saul, his hands extended in front of himself.

"I didn't know Shira was one of them," he explained. "My wife blames me for her being stolen from us."

Saul nodded. "I don't blame you, sir," he offered. "If it's any help at all, I went after her today. I spoke with her."

Nitza brightened. "You did? Where is she?"

Saul's eyes filled. "She refused to return."

Caiaphas couldn't believe what he was hearing. "What?" he asked. "Why didn't you force her to renounce her beliefs and bring her with you?"

"Because she wanted me to rescue everyone else as well," Saul sighed.

Caiaphas snorted. "Well, *that's* not possible."

"Why not?" she exploded to her husband. "Isn't the life of our child worth the cost of your..... your *operation*?"

"She is," he replied carefully. "However, my responsibility to the nation of Judea before *God*, is to protect the purity of our faith. The Ecclesia destroys that faith in the Law, and pulls good people into deception."

"And is our daughter one of those 'good people?'" she demanded.

"Nitza," he cajoled. "Please, believe me. There is *nothing* I can do to fix this."

"Why not?" Saul asked. "If we go after them, and pull her off the ship, and leave the others, who is to know?"

Caiaphas looked at the younger man. "And how do you propose we find the ship, exactly?"

"What ship?" Nitza asked.

The High Priest sighed. "The Temple commissioned the building of a specialized vessel, just for the purpose of exiling the members of the Jerusalem Ecclesia," Caiaphas told her. "It has no rudder, or sail, and was set on the Great Sea without oars. It will sink in a matter of hours when it hits the circular water currents."

Nitza's mouth fell open. "You sentenced those people to *die?* Without even knowing who you were condemning? You just rounded them up like you pulled in a fishing net? How could you be so cruel?"

Caiaphas shrugged. "It was business."

"I came here to tell you what happened with Shira today, and to ask permission," Saul interjected.

"Permission? For what?"

"Well, I put a lot of thought into this as I was riding home. The fault in our losing of Shira should really be placed at the feet of the leaders of the Jerusalem Ecclesia. She felt alone because I was so busy. That made her vulnerable. She went with her friends to the prayer meetings and teaching sessions. She really believes she is following ElShaddai. She told me she believes Jesus the Galilean is actually ElShaddai come in human form."

Nitza reacted. "She *said* that?"

Saul nodded. "She did. Just before she said she would rather die than renounce him."

Caiaphas was shocked. "I thought we had trained her better."

Saul continued. "I want to propose something. If stoning Stephen was designed to make a statement, I believe it was successful. To follow his death with the disappearing of such a large group of Jesus' followers was brilliant."

"Thank you," Joseph replied.

"It's true," Saul offered. "But we need to do a little more. I want permission to go to the homes of those who are known members of the Ecclesia, and arrest them as religious criminals. Then, we can either kill them, or exile them from the city. It's the only way to protect other young men and women like Shira."

"That's not a bad idea, son," Caiaphas responded. "It will be a long and tedious exercise. Are you sure you want to do that?"

Saul sneered. "Believe me, I have enough energy stored in myself due to this whole situation…. I could go for years."

"Well then," the High Priest responded. "That's settled. We are on to the next step. We can bring your idea to the Council first thing in the morning."

The two men took food from the workspace where Nitza had been working when Caiaphas arrived home. They exited the room in conversation, planning how Saul might begin the "Purification of the Faithful" in Jerusalem.

Incredulous, Nitza called after them as they walked. "That's it? That's how you are going to end this? What about *Shira?*"

Joseph Caiaphas looked over his shoulder.

"She's dead to us, Nitza. Let it go."

Silenced and amazed, Nitza stood, watching the two priests retreat. Then, she turned and went back to preparing the food dish she had begun.

"It's a pity I didn't tell them I have become one of them too!" she said, as the tears began to fall.

In Edessa, Thaddeus Adai, Kahina, and Mari were in the midst of a planning conversation with King Abgar and Queen Helene. The Edessa Ecclesia had grown exponentially in the last couple of years. It was time to appoint new leaders for house meetings.

Hanging from a nail in the wall of the throne-room was a large wooden box-frame. Inside, a sepia-shaded image of a man's face was centered on a background of cream colored fabric.

A little over three months ago, Thaddeus Adai had received a scroll from Jerusalem, along with gifts from his brother, Simeon, and his family. Among the gifts were three scrolls. A letter with the scrolls described them as having been sent by the Capernaum Ecclesia.

Levi, who was now going by his Roman name, Matthew, had compiled an account of the life and teachings of Jesus. He had written the account down, having sensed a leading of the Holy Spirit to do so. The entire story was written in Greek, the language used for literature of the day. As such, it would be the most easily understood language in the entire Roman Empire.

Simon had been so excited to see his brother receive Matthew's record, he had purchased three copies for Thaddeus Adai and the Edessa Ecclesia. Simon also told his brother of other copies of Matthew's account being sent to each of the known Ecclesias as the copies became available.

King Abgar had commissioned several scribes in the past few months, who were now working on the tedious job of creating more copies of Matthew's record. It was Mari who had suggested it be titled "The Book of Matthew," using the Roman name, in order to increase its appeal to those who weren't Jewish.

Since that time, several leaders in the Edessa Ecclesia had expressed the desire to travel to other parts of the nation of Osroene, sharing the news of new life in Jesus. Thaddeus Adai wanted the king's permission to provide these men with copies of the scrolls, and to train them as leaders as well. He felt it was vitally important to make sure each of the leaders upcoming were well-rounded, briefed in how to give spiritual care with solid and ethical skill.

In Capri, Pontius Pilate was midstride, dictating a letter to the new Caesar, the "Mad Dog," Caligula. Close by, Pilo played with wooden blocks with his nursemaid, Yasmina. As soon as one of them completed building a tower, the other would knock it down. The resultant giggles and peals of laughter brought smiles to the faces of both the retired general and his scribe. Darting in and out of the playtime fun was Pilo's little white dog, who punctuated the air with short barks, directed at the falling wooden cubes.

Claudia Procula and her handmaiden, Candace, were folding items they had laundered. Everyone in Pilate's family group anticipated moving from the villa within the next few days. They had become comfortable living here. Packing would be a rather large undertaking.

After the scribe left, Pontius looked at his bodyguard. "Quintus, would you please ask Valerius to join us? We have some plans to make."

Before moving, Quintus smiled. "The older or the younger, sir?" he asked.

"Both of them, please," Pilate returned his smile. Quintus gave a chest salute and went to summon the men requested.

When he was gone, Pontius looked at Claudia. "Would you like to hear it?"

Claudia Procula laughed. "You didn't want Quintus to hear it?" she asked.

"He already has, as I was dictating," came the answer, with a chuckle.

"Did you say all the things you said you were going to?" she asked.

"Yes, I did," he answered. "And we will not need to go back to Rome." He looked up to meet her gaze. "Can you live with me another twenty years?"

"Well," she said, relieved, "I should think so. I will never be bored."

He smiled, and unrolled the scroll. "I wanted to read it to you before I seal it."

At that moment, Quintus returned with both generations of Valerius Gratus.

Pilate looked up. "Oh good," he said. "I was just about to read the letter to Caligula to Claudia. I want you both to hear it as well."

"From Pontius Pilate, former Procurator of Judea, husband to Claudia Procula, your beloved cousin, and loyal friend to Caesar. To Caligula Caesar, Emperor of the Empire, Conqueror of all lands between the seas, declared god by the Senate of Rome.

"Greetings, most excellent Caligula.

"Gaius, your loyal friend and emissary, has provided me with your choices for me to choose from in my transfer in service to Rome. I am grateful to have the opportunity, and for your gracious mercy.

"I have chosen to receive the station offered in northern Gaul, in the land of Helvetia, in the Alpes Poenaie; the Celtic village of Lucerne by the River Rhones. By the time you receive this, we will have arrived with the battalion stationed there.

"As instructed, I will communicate with the Senate through Gaius, as to our needs and requests. And, as commanded, you will never have to hear my name again. Thank you. Goodbye."

As Pilate finished reading, the older Valerius cheered. "Perfect!" he cried. "You give his ego nowhere to go. There is no conflict stirred. You have given him his heart's desire and asked nothing in return."

"What is your plan, Pilate?" the younger Valerius asked.

Pilate finished rolling the scroll, and heated the wax for its seal. He tied a red ribbon around it, and closed the ribbon with a second seal. When he was finished, he spoke.

"Sit, please, my friends," he urged. "Claudia, come join us. Candace, please help Yasmina with Pilo. I would like you to take him to the gardens and take a nice long walk." He looked at Quintus. "Please have one of our party follow them as a bodyguard."

"Yes sir." Quintus saluted once more.

"Oh, and Quintus?" Pilate continued.

"Yes?"

"When you are finished, come back and join us, please." The general wanted to be sure his instructions would be followed.

The centurion nodded, as he left the room once more. A few moments later, he returned with one of the younger Valerius' attendants. After receiving instructions from Pontius, the two female slaves and the young boy left for an outing in the gardens.

Pilate looked at the centurion. "You have been on your feet a long time, Quintus," he said kindly. "Why don't you sit down and join us?"

Quintus wasn't sure what to say. "I'm used to standing, sir. It's my job," he said.

"I realize that," Pontius answered, "but we are going to be talking about your life, and I'd like you to be involved without feeling obligation."

Obediently, Quintus moved to a nearby bench. At Pilate's hand motion, he removed his helmet.

"Here is my proposal," Pilate continued. "I want each of you to feel free to say 'no,' as I have no idea what the Emperor will do in regard to providing living conditions, or personal needs. Claudia has warned me her cousin, Caligula Caesar, is prone to mood swings, and tends to be unexpectedly violent when he is displeased."

341

The older Valerius spoke. "But, there *are* many good things going on here, which convinces me God is watching over all of us. There is no need to return to Rome, so you will not be executed. Caligula has offered you a choice of commissions, which is rare, and I believe you have chosen wisely."

"Thank you for your wisdom in walking through that, by the way," Pontius said to Valerius.

"Glad I could help," the man replied. "Now, what are your requests for the Roman Senate?"

"That is why I called you here. What would you ask if you were in our position? And, secondly, how many of you are willing to go with us to the Alps?"

Everyone in the room looked at Pontius and Procula in surprise. One by one, each person in the room spoke.

"Tiberius wanted me to take care of you," the older Valerius answered. "It has been my plan since the beginning."

"Me as well," his son offered.

Pontius looked at Quintus. "Me?" the soldier asked. "Sir, I am your servant. I have no family. Where you go where I go."

"I have been able to pay you until now," Pilate told him. "Do you want to remain with us, if you have no income? I am unsure whether the Senate will provide the allowance I am requesting. Quintus, you are relatively young. You could make a second career, and do it well."

Quintus returned his gaze. "I am your servant, Pontius. I would remind you we are also brothers in Jesus. I go where you go."

"We are your brothers also," the younger Valerius offered.

Relieved, Pontius and Procula both let out sighs, as though in unison. In response, everyone laughed together.

"So, sir," the younger Valerius repeated, "what is your plan?"

Grasping his wife's hand, Pilate answered.

"I would like to board the royal vessel to take us from here to Massilia, at the mouth of the River Rhones. From there, we will travel up the river as far as the waters will allow and rest at the Roman city of Lyon. We will wait in the city for an escort to our outpost."

He paused, looking around the room for concerns or suggestions. None were offered. "We are agreed, then?" he asked.

Almost in unison the five adults in the room answered. "We are agreed."

Pilate continued. "Then I will prepare dispatches regarding our plans. We will leave one week from today in the early morning. As there are seven days remaining in the period of time Caligula provided for our decision, I want to give us the next seven days to prepare. At the end of that seven days, Valerius and I have decided we will leave the palace as soon as the emissary's vessel is out of sight. If there are purchases you need to make, or letters you wish to write, please take care of those things in this amount of time.

"Pack only what you need. It is my understanding the Alps are a much cooler climate than we are used to. When you have a bag or box ready to go, please let Quintus know. Quintus, I will need your help and that of the bearers to begin loading the ship in the night hours over the next few days. I don't anticipate an issue, but please let the bearers know; if anyone speaks of our plans, they will lose their life.

"Say nothing to anyone. We will speak again: here, at this time tomorrow."

The home of Ampliatus and Maria was the first house of cleansing visited by Saul and his henchmen, with torches and clubs.

Just before dawn, Saul stood outside the door, and motioned for three of the Temple Guard to sneak up the outside steps to the rooftop. When everyone was in place, the priest pounded on the door.

Taking a deep breath, he shouted in a loud voice. "Followers of Jesus! Open the door and come out! You are under arrest!"

He stepped back, making room for the battering ram carried by six of his men. With one swing, the log shattered the door. In the middle of the large room just inside, a startled Ampliatus stood looking blankly at the men swarming in through the front door.

"Oh, the architect!" Saul sneered at the man. "I'd forgotten! You are part of this conspiracy against our God?"

"Saul? What conspiracy?" Ampliatus spoke, dazed. "How is your wife?"

At the mention of Shira, Saul took three steps towards Ampliatus, and struck him across the face. The force behind the priest's fist was so great, the older man fell to his knees. Blood dripped from a gash on his forehead.

"Oh, I'm sorry," Saul said sarcastically. "My ring appears to have cut you." He pointed to the man's forehead. "You might want to take care of that."

As he was speaking, a guard emerged from the couple's sleeping chamber with Maria, holding her by her hair. Another came from the outdoor cooking area, with John Marcus, with hands bound in front of him.

"Apparently, the boy thought he could run for help," the soldier explained.

Saul smiled. "Bind all of them." He pointed to the soldier who held John Marcus. "You, take them to the prison. We will meet you there."

With that, Saul marched out of the house, back into the street. He motioned to his men. "Let's go!" he shouted.

On the door of the next home, he pounded his fist and shouted the same warning. A surprised John opened the door before the battering ram could be used. As soon as his face was visible, Saul grabbed him by the fabric at his throat, and dragged him out into the street.

"You are under arrest!" He pulled on John's robe, and threw him to the ground. "You killed my wife! She is dead to me! You stole her from me!" As he was screaming, he kicked the man in the ribs, emphasizing the words timed with his feet's movements.

He looked at the man on the ground. John was huddled into a position to protect himself.

Saul looked at one of the guards. "Bind him, and take him to the prison. Are there any others?"

"No, he's the only one," came the answer.

Saul raised his hand, and shouted. "Let's go!"

In the Essene Quarter, the pattern was repeated. Scores of men and women were dragged into the main street, beaten with clubs, bound, and taken to the prison in the lower level of Joseph Caiaphas' palace.

By evening, the cells were filled.

The guards on duty commented how different these people were from most criminals who had been imprisoned by the High Priest. These people seemed to care about each other. They were tearing their cloaks into strips to create slings for broken limbs, and bandages to bind up bleeding wounds. Everywhere, comfort was taking place.

After some time, a man's voice began to sing from one of the Psalms in David's songbook. One after another, voices joined, until the entire prison was filled with song.

Upstairs, Nitza heard the words, and went to investigate.

She questioned the guards on duty. "Who is in the prison?" she asked. "Why are there so many?"

"My lady," the man on duty replied, "they are followers of Jesus, arrested by Saul of Tarsus."

"Who is in there?" she questioned.

"Do you know want to see if you know anyone, Mistress?" the guard asked. "Prince Caiaphas is gone. I would be glad to let you go down there," he told her.

Suddenly hopeful, Nitza nodded. "Could you, please?" she responded.

Smiling, the guard unlocked the door to the steps leading to the lower level. Returning his expression, she passed him and made her way down the steps.

As she rounded the corner to the cells, cries of recognition could be heard. "Nitza!" "Have you been arrested too?" "Why are you here?"

Without a word, Nitza returned upstairs, where she gathered food and water. She began making trips; bringing baskets of bread and fruit, with full water-pots of water to those in the cells. Serving through the night, she was a source of encouragement for those in cages.

After Caiaphas left for the Temple the next day, she sent for a physician to treat some of the more damaging wounds.

At midday, Caiaphas returned home, with Saul and several other Sadducees. Nitza warily followed them downstairs out of curiosity. After rounding the corner, she watched as her husband stood where everyone would be able to hear his words.

"Men and women of Jerusalem! We, the Sanhedrin have met together to discuss your fate. You all have aligned yourselves with the heretic, Jesus of Nazareth! We, as the protectors of the purity of our national heritage and faith, will not tolerate your deception sweeping through our country. Now, not wanting to execute so many of our own countrymen, we have decided to give you a choice.

"You may stay in Jerusalem, and eventually be arrested and stoned, or worse. Or, you and your families can leave Jerusalem before the week's end, and continue to live. We will release you all now, and allow you to go to your homes.

"There are four days until the week's end. Should any of you be in your homes at the beginning of next week, please know we will find you, arrest you...... and..... *we will kill you.*"

Caiaphas finished his sentence with a somewhat dramatic flair. At his nod, the solders made their way down the row, opening the prison doors, and releasing the captives.

For the next six days, the pattern was continued, until everyone in Jerusalem became aware of the Temple's "Purification of the Faithful."

A mass exodus of thousands began. Horses and oxen pulled wagons and carts. Families packed what they could carry and walked away from their homes. Stunned at the fierceness of the Temple's condemnation of their neighbors and family members, Jewish and Roman citizens of Jerusalem alike were sympathetic and helpful to those they knew.

Over the two weeks following the dispensed judgment against the Jerusalem Ecclesia, long lines of displaced persons made their way out of the city. Refugees without hope or destination, most sold everything to fund travel to another, as of yet unknown, home.

A place where they would be free to worship without fear.

Yet, some chose to stay in the city, simply because the Holy Spirit asked them to stay. Among those were members of the twelve, the household of Ampliatus and Maria, Nicodemus, Judah and his family, Lucius who owned the weaving house, and the business owners who travelled from Galilee.

One afternoon, during this two week period, Gamaliel was standing on the steps of the amphitheater in Solomon's porch. He and several others were discussing the Law of Moses, and the responsibility of those who believe in ElShaddai to show their beliefs by how they live.

"It is simple," Gamaliel was saying. "To live intentionally, doing the right thing, brings honor to God. There is no purity without this."

"But I cannot *earn* the acceptance of God," James the Just (Jesus' half-brother) debated. "I must live honestly before my God, in relationship, or my works mean nothing. Without open relationship, my actions are just that; they are empty."

The conversation became strong, heated with emotion, as each man tried to convince the other, debating in true priestly/rabbinic fashion.

The conversation continued to gather steam, as well as observers. Unnoticed, Saul of Tarsus stepped behind James the Just. With a strong thrust of his dagger, he stabbed the leader with a knife. Fortunately for James, the priest missed the man's ribs, and instead, put a knife through his right arm. Frustrated with his own poor aim, Saul then pushed James down the stone steps of the amphitheater.

Miraculously, and to everyone's surprise, the disciple had no broken bones upon landing, only bruises. Additionally, the knife wound was not mortal, but had accomplished its strategic purpose.

After being treated by Luke the physician, James escaped from Jerusalem, stitched and bandaged, with arnica oil in hand. He had associates living in Jericho, and at the EnGedi wadi. He knew he would be welcomed by his friends.

News of James' assassination attempt was followed by more members of the Ecclesia fleeing Jerusalem. This time, the majority of those leaving the city headed south, towards Jericho; following James. For his part, the leader had decided he would stay in Jericho until he healed completely, and then return to the Jerusalem Ecclesia when the present uproar had subsided.

In Capernaum, Simon Peter and Elsbeth were working in the large room attached to their home. For the past three years, it had been utilized as a classroom, where members of the twelve had taken turns teaching and training those who desired to be equipped to help others. It had been used as a meeting place for the Ecclesia.

Now, it would be also used as temporary housing.

Simon Peter's students had been working to help with the project all day as well. Working inside with them today was a particular young man, who had sought Simon out just after the day of the Great Wind in Jerusalem. His parents had followed Jesus' ministry from the early days in Galilee. Recently, they had moved to Capernaum, to be a part of the Ecclesia.

But Simon Peter and Elsbeth had known the family longer than that. In fact, Simon remembered a time when Jesus picked him up as a little lad, and placed him in the middle of the twelve. Ignatius, the boy, still spoke of his memory of Jesus' words. Peter knew Ignatius had been used to halt an episode of the twelves' seemingly inexhaustible conflict over their own importance.

"If anyone wants to become a part of the Kingdom," Jesus told them that day, "they will need to change and develop a heart like a little child."

The young man had now seen twelve summer seasons, and would celebrate his BarMitzvah in a few weeks. He was excited to be able to attend the Feasts in Jerusalem for his first time this year.

Watching Ignatius struggle to help repair broken plaster spots, Elsbeth smiled. The boy had developed a close relationship with Simon Peter. It was good to see him working alongside their own children.

Also working with them to set up the shelter, were several unusual allies. Jairius, the ruler of the Capernaum synagogue, and his wife, Gedalia, had followed Jesus since the Master had raised his daughter from the dead. Her name was Amita. It had been five years ago, now. It was amazing, Elsbeth considered, how she had grown up since then. The beautiful young woman was now of marriageable age.

Although he was watched carefully by spies from Jerusalem, the priest's and his family's loyalties rested with the twelve.

Another unexpected supporter was Justus Flavius, centurion commander of the Capernaum Roman battalion. Jesus had healed his servant, Adelphos, with just a word. Justus' wife, Julia, and daughter, Helene, had become close in relationship with Zebedee and Salome. In fact, Zebedee had become more like a father to Justus in the past few years, having helped him accept and grieve the death of his twin sons.

It had been three days since James and John, Zebedee's sons, had arrived from Jerusalem with news of what had occurred in the capital. Capernaum was proving to be a refuge for many.

Sadly, Mary and Salome would not be coming home.

It had been difficult to break the news to Zebedee. He had been grieving since his sons' arrival, intermittently weeping and unable to speak.

John had arrived in Jerusalem in the late afternoon the day of Stephen's murder. He had returned from teaching in a nearby village. Upon arriving, he went to the family's Jerusalem office home, and found the house empty. A neighbor informed him of what had happened to his mother and Aunt Mary.

Apparently the sisters had gone to the market that morning, with Salome's handmaid, Sarah. They had not returned home. Concerned for the three women's safety, he went to the marketplace, looking for them.

Then, after learning how the group of believers had been rounded up by the mercenaries in "Potter's Field," John sought eyewitnesses living in that part of the city to tell him what had happened.

Yes, his mother, Sarah, and Aunt Mary *were* in the group taken away.

The Nobilius Decurio had also been seen, with Mary the Magdalene, her sister Miriam, and brother Eleazar.

John returned from his investigations, and immediately decided to head to Capernaum. But, before he could pack his bag the next morning, Saul and his Temple detail had found the disciple alone at the office, and arrested him.

After Caiaphas' warning and releasing of the prisoners the next day, John arrived at the Jerusalem office to find his brother, James, and Achaicus fresh off the road from their mission to Sardinia.

The two men had come home with reports of an Ecclesia established on the small island, as well as news of a group of believers in Saragossa in the land of Spain. James had so many stories to share, it was difficult to allow him to rest.

Many miraculous events had taken place. Each time they shared about their journey, they each portrayed fresh accounts of the Holy Spirit's power.

In contrast, the news from Jerusalem was difficult to hear indeed. Everyone working to set up the shelter was serving with a sad and heavy heart.

"How many more beds do we need, Elsbeth?" Julia asked.

"As many as we can fit in here comfortably," Peter's wife answered.

"We can set up space in the synagogue as well," Jairius offered. "After all, the Law teaches us to open our hearts to the poor and needy."

Peter chuckled. "But you know who made them that way, brother," he warned. "Are you sure doing so won't damage your standing with the Temple?"

Amused, Jairius replied. "How long do you really think I will be allowed to maintain my status when Caiaphas advances his "Purification of the Faithful" to our little town? Everyone here knows I follow the Master's teachings."

He looked his friend squarely in the eye. "Anyway, Gedalia and I anticipate relocating somewhere in the near future as well."

Morning sunrise marked ten days the ship of refugees had been on the waters of the Mediterranean. Life aboard had settled into a vigil of waiting. Quarters were cramped, with one person sitting on top of another.

Construction of the boat's hull was like that of a barge. However, even though it appeared sturdy from a distance, no benches had been provided for seating or storage in its construction. This meant any movement by the passengers would cause it to rock on the water. It only took one slosh of seawater into the ship over the railing for all of the refugees to realize how perilous their situation could become, and just how quickly.

The first day, everyone on board had fallen asleep after being towed out onto the open sea. Exhaustion simply overtook them. They had walked for nineteen hours, with minimal fifteen-minute stops. They had received only a few ounces of water to drink during those rests. It was evident to all, through the actions and attitudes of the mercenaries, the intention was to cause all of them to die a slow and suffering death; to force them to watch their lives drain away under the most distressing of circumstances.

Upon waking, most had begun to pray; some in the language of angels, some in their own tongue. No land was in sight, and they were completely surrounded by the azure waters of the Mediterranean. Without sails, or shade, those who still retained their outer wraps or cloaks shared with those without, creating handheld, makeshift tents to prevent sunburn.

The second day, a cloud formation rolled up from the east. A short rain shower provided fresh water, much of which pooled in the bottom of the ship. Several of the women used their wraps to either sop up the water, or catch the rain. The wet cloths were then passed around the group, and they took turns pulling water from them through suction, or squeezing what they could into their mouths.

The same occurrence took place the third day. Just enough water fell from the sky to quench their thirst.

Then it stopped.

"It's like when our forefathers were in the desert!" one of the men observed. "ElShaddai is taking care of us!"

Joseph of Arimathea looked at the man who spoke. "I don't know you yet," he said. "What is your name?"

The younger man looked at him and smiled. "My Roman name is Maximus. I first met Jesus when he came through our city. I was a synagogue ruler in Bethlehem. One day, I asked him what I needed to do to become his disciple."

Joseph looked at him with interest. "What did he tell you?"

"He said, 'Love the Lord your God with all your soul, all your heart, all your mind. The second commandment is like the first; love your neighbor as yourself.' When I told him I had kept those commandments since my childhood, he told me to go and give everything I had to the poor, and come follow Him."

"That sounds like something he would say," Joseph responded. "What did you do?"

Maximus looked down. "I was offended. I walked away pouting. My family was very wealthy, and I was so proud of that. We had the best of everything." He paused, looking around the ship. He suddenly realized everyone was listening to him. "When I walked away, I felt like what he asked of me was too hard for me to do. I heard him tell the twelve as they walked away that it was harder for a rich man to enter the Kingdom than for a camel to walk through the eye of a needle.

"I started to feel afraid, and then rejected; like I wasn't good enough to be his disciple because I was wealthy. Then I heard him say that with men this is impossible, but with God everything was possible.

"After a time, I realized he was telling all of us we cannot earn or buy our citizenship in his Kingdom. We are all on the same level, and each of us come to him holding nothing. But we must bring all of ourselves."

Joseph smiled. "I am Joseph of Arimathea. I used to serve on the Sanhedrin in Jerusalem. It's nice to meet you, Maximus."

Similar connections were taking place all over the ship. Quietly, people were telling their stories, finding comfort in common experiences. It was during this time the boat hit one of the many dangerous, circular water-flows in the Mediterranean. This particular flow was on the eastern side of Egypt, and was caused by the discharge of the mighty Nile River. As the waters flowed through its delta, the river continued to cut its riverbed bed even further into the Sea.

The refugees' little ship suddenly went from a lazy, directionless drifting, to bobbing and weaving under the influence of a great flow of waters. Involuntary screams rose from a few of the younger women.

Instinctively, Joseph called them all into action. "Quickly!" he shouted. "We need to turn the boat around! All of you on this side, put your arms into the water and paddle us into the middle of the Nile's current, or we will be caught in a cycle. We want to go further out to sea."

Immediately, those on the left side reached over the rail, beginning to paddle with their hands. The former beggar, Uri BenLevi, began to count. "Paddle at the same time!" he yelled. "One, two, three, four! One, two, three, four!"

The count was taken up by those working to right the ship.

As soon as it was turned, Joseph shouted more instruction. "Now, we want to get *through* this current, to the westwardly circular current on the other side. It will take us toward the African continent! Everyone who is at a side rail, put your arms over the side and paddle the boat in a straight manner!"

As Uri continued to count, the entire group began to work to maneuver the ship with their hands in the water. It was difficult at first, but after a few adjustments, they began to work together as a team.

"Abba Father, please help us!" Mary Magdalene prayed out loud.

Everyone around her echoed her prayer.

Then, out of nowhere, a strong breeze began to blow, pushing the little ship into the western side of the river's current coming out of the Nile River's delta.

"That's good, everyone! You can take a rest!" Joseph said. Then, he added. "We need to give thanks for the wind. Without what we just did together, we would be in the middle of the Great Sea, without the direction we were given by that wind."

Prayers of thanksgiving began to go up all around.

A little while later, two of the men emerged from quiet conversation. Then, one took off his head covering and put it in the seawater, holding two corners with his hands. The other man held the top and bottom open on the other side. For a short time, they held the head covering in the rushing water, and then, abruptly scooped water into the boat with the square fabric. The splash wetted everyone around them, and several reacted. But then, looking down at the puddle, Salome realized, "Look! They caught a fish! It's a fish!"

At that point, a few others began copying what the two men had been doing; using their head-coverings like a net. Before long, there were ten or so good-sized fish in the bottom of the boat. Several of the men pulled daggers from leg sheaths, and cleaned the fish, cutting them into chunks, which could then be held by the skin and eaten.

"I've never eaten raw fish before!" Libi said out loud. "I'm so hungry, I don't even care if it's cooked!"

"Me either," agreed Shira.

Everyone seemed to agree, as they bit into the unusual texture of the piece of raw fish they had been given. There was silence on the ship, as each one considered the changes lives had experienced in just five days.

As the days progressed, a routine to set in. Each morning, like manna in the wilderness, a short period of rainfall provided the travelers with fresh water. Each day, they fished in their rather unorthodox method, and ate chunks of raw fish, knowing the provisions came from ElShaddai, keeping them alive. Late each evening, short bursts of rainfall occurred once more, providing just enough cool water to quench their thirst before it was time to sleep once more.

In an older section of Jerusalem, Nicodemus sat in the large gathering room in his home. He had lived there alone for over seven years, since the winter his wife had died. His housekeeper came every other day, to maintain his home, and food stores.

Sometimes, she was his only company after he left the Temple each day. But today was different.

It was a rare moment when Nicodemus opened his small house for guests. This evening, the group of Pharisee priests who served with him on the Sanhedrin, who had also chosen to follow Jesus, had come for an evening meeting.

"How can we protect our members from this kind of persecution being repeated?" Gamaliel asked. "If we had put a strategy in place beforehand, perhaps the kidnapping could have been prevented."

"Do you remember what Jesus said about persecution?" Nicodemus asked. "We are supposed to expect it."

"Yes," Judah answered. "But Gamaliel could have a point. We don't have to invite it, or go looking for it."

"I would just as soon help as many of our people stay alive and safe as long as possible," Simeon said. "What are you thinking, Nicodemus?"

The older priest paused, his voice lowering unconsciously. "I think there has to be a way to help prevent people falling into a trap the way our friends did." He looked around the room. "What about a signal of some kind?"

"Like a code word or something?" Simeon asked.

"But if someone found out the word, they could create a trap. That could be dangerous for people as well," Judah offered.

"What if it were like a drawing that needed to be completed?" Nicodemus asked.

"Like a symbol, you mean?" Simeon asked.

"It could be," Judah responded. "But I'm not sure how it could happen."

"A sun maybe, or an arrow?" Nicodemus suggested.

"How would *that* work?" Judah asked.

"I don't know, exactly," Simeon replied, beginning to walk back and forth in the room, thinking. "It would have to be something which could be offered, and replied to, but then go unnoticed if the other person were not a disciple."

"A sun, or an arrow?" Nicodemus repeated.

"The arrow *might* work," Simeon mused. "One person could draw a straight line in the sand, and the other could finish it."

"And it means we are to stay focused on living our lives with direction and purpose," Nicodemus completed.

"That's fine," Gamaliel said, "and it could *work*, except the purpose sounds as though the final outcome rests on what *we* do, instead of on what the *Holy Spirit* does. It's too easy for us to slip back into trying to earn relationship with Abba Father. And isn't that what the requirements of the Law did to all of us? And didn't Jesus come to free us from that kind of performance?"

"All right, then," Simeon responded. "The idea of one person beginning a symbol and another person completing it would actually be really effective and still simple. But it can't be as distinct as an arrow. It needs to be something that could be mistaken for pointless doodling during a conversation."

Silence hung in the room, as each man strained for a symbol to represent the entire movement.

During the discussion, Judah had been silently tracing images on the tiles in front of him. Without raising his head, he murmured, "Joseph of Arimathea and I had a conversation about this idea a few months back. He suggested using a fish. A fish would work."

"What did you say?" Nicodemus asked.

Judah looked up. "A fish would work. Look." As he spoke he drew an arc with his finger on the ground. "The first person is looking down at the ground, and draws an arc. The second person turns the arc into a fish by drawing another arc, like this." As he spoke he drew a second arc, its beginning forming the front of the "fish," and the ends extending past the closure point, to resemble the profile of a fish.

"If the second person doesn't respond, then it is just a mark in the sand," Nicodemus remarked.

"And Jesus told us we would be fishers of men!" Joseph cried. "The fish is a perfect symbol. It speaks of our identity as well as our mission."

Nicodemus smiled. "We will need a way to communicate it."

Simeon looked at his father. "Abba, what if we used an acrostic to help people remember?"

"Like what?" Gamaliel asked his son.

"Well, when I was in school, you taught me to remember things by using code words to describe what I needed to remember," Simeon answered. "We could use the Greek word for fish, *ichthus,* and use the words "Jesus, Christ, God's, Son, Savior."

His father nodded. "I like that," he said.

"I do too!" Nicodemus declared.

"As do I," Judah added, patting Simeon on the back. "Thank you, Simeon." He looked around the group.

"I wish Joseph was here to see this, don't you?"

Inside the Weaving House, in the business section of Jerusalem, its owner, Lucius, was in deep conversation with a businessman named Babur. Babur was moving to Jerusalem from Macedonia, due to his wife's need to live in a dryer climate. A weaver of fabrics and carpets, he had approached Lucius several months prior to make a purchase. Lucius had told the man repeatedly the property and business were not for sale, at any price.

"I am about to marry the only woman I have ever loved," he told Babur.

"Then I am sorry I asked," came the reply.

But this morning, Lucius had experienced a change of heart. A few weeks ago, he had learned of Miriam's abduction, and that of her siblings, in the Potter's Field. Apparently, based on eyewitness accounts, as well as unfounded rumors, the persons carried away by the mercenaries should be assumed dead.

No one would be coming back.

His heart was broken. He was in his forties now, and had never married. Miriam had been the one. He had watched her recover from the death of her first husband, Abiel.

She had been so gifted in the healing arts. And her laugh! She loved to laugh. He had loved to laugh with her.

He would miss her so greatly!

After the flax harvest this year, they had planned to marry. The sale of linen woven this year would have funded the business; would have built a house, and done much more to help them to accomplish many of their plans to provide a home for the sick and recovering.

Lucius put aside his grief for the time being. But he had decided he could not remain in Jerusalem, especially since he had made the decision to follow Jesus. Everywhere he looked, he saw her face.

He had purchased the Weaving House from her father years ago, and watched her grow into womanhood.

He had held his love until the proper time.

And now she was gone.

When he heard the news, he immediately sent word to Babur, who had been staying at a local inn. "Come this morning," he wrote. "I am ready to sell."

And here they were, settling on a price. It seemed Babur wanted to convert one room into a weaving place for thick rugs. He had come from the mountains of Macedonia, where the goats grew long, soft wool. He showed samples to Lucius.

"This is called 'cashmere,'" he told the present owner. "We use it for blankets, rugs, and clothing. It is very warm in our mountain climate."

Lucius had smiled at the man's enthusiasm. "It doesn't get lower than 30 degrees here, Babur," he answered. "But it might be worth a try for sale in the winters." He rubbed the cashmere against his hand, then his face. "So soft! It is like feeling a cloud!"

Babur was close to making an offer, but decided to add something to his acquisition. "Do you want to continue running the Dyeing House, or are you selling both?" he asked.

Lucius was surprised. "Are you wanting to buy both?" he asked. "I was ready to make two different sales, but I would be more than happy to sell both to you. I'm getting ready to relocate."

"Has there been a death in your family that you have to move? Are your parents ill?"

Lucius looked him in the eye, squaring up his gaze. "Something like that," he answered vaguely, and then thought better of it. "I made a decision about three years ago to follow Jesus the Galilean, and my life has never been the same. I find I am no longer welcome in Jerusalem."

"Really?" Babur wanted to know. "Tell me about this Jesus. Surely a man who has caused such a stir in the angry Caiaphas even *after* his death, must have been very special indeed."

Lucius invited the man into his private resting quarters at the back of his business place, where they shared a short lunch together. As a result, Babur gained a new life, and spiritual family. And, Lucius sold both businesses, making more of a profit than he had anticipated.

"Where will you go now?" Babur asked him.

"I have been feeling drawn towards Antioch," he answered. "But I have a few stops to make along the way first."

"You have changed my life, Lucius," Babur told him. "Can I come by tomorrow, and we can complete our business?"

Lucius smiled. "Absolutely!" he answered. "And I will let you know where to find the scrolls and codex I told you about!"

That evening, Lucius travelled to EnKarem. He had been invited to share the evening meal with Eleazar, the father of Mary Magdalene, Miriam, and Eleazar the younger. When he arrived, he discovered the presence of new friends who had been invited as well: the wife of Simeon of Cyrene, Ramona, and her sons, Rufus and Alexander.

As Lucius arrived, the older Eleazar saw him, as he was working in the vineyard in the steppe-cut hillside. "Greetings!" he cried. "Come on up and see me!"

Lucius made the trek to the vineyard steppe where the older man was working. "What are you doing?" he asked.

Eleazar didn't look up. "Pruning the vines," he answered.

Lucius was surprised. "It's a little early, isn't it?" he asked. "I thought you didn't do that until next month." He looked around and made several observations. "You didn't plant your barley this year."

The older man stopped working, and looked at him. "I am selling the property. It's time to move out of the area."

Lucius assessed his friend and employer. "That's funny," he said. "I am about to sell the Weaving and Dyeing House as well."

"I remember when I built that building, and we purchased the loom," Eleazar said, reminiscing. "I miss my Rachel, even now." He went back to working. "I want to prune the vines so the new owner will get a good harvest of sweet clusters."

"That's kind of you," Lucius observed. "What are your plans?"

The landowner stopped working, and leaned on the fencing in front of him. "The Holy Spirit has made me aware it is a matter of time before my life is to end. I don't want it to end at the hands of the Sadducees. It seems pointless to continue to tend this entire place alone. I am certain now all three of my children were in the culling of believers the day Stephen was murdered."

He sighed, and began pruning once more. "I am sensing a calling to help in the Antioch Ecclesia in Syria. I made a journey there some time ago, and the landscape is similar to here. I have no plans as of yet, but I would like to purchase a small home, and be of some help if I can."

Lucius was amazed. "I have the same direction from the Lord!" he exclaimed. "How soon are you planning to leave?"

Eleazar grabbed his friend's arms. "Really? What a wonderful coincidence!" he cried. "I am so excited! Come! Let's go into the house. Baruch and Leah are preparing the meal. There is so much to tell you!"

In the late evening, four men sat around a fire. They were almost a mile outside the city of Jerusalem, and had set up camp for the night. Over the fire, two held meat, skewered and roasting, for their meal. Not far away, the fifth man in their party was unpacking cheese and fruit from his saddlebags.

"I'm still not sure," the youngest man, named Ofek, was saying.

His leader, Yaniv, was frustrated. "I thought we were all agreed," he said.

Ofek looked up. "I just don't know if taking things into our own hands is a good thing. Can't we just watch and wait? Circumstances like these always pass, and life just goes on."

Daniel, the man preparing fruit and other additions to the meal, interjected. "This situation won't just pass, Ofek. It is *building*, and it doesn't calm down

357

before something else takes place. We have to do what *we* feel is right. All of us have seen the war with Rome escalating. These things are just happening too fast. We have to *do* something. Weren't *you* the one who came to me, and started this ball rolling in the first place?"

Ofek sniffed. "I know," he responded. "But I was angry over the death of my Abba. I wasn't ready to be alone, and there was no one left in my family to help me. I'm only thirteen, you know."

Yaniv patted his back. "And now you have all of us," he said. "We have become your family. But that doesn't change the truth, does it? There have been enough uprisings in the past few years to cause Caesar to send troops here. They will sweep away everything we hold dear to us. It's scary, the way they keep changing the governors, and the Prefects! Think about it! Pontius Pilate wasn't afraid to crucify a man, and yet Caesar has recalled him!

"Those of us who knew Moshe well have had enough. First, Jesus came and people said *he* was the Promised One! But he was crucified and the government didn't change. Then, Moshe came and said he was Moses returning to change the system. And Rome squashed him completely! Now he is dead, along with more than half of our brothers in Samaria."

"That's why I'm afraid, Yaniv," Ofek answered. "I don't want to lose any of you in this thing we are saying we are about to do."

The fourth man, Ethan, was sitting next to the thirteen year-old boy, holding a long skewer over the fire as well. For the first time, he spoke up; his voice quiet. "Ofek, we are all afraid; afraid to take steps; afraid *not* to take steps; afraid the steps we take will be the *wrong* steps. Listen to me. You are not alone in what you feel. We all want the security of our nation. The disruptions happening around us are sure to bring the Caesar's wrath down upon us, just like in the days of the exile, and Nebuchadnezzar of Babylon."

Yaniv spoke once more. "We know there are Sicari and troops training in Qumran. At some point, it will be the proper time. But this is not that time. I thought we agreed!"

Yaniv pulled his stick out of the fire to test his meat. "It's perfect!" He nodded to Ethan. "Try yours. I think we could eat now." He raised his voice, calling to the fifth man who was unpacking the foodstuffs they had brought with them. "Come and bring the cheese, Daniel! The meat's ready!"

"I'll get the wineskins," Malachi, the fifth man offered, getting up to gather two full wineskins from where they were tied to the horse saddles.

After each one had portions on individual oilcloths in front of them, and they had begun to enjoy the meal, conversation returned to the former subject.

Ethan was the first to speak. "Before we abandon everything we have agreed on; and all of us walk away from the values we have finally chosen, I would like to make a couple of observations."

He paused. "Go on," Yaniv urged.

"If these uprisings continue, and our people continue to be turned against each other, the inevitable will certainly occur. And, if the men of the High Court continue to violate the Law, and disregard the Romans, we will all most certainly lose our faith, and with it our identity as well. We all came to these values separately, which suggests to me that God has been speaking to us. Why would we abandon what we each felt was an assignment from God himself?"

Ofek considered Ethan's statement, and then answered. "It isn't that I question our values. I just have questions about how we are planning to carry out our mission. I'm not sure about the taking of human life. I don't think I'm ready."

Yaniv looked at him carefully. "Is it just you are afraid you might get hurt, Ofek? Do you want more training? I can give you that easily enough."

Ofek returned his gaze. "I… I don't know exactly," he answered. "I just don't want to break the Law of Moses…."

"But didn't Moses lead our Fathers into battle," Malachi asked. "And weren't those he fought seeking to oppress our ancestors, to rule over them like the Romans rule over us?"

"Yes," Ofek answered carefully. "I agree with that. I just don't see how that has anything to do with culling our own countrymen in the name of patriotism. How is that right before God? And we are not Sicari…. Are we? And if we are not, and this mission is not a vow to God, then why are we doing it?"

Yaniv sighed. "I can do no more of this tonight," he said. He stood up and went into the woods, then came back and laid down to sleep for the night.

One by one, the men in the group readied themselves and went to sleep for the night around the fire.

Finally, Ofek sat alone, gazing into the embers.

Would he have the heart and will to take a life when it came his time to do so, he wondered? Perhaps Yaniv was right. He would have more confidence if he had more training.

Summer, 37AD

In the Court of Hewn Stones, the sitting Sanhedrin was listening to a report and summary of the present operation, "The Purification of the Faithful." Presently, Saul of Tarsus was giving a summary of his activities, and the success of exiling of the followers of Jesus from Jerusalem.

"We have not been completely successful," he was saying. "But, at least for the time being, the huge gatherings in the Temple Courtyard should be deterred. Speaking of which, I took steps to rid the city of James, the brother of the Galilean. The man had the nerve to debate publicly with Master Gamaliel, and he isn't even a priest. He has had no training." He smiled. "It is my hope he will stay in Jericho, and find some purpose to keep him there."

Murmurs of approval rippled through the room.

Gamaliel and Nicodemus observed the other High Court members, taking note of their responses. It appeared even some of the Pharisees were now in agreement with Caiaphas. Nicodemus noticed their friend Judah was also watching, making mental notes.

Saul continued. "Prince Joseph," he spoke dramatically, "I would like to make a request. I feel I have a mission from ElShaddai himself, and I want to follow correct protocol in order to see it through."

Caiaphas smiled; a perfect, practiced mask of humility. Everyone in the room knew the drama being played out before them had been well-rehearsed in a private setting.

"You know, Saul," he began, "if you continue to serve this Court with the same dedication you have shown these past weeks, it will be a matter of time before you become a full-fledged member of this Court."

Saul feigned surprise. "It is my honor to serve our God."

"Those who are widowed are eligible to serve the matters of the Law with us, but not unmarried men." The High Priest paused for effect. "You are too young to live as a widower, young man."

"Yes, sir." Saul answered.

"But I have taken you away from your request. Please speak freely."

Saul took a deep breath, and shifted his attention to the members of the Court.

"Fathers and rulers of Israel, I come humbly before you. As you all know, there is a sect operating in the city of Jerusalem, seeking to undermine and destroy everything our God, ElShaddai, has given us. Their teaching is spreading like a poison, and has brought division to so many homes. We are engaged in a struggle for our very survival as a nation. We are facing the Roman and Greek influences. These seek to deter our children from becoming contributing and faithful adults. Now, we have the teachings of this Jesus, which have undercut our beliefs even further.

"As most of you know, I have lost my wife, Shira, to the Followers of Jesus just recently. I am a young husband, but I have been a good husband. I have been obedient to the Law. But now, because of *their* influence, my wife became disobedient and rebelled against me publicly. In my effort to rescue her, she became resistant, claiming this Jesus was ElShaddai come in human form. Then, when faced with a choice of returning home with me, or facing death, she told me that Jesus had given his life so that she could live."

Murmurs of concern and sympathy for Saul were heard through the room. He continued.

"I had ridden on horseback more than six hours to save her. I was devastated by her response. I loved my wife. My life will never be the same without her." His voice choked with real emotion. He regained his control.

"As I traveled back to Jerusalem, alone, I feel I received a revelation. I would like to avenge the life of my wife. Jerusalem has undergone a tragic loss of clarity in our religion. And, other cities where our countrymen worship in synagogues, without this Temple, are in danger of the same repeated pattern."

Caiaphas moved to the edge of his large chair. "What are you suggesting, son?" He glanced around the courtyard, taking note of the faces of the priests in the Court. He smiled to himself. They were all obviously invested.

Saul responded. "I have a trained group of men, who have worked with me in this city. We have been successful in bringing about the "Purification of the Faithful;" the cleansing of Jerusalem. I have heard from many sources of an Ecclesia in Damascus of Syria. From what I understand, the same kind of miracles, the same growth in numbers is taking place in that city as took place in this one. The synagogue ruler there has appealed to us for instruction as to what actions he should take. He has asked our permission to take steps to protect what he has built there."

He looked around the room, his voice rising in intensity. "Please give me letters of permission. My men and I will go to other cities, beginning with Damascus. We will continue the "Purification of the Faithful" in every city where we find this sect. We will destroy it. We will drag them into the streets and stone them. We will see our traditions restored, and the name of this Galilean ground into the very ground from which he came."

361

Saul's voice rose to a feverish pitch by the time he finished his oration. As he came to completion, a large portion of the Sanhedrin rose to their feet, with cheers and applause.

Joseph Caiaphas beamed at Saul. He waited for a moment or two, allowing the angry emotion and zeal to be expressed. Then, regally, he rose from his chair, making motions for the shouting and clapping to come to quiet.

"Please, please, sit down," he urged. He waited for the men to still once more. "By this response, I would say we are agreed, by a large majority." He made sure his eyes met with Gamaliel, Nicodemus, Judah, Simeon, and all others who had remained in their seats.

"It is decided then, by the power of God invested in this Court, that Saul of Tarsus shall bring an end to the sect of the Followers of Jesus. We will equip him with tools and weapons, horses, and attendants." He looked at Saul with genuine sternness.

"You and your men will be heading into harm's way. We have no idea what these Ecclesias are capable of doing. It is my private opinion; either you will bring an end to this sect, or this sect will bring an end to you. Go with God, Saul."

"Go with God!" the rest of the Sadducees repeated.

"Thank you gentlemen," Saul replied. "It is my desire to serve God with all of my heart, soul, mind and strength. My men and I will leave in the morning, two days from now."

In the port of Massilia, a city in the Roman province of Gaul, the private, royal vessel belonging to Caligula Caesar was putting out anchor. Quintus, and two of Pilate's Guard were making ready to board a rowboat with the younger Valerius Gratus, the first mate, and one of the sailors.

Having served as a soldier during the ongoing conquest of northern Gaul, Valerius had friends in Massilia. It had been in this rather large Roman city he had spent prolonged time, recuperating from injuries received on the battlefield. So, while the first mate delivered dispatches to Roman authorities in the city, and waited for replies, Valerius and his bodyguards sought passage up the Rhone River for Pilate's entire party. They also hired a guide to take them to the battalion in Helvetia, to a Roman settlement called Lausanne. In Lausanne, they would hire a second transport party, hopefully with wagons to then travel the rest of the distance into Helvetica.

"The present commander has been ordered to meet us in the mountain village, and the army will provide protection and transport belongings from there," Valerius told Pontius. "But we are responsible to get our belongings to the Lausanne."

"Do you speak the language here?" Pilate wanted to know.

"Oh, yes," the younger man answered. "I was stationed here for several years, and served part of that time as a liason officer. The Celtic language is not that much different from the Latin we speak in Rome. Come to think of it, you and Mistress Claudia should have no difficulty."

Valerius unrolled a scroll, disclosing a map of the mountainous region. For the first time, Pontius noted the area was almost entirely made of mountain ranges, with three plateaus between the highest peaks. On the largest plateau, a large river cut its way through the center. The waterway pooled into a great lake midway; with differing names on either side, he observed; Rhone to the west, and Rhine to the east.

As expected, Alpine villages and cities were constructed along this great river.

"We are traveling here," Valerius informed him, pointing to a location to the easternmost region of the mountains. "We have a long journey to arrive here. There is a small village close to the battalion. There is a military outpost in the Alps not far from the farthest edge of our assignment. It is a stone fort.

"As we negotiated with the Senate, you are to choose the city from which you will rule. You are the first Roman official to be placed in the area, and we will be setting up the new government for the conquered areas of Gaul; reinforcing the Senate's will. Your family can be centered anywhere on the western side of Lake Lemannus. I'm sorry to tell you the western side is much colder than the eastern; the lake begins with a glacier at its northernmost point. You don't have to decide now. If you wish, you can wait, and observe which location Mistress Claudia prefers. Should you ask for my suggestion, I would suggest Lapidaria."

"How long will the journey take us, Valerius?" the general asked.

The older man paused. "It is more involved than a simple military venture," he answered. "Because we are moving a *household,* and setting up living conditions, it will take twice as long. I will arrange for water coaches to take us upstream. We will be either under sail, or pulled by horses against the current.

Our belongings will be transported by water barge once we have come to your final destination.

"Because we will be traveling upstream the entire way, it will take almost a month to arrive at Geneve, the city on the lower west side of the great lake. Past that, the travel time will be determined by your choice for a center of operations."

It was evening. In the Court of Hewn Stones, Joseph Caiaphas was in session with Saul of Tarsus, Saul's Purification Team, and several members of the Sanhedrin.

Emotions were running high.

It had been several weeks since reports of Tiberius Caesar's death The subsequent enthroning of the insane and cruel Caligula, had also reached Jerusalem. With the news had come many changes. The new emperor apparently was quickly depleting the vast, 2,700,000,000 sestarcii treasury left in Tiberius' wake. It was rumored he was using much of the money to entertain guests, enlarge buildings, and build bridges. It seemed he couldn't spend it fast enough.

Gauis Julius Caesar Augustus Germanicus, was called Caligula by those who knew him. "The Little Mad Dog," was fourth ruler of the Empire, following Julius Caesar, Augustus and Tiberius. He had lost touch with the principles which had guided the former leaders. His predecessors' goal of expanding the Empire through warfare, and living frugally to save for future needs was abandoned.

Caligula set his sights on fulfilling any and all of his own personal desires.

It was rumored there was to be a new tax levied against the Jews.

Reports had also been received just today from the synagogue rulers in Syria. Rather than assigned a political officer to the region, Caligula Caesar had appointed a new provincial *military* governor to rule from Syria. This military governor had been given more authority by the Senate than his predecessors. He was charged with the task of completely subduing any and all signs of rebellion against the Empire.

His name was Lucius Vitellus, and his ambition would one day make him father to a Roman Emperor. Any complaints to his office would result in harsh punishment upon those making the complaints.

Caiaphas' era of diplomacy with Rome had ended.

There would be no more leniency.

Today, this non-negotiating governor had dispatched his military assistant to Jerusalem, replacing Pontius Pilate's more judicious rule, with one void of compromise and communication. This man was a *representative* authority, an extension of Rome's military arm. He had been chosen by the governor, Lucius Vitellus. Rather than seeking permission for politically intricate decisions, the new Prefect, if you could call him that, was given *complete* authority to dole out Roman rule.

For the general population, it meant no real changes would occur. But for those in leadership positions, freedom to exercise unsupervised judgments had ended.

The Sanhedrin no longer had a voice with Rome.

Like an assassin, the new Procurator went by one simple, Roman name, rather than the customary two for members of the Royal House.

His name was Marcellus.

In one swift, abrupt moment, the balance of power had shifted.

Gone were the days of complaining to Rome regarding harsh treatment. In a fit of temper, Caiaphas expressed to Saul his understandable rage. He was angry at being "cut off," as he put it, from "fair and just treatment." How were they to survive, he demanded, when the Temple's financial reserves were already lower than they had been in a hundred years?

To him, the solution was simple. It was time to raise the Temple tax, and the prices for sacrifices. It was time to seize properties in the name of God. It was time to go after the Followers of Jesus in a greater way. After all, he reasoned, difficulties in the city, and the nation for that matter, had begun when the troublesome sect had declared their existence.

It was time to truly empower Saul, he decided.

The day before, the letters the young priest requested had been completed. Copies for various locations had been scribed. The wording was edited and recopied until it was perfect. In fact, anyone who read even one of the three variations of the letters would be led to one conclusion. The Jesus Sect was deceptive, heretical, divisive, and treasonous to the Roman Empire.

In short, "these people" represented a nameless, faceless evil. They were to blame for all the ills coming against the Jews. They should be executed, their properties seized and given to the Temple.

If a reader was faithful to ElShaddai, they would agree, the High Priest concluded. And, he believed, they would also further agree to payment being extracted to compensate for all the trouble these individuals had caused.

Caiaphas ended the meeting, and remained in the Court alone with his thoughts. It was then he decided to open the scroll from the Roman governor,

Vitellus, which had arrived the day before. He was sure it would be a mandate for the excising of a new tax, or yet another regulation to be enforced.

It was becoming difficult to maintain a truly Jewish identity, he reasoned. Breaking the Red Eagle's wax seal, he unrolled the ornate sticks, and began to read.

"To Annas, former High Priest of the Temple in Jerusalem, and Joseph Caiaphas, acting High Priest of the Temple in Jerusalem.

"From Lucius Vitellus, governor of the provinces of Syria and Judea, serving the Roman Empire

"Greetings. In light of the appointment of a new Military Procurator in Jerusalem, having deposed Pontius Pilate, who so harshly dealt with your countrymen in Samaria, we are making changes in all leadership positions of those formerly serving the Roman Senate.

"It is our command that due to the many difficulties and intrigues surrounding him, Joseph Caiaphas is permanently relieved of the office of High Priest, by the decree of the Roman Senate. We have had enough of his high-handed methods.

"It is further our command, upon Caiaphas' removal, that Annas stand in the office of High Priest until such time as we have had opportunity to review his recommendations for a replacement for Joseph Caiaphas.

"I will visit Jerusalem within the next two weeks. Please make preparations for our time together."

Stunned, Joseph looked around the room. He would no longer rule. He would no longer be permitted to plan or direct the "Purification of the Faithful."

What had made the Romans come to this decision, he wondered?

He knew Pilate had been recalled. Had the former Procurator complained against him? Would there be a trial?

Suddenly, Joseph experienced an unfamiliar emotion. It began to grow, with accusations, and fears of anticipated judgment. He had never felt intimidation before. Was this the inward response those he had exercised power over had experienced?

It was disconcerting indeed.

He sighed.

Standing, he stretched. It would be difficult to go home this evening, he considered. In addition to causing the loss of their daughter this month, he now had to tell her of the governor's message. After deliberating, he decided to take the letter home.

Nitza might feel sorry for him if she read the scroll. He rerolled it and took it with him. He needed all the help he could muster if he were to regain her support.

Losing his position didn't help.

Taking a lamp from a nearby shelf, Joseph lit it, and used it to light his way as he left the Temple Mount.

As he made his way through the streets to his home, a shadowy figure followed him. When he turned a corner, the shadow turned the same corner. When he stopped to look behind him, he saw no one. Was there more than one, he wondered?

Perhaps he was only paranoid.... Imagining plots and counter-plots. But then, when he arrived at the gates to his own home, he knew there were at least three of them. Suddenly, the lamp he carried was knocked from his hand, extinguished on its way to the ground.

From behind, someone grabbed him, holding his shoulders. Hands went over his mouth, and a black sack was put over his head. Then, he sensed a rather large presence in front of him.

Someone punched him in the face, and then in the stomach. He lost count of the blows which followed.

Without warning, he felt a sharp pain in his side. And then another. Unexpectedly, his legs buckled. Reaching out to grasp the man he was sure was still standing in front of him, he found nothing, flailing at the air.

He fell to the ground.

Several hard kicks hit him in the lower back and stomach. One landed near his head. He tried to scream, but a groan was all to emerge from his lungs.

Then, he heard footfalls retreating. The self-appointed vigilantes were running away. They were thrilled their mission had been successful!

Later, Ofek, Nathan, Yaniv, Ethan and Daniel congratulated themselves. They had planned and executed it so well, no words had even been necessary!

At first, Caiaphas struggled to stand after he sensed his attackers had retreated, but weakness prevailed.

Overcome, he found it hard to breathe.

Finally ..... everything went black.

16 – Adrift

Autumn, 37CE

About a half-mile off the coast of Egypt, the small ship of refugees was still drifting along, carried by the unpredictable circular coastal currents of the Mediterranean Sea. Joseph of Arimathea squinted his eyes in the morning sun. He had sailed on many voyages in his life, but never a journey taking as long as this one, or with so few supplies.

Military, trade and merchant vessels all ventured into the deeper waters of the Great Sea, he considered. They had the advantage of choosing their destination, navigating their way by the stars. But, this little ship was at a unique disadvantage. It had been Providential indeed, they had been held to the swirling coastal currents, moving along at a consistent rate of speed.

By the priest's estimation, they had traveled at an average of four miles an hour, relying on the serpentine currents caused by the Nile River's emptying into the Sea. They had been on the sea for over ninety days. By his observation of the night stars, they were a little over half-way to the Roman city of Cyrene, on the tip of the African continent. Without rudder, anchor, oars, or sails, they had had no control over their direction.

"Where are you taking us, Lord?" he questioned in his prayers. "Please help us come to a port soon."

He had never been so tired.

Still, he reasoned, it was evident to everyone on board ElShaddai was sustaining them. They were tired of rainwater, and raw fish, to be sure…

But they were all *alive*….

No one had become ill.

The inevitable human conflicts occurring due to fear, anger, inconvenience, hunger or weariness, had surely shown themselves in the past three months. Clashes had been resolved, relationships had deepened. He had watched as the leaders among their small group of seventy-two had emerged.

The combination of persons aboard amazed him. This too, was proof of Abba Father's interest and involvement in even the tiniest of details. He realized now, in retrospect, they had all been in shock after Stephen's murder.

How had each of them not *heard* the warnings of the Holy Spirit that day?

It had been discussed many times since they had put out to sea, just how intricate the Sadducees' plan had been. How long had it taken to construct the ship they were floating in, for example? It was obvious they had conspired to stone a man when Roman government influences had been lessened. How was it, in a group this size, no children had been captured?

It had taken more than a week for the company to acclimate to living on the sea; to making the most of a difficult situation; learning to be thankful instead of complain. They had chosen to use their Roman, or Latin, names from this point forward, realizing the need to preserve their lives.

It had become obvious to each individual, and to all corporately; they had been chosen, and now had been sent out by the Holy Spirit.

Joseph looked around at his fellow travelers, and noted the friendships blossoming in the midst of great difficulty.

His niece, Mary, who had been his ward since the death of her parents in early childhood. He had taken care of her until she had married Joseph of Nazareth. Those not in her family knew her as the mother of Jesus.

Salome, Mary's sister, and wife of Zebedee; mother to James and John of the twelve. Her hand-maid, Sarah, was with them.

Philip, another of the twelve, who had traveled with Jesus, and then served the Jerusalem Ecclesia with Stephen. He was now separated from his wife, Tahlia, and four daughters.

Simon Zealotes, who had also travelled with Jesus. He had experienced an entire changing of his life's motivation and personal sense of destiny when he had accepted and believed in Jesus' true identity. A zealot, his purpose in joining the twelve had at first matched that of Judah the Sicari. But unlike Judah, somewhere along the line, he had chosen the True Source of power.

Eleazar, whose Latin name was Lazarus, who had been raised from the dead, by Jesus, in the town of Bethany.

Miriam, whose Latin name was Martha, sister to Lazarus. She had welcomed Jesus and the seventy disciples into her home in Bethany. Her hand-maid, Marcella, was with them.

Mary Magdalene, sister to Lazarus and Martha. She had been the first person to see Jesus after his resurrection. She had travelled with Jesus since the beginning of his ministry, when he had cast seven demons out of her being. She and several other women had stayed with the company during the Master's three-year ministry, supporting all of them many times from her own purse. Simon Peter often referred to her as "the first apostle to the apostles."

Zaccheus, who had formerly lived as a dishonest tax-collector, in the service of Rome. Jesus had come to his home for a meal, and changed his life. So much so, he had repaid those he had cheated seven-fold.

"Little Mary," daughter of Cleophas, and step-daughter to Mary, the mother of Jesus.

Joanna, whose husband, Chuza, served in Herod's palace as a steward. Joanna had been with Salome and Mary Magdalene in Joseph's garden tomb the morning Jesus' resurrection had been discovered.

Maximin, who had been a synagogue ruler. He had run after Jesus and asked which commandment was the greatest. Zebedee's John had nicknamed him "the rich, young ruler."

Uri BenLevi, the former crippled beggar who had been healed at the Temple's Beautiful Gate in Jerusalem when Simon Peter and John were heading for a prayer gathering.

Sidonius, who had been born blind. Jesus had healed him by placing mud on his eyes, and instructing him to wash in Jerusalem's Pool of Siloam. The sockets where eyes had not existed were filled with new eyes which could see clearly.

Simeon, the dark-skinned man from Cyrene, who had helped the Master to carry his cross the day he died. He was now separated from his wife, Ramona, and his two sons, Rufus and Alexander.

Clementos Romanus, who had been visiting with Simon Peter, and somehow ended up at the Temple that day. Most of the company in the ship referred to him simply as Clement.

Clemon, who had been travelling with Clement.

Trophimus, who had served in the Jerusalem Ecclesia. He was a strong man, with a heart to serve.

Eutropius, Martial and Saturninus....

Shira, Libi, and Sarah....

There were so many more in this group, he considered. It would be interesting to see what the future held.

An adventure had begun.

He realized now; he would never return to Jerusalem.

Late that afternoon, something rare took place. A royal recreational vessel sailed through the waterway common to the little ship of refugees. It belonged to the Roman governor of the African province. As the great vessel sailed by, the governor's young daughter spied the floating little.

"Tata! Tata!" she cried. "We have to stop our boat!"

The governor, widowed the year before, was in the habit of responding to his child's every wish. Powered by hired galley oarsmen and sails, the large ship came about and dropped anchor.

"Can you send up a spokesperson?" the first mate called.

After a few moments deliberation, Joseph of Arimathea was chosen to board the ship and speak to the governor. Upon discovering Joseph's identity as the Nobilius Decurio, the governor made the assumption the group had suffered a shipwreck, and were drifting in a damaged boat.

He promptly gave orders for a tow rope to be provided, and attached to the back of his vessel. The ship's crew attached two ropes, which provided stability the group aboard had not yet experienced.

"I can take you as far as Cyrene, near Carthage," he offered. "We are just three days' journey away. I have a home there. We are putting in for more provisions, and meeting my brother, before we set sail to Hippo. I can put you in touch with a shipbuilder when we reach port."

Joseph was grateful. "That would be wonderful, sir," he replied. "We have been drifting for three months now."

"How have you survived?" the amazed governor inquired.

"We have caught rainwater from the sky, and fish from the sea," Joseph answered, with a smile. "We are glad just to have had all remain alive."

"The gods were certainly with you," the governor answered. "That is truly amazing. Raw fish? Just raw fish? We will have to see about that. Let me see what our cooks might have left in the galley. I'm sure we have some bread we could share."

Joseph was overjoyed.

A little over an hour later, the weary group of refugees was giving thanks, laughing and talking together, as a rather large basket of bread, cheese and fruit was passed from person to person. Also in the basket were water-skins and an ampora of wine.

Shira looked behind the boat. "Look," she told Libi. "Our boat is creating a wake. That means we are now moving faster than the current!"

Libi smiled excitedly. "We will be landing somewhere soon, then."

"I think so!" Shira answered, taking a bite of bread. "Somehow, I think I will be staying away from raw fish for a while."

That night, the passengers aboard the great Roman ship were serenaded by the singing of the refugees inside the little boat.

For the first time in more than ninety days, each person was feeling hope.

Yes, there would be a future after all.

In Jerusalem, Annas was inspecting the newly emptied palace of the High Priest. His own son, Jonathan, had been appointed as High Priest by the Roman governor's new assistant, Marcellus. He and his family would be moving into the house this afternoon.

Joseph and Nitza had left by wagon this morning. It would be a long trip to get to Beth-Shemesh, where their son, Joshua, served as ruler of the synagogue. In fact, the Caiaphas family still lived there, with many members spread out over the valley of Elah, in the Shephelah region.

Nitza had finally smiled when she heard Annas speaking of her grand-daughter, Mariamne.

Annas cried when he had said goodbye to his daughter.

It was probable, he realized, he would never see either of them again.

On the road from the city, Joseph winced each time the wagon wheels went over a bump.

He had been stabbed six times the night of his attack.

Apparently, he had cried out in pain when the first blade cut through him. The household steward, Micah, had heard a noise and looked out through the shutters. He had seen five men running away from a hooded man they had attacked in front of the house. He had run outside to help the man, and discovered it was Joseph.

Nitza had immediately sent for a physician.

It was Luke who had treated and bound up the man's wounds. The entire time, he had prayed with Nitza in the language of angels. Micah, now also a follower of Jesus as well, had joined with them.

Caiaphas couldn't remember anything about that evening. He had even forgotten the scroll, and what had been written on it. Dumbfounded, he had listened when Annas read it to him the next morning.

"I'm not High Priest?" he asked, not once but many times.

Each time, Nitza answered him carefully. "No, my love. Not anymore."

That had been ten days ago.

Today, they had departed from the home where their children had been raised. Now refugees themselves, they would begin again, in a new place, with different responsibilities. It would take time to adjust to a new place, they realized, but they were willing.

"At least we are alive," Joseph told her.

About one hundred and seventy miles north of Jerusalem, a caravan of men, travelling on horseback, headed toward the Syrian border. They had been traveling for almost two weeks now, camping by the side of the road each night. From all appearances, they were merchants, in route to the northern cities of Syria, perhaps even Pontus near the Black Sea.

All were dressed in traveling attire, except for the leader.

He was obviously a Jewish priest. He seemed focused, intent on his travel, his thoughts elsewhere. Occasionally, he shouted an order to the men behind him, and they would respond.

For an observer of details, this group was different from many traders seen in the area. They did not speak to each other, except in the midst of their evening meals around the campfire. During the day, it was obvious they were determined; resolved on a unified purpose.

At second glance, the leader drew attention. It was curious, indeed, to see a priest in the presence of men involved in an apparent mission.

Yes, the man was unique.

In his saddlebags, he carried authorizations from the Temple in Jerusalem. He would show these to the rulers of every synagogue in Damascus. These documents would give him permission to arrest all members of the Ecclesia in Damascus, using any method of force he chose; seizing their property in the name of the Temple; bringing all of them back to Jerusalem in chains for execution.

Saul of Tarsus was tired of traveling. He had forgotten how far away Damascus was from Jerusalem. Oh well, they were less than a mile away now.

Saul was fervent in his passion. He was dedicated to serving ElShaddai with all of his heart, soul, mind and strength. He wanted to see the Plan and Purposes of God come into reality.

He was ready to begin his mission. Damascus would be the first place where he had been trusted to take his Purification Team, without having to report back to the Temple each evening.

It felt good to be trusted, he considered. He would be sure to pray. Surely this would seal his reward with ElShaddai.

Saul considered his good fortune. He had advanced quickly in leadership for a man of his young age.

Suddenly, and without warning, a force like a bolt of lightning stretched out of the clear sky. All around the company, the earth shuddered. Horses reared and bolted. Men were thrown from their mounts.

Saul found himself on the ground.

Just ahead, in the roadway, a brilliant, blue-white light shone, illuminating the entire area. From his crouched position on the ground, Saul squinted, shielding his eyes. He looked up, trying to peer into the center from which the light still streamed. In the middle of its brilliance was the form of a man. Afraid, the priest looked away, checking to see if his companions were also experiencing the same incident.

They seemed dazed, confused. He looked back toward the light.

A voice emerged from the man in the center of the brilliant beam. "Saul! *Saul!* Why are you persecuting *me*?" he cried.

As he spoke, the light grew even more intense. Saul could not tear his eyes away.

"Who are you, Lord?" he asked. Hadn't he heard this voice before, he wondered? But where? He couldn't quite place who it belonged to.

The man answered. "I am Jesus," he said. "By hurting my Body, you are persecuting me!"

The strength of the light's burning stream, suddenly struck at Saul's inner core. Was this *real?* Was he having a *vision?*

Jesus spoke once more. Saul was startled by the kind compassion as well as strength he sensed emanating from the risen man's being. "Go into the city, and you will be told what to do."

Then, just as abruptly as it appeared, Jesus and the light around him disappeared. Struggling to stand, Saul realized he could not see. He reached his hands out in front of himself.

"I can't see anything!" he cried. "Help me!"

He flailed around, until his hands came into contact with one of his companions. "Who are you?" he asked, desperately grabbing the man's arm.

"This is Gilad," the man answered. "What has happened to you?"

Saul was in a form of shock. "Did you hear the voice? Did you see the light?" he asked.

"*I* didn't see a light," Gilad replied. "But we all heard the *voice* speaking. Who is Jesus? Is that the man whose followers we have been assigned to bring to Jerusalem?"

Stunned with the beginnings of revelation and understanding, Saul nodded. "He said to go into the city, and I will be told what to do."

"I heard," responded Gilad. "We will help you get to a place of safety in Damascus."

Gilad remounted his own horse. Then, he helped Saul back into his saddle. Placing the priest's hands on the leather for balance, Gilad took hold of Saul's reins. He pulled ahead to lead the priest's horse into the city.

Reuben, another soldier, mounted his horse and moved in behind the two men. "I'll go with you, Gilad," he stated. "That way you have someone with you on the return ride."

"Thanks," Gilad replied. He spoke to the rest of the company. "I don't think we will be doing anything tonight," he announced. "Priest Saul is now blind. We are going to take him into Damascus and get him some help. Set up camp here. Reuben and I will be back after we find him a place to stay."

Grumbling broke out as the small, private army, once more dismounted, and began to make preparations for an overnight stay.

In Capernaum, Simon Peter was teaching a class in the large room added to his home. As of late, his life had settled into a somewhat predictable pattern. At night, he and his sons fished, providing income for the family. In the afternoons, he taught classes to those who wished to learn of Jesus, and how the Master had taught his followers to live.

For the past weeks, Zebedee's brother, Joses, had joined him for classes, although no one referred to Joses by his given name anymore. He was now consistently answering to "Barnabas," a nickname meaning "the son of encouragement." For the past few months, Zebedee's nephew, John Marcus, had also been visiting from Jerusalem. Ampliatus' son was fascinated by Barnabas' stories of his exile on the island of Cyprus.

Today, Simon Peter was sharing the account of Jesus' healing of a man with leprosy. It was strange, John Marcus considered, how when Peter told the story, a person felt like they were there, experiencing life with Jesus all over again.

Many in Capernaum had begun referring to Simon Peter as "The Big Fisherman." The nickname had begun in Jerusalem, but now, it seemed to have followed the man to his hometown.

Having followed Jesus in his early years, John Marcus remembered the story Simon Peter was sharing. He closed his eyes, and could picture the situation, just as if it were happening at that very moment.

"I remember that," Ignatius whispered to John Marcus. "Weren't we together that day?"

John Marcus nodded. "We always seemed to find mischief, didn't we?"

376

Barnabas leaned over to him. "We really need to write down Peter's stories about Jesus, Marcus," he confided. "He remembers some things that Matthew didn't. The way Peter tells shares the accounts, it's like I'm there with Jesus.... Right now.... He talks so freely about the power of God."

"I was thinking how we need to write down the things he's been saying just this morning," John Marcus responded. "The codex of Matthew's remembrance is being recopied for the new Ecclesias springing up. Why not tell the story from Peter's viewpoint as well?"

Barnabas smiled. "That's exactly what I was thinking, my boy," he answered. "You are a gifted scribe, at your young age. You could write down what Simon is saying, and then we can put the accounts in order later."

"I think that might be what I've been searching for, what I can do to help in the Ecclesia. It would mean a lot to me," John Marcus responded.

"And to the rest of us," Barnabas nodded. "Let's get some tools together and some papyri as soon as we are finished with this meeting."

"That's a great idea," said the younger man enthusiastically. "You will help me too, won't you?"

In the late morning, the Roman governor of the province of Cyrenaica, sailed his recreational vessel into the Cyrene harbor. The hired galley-men, who had powered the great ship with oars, were immediately given food and water.

Hired galley-men were among the highest paid workers in the Empire.

As members of the crew of the great ship lowered the anchor and sails, dock workers attached the great ship to its moorings, and pulled the smaller craft next to the quay as well. Slowly, those who had been cramped into the small boat, straightened from stiffness, seeking freedom from the survival positions they each had held for more than three months.

Joseph stretched. His legs were painful. He looked around at the rest of his company. Each one was taking tiny steps, seeking to restore flexible movement to their limbs. As he walked, he realized the smell emanating from his body. Suddenly aware, he assessed himself and his companions. Not one had bathed in more than a hundred days. And, although they had sought to help each other in daily waste elimination, he realized, it was ludicrous to think anyone among them were without the residues of excrement on their garments.

He noticed the streaks of dirt on the faces of his Mary and her older sister, Salome. How tired they looked! His eyes went to the faces of the others.

Magdalene, Martha and Joanna were in deep conversation, looking around the shops near the docks. Martial and Sidonius were seated on the dock, with their feet dangling over the side.

These were the courageous! How far they had come!

What was Abba Father planning?

His heart skipped a beat, in anticipation and excitement to learn what God had in store.

"Help us, Jesus," he prayed. "Show us each the next step, please. I don't want to miss your plan…"

A few moments later, the first mate from the governor's ship approached Joseph where he still stood on the docks.

"Are you Joseph?" the man asked.

Joseph looked up to meet his gaze. "Yes, I am Joseph," he answered. "How can I help you?"

The seaman shook his head. "Oh no, sir, not me," he replied. "The governor wants to see you. He said you should come to his ship this evening, with all of your friends, as soon as you have had a chance to clean up."

His mental fog lifting slightly, Joseph smiled. "Thank you! We will be there this evening," he answered. "Please thank him for the invitation… And what is your name?"

"I am Nassef," he responded. Surprised, he smiled.

Joseph repeated his name. "Nassef, can I ask you to help me with something?"

"That's why the captain sent me," he answered. "He knew you and your people would have needs, and might be a little lost."

The priest laughed. "That is absolutely true, my friend! Let me ask you to run a couple of errands for me, while I am taking care of my people?"

Nassef nodded. "Sure. What do you need?" he answered willingly.

The two men went into detailed conversation, at the close of which Nassef moved into the mainstream of traffic on the columned street. "I will see you soon," he said.

"Yes, you will," the priest agreed.

As the messenger walked away, Joseph called to his companions. "Everyone! Come and gather here with me. We need to meet together."

Hearing his voice, the group began to assemble themselves around Joseph. Looking down, he found a wooden box on which to stand. He stepped up on it, so he could be seen, heard, and understood.

"Is everyone still here? Simeon?" he looked through the crowd until he found the African. There he was, next to Uri BenLevi.

"Right here!" Simeon answered.

"Good," said Joseph. He turned his attention once more to the entire group. "I have an announcement to make. It's taken me a few moments to gain my footings, so I am sorry for the delay. We have been invited to dine with the governor on his ship this evening."

A joyous murmur rippled its way through the group, followed immediately by comments of concern.

Joseph glanced at Simeon. The two men chuckled. They had been in conversation for several days about this very moment. Joseph raised his hands, motioning for silence.

"Let me help you a little," he said. "I have a small home here in Cyrene. I have used it many times on business. It has a bathing area. I think you ladies might like to use it to rest and refresh yourselves. I have sent someone to gather the couple who serve as my stewards here in the city, and they will help you."

Relieved responses were heard, along with a few giggles.

Joseph continued. "Simeon, who is among us, has parents who live just outside the city. He has graciously offered to take the men to his childhood home, where you will also be able to bathe and rest. We all need to meet back here just before dusk this evening."

"Uncle Joseph?" Salome asked, standing next to him. "Will you be resting as well?"

Amused, the priest chuckled at her. He put his arm around his niece, giving her a squeeze. "I have a few errands to run, and then I will join the men at Simeon's parents' home," he told her with a sideways glance. "Thanks for being concerned."

As they were speaking, an older man and woman joined the small company from the street. They were accompanied by the Nassef.

"Master Joseph!" the man cried, incredulously. "We had no idea you were coming this way!" He moved forward to greet his employer with a hug.

"Cynifrid!" came the reply. "To be honest, I had no idea I was coming, either." He smiled at the woman. "It's good to see you, Romilda."

She smiled, and then pinched her nose, raising her eyebrows. "Welcome home, sir," she replied, with an involuntary frown. It was obvious the odor accompanying the group had overpowered her senses.

Laughter erupted from the group.

Cynifrid smiled. "It looks like all of you had a surprise voyage."

"I will fill you in," the priest told him. "It's a rather long story." He looked around at the company. "For now, though, we have all been invited to dinner on the governor's ship this evening. We have each gained a stench, and probably look as disheveled as we feel. I have asked the ladies to return to my home with you and Romilda. If you will help them, please. Each one of them has had a difficult experience. Take good care of them for me."

Cynifrid nodded, but it was Romilda who spoke. "Absolutely," she answered. "May I enlist a few others to help me?"

Joseph smiled. "As you usually do, Romilda, do your best."

"Well then," she replied. She looked at her husband. "Will you guide them, and I will gather what we will need?"

Cynifrid exchanged a glance with Joseph. "Thanks a lot, sir," he jibed. "You just had to give her a free hand as soon as you arrived, didn't you? There will be no living with her now....."

Joseph slapped him on the back. "You'll be fine, my friend," he chuckled.

Cynifrid smiled good-naturedly. "Ladies, if you will come with me," he invited with raised voice, "we will go to the apartments of the Nobilius Decurio of Rome."

For her part, Romilda was scurrying about the marketplace. She first hired two older boys to help her carry items home. She then went to a local slave vendor, where she rented seven ladies' maids, giving specific skills be provided by their services. Next, she arranged for a selection of *amporas* of sweet wines, as well as baskets of fruit, cheese, breads and lighter foods to be delivered to Joseph's home. Then, she purchased fragrant cleansing oils, *datuns* (or Neem tree twigs for cleaning teeth and breath), as well as several bars of *nitre*, (a fat-based soap).

Finally, she purchased twenty sets of women's clothing, and asked a shoe merchant to send a selection of sandals to Joseph's home.

And everywhere she went, the charges were signed for by the stewards of the Nobilius Decurio.

After Simeon arrived at his parents' home, his mother sent two house slaves to the marketplace to make similar arrangements for the men, per Joseph's specific instructions.

These charges were also signed for in the name of the Nobilius Decurio.

It had been the hand of God, Joseph considered, he had been allowed to maintain his holdings. How merciful of ElShaddai to bless him with belongings, that he would be enabled to care for these desperate souls! Once again, he gave thanks for his financial steward, Janaus.

Before heading to Simeon's family home, he stopped at the largest inn in Cyrene, and made arrangements for each member of the party to be housed for the evening. He also informed the owners that some of the refugees would be staying at the inn over the winter season. After all, he reasoned, it would take at least a couple of months for the modifications required to be completed on the small ship.

And not everyone would want to remain in Cyrene, or travel on with him.

It was a perfect time of year, he realized. Those who wished to return to their homeland, could do so, booking a passage before the winter arrived. Those who wished to stay, or travel to other destinations, could also do so and arrive safely before cold weather would make travel dangerous.

His own final errand was to purchase clothing and sandals for himself.

He was confident Simeon's parents had taken care of the details in caring for his friends, in regard to food and clothing.

With clothing in hand, he entered a private bath-house in the city, designated for male Roman government officials. He washed, received a massage, and bathed. Within the bath-house was a barber shop, operated by slaves. Here the priest received a trim, his hair and beard groomed for the first time in six months.

After his bath, Joseph visited the bank in the center of the city, where he created several dispatches. In his letter to Felix, his financial agent in Pompeii, he described his current situation, and explained he would be living in Cyrene for now. All correspondence should be sent to him at his address in the city. He sent a similar letter to his representatives in Jerusalem.

Finally, he sent a letter to Arviragus, the king of the Dumnoni, with whom he shared two grandchildren. He knew he would be visiting his old friend sometime in the near future.

As he wrote, images from the dream he had experienced some months prior, repeated their presence in his mind.

By late afternoon, Joseph arrived at Simeon's parents' home, where he found solace in an outdoor settee, and for an hour or so, fell fast asleep.

Across town, Cynifrid and Romilda were caring for the thirty-four women who had been on board the small vessel. Throughout the entire house, female voices and laughter could be heard.

"It's like having the children at home again," she confided to her husband.

"Yes, but ten times louder," he shouted to her across a room so he could be heard.

"It's like they've just been released from a prison cell," she muttered, "and they haven't seen each other in weeks! Still, it is pleasant to see each of them so happy."

As the women bonded that afternoon, many realized this was the first time since their abduction months prior, when anyone had felt a sense of safety. It was so good to have one's feet on solid ground again.

Relief was also part of the emotional expressions of these women.

Finally dressed and readied for the evening's events, Shira sat in the small courtyard near the household's private well. As she considered the past months, the young woman thought back to an afternoon a few weeks prior, when Libi had tried to climb out of the small boat, seeking to drown her inward torment; ending her life in the Mediterranean.

"No one will miss me," a sorrowful Libi confided to Shira and Salome. "I have lost everything. Please. Just let me go into the water and die."

The older woman had hugged her. "Nothing doing," she had answered. "*I* would miss you…. And besides, you are in the perfect place for a brand new beginning!"

Salome had taken Libi under her wing from that moment forward… and Shira too. Mary Magdalene and Martha had also been drawn into their conversations. Why had Abba Father allowed this to happen to them? Had they been disobedient to him in some way? Was the way people had treated her when she was growing up an indication of how God felt about her? What was the right thing to believe, she wanted to know? Should she hold onto what her mind remembered from Jesus' teachings, or to what her emotions spoke in the middle of the night?

Were her emotions wrong?

What was truth?

What was right?

"Emotions change," Salome told them. "They are based in my own sense of comfort, and in my circumstances. If my station is good, then my emotions tell me everything is fine. But if my circumstances are difficult, my emotions try to overshadow the love of Abba Father, seeking to convince me I am alone. And didn't Jesus promise to always be with us, no matter what happens?"

"But isn't that just making myself act out a lie?" Libi asked.

Magdalene laughed. "Not really," she answered. "When I am struggling with being selfish, it can feel that way. It's reminding myself what the truth really is. I can remember a lot of times in my life when circumstances in my life were telling me to just give up; that there was nothing left. But then, when my circumstances changed, my emotions told me that life was worth living again."

Martha added, "Truth doesn't change, no matter what my circumstances *or* my emotions tell me."

Libi looked at them strangely. She had never considered her life this way before. "So then," she asked, "are you saying there are two parts of me, and only one part of me wants the right thing? That I have to choose which part I believe?"

"That's it," Salome told her. "When I became a follower of Jesus, it became important to me to live my life with his example in mind. My own emotions tend to complain, and get offended. One part of me wants to take care only of myself, and the other part wants to obey Abba Father. When I listen to the Holy Spirit, he teaches me how to live the way Jesus did. When I decide to obey him, my emotions follow."

"But I don't know what the Holy Spirit says. I don't hear him," Libi protested. "Am I supposed to?"

Salome smiled. "Jesus told us we would know his voice when we follow him. Have you opened your heart to the Holy Spirit?"

"I don't know," Libi replied. "But I want to."

"Just tell him. Talk to the Holy Spirit. He is a person, just like Abba Father, and Jesus. His purpose is to explain Jesus to us. When he is filling you, and teaching you, he will speak inside your heart, and give you direction."

At that point, Shira asked a question. "Has anyone prayed with you to experience Jesus' baptism with the Holy Spirit?"

Libi shook her head.

Shira looked at Salome inquisitively.

The older woman smiled, and looked around the circle. "You want to pray right now, Libi?" she asked.

"I would," she replied.

And so, they had prayed together, first in the languages of men, and then, as the Holy Spirit enabled them, in the language of angels; in the middle of the Mediterranean Sea. And the Presence of the Holy Spirit had visited them all, in the small ship.

Libi had been free of depression since that day.

She too, had prayed in the language of angels.

Now, Shira could hear her friend's laughter from another room.

How had the Holy Spirit made such a change in her, she wondered?

Have you made changes like that in me as well, Holy Spirit, she asked inwardly? She hadn't recognized how greatly she had questioned her own personal significance, until this very moment.

Then, she waited, as the realization became real.

Unexpectedly, a sense of peace washed over her. She was reminded of instances and attitudes she had carried before knowing Jesus. Somehow, they were contrasted with her present values. Yes, there had been change.

She was encouraged.

Her thoughts returned to the women inside, who were readying themselves for the evening's dinner. A stranger might have thought they had not seen each other in weeks!

Two of the rented ladies' maids were working to massage the pain out of stiff joints and backs. Four were helping with clothing selection, bathing, haircuts, manicures, and facials. The one remaining was serving the ladies refreshments.

It wasn't long before Libi was finished with the procedures, and came looking for Shira. "I feel so much better," she cried. "What a wonderful spa Romilda created for us! I've never had such a wonderful time!"

Looking up at her friend, Shira said, "Let's find somewhere to rest for a few moments? You want to?"

"Oh, yes," Libi answered.

And so it was the two friends found a quiet corner in the outdoor courtyard, to try to take a short nap.

"Just a few minutes," Shira told her friend. "I just need a few minutes. It feels so good to be clean again."

But Libi didn't hear her. Her head was resting on a pillow; eyes closed; breathing deep and even; already sleeping soundly in a place of badly needed rest.

In Galilee, Zebedee was working in the outdoor kitchen in his Capernaum home. John was nearby, reading through a codex of Matthew's account of the life of Jesus.

"Abba," he said, "can I ask you something?"

Zebedee was chopping vegetables for the evening meal. "Sure," he answered.

"Can you tell me what it was like to watch Jesus grow up as a child? I didn't see him the way I do now. Was he always doing miracles? When did he start to be the Promised Deliverer, and stop being your nephew?"

His father stopped working, and wiped his hands dry on the hand towel on the table top. He looked at his son thoughtfully.

"He was always my nephew. He was a baby. He was a toddler. He was a little boy. He was always responsive, and wise beyond his years. But the miracles didn't begin until after he was filled with the Holy Spirit; when the dove came upon him during his baptism. I remember when Joseph and Mary left Jerusalem after Passover the year he was twelve. He went to the Temple, and ended up going home with the priest, Judah, and his son, Simon. (We know Simon as Simon the Leper, whom Jesus healed.) Jesus was with the priests and elders for three days before they found him. At first, Mary was angry. She thought he was being disobedient."

"*Was* he being disobedient?" John asked.

"No," Zebedee chuckled. "Matthew wrote about it in his codex. We assumed he was with us. So that was *our* error. But he went to his *Father's* house; the Temple. When Joseph chided him, he said, 'don't you want me to be doing my Father's business?'"

John smiled. "You have thought about all of these things for a long time, haven't you?"

"I have held many things," his father answered. "Someday we should talk more about it. But Jesus' life was always filled with the evidences of Holy Spirit. I remember thinking about the depth in his eyes, even when he was a child. He was different from other children. Completely."

There were a few moments of silence.

"Abba?" John asked.

"Yes?" he answered.

"Do you miss Mom?"

Zebedee looked at his son, his eyes welling up. "I do," he answered. "I wish I had gone to the Temple with her that day."

"No," John told her. "It would have been too much for you. I'm glad you didn't go."

"We all miss her," the older fisherman said wistfully. "I wish she was here."

"Me too," John sighed.

Zebedee turned and picked up his chopping knife once more, returning to the preparation for the evening's meal.

385

It was the following morning when Joseph made his way to the shipyard in Cyrene for a scheduled meeting. The owner was a dark, swarthy man of Macedonian descent, from the city of Philippi.

His name was Duruk. As he approached the dock, he stopped to remove his turban and wipe sweat from his forehead. Looking up, he saw Joseph waiting. "I seem to sweat more and more the longer I live here," he panted. "How are you Master Joseph? When we are finished here, we need to go over the specifications for the new merchant ship you commissioned last year. We have the hull finished. We are ready to know what you want in the storage areas, and the galley areas."

Joseph smiled, patting his old friend on the back. "Thank you, Duruk. I'm sure your men have done a tremendous job, as usual."

He paused, and pointed to the ship without a sail.

"This is why I asked you to meet me here," he said. "Some friends of mine were in this little ship for many days. I would like to see what we can do to make it usable."

"I will have to get it out of the water," the shipbuilder was saying. "That's the only way to tell if we will be able to do what you want."

"That's fine," Joseph told him. "I anticipate it will take a few months to outfit it properly."

Duruk looked at him. "It's obvious whoever put this vessel on the sea did not expect the passengers to survive. Look! There are no oar mounts, or even benches! Who built this? There are no sails!!" Incredulous, he looked back at Joseph. "Who builds a boat with no sails? Or rudder?"

He paused, looking at Joseph in deep thought. "Were you on this boat, sir?" he asked.

"I was," came the answer.

"Who would dare to…," Duruk began, and then caught himself.

"It doesn't matter," Joseph answered. "My God is taking care of my needs. I am here, as you see, and so are my friends."

"Did anyone die in the journey?"

"Not one," the priest answered.

Duruk's mouth hung open. "It is a miracle," he whispered. "Who did this to you?"

Joseph smiled. "Let's just say I am no longer part of the Jewish Sanhedrin. We came to a difference of opinion on some matters of importance."

The shipbuilder nodded. "I have heard stories of riots in the last couple of years. And someone told me about a ship like this put on the Mediterranean. That they kidnapped over seventy people, who they now think are dead. They said these people all had become followers of a man who claimed to be their Promised Deliverer. The rulers were angry because the belief, "The Way," was becoming too popular. Is that true? Did *you* hear about the Galilean they crucified?"

"I did."

"Is it true he rose from the dead?"

"It is," the priest answered. "He was buried in my own tomb."

Silence hung in the air for a moment. Then Duruk spoke quietly. "This is that ship, isn't it?"

"It is."

"And the people who came here were the ones sent away."

"We were."

"I would like to hear more," Duruk said earnestly. "Could we speak later?"

"Absolutely," Joseph replied. He noticed Duruk was still assessing the small ship. "I consider this little boat a gift. I would hate to see it go to waste. Other than the obvious difficulties, does it look sound from what you can tell?"

Duruk pursed his lips, walking from one end of the boat to the other. "Mmm," he said. "I think we could make it work for you. I'll have it put in dry-dock so we can get to work on it." He looked at Joseph. "I assume you want sails and riggings, benches, shade, storage, oars, rudder…. Anything else?"

Joseph shook his head. "That should be good," he answered. "We will put into ports to rest along the way, after we leave here."

"I'll have some drawings for you, say, by the end of the week?" the shipbuilder offered.

"That would be wonderful, Duruk," Joseph told him. "Would you like to come by my home here in Cyrene sometime tomorrow morning? If you want to know more about Jesus, I would love to have you meet some of my friends, and hear their stories."

Duruk was overjoyed. "Thank you! I will see you tomorrow."

That evening, the entire company met together, after eating together in Joseph's home.

Assuming the leadership role, Joseph spoke to the group.

"Friends, we have come through a difficult time, and I know we are all thankful to ElShaddai for bringing us through. Does anyone have something you would like to share?"

One by one, several members of the group shared their experiences of the past two days. Some told of experiences showing the hand of God in their day; some told of relationships promising an opportunity to share the truth of Jesus; others were simply thankful to be alive.

At the close of the sharing time, Joseph spoke once more. Passing a plate of unleavened bread, and a small, blue bowl filled with new wine, he began an invitation.

"When Jesus was alive, he told us to remember him, by sharing bread and wine, the way he did on the night before he died. These are symbols; the bread of his body, the wine of his blood. Now, they also remind us of the power of his resurrection. We experienced the power of His Spirit sustaining our lives as we journeyed here. We all know in our hearts that without that sustaining, we really would be dead. We had no rudder, no sails, no oars, no shade, no water, no food.

And yet, unexpectedly, unexplainably, here we are.

"It would appear Jesus is not finished with any of us. Apparently, each of us have a new adventure ahead. For my own part, I am seeking him for direction.

"I am going to celebrate the Lord's Supper with you, and then I will fast for three days and nights. I am going to ask God what He has prepared for my life, and how I am to proceed. All I know at the moment, is that I am to have the small ship outfitted for travel. At this time, though, I don't know why. It was like that with the tomb in our Jerusalem house. Eshca and I had a tomb on our estate in Arimathea, but we sensed we were supposed to carve out the cave in the garden. Later, it became Jesus' tomb.

"Each of you have a story. It is not finished. God is writing your story. What will be your next adventure? I invite you to join with me in my fast. Pray and seek God for the next step in your own journey. Jesus said we would go into all of the world with the good news of his coming. It appears we have been sent, even if it was unexpectedly."

A ripple of agreement moved across the room.

Joseph continued. "After we break our fast, we will have supper together here. We will meet again, and share what we have received from the Holy Spirit in prayer. We will also share the Lord's Supper once more. If you are unable to fast, Cynifrid and Romilda will have a meal here for you each night. Even if you don't fast, please pray for direction."

As the group parted ways that evening, heading to the city's inn, and Simeon's home, each person found a sense of excitement and anticipation rising in his or her heart.

Inside the house, after everyone had gone, the two sisters, Mary and Salome cornered their uncle. "Do you know where you will be going from here, Uncle?" they asked.

He smiled at them. "I wish I did," he answered. "I thought I was dead several times in the past three years, but now, here we are."

"I just wondered whether you see us as being on short mission, or making a permanent change of address," Mary told him.

Joseph shrugged, and looked at her with a smile. "I can't say that I have a definite answer. But we have been here before, haven't we? For myself, I am finding new areas where I need to trust Him every day."

Mary Magdalene and Martha came into the house from the outdoor courtyard. "I can't wait to see the next step!" Magdalene exclaimed. "Just when I think things are just horrible, Hope arrives!"

Suddenly, Martha hugged Joseph tightly. "Thank you, Joseph! Thank you so much!"

Startled, Joseph looked at her. "Whatever for?" he asked.

"You helped me so much tonight. I needed something to focus on, so I didn't continue to feel sorry for myself," Martha declared. "Thank you, too, for the provisions you have given us."

Characteristically embarrassed, the priest smiled. "I'm thankful I was able to help. Thank you for your heart to help us all as well, Martha."

Magdalene poured herself a cup of water. "Do you mind if I take this to our room with me?" she asked Joseph.

"Oh, I always take water to bed with me," he answered. "So please do! Is your and Martha's room adequate for your needs?"

Martha replied. "Oh, yes," she said. "More than adequate! We are blessed!"

Magdalene nodded in agreement. "I am heading there now, if you all don't mind. I am still catching up on my sleep."

Salome yawned. "As am I." She poured herself a cup of water and prepared to leave the room. Her sister, Mary, followed suit.

Martha looked at her sister. "I'll be there in a minute, sis. I just want to sit under the stars by the well for a little while, if you don't mind."

Joseph stood and poured another cup of water, and headed quietly towards his own bedchamber.

"Good night, ladies," he said gently. It was good to have someone in the house, he realized. He had been alone much of the time in the past few years.

"Sleep well, Uncle," Mary and Salome each replied. "I love you."

"Love you as well."

It was late when Martha retired that night. She knew she would wait for confirmation to come in one form or another, but her path would take her to the west. She didn't know how she would get there, but she knew she would be in a place completely unknown to her.

As Joseph slept, he dreamt once more, as he had during his time spent alone on the estate in Arimathea.

The first night images revisited his first dream some months ago. This time, as he dreamt, however, he sensed a hand on his shoulder, and heard Jesus' Voice explaining what he was seeing.

As before, he stood on the white cliff, in bright sun, overlooking a sandy beach. As in the first dream, the edge of another continent could be seen in the distance over the sea. Somehow, once again, he knew this distant continent was remotely attached to his homeland.

The Voice spoke, "You are about to visit that land, and then you will go to Briton. You will be brought before the kings of the Dumnoni, the Canti, the Regnenses, the Belgae, and the Durotriges. Do not be afraid."

Then, as before, he was no longer on the cliff, but standing in the sailboat.

This time, however, he recognized it as the little ship they had drifted in for three months.

The shadow, originating in the far land, began to fall. When he looked up to find its source, he once more saw an immense, black moon rise and block out the sun. As Joseph watched, he saw the shadow had taken a shape over the land of Briton. It became a solid image filling the entire land where he stood. As far as he could see, the moon had blocked out the sun's rays. All of each land now was hidden in darkness.

The Voice spoke again. "Many of my people have been lost, and have wandered to these lands. They have become deceived and chosen wrong paths. They worship many false gods of darkness rather than the Source of Light."

Again, Joseph watched, and the woman appeared. Dressed in white, at first, he assumed she was working to restore the light. But then, her face drew close to him, and he felt icy fingers around his neck. It was hard to breathe. Her eyes grew black and then turned to glowing red. Her lips grew black, as did her teeth and the inside of her mouth.

The Voice went on. "The worship of the goddess draws many, but brings death. She will try to silence you, but you will prevail. Have no part with her."

Joseph looked down at his hands, and realized he carried his walking stick in his right hand. Still struggling to breathe in his dream, he took his staff with both hands, and drove it down into the ground where he stood. Immediately, the atmosphere exploded into bright light.

"I will do miracles. Don't be afraid."

Again, the priest stood alone inside a mining cavern. He could see veins of tin, silver and copper running through the stone. Inlaid with the metals were precious stones, waiting to be picked up.

He looked once more at his hands, and saw a codex, and a crown.

The Voice he recognized, and had known oh so well, spoke.

"The people are my gold and diamonds. Be patient, and allow my Spirit to form them. Don't be afraid. Mine them well. Teach them. Tend them well. Remember Me."

Then, still dreaming, Joseph sensed himself being lifted up. He could see a huge ball suspended in a night sky. He knew it was the entire earth. Then, from Jerusalem, a flame began to flicker and grow. As it grew, it sent sparks out from its center, with the largest spark landing on the lands where Joseph knew the Dumnoni lived. From Briton, the flame moved northward to a tiny island. Finally, sparks came from that island and lit the entire ball, until it burned white hot with flames. A lion emerged from the flames, and a glowing city appeared in the heavens.

Then the man awoke.

Stunned by the intensity of his dream, he rushed from the bed, to find a clay tablet, or papyrus on which to record the vision he had just seen. The record of his first dream was still in Arimathea.

"Help me to listen, Lord. Please help me to understand," he prayed. As he opened his eyes, they fell upon an old scroll he had left in his apartment more than a year before; the writings of Jeremiah. As he had the night he had first received the vision, he opened the scroll and began to read the same lines of Scripture he had read so many weeks before....

The LORD gave me this message:
"I knew you before I formed you in your mother's womb.
Before you were born I set you apart
and appointed you as my prophet to the nations."
"O Sovereign LORD," I said, "I can't speak for you! I'm too young!"

The LORD replied, "Don't say, 'I'm too young,' for you must go wherever
I send you and say whatever I tell you. And don't be afraid of the people,
for I will be with you and will protect you. I, the LORD, have spoken!"
Then the LORD reached out and touched my mouth and said,
"Look, I have put my words in your mouth!
Today I appoint you to stand up against nations and kingdoms.
Some you must uproot and tear down, destroy and overthrow.
Others you must build up and plant."

Joseph looked up from reading, and smiled. "I think I am beginning to understand now," he said aloud. "Thank you, Lord, for teaching me."

During the days of prayer and fasting, similar experiences to Martha's and Joseph's took place with almost everyone. When the small band gathered together once more, everyone was excited to share what they had received from the Holy Spirit, comparing their experiences.

Philip, who was one of Jesus' twelve disciples, as well as a few others, felt a need to complete a task begun before their kidnapping; the reaching of the Samaritans. This meant the group feeling called in this way, would need to travel home by way of a commercial vessel. They would harbor at Caesarea, travel by land to meet up with family members, and then begin the process of planting an Ecclesia in Samaria.

Trophimus, a young man who had worked in the Jerusalem Ecclesia, then shared he had received a dream of people in a land to the west. He wasn't sure which land it was, but knew its shores were on the Mediterranean Sea. Surprised, Maximus shared a similar experience, as did Eutropius. No sooner had they shared, when others, including Mary Magdalene, and Martha ventured to say they had sensed the same direction, either through a dream, or a non-fading, strong impression which had remained without weakening.

Then Mary spoke. "Uncle Joseph," she said, "the Holy Spirit's instructions to me were to stay with you, wherever you are headed."

"As am I," Salome rejoined.

Sidonius spoke up. "I had a dream, and a man in white told me to follow you; that I was to help you where he sends you."

"I have the same directions," Uri BenLevi declared.

Amazed, Joseph looked at Clementos Romanus, and his friend, Clemon. "What has the Holy Spirit said to you men?"

Clementos responded. "I am to go back Galilee with Philip, and find Simon Peter. My mission awaits with him."

Clemon agreed with a nod. "Me too."

Joseph smiled. He looked around the room. "Who is headed with Philip?"

A group of hands were raised.

"Who is coming with me?"

Another group of hands were raised.

"Is there anyone who is supposed to go to another location, other than these two locations?" Joseph asked.

A few hands went up.

He looked at each one. "What is your destination?"

Simeon of Cyrene answered. "I am supposed to stay here, and send for my wife. I know we are supposed to reach people here in our own country."

"I'm still not sure where I should go," Shira spoke shyly. "Hearing the voice of the Holy Spirit is new to me, and to be truthful, I'm a little afraid. There is nothing left for me in Jerusalem. I want to believe Jesus has something for me, but so much has happened….." Her voice trailed. She looked around. "What does that mean? Am I the only one?" Tears streamed down her face.

Joanna, who was sitting next to her, put her arm around her. "No, you're not the only one, Shira," she soothed. "I am not sure where I am supposed to be either." She looked up at Joseph. "What does that mean; when we don't know?"

"We have time, Joanna," he answered. "I am staying here until the ship is ready, which means we will probably be here through the winter."

"Oh good," Shira breathed out a sigh. She whispered to Joanna. "I was afraid perhaps I wasn't hearing because my father had murdered Jesus. Or because of my husband's part in this whole situation."

"Shira," Joanna whispered the young girl's name reassuringly. "You and I both know that is an accusation against ElShaddai. He made you, and he loves you more than that. He *wants* to help you hear his voice. You'll discover what you are to do. It will come unexpectedly; like it's emerging slowly from a fog. That's what I'm waiting for as well."

Joanna took Shira's hand in her own. "We'll wait together on this. I'll pray for you, and you pray for me. Deal?"

Comforted, Shira looked at her and nodded. "Thank you, Joanna."

As the women had been whispering, the meeting had continued around them. Joseph's mention of the ship's refurbishment generated expressions of curiosity in the room.

He continued. "It is so amazing to me that my grandfather and father chose the shipbuilders here in Cyrene, to construct the merchant vessels for our family's business. How did we just *happen* to harbor here? That being said, my friend, Duruk, is working on a design for those of us who will travel in a few months. Our little ship will be like new, and hopefully, completely different. It will have a rudder, sails, shade and oars, and we will be able to steer into ports on the way, to rest and purchase provisions.

"What is your family's business, Joseph?" Libi asked.

"My family has owned interests in the tin mines past Land's End in Briton, since the days of the Phoenicians, before King David. Because of this, the heir in each generation has become the one in charge of trade. In this present generation, the man in charge seems to be me. God has prospered us. It seems our mines, and the tribes who live in there, are now the only mines willing to trade with the Roman Empire.

"Everyone who works with metals needs tin. Bronze cannot be made without it. Coins are made with this metal as well. Additionally, the Dumnoni tribe only partners with my family. Now, because of Rome's invasion of Briton, the tribe is paid to mine the metals. And, they pay us to ship what they sell. Working together has blessed us all."

"He will not tell you this," Simeon began, "but Joseph also carries a title with the Roman government. Seneca said, 'it is difficult to become a Roman Senator, but it is almost impossible to become a Decurio.' This humble man who stands here, helping all of us without complaint, has the title Nobilius Decurio of Rome. He is an esteemed counselor to Caesar himself, and many other kings."

Shira was confused. "How were you a member of the Sanhedrin? Are you allowed to do both?" she asked.

"I was born to this. I did not have a choice," Joseph replied. "And yes, I am allowed; it didn't really become a threat to my own countrymen, until Rome annexed Judea into the Empire. Your father and I began to have conflict after that."

"You said your family was running the business," Libi asked. "Did you lose your family when they kidnapped you, like we did?"

Joseph smiled wryly. "My family is gone somewhat at this point. To tell the truth, Jesus was, or is, rather, my great-nephew." He pointed to his nieces, who were sitting together.

"Mary, his mother, is my niece. She and Salome are sisters, from my own sister, Anne. When Anne and her husband died years ago, I took Mary as my own child. That's why Jesus was buried in the garden tomb at my home in

Jerusalem. My friend, Nicodemus, and I buried him, with a little help from Pontius Pilate, and Salome's husband, Zebedee."

"Life changed for me, as it did for all of us, when Jesus rose from the dead. I am the last member of my family's direct line. I have no son, but my daughter, Anne, is married and has a son. I don't know what will happen to the business now, or in the future." He looked around the room, his eyes ending their gaze with Shira and Libi. "I hope that helps explain things a little."

Both girls nodded.

They had had no idea the quiet man who gently encouraged all of them, guided them, fed them, and cared for them had been carrying such great responsibilities all this time; and lived with the history of such deep pain.

Yet, this man was always so concerned for everyone else. He had always put the concerns of those around him ahead of his own.

As she listened to Joseph sharing, Shira fell into deep thought. Spending the past few months in the small ship had changed her, she realized.

Caiaphas, her father, had always been more concerned for his own plans. She had drawn the conclusion, even in childhood, her own needs were not important. It was clear to everyone, her father's wishes had to be the center of her world. There was no surviving otherwise.

She had been afraid of him for many years, hopping around to avoid his anger. Later, she had resented him, doing her best to stay out of his way.

Stay quiet and invisible – that had become her motto.

Now, she realized, she had viewed Saul the same way.

And, he had treated her the same way her father had treated her mother. Watching Joseph of Arimathea now, though; she considered the difference between the two priests; men named Joseph. She had never met a man who cared for others without persuasive charm, or personal agenda.

Or even strings attached.

Was this what Salome had meant in telling her that Jesus came to show people how to live in God's love?

"I have so much to learn," she said quietly. "Holy Spirit, would you teach me?"

A Voice spoke into her reverie.

I will.

In the Syrian city of Damascus, a confused Saul sat in darkness. It had been three days since his companions had abandoned him here. They had delivered the letters from the Sanhedrin to the synagogue rulers in the city, and left him in the hands of one of them; a priest named Judah.

Was the blindness permanent? Would he heal in a few days?

He was afraid.

And no one knew an answer.

Galad, and the other men on his Purification Team had heard the Voice speaking just before Saul fell off his horse. They looked around, trying to find a man hiding behind the rocks, or the trees.

There was no one to be found.

Then, after waiting a day, it had become obvious Saul would be blind for a much longer time. His eyes had suddenly glazed over, white, like an old man with gradual onset blindness.

When this was discovered, his men had returned to the rest of the company, who had camped at the city's outskirts. The entire Purification Team had headed back to Jerusalem. Caiaphas and the high council would need to know of these developments. A new leader would have to be appointed.

It had been three days.

Judah, the synagogue leader in Damascus, had become deeply concerned for Saul. He watched the priest; the endorsed purifier who represented the High Council.

The man said nothing, ate nothing, and would not sleep.

He wept constantly.

What had happened to him, Judah wondered?

Whatever it was, it must have been traumatic, he concluded.

In the midst of his blackness, Saul found himself in deep contemplation. The anger he had tried so hard to keep under control; the harsh attitudes he had made room for in his soul; his addiction to judgments and control. These things had always served him well, and helped him to succeed.

Now, they were simply ineffective elements of the shattered wall, no longer covering his naked soul.

From the moment Jesus had appeared to him in the middle of the road, Saul's life turned upside down. Inside, he was receiving understanding. The Holy Spirit was weaving the training of his youth with the teachings of Gamaliel. An ability to grasp what was happening in his life was beginning to dawn on his inner awareness.

Broken before God, he could take ownership of his failings, of his misplaced zeal.

He had truly believed he had been on a mission from God.

His anger had substituted for actual strength.

His pride had deceived him.

His mind went to Caiaphas. When it did, the Holy Spirit began revealing to the self-appointed vigilante, the differences between the religiosity of man with the reality of healing relationship with God.

How could he have sold his soul for a substitute?

"I have truly been blind, Lord," he whispered through his tears. "Show me. Teach me to see what you see. Help me, please. I don't even know what questions to ask."

Suddenly, in his understanding, he saw a man in a brown robe and lighter cloak standing in front of him, with hands on Saul's eyes. Then, the vision ended. Somehow, Saul knew, he would receive his sight.

"His name is Ananias," Jesus told Saul.

Across town, another man was in prayer. It was his daily discipline to spend time praying in the language of angels every day. As he was praying, a man appeared to him, bathed in a white light. He recognized the face of Jesus from the days when he had traveled as a member of the seventy.

Jesus called him by name. "Ananias!"

The startled disciple responded. "Yes, Lord?"

"I have something I need you to do," Jesus answered. "Go over to Straight Street. Judah, the synagogue leader, lives on that street. I want you to go to his home. When you arrive, ask to see a man named Saul from Tarsus. He is praying, just as you are, right this moment. I appeared to him on the road to Damascus, and he has become blind. I have shown him you will be coming to pray for him, and he will receive his sight."

"Are you sure about this, Lord?" Ananias asked before he thought. "I have heard so many people talk about the horrible things this man has done to the followers of Jesus in Jerusalem! And now, they said he was coming here with authorization from the High Council to arrest everyone who calls on your name; everyone who chooses to follow you."

Jesus smiled. "Just go, Ananias. There is no need to be afraid. Saul is the man I have chosen to take the message of my coming to non-Jews, to kings, as well as to Israel. I will show him how much he will go through because he is choosing to trust me and follow me."

Looking at the Master's face, Ananias realized just how much he had missed seeing Jesus' smile. "I will go right away, sir."

The light began to fade away. Just before the last remnants of the glow disappeared, he saw a clear view of Jesus' form. In his eyes, the same compassion and understanding that had drawn him to follow the Lord in the first place looked deep into his soul.

Suddenly, Ananias stood in the room alone once again. Grabbing his cloak and head-covering, he left immediately to find Judah's house on Straight Street.

The synagogue leader opened his own door. "Can I help you?" he asked.

"I came to see Saul," Ananias answered. "My name is Ananias."

"Oh, yes," Judah replied, moving aside. "Please, come in."

Following the priest inside the house, Ananias was led into a small, lamp-lit room. Judah looked at Saul. "He is in here. He hasn't eaten anything since he arrived. I have offered him water, but he hasn't taken much of that either...." He turned his attention to the blind man seated on the cushions in the corner. "He hasn't spoken either."

Ananias touched Judah's arm. "He will be all right. ElShaddai sent me to find him."

Judah's eyebrows went up. "Oh," he said. "I see. Then, I will leave you both to talk. If you need anything, I'll be in the courtyard in the back."

"Thank you, Judah," Ananias answered.

After the synagogue ruler left the room, Ananias sat down next to Saul and spoke quietly.

"Saul? Are you awake?"

Saul did not answer.

"Brother Saul, the Lord Jesus, who appeared to you on the road, has sent me so that you might regain your sight and be filled with the Holy Spirit."

Hearing these words, Saul turned his head towards the voice he was hearing. Ananias noticed his sightless eyes were red and swollen from weeping.

"Are you Ananias?" he said. "Jesus told me you were going to come and lay hands on me to open my eyes."

"Yes, that's me," an amazed Ananias responded. "Are you ready for me to pray for you?"

Saul nodded, keeping his head up, facing the one who had spoken.

Carefully, Ananias laid his hands on Saul's head, and stretched his thumbs to cover the blind man's eyes. Suddenly, Saul opened his eyes and blinked. Once, twice, then three and four times. Without warning, a thick, filmy, white scale peeled away from Saul's left eye; and then one peeled from his right.

Saul felt an itch in his eyes, so he rubbed his face. He blinked several more times, as streaming sunlight developed into blurred shapes, and then gradually came into focus.

"I…. I can see!" he declared. Jumping up, he grabbed Ananias by the arms, and looked him in the eyes. "I can see! Look! I can see! Are you Ananias?"

Smiling, Ananias nodded.

Saul continued, without a pause. "I didn't understand. I thought I was doing what ElShaddai wanted me to do. But I wasn't. I destroyed my marriage. I rejected my teachers. I went my own way."

"We all have done that, Saul," his new friend offered. "That's why we need to be rescued. Jesus came to show us how to live. We cannot know God without knowing him."

Saul was looking around the room, his mind speeding forward. "I wonder if I can find Shira, to tell her. I need to be baptized. I've been so wrong. I want to be his disciple. I want to learn. I see things differently now. These past three days I realized how truly blind I have been. How could I have closed my heart to him the way I did?"

He looked at Ananias. "Did you know? Jesus is the fulfillment of all of the Law and the Prophets!"

Ananias chuckled. "Yes, he is," he answered.

"I began to understand during the days I was blind. Oh, I have so much to learn!" He paused, looking around the room. "Do you have a place where I can be baptized?"

"There is a place just in the city, where the Abana River flows through city gardens. We can go there tonight if you wish," came the reply.

Saul clapped his hands. "Can we go *now?* And are there people I can speak to? I want to share what has happened to me! I *saw* him, Ananias! I saw *Jesus!* He *stopped* me! I was coming into this city to kill people, and he knocked me off my horse!"

Ananias smiled at Saul's exuberance. His excitement was contagious! He slapped Saul on the shoulder. "This is how it should be, my brother!" he exclaimed. "If we are going to be able to talk freely, I would be more comfortable if you would allow me take you to my home. That way, you will be with other believers in Jesus. I'm not sure how Priest Judah feels about us just yet; and the Jews have been looking forward to your Purification Team getting rid of us all."

"Oh, yes," Saul said. "I had forgotten."

He glanced at Ananias, assessing him. "It seems I have changed sides."

"Yes, it does," the older man replied. "Let's get you to a safer place."

"Excuse me," Saul said. He left the room. As he walked towards the house's outer courtyard, he called for the priest. "Judah? Master Judah?"

The synagogue ruler had been seated just outside the door. "I'm here, Saul. Don't come, I'll come and guide you," he offered.

As he rose to make good on his offer, Saul walked through the archway to greet him. Upon seeing Saul's steady steps, and hearing the change in his voice, he was shaken, and sat back down.

"Are you all right, son?" he asked.

"Never better, Judah! I can see!" Saul answered. "Look in my eyes! Jesus healed me!"

"How? Wh-a-...?"

Excitedly, Saul sat down next to Judah, and began to share his experiences of the past four days, beginning with his being dispatched from the Temple. He shared his encounter with Jesus on the road to Damascus. He explained how fresh understanding was beginning to unfold itself in his heart and mind regarding the Law and the Prophets. As he shared, Ananias emerged from the house and sat down in the courtyard as well.

Amazed at the miracle which had taken place, the Damascus priest said nothing, and listened in stunned silence. When he finished, it was Ananias who spoke.

"Master Judah," he began, "you have been so gracious to house and to feed this man for the past three days. He wants to be baptized as a disciple of Jesus, so I thought you might want to send him with me, rather than allow him to stay here. I'm sure there will be no small uprising when his life-change decision has been made public. I would like to make your life as easy as possible."

Judah looked at Ananias. "Thank you," he said quietly. "Although, I myself have been conflicted over this new teaching about Jesus. I was in Jerusalem for Passover the year he was crucified. I heard the stories about his resurrection. I saw the hundreds of people who walked into the city out of their tombs that day. I had to come back here because of my responsibilities in the city, and I wasn't able to return when the Great Wind blew on Pentecost."

Ananias was surprised. "I was blessed to be able to travel with Jesus before he ascended back to heaven. I could try to answer any of your questions, if you like."

Judah's eyes brightened. "I heard there are members of the Sanhedrin who have become his disciples as well."

"Yes, several," Saul murmured. As he spoke, Gamaliel's face presented itself in his mind. "I'm afraid I have wounded a few of them with my poor choices."

Silence hung in the room for a moment.

Finally, Ananias stood and dusted off his cloak. "Well, Master Saul," he said, "I am going to return to my home, and I would love to have you come with me. Do you have any belongings you need to gather?"

"I don't know," the young man replied.

"I'll get them," Judah chuckled. "He doesn't know where I put them. He was blind when he came." With that, he moved into the next room, and returned with a satchel, a purse and several small scrolls.

"The letters are for you," Saul told him. "Dispatches from the Sanhedrin, giving me full authority to…." He sighed.

Judah walked to him, handing the younger man his things. Taking one of the scrolls from the pile, he broke its seal, and began to read out loud.

> *"From Joseph Caiaphas, High Priest of the Temple in Jerusalem, and prince of Israel; from the Sanhedrin, priests and High Council of Israel*
> *To all faithful members of the priesthood, within the city of Damascus and its environs;*
> *Greetings!*
> *This letter is to introduce to you a rising star in the priesthood, Saul of Tarsus. As you are aware, several years ago, a dissident named Jesus, from Galilee, was crucified for claiming to be the King of the Jews. Since his death, there have been many false claims of his divinity; including his resurrection, and his continuing to live through those who following him.*
> *This sect, which we refer to as "The Way," has now become organized and structured. It is a threat to the Jews living peaceful lives. We received consent from Roman authorities to do away with Jesus, as he caused an uprising, and led people away from the True Faith.*
> *Saul of Tarsus has come to your city with our authorization to purge out those who claim to be part of The Way, and spread their heresies. Those who are found by him to be disloyal to ElShaddai, will be chained and brought back to Jerusalem for trial, then executed by stoning.*
> *The Temple will seize their properties.*
> *Thank you for your faithful and obedient service to God, and to Israel."*

Saul had not read the letters. He had some idea what was in them, due to the tone and demeanor Caiaphas had utilized in commissioning him. He knew the man's rage over the sect's growth had fueled them. He felt shame for his part in furthering what he now realized was a purely political agenda.

How could he put into words what he had experienced; the life-altering, cataclysmic encounter on the road to Damascus?

"What do we do now?" Judah asked, as he rerolled the letter.

"I would say that would have to be left to your judgment," Ananias replied.

"I have no idea what to do with this," Judah replied. "The man who was given permission to imprison these people no longer has a team of men with him. And, unless I miss my guess, he has abandoned his mission for personal reasons. I think I will have to reflect upon this matter later, anyway, since I'm going with Saul to be baptized," Judah replied. "I know in my heart this is real, and I want to be part of what ElShaddai is planning to do."

Ananias smiled. "Well then," he said. "Let's all go to my house. I think we will be having a meeting tonight."

That evening, several people in addition to Saul and Judah were baptized in the Abana River, where the waters flowed through the city's gardens. Each person attending carried a lamp, and the group sang as those baptized went into the water one at a time.

Before each one went under the water, he or she repeated a statement regarding their choice to believe in Jesus. Ananias had worked in the Jerusalem Ecclesia, and was familiar with the statement used by Peter and John when they baptized new followers. So, he led each person in the statements which would eventually evolve into the Apostles' Creed:

I believe in God, the Father Almighty, Creator of heaven and earth.
I believe in Jesus Christ, his only Son, our Lord,
    who was conceived by the Holy Spirit and born of the virgin, Mary.
He suffered under Pontius Pilate, was crucified, died, and was buried;
He descended to hell.
The third day He rose again from the dead.
He ascended to heaven and is seated at the right hand of God the Father
    Almighty.
From there He will come to judge the living and the dead.
I believe in the Holy Spirit, the communion of saints, the forgiveness of
    sins,
    the resurrection of the body, and the life everlasting. So let it be now,
    and forevermore.

Two days after his baptism in water, Saul of Tarsus experienced a baptism with the Holy Spirit and fire. He had been reading from a scroll, on loan from Judah. The writings of Moses; Exodus, the second book of the Torah. As he read, he began to understand the account of Israel's redemption from Egypt in an entirely fresh light.

"I want to know you the way Moses did," he found himself praying. "I want to be the friend of God. Like Moses, like Abraham. Holy Spirit, I need your power in my life."

A set of phrases went through his mind, almost as though someone was speaking to him.

Ananias had laid his hands on Saul's head the day before, and prayed for him; requesting Jesus would baptize him, immerse his soul, into the Holy Spirit and His purifying fire. The older man had prepared Saul for this very moment.

"When it happens, you might have doubts because it is a new experience. You might even experience threats from fear. But if you push through those doubts, and repeat the phrases, an entirely new language will begin to pour through you. It is the language of heaven; the language of angels. It is the empowerment Jesus told us to wait for. He said we would need the relationship it opens with the Holy Spirit, if we are to be effective. We are called to be people who can tell the nations what we have seen and heard as his followers. So, when it happens to you, just yield."

"I will," Saul replied. "Thank you for preparing me."

And now, the moment for which Ananias had equipped him was taking place. Silently, Saul considered the phrases presenting themselves. Should he repeat them? Was this really the language of angels showing itself in his mind? What if he was making it up? What if it wasn't real? Could he be deceived the same way he had been deceived by Caiaphas?

Ananias' words came on the heels of that thought. "If you push through those doubts, and repeat the phrases, an entirely new language will begin...."

Swallowing hard, with eyes closed, Saul shakily spoke out a part of the first phrase. As he did, something constricting around his chest was loosened. It was as though something broke open inside of him. A warm torrent of the overwhelming, overcoming love of the living God rose like a tidal wave, filling his heart with knowledge and awareness of acceptance and approval. As his confidence in his relationship with Abba Father increased, fluency in the language of angels rose. Wave after wave of ElShaddai's understanding and compassion released wave after wave of inward realizations.

He prayed for over two hours, in the language of angels; his mind unfruitful, the Holy Spirit breathing life and depth into his heart and understanding.

How had he lived without this experience, he wondered?

Saul knew he would never be the same.

He began to utilize his new prayer language every day.

A week later, at an inn in the city of Damascus, a group of religious Jews sat in conversation over a meal with Galad, one of the members of Saul's Purification Team. When the rest of the men had returned to Jerusalem, he had decided to stay in Damascus just in case he might be needed by a blinded Saul.

But now, he had received news. Apparently, not only had Saul changed, having begun to follow the teachings of Jesus, but now the local synagogue leader had chosen the same life-path as well! And now, there were rumors of plans in the making to begin a more public form of an Ecclesia in Damascus.

Such news was devastating to the men with whom he was meeting. They had come, seeking him out; hoping for answers.

"What hold does this Jesus have on these people, Galad?" one of the men was asking. "What has taken their loyalty from our God?"

"They believe Jesus was our God, come in human form."

"Is there any substance to their beliefs? I mean, what happened to cause Saul to change so drastically?" another man wanted to know.

Galad shrugged. He really didn't know how to answer the question. So, he just began to speak.

"I heard a voice speaking around Saul, just after his horse reared," he told them. "He acted as though he was talking with someone, but I didn't see anyone. He was afraid, and kept holding his hand up over his face, like they were going to hit him."

"What did the voice say?" the man asked.

"I didn't hear the words exactly," Galad replied. "But when Saul stood up, he said he had been told to go into the city. So we took him to the home of Judah, the synagogue leader, as had been arranged."

"Arranged?"

"Saul of Tarsus is a priest from the Temple in Jerusalem," he explained. "He had letters of authorization to arrest members of "The Way," here in Damascus, and bring them back to Jerusalem in chains. I am one of the men hired to help him accomplish that task."

"What is 'The Way'?"

Galad smiled. "It's the term Joseph Caiaphas, the High Priest, uses when he refers to people who follow the teachings of Jesus, the Galilean."

"Oh," the third man answered. "We've had difficulty holding on to people in our synagogue as well. I've never seen anything like it. Do you think it might be a mental illness of some kind?"

"I don't know for sure," Galad replied carefully. "There has to be some sort of power attached to it. Saul was suddenly blind when he stood up after the encounter. He said he had been told to go to the house of a man named Judah on Straight Street. So we brought him there."

"What do we do?" the men asked each other. Finally, it was decided they would send Galad back to Jerusalem with messages for the High Priest, communicating the results of the Temple's latest attempt at getting rid of those who followed The Way.

It was a matter of days before the news of Caiaphas' stabbing and demotion by Rome reached the religious Jews in Damascus.

"It's safe, then, for me to share about Jesus," Saul decided aloud to Ananias. "He can't send anyone else if he is no longer there. Do you think it would be all right for me to share what has happened to me in some sort of meeting?"

Ananias smiled. "You do understand some of our community might think you are setting a trap; that you have a small army in hiding somewhere in the city?"

Saul gave this consideration. "That would be understandable," he said. "But they can't continue to believe that if I stay, and prove myself to be an honest man. I really want to share the changes Jesus has brought in me. I mean it. I haven't ever felt this way before."

"It *might* be a good idea," Ananias answered thoughtfully, tapping his chin. "It's possible many of our Ecclesia will be interested, and want to be of help to you. In fact, I'm sure you will draw quite a crowd, even if they are just curious to know what happened."

Suddenly hopeful, the young man looked at Ananias. "You really think so?"

"I do think so, Saul," he responded. "But we need to begin slowly. We both know, by the Holy Spirit's word to each of us; ElShaddai has appointed you to reach many more people than just those in this city. Be careful you don't allow your newfound zeal to place you in dangerous situations. Recklessness is not a sign of wisdom. I'm sure you will encounter difficulty that serves God's purposes at a later time in your life. But it shouldn't happen just yet."

"What do you mean?" Saul countered. "Should I hold back my words just because what I have to share is new? Or because it might put me in danger? I have endorsed the deaths of many! I have been responsible for exiling my now brothers and sisters in Jesus from their homes, and their country! Surely, you are not telling me to be quiet!"

Ananias put his hands in front of his body, and motioned for Saul to calm down. "Patience, Saul." He waited a moment.

"No, son, I'm not saying that at all. And I will speak with Judah to see if he would be agreeable to you reading from the Torah and speaking on the Sabbath. He has chosen to follow the Master as well, and he is still the ruler of the synagogue. It might just be the perfect place for you to begin."

Saul sighed. Ananias' offer wasn't good enough. He wanted to make a real difference.

Quickly.

Ananias continued. "I just know from my own experience, your zeal must have substance and depth for you to be truly effective. Only you know within yourself the places of your being just now opening to His touch. There is a substance and depth yet to be developed in the days and years to come. Such a thing does not happen overnight."

The younger man slumped. "I know what you're saying is true. I just don't want to waste any time," he admitted.

"Saul, true seasoning takes time. There is no substitute for maturity. In the same way we wait for wine to become ripened and full-bodied, the ways of the Holy Spirit must be worked into your *nature,* your *core;* becoming habit, becoming character. The Spirit will develop you, strengthen you, teach you to live this life as Jesus did. When you are obedient to the Spirit, no time is wasted. He cultivates you."

There was silence as Saul reflected on Ananias' words.

"What should I do then?" he asked.

Ananias stood to his feet. "I don't know, son," he answered. "In fact, why don't we go together right now to find Judah, and ask his input on this idea?"

Saul jumped to his feet. "Yes, let's go," he replied impatiently. "I can't wait."

Saul *did* share his story at the synagogue that approaching Sabbath. In fact, he shared not once, but many times. His years of study with Gamaliel helped him to explain the life of Jesus in ways the people of Damascus could understand. Those who had chosen to believe Jesus was the Christ, the Promised Deliverer, found his words fortified and developed their ability to persevere.

As the weeks passed, Saul's sharing became a daily event in homes, in addition to the days he was invited to read at the synagogue on the Sabbath. From the first week, blind eyes were opened, deaf ears were opened, and cripples were healed; restored to walk in strength. In fact, so many of those in the Jewish community were choosing to believe in Jesus, those who were being baptized began to outnumber the religious Jews.

"Jesus is our God, who has come in human form to rescue us from the kingdom of darkness! He is alive forever!" Saul could be heard shouting his message in the street on many days.

In the Jewish community, the reaction was one of amazement.

All who heard him were astonished. Even those in the religious opposition were repeatedly stunned. No one was able to disprove his words or his actions. It was evident to everyone. God was indeed moving through the life of this energetic, young man.

"Isn't this the same man; the priest who caused such damage in the lives of Jesus' followers in Jerusalem?" they asked. "Wasn't he endorsed by Caiaphas to come to this city to arrest them? Wasn't it his mission to come here and kill Jesus' followers? Wasn't he supposed to chain them, and take them back to the Temple?"

Over the weeks, the questions among the religious Jews and Greek speaking Jews in Damascus turned into complaints. The complaints turned into resentments. Resentments built, until the two groups began to network together, secretly plotting to kill Saul.

Those involved in the scheming began to watch his daily activities. As they did so, they noticed it was Saul's habit on many days, to walk outside the city's gates. He ventured into the farming centers just outside the city, speaking every day with anyone who had a question.

Finally, it was decided the would-be assassins would lie in wait for him at the city's gate.

But someone overheard the plan.

That someone confided what they heard to Ananias.

So, one night, under cover of darkness, just before the plan was to be carried out, Ananias, Judah, and several other disciples of Jesus in Damascus, hid Saul in a large basket. With ropes, they lowered him through an opening in the city wall.

Fleeing from Damascus for his life, Saul made his way south.

At first, he thought he might head back towards Jerusalem, but then had thoughts of perhaps avoiding the city. He would go through Qumran. Surely, someone somewhere could answer his unspoken questions. If he admitted his deepest concerns, he would have to say he felt like an orphan. He could see now, he had covered his weaknesses with anger. In fact, he had mistaken his anger for manly strength.

Was there anyone to help him? Was he truly better off now?

He had been in control of his life and his emotions before Damascus. But, then, he wouldn't trade the comfort and compassion he had sensed the day Jesus appeared to him. And the power of that kind of love had changed him.

Ananias was right, he considered. The *right* things done at the wrong *time* would become the *wrong things*. So how could he mature in ElShaddai's wisdom more *quickly?*

And somehow, he knew no matter where he went, his life would eventually be in danger.

"What should I do, Holy Spirit?" he prayed. "Where do I go?"

I will lead you.

"But where, Lord?" he asked, in response to the now familiar Voice.

Fearful images began to present themselves. His mind began to fill with memories of his sea voyage alone from Tarsus to Jerusalem. Emotions rose from nowhere. His pulse quickened. Suddenly, he was eight years old again and the evening sea was angry.

Saul, don't be afraid. Trust me.

"Strangely, I do. Help me, please," he answered. He walked in silence, contemplating his fears, somehow seeing them for the first time as separated from himself.

"You know I've never trusted anyone since that voyage, Lord. Are you sure you can trust *me?* What if I miss what you have for me?"

Prayer will keep your heart open. I chose you for a reason.

And so the conversation continued. Not knowing where else to go, Saul headed back towards Jerusalem.

Perhaps he *could* travel. He could find Shira…. He could mend his marriage.

If she would have him.

But then, before he knew it, following one instructed step at a time, the young, former priest and Pharisee attached himself to a caravan headed into Arabia.

It had two weeks since the celebration dinner on the governor's ship in Cyrene. For most everyone in the little band of refugees, life had settled into some sort of temporary routine. Each morning, those who could, met together for prayer at Simeon's parents' home. Each evening, a meal was shared in Joseph's home, as well as worship, prayer and teaching.

Tonight's evening's meal would be the last one they would all share with everyone present. Philip, and several others felt a need to return to Judea. The last vessel to sail before winter was putting out to sea at dawn. The 1800 mile voyage to Joppa would take almost three weeks; much less time than the more than three months it had taken them to arrive in Cyrene.

Tonight would be a commissioning time. They would eat together, spend time sharing communion. They would worship in song, and then pray for one another; laying hands on those who were leaving; sending them out from their midst with blessing.

The entire group would pray for Philip, Clementos, and their companions.

Additionally, Philip had taken Joseph of Arimathea and Lazarus aside during the prayer time that morning. The Holy Spirit had been talking to him, he said. He had been instructed by the Holy Spirit to commission both men as apostles, by means of prayer and declaration.

"It is similar to what the Temple priests do when they ordain a new priest. He receives his *semichah.* Just as Jesus laid his hands on us, we were instructed to lay hands on those we commission and ordain. We are simply agreeing with what Abba Father is already doing through you, you understand," he had explained to both of men. "We are all confirming what we see the Holy Spirit doing in your lives. This is what Jesus told us to do, to impart an office of ministry, when a person's call has become evident. I want you to have every advantage. So we will ask the Father to increase His anointing in you and on you."

Over the past few weeks, it had become clear in Joseph's heart and mind he was eventually to begin an Ecclesia in Briton with those who were called to follow him. It appeared there would be several from the group who felt drawn to the same regions. They would be traveling with him.

In fact, Joseph had sent a second letter to Arviragus this morning, expressing his desire to see his old friend. His message was simple. "I am coming to see you, very soon, with friends. We will arrive by summer. I have many things to tell you."

Then, he had sent a letter to the Jerusalem Ecclesia, bringing James and John up to date with all that had taken place. He was sure they were aware of some of the facts by now, but he wanted to share with them firsthand how the group was responding. He also asked John to make sure Zebedee was not left alone. "I am concerned for him with the loss of his wife. Please keep him in your care," he wrote. He also included a list of those who had been kidnapped by Caiaphas' hired mercenaries.

A third letter went to the Ecclesia in Capernaum. He smiled as he remembered the rough but kind personalities of the people who fished the Sea of Galilee. Peter would need to know what had happened, and he knew Zebedee and his sons would be comforted to know where Salome was.

They needed to know she was still alive.

17 – Seedlings

Spring, 38 AD

It had been a little over a year since Pontius Pilate had departed Jerusalem for his new assignment in the imperial province of Alpes Poiniae, just north of Italia.

The family had settled into a family home in the Roman capital settlement of Aventicum. A walled city in the Alps, the settlement was home to the legions of Roman military and construction slaves charged with maintaining the borders of conquest. Currently, the Senate referred to the entire region as Helvetica. Development of the area had begun during the reign of Augustus Caesar, and continued through Tiberius' reign.

Since Julius Caesar had begun conquest of the area more than eighty years prior, Roman roads were now established for trade and development, spanning the mountains from Massilia northward. Wherever Rome advanced, aqueducts, gymnasiums, temples, amphitheaters, and bath-houses were erected in systematic fashion. In short, Roman culture was creeping up, attempting to gradually replace the life-styles of the indigenous Celtic and Germanic peoples.

It would be a difficult task, if it would be possible at all. Weathered, hard-working farmers, and herder-gatherer tribes had inhabited the area long before militia arrived. They were used to the harsh climate, with centuries of survival experience. By comparison, the Romans were inexperienced newcomers. Privately, many of the indigenous peoples wondered how long these people could last in the mountains.

"It is impossible to force the mountain to change to fit *you*," they laughed, reminding each other. "*You* must change to fit the mountain."

Why would anyone try to build a stone fortress during an Alpine winter season?

Located near a secondary lake, Aventicum was a typical Roman city. It was fortressed, surrounded by a great wall, three and a half miles long, which protected and provided shelter from the harsh winter winds, as well as from its potential enemies.

Even in spring, the weather in the Alpes Poineae was chilly. As the company had climbed upward from the warm Mediterranean beaches in the developed Roman city of Massilia, temperatures slowly descended.

As the outside chill factor increased, the older Valerius Gratus had insisted each member of their party put away their sandals and begin to wear locally-made, fur-lined boots. Additionally, he told them, the thinner clothing they all had worn in warmer, balmy weather provided no protection from the cold. So, in place of those lightweight linen garments, each person now donned a leather loincloth and custom-made leggings. The leggings were made of strips of tanned leather stitched together with sinew, personally tailored to each person.

Designing custom clothing for a company as large as theirs had taken over two months. But now, men and women alike were thankful for the warmth. Claudia and the female servants were all amazed at how much better they felt when cold air was prevented from drafting through their thin togas.

Then, when they had arrived in the higher altitudes, bearskin hats with leather chin straps had been added to each person's ensemble, along with fur lined mittens. Snow shoes were also purchased.

Now, when they walked outside, each person wore a fur-lined, leather jacket with a belt, or a heavy cloak, made from woven grasses and reeds.

As they settled into their new environs in Aventicum, Claudia Procula found herself unexpectedly excited about her husband's new assignment. She loved the crispness of the air; the openness of the countryside. With each new relationship she forged during their journey, Claudia realized she was coming closer and closer to a discovery.

The Helvetic culture was different from any she had ever encountered. She had never lived in a rural area before, she considered. In the cities where she had lived, she had felt alone; out of place. But here, the values of the people were centered on working the land.

Not only that, but family relationships came first in the considerations of those she talked with. What would it be like to feel that kind of closeness with *her* father, or *her* mother for that matter, she wondered? Would she have been as sad as a child if she had lived here sooner?

And yet, she considered, in her early years, she had been told every day how lucky she was to grow up a princess. She had come to believe every child felt worse than she did.

Even Pilo was more settled, she considered. In Jerusalem, and even on the island of Capri, he had stayed inside, unable to entertain himself, silently demanding Claudia, Yasmina, and Candace entertain him with games and stories.

He had always been so afraid, she considered.

But now, he played outside with other children, and came in with sparkling eyes and rosy cheeks. He was laughing more, talking constantly about his encounters. Each day, a new friend came home with him. Each night, the family meal was punctuated with precious souvenirs of his daily adventures; a rock, an arrowhead, a plant. Truthfully, it could be just about anything.

Was it the fact they all lived in a smaller settlement now, without the stiffness of Roman protocol?

They were all happier.

Pontius was certainly less pressured, it seemed.

She knew her husband would be charged with maintaining the perimeters of the province at some point. He would need to travel.

But for now, she was enjoying their new life.

Their home was built of stone. She noticed the construction was similar to homes she had seen in the countryside near Jerusalem, and Rome, in the less prosperous areas. In Rome, and in Jerusalem, areas where she had lived before, it had been customary to plaster over the rock skeleton of a home, making its final surface smooth. In some of those homes, where the owners could afford more, dyes were applied for decoration. But here.....

Having the bare stone was a luxury. Being shielded from the weather was more than good enough.

She was grateful they were all alive.

Her father had done well. Valerius had done well.

Things were so different here. The values of the people living in the area were centered on working the land and on family relational structure. So saying, the household's servants and staff were settling in to new duties.

Gold meant nothing here.

Relationships meant everything.

It was strange, Claudia considered. She had always loved being outdoors, and had avoided the women who loved to visit the spas and gossip with each other. There, she had felt ostracized, virtually alone.

Even in Jerusalem.

Now, however, she felt hopeful she might develop relationships with other women, no matter their station.

Here, trade prospered in the form of bartering. Meat was traded for services. Grains were traded for goods.

Here, life was not about what you possessed.

It was about who you knew.

And what skills you had mastered.

413

Over the past few days, Claudia and Pontius had been sitting together with Valerius Gratus, the older, each afternoon. Also attending the meetings were their military attendants; Quintus, and the Legion Commander of the fortress in Aventicum. In the past few days, all of the family's servants had also been expected to join.

Pilate considered the meetings a necessary cultural education to ensure the family's future. As a result, a new way of thinking about their lives was emerging.

Having been stationed in the area during his military career, Valerius Gratus, the older, instructed them on the culture and language of the Helvetii. How were they to insure a long and healthy governorship? What provisions would they need to make in regard to their son's education? Did the citizens in this region recognize Rome's rule, or did they resent it? What would wise behavior be in regard to those who had lived here for generations? Who were the leaders?

It was time to learn a new language, if they were truly to fit in.

It was late each night when they were headed to their bed.

One night in particular, Pontius was reminded of the dream he had experienced the night Jesus was crucified.

Thinking about it, he realized the dream had been prophetic in nature.

The eagle had represented Rome. The black cobra had represented Satan, and the hordes of evil which sought to destroy not only Jesus, but anyone who followed Jesus. In the dream, Pilate realized the cobra had made him its target; threatening him.

The new governor thought back to his state of mind during those years. He had felt powerless to act, trapped between Caiaphas, Herod and Rome. He had felt as though his feet were made of sand.

He hadn't understood the meaning of the grain replacing the sand until this very moment. Now, it meant the potential of a harvest.

Had moving from Jerusalem to Helvetica presented him with that opportunity, he wondered?

Then there had been the image of his hand melting, and turning into blood. Even the morning after the dream, he had realized it had represented Jesus' blood, which he had tried to wash off his hands the day before. The melting wax had indicated his own inability to hold his resolve. When the time had come to voice his resolves; to speak his mind, maintaining a boundary; his strength had melted like wax.

How weak he had been in those days, he considered.

But now, he remembered the dripping blood falling into the grain. As it touched the grain, flames emerged, scaring him. He had reached to Rome to rescue him from what he feared in the dream, but Rome had been consumed by the cobra. But then, the snake's belly had begun to glow, and it opened its mouth to pour fire down on him.

What did that mean, he wondered? Was Rome about to be consumed by evil? Was the greatest Empire ever seen going to fall?

He understood now, the attacks threatened against himself and Claudia by Caligula had been sourced by a greater evil that an insane Caesar.

Then, in the dream, the serpent had exploded, causing the mountain Pilate stood on to split. Suddenly, a golden eagle appeared, and picked him up with its talons, carrying him up into the clouds.

What did the mountain represent, he questioned?

What was the difference between the eagle that was Rome, and the golden eagle?

Did the golden eagle represent the manner in which he would die? Or did it represent his newly discovered, Unseen Abba Father?

He knew he would need to find a place of solitude to pray. It would take time to understand. He needed answers. Perhaps he could take some time away in the mountains when he inspected the military settlements.

He would be leaving in a few weeks to inspect the troops in Augusta Raurica and Vindonissa. He was now responsible for the one hundred mile radius of settlements around Avendicum; including all military, citizens, population, slaves, and development.

He knew Rome would expect the same level of communication he had provided in his former, warmer assignments.

Still, he reasoned, the fear was gone. Something within him had shifted. He was now firmer in his convictions. He saw a greater potential.

He prayed inwardly. *What are you saying to me, Holy Spirit? I didn't realize the dream had such a deep meaning. Please help me understand.*

He could feel his awareness of the Holy Spirit deepening in his inner man.

In Jerusalem, Marcellus was packing up to return to Syria. His military replacement, Marullus, was on his way. It seemed the Judeans needed a firmer hand than Marcellus had provided, and concerns for the continuity of the Empire in the region had been roused in the Roman Senate. Everyone in a leadership capacity had been warned to stay on the less dangerous side of Caligula Caesar.

The Syrian governor, Vitellus wanted to make sure he drew no attention to his post. "Let the Caesar keep eating his weight in gold," he said to his bodyguard. "We need no interference here, just now. Let us just bide our time until he is no longer on the throne."

In Jerusalem, conflicts continued within the Sanhedrin. Dissatisfied with the present High Priest's performance, and determined to make his displeasure felt and heard, the new Procurator, Marullus, hastily deposed Annas' son, Jonathan, from the office of High Priest, and replaced him with another son of Annas; his youngest son, Theophilus.

Late one afternoon, a commercial travel vessel arrived in Joppa from Cyrene, Africa. Disembarking from the ship were ten persons from the rudderless ship; Philip, Clementos, Clemon, as well as Shira, Libi, Joanna, and several more women. To the observant eye, it was clear they had all traveled together, perhaps from the same locality. They gathered to confer together after walking the gangplank.

After prayer, they all headed north together.

It was two days later when Philip and his party arrived in Capernaum. A flurry of energy rippled through the entire area as the news of their return made its way from home to home. Simon Peter had been the first to notice them. He was sitting on his rooftop, in the cool of the early evening, when he heard a large group of people approaching in the road below. Glancing down, he recognized Philip, but thought his eyes were playing tricks on him.

Then, he recognized Joanna.

Surprised, he bounded to his feet, and ran down the outdoor steps. "Philip! Joanna!" he cried. "Is that you?" He looked around the group. "Clement! Clemos! How did you...What..."

He stopped, realizing his heart was stuck in his throat. His eyes filled with joyful tears.

"Zebedee will want to know!" He looked through the group once more. "Where is Salome?"

Joanna hugged him. "It's good to see you too, Simon! Salome didn't come with us. But she sends her love, and a message. We are headed to her house now. You want to come with us?"

"Yes, I do," he replied. He looked at Philip. "Does Tahlia know you're coming home?"

Philip smiled. "No, not yet. I'm going to Bethsaida from here. I can't wait to see them!"

"She came to see me a week or so ago," Simon Peter told him. "She said your daughters and their husbands all still want to begin an Ecclesia in Samaria. She wanted to know what could be done about it. Were we sending someone else, and could they be a part of the planting...."

The traveler was surprised. "When we were in Cyrene, the Holy Spirit showed me a building in Samaria in a dream. That's how I knew I was to come back here. I wondered how long it would take before our family could actually move there, and how many of our daughters would want to go, or if their husbands would feel the same way towards the mission."

Joanna smiled. "It sounds like Jesus was working on all of your hearts, even while you were apart."

"It does," Philip agreed, somewhat relieved.

Zebedee and Barnabas were up on the rooftop of the family's home when the group arrived at the door. It was Philip who bounded first up the steps. The entire group followed.

"Zee?" he called. "Are you home?"

Zebedee didn't recognize Philip's voice at first. He turned his head towards the top of the stairs. As Philip moved closer to him in the shadows, Zebedee jumped up. "Is that you, Philip?" he asked. "I thought you were at sea on Caiaphas' boat. We were told you all were dead."

"Well, not *totally* dead. Not yet, anyway," Philip said dryly, moving into view. "Hello, Zebedee," he said.

"Oh, my!" the older fisherman cried. His hand went to his heart. He looked around the group. "Where did you all come from?"

"Joseph send a letter before we set sail," Joanna told him. "Didn't you get it?"

Surprised, Zebedee shook his head. "Dispatches usually go to Caesarea first," he told her. "It will probably be delivered sometime next week. But this is amazing. It is wonderful to have you all here."

"Well," Philip said, "I have a letter for you from Salome." As he spoke, he drew a small scroll from his cloak pocket, and handed it to Zebedee.

The man's eyes grew wide in surprise. "She is *alive?*" he whispered. "How? What happened?"

The disciple slapped his shoulder. "Sit back down where you were. There is plenty of time to fill you in, brother. First however, I know you will want to read this."

As a stunned Zebedee sank back down into the cushions with Salome's scroll, a suddenly energized Barnabas moved into action. He clapped his hands together. "So!" he said. "Who is hungry? I think we might have some food around here somewhere."

"I would love some water, and perhaps some bread?" Clement offered, looking at Simon Peter.

"Oh, we can do better than that!" Barnabas replied. "Come with me. Let's go downstairs, and all of you see the boys. Both James and John are home, and have been working on some teachings for the Ecclesia school." With that, Zebedee's brother walked to the steps and made his way down. As he went, he called up. "We actually had chicken for dinner this evening, and I know for a fact there is still some pita bread left. And James made tzatziki to go with it all."

Peter made a lurch after Barnabas. "What? No fish? I'm in," he called, "even if no one else is."

"Oh no you don't!" Philip interjected, laughing, running down the stairs after him. "I'm sure Elsbeth cooked for *you* tonight! None of us have eaten. I'm so hungry I think my stomach is about to send up messages to my mouth for help."

James and John heard the noises of visitors from the outside. As Barnabas reached for the front door, John pulled it open, and stepped outside, bumping into his uncle. "Oh!" he said, startled. "I'm sorry, Uncle."

About that time, Peter darted between them with Philip on his heels. Joanna and Clement were not far behind, as were Shira and Libi. John looked at his uncle, who smiled.

"An entire group of our friends is home again," he told them. Philip has returned with Clement and Clemon. It seems Peter saw them before we did, so he came with them. Your father is upstairs, reading a letter from your mother."

"A letter from Mother?" John echoed. "She's *alive*? Is she all right?"

Barnabas hugged him. "Apparently. I'm sure your father will fill us in when he comes down. But for now, these poor people have been through so much. We need to feed them, and give them a place to sleep for the night. Philip plans to go home to Bethsaida tomorrow. I think Clement will want to go home with Peter, because the Holy Spirit told him to commit himself to schooling here in Capernaum."

John nodded. "I'm going to check on Abba," he told Barnabas. "It must be hard for him to know these friends have returned and our mother didn't. Do you know why?"

Barnabas patted his arm. "I'm sure that's why she sent a letter, son."

"Thanks, Uncle," John replied. He went up the stairs to the roof.

In the main room of the house, Philip greeted James. "What happened?" he asked. "How did you come here?"

He took a pita chicken sandwich from Barnabas. "Thank you," he said, looking at James. "We were in a ship without sails or a rudder. They set us onto the sea, and we drifted for three months. ElShaddai sent fresh rain every morning, and we learned how to fish for our food. We lived in a miracle! Even though it didn't feel like it at the time. Your great-uncle Joseph was amazing. He taught us to paddle with our hands. He helped us to stay near the coastal currents, as he called them. We finally came to Cyrene."

"In Africa?" James asked.

"Yes. Simeon, who helped Jesus with his cross, was also in the ship, and his parents lived in Cyrene. They helped us. Joseph has a small home there as well, because of his mines. It just happens to be the port where all of his merchant ships have been built. He and the rest of the group are wintering there, while the little ship is being repaired."

"Repaired?"

Philip continued. "Well, the men who kidnapped us, made us walk through the night to a port. I think we were just outside Appolonia. Anyway, someone paid to have a ship constructed without a mast or benches, or sails, or rudder. It was impossible to govern it on the sea. But by the miracles of ElShaddai, we made it to Cyrene. Joseph feels it will serve a purpose, so he is having it outfitted to make it usable. He intends to sail to Massilia with those in our group who feel led by the Holy Spirit to go with him.

"There were several who had dreams or visions of lands and peoples in Gaul or Briton; Martha had an amazing vision of Abba's purpose for her, and so did Joseph. Magdalene, Martha and Lazarus sense the Holy Spirit has instructed them to teach in the country near Massilia, at least for a time. Several sense they are to stay in Cyrene. I heard someone else mention Rome.

"For his part, Joseph intends to go around Land's End, sailing in that little ship, eventually reaching the Tin Islands, where his family has holdings. He has had several dreams of Abba Father's plans for the tribes there."

"And what did the Holy Spirit say to you, Philip?" James wanted to know.

"He showed me pictures in the night – I still can't tell whether I was dreaming or not. Would you call such an experience a dream, or a vision? I guess it doesn't really matter. All I know is he has poured an understanding into my heart of what he wants to do for the people in Samaria; things only God can make happen. I know I am supposed to plant an Ecclesia there. In fact, I was a little worried my wife and daughters, and their husbands, would take a long time to persuade, but from what Simon Peter tells me, they are already planning to move there, whether I come home or not!"

"It amazes me how the Holy Spirit works," Clement offered. "Each time I anticipate in fear I will encounter problems, he has already worked through the puzzle. How does that happen?"

Simon Peter patted his shoulder. "I know what you mean. It *has* to be the Holy Spirit," he answered. "When I begin thinking I can do things in my own strength, he becomes quiet. When I ask him to lead me, and trust him, I hear him speak." He paused, and then added. "And, when I pray in the language of angels, I know He understands what is being spoken. I know that helps me stay focused on the spiritual realm instead of the natural."

"Well said, Simon," Barnabas replied, handing him a sandwich. He moved to the storeroom. "Hey! There's a full wineskin in here. Anyone thirsty?"

On the rooftop, John was lighting a lamp to illuminate the evening darkness. His father had broken Joseph's seal on the scroll, and was reading the letter out loud.

> *From Salome, your loving wife and sister in the Lord Jesus;*
> *To my beloved friend, husband, and partner, Zebedee;*
> *Greetings!*
>
> *I am sure this letter has come to you unexpectedly. We were told in Cyrene that all who were put on this little ship were considered dead. But, by the miracle of our God, I am alive and well.*
>
> *Our uncle, Joseph of Arimathea, has helped to secure safety for all of us, with the help of the Holy Spirit. After prayer and fasting, each one has sensed a calling of the Lord to obey the commandment of Jesus to go into all the world, to preach the good news to everyone who will listen.*
>
> *When we prayed, several of the women felt led to come back to Jerusalem, to serve in the Ecclesia there. Along with my sister, Mary, I was compelled to travel with Joseph to the Tin Islands of Briton. Although my heart longs to see you, to hold you, my desire to obey the Holy Spirit is*

greater. I am not sure why I have received the leading I have; perhaps because you have remarried, or been sent by the Lord elsewhere. It would be understandable, since I am sure you thought I was now with the Lord.

Uncle Joseph believes we will be in Briton, with King Arviragus and the Dumnoni tribe by the summer season. If you are able and willing, I would love to see your face.

Please care for the young girls, Shira and Libi, who are new to the faith, and have suffered much.

If you cannot come, I will understand, and will remain faithful to our covenant to each other until death. I know I will see you again.

Zebedee finished reading the letter and looked up at John. His eyes were filled with tears. "I'm so proud of her," he said simply.

John looked at his father with admiration. "Her decision doesn't anger you?" he asked. "Like she chose *this* instead of *you?*"

His father smiled. "That would be selfish of me, wouldn't it?" he asked. "It is obvious ElShaddai ordained her presence on that little ship, as she calls it. In his mercy, he has kept her alive. Only he knows what she has been through. It took more courage for her to write this news, than it would for her to have simply returned home. Who would I be to assume God had made a mistake?"

"But can she be effective as an apostle, or an evangelist, without a man to protect her?" John asked.

"Because she is a *woman?* Or is it something else?" Zebedee was surprised by his son's prejudice. "Come sit, and let's talk about this."

John stood, caught off guard by his father's responses. He had not considered his attitude toward women before as something the Holy Spirit might address in his discipleship. As most Jewish young men of the day, he had adapted the attitudes portrayed in the culture of living around him. Stunned, he wondered.

How would Jesus' teachings affect the world's cultures, and change the status of women? What had he missed?

"I suppose I hadn't given it much thought," he told his father.

Zebedee patted the cushions next to him, where Barnabas had rested earlier. "What is it? You think she will need added credibility because she is a woman? And that may or may not be true. Or perhaps, because I am not there with her, she is somehow less; incomplete?"

He waited for a deeply thinking John to respond. "I know what Jesus taught us about women, and how they should be treated," his son began slowly. "But I also know what the priests and rabbis teach. *Shouldn't* she have come home to *you,* because she *belongs* to you? Isn't she violating the Law to stay with Uncle Joseph?"

"Oh," his father responded. "I see. You are mixing two cultures in your thinking, John, rather than choosing one or the other. It isn't wise to mix two wells. Either we are living according to the values Jesus provided us, or we are not. Our cultural law must be traded in for the Law of Life in the Holy Spirit when we enter the Kingdom of God."

John sensed a teaching moment was about to begin. He sat down on the cushions.

"But isn't our view of women something passed down from Moses?" John asked. "If not, then *everything* changes when I follow the Master."

Zebedee looked into his son's eyes with a steady gaze. "Didn't everything else change as well? And did Jesus say he was the fulfillment of the Law?" he asked. "For example, consider this: Did God tell Moses that Israelite women were not allowed to enter into the Outer Court of the Wilderness Tabernacle?" his father asked.

"No," John responded. "Everyone could enter and approach to worship."

"And in David's Tabernacle, were the women excluded from participation?" his father asked.

"No," John replied. "In fact, they enhanced the worship with dance and musical accompaniments."

"Then why does the present Temple of Herod, have a Court for the Gentiles, a Court for the Women, and then place the Altar of Sacrifice in the Court of the Men? Doesn't this communicate that a woman is less worthy of His presence than a man? Do you think it was ElShaddai's original plan to prevent a woman from approaching the Brazen Altar?"

John thought, and then shook his head. "No. Not at all."

Zebedee continued. "Then we have to think this through. To think of your mother as being my *property,* the way the Egyptians do, or the Syrians do, or even the priests do, is to reduce her *value* as a person in the eyes of God. It means I see myself as superior to her. That is male pride. God sees us all as equally important. To reduce her this way destroys the significance of her heart and mind. It means I somehow believe he cannot speak to her without going through me first. Do you follow?"

"Yes," John nodded. "But what about authority? Doesn't the man have the final authority in the home?"

His father smiled. "Not authority, son," he answered. "Jesus told us we are to serve. If a man is to be one with his wife, he won't bully her into agreement.

422

He will love her. In my experience, I have never seen a woman who could resist being loved by a man. When we serve each other in love, it amazes me. I have had your mother yield her views for the sake of unity, just because I loved her."

"I can remember that happening," John noted.

"For example," his father explained, "when Adam was first created, man and woman were together in one being. This was the complete image of ElShaddai. Would you agree?"

John nodded. "Yes. I follow."

"So, if I deny her significance, then I lose a portion of myself, don't I? I cannot appreciate perception, then, or intuition, or emotion. And these are the parts of our humanity which relate well to the Holy Spirit's nature."

"That's true," John replied. "But what do you do with an unmarried man? Is he then incomplete without a woman?

Zebedee raised his finger once more. "No, because we are each completed in Jesus! He has covered our deficiencies."

"Then why would a man become married?" John asked.

"Ah," his father replied. "For companionship. Remember, our God separated the man from the woman, and created the concept of human relationship. Before he took her out of the man, Adam was living alone; isolated. This was the only part of his creation our God deemed as 'not good.' So, he amended his creation, and presented a counterpart to the man. Would you say this is true?"

"Of course," John answered. "All of the priests and rabbis teach this. I have heard it since childhood."

Zebedee lowered his voice, and instinctively raised his forefinger in making a point. "So, then," he said. "Since she was taken *out* of the man, does she lose her ability to stand separately and alone, or does he? And if she does lose that ability, wouldn't the man lose that ability as well? Which part of the relationship has more significance and value; the man or the woman?"

John considered the question. "I would have to say they both have equal value."

Zebedee chuckled. "And that was the *original* plan of ElShaddai! To reduce the inward parts of Adam to the level of an ass, or a wagon, is actually a demeaning of the image of God himself. By his very words and actions, Jesus himself showed us ElShaddai's attitude towards women."

John looked at his father in surprise. "I would agree, but I need an example," he answered.

"Think of Magdalene sitting at his feet like a student; as only a man would be allowed to do under the oral, Tanakh Law. Or, the Samaritan woman speaking to him alone at a well; as only a man would be allowed to do under the Tanakh. Or, Jesus' relationship with Martha. Or, even the fact that in Eden, after the fruit was consumed, he told them the Promised Deliverer would come from the 'seed of the *woman*.'"

John was digesting what he was hearing. "This would put women in a completely different place in the culture," he responded.

His father smiled. "Yes," he replied. "I believe it puts them where they belong. Of equal value and significance to men. This means in Jesus, they are allowed to think and speak and learn; to have minds and hearts of their own. A woman chooses; just as the man chooses. The role of women has been redeemed as well as everything else!"

"And that's why you are not offended with Maman's choice?"

His father's eyes twinkled. "No, son. I am challenged. God has made your mother an arrow to show us the way. I'm going to seek the Holy Spirit's permission to move."

"Move?" his son questioned.

"To the Tin Islands. The Holy Spirit would not have spoken to her to stay with Uncle Joseph if he wasn't going to make us both a part of what he is going to do. He is the one who brought us together. He is leading all of us." Zebedee began to reroll the scroll.

John nodded. "I agree. I have wondered what it will take for all of us to actually make the changes Jesus instructed us to make. He told us to go into all the world, and it seems many of us are becoming stuck in one place. Something has to happen to help us 'go to all the world.'"

His father nodded. "I have felt for some time there is a change coming for all the Ecclesia in Israel. We will eventually be involuntarily *required* to leave Judea. I don't know why. Now, after reading and considering your mother's letter, I am convinced it is the Lord speaking to me. You see, I've had to discern between his voice and my own fears. Perhaps it would be better to relocate before we are forced out. That way we could sell the business, and move at our own pace, rather than rushing out in fear."

Something inexplicable stirred in John's chest. He smiled. "For some time now, I have sensed a need to go to Ephesus, but haven't known the timing of making such a change." He looked at Zebedee. "Perhaps this is my clue to leave as well."

424

"This is certainly an arrow to show us all the way. I am amazed at the goodness of God," Zebedee repeated. Then he added, "I can't wait to see what the Holy Spirit is going to do."

In the city of Cyrene, a group of more than thirty were packing their belongings, readying to set sail. It had been two months since Philip and his party had sailed for Caesarea. Since that time, a group had sailed to Cyprus, another to Rome, another for Ephesus, and another for Thessalonica. Most had family members in these cities, and felt drawn to reach them with the message of Jesus' love and the freedom of the Holy Spirit.

Over the past two weeks, Joseph had helped each of them to streamline their needs to fit in the small ship. As far as they knew at the moment, the plan was to row against the coastal currents from Cyrene to Carthage. From there, they would determine whether to remain in waters under Carthage control, and head north to Sardinia, and then finally to Massilia, or, to simply follow the coastline to the Straits of Tangi.

There, the waters separating the lands of Espania and Mauritania were less than ten miles wide. Ships sailing into the Mediterranean from the Oceanus Major and the Celtic Sea were propelled into the smaller Mediterranean Sea by a mighty current, which ancient legends taught was actually a river, still forging its path from the days when the Great Ice had covered the area.

It was said it was impossible to sail out to Oceanus Major by way of the straits. Many men had lost their lives seeking to tame the oppositional waters and winds which worked against them.

Seasoned sailors, who called the western end of the Mediterranean their home, avoided the straits, making it their custom to sail to Narbo or Massilia when they wished to travel outside the lesser waters to Briton or elsewhere. From there, the standard practice was to pay one of the two Transport Services, whose slaves would pull the vessels by river or on wheels across the continent to the other side. From there, they could set sail for the northern lands of the Vikings, to the Tin Islands, or to the recently discovered western land of Eire.

Mary and Salome had gone to the market in the early morning, with instructions from their uncle to purchase dried meats, fruit, and bread. He had already loaded fresh water-skins and wineskins onboard.

The changes Duruk and his workers had made in the little ship were amazing, Mary considered. There were now benches on which to sit, with

425

available storage under their cushions. A mast had been added, with adjustable sails and riggings. The shipbuilders had added a rudder, three sets of oar holders with oars, and an anchor. In the aft, or rear, of the little ship, they had also created two canopied areas for shade, each one with a curtain which could be drawn for privacy. Two boxes with hinged lids for more storage had been fashioned inside each of the canopied areas. And another single box had been added at the bow. All additions had been fastened to the hull, and sealed inside and out.

Duruk had water tested the vessel, and found it to be sound.

It was beautiful, Salome decided. The fabric of the sails matched the cushions and the canopy. The colors of all the additions were coordinated. The entire craft now looked as though it had been created as a family's recreational excursion vessel for a day at sea.

How had an instrument of destruction and torment, become now a tool for their God-given mission, she considered?

After placing purchased foodstuffs under canopy, the two women took in the newly acquired beauty of the vessel. Thankfully, Mary tried to remember what the little ship had been before Duruk and his workers had begun its refurbishing. Amazed at the changes, she realized the travel from Cyrene to Massilia would be much more comfortable than the drift-and-tow method they had experienced on the first leg of the journey.

But then, in her assessments of the little ship, she discovered a concern, which she voiced to Salome.

"Do you see a privy pot?" she asked.

Salome laughed. "No," she replied. "I didn't think of it. Leave it to you to be practical." She viewed the interior of the boat with pursed lips. "I don't see any cleaning cloths or towels either..... And we will need to purchase enough *saipo,* or soap, to get us through the next few weeks of travel. Do you see anything else we need to mention to Uncle Joseph?"

Silently, the two women contemplated the missing detail outfitting of the boat.

"What about a small water-pot on a rope to draw water from the sea for washing hands and such? What do you think?" Salome offered.

"Good idea," came the reply. "Do we need to find a way to keep our foodstuffs separated from all the other belongings people will be travelling with? We could purchase a deep basket to keep under one of the canopies. Or even a series of baskets we could stack on top of each other. What do you think?" Mary replied.

Salome had been investigating the added benches on the sides and middle of the boat. Each cushioned top was resting on what appeared to be a wooden block. As she investigated, she discovered the top of each cushion was removable. Additionally, what appeared to be a wooden block, was actually a box created for storage.

"Mary! Look!" she cried. "We can each put our belongings inside the benches under us! We could assign each person a space to help us stay organized!"

"So, that will free up the canopied spots for group needs!" the younger answered. "If we designate one area for food, and put the privy pot in the other; we could designate that side for cleansing. I think it would help us all. That way the curtain can be pulled closed when someone is using the pot, and it can be emptied over the rail."

"We had better hurry, if we are going to accomplish these things before we sail," Salome said, looking up at the sun's position in the sky. "How much time do we have until we are to sail?"

"I think about two hours," Mary answered.

Salome moved into action, turning to go. "We had better get a move on then," she said. "I still have to go back to the house to gather my things."

"Me too," her sister agreed.

As they walked back to the marketplace, the two women strategized regarding fine points to help make the sea journey more comfortable for everyone involved. In the marketplace, they each went separate ways to purchase the items needed. After making their way back to the ship to stow away the purchased goods, they returned to the house to retrieve their possessions.

In the midst of their errands, Mary realized for the first time she was actually looking forward to the days ahead. A sense of anticipation and excitement had overtaken the great sadness she had been carrying since Cleophas had died. As she considered the change, she discovered she was looking forward to seeing her friends in the Tin Islands as well. She had visited many times in her life, traveling with her Uncle Joseph.

As they walked together, Mary fell silent, remembering her visits to the villages of the Dumnoni. She had been there with Uncle Joseph and Aunt Escha as a child, to be sure. But in particular she was considering the trip she and Joseph had taken with her uncle to see the mines. Jesus had been in his tenth year then. Then, she had returned four years later, when it was time for Jesus to begin his schooling at the Academy. It had been just after her first husband, Joseph's death.

They had travelled almost a month prior to the school term's beginning, she remembered. Her uncle had been helping the workers choose a new vein of tin to follow down into the earth from the surface. Most of the mines had been in operation since the days of the ancient Phoenicians. Some of the digs had become too deep to lower a man into without danger of suffocation or illness. So, Joseph had decided to take the challenge personally. As the oldest of Mary's sons, he had invited Jesus to help in the process.

She had made many lifetime friends during that summer, she decided.

She smiled, considering the enormity of the projects Jesus had undertaken during his years there. Was the building he constructed still in place, she wondered? He never had been one to shrink away from a task. Were they empty now, or had the Druid priests, and the king repurposed them?

It wouldn't be long until she had the opportunity to learn the answers to her questions for herself, she realized.

It had been more than fifteen years since they had visited for his graduation ceremonies.

In the city of Antioch, in Syria, Simeon of Cyrene's two sons, Rufus and Alexander, were sharing a meal with Lucius, the former owner of Jerusalem's only Weaving and Fabric Dyeing Houses, and an older man from EnKarem, named Eleazar. Across the table from these men were two of the leaders from the Jerusalem Ecclesia; Simon Peter and Barnabas.

"Do you have a meeting place yet?" Simon Peter was asking.

"We have been meeting in the synagogue during the week," Lucius answered. "But our group is becoming too large to fit in the building."

"How about house-to-house meetings?" Barnabas asked.

"My wife and I have a group meeting in our home two nights each week," Rufus answered. "There are such wonderful things happening. People are being healed, and coming to the knowledge of who Jesus really is. We are seeing families brought back together, too. So many of our brothers are coming to believe."

"What are the Jewish religious leaders in the city doing in reaction to these things?" Barnabas asked.

"What do you think they are doing?" Eleazar chuckled. "The same thing they did in Jerusalem. The same thing they did to my children. They want to kill us all!"

Lucius laughed, stroking the older man's arm. "It's all right, Eleazar. Remember, your children aren't dead. They were all on the little ship commissioned by Caiaphas."

"Joseph of Arimathea sent word to us at Capernaum that they are all alive, and following Jesus' commandment to travel to different nations to share the story of Jesus with our Jewish brothers who haven't heard yet." Simon Peter told him.

Eleazar shook his head. "That's right. I remember now. I'm having more and more of these lapses happen these days."

Rufus spoke up in an effort to redirect the conversation. "Our parents, Simeon and Ramona, are back in Cyrene now. Father sent word of an Ecclesia beginning there. Our grandparents have chosen to follow Jesus' teachings. And so have many others. So far, they have more than twenty meeting together in their home. They have one of the copies of Matthew's Codex of the story of Jesus, and they are working through it; teaching anyone who will listen."

"There were several of us in the marketplace last week," Lucius said. "I've been looking at several buildings where I could set up a weaving house here. Rufus was praying for a man who had been crippled since birth. When he stood to his feet, and began to walk back and forth in the market, one of the Greek-speaking Jews began to heckle him."

"What did he say?" Peter asked.

"The same kind of things they said in Jerusalem, and Samaria," Rufus answered. "He called me a *'little Christ.'*"

"A Christ-ian?" Peter echoed, a smile emerging on his face.

"That's the word!" Rufus replied. "I think I've decided I like it. Isn't that our final goal as followers of Jesus? To become like the Christ; in how we live and treat others; in our personal values and character?"

Silence hung in the room. It was Alexander who spoke first. "I am a *Christ-ian.*" He looked around the room. "I like the sounds of that. It's like a badge of honor!" He looked at Simon Peter. "Are you a Christ-ian?"

Peter smiled. "I'd like to think I am. It's certainly a goal I'd aspire to. How about you, Eleazar?" he asked.

"I am a Christian, too," the older man declared. He looked at Rufus. "I like this! How many of those coming to study with us would want to adopt that name as our own?"

18 – Massillia

Spring, 39 AD

When a person has experienced extreme hardship, subsequent hardships seem manageable.

Before setting sail from Cyrene, Joseph had investigated the currents of the waters they would be encountering, interviewing several of the city's most seasoned seamen. The next segments of travel involved sea voyages from Cyrene to Carthage; from Carthage to Sardinia; from Sardinia to Massilia.

As he walked through the process of learning, Joseph created a map of sorts, based on the descriptions of the area fishermen. It was during these discussions, the group had decided to travel to Sardinia from Carthage, avoiding the Straits by Espania completely.

Setting sail at dawn one Tuesday, the group was thankful for a calm sea and a strong breeze from the east. For everyone involved, the passage felt luxurious compared to the days of kidnapping and being set adrift.

Thinking about it now, Lazarus decided it was the leg to Carthage which had been the most difficult. Oppositional currents, whirlpool-like eddies, and strong winds presented themselves daily. Reduced to rowing constantly, the travelers found themselves hugging the coastline for more than two thousand miles. Rowing in shifts, each evening still found them all exhausted, hungry and ready for sleep.

Still, they reasoned among themselves, they had an option on this journey they hadn't had before. They could always put into a port or pull to the shoreline to rest when they were desperate and felt weary or hungry.

Joseph and Lazarus discussed what they appreciated most in the journey. They found agreement in the fact; each of them appreciated the opportunity to walk and stretch every day. Joints didn't become nearly as stiff as they had on the way to Cyrene.

Every few miles, a new freshwater creek or small river fed into the Mediterranean from the mainland, adding to the sea's unique circular currents. Built on the banks of these waterways were innumerable farms and fishing villages. As they travelled, the group discovered lodging was not readily available in every village. As a result, several nights in a row had required sleeping near a campfire.

Every person in the group loved sleeping outdoors. And, during this season of the year, the nights were cool, but not cold. The days were warmer, but not stormy. For each of them, there was much to give thanks for.

Finally, they arrived in the ancient city of Carthage.

Carthage had been built in the days of the Phoenicians, and pre-dated the Roman Empire. The Carthaginian military had set the standard for fierceness in battle in the days of the Punic Wars. As such, in spite of all efforts, Rome had been unable to conquer the city. In 500BC they had signed a peace treaty with the Carthaginians, giving them the provinces of Sicily, Sardinia and Corsica. With individual independence, little in Carthage's lifestyle was different from that in the Roman provinces.

Carthage paid no taxes to Caesar, and maintained its own cultural traditions. Peace by deterrence had worked for this small country – at least for now.

After resting a few days in the city of Carthage, and restocking their stores, they turned northward. Setting sail for the city of Caralis, they began the next leg in the journey, crossing the open sea to the island of Sardinia. Carried by the favorable Scirocco Winds, the miles seemed to melt away.

From Caralis, they sailed on the high tide, using the Marin Winds to reach Massilia. The last two jaunts of the voyage were actually enjoyable, refreshing to everyone, even though several nights were spent on the open sea.

They hardly had to row at all!

Duruk's sails had filled with the favorable winds, kindly propelling them to their destinations.

An experienced sailor, Joseph was now outfitted with lanterns, a compass and a map of the night sky. It was amazing, he considered, how the right winds had just presented themselves the closer they came to their first destination of Massilia.

It had to be the hand of God.

Massilia was a Roman city on the southern coast of the continent. Presently, the settlement served as the capital of the Roman province of Bouches-du-Rhone. On its western side, sandy shores and a rock harbor provided safety for the dry docks and armory housed there.

In its center, the local Temple to Diana of the Ephesians, called the *Ephesium,* was equipped with more than a thousand temple prostitutes. Within walking distance from the Ephesium was another Temple, dedicated to the Delphians of Apollo. The Romans believed Apollo was the god of light, and provided chambers for temple psychics to give "holy readings" to the faithful, but only after the acceptable amount or its equivalent had been placed at the feet of the god's sculpted image in the main atrium.

Such religious provisions and practices were common throughout the Roman Empire. The Romans were poly-theistic, meaning they worshipped many gods. Devoutly religious Romans lived with tremendous levels of anxiety; most had sleep issues. The majority of those raised in the Empire suffered with a constant fear of displeasing any one of the many gods. There was a god in charge of the harvest, a god who ruled the weather, a god who gave favor in war, a god who made one fertile, a god who provided the safety and security of the home, all of which required sacrifice and homage.

Just to name a few.

So many gods existed in the minds of Rome, a person could choose a god based on whatever need presented itself. After centuries of these practices, most Romans had given up on their prayers or sacrifices receiving any answers.

Not only did those of the Empire worship the Roman gods, they gave tribute to the Greek ones as well. Diana of the Ephesians was an evidence of one such goddess. The Greeks believed the gods had come down from heaven on Mount Olympus, and had cohabited with earthly women, producing men like Hercules and Achilles.

Since Massilia was a center for trade and commerce, the city was also filled with typical Roman establishments, as were larger cities in the Empire. Bath-houses, brothels, several inns, drinking houses, spa salons, fabric houses, clothing stores, sellers of cooked foods, and innumerable merchants in the marketplace from all over the known world.

Near the Ephesium, a large boarding school had been constructed for the sons of wealthy Roman citizens. Although small when compared to Roman learning centers in other cities, those whose families served the Empire on the western side of the Mediterranean considered the school a lifeline to civilization. The people of Massilia were proud to consider their school comparable to those in Ephesus, Athens, and even Rome.

In fact, Massilia's government was controlled by a well-regulated council of six hundred, called the Tumichi. It was also an entry port for the Empire.

Joseph of Arimathea, as the Nobilius Decurio, was well known to port officials here. Much of the tin mined over the centuries had passed overland, from the cities of Morlaix and Calais on the coast of the Bristol Channel, to reach the coastal waters of the Mediterranean in Massilia.

On the western outskirts of the city, a synagogue had been built in the past ten years. A large Jewish Community made up the population for more than twenty miles along the coast. Knowing they would be welcomed into the community, Joseph and his companions rested there.

For several weeks, it was almost as though they were back in Jerusalem. The small ship's company filled the local inn in the Jewish Quarter. This caused no small stir among the synagogue leaders.

Word spread like wildfire....

A member of Jerusalem's Sanhedrin was present in Massillia! And, it was the man who was known by the Romans as Nobilius Decurio! On the Sabbath, the priests asked Joseph to read from the scrolls and make comments, teaching from the chosen reading.

Following the meeting, many stayed to speak with the newcomers.

Were they here to stay?

How had they come to Massilia?

Who was the Jesus this man had spoken of in the meeting?

What did he mean, 'the Promised Deliver has come?'

"I was dead for three days," Lazarus offered. "Jesus raised me back to life."

Kfir, the Pharisee priest who served as synagogue ruler for the settlement, was stirred and amazed at the statements being made. He took Joseph and Lazarus aside.

"Sir," he began, "I want to invite your company to my home. I want to hear more of what you are saying. I have heard rumors of a man dying on a cross in Jerusalem some years ago; the year darkness filled the earth in the middle of the day."

"Yes," Joseph said. "That man was Jesus; the man I spoke of."

"He had power over the winds and the sea? Is that what you were saying?" Kfir inquired.

"He did; and he does still," Joseph smiled.

Kfir looked at Lazarus. "And he raised you from the dead?"

Lazarus nodded. "Yes sir," he replied. "And many others as well. My sisters are here and can tell you about it as well."

Overhearing their conversation, Zaccheus added a comment.

"He changed my life completely," inserted Zaccheus. "I was a thief who collected taxes and now I am an honest man. A clean man on the inside."

"I must know about this man," the synagogue leader responded. "Can you come to my home tomorrow? Say around midday?"

"We would greatly enjoy that," Joseph answered. "Thank you for the invitation."

The next day was full of surprises.

Several in the company had been concerned about attending the meeting with the synagogue leader and his family. What if his questions were only setting another trap for them? Was it possible Caiaphas had sent word ahead of them? Or, that they would be arrested and executed on the spot?

In spite of their fears, everyone in the company sensed the peaceful leading of the Holy Spirit to attend the meeting.

And, true to the Spirit's leading, their fears were unfounded.

The gathering that day would prove to be a hinge pin; a turning point in the plan and design of each of their lives.

As they arrived that midday, each person was greeted kindly and provided a towel. Then, house slaves busied themselves with washing the dust off their feet. Then, after insuring their comfort while waiting for the meal, the discussion turned to the current news from Jerusalem. As it turned out, the priest and his wife were aware of more news of current events in their home country of Israel, than the travelers.

Joseph was surprised and saddened to hear of Caiaphas' stabbing, and the injury to James, Jesus' half-brother. It seemed strange to him, he realized, two different High Priests had served in that office in the past year. And yet, Caiaphas had been in power for more than twelve years.

Perhaps it was a sign of growing unrest in the nation.

Or, perhaps it was a manifestation in the physical, visible realm, of something which had taken place in the spiritual, visible realm. The real High Priest, Jesus, had taken his place in the spiritual realm.

He had been the Lamb of God.

There was no need for further sacrifices.

Kfir told them Pontius Pilate and his family had come through Massilia on their way to a new post in the Alpine region. Pontius was now the governor of the district just north of the one in which they were presently standing.

There had been no uprisings or mass executions as far as anyone knew.

Kfir proved to be a welcoming host, who was truly spiritually hungry. He and his wife, Eliana, served truly ethnic foods.

This was their first taste of Jewish cuisine since leaving Jerusalem, Mary realized!

The entire group ate until they could eat no more. Salome and Martha helped Eliana and her daughters, Jasmine and Deborah, in cleaning up after the meal.

"I haven't had good stuffed grape leaves since before we left Jerusalem!" Salome told her. "Those were so good, Eliana! What do you put in them? They were absolutely amazing!"

Eliana smiled, and recited her recipe.

Martha looked at Salome. "That sounds like the recipe I use," she said. "But honestly, it's been so long, I will have to work at remembering for sure."

It was after the meal when discussions began in earnest. During conversation, Joseph learned Kfir had been a student in Gamaliel's school for boys. He was a Pharisee, and had come to Massillia to serve Jewish families who had fled Judea to avoid political unrest. He had heard of Jesus, but had not been told of Jesus' true identity as God come to earth.

He had no idea that Jesus had come as the Promised Deliverer.

The synagogue ruler had many questions regarding the group and their purpose in traveling together.

"How did you come to be in such a small ship, so far from home?" Kfir asked.

Joseph smiled. "Because we have chosen to follow Jesus," he answered simply, with a shrug. "The love and real power of our God seems to intimidate those who only want to be religious."

Kfir nodded. "There are many like that here as well," he answered. "In my placement here, I have observed a similarity between the Gentile worshippers of Diana and Apollo, and the religious members of my own synagogue."

Joseph was surprised at the man's perception. Such thinking was rare indeed. "What do you mean?" he prodded.

"Well, those who walk in religion only, seem to trust their own ability to do good works, and to follow schedules. But those I have had the opportunity to speak with, tell me of a dark cloud they sense hovering over them, even when circumstances are going in their favor. The same cloud seems to haunt Gentile and Jew alike." The priest shook his head. "I don't understand it completely."

"But something has occurred to you," Joseph noted. "What have you learned?"

"The difference seems to occur when one has a relational experience with the person of ElShaddai," Kfir answered. "These are people who seem to know their God and not live in fear of failing him." He paused. "I see such a nature in you, Joseph," he said with directness. "And in those in your group I have spoken with."

"Thank you," Joseph replied.

"What has provided this confidence in you; this strength?" the synagogue ruler pressed. "Does it have something to do with this Jesus?"

Joseph smiled. "It has everything to do with him."

"Tell me. No, wait." Kfir looked towards the cooking area. "My wife and daughters are experiencing the same yearnings I am. I want them to hear as well. Can we wait until Eliana and the women are done working?"

"Surely," Joseph responded. "Tell me, do you have a scroll of Isaiah?"

"I do," the priest answered excitedly. "Do you want it?"

Joseph nodded. "It will help us when we talk about parts of the story. So many of the prophets foretold Jesus' coming, and the way in which he would come. Every one of them came to pass, just the way the prophecies promised."

"I have read all of the prophets' scrolls in the synagogue, several times," Kfir offered.

"I'm sure you will be reading them again soon," Joseph told him, smiling. "There are more prophecies fulfilled in Isaiah's scroll than any other. So this would be a good place to begin."

"I'll be right back," the priest told him.

On his way out of their home to the synagogue, he stopped to speak with Eliana. "Joseph and his companions are going to tell us how to develop a personal relationship with our God," he told her. "I'm going to get the scroll of Isaiah from the synagogue. Do you think you will be done out here by the time I come back?"

His wife responded with excitement. "I can be done right now, my love," she told him. "Are the girls and I allowed to be part of the teaching time?"

He hugged her. "Absolutely! I want you there!" he told her.

"I know you do," she answered. "But Joseph is a member of the Sanhedrin. I was sure he would want to reinforce the law of the Tanakh."

Kfir hadn't considered her point of view. He looked at Salome and Martha. "What is the practice in your group when it comes to allowing women to learn with the men?"

Martha laughed. "I can tell you what Jesus thought about teaching women. I once caught my sister sitting down at his feet like a prized pupil, asking questions and learning during the time I was preparing a meal for the more than seventy people he had travelling with him. When I told him she was supposed to be helping me, you know what he did?"

"What?" Eliana asked.

"He told me I was too worried about the little details, and they were more important to me than my own inward development," Martha answered. "He would have preferred it if I had joined them for a few moments, to learn as well. Now, looking back, I'm sure he would have helped us finish the preparations if I had asked without making demands."

Kfir was impressed. "I have wondered many times why the Tanakh took away the wonderful contributions women can make in our group settings. I could not serve the people in my care without my wife's help. And I cannot even begin to see things the way she does. What she feels is important, especially when it comes to the women and family matters."

Salome spoke up. "Jesus was always giving us dignity," she said. "I can't remember a time when he spoke down to any woman. Not once in his 33 years. I remember one time when we were all traveling together and a group of women with children pressed in to ask him to bestow a blessing on their little ones. The twelve were offended, and tried to shoo the women away. They said, 'he's too busy today. He doesn't have time for this.' But Jesus corrected them. He said, 'let them some to me. These are the people who make up the Kingdom of Heaven.'"

The priest looked at his wife. "That settles it for me," he told her. "I want you all in the teaching time, and every teaching time from today onward."

An hour later, the private outdoor courtyard of Kfir and Eliana's home was filled with the synagogue leader's family, Joseph and the entire company from the little ship, and two or three additional friends of the priest and his wife.

In thinking about how to proceed, Joseph considered the training he knew Kfir had received, and the areas of struggle he had watched Nicodemus and Gamaliel walk through when it came to walking away from areas of legalism and religiosity.

He knew it would encourage the man to learn that his mentor and instructor, Gamaliel, had become a follower of Jesus as well.

While they were waiting for Kfir to return with the Isaiah scroll, Joseph spoke with Mary, his niece.

"They want to hear the story of Jesus, and hear how all of us came to be on that little ship," he told her.

Mary laughed. "We will be here all night, Uncle! Where are you planning to begin?"

He looked at her in his fatherly way. "I thought we should do what Matthew did in his codex."

She looked back at him. "What do you mean?"

"I think *you* should begin the story."

In shocked surprise, Mary was speechless. Her eyes grew wide.

Joseph stroked her arm. "It began with Gabriel's declaration to you, and Elizabeth's pregnancy. I know Matthew didn't include those two things, but they are extremely important. I know he wanted to protect you from persecution as his step-mother."

"That's true," she answered.

"But we don't have to be concerned with that type of persecution here. We can tell the whole story, with each of us telling our own part of what happened in our lives because of Jesus," he told her.

"I've never had to speak to a group before," she said.

"It's easier than you think," Joseph instructed. "Just focus on someone in the group you are most comfortable speaking to. Talk to that person as though the two of you are alone. Secondly, remember it is important everyone hearing you understands what you mean to say. If you become uncomfortable, ask those who are listening if they have any questions about what you are saying. Those things have always helped me, even in front of kings."

"So you're serious. You want me to speak, even though I'm a woman," she clarified.

"I want you to speak because you are the best one to describe what happened to you and your Joseph," he answered. "Male or female is not an issue in the Kingdom. Of everyone on our little ship, you of all people should know that."

She smiled. "Thank you, Uncle," she said. "I guess I just haven't ever seen myself that way. We are part of something entirely new in the world, aren't we?"

"Yes, we are," he answered. "Jesus coming changed everything. The world will never be the same."

439

Close to a month later, the company met together in the same courtyard. The inn owners in the Jewish Quarter had been very kind. It was almost like having a new home, Mary considered.

The Holy Spirit had been busy among them.

Lazarus had developed a fast friendship with Kfir. The man's family worked as trade merchants, and owned several caravans. Lazarus had operated his own caravan trade business during earlier years in EnKarem. In fact, it had been a caravan camel's bite which had caused his death.

The two men found they had much in common. This past week, Lazarus had experienced a night-time visitation. As with most experiences which are truly divine in nature, the man wasn't sure if he had been dreaming or awake.

In his night vision, Jesus had stood next to his bed and called him by his Hebrew name. "Eleazar, I want to speak with you."

Sitting up in his bed, he had rubbed his eyes.

"Yes, Lord?" he asked.

"You are to stay here in Massillia and establish an Ecclesia here. I will bless you and prosper your efforts. Don't be afraid. My favor rests on you."

Lazarus had awakened the next morning, rested, but with vivid memory of Jesus' words the night before.

The next day, before he could tell his sister, Mary Magdalene, she greeted him eagerly. "Brother, I had a dream! I know what I am to do now. I am supposed to stay here and work with these people. I think I will be rescuing women from the brothels here. At any rate, I am so excited to finally have a clear word. Jesus came and spoke to me as I was sleeping."

As she was speaking, Martha interrupted. "You too? He came to me as well! I am supposed to stay here as well!"

Lazarus looked at both of them, his face breaking into a great grin. "Here we go again. He appeared to me as well last night. I am to establish an Ecclesia here. I think we will all be working with Kfir."

"Did you know he and Eliana want to be baptized?" Magdalene asked. "Deborah and Jasmine too." She unconsciously clapped her hands together. "This is so exciting!"

As the group came together, several others spoke excitedly about visions and experiences they had the night before. Zaccheus expressed a desire to stay in Massillia, having experienced a calling from the Lord as well.

Trophimus, who had served in the Jerusalem Ecclesia, sought out Martha as soon as he arrived.

"I had a dream last night. Or it was a vision. Anyway, Jesus spoke to me, and told me he has called you for his purposes. Then, I saw a huge creature, like a dragon. It faded away, and I saw you standing there. He told me to take care of you. To serve as you care-giver, and protector, because you will be very busy."

Martha's head cocked sideways. "Like a *paranymphos?*" she said. "That's funny, because Jesus spoke to me last night as well. I am supposed to stay here in Massillia. At least for a while."

Trophimus let out a long breath. "I am so relieved. I wasn't sure how you would respond. The Lord let me know you will need a helper, and somehow, I have a sense we will be very busy."

"I have that understanding as well," she told him.

A similar occurrence took place when Maximin came outside for breakfast. He walked right to Mary Magdalene, and said, "Mary, can I talk to you?"

Smiling at him, she answered. "Good morning, Max."

"Mary," he began. "I had a dream last night."

Having heard the other conversations taking place around them, Mary thought it might be fun to give him a hard time. "You saw Jesus, didn't you?" she asked. "And he said you were supposed to stay here in Massillia."

Maximin's jaw dropped open. "How did you know?" he asked.

She was instantly sorry. "Forgive me," she said. "I've heard several people say they had the same dream last night. It seems Jesus appeared to many of us, and instructed those he spoke to that we are staying in Massillia. The same thing happened to me, to Martha, to Trophimus, to Lazarus, to Marcella. For each of us, Jesus appeared, and told us we would be staying here, and beginning an Ecclesia in Massillia.

Maximin's face broke into a smile. "What do you think Jesus said to me, Mary?"

The Magdalene looked at him with surprise. "I'm not sure I could say," she answered. "I was just trying to tease you a little, that's all."

"Oh, it's fine," Maximin soothed. "Actually, it is kinda funny. But seriously, the Lord told me that I am to serve you, as paranymphos. I don't know where that means we will be, but the Holy Spirit wants me to take care of you and protect you."

"Why?" she asked.

In earlier days, Mary Magdalene had experienced the worst side of men seeking her company as a single woman, mostly in environments far from healthy. At the end of that life season, she had encountered Jesus. That had been the day he cast seven demons screaming from her being.

441

Over the years, she had been the target of abuses and exploitations of many kinds. There were only a few men in her life whom she felt were truly trustworthy.

As she listened to Maximin, the Holy Spirit began to help her to discern and respond, rather than react in suspicion, to his words.

There had been a time early in her days of following Jesus, when Mary had been afraid sharing her personal history would cause difficulties in developing relationships in her future. And even though she had thought about it as a threat back then, and wondered what she would do if it happened, the possibility had not presented itself until this very moment.

Yet, unexpectedly, like a mystery, God was giving her his peace.

Assessing him as he spoke, she decided she liked Maximin.

After all, she reasoned, he also had lost everything, had been kidnapped, and was seeking direction for his future as well.

She decided it was time to learn to trust once more.

Inwardly she prayed. *Thank you, Jesus, for taking me deeper to heal me.*

A week later, Joseph and eleven others set out from Massillia to cross the continent towards Briton. The little ship had been loaded on an oversized wagon, wedged in its place with poles. Two other vessels were part of their particular transport group, which would make its way over 1300 miles to Calais, the only harbor city providing ferry service to the southern part of Briton. Passage to Calais also enabled travel to the northern coastal cities in Denmark, Norsk, and Finlandia.

Rome had been building up the transport system from Italia and across the continent for the last five years. The ship transport to the Bristol Channel was no exception. The facilities for boarding horses and oxen, and their keepers had more than doubled since Joseph's last trip to the mines.

"If Land's End exists where we are going, why are the Romans going to so much trouble to enlarge travel to the Channel?" Mary asked her uncle.

"Trade, for now," Joseph told her. "But we all know they will go to war against the tribes eventually. This is the first step in building the Roman war machine."

Mary had not considered the effect of Roman conquest on lands outside of Judea. Watching the slaves prepare the wagons, she began to wonder what their lives had been before conquest. How long had the men she was watching been slaves, she wondered? Where were their families?

Suddenly, a wave of compassion overwhelmed her.

These were the lost ones. Even as Gentiles, they needed to hear the story.

They didn't know. They hadn't heard.

Who would tell them?

Silently, she watched her uncle. He was negotiating and paying the service fees for their relatively small party of twelve to ride rather than walk across the continent. Due to the terrain, travelers were ill-advised to walk. Most travelers chose to pay for passage, especially since the fees included food and lodging for the forty days of travel.

Massillia's Transport Service was no longer a private business. Now, it had become property of the Roman government. Mary became aware of the newly organized, less relational feel she was sensing, compared with her previous experiences in Massillia.

As usual, she considered, they would not be able to utilize the ferry from Calais to the Briton coast. The Dumnoni tribe was to the far southwest on the large island. As many did when they reached the Bristol Channel's waters, the little ship would put out to sea from Calais.

This was her first time to sail in a smaller vessel, she realized. She imagined their travel would somehow be easier to manage at Land's End than was possible in the large merchant vessels her uncle was used to navigating.

"What is Uncle Joseph doing?" Salome asked.

"He is negotiating," Mary told her. "We don't want to walk to Calais from here, and the travel fee includes food and lodging."

"Does everyone who travels have to pay a travel fee? And is this the only way?" her sister wanted to know.

"It's just a better idea," came the answer. "It's 1300 miles from here to Calais, but it's the only route available for the ship to go. If we were sailing the other way, we could use the winds of the Straits, but it's too dangerous to go against the currents, even for the large ships. So, anyone wanting to travel to Briton or the northern lands by water, has to go this way."

"Will we be safe?" Salome asked.

Mary smiled. "I hope so," she answered.

"Me too."

Salome looked around at the group waiting to travel. How close she felt to each of these people, she considered. Thinking along these lines, took her mind to Zebedee. Had he received her letter by now, she wondered?

Had he forgiven her?

She felt a gentle squeeze from Mary on her hand, and looked to her sister.

"Are you all right?" Mary asked. "I've done this before with Uncle Joseph, and things will be fine. I promise."

"No," Salome answered. "I was just thinking how close I feel to everyone in this group, and that made me miss Zee."

Mary reached up with her free hand, and brushed an unconscious tear from her sister's face. "God will help us," she said.

Salome nodded, and looked again around the group.

Sarah, her handmaid, was close by, talking with Cleophas' daughter, Mary, and Martial, one of the men who had remained after the group's dispersion in Cyrene. She didn't know his Jewish name, since all of them had agreed to go by their Latin names.

She had always been close to her sister, Mary.

Saturninus, a member of the Jerusalem Ecclesia, whom she had never met, or spoken with until the journey to Cyrene.

Eutropius and Cleon, two of the younger men from Jerusalem, were sorting through their baggage, ensuring they had everything they might need for the journey. For a moment, she thought of James and John, and contemplated what they might be doing at this same moment.

Restitutus, who at present was still resisting his Roman name, and demanding to be called by his Jewish name, Uri. He was the crippled beggar healed at the Temple's Beautiful Inner Gate, as Peter and John walked to prayer several years prior.

Sidonius, who also refused to go by his Roman name, had been born blind, and healed by Jesus near the pool of Siloam. The group had nicknamed Jacob. At the moment, he was busying himself re-checking the waterskins they had purchased for the group's usage.

And finally, there was Simon Zealotes, already well-travelled as an evangelist, who was one of the twelve.

Autumn, 39AD

In the desert city of Petra, made green and lush by the Nabateans, Saul of Tarsus struggled to push a bone needle, threaded with sinew, through two layers of tanned goatskin. His fingers were bruised.

His hands hurt.

His head hurt, and his eyes were tired.

He had not slept well in more than a week now.

He had broken two needles just this afternoon.

For the first time in his life, he was face to face with his own inability. He thought he had heard the instructions from the overseer, Hasim.

He watched his classmates, trying to copy their methods.

Apparently he had missed something somewhere.

He had only been allowed to join the class late because the Bedouin caravan he travelled into the desert with had vouched for him. Their business completed, they had stopped in Petra to enjoy the water-pools and rich foods.

Saul was surprised when the Holy Spirit directed him to stop in Petra. He was even more surprised when his friend, the caravan owner, introduced him to the headmaster of the tent-making and building school.

Constructing tents was an easy profession to learn, they told him. It was a respectable profession. Everyone wanted a tent. And business owners always wanted awnings to provide shade for their booths in the marketplace.

Saul had been to school. He had seen thirty two summers. He had earned a priestly ordination. He had known many academic successes.

But he had never learned how to make tents before.

Why was this so hard for him, he wondered?

He was failing. Miserably.

He was so hungry. And he would only be allowed to eat if he finished his section of the tent they were working on.

He hadn't eaten yesterday, either.

Discouraged, Saul looked around the compound, where other students in his class were also working on assigned segments of the tent. He noticed many of them were close to the center, where their work would intersect with the work of the student on the opposing side.

"Hadi, I am too slow at this," he told his neighbor, who was more than a foot in front of him. "It is clear I was not made to make tents. I will never be able to finish this way!"

Hadi laughed, his white teeth glistening in contrast against his dark skin. "You will not fail, Saul of Tarsus. Every man must have a trade. Even if he is late in learning!"

"How do you work so quickly?" Saul inquired. "Show me, please."

"A question is the way we learn," Hadi told him. "Is this the first time you have asked for help? How can anyone teach you if you don't ask a question?"

His innocent words stunned Saul to the core. He realized suddenly why the Holy Spirit had placed him where he was. He nodded and hung his head. "Yes," he said.

"Why are you so ashamed?" his co-worker asked. "There is no shame in not knowing something one has never known before. In fact, you cannot learn unless the teacher can see what it is you don't yet understand."

He sat down next to Saul once more. He spoke kindly.

"Here Saul. You sew for me first, and let me see what you are doing," Hadi told him. "That is easier for me."

Silently, Hadi observed as Saul tried to push the needle through the layers of leather. "Hmmm, yes, I see what you are doing," he said. "Part of the problem is you are not working with protection for your fingers. Here. I will get you something."

Hadi was gone for a few minutes. When he returned, he had four, small cups made of dark wood in his hands, with a pitted stone. "You need thimbles and a needle pushing stone. You are working slowly because you have no tools to help you do the job."

He put the thimbles and stone into Saul's hand. "Put these on your thumbs and first fingers on both hands to start. Then, as you work, you can move them to your fingers which need more protection. This will help you to be more effective. Or, if you need to add more thimbles, there is a basket full of them in the stockroom."

Saul was amazed. "Why didn't *I* know about the thimbles?" he asked.

"Well, you came late to the class. It's something he covered in the first couple of days. I know Hasim tried to catch you up, but he doesn't like to do much instruction, even at the beginning of the class. And when we gain late students, he only tells new students about the tools one time. I had to learn from a second semester student when I was learning."

"Really?" Saul asked, feeling a little encouraged.

"Yes," Hadi spoke with a chuckle. "He says he thinks developing calluses is good for you. But it is my opinion that if your hands are sore, and if your fingers are bleeding, you won't be able to buy bread."

He laughed again. "You should have seen my fingers when I began."

Saul smiled. "I've been so pre-occupied, I didn't notice the thimbles on your fingers before. Even though we work together every day," he admitted. "Besides, they are the same color as your skin!"

Hadi laughed out loud, looking down at his hands. "They *are* the same color as my skin!" he kept repeating, until there was nothing Saul could do but laugh with him.

Later, when Saul considered the discussion, he realized just how self-absorbed he had been living in his life. How had he begun to only notice the things in his life which had to do with himself? How had he missed the fact the man who sat next to him day after day wore thimbles and used a stone needle pusher?

Had he always been so selfish?

As his laughter subsided, Hadi wiped tears from his eyes. "Oh, I needed that. Thank you!" he said. "Oh, and Saul. I forgot to tell you something. I think you are sewing the wrong edges. You are supposed to only sew the leather sides that are already punched. You cannot really make holes with the needle. That may be why some of your work is uneven. The tanners bring the hides to us with holes punched on the sewing edges for putting them together. When our job is done, the workers outside seal the tent seams with pitch. No wonder your hands hurt."

Saul was embarrassed. How had he missed the instruction? When would he stop being so stupid?

"I'm sorry," Saul admitted. "I'm not good at this; at working with my hands. I don't understand why I keep missing things like this. I am a *teacher*, not a *laborer!*"

He threw down his segment of the tent in frustration. He looked at Hadi.

"I don't know why I have to learn this! I'm not convinced I'll ever use these skills again!"

Hadi looked at him. "Wait a minute. Didn't you tell me your God brought you here?" he asked. "Do you think he has changed his mind so quickly? I don't want to offend you, but I don't think you have learned all there is to learn here."

"Well, no, I haven't," Saul admitted. "It's just so hard! I guess I'm questioning whether it really *was* God who put me here. Surely I made a mistake!"

"So, Saul of Tarsus, do you think your God puts no value on men who work with their hands? Does knowing how to read and teach make you more *valuable* than me?"

The words stung Saul's heart to the core.

Hadi had as much value as he did, as had Shira, and many others he had snubbed over his lifetime.

Tears smarted Saul's eyes. "No, Hadi," he replied. "You are very valuable. I think I am finally learning how entitled I have been. I always thought I was better than other people; destined for some great task. But I am ordinary; just like everyone else. I seem to fail at most things. What do I have to show for my life? Look at all of these people around us. All of you are younger than I am."

"But you haven't even been here two weeks!" Hadi reproached him. "You're not giving yourself a chance. You've worked very hard, doing things the wrong way. There is no telling how well you will do, or how fast you will be able to work now you know how to do things the right way."

He paused, assessing Saul. "Give yourself time. Be encouraged, and keep putting one step in front of the other. Keep working to learn, my friend!"

Saul sighed. Would he ever get this?

But Hadi was right, he realized. He hadn't given himself the opportunity to make a tent with the proper tools. And, he had expected himself to *just know*, without being taught. Had he always been so unrealistic in his standards for himself, he wondered?

Had he set the same kind of expectations for others as well?

Thinking about it, Saul realized Hadi was a good teacher. The man had slowed the teaching process down from Hasim's method of instruction. He had slowed the lessons to the pace of Saul's ability to absorb and understand.

Saul realized a difference in his two instructors.

Hasim had taught a lesson, in order to meet his own goal of completing a task. In his mind, it was more important he complete the task of verbalizing the entire lesson. He did it to get it done.

On the other hand, Hadi was more concerned with connecting with Saul, and making sure he understood each step at the pace he could absorb the information.

Hasim told him the "what" and walked away, he realized. Hadi had invested himself, stayed with him, and showed him the "how."

He would be grateful to Hadi for the rest of his life.

Then the Voice spoke inside his heart.

That is what I did for the twelve. I want to do that with you as well.

The remainder of that day, and for two days afterward, Saul of Tarsus could not stop weeping. Each time he lifted the needle, he wept. Each time he pulled the sinew strands through to connect the leather layers, he wept. When he walked, ate, bathed, or read, his mind returned to instances in his life which had been void of the love of God.

"You are mending me," he prayed. "Aren't you?"

448

And, faithfully, gently, filled with mercy, the answer came.
I Am.

19 – Land's End
Autumn, 39 AD

In Calais, a small ship was being floated into the harbor by the Transport Service from Massillia. Just a few feet away, the Bristol Channel waited to serve as their waterway to carry them beyond the continent, around Land's End, and through the Islands to the lands of Arviragus.

The channel had once been a river, according to the ancients, flowing through the unified continent of Pangea. According to the legends, as the Great Ice Shelf had melted away, the land of Briton and the newly discovered land of Eire, had broken away from the mainland, drifting to their present locations.

Celtic scholars taught the lands were still rising from being pressed down by the ice shelves for so long. As the weather warmed over the centuries, changes had taken place.

Much of the land in Briton was interspersed with marshes, bogs, and low-lying areas covered in fog most of the time. Woodlands were prevalent in these areas. Some of the marshes ran in long lines along the land, connecting inlets, sometimes all the way to the sea. These long lines traced the retreating path of the ancient glaciers.

In such areas, low tide revealed the mushy earth beneath the brackish waters. High tide greatly reduced the ability of the inhabitants to walk across from east to west of the large island.

Travel between tribal territories required experienced guides.

Those untrained individuals who unwisely tried to row through the marshes at wrong times, found themselves mired at low tide. Many had died, or suffered the insanities of Marsh Fever.

And the inhabitants of the large island were many.

The highest grounds on the large island could be found in the north and in the east.

In the mid-west of coastal Briton, the area to which they were heading, the tides affected the land, by creating islands at high tide. From the Island of Apples, called "Avalon" by the inhabitants, at the village of Glaston, to the

449

outskirts of Land's End, the lower levels of the marshes disappeared every twelve hours, rendering the ground uninhabitable.

Salome watched as those who were not boarding vessels traveling the Channel boarded the ferry between Calais, headed to *Portus Dubris*, meaning "White Harbor." The name came from the color of the chalk cliffs visible from the sea.

Some years prior, a heavy rope had been threaded through iron rings between two tall stone pillars, one in Calais and the other in Portus Dubris.

"What will they do to get over to the other side?" she asked Mary.

"There is a hook in the middle of the ferryboat," Mary told her, pointing to indicate the item of which she spoke. "See it?"

Salome nodded.

Mary continued. "One of the ferryman will put that hook around the large rope. It is connected across the waters to another stone pillar like this one. The rope falls under the water so ships needing to come through from the north to Espania can do so. But when the rope is in use, it takes three workers of them to manage it. Using the rope prevents them from being carried northward by the Channel. The current is very strong. So, they have to pull themselves across. It will take more than a full day, and three ferrymen working day and night. The problem for us is, that we *could* take the ferry, but from where it comes to land, it will be impossible to cross to the Dumnoni Tribe."

"Why?" Salome asked.

"It's too dangerous," came the answer. "In the southern part of the island, the marshes change in depth because of the tides."

"What is a … a tide?" Salome asked.

Mary looked back at her sister, realizing this was a new concept for her sister. There had been no rising and falling of sea waters every six hours on the Sea of Galilee. Nor did the Mediterranean Sea experience tidal changes.

Mary had learned of tide changes from her travels with their uncle.

"One of the sea captains explained it to me. They don't know why it happens. Some people think it has to do with cycles of the moon. But this man explained it to me as though the Oceanus Major is a living thing. He said 'every six hours she breathes in, and every six hours she breathes out'." As she spoke, Mary imitated the guttural drawl of the sea captain she had befriended in childhood. As she did, both sisters laughed.

"I see," Salome said, trying to imitate her tone and facial expression. This caused them both to dissolve into giggles.

Inwardly, Mary smiled. It was so wonderful to be spending time with Salome like this. It was as though they were young girls once more.

A few minutes later, Joseph's little ship was in the water. Then, the group was boarding.

As the Calais harbor slaves pushed them out to deeper water, the men unfurled the sails to catch the wind. Simultaneously, the group began to row in the same rhythm they had used from Carthage to Sardinia, and then to Massillia.

Here, as between Cyrene and Carthage, they were rowing against the current once more.

Thankfully, the winds were favorable.

"The waters will become dangerous as we near the place where we have to go around the island," Joseph told them. "As the wind carries us forward, we want to steer closer to the land on the other side."

He continued. "Let's work in shifts, because once the winds change, we will need to make sure we stay as close as we can to the land. We don't want to become stuck between the islands. It will be too easy to be carried out into open water, or pushed up to the Channel."

This could very well become the hardest part of the journey so far, Mary decided.

Every prior journey she had made to Briton with her uncle had been taken in a merchant vessel, the weight alone of which had helped to offset the currents. Additionally, with eighty hired oarsmen, each of Joseph's galley-powered ships had travelled the waters much faster than the little boat they were navigating at the moment.

They rowed hard for almost two hours, finally crossing the Channel waters. And, as soon as they passed the edge of the current, the coastal waters turned calm, as those corresponding on the other side had been.

Immediately, Joseph called for a rest, and a changing of rowers.

As the water-skins were passed, Joseph instructed the group regarding the next step of their journey.

"We want to turn left now, and head around the southern end of the island," he told them. "There are too many marshes for a merchant vessel to get through without becoming mired. I haven't navigated those marshes before, so we will follow the path of the larger galleys that I am familiar with.

"As we travel across the southern end of Briton, we will come to the other end of the island, but we will need to go farther; beyond what is called Land's End. For many years, it was considered the end of all land created by our God.

"There are several large islands there, called the Scilly Islands. The largest one is called Lyonesse. The second largest is called EnNoer. The third is called Scillonia Insula.

"If we arrive at high tide, the waters will be easier to manage; they could be as much as 19 feet above the low tide. For use at low tide, the people have built land bridges to connect the islands. They can walk between them. Even at high tide, you will be able to see the road between the two larger islands. There are farms and herds on Lyonesse, and farms on EnNoer and Scillonia Insula."

"Is that where we will be staying? On the islands?" Martial asked.

"No," Joseph answered. "Those are the islands we will see just before we get where we are ending the journey. The Phoenicians called this place the Cassiterides, or Tin Islands. So did the Greeks. But tin was never found in the islands. It is actually in the mines where the Dumnoni Tribe lives. That is where we are going. We need to continue to row *past* the islands, and then turn right and head north to the islands near Avalon."

Joseph looked at the sky, assessing the sun's position. "We only have a few hours of daylight left. Let's change to the second team of rowers, and keep going. We can probably go another ten miles or so before we stop to sleep."

The second set of six took the rowing seat positions from the first set. And the ship embarked once more, with renewed energies.

We will all sleep well tonight, Mary thought to herself.

"Uncle," she asked, "how many days will we be rowing like this?"

Joseph looked around the boat at each of the travelers. "As we decided in Calais, we will be sleeping in this little ship for the next several days. We will be eating the dried fruits, salted meats, and breads we purchased in Calais. And, please don't worry. There are plenty of water-skins, and I purchased an ampora or two of wine, as well as two barrels which are under the food storage canopy. We should arrive in Dumnoni in ten days or so. We have a 400 mile trip ahead of us."

Simon Zealotes smiled. "That seems like nothing in light of how far we have come so far. For myself, I want to say I am thankful we have water and food on this leg of our journey."

He paused. "And we have oars; and a rudder; and a sail; and shade; and we have more room in the boat." He looked around the group. "Does anyone remember how hard it was to sleep in this little ship from Jerusalem to Cyrene? I had to squish up against Trophimus and Restitutus. I woke up every time one of them moved."

Restitutus interrupted him. "Hey! My name is Uri," he declared. "I am a Jew, and proud of it. Why do I need a Roman name?"

Several of those next to him reacted with humorous comments.

When the chatter calmed, Sarah, Salome's handmaid looked at Simon Zealotes and spoke up. "I *needed* to remember where we came from Simon," she said. "I had forgotten how hard it was for me when we were captured. Thank you. You have helped me to remember to give thanks."

It was twelve days before the small ship rounded the western edge of the large island of Briton. As they neared Land's End, several islands came into view, with a great bit of water between them.

"We have arrived at high tide!" Joseph exclaimed. "That means we can cut close to 100 miles of extra rowing from our voyage. We can turn right here, and travel over the tops of the islands that sink below the surface during high tide."

As they rowed around Land's End, Mary noted the land bridges her uncle had said would still be visible at high tide. They had built up one or two land bridges since she had visited the area when she came for the graduation ceremonies?

Her mind went back to Jesus' days in Briton. It had been her Uncle Joseph who had been the first to offer the opportunity of the Celtic University to the ten-year old boy. He would not begin until his fourteenth year, but Joseph knew it was a good idea to communicate with the school as soon as parents knew they wanted their son, or daughter to attend.

The Celtic University offered the best schooling outside of Rome. Wealthy families, especially those in the ruling classes of many nations, were eager to have their children attend school in Briton. The teachers were world-renowned for their knowledge, as well as their abilities in the arts. Nobles who were concerned their sons learn to read, and gain a full understanding of world history, sent their sons here.

Additionally, it was considered a benefit by most that the School of Druid Arts operated on one of the islands, separated from the Celtic University proper. Most students attended one school. The privileged attended both.

Mary considered Jesus' education. As the years of his learning had progressed, it had become obvious to everyone the Celtic people group had descended from Israel. History classes went back to the teachings of Moses; from which were drawn their lessons on ethics. Medical practices seemed to stem from the Torah as well. Additionally, they taught of the northern tribes' dispersion and displacement in the days of the Babylonians; even tracing the development of people from Israel to northern Gaul, and then finally to the Isles of Briton.

Were these people more of "the lost sheep of the House of Israel," her son had referred to? Were these the "sheep of another fold" he had spoken of?

Something of anticipation within her heart began to stir. Understanding began to frame a network within her soul. She could sense pieces coming together; pieces she had considered to be useless trivia until this very moment.

As they rounded Land's End, Mary looked forward, hoping to see the area where they would finally put the little ship onto land. Thinking about it now, she realized why her uncle had held on to the vessel.

In Briton, the tool of their combined exile would become a valuable commodity. It would help them to travel along the rivers and through the marshes. They could now travel where the much larger vessels could not go. And this little ship was just the right size; not too large. Yet, it was bigger than the wooden, barge-like rafts used by Briton's inhabitants.

Stunned, she pondered.

El Shaddai *had known.*

Her mind went to Abba's words to the weeping prophet, Jeremiah: "My plans for you are for good, and not for evil; plans for a future and a hope." Then, she remembered the phrase Joseph, the son of Jacob, had spoken to the brothers who sold him into slavery: "What you meant for evil against me, God has used for good."

Holy Spirit, she prayed inwardly, *You are speaking to me aren't you? You are reminding me of the bigger plan here, aren't you?*

Instantly, she sensed an inward rush of greater hope and anticipation, somehow mixed with joy.

They had come so far. That night, when they dropped anchor and prepared for sleep, conversations took a turn towards learning.

"Joseph," Simon Zealotes asked, "what will life be like with the Dumnoni Tribe?"

"It will be a little different than what we are used to," Joseph answered. "There are some who hold to our health laws among them. The king's chief steward is a son of Judah and Judith of Gamala. He was one of the 4,000 taken from Galilee."

"Do you know him?" Martial asked.

"He is a good friend," Joseph replied. "He is married now, and keeps the Sabbath. I brought him copies of the Torah and prophets some years ago."

Sarah, Salome's handmaid sat up from her resting place. "So, does that mean the king.... What's his name again?"

"Arviragus," Salome told her.

"Arviragus," Sarah repeated carefully. "Does King Arviragus do that too?"

"Do what?" Joseph asked.

"You know," she answered. "Keep the Torah, and eat like we do?"

"How do they dress, Joseph?" Cleon asked. He had chosen to follow Jesus on the day of the Mighty Wind in Jerusalem.

"What do they eat?" Sidonius wanted to know.

"One at a time, please," Joseph chuckled. "I have only been here as a representative of Rome, doing trade in metals. I have always been treated kindly, I suspect partially because of my position. They have served food, and I have eaten what I was allowed to eat. My position as a priest was never considered in my dealings with Arviragus. I think he respects me."

"Will he expect us to let go of our customs?" Martial wanted to know.

"I don't know," Joseph answered simply. "All I know is we are being led by the Holy Spirit. He has provided for all of us, and I know He will continue to do so. He has given me dreams, since the day of my great-nephew's resurrection. He showed me this ship. He showed me the great white cliffs of Briton. So I trust him."

There was silence for a moment or two.

"What did he show you?" Cleophas' daughter, Mary, asked.

For the next hour or so, Joseph shared the repetitive dream he had experienced, and the meaning he had been given during its second visitation. The group found it encouraging they were resting in a ship he had seen just after the resurrection.

"Does the woman in the dream mean there will be danger ahead?" Sarah asked.

In the darkness, Salome reached to comfort the younger woman.

"Perhaps," Joseph told her. "But what could have brought us closer to death than this little ship? We don't really need to be afraid. There are unfulfilled events in the dream; which means, the promise of the Holy Spirit is in the dream. Abba Father is showing us all His plan."

Sarah contemplated this for a moment.

"What was the shadow that fell over the continent, and then over Briton?" The question came from Uri (Restitutus), who had been healed at the Temple's Gate.

"I think it has to do with the worship practices of the Celtic people in the region," Joseph answered. They worship the moon, and believe in sorcery. They even have a school to train those who wish to become a Druid. The Druid masters mix witchcraft with the worship of the trees. They have mixed wrong beliefs in with their original worship of ElShaddai. It's almost like the days of Jezebel and Ahab with Elijah."

"What do you mean, 'mixed'?" Uri asked.

"Well, the Celts can trace their ancestry back to the ten lost tribes of Israel," Joseph responded. "When *they* teach world history, they include the dispersion of those tribes. They are the only school on earth to explain where our lost countrymen ended up."

"What do they teach?" Jacob (Sidonius) inquired. "Where *did* those tribes end up?"

"Here," Joseph replied simply. "And in Rome. As well as through all the nations across to the iced-lands of the Nordsmen."

It was a thought unconsidered.

In the morning, conversations continued. As the rowers took their places for the first shift of the day, Salome whispered to Mary.

"What do the women here wear?"

Mary laughed. "It's about the same, except they wear shifts over a topshirt. Most of the women wear a leather girdle or belt on top of the tunic. But the end effect is the same. The men wear something called *braccae,* which divides into two parts down the middle to allow them to ride horses. When they are not riding, they wear shifts with a loincloth."

"So we won't seem *totally* out of place," Salome said, relieved.

"No, just a little different for a while," her sister answered.

Two days later, they had their first, distant view of the Tor, the largest of the islands in Briton's Uxella Marsh. It would be a little longer before they experienced the flow of the two rivers; the Parret and the Brue, each flowing through the islands to the sea. Near the Tor, the Mendip Hills would also soon be visible.

As her anticipation rose, Mary began to point out areas of interest to the rest of the group. "We are really close now," she said, her excitement growing.

Little by little, the anticipation began to spread within the group.

"We really are," her uncle agreed. "Can you see the Tor?"

"I can," she answered. "Come to think of it, did you notice the new land bridges they have built when we rowed past Land's End?"

Joseph nodded. "I did. I wonder if they have enlarged the staging posts for merchants purchasing metals as well. We will have to see."

A few hours later, the group was pulling the little ship onto solid land. Having finally arrived at their destination, the men worked to guarantee the ship was secure. At the same time, the exhausted women clambered on hands and knees higher up onto the uninhabited hill. After a stake had been driven into the earth, and the boat had been tethered, Joseph and the others joined them.

In the late afternoon, they all fell asleep, too weary to worry what tomorrow would bring.

The landscape had completely changed when Mary awoke the next morning. The waters had receded, risen again, and begun to recede once more before the need for sleep had left her. As she came to awareness, she realized someone had covered her with a blanket, covered her face with a lightweight fabric of some kind, and removed her sandals from her feet.

Stirring, sleepily, she looked around. Salome was close by, still asleep, as was Sarah. Someone had covered each of them as well. Close to where Sarah rested, another blanket had been abandoned, possibly by her step-daughter, Mary.

Where were the men, she wondered?

She looked for the little ship, and saw it was still moored to the stake from the night before.

"Mistress Mary?" a man's voice behind her spoke quietly.

Startled, she turned. "Yes?"

"I was told to wait here until you ladies awakened. Your uncle is with the others with King Arviragus and his steward. I am to take you to them when you are ready," he said.

"What is your name?" she asked.

"I am called Caedmon," he answered. "I am Master David's assistant in the management of the mines."

Working to straighten her head covering, she smiled at him. "It's good to meet you, Caedmon. It's been a long time since I was here last."

"I think I remember you," he told her. "You came once when I was a boy, with your son, as I recall. Is that right?"

"Yes! That's right," she answered, surprised. "His name was Jesus."

"I remember, because I heard your husband and your uncle talking about Jesus attending the University and I thought he was too young at the time. He was just a few years older than me." He laughed. "Then my father explained it to me. There was a reservation list."

"He would have been a little young at ten to go to school here," she agreed, suddenly smiling, with the image of a small, confused Caedmon presenting itself in her mind.

"And then you came back when he started classes at the University," Caedmon reminisced. "But you seemed so sad."

"My husband had just died that year," she confided. "I wasn't sure what life held for me."

"Are you better now?" he asked.

She nodded. "ElShaddai has been working in my life. My God takes care of me."

His eyes widened. "Master David tells me that all the time!" he exclaimed. "Don't you share the same beliefs he does?"

Not having met David, Mary answered carefully. "My Uncle Joseph has told me Master David reads the Books of Moses and the Prophets. I do as well," she answered.

Caedmon let out a low whistle. "That's amazing," he said. "I have had so many questions about your God, and I think I must wear Master David out sometimes."

"I'd be glad to speak with you, Caedmon," Mary told him. "Anytime."

"Really?" he asked. "That would be wonderful."

There was a brief moment of awkward silence.

"The hut your son built is still here," he told her. "They have been repairing it, and preparing places for your company since your uncle's letter arrived a couple of months ago."

Mary was astonished. "What?" she asked. "I didn't know he sent a letter. When did it come?"

"Oh, just at the beginning of the winter months," he replied.

"We wintered in Cyrene," she explained. "Our little ship needed repairs."

"When I saw him today, Master Joseph said there was a story he would tell me later," Caedmon nodded. "I can't wait to hear it."

"There certainly is a lot to tell," she said.

Hearing a stirring from Salome's direction, Mary turned her head. "Good morning, sister!" she said. As Salome moved, Sarah did as well.

"Good morning," Salome answered. "Where is everyone?"

"They await us in the King's courtroom, Milady," Caedmon answered. "When you are ready, I am to take you there in your little ship."

Salome looked at Mary. "Are we the last ones to wake?"

Mary smiled, and nodded. "I actually slept until I woke up on my own. It feels wonderful."

Salome's eyes sparkled for the first time in long time. "How glorious!" she declared, looking to Sarah. "How did you sleep, dear?"

The handmaid looked at her with a drowsy smile. "I feel so much better," she said. "The best I have since we left Cyrene."

"I'm so glad," Mary told her. "I knew *I* was tired, so I was sure you were."

Sarah had pulled her hair back and put on her head covering. She then helped Salome with the same task. Salome looked at Mary and then Caedmon.

"Ready?" she asked.

"Let's go!" Caedmon replied. He stood up and walked down the hill to the little ship, where he began readying it to be boarded.

One by one the women stood to their feet. Salome folded the blankets and carried them to the boat. "We will want to return these to the person who covered us," she told Sarah.

Mary was the first one to board the little ship. As he had been instructed, Caedmon took her hand, and helped her as she stepped from the ground into the vessel. Next, he helped her to find a bench to sit on. He then turned to help Salome and Sarah in the same way. After they were seated, he pushed the ship away from the shore, moved to the bow to steer the vessel from a standing position.

"Caedmon," Salome asked, "are you pushing the oar on the bottom of the water and pushing us along?"

Caedmon nodded without looking back at her. "Yes ma'am," he replied. "We are at low tide, and this little ship is perfect for moving between the islands. I'm sure what I'm doing is not what the stick was made for, but it is the only way I know. Here, we push barge rafts from place to place this way."

"Oh," Salome answered. "I just hadn't seen anyone do it that way before. It's interesting. I'm learning, just watching you."

Caedmon wove through a labyrinth of waterways until they came to the mainland, where he steered the boat into a slip next to a dock. After assisting his charges' feet to find solid land once more, Caedmon tethered the boat. He then led them up a gentle slope to a large wattle-and-daub building with smoke-escape holes punched in its roof.

As they entered the building, Mary's eyes took a few moments to adjust. A small amount of light entered through the cut window above the door. Inside, she found a long table with benches on either side. Lamps lit the room very well.

In the middle of the room was a raised hearth, with a blazing fire, and a lamb roasting on a spit. A man was turning the spit. A large metal funnel shielded the inside ceiling from the cooking flames. Did her eyes deceive her, or did smoke from the fire seemed to go up the funnel rather than into the room?

Mary realized she had never seen a cooking fire *inside* a home before, even in colder weather. She squinted. How had they fashioned the roof over the fire, so it could provide warmth for the room, cooking the meal, and yet not cause coughing spells? She stood gazing, fascinated, until her Uncle Joseph came to greet them.

"Welcome, ladies!" He exclaimed. "Did you sleep well?"

"We did, Uncle," Salome replied. "Thank you."

"Are you hungry?" he asked. "Come and eat something."

He led them to the table, where everyone in their travelling party was already eating. Two additional men, and three women were seated at the table also, at the same end as their Uncle Joseph.

The older of the two men stood, and came to greet Mary before she had a chance to sit down.

"My dear lady," King Arviragus said, taking her hand in his own. "I am so glad to see you once more. How long has it been? The last time I saw you, Jesus had just finished his classes at the University."

Mary looked to her uncle for confirmation. "Ten, eleven summers?" she asked.

"Jesus had seen twenty-four summers when he graduated," Joseph nodded, answering. "He was about to enter his thirty-fourth summer when he died. It has been four summers since then."

"You are well?" the king inquired.

Mary smiled at him. "You are kind. Thank you for caring. I am doing very well, now that we are once more on solid ground."

Arviragus clapped his hands, which apparently called two serving maids from behind a door. "We need food for these ladies," he ordered, "and some warm wine."

The servers nodded and then disappeared for a few moments. When they reappeared, they carried plates of fresh breads, fruits, sliced cucumbers, white cheese slices, and hard boiled eggs. Another server came behind them with three steaming mugs of warm, honeyed, fruit wine, and table linens.

Content his guests were well taken care of, the king moved back to his former chair. "We have been talking about your accommodations," he said. "We had just finished making introductions, and I had mentioned to your Uncle Joseph that we have been working to design a settlement for you all.

We want you all to feel welcome, but not intruded upon.

"I was just telling my friend, Joseph, here, that his daughter Anne, and my son, Prince Beli, have been with us for a little over a year now. Since Tiberius Caesar's death, and the installation of Gaius Caligula as emperor, they have chosen to stay here. They received news of the new Caesar's mental instability, and formally requested sanctuary, which of course, we have given them.

"So, I know you will want to see your grandchildren, Joseph. They are beautiful! I didn't tell my son, Beli, you were coming, so I would like it to be a surprise when we eat together next week. We have made loose plans for a state dinner when our foreign dignitaries arrive. That is who they believe you to be, at the moment. Now that you are here, we begin planning for that event.

"They are living in the Roman villa which Tiberius had built in the countryside not far from here."

"That sounds wonderful," Joseph answered. He paused. "Your majesty?"

"Yes, Joseph?" the king answered.

"The foods we are served this morning are different from what I have had here in the past. Did you go to special trouble to create a menu for us?"

Arviragus chuckled. "Not really," he answered. "But you see, I have new cooks, and David has made sure to train them to follow the health laws in Moses' books of Leviticus and Deuteronomy."

Joseph's eyebrows went up. "Really? Why would that be?" he inquired.

The king motioned to the younger man at the table. "This is David, my steward," he said. "Augustus sent him here as an exile, to make way for Rome. But he has become my friend. I trust him like none other. He has saved my mines, my family, and now my life."

Arviragus indicated David should share. "I *hope* I am a trustworthy man," David said. "I seek to be so."

He glanced at Joseph before beginning his story. "There was a plot to assassinate the king. Some of the Druid leaders were offended with him as a leader, because he began questioning the need for human sacrifices. He has now limited the activity of the Priests and Wikka during the Festival of ShroveTide, and at other seasons of the year as well. The chief of the Druid Priests is a mage. He uses alchemy and witchcraft to see his purposes come to fruition. When his anger is aroused, he can be a dangerous man.

"When the king brought limits to his activities at the Tor, the man appealed at first. In his alchemy classes, he teaches that Avalon, the island where the Tor

461

was built, is Meeting Place of the Dead. It is, according to Druid teaching, the point where a person's soul passes to another level of existence.

"His name is Asarlai Draoi, which means 'wizard.' The Druids believe the Tor to be the entrance to Annwfn. That is the name the Celtic people give to the spiritual realm. Asarlai believes the Tor to be hollow, holding the palaces of the Lord of the Dark Underworld, Gwyn-ap-Nudd, and his brother Avallach, the Fisher King.

"He also teaches the Tor is the place where fairies dwell. Fairies are tiny, unseen creatures, who many times have wings. The Druids believe the oldest and strongest of the fairies were once fallen angels. He teaches that it is dangerous to accept a favor from a fairy, as they will always want something valuable in return. He believes they are the inhabitants of the unseen realm, and they love music. All of the Druid teachings focus on the unseen realm.

"He also believes in tiny men called elves.

"The Ancients of this region created a trail on the surface of the Tor, in the same pattern as those fertility paths followed by the Moabs and Philistines in our own land of Israel in the days of Joshua. The Druids believe a person can appease the Underworld rulers, or gain power, by walking the paths of the Tor, and conducting fertility rites on its peak. This means they have public sex. Many babies and virgins have been sacrificed there, in order to appease the entity the Druids refer to as Mother Earth. She is also called the Water Goddess, Vivien, or sometimes, Modron. She is considered the mother of Gwyn-ap-Nudd and Afallach. Some in the School of Alchemy refer to her as 'The Lady of the Lake.'

"When King Aviragus began to question the practices of Asarlai, the Druid Priest sent him a warning message by beginning the poisoning process of Izolde, our beloved queen. Not realizing he was asking her murderers to help him, Aviragus went to Asarlai and asked for the healing arts of the goddess to be performed in her behalf. When she did not recover, and instead worsened in her symptoms, the king began to be suspicious of Asarlai's loyalties.

"Then, at ShroveTide, which is a sacrifice holiday, the king realized he himself was experiencing the same symptoms as his wife, but only after he ate the food prepared by the Druid priests on the national holidays.

"It was then he decided to ask me to help him. I have done my best to serve, but I have not been to my homeland since I was a boy. There are many things I'm sure I don't know or don't remember.

"King Arviragus has asked me many questions about ElShaddai; a great number of which I cannot answer. But, in the process of what has become a learning experience for both of us, he has decided to follow our food laws. He is now undergoing an herbal cleanse on a regular basis."

"And I feel great!" Arviragus interjected. "And David is teaching me to pray and meditate! And I do! Every day! And I am reading the Torah, Joseph."

"So have you become Jewish then?" Mary asked him.

Arviragus shrugged, and laughed with a degree of irony. "I don't know what I am! Druid, Jew, Dumnoni…. All I know is that I am alive, and I feel great!"

Joseph smiled, and patted his friend on the back. "You are in the middle of a journey, then," he offered.

Arviragus looked at him. "You are very perceptive, my friend," he said.

Silence held them all for a moment. It was finally broken by the king's redirection of the conversation, utilizing a question aimed towards Mary.

"Mary," he began, "I was *hoping* you would be coming with Joseph this trip."

"Yes?" she replied, smiling at him.

"Do you remember the little house your son built years ago, when Joseph brought him to attend the University?"

"I do," she said. "I had never seen anything like it."

"Nor had I," the king replied. "So, when Joseph's letter arrived, I had it refurbished, thinking at least he could stay in it. It has a new thatch roof, and has been thoroughly repaired. It is a round house, as you remember, I'm sure. We didn't know how many of you would be arriving, but it has been furnished for your needs for as long as you all may choose to remain here."

Mary was overwhelmed at the king's kindness.

"Thank you, sir," was all she could manage, her throat suddenly becoming constricted. An image of her son as a young man, standing in the doorway of his Brittonic home, had flashed across her heart and mind. She coughed.

Joseph spoke at that point. "King Arviragus," he said. "That brings us to a point we must discuss with you. But, in order to be able to discuss the problem, I must…" he looked around the table, pausing. "*We must* tell you a story. Do you have time, or should we set a time later today?"

Nonplussed, the king assessed his friend. "You are here to stay, aren't you?" he asked. "I surmised as much, when I saw the method by which you arrived. Who travels across the seas in such a little ship?"

"Yes, that is true," Joseph said humbly. "We seek sanctuary."

Arviragus laughed. "That is yours without question, my friend," he said. "But I am intrigued to hear this story." He looked at his steward. "Please rearrange my day, David. I will be with these good people the rest of the day."

Then to Joseph and the others at the table, he said, "Let us go to my home, where we can sit comfortably, without fear of being overheard."

As they left the Feasting Hall, the king's personal staff followed the company, ready to help with meeting the needs of their guests.

Later in his years, King Arviragus would look back on the day Joseph arrived in Briton, and remark his life had changed completely that afternoon. In rapt attention, he was fascinated by the story each of those in the company told. As before, in Massillia, the account began with Mary receiving a visit from the angel Gabriel.

"What do angels *look* like?" the king wanted to know. "*Are* they like fairies? Did the room change when he appeared? Did he have wings?"

"He looked like a man, and spoke like a man. He was a little taller than a man. He had light emanating from inside of him," she answered. "In fact, he was so bright, I almost couldn't see his face. He didn't have wings at first, and then, just before he disappeared, they grew from the center of his back."

"What did they look like?" Arviragus asked.

"Very feathery," she answered. "And almost golden. They must have been twice has tall as he was. They glowed and reached way up into the sky. And then he was gone."

She finished her part of the story; telling of Zacharias and Elisabeth; of her courtship with Joseph; of the dreams; of Bethlehem; of the shepherds; of the heavenly host; of the wise men; of her Joseph's dreams; of Egypt; and finally of coming home to her husband's home in Nazareth.

Then, her Uncle Joseph took up the story. He told of Jesus' early visits with his brothers to Arimathea. Then, Mary told of her husband's death, and the journey to Briton she and Jesus had taken with Joseph.

Cleon had been in the crowd when Jesus was baptized by John the Baptist in the Jordan River. He had watched the dove land on Jesus' shoulder. He had heard the Voice speak from heaven.

Others then told of their journeys with the Son of God.

Simon Zealotes told of his discovery of the True Kingdom, and his years with Jesus. Salome and Sarah told of Jesus' years in Capernaum, and the calling of the fishermen to become disciples; of his turning water into wine at a wedding.

One by one, each member told how Jesus had changed their lives. They shared the parables and key teachings they remembered.

Then, Joseph told of the conflict against his great-nephew. How Jesus was tried unjustly, beaten and crucified. He told of the deep darkness which had filled the entire region.

"There was a day in April some years ago," Arviragus told them, "when there was a great darkness over our entire country. It was not the periodic hiding of the sun by the moon, as the Druids thought at first. We all were concerned the world was coming to an end. It was a deep darkness that lasted for three hours. The earth's shaking and the wind were terrifying.

"But, as they always do, the priests told everyone they had divined through blood sacrifice, they said, the event could be explained as a warning and a curse. The three hours of blackness had come because the people were not sacrificing enough; not supporting the Tor enough. They threatened the people with death and plague if they did not sacrifice more. They convinced them all it was a curse from Vivien, the Mother Earth goddess."

"But they *didn't* convince you," Joseph observed aloud.

Arviragus shook his head. "I had already grown tired of their superstitions," he replied. "And the human sacrifice. But I still feel so empty. I just don't know what is real anymore, or if there really is a spiritual realm."

He looked at Joseph. "Now you are telling me the sun was hidden from sight because *our* Jesus was tortured and hung on a cross? That *is* what you're saying, isn't it? That the whole earth was in darkness because he died there?"

"Yes, that is what happened."

"Who *was* he? That the entire earth was thrown into darkness because he is dead? Where was their respect? Who would kill an innocent man like this? What has been done to them?"

"Oh, but the story is far from over, Arviragus," Mary interjected. "In fact, it is still being written."

"What?" the king responded, surprised. "How? But he died. What happened next?"

Joseph then shared of the day they had buried Jesus; of Nicodemus; of Zebedee. He told of the burial in his own tomb, and the events surrounding Jesus' resurrection three days later.

Simon Zealotes shared what it was like to watch his friend, Judah Iscariot, betray and sell Jesus for silver coins, and then refuse to accept the free gift of the Kingdom after he was proven wrong through the resurrection. He also shared his own amazement to see Jesus rise into the cloud of witnesses who had also come alive when Jesus had resurrected.

Arviragus was amazed when he heard of the miracles, and became astonished when he heard the wisdom Jesus had shared. But the king became even more filled with wonder as they shared about the Mighty Wind in Jerusalem, and the miracles which had continued to occur after Jesus' ascension into heaven.

"This is the *same* Jesus… the boy who came here with you to the mines?" he asked Joseph. "The boy who hugged me; this is the one?"

"The same one," Joseph nodded.

"This is one who came to the University, and *lived* here?" Reality was sinking in. "So *who is he*?"

Joseph smiled. "He is ElShaddai, Arviragus. He created the earth," he said. "He made Adam, the first man with his own hands, and breathed his own breath into him."

Arviragus stared at him, beginning to comprehend. "Is *he* your God? I mean, like the God that David has been telling me about? Is he the same one?"

Joseph nodded. "He made us in his own image, and then he came to teach us how to live."

"He builds us with his own hands; just like he did that hut?" the king clarified.

"Yes, he does," Joseph smiled.

There was silence for a moment, as the king lapsed into thought.

"He was so careful with that little house, too," Arviragus mused aloud. "He checked his measurements three or four times. It had to be just right. I teased him about it one day, and he told me it takes a lot of work and time to make things right in this realm. He said the only place things were already right was in the Kingdom of Heaven. I didn't understand what he meant at the time."

He looked to the window opening above the door. "It's dark outside," he said. "I have kept you too long. There is no way to take you to your lodging places now. It's not really safe after dark to travel unless it is on the same island, or on the mainland."

"Are there robbers?" Sarah spoke up.

Arviragus chuckled. "No, not here," he said. "No, our danger is from the wild animals and the miry areas of the marshland. Also, the Marsh Fever

466

mosquitos come out in full force when the sun goes down. If a person is bit, it can be deadly."

"What's a mosquito?" Sarah asked.

"It's a tiny, very fragile insect," David told her. "It flies silently and drills into the skin for blood. Not all of them carry Marsh Fever, but many do. They leave behind a nasty bump that itches. When a Marsh Fever bug bites, the person is never the same; something changes in the head. One of our miners was bitten, several weeks ago, and went to sleep. He has been sleeping for a month now. He only wakes every two or three days, and takes long drinks of water."

"I would like to see him, and pray for him," Simon Zealotes said simply. "Would his family be open to that?"

Surprised, the king looked at him. "I'm sure they are open to anything at this point. He has not eaten anything. I'm convinced the water is the only thing keeping him alive. He has lost a lot of weight." He paused, thinking. "I would love to take you there."

"Thank you," Simon said.

"I would like to go too," Mary ventured.

"And me!" Eutropius and Saturninus added, not quite in chorus.

"I'll take all of you!" Arviragus offered. "In fact, it would be good for you to meet everyone living and working in the mining region. I want all of them to hear the story I have heard today."

He paused, looking around the room. "This is not the way I wanted to do this. We have had lodging prepared for all of you, but we have waited here past the sun's setting, into the hours of darkness, and I cannot take you there. Would you be willing to sleep one more night like Culdees?"

Joseph was intrigued at the word. "What is a Cul-dee?" he asked, pronouncing the word slowly.

"It means you have been displaced from your home. You are waiting for safety," the king explained. "We use it to describe those of our people who lose their homes when the tides rise too high."

"In our language, we use the word 'refugee,'" Joseph told him. He thought for a moment. "Culdee. I do like that word. It describes me perfectly."

"We will be the Ecclesia of the Culdees!" Martial exclaimed excitedly. "We are *all* refugees, waiting for Jesus to return!"

"Wait! What do you mean? He's coming *back?*" Arviragus reacted, somewhat startled. "There's more?"

"So much more," Joseph answered. "But now we have time."

467

"We do have time," the king responded. "I can't wait to hear the story. But it is time for sleep now. I will have the maids bring you coverings and cushions. There is another large room if you would like to spread out a little."

Mary beamed. "Thank you, your majesty. I think I would like to sleep in another room from the men, if you don't mind."

The other women nodded in agreement. "Me too," Salome said.

Sarah and little Mary were smiling as well.

"King Arviragus?" Sarah said shyly.

"Yes, little one?" he answered.

"Could I get a cup of water, please?"

A ripple of realization made its way through the room.

"It's late, and you haven't eaten!" the king cried. He hit his forehead with his open hand. "What am I thinking!?"

He called for an attendant. When the man arrived, Arviragus gave instructions for food and drink to be brought. "And ask the maids to prepare the large rooms for sleep. Our friends will be staying here tonight."

"Yes, sire," the servant replied. "We were wondering if you might all be fasting tonight!"

The group laughed spontaneously in relief.

It was the king who replied. "I'm too hungry for that tonight, Belenus. What do we have we can feed these new friends?"

"I don't know, my king," Belenus answered. "I know the women brought some supplies from the Feasting Hall earlier today. I will let them know you are ready for a meal."

"Thank you," Arviragus replied.

After Belenus left, the king rubbed his hands together, warming them. "It's a little chilly in here, too," he noticed. "I was so interested in what you were all telling me about Jesus, I didn't realize it." He stood and stretched. Pointing to the door, he spoke. "Martial?"

"Yes sir?"

"Is that your name?"

"Yes, sir."

"Oh, good," the king replied. "There is firewood stacked just outside that door. Can you bring some in so we can get our fire stoked?"

"We'll take care of it, your majesty," he answered.

Martial moved into action, with Cleon just behind him. The two young men worked for the next few minutes to revive and stoke the fire.

Observing them, Mary was amazed once more to see the smoke rise through the metal funnel going through central point in the round roof. Who had thought of such an idea, she wondered?

The next morning, Belenus awakened them with a call to breakfast. The cooks had prepared food according to the king's new customary eating style: fresh boiled eggs, bread, cheese and apples.

Sarah and Salome had never had an apple before. "What are these?" Sarah asked Belenus, pointing at the basket filled with the fruits.

"We call those *avvalls*, milady," he answered. "They are a fruit grown here on our Tor, which we call *Avalon,* or Apple Island."

"How do you eat them?" she inquired.

"Like this, mum," he answered, smiling. He then picked up an apple, and holding the ends in one hand, buried his top teeth into it, and took a bite. As he pulled the fruit away, juice ran down to his chin. "They are so delicious!"

Sarah promptly picked up an apple and took a bite. In a moment, she too had apple juice dripping. "They are really good!" she told them all. "But you will need your sleeve when you eat one!"

"Is it as juicy as the pomegranates back home?" Saturninus asked.

"Not quite," Sarah told him. "Just try one. I'm going to take another for later. I can put it in my pouch."

Belenus smiled at her knowingly. "We all do that here, milady," he said. "The miners take them along to stave off hunger during the day. We bake them as well. My wife likes to stew them with raisins and honey."

"Your wife?" Sarah asked. "I thought you lived here with the king."

Belenus chuckled. "No ma'am. We live just next door," he answered. "That way, if he needs me, he can call my name and I come straight away. My wife is in charge of the food preparation for the workers' Feasting Hall. She oversees the cooks and workers at the Hall, every morning and every night. Just recently, she has become King Arviragus' personal cook as well."

"Does she have help?" Sarah asked, wide-eyed, picturing the man's poor wife overloaded with such huge tasks.

Belenus smiled at her. "Yes, milady," he answered. "Our king is a kind ruler. My wife has an entire staff of helpers. Some in the fields, and some in the pastures, and many in the *cisten*."

"What is a cisten?" little Mary asked.

"We call it that, because it is the place where water is available for cooking. It is where we prepare the food," he told her.

"It sounds like our word for a well," she said. "We call a private courtyard well a 'cistern.' I wonder what other words we speak that are related."

After breakfast, Arviragus summoned his steward, David, to join them. "Joseph," he said. "I want to lead you to your new home. That way, you can unload your ship before we go out to the mining communities. As I said before, I was unclear how many of you there would be, and did not know how long you would be staying. But now, I think I have a plan. I'll know more after I speak with our builders."

As they boarded the little ship, Mary looked around, taking in the surroundings. In her homeland in Galilee, beaches of soft sand eased a person down to the water. It was not so here. Mossy banks over black earth went down into the waters. And, all of the ground here had a sodden feel, as though a little more water would cause it all to turn to sloppy mud, all the way through.

Here, near the confirmed mainland, the islands were closer together. Here, she observed, platforms had been constructed for passage between some of the islands, connecting them to the mainland. In parallel rows between the islands, poles had been driven deep into the mud. Wooden bridges of horizontal planks then had been constructed, and were resting on the tops of the poles. In the light of day, people were walking on the walkways. Some appeared to be merchants, pulling carts filled with items. Here and there, men stood in the mire, harvesting something where the waters had receded. In some places, reeds were being cut. Elsewhere, fishing nets had been hung to dry.

She turned to the king's steward, who was helping her board the boat safely. "David, what is used for trading exchanges here?" she asked. "At home in my country, we trade with fish, vegetables, and flax. Sometimes, we work for coins, but only for what is needed to purchase in the marketplace or for taxes."

"I remember," the steward answered in Hebrew, surprising her. "My family lived in Gamala. We fished in the river by my home all the time! You are from Galilee, right?"

She replied in Hebrew without thinking. "My accent gave me away, didn't it?"

Then, stunned, she stared at him for a moment. "*You* are the one who was exiled!" she exclaimed, her mind making the connection. "You are Judah of Gamala's son!"

"Yes, ma'am," he answered. "I was his middle son. Two of my grown brothers were crucified with my father, the day I was taken from my home. My brother, Simon, was their age, but had refused to fight with my father."

Salome's interest had been piqued when she heard her native tongue. "My husband's brother, Barnabas, was exiled from Galilee at the same time," she told him. "He was schooled in Rome."

"I was as well!" he answered, "Along with my brother, Micah! I wonder if I might know him…"

"I think I knew your nephew," Mary told him. "Although Simon must have been quite a bit older than you, because Judah was younger than you are."

"You know Judah? He was so little when I was there," David reminisced. "He couldn't have seen more than two summers. How do you know him?"

Mary and Salome exchanged glances.

Mary answered. "He was one of the men who travelled with my son, Jesus. Just after the four thousand young men in Galilee were exiled, your brother, Simon, decided he wanted to fight like your father had, for a free Judea and Israel. He continued your father's movement in Judea. The men he trained are now called 'The Sicarii.' When one walks alone, we call him 'Iscariot.'"

"I heard rumors," David told her. "In fact, I think it was your Uncle Joseph who told me. Each time he comes here for trade, he fills me in on the news from Judea and Galilee."

"They are all Zealots," Mary told him. "But the Sicari take their idea of patriotism further. They are willing to lay in wait for their prey; setting traps for Israel's enemies. They have been known to hide in a crowd, stab a man in the back, and then just walk away before the man hits the ground. They see it as their mission before God to develop an army of assassins to fight for Jewish freedom. They even have training camps now, at Qumran. Your nephew, Judah, was called Iscariot."

David looked at her, his mind slow to grasp what she was saying.

Salome spoke. "Simon Zealotes," she said, indicating Simon to David, "was his partner when Jesus sent out healing teams. You should speak with him. He probably knew Judah better than anyone."

"Yes, you should," Mary interjected. "I liked Judah. It was hard for him to grasp the meaning behind what Jesus meant by the words 'kingdom,' and 'freedom.' To Judah the words had a different significance than they did to Jesus."

"You are speaking about Judah in past tense," David observed. "What happened to him?"

Mary looked down at her hands. She paused, not wanting to hurt the man during their first conversation. "Um…he died around the same time as my son," she told him. "When we have more time, I will tell you the complete story."

"I would like that," he replied. "Although I think King Arviragus has something else in mind for all of us today."

She smiled at him. "Shall we change the subject, then? Can you tell me what your people use for trade?"

He turned to face her, and smiled in return. "Well, you know our main export is precious metals," he said. "We are the only mines contracted to trade with Rome for Tin. But we also mine other precious metals. The Mendip Hills, just above our border are filled with lead. Our mines also produce some copper and silver. After centuries of mining, here, there is only a small amount of iron, but we still have an Ironworks."

He pointed to the fishing net. "We fish for eel, and many times get larger fish from the rivers flowing through the Uxella Marsh. We raise sheep, so we have wool products. Many of our women weave. We grow flax, so we also have linen."

"The men standing in the water are harvesting oysters from the water. See the knife in his hand? He breaks them away from the rocks and then throws the oysters in the big basket on his back. When he arrives home, he will steam them. They open then, and give up their pearls. We have harvested pearls in all sorts of colors. They bring in a lot of revenue. We also use the meat and the shells for trade."

He looked at her. "Have you ever seen a willow tree?" he asked.

She nodded. "Just a few times. I think they are beautiful."

"I do as well," he answered. "When we plant one by the water, its roots grow, making the ground firm. Our people use the branches to make baskets for trade. We also harvest reeds from the Uxella for making mats of all sizes."

Salome pointed to two women on a far island, who were on their hands and knees, digging in the dirt closest to the water. "What are they looking for?" she asked.

"Oh," David replied, "they are harvesting peat moss. We use it in our gardens, and to wick away moisture in our homes." He paused, thinking. "Oh, and we dig roots and herbs for medicinal purposes. My wife makes a wonderful tea I drink when I begin feeling badly, and it helps me heal more quickly."

"Speaking of herbs," Salome began, "what spices do you use here?"

David smiled at her. "It's not like the food I had when I was a boy. The food is not highly seasoned here. Although, in the past few years, the Romans have shown us how to harvest sea salt from the Celtic Sea. And, your uncle has brought my wife spices from Jerusalem over the years."

"At home, we harvest salt from the Dead Sea," Salome told him. "You mentioned having a garden. Do families here grow food as well?"

He chuckled. "Yes, we have to. Our nation is somewhat remote, you see, compared to the countries in the Mediterranean. We only have about 3600 square miles when we combine our lands with our neighboring tribe, the Durotriges. They are mostly farmers and pasturers. For that reason, much of our food trade is made with them."

"Do you grow herbs?" Salome asked.

"We do," he answered, "in many varieties. The Marsh yields a treasure trove of roots and herbs. Many of our people have learned to harvest them for their healing properties over the centuries. My wife especially loves to grow and harvest mint."

Mary had been thinking. "We have close to the same amount of ground, if I count all of Israel's provinces," she said. "It is amazing your people have been able to do all this in this small amount of land."

"I know it," David agreed. "And much of this area is under water most of the time."

As they worked their way through the Uxella Marsh, following King Arviragus's Royal Barge, Mary noticed several more things.

The waters were quiet this morning, with an occasional humming of a frog, or the singing of a bird. They were once again close to high tide. In the distance, Mary could see the Tor; the center of worship for the Dumnoni and other tribes. At the Tor, sacrifices were offered; fertility rites were carried out; candles were lit; funeral pyres were set aflame.

An oval shaped island, the Tor rose more than 500 feet above the water. Looking at the island's reflection in the still waters, she could understand why the Celts called it *Ynys Gyrdyn,* or "Glassy Island." When she had visited during Jesus' graduation, she had heard another name, one the king's manservant, Belenus, had used that morning: Avalon. David had also told her the area was called *Glas Ton,* or "Green Hill," by the other tribes in Briton.

As they drew near the Tor, Mary could see the fires from the smelter's earth furnaces by the ironworks on another island across the water. She remembered watching the blacksmiths work in her homeland. The process of softening rocks with fire still fascinated her. She had realized a symbolic corresponding of the softening of rock, to how the heat of difficulties had softened her own heart.

For some reason, she had been drawn to the metaphor. Even now, hearing the blacksmith's hammer echo across the water, she was reminded of Abba Father's process of creating something usable from an unusable piece of hard, stubborn rock.

She was still thinking about these things, when they pulled into a slip, on the same island as the Tor. After disembarking, they walked through a row of willows, to discover an apple orchard. In the corner, near the edge of the island, a small vineyard had been planted.

As they moved into more open land, King Arviragus turned to address the group.

"When Jesus went to school here, at the University," he explained, "he built a hut for himself to live in. He asked for permission to build in a quiet place. Knowing he was your nephew, Joseph, I knew I could trust him. I told him he could build anywhere he wanted to. He came here."

Arivagus smiled, as they approached a large, round hut. He looked at Mary. "Would you like to be the first to enter?"

He opened the door for her.

Mary stepped through the door, and immediately remembered the house where her son had lived during his years at the University. It was built in a circle, with windows slits cut high to allow the light inside. In its center, a stone fire-pit had been built, with an outer ledge two feet deep, and one foot across. Across the top of the pit, a metal lattice was laid, like a shelf. The lattice rested on the top of the fire-pit's ledge. Above the fire-pit, was a huge, metal funnel.

At the funnel's edge, a second rim of metal had been fused to its slanted body, overlapping the space where the smoke would rise. As she had observed in the construction of the funnel in the king's home, the center of the funnel was vented through the root.

Arviragus pointed to the fire-pit, and looked at Joseph. "I have not been able to completely copy his design. This one does not allow *any* smoke into the room…. at all! But *my* copies still do. Perhaps you can help me discover what to do differently."

Mary involuntarily chuckled. "I have felt that way with the things Jesus did around the house, more times than I can count," she told the king.

"And look!" the king declared. "He also put in two doors, instead of just one. "It is good for airflow in the summertime. And, as I was trying to decide where to put you, Joseph, I decided it would be good to put you here in this house, since a member of your family built it."

"Thank you," Joseph replied, amazed.

Mary had been taking in the details of the little hut. Like the homes in her native land, her son had lined it with plaster inside and out. He had then whitewashed the walls as well, inside and out.

"Did he use wheat to make the plaster?" she asked.

"In our culture, we had always done it that way, but Jesus travelled to the Great Chalk Cliffs, and dug out the powder himself. He borrowed a cart from David, and a mule. He was gone about two weeks during the summer break between his classes.

"I sent my brother's sons with him. They were both home from Rome for a visit that year. They had a grand time, living like traveling miners for a few days. Caractactus' boys came back bragging about what tough men they were. It was good for them."

Joseph chuckled. "It's good to think of him as a young man." He looked at Mary and Salome. "Can't you just see him?"

They both returned his gaze and smiled. Mary nodded.

"I can," Salome told him.

Arviragus continued his story. "Well, when he came back from the cliffs, he had bags and bags of white gypsum powder. He then built the daub-and-wattle frame on top of a short stone wall.

Our builders have always built with a wooden frame in a circle, and then leaned poles to the center. We have always punched holes in the roof for smoke to escape. But Jesus did it differently. He built a stone wall in a circle, and then added poles as a frame for the roof."

"Why did he do that?" Simon Zealotes asked.

"He said it needed a good foundation. He dug down into the ground all around, and laid a three-foot stone wall as a base for the wattle-and-daub walls. He covered all of it with the plaster and whitewash.

Our builders only put plaster between the main beams."

He tapped the floor with his foot. "And look at the floor! There is no dirt here! He put wood planks down and mortared them together! I have never seen such a thing!"

Mary noticed a wooden ledge inside the wall, running under the large window. Arviragus followed her gaze.

"He used to sit there on something like a bench, but it had a back to it, with a place to rest his arms. He would read, and look out of the window."

The king moved to a large willow basket next to a pile of cushions. "And look here!" he exclaimed. "He left these scrolls behind. David says there is a complete set of the prophets, and two sets of the books of Moses."

The house had certainly been well-furnished recently. Joseph noticed the cups and plates on shelves that had been built into the walls. There was a water pot next to the door. Several cooking pots were lined against the wall under the shelves.

"Who is to live here, Arviragus?" Joseph asked.

"Well, here is the plan," the king replied. "And yes, I now have a plan. Let's go outside. I want to show you something."

He walked to the back door and opened it, stepping out onto a level, stone piazza. "Your nephew laid these stones, as well. And planted the flowers. All we have done is trim them.

"Now, this hut is twenty-five feet across, and perfectly circular. I have an idea we could surround this larger hut with twelve smaller ones just like it, one for each of you. We can lay stone walkways between them, with stones like this piazza. That will help you to deal with the seasonal mud we have. We could complete them in the next few months if I have my builders study the design. They are very thorough.

"Here is my idea. This middle building could be lived in until the other buildings are finished. As you each move into your homes, the center hut could be used for group gatherings. I have measured the grounds here, and I think we could surround everything with a stockade of sorts to protect all of you from wild animals. There is a small space over by the orchard receiving sunlight most of the day, which would be a perfect spot for a garden."

"Do we draw our water from the marsh?" Sarah asked.

"Not any longer," Arviragus answered. "There are several fresh water rivers to draw from. But because of the rising and falling of the Uxella Marsh, when our people draw water, we always boil it before we drink it. This seems to cleanse it. But there are many fresh water sources in our area. And none of you will have to worry about that. There is a well flowing from a spring, some feet away."

He pointed to a location not far from the large round-house.

"Jesus was the one who found this spring. None of us knew it was here. My steward, David, had come to visit him, and noticed him digging one day. When he arrived, Jesus was digging below the surface. All you could see was dirt flying up from out of the hole. Apparently, he had dug deep down into the ground.

"When David first told me, I thought he might have been trying to create a place for cold storage. In fact, I still have questions about this. Inside the well, there are two underground caverns. They are limestone caverns. But in the center of the two, Jesus had laid a pattern of precious stones, in the shape of a cross. He inlaid them into some sort of stone.

"Somewhere close to ten feet in depth, he hit this spring. The waters filled the two underground caverns here, and still it keeps flowing. And yet, it doesn't flood the grounds."

"Jesus dug this well?" Eutrophius asked.

Arivagus nodded. There was silence, as each one contemplated.

Unbidden, Joseph was reminded of words Jesus had spoken. *When a person is reborn, he will experience springs of living water bursting from within.*

Joseph's thoughts went to his friend, Nicodemus.

Leaning in to gaze at the stones, Joseph noted the shape they had been placed in. He couldn't be sure, and the order had been altered.....

But the stones used to form the cross, appeared to be the same stones used in the Jewish High Priest's breastplate.

Had that been Jesus' plan all along? he wondered silently.

"It is a bountiful spring," the king said. "The water tastes sweet, and it is always cold and refreshing."

20 - Confrontations

Early the next morning, the entire company of Culdees met King Arviragus to travel to the mining district. They were joined by David and Belenus.

"The travel is demanding, milady," David told Mary. "Are you sure you want to make the trip? My wife tries to avoid it whenever possible."

Mary looked at him, suddenly remembering how fragile she used to feel. Somehow the events of the past two years had made her stronger, more resilient.

"I think I will be all right," she answered. "After all, when will there be another time to go with you and the king?"

How would they have survived in Glaston without the little ship, Mary considered? The larger vessels her uncle owned would never have worked for travel here. And how would twelve of them have been to move about the country without this especially prepared boat? How had it happened this way? Even in the difficulty and persecution, Abba Father's plan for their future had been in the works.

What they had meant for evil, ElShaddai had used for good.

Several of the Culdees travelled on foot into the southern part of the Island. There was only one safe pathway to take if a person was walking from Uxella

Marsh to the South. Due to the swift and strong currents of the Brue River, a stone bridge had been built to provide safe passage.

But, the bridge wasn't always reliable. Even though it was made with four stone archways, the bridge was underwater much of the time, and slippery from algae when not. Over the years, it had been aptly named, "The Perilous Bridge."

After crossing the Brue River, the travelers could either continue to walk, or ride in one of the wagons which were kept on the mainland to the south of the middle islands.

The next fourteen days were filled with new sights and experiences for everyone in the group. As they travelled through the countryside, they moved from village to village, mine to mine, greeting the workers and their families, sharing meals, and telling the story of Jesus. It became a pattern to tell the story, and then ask if anyone present was in need of prayer or in need of healing.

"What do I have to sacrifice to you to get healed?" was a common question.

"Nothing. Jesus wants to heal you. He already paid the price," became Joseph's common reply.

And when prayer to *this* God was offered, results took place. Stunned and awestruck, the people were not used to their prayers receiving a reply. There had never been truly supernatural healing power present among them before. But these days, blind eyes were being opened, and cripples' legs were strengthened and made to walk again.

Who was this Jesus?

And, when they discovered he was Jesus; the same young man who had lived among them, they were overwhelmed.

The Britons had never experienced Hope before.

Something was happening. Something good. It was amazing, they said to each other. When prayers were offered to Jesus, changes took place.

With everyone else in his land, Arviragus was caught up in the discoveries coming upon his people. A diligent ruler, he had never been away from his governmental duties for this period of time before.

Then, when the Holy Spirit continued to move among his people with power after a week, the king sent David home to Glaston, with a message for his advisors.

The journey with their new friends was taking longer than anticipated. He would return in another two weeks time.

In the third week, the group arrived in the southern mining districts, one day in the late afternoon. It was here the man suffering from Marsh Fever lived

478

with his family. After asking directions, one of the townspeople led the group to his home.

When the door opened, they were greeted by a woman with tear-streaks on her smudge-covered face. She was holding a little girl, who was rubbing her eyes. Smoke from a cooking fire billowed out the door, and escaped through punched holes in the thatched roof.

"Yes?" she said. "Can I help you?"

"Is this the home of Lugus, the miner?" the king asked.

"It is," the woman answered. "Or was. I am his widow, Bella. And this is his daughter, Inastasia."

"Who is it, Mama?" a small boy pushed his way to stand by his mother. With one hand he held to her tunic. His other thumb was in his mouth.

"I don't know, Arwyn," she told him. She looked at Arviragus. "Who are you?"

"My lady, I am here to help you," he answered. "When did your husband die?"

She looked at him strangely. "*Do* I know you?" she asked.

Arviragus didn't answer right away. He looked into her eyes. This woman had been struggling a long time, he realized.

"When did he die?" he asked.

She looked away, her tears beginning once more. "Just this morning," she choked out. "The Priest and that Wikka lady were here already. They said they would be back for his body this afternoon. I haven't had the energy to do anything with him yet. I've had no sleep for weeks, what with his losing his mind from the fever and all."

Simon Zealotes had made his way forward to stand behind the king while she was talking.

"Mistress Bella," he began. "My name is Simon, and I came because God told me to pray for your husband."

Not comprehending, she stared at him. "God," she echoed. "God who? Which god?"

"I serve the only Living God," Simon told her.

"There is nothing to be done now, by any god," she told him. "My husband is dead."

"I believe you," Simon answered. "But God sent me here to pray for him. Can I come in anyway and pray?"

Bella looked past Arviragus, still not recognizing him.

She spotted Mary and Salome, and nodded in indication. "Only if those two come in with you," she said, looking at the king suspiciously.

As Simon, Mary and Salome entered the house, Joseph and the king exchanged glances and grinned. Bella was in for a surprise at some point. That was sure.

Once inside, Mary and Salome busied themselves making friends with the woman's children.

How could anyone live, or even breathe in such a smoke-filled home, Mary wondered?

And yet, she understood. Winter was coming. A mother would want to keep her children warm. *How could they help Bella not live with such soot everywhere,* she wondered?

"Would you like some water, or some bread, Inastasia?" Salome asked the little girl.

Bella smiled at them. "She hasn't said anything since her father got sick," she said. "Her papa has only taken water for weeks. I've had a hard time getting *her* to eat anything at all. I do have some stewed apples from last night over on the shelf there."

Salome reached to take Inastasia from her mother. "Would you like some apples?" she offered. "Here, let me hug you for a moment."

Hearing the conversation, Mary found the apples, and moved to create a snack for the children. Abruptly, she felt a tiny tug on her toga. She looked down, and little Arwyn's big blue eyes met hers.

"Pweez?" he said, his mouth already filled with thumb.

She laughed, remembering her own sons at this little one's age. She crouched until her head was at his eye level. "Are you *sure?*" she teased, gently tugging at his thumb. "It looks like you are already chewing on something else!"

Bella watched the two women with her children, making sure they were truly trustworthy. Momentarily forgotten, Simon Zealotes made his way through the house, and found Bella's husband, Lugus, still in his bed.

Stone cold.

He felt the man's neck for a pulse.

Bella was right. He *was* dead. In fact, the stiffness of rigor-mortis had set in sometime prior. "You moved my heart to come here, Jesus," he prayed. "What do you want me to do?"

Pray.

Simon began to pray in the language of angels. As he did, he became aware of a great sadness in the house; a sense of heaviness filling the environment. As he continued to pray, the atmosphere began to change.

Bella came to check on him. She watched him for a moment, and then left again. Simon continued to pray.

Then, after a short time, he sensed a direction in his heart.

Place your hands on his head and his heart.

Simon obeyed the Holy Spirit's voice, and continued to pray. After another few moments, the Voice spoke again.

Call him to life in my name. Call him by name three times. Shout.

Feeling a little self-conscious, Simon paused. What if nothing happened when he prayed? What if he was just making all of this up in his own head?

What do you have to lose?

That's true, Lord, he acknowledged.

He continued to pray in the language of angels. As he did, his heart felt encouraged. Unexpectedly, confidence stirred in his soul.

All right, Lord, here we go, he prayed. *Help me.*

"Lugus!" Simon shouted. "Lugus!" Lugus!" I call you to come to life in the name of Jesus, the Living God, the Resurrected Lamb!"

He watched. Nothing. Had this been a training exercise, he wondered?

Wait.

Simon began once again to pray in the language of angels. He was so focused on prayer, he forgot about watching Lugus. With his eyes closed, he began to walk back and forth, praying aloud in the language of angels.

Suddenly, out of nowhere, startling and surprising the disciple, a deep voice spoke.

"Who are *you?*"

Simon nearly jumped out of his skin. He looked around to find the source of the voice. He was actually surprised to see Lugus sitting up in his bed.

Lugus repeated his question. "Who are you? What are you doing in my house?"

Bella appeared in the doorway. "Simon," she said, "I think I'm hearing things." A movement from her husband drew her attention. Her mouth dropped open. She was speechless, unbidden tears filling her eyes once more.

"Bella?" her husband asked. "What's wrong?"

Stunned she looked at her husband, and then back to Simon.

"Lugus? Are you …. *alive?*" she whispered.

"Woman, I'm right here!" he answered. "What's going on?"

At that point, Mary and Salome showed up at the door, with Inistasia and Arwyn in tow. When Inistasia saw her father sitting up, and heard his voice, she screamed and giggled, running to jump on him. "Poppee!! You're awake now!"

He rubbed her head. "Yes I am!" He looked at Bella. "And who are these people?"

Simon put out his hand in greeting. "I am Simon Zealotes, sir," he told Lugus. "God sent me here to pray for you."

Surprised, the man looked to his wife. "God?"

"You were dead," Bella said simply.

"What?" he asked.

"Dead as a rat in a trap," Bella told him.

"What is the last thing you remember?" Simon asked.

"I was at the mine. I took the two-day shipment of bricks up to Glaston for Master Caedmon. On the way back I got caught in a swarm of mosquitos." He paused as awareness struck him. He continued his recounting of the events a little more slowly. "I started feeling sick and had a headache. I took to my bed, and then I fell asleep."

"Is that all you remember?" Simon prodded.

"No," Lugus told him slowly. "I remember waking up and drinking water, several times. But my head hurt so badly."

"It was weeks," Bella told him. "And then, this morning, you were cold and not breathing. You were already stiff when I woke up. The Druids came to check you. And then, I tried to get the children to eat. I built the fire, and these people came."

"I had a dream just before I woke up," he said.

"You did?" she asked.

"I had three creatures holding on to me," he told them. "They were dark fairies, like the Druid priests talk about. Except they were bigger than I am, and had red eyes. They were black, and had wings like a bat. They had long claws and teeth, and skin like a snake. They were taking me somewhere, and I felt hot, like my skin was burning.

"Then a man came and called my name. He was dressed in bright white. He had a golden sash. There was light coming from him, and the creatures tried to hide from him. Each time he called my name, one of the creatures let go, and backed away from me. Then, the man said, 'I call you to life in the name of Jesus, the Living God; the Resurrected Lamb.' I felt myself pulled away from where I had been.

"Then, another man came and stood with the man who had been talking. He was dressed in white as well, but not as bright as the first man. He extended his hand to me, and I took it. Then I woke up."

He looked at Simon. "What *happened* to me?"

"The man you saw in the bright white light with the sash was Jesus," he told Lugus. "He has raised you from the dead. How do you feel?"

Lugus looked at him strangely. "Fine." He paused. "Say, *you* were the *other* man in my dream!"

"Those are the words Jesus told me to pray," the disciple answered simply. "When I do what the Holy Spirit tells me, he honors it. I was just obedient to him. He wants to give you life; the best life you have ever lived. He wants you to be here for your wife and children. He has a purpose for you."

Bella walked over to the bed, and sat down next to her husband. She reached out to touch him. He hugged her. There was silence in the room for a moment, as Bella put her head down on her husband's shoulder and burst into tears.

"There, there, now, *gra-mo-chroi*[1]. Sha, now. It's all right, my Bella," he told her. "I'm here. There now." He stroked her hair gently as he spoke.

Seeking to give the couple privacy, Salome made her way to the outdoors, where she shared the news of Lugus' resurrection with everyone who had come with Arviragus.

As she walked back into the house, the entire company followed.

Quietly, they made their way to the door of the bedchamber where Lugus was holding his wife. When Bella's tears had subsided, she began to apologize.

"I'm sorry," she said, "I guess I've just been pushing it down for a while now."

Blowing her nose into her apron, Bella became aware of the presence of others in the room. She looked up and saw Arviragus. Seeing her concern, Lugus also looked at the king. But the miner recognized the ruler, and reacted accordingly. In a sudden response, he pushed his wife back, and struggled to stand. "Bella, you have to move," he ordered. "I have to get up."

"You need the privy?" she asked.

"No, woman!" he said, exasperated, "the king of all Briton is standing in our bedchamber."

"The king?" she echoed. "Where?"

Lugus pointed. "Right there!"

---

[1] love of my heart

At that point, Arviragus put out his hand in greeting. "Good day, Mistress Bella. My name is Arviragus."

Bella fainted on the spot.

Having visited all of the mining districts, Arviragus headed home once more with the twelve Culdee newcomers to Briton. It was during this trip he shared a decision he had made during a conversation with Joseph.

"I am completely convinced now that Jesus is who you say he is," he told his friend. "I'll admit, I was willing to grant you sanctuary based on our friendship, but now, I see a greater good in your coming to our shores. I want to give each of you a Land Hide, and bestow upon you titles."

Surprised and not just a little curious, Joseph responded. "What does that mean?"

Arviragus explained. "Well, you see, for a long time now, the powers of decision and moral change have been shifting in our land. Over time, the Druid Priests and Wikka have become more independent. As a result, I have come to trust their motives less and less. My people are sickly, and down-trodden. They have lost all hope for their future. When sickness comes, they don't fight to become healthy. When trouble comes, they are weak. I have been concerned for the future of our entire island.

"But in the past few days, I watched a shift in my people. There is a power in your God; greater than anything I have seen; He is so great I had begun to believe even *before* I had learned Jesus was sent by Him; that Jesus was your God... *our* God.... Come in human form.

"My steward helped me to heal after the priests tried to poison me. I have no idea what would have happened to my people had they succeeded with their plans. That being said, I am not sure what state my ability to rule will be in when we return to Glaston, or whether my throne will still be intact. So, I want to empower each of your company to help us."

"I am sure that is why God sent us here," Joseph told him.

"Additionally," the king continued. "I want to give each person in your company a Land Hide.

"What is a Land Hide?"

"Oh, it's just a term," Arviragus answered. "A Hide is a measurement. It is 160 acres of land laid out in a tract of 16x10 acres. I will be giving each of you a Hide of land. And, with each gift, I will attach authority. You will have the power to govern and make decisions. Your group will, in effect, become my Personal Council. I would like you to become my Chief Counsel, if you are willing."

"That is very gracious, your majesty," the astonished Joseph responded.

"I also want to be baptized," the king told him. "I am going to call a meeting when we return, so you can tell the story you have been telling these weeks to the rest of my Court, and to our tribal leaders. I want Briton to become a tribe, and a family of tribes, ruled by the will of the Living God, and none other."

"I know we all would love to be a part of that," Joseph replied.

"My present Chief Counsel is the Chief Druid priest," Arviragus said. "You remember David told you. His name is Asarlai Draoi, which means 'wizard'. Another responsibility he carries presents itself. He is also the overseer of our armies. He is powerful as a mage and in alchemy. But, as I'm sure you have discerned, a discovery has been made of late. His agenda is to rule in my place. Hence, the poisons.

"It is my hope *he* will see what *I* have seen in the power of ElShaddai. I want to see him discover the hope I have found for himself and his family."

"And what will you do if he isn't convinced?" Joseph asked, thinking of Caiaphas and the Sadducees. "Will you punish him for the plot to kill you and your wife?"

Arviragus shrugged. "I don't know about that yet. I do know my course is set, Joseph," he looked at his friend with a steady gaze. "I have seen enough to know I can trust ElShaddai. Since I am not given to trust easily, I know something inside of myself has changed. All I know is I must to do what is right.... For me, my family, and my people."

"Can you exile those who oppose you from office? Remove them somehow?" Joseph asked.

"Only if they die," the king answered, with an ironic chuckle. "Decisions here are made for a group of tribes, and so come about by means of a Council Meeting. Granted, I am the Pendragon, 'the chief of chiefs,' which means I do have the final say. But resentment builds in the chieftains when a lesser chief is ignored, or countered. I would like to see change come without conflict. That is why we need everyone to be there."

Joseph nodded. "What are you asking *me* to do?" he asked.

"Your God seems to have planned for this long ago," the king answered. "The more I consider how well the pieces fit, the more amazed I become. For example, you are the Nobilius Decurio of Rome. And for now, even though you have been displaced, it is important you continue to conduct yourself in those duties."

"Yes, I agree," Joseph answered. "I was going to speak with you about that."

"Do you realize how very much ElShaddai must care for me and my people?" Arviragus asked. "And this is secondary to seeing my people freed from the Druid beliefs. Have you considered how you, being a Roman Consul, is relief to the Dumnoni? Your position and presence here might very well save all of us from a Roman assault."

The king waited for a response. When Joseph appeared to be only listening, he continued. "When we present this, however, I don't want it to be a political decision. It is my hope each of my tribal chiefs will recognize the wisdom of choosing to follow Jesus, or at the least come to an agreement to do no violence against those of their people who choose to do so."

He paused, thinking. "I do, however, have concerns about my father, Cunobelin. He put me on the throne, but occasionally he sides with Asarlai against my decisions. And his health has been failing of late."

"You might have a battle on your hands, if Asarlai and your father are determined to do battle with Rome," Joseph advised.

"I am sure we will have *some* sort of conflict, at least with Asarlai," Arviragus informed him with a determined smile. "Especially since the land I intend to give to you will include the Tor."

"Oh," he added. "Do you think we should invite my son, Prince Beli, and your daughter to the meeting as well? I think my plans for a formal dinner have been somewhat altered by our God."

When the group arrived in Glaston several days later, Joseph was greeted by his daughter and son-in-law, Anne and Eubulus Beli, with Gwynth and little Eubulus Joseph.

As the little ship pulled to the shore of Avalon, little Gwynth rocked back and forth in her white tunic.

"Scooz mee," she said to Cleon, as he jumped out of the boat to tether it.

Cleon crouched down with his hands on his knees. "Yes, miss?" he answered.

"Are *you* my grandfather?" she asked carefully.

Cleon laughed. "I don't think so," he said. "*You* must be looking for Master Joseph."

Hearing the conversation, Joseph stepped to the side of the boat, to disembark. "Cleon, would help the others?" he asked.

"Certainly," Cleon replied.

"Thank you," Joseph said. He directed his attention to his grand-daughter. "And who are *you*?"

"*I'n* Gwyn," she answered, rocking back and forth. "Mama says you need to come to your house when you get here."

Chuckling, Joseph picked her up and tossed her up in the air quickly and then caught her.

"Whee!" she exclaimed. "I like *you!*"

Joseph made his way to the large round-house, where his family was waiting to reunite with him after almost five years.

Gwynth put her hand up to play with her grandfather's hair. She twirled it in her fingers. "You d'ot curls too!" she noticed.

"Yes, I do!" Joseph said. "Mine are shorter, aren't they?"

Gwynth flipped her hair. "Mine's longer."

Joseph chuckled. "Is Mama at my house?" he asked.

"She had to take Eubie in. He d'ot dirty agin'," she informed him. "Not me. I stayed *kween*. See--ee?" she looked down and fluffed her tunic.

As Joseph and Gwynn approached the large round-house, Joseph noted the king's builders had been busy while the Culdee company had been away. Several new smaller buildings had been added. And now, he was walking on a walkway made of flat stones, which led to the entry door.

He would have to investigate those things later, he decided.

As he entered the round-house, he looked for his daughter. "Anne?" he called.

"Abba?" a female voice answered. "We're back here, outside the house. Eubie got mud all over himself. I'm trying to save his good toga from the marsh mud."

By that time, Joseph and Gwynn had arrived at the open back door. The sight meeting them caused both of them to burst into simultaneous laughter. Eubulus Joseph had apparently gone wading in the marsh at low tide. The boy was covered in black muck from head to toe. The only parts of him not covered in mud were his eyes, and teeth. Black muck dripped from his tunic and hair.

"Hi! Poppee!" the little boy giggled in delight. "I got dirty!"

"Yes, you certainly did!" Joseph chuckled.

Next to him, his now, rather muddy mother, was working unsuccessfully to clean him with well water from a bowl and a small cloth.

Anne looked up at her father. "We left the villa early this morning. I didn't pack any extra clothes. I should have planned better. And he lost a shoe!"

She threw the rag into the water. In a deep clay pot nearby were two rather large full-grown frogs, also covered with marsh mud. The frogs jumped in reaction to the rag's splash into the water.

"You weely durty, Eubie," Gwynn volunteered.

Joseph moved over to view the frog specimens in the pot. "These are beauties, Eubie!!" he exclaimed.

"Yes, day are!" his grandson replied, exultant.

"Abba! You're as bad as Beli! Don't encourage him!" Anne wiped the back of her hand across her forehead, leaving a trail of mud behind, streaking her face.

"Not to be a boy?" Joseph asked. "This is great stuff! *Great* stuff!"

"That's all very well and good, Abba," she sighed. "But now we will have to leave early because he has nothing left to wear. I can't very well let a boy in line for the throne of the Dumnoni run around naked the rest of the day, can I?"

Mary and Salome had been standing in the back entry doorway, watching in amusement. As mothers of grown men, who had been boys at one time, they exchanged glances.

Anne really needed to relax.

It was Mary who spoke first.

"Hi Anne! It's good to see you!"

Joseph's daughter looked up. "Hi, Mary! I've missed you! I have no idea what to do here. Beli is waiting for his father, with several other gentlemen in his home. I can't go anywhere until he is ready to leave. Meanwhile, Eubulus is covered – again! – in black muck! Now, I have dirt all over me.... and I didn't pack any ...." Her voice trailed off. Tears of frustration spilled over. "The villa as over an hour away."

Mary moved over to her cousin, and put her arm around her. "It will be fine, Anne," she said. "Eubulus is a strong, intelligent, active boy. And he will be a man someday. Every time he does something like this, he is developing his sense of leadership; his creativity. He is learning."

"That may be, Mary," she answered. "But that doesn't solve my problem. I don't mind if he does things like this at home. But I do mind when we are in a situation like this!"

"It's going to be fine, Anne," Mary told her. "I raised four boys of my own. Salome raised two. Let us take care of Eubie, for you... I know. What if you come inside with me? I brought a couple of things you might be able to wear."

Anne nodded. "I'm not sure I'm cut out for this," she sighed.

"You just need a little support," Mary told her. "You're going to be just fine."

Salome stepped towards Eubulus. Pulling his tunic up over his head, she began stripping the boy down to his little loincloth. She looked at her uncle.

"Uncle, can you keep Gwynn here?"

Joseph nodded. He looked at Gwynn. "How's that sound? We go inside with Mama, and get a snack?"

"Tounds dood to me!" Gwynn declared. She looked at Joseph. "You d'ot anee avells?"

Salome spoke next. "Sarah, can you help me, please?"

Sarah stepped next to her. "Yes ma'am?"

"I'm going to go down to the market. Would you please take Eubie over to the well and give him a good bath?"

She looked around the room. "Cleon? Martial?"

The two young men responded. "Yes?"

"Would you mind drawing water from the well for Princess Anne? She is going to want to wash her face and hands." She looked around. "Is there anyone here who could show me where to purchase children's clothes and shoes?"

It was David who took Salome to the marketplace for Anne and Eubie. She purchased tunics for both children, a clean tunic and topshirt for Anne, and shoes for Eubie. True, the items were not as finely made as the ones which had been destroyed, but they were clean, serviceable, and would help Anne to meet her husband for the evening meal at the Feasting Hall.

Three weeks later, just after the morning meal, a large group gathered in the Feasting Hall. Tribal Lords had been arriving for the past two days. David was extremely busy, arranging lodging and amenities for each one. A few leaders brought their wives, and, since King Arviragus was a widower, David enlisted the help of his own wife, Eiless, to entertain them. As the king's cousin, she had been trained from the days of her girlhood in the arts of communication and hospitality. She was thrilled to be asked, and was enjoying a chance to spend time with other women her own age.

In the Feasting Hall, the servants moved the long tables away from the room's center. Benches were placed, in a hexagon, encircling the central fire-pit. Enough room was left between the fire-pit and the first row of benches for those who wished to address the group to stand, and even pace while speaking, if needed.

Lanterns were lit all over the great room. Great urns of water were placed on benches throughout the hall, with clay cups set nearby. The custom was to share the cups, so each urn had been allotted a maximum of three cups.

King Arviragus had invited chiefs from districts as far away as the North Country, as well as leaders from the Cymru peoples across the waters from Glaston. A leadership *ionadai,* or representative, was present from each of the mines, as well as many villagers who had experienced healing and change during the recent month of visits made by Joseph and his company of Culdees.

Lugus and Bella had arrived as well, with Inastasia and Arwyn.

On the Isle of Avalon, the twelve Culdees met together in the large, round house. Six of the smaller, round houses conscripted by the king had been completed so far. Three were finished when they arrived home from travelling to the mining districts. As had been true in all of their dealings with Arviragus, the king was generous to them. The houses were each furnished with bedding and dishes, cushions and water-pots.

As the smaller huts were completed, members moved from the central hut, a few at a time. The first to move into the smaller huts were Cleon and Martial, then Simon Zealotes and Joseph, then Sarah and Cleophas' daughter, Mary. Restitutus and Sedonius (Uri and Jacob) moved into the fourth hut; Eutropius and Saturninus into the fifth. When the sixth hut was finished, Mary and Salome moved into it. This would be their housing arrangement for now. As each smaller hut was finished, one would choose to inhabit it, until all twelve were completed.

Mary found it difficult to leave the larger round-house. It was strange how easily she had been able to imagine Jesus living there. She felt close to the boy she remembered mothering during the time they stayed there. But when she and Salome entered the smaller hut, it was constructed after the template of the larger round-house. The king's builders even installed a plank and mortar floor.

"Thank you for this little house," she whispered in her prayers; many times since she and Salome moved in. "Thank you we are no longer awakened by snoring."

This morning, they were meeting together in the round-house to pray together, in preparation for sharing their stories once again. Today, they could feel it would be different from visiting the mines.

It would be completely different from Massillia.

As they boarded the little ship, every member of the group continued to pray in the language of angels.

Each of them could sense it.

Today held the potential to change the face of the entire island of Briton.

Steering the rudder, Joseph thought back to his younger days in Jerusalem. This meeting held the possibility of becoming like his hardest day in the Sanhedrin; when opposing arguments continued all day and into the night hours. When men had come to blows.

He could feel it in his bones.

There would be difficulty today.

As they pulled the little ship up to the bank of the mainland, Mary noticed a group arriving at the Feasting Hall. They seemed to float across the ground. With their heads hooded, and their manner intimidating, she surmised they must be the Druid contingency.

There are so many of them, she thought.

Were all of these people leaders among the Druids? Which one was Asarlai Draoi, their leader?

Then, she noted the first man in their procession carried a walking stick. And, although he was tall, the walking stick was a foot taller. A large, golden, flat disc was mounted on its top. As she observed the disc, she realized it was etched with a circular pattern, similar to a labyrinth. In the center of the disc, in the middle of the design, a shining clear crystal was fused. It seemed to emanate a light all its own. Or was it reflecting the sunlight, she wondered?

He must be their leader, Aslarai.

Following the tall man, were the Druid Priests. They were clothed in long, flowing robes, with hooded cloaks, pulled up to hide their faces. Their feet were shod in fine sandals. Their necks were adorned by feathers and human bones strung on golden chains, or woolen cords.

Behind the Priests, came a group of women.

These must be the Wikka, Mary concluded.

Moving seductively, they made their way along the path. Each woman was dressed in a sheer, belted tunic, with multiple slits opening the tunic from the edges trailing on the ground, all the way to the waist. Bare legs showed above the thigh as the women walked, with geometric markings tattooed or cut into their flesh. Astonished, Mary stared at them. The upper torso fabric of each robe's front was cut into a "V," with the narrowest point of the neckline disappearing somewhere under the golden belt. And, although there were several layers of the sheer fabric making up each woman's tunic, nothing was really covered. Every detail of each Wikka's body was visible, or at least discernable.

Following the Wikka, came a group of men and women, who were dressed in ordinary linen tunics, with hooded cloaks, similar to the Druid priests. Many of them carried small lyres, or pipes. Many were adorned with feathers of differing variety. These were the Bards and Ovates, the Druid poets and seers; the teachers and scholars. Leading this contingency was Maedoc, Caedmon's assigned mentor.

Many of those in the four groups had painted their faces.

Mary was sure those who had done so, honestly believed the markings provided them with an unseen power.

Unconsciously, she shuddered.

They had never seen power, she surmised, smiling.

Not True power.

Inside the Feasting Hall, King Arviragus stood near the fire. Standing with him was his brother, Caractacus, who was a king in his own right, ruling the Catuvellauni tribe. Nearby, their ailing father, a retired Cunobelin, sat in a chair with cushions, attended by a slave.

There were no seats of distinction here, he considered. Every person could sit where they wanted to sit. In fact, each person here today was considered a leader by the general population of Briton. And, even if they might disagree with what would be shared today, they could never say they were unaware of what was happening, or had not been given a chance to choose.

There would be no secrets in this assembly. He knew each one would speak their mind, even if it prolonged the gathering into the midnight hours. Silently, he prayed.

"Lord Jesus, prepare us. Holy Spirit, speak through us. Help us. Please help us."

David and Eiless were seated on the first row of benches, near the place where the king stood. Caedmon had come up from the mining districts, and had taken a place next to David.

When the first of the Culdee party entered the Hall, the room quieted somewhat. Many had heard about the group, and wanted to get a first glimpse. Some knew of the journey they had taken through the mining districts.

Most knew Joseph as a representative of Rome, as the Nobilius Decurio; as the man who was part owner of the mines providing their livelihoods.

Whispers could be heard throughout the great room.

What was the purpose of the meeting?

Why had the Pendragon called them all together?

Why were the Druids here as well?

Who were these Culdees?

As was customary, the group was called to attention by the leader of the Ovates, who gave thanks to the Goddess for their safety and the good weather. He then welcomed them all in the names of Gwyn-al-Nudd, Lord of the Underworld, and Avallach, The Fisher King. He then introduced the Pendragon, Arviragus the Great, the Druid prince who had drawn them all together.

When Arviragus stood, he lifted both his arms above his head and shouted to them, "Brothers, Sisters, and good people all! I have called you here because I have heard a story. It is a beautiful story of life and death; of love and battle; of betrayal and healing. I have heard it many times in the past month, and each time I hear it, something inside of me has a fresh glimpse of perfect light.

"It is a story of power; of common people becoming extraordinary. In fact, twelve of those common people are here today. They are Culdees, and, as it is your generous nature to do, I have extended our hospitality to them; the gracious warmth of Briton. *We* have; *you* have; *together* we have provided a home for them.

 He nodded at Joseph, motioning for his friend to join him. "All of you know Joseph of Arimathea, the Nobilius Decurio of Rome. In fact, many of us can remember when he used to come here on business with his great nephew, the daughter of his niece, Mary. She and her sister are here as well."

He nodded at Mary and Salome, motioning for them to stand, and Mary to join him where he stood with Joseph. When she stood, she turned to view the crowd. The room was filled. People stood in the back and against the sides two and three deep. Even the tables on the sides of the Hall had been used as places to sit. Looking over the crowd, there were a few people she thought she might recognize. As she met their eyes, many smiled and gave an acknowledging wave of greeting.

So many friends are here, she realized. There was no need to be afraid.

I have brought you this far. I have you in my Hand.

493

A wave of comfort washed over her, and she found herself smiling and surreptitiously waving back at several of the women, greeting them.

Joseph was speaking now.

"Last month, our group travelled with King Arviragus through the mining districts. We told our story first to him when we arrived. At his request we shared it many times last month. Some of you have heard what we are about to share already.

"I'd like to hear it, as many times as you'd like to tell it, Joseph!" a man shouted from the back of the room.

"Tell us about Jesus!" a woman in the front called out.

"I want to hear again from Uri!" a man whose leg had been healed cried.

Throughout the room, ripples of similar responses began to rise. Surprised, the king motioned for a stilling of the noise.

"Now, now," he soothed. "You will get your chance to hear it all. That is why we have begun so early today. We are here until decisions have been made."

"What decisions?" one of the Ovates asked.

Arviragus chuckled, and glanced at Joseph. He raised his voice and spoke. "When my sons' children do this, we never get the story told," he said. "You must hear the story in order to make a correct choice." He smiled at the Ovate who had spoken. "How can we ask you to make a decision without complete information?"

"Yes, Your Majesty," the Ovate replied. "I guess I was caught up in all of the excitement. I'd like to hear this story as well!"

Arviragus motioned to Joseph once more, who looked around the room, and then began to speak.

"Friends, many of you know my niece, Mary. The story really begins with an experience she had. So, I will allow her to begin, and then each of us will speak to you in turn. Can we hold questions until the end, please, since there are so many of us here?"

People nodded in assent.

"Can everyone hear well enough?"

It was obvious Joseph was speaking loud enough to be heard, but a good-natured voice of an old man erupted from the back of the room. "What?"

This was followed by laughter.

Joseph turned to Mary, who began to share.

As she had done many times before, she told of Zacharias and Elizabeth, of Gabriel, of her courtship with Joseph, of the nativity, of Herod, of Egypt. She told it all, in fine detail.

Then, like a well-oiled machine, each of the Culdees shared their part in the story of Jesus' birth, life, ministry, death, resurrection and ascension. But this time, Joseph also shared about his own experiences during the week of Jesus' crucifixion. He shared how Jesus had appeared to him in Caiaphas' prison. He shared of his friendship with Pontius Pilate. He shared about the resurrection of Simeon BenGamaliel's sons, and their separately agreeing accounts of Sheol, or what the Celts called the Underworld.

He shared his experiences the day of the Mighty Wind in Jerusalem, and the birth of the Ecclesia in Jerusalem. Of miracles. Of healings. Of supernatural events brought about by the power of God. He shared briefly regarding the division between the Pharisees and Sadducees, and the subsequent persecution.

Then, he came to the day of Stephen's murder by stoning, and the vision Stephen shared seeing just before he died. Finally, he shared of the seventy two persons who had been rounded up; had been made to march over eighty miles in two days' time; had been forced into a little ship designed to bring about their deaths at sea. He shared of their miracle journey; of rainfall every morning for three months, and raw fish; of the refurbishing of the little ship, of the party left in Massilia and their arrival in Glaston.

At that point, it was time for the midday meal. Joseph invited everyone to view the little ship, which was moored outside, during their repast.

Two hours had been budgeted for the meal.

As she watched the faces of those in the room, Mary was amazed. Most of the women had tears streaming from their eyes. Furtively, she observed the Druid contingency. She was surprised. Somehow, the spiritual nature of the story had intrigued them. Many were weeping. She saw confusion on a few of the older men's faces, and anger in one or two. But, for the most part, the first, silent responses seemed to be positive.

During the break, many of the delegates took time to inspect the little ship. One of the Ovates had attended the Academies in Rome, and recognized the pattern of the fabric Duruk had used.

"That pattern of fabric is made in Cyrene," he told Joseph.

"That's true," Joseph answered. "We had the ship outfitted there."

"What are these wood planks criss-crossing the hull?" a man who owned a ship-building business asked. "And why is the rudder mounted the way it is?"

Joseph chuckled. "Do you remember what I said this morning? It originally was made *without* a rudder or sail? Those planks are the only method Duruk could use to give us a sail and a rudder. He also built and mounted the benches and their cushions."

495

The man nodded in approval. "I've heard of Duruk," he said. "And I recognize his work. This was well done."

"Thank you," Joseph replied, with a small nod.

And so went many other conversations during the meal break.

After lunch, the meeting resumed once more. This time, King Arviragus welcomed everyone back to the meeting, and then asked for the stories of those in the mining districts who had experienced healing or change in their lives due to the ministry of the Culdee team. Many responded. In fact, there was a line around half of the room of those who wanted to share.

There was a child who brought a crutch made by her father from a tree limb. She no longer needed it. She ran and skipped through the room.

A man born with balls of flesh for feet stood barefooted, with toes showing, sharing about the afternoon he had been prayed for.

Deaf ears had been unplugged. Blind eyes had been opened.

Discoveries had been made. Souls had been made aware.

Hope had been restored.

When those in line were finished sharing, Joseph invited Bella to come up. The shy woman answered his questions, and with Joseph's help, told the crowd how her husband had contracted Marsh Fever, and lain in a semi-coma for weeks, only waking for a drink of water every few days. When she got to the part of the story when Lugus died, there were gasps through the room.

Then, King Arviragus shared his account of the arriving of the Culdee group, and how Simon Zealotes had asked whether he would be allowed to pray for the man sick with Marsh Fever.

No one had known Lugus would be dead when they arrived.

At that point, unbidden, an Ovate from within the Druid group stood, as did one of the priests.

"Yes? You have a question?" the king asked.

"No, your majesty, but we have something to add to this story," the priest announced. "Mistress Bella asked me.... I mean us, to come to her home, and confirm her husband's death. We did confirm his death, and told her to prepare her home and his body. We told her we would return to gather him for the pyre in a few hours."

Joseph looked intently at the two Druids offering this information. Something had stirred in each of them, that they would stand in this gathering and publicly confirm Bella's story.

Sensing something ha not yet been told, a woman in the front stood up. "Bella, what happened?" she asked. "You wouldn't be telling a story here if something hadn't happened!"

Bella's face broke into a great smile, and she looked for her husband's face in the crowd. She raised her arm and pointed.

Lugus stood to his feet, tears streaming down his face. "I'm right here!" he managed to croak out through deep emotion. He made his way through the crowd, stepping over benches, between those in his way.

"Jesus brought me back to life!" he shouted, his hands raised high.

A thunder of applause rose without prompting. Even the Druids were expressing their approval. Who would have thought the boy who had lived among them would have been sent by God, and had power over death itself? What was to be thought about the round-house he had built, or the well he had dug, or the questions he had asked in his classes?

As the applause died down, Joseph gave an invitation, to discover how many of those present felt they wanted to choose to become followers of Jesus and his teachings. A majority of hands were raised in the room.

"Then we will plan a baptism tomorrow morning at high tide," Arviragus announced. "If you would be pleased to stay, we will prepare sleeping places for all of you."

A thankful murmur made its way through the room. It looked as though there would be many opening their homes in Glaston that evening.

"Now," said Arviragus to the entire hall, "I need to speak with you about the decision I mentioned." He looked at Joseph. "Thank you, my friend. You have been standing and speaking most of the day. Take a rest now, if you will."

Joseph sat down on the bench next to David. "Can we speak later, Master Joseph?" the steward asked.

Joseph patted his knee. "Absolutely, David," he answered. "I'd love to speak with you."

They both turned their attention back to the king. He had raised his voice once more. "As you can see, and now know, there is something different about these Culdees. And, you should know, they have adopted our name for them as their own. They have come to live among us, being persecuted, cast out of their own country, because they have each chosen to follow Jesus, as many of you have this day.

"I have known Joseph of Arimathea for many years. I knew him as the Nobilius Decurio of Rome, and have conducted trade with him for the sake of our tribes. Only recently have I learned he was considered a sage and advisor in his own nation. His experience has been first-hand in dealing with spiritual and judicial issues as a member of the Jewish Sanhedrin in Jerusalem.

"Many of you are aware of the scholarship we utilize in our own Celtic University; and that in our own history, we recall the exile of our forefathers from the nation of Israel. Many of our ancients, and even some of you here today, are able to trace your own family roots back to the days of King David."

"For this reason, I believe the Living God has sent Joseph and the Culdees among us. I, myself, have come to believe in Jesus as the only Living God."

He paused. Looking around the room for confirmation or denouncement.

Either were acceptable in this assembly.

But neither came.

The entire gathering was absorbing the information of the day. Arviragus' decision was apparently just another fact added to the momentous disclosures made over the past eight hours. The king licked his lips, and took a sip of water before continuing.

"Because of my relationship with Joseph, I have asked him to become my Chief Counsel. I believe he will be able to help our tribe avoid the inevitable war with Rome, and still maintain our identity as Britons. I also have come to believe in the true spiritual Power of this God. If we align our loyalties with him, our future will be secure, for eternity.

"Does anyone here object to my choice of Joseph as Chief Counsel? I have had no one serve in that position for some time."

He waited. No one spoke.

"Well?" he prodded. "Are you still here?"

"I have no problem with your choice, King Arivargus." The voice belonged to Asarlai Draoi, who was standing to his feet.

"Good," Arviragus spoke, meeting the man's eyes. He extended his hand to the wizard. "There is more."

The Chief of the Druid priests spoke once more. "And that is?"

"The round-house which Jesus built during his years here still stands. The well he dug still pours forth fresh waters, some 25,000 gallons each day. His mother sits here with her sister, his aunt. His great-uncle has stood before you today. Since many of us have come to believe Jesus is the only Living God in this Council, then it is not a small stretch to believe he would want us to care for those who cared for him in his boyhood. I have given the round-house to Mistress Mary, his mother, and Master Joseph of Arimathea, his great uncle. We are in the process of constructing additional homes for the rest of the Culdees, because it is only reasonable they should dwell in close proximity to each other. I also feel it is within our province and duty to provide each of these with a Hide of Land."

"But sire," Asarloi objected, "the round-house was built on the Isle of Avalon! The well you speak of is also on that island! Is it wise to give this precious property to the Culdees, when it is the entrance to the Underworld? When it is the place of the Goddess? Will these newcomers adopt our beliefs, then? Will they merge our teachings with their own?"

The wizard looked around the room, for agreement.

Mary watched as many of those in close proximity to the wizard looked away, or down at the floor.

"Oh, I see," he spoke to the Druid contingency around him. "Am I the only one who believes our sacrifices and way of life should continue as they always have?"

The female Ovate from Lugus' village spoke. "When has the Goddess brought someone back from the dead?" she asked, pointing at Lugus. "When have you heard our people speak with this kind of hope, this kind of life-giving energy? When have our spells, or chantings, or divinings, or even prayers to Avallach caused this kind of change to happen for our people? And in one month? This kind of thing has not happened among us ever before – no, not in centuries!"

She looked around the room. "For myself, I choose to follow Jesus!"

The Druid Priest of Lugus' mining district stood as well. "And I," he declared.

"And I."

"And I. I choose to follow Jesus!"

One by one, the majority of the Druid contingency stood, renouncing their allegiance to the Mother Earth Goddess, to choose to become followers of Jesus.

Chagrined, and not yet willing to yield, Asarlai raised his voice.

"Then, let us issue a challenge! Those who still hold their loyalty to Vivien, the mother of all things, the Lady of the Lake, come to me. On the morrow, at dawn, we will have a contest to see who the real God among us is!"

He raised his staff and pointed it's flattened, golden disc and crystal towards Joseph of Arimathea. His eyes were simmering with rage.

For a moment, Caiaphas' face flashed across Joseph's mind.

What is the comparison you are showing me, Lord?

He became so focused on the fresh understanding he was receiving, he almost missed the wizard's next words.

"Joseph of Arimathea!" he bellowed. "Tomorrow at dawn you will present yourself for the judgment and punishment of the Goddess! You, and these who have invaded our land with you! At that time, we will see who the True God is! And you will yield when the rulers of the Underworld make their presence and power known!"

Watching his outward dramatics, Joseph smiled at him. Quietly, he answered. "And what will you do when Abba Father, Jesus and his Holy Spirit prove to be more powerful than your Goddess and her sons?"

Enraged, the wizard leaned forward to scream at Joseph. "Then we will give up our beliefs for yours. But! When Avallach shows himself, *you* will have to yield!"

With that, Asarlai Draoi stomped his foot, and banged his walking stick on the ground. Flourishing his cloak, he pushed his way over the benches in front of him, and pompously stormed out of the room.

Behind him, three Priests, one Ovate and two Bards followed.

As they left the room, the Feasting Hall burst into spontaneous applause and cheering.

As the cheering died down, Joseph turned his attention to the crowd. "My friends," he began. "Let me ask one thing of you today. We need the power of Abba God, of ElShaddai, of Jesus and the Holy Spirit to help us. The power of our God is real, and I have no doubt He will prevail. However, my deeper concern is for the souls of Asarlai, and those who left with him. They are angry now, because their pride is wounded.

"I remember when Jesus dealt with me about my own pride. It is no easy thing. Can we pray for them before we finish today?"

As he had been speaking, Arviragus stood. "Joseph," he said, "will you lead us? Teach us how to pray."

Without thinking about it, Joseph began to pray aloud in the language of angels. Then, as his mind began to sense what the Holy Spirit was saying to him, he prayed so as to be understood. When he was finished, he looked up.

A man stood up in the center of one side. "Master Joseph," he asked, "what was the language you were praying in?"

"It is the language of angels," Joseph answered. "It is a gift of the Holy Spirit. It is what happened to each of us who are Culdees on the day of the Mighty Wind in Jerusalem."

"Can I get that too?" the man asked.

"Yes, you can," Joseph told him. "It is a free gift from Abba Father."

Arviragus stepped forward, patting Joseph's arm, and motioning with his hands. "But that will take another entire day, I am sure." He looked at the man who had asked the question. "Is it all right with you if we let our guests rest now? They have worked hard today, and I am sure they are tired."

The man smiled at Joseph and nodded. He sat down. After all, these people would be living here from now on, he realized. He mentally made plans to speak with one of them and make an appointment when the meeting concluded.

The king spoke once more. "There is one more thing I want to do before we leave," he said. He surveyed the room once more. "Is there anyone here in this delegation who disagrees with the choices we have made as unified tribes today? Is there anyone who still wants to give loyal service to the Mother Earth Goddess Vivien?"

He paused, waiting for a response.

"If you don't agree, you won't be judged or punished. Please don't be afraid."

Still nothing. He waited a few more moments.

"Anyone?"

"So are *all* of you wanting to be baptized tomorrow?" he asked.

A murmur of assent rippled through the room.

"All right then," the king replied to the crowd. Quietly, he looked to Joseph and Simon Zealotes. "We will be busy tomorrow!" he whispered.

Then, he turned once more to the delegates. "As I said before, we still have an agenda to pass together."

He paused, and raised a finger to indicate a first consensus. "Number one! Does it seem good to you, and meet with your approval, that I give a gift of sanctuary to each of these Culdees who have come to peacefully live among us? If you agree, say 'aye.'"

The entire Feasting Hall responded "Aye" in unison.

"Number Two! Does it seem good to you, and meet with your approval that 160 acres, a Hide of Land, be deeded to each of these Culdees, to provide their livelihood and legacy? If you agree, say 'aye'."

The entire Hall responded "Aye" again in unison.

"Number Three. Does it seem good to you, and meet with your approval that the parcel of land deeded to them include the Isle of Avalon, as well as the Sacrificial Tor? If you agree, say 'aye'."

Surprisingly, at this question, the Feasting Hall responded even more intensely with "Aye!"

"Number Four! And does it seem good to you, and meet with your approval that I appoint each of these Culdees to serve you as Masters of Instruction, helping in all judicial and spiritual matters for our entire tribe? If you agree, say 'aye'."

But this time, most of the delegates were on their feet, ready to shout out their answers.

"Aye! Aye!" the word thundered through the room.

King Arviragus raised his voice above the crowd. "Then we are agreed! Before you leave today, come and welcome these friends, our new leaders!!"

The Hall erupted with movement. Only a few of the delegates moved to leave the room. Most stood, and began talking with others around them. Many made their way to where the company of Culdees was seated, not yet preparing to leave. For the next hour or so, greetings and connections were made, needs were expressed, prayer was given, questions were answered, and appointments were made.

After making his way outside the Feasting Hall, the king greeted those exiting the meeting. To his right, David and Eiless coordinated sleeping quarters and evening meal arrangements for the delegates.

Across the way, some fifty yards or so from the Feasting Hall, Asarlai Draoi and his companions stood together in a circle. They were making plans for their prayer vigil to the Goddess the next morning. Stunned, they now realized *they* were the ones in need of a sign to convince the people of the authentic power of their belief system.

"What alchemy do you know to sway them?" Amren, the Ovate, asked Asarlai.

Asarlai shrugged. "We could use some powder and appear in smoke," he offered. "Much of what we do is all illusion, after all."

"What about a spell? Or a potion?" Fercos, the Priest, asked.

"To do what, exactly?" Asarlai asked.

"You could cast a spell on the apple trees, and cause them to die overnight," Fercos offered.

"That's actually a good idea," the wizard answered. "It's just that we worship the trees. And killing even one goes against what we believe about preserving the Earth. How can we dishonor something the Goddess Mother has provided, and expect her to honor us?"

"That's true," Amren said. "We need a demonstration of her power, *and* the power of Gwyn-al-Nudd and Avallach. She has the power to give life: and her sons take it away. So, we need to ask for something to prove both of those things."

"Isn't she the one who rules the air over the Tor?" asked Fercos. "We need to beseech Avallach to kill one of these Culdees with lightning from heaven. And then, we should ask her to send rain on the Tor; and only on the Tor."

"That could work," the wizard answered. He paused, thinking, "In fact, it is a brilliant idea!" the wizard answered. "We will need to return to my classroom to reference which sacrifices are required for such a display. We can do that!"

"Are there any babies or children, or perhaps, a virgin already marked and consecrated for sacrifice?" The question came from Huelfwen, the Bard. "We will need a sacrifice, *and* a spell if we are to see a strong enough result."

"That being said," Asarlai offered, "we need to meet at the top of the Tor just before dawn to light the sacrifice fire." He began pointing at delegates. "You, bring firewood." "You, bring the sacrifice; an animal or a child." "You, bring the cauldron." "You, bring the supplies for the spell." "And all of you, bring your wands if you brought them with you for these meetings."

As they broke from their short council, Asarlai noticed Joseph and the Culdees loading into their little ship. On a whim, the wizard walked over to speak with them.

"Joseph?" he called. "Can I speak with you a moment?"

Surprised, Joseph looked at him. "Yes. What do you need Asarlai?"

"I just wanted to wish you luck tomorrow," the wizard said with a false sincerity. "We are beseeching the Goddess Mother and her sons to show the full strength of their power."

"In what way?"

Asarlai smirked. "Vivien is the Mother Earth Goddess. We are asking her for a sign of the life she gives, by pouring rain on the Tor, and only on the Tor. Her sons are the rulers of the Underworld. We are asking for a bolt of lightning to strike one of your group, and kill them."

Joseph's gaze became clear and steady. Looking into the eyes of the wizard, he recognized the same spiritual influences he had seen in Joseph Caiaphas' eyes in Jerusalem.

This is the religious spirit. It is a demonic entity.

The Voice of the Holy Spirit surprised him at that moment. Suddenly, he realized a correlation between the zealous, ritualized traditions Caiaphas had defended. He saw a man's heart, closed to Truth, intent only on his own intellectual pursuits in the name of God.

This is the entity that crucified Jesus. It wants to kill the Life of Jesus in you.

503

As this awareness became real to him, Joseph gazed silently at the wizard. Suddenly, his heart was filled with compassion for the man. In the few moments spent, he saw a deep insecurity in the man's eyes.

Silently, Joseph prayed inwardly. *Let this man discover the truth tomorrow, Lord.*

Outwardly, he looked around the little ship for his walking stick.

"Asarlai?" he said. "What name did your mother give you?"

"Excuse me?" the wizard asked.

"What name did your mother give you?" Joseph repeated the question.

"Uh – she named me Waljen. It means 'chosen.'" The man stuttered as he responded.

Joseph picked up his walking stick, and stepped out of the little ship. "Waljen," he said. "Do you realize Abba Father chose you? Even now, before you ever have known him, he wants you. Did you know He cares about you? Jesus told us the Father has numbered the hairs on our heads, we are so important to him."

"So, you're saying this Abba whatever, cares about me. Even when I walked out today?"

"Yes, even then."

"You know, Joseph," Asarlai said. "You seem like a good man, and like you will be a helpful asset to the king. You're just a little misguided, that's all. I'm not sure about your beliefs."

"What did you think about Jesus?" Joseph asked.

"Oh, I agree this promise of a New Life sounds wonderful. And who doesn't want their quality of life to improve? But it's too good to be true. In fact. I'm sorry, but unless I see a miracle of my own, I can't let go of what I have always known."

"Jesus does miracles all the time, Waljen. Why don't you ask him for a sign?" Joseph patted the man on his shoulder.

"Like what?" the wizard wanted to know.

"I don't know," Joseph replied. "Perhaps something that means something special to you."

"I will have to think about that," Asarlai answered. Suddenly, he noticed the others on the little ship, were hearing his conversation with Joseph. Were they waiting for it to come to an end? "You had better go before the sun sets."

"Don't worry," Joseph comforted him. "We'll make it to the Island." He turned to board the boat once more.

"Can I ask you something totally off the subject?" Asarlai started. "Your walking stick is really amazing, with the polished burl on both sides. How did you get it to be so smooth?"

Joseph laughed. "Lots of use, I suppose." He looked at the rod. "It's actually cut from the center of a fig tree. In my nation, the fig tree is a symbol of our national identity, as well as the spiritual condition of her people.

"When I received my *semichah,* or my ordination as a Jewish priest, my father had this walking stick carved for me from a fig tree's core. The burls happened to be buried in the middle, by the trunk. The fig tree had just grown around them. So the woodcarver who prepared it for me, sanded it, and polished it. It became this wonderful walking stick."

"Fig-wood," the wizard mused. "Well, it certainly is beautiful. I hope you have a good rest this evening. We will all meet at dawn."

"Sleep well, Weljan," Joseph answered, stepping into the ship. "And remember, Jesus chose you, before he even created the earth. That's what your name means."

When the little ship was brought to the shore at Avalon, each one in the weary group went to their homes, with the exception of Joseph.

"I have an errand to run," he told his friends.

When Simon looked at him questioningly, he smiled and shook his head.

"It's something I must do alone," he assured his roommate. "Go and rest."

Pulling away from the bank once more, Joseph followed the inner urging he sensed from the Holy Spirit. As he pushed away from the bank once more, he knew he was heading to the small island where the little ship had been tethered the first day, just a little over a mile away from the Tor; and the round-house, and the well.

Upon his arrival, he climbed carefully to the top of the little hill, praying aloud in the language of angels. "Speak to me, Lord," he prayed. "Please help us to be ready tomorrow."

I will endorse each of you. As I did Aaron. Plant your walking stick in the top of the hill.

At first, Joseph wasn't sure he had heard right. Then, he remembered Asarlai's interest in his walking stick. Abba Father must have a plan he was unaware of. Yes, it was always better to obey when the Spirit spoke rather than procrastinate, he decided.

Considering this, he walked to the center of the hill's peak. Lifting the fig-wood staff up above his head, he drove it down into the soft ground with both hands. When he removed his hands, it stood firm.

"It's done, Lord," he said aloud.

Rest well, Joseph.

"Thank you." He spoke aloud once more.

The weary man made his way down the incline, and headed toward the little ship. From there, he made his way back to Avalon. He would sleep in the large round-house tonight, he decided. Simon was good company, but for some reason, he didn't want to talk to anyone this evening.

After the events of the day, his brain was tired.

He wanted to be rested enough to hear the Holy Spirit accurately, he reasoned. Truthfully, the dawn was now only a few hours away. He needed time to pray, and re-gather his scattered sensibilities.

When dawn arrived, Joseph rose and washed his hands, feet and face. He combed his hair, and put on his sandals. Gathering up his outer wrap, he left the round-house to meet the Druids on the top of the Tor.

Upon approach he noted a crowd gathering at the base of the Tor. Mary, Salome, Simon, and several others were already climbing the great hill.

On its peak, flames were beginning to emerge from beneath a great cauldron hung over a fire-pit. Shadowy figures danced around the large pot. Joseph counted nine females. Nearby, wood pipe and lyre music played, reverberating down into the valley, some 400 feet below.

Standing before the cauldron, with arms raised over his head, Asarlai Draoi had begun a show of religious ritual. His deep voice was raised to a shout.

"Great Goddess Vivien! Giving Mother of all the Earth!" he cried. "Lord Gwyn-al-Nydd!! Lord Avallach! We call upon you to show us your aid!"

He dropped a small bag of yellow powder into the cauldron. A great cloud of yellow smoke billowed up in front of him.

"We stand before you, to summon your powers," he shouted. "We honor you with a dance for each of the cycles of the moon in the birthing months! We praise you for fertility, and for the expression of love! We bring you music! And we bring you sacrifice! We beseech you to manifest your great power! Let the rains come upon the Tor and only upon the Tor as we express our worship!"

He took several strange looking pieces of wood roots from the student helper standing near him, and lifted them over his head.

"We beseech you to hear us now! We bring you the power and authority of these Culdees! We curse their origins, and beseech you to destroy the threats they have brought against your mighty powers among our tribes. We bring you fig-wood roots to represent their leader, Joseph of Arimathea, to show you the pathway to his person. Strike him down and stop their deceptions, O Great Goddess!"

Asarlai dropped the roots into the cauldron with another pouch of powder.

The spell and its sacrifice were now well underway.

"We offer you the blood of this rooster, our trumpeter of the sun, to dispel the dark and negative forces set against your combined greatnesses."

As he spoke, Asarlai plunged a dagger deep into the chest of a rooster, held by a Bard. As the Bard held the poor bird over the steaming cauldron, the wizard pulled the blade through the body, causing its blood to gush into the cauldron. Pulling another pouch filled with powder from his robes, he tossed it into the boil with a hidden motion. More smoke billowed.

A Wikka stepped up to Asarlai's side. She shouted, "Lord Avallach, we offer you the blood and body of this river otter. We ask you to give us wisdom, faithfulness, and to bring us victory in the middle of this terrible crisis!"

As she spoke, the wizard chopped the head off a river otter, and added its head and body into the cauldron.

Asarlai was then handed an owl, which he held by holding its wings to its sides. "Lord of the Underworld, we offer you this sacred owl. We pray its blood will open up the door under the Tor, to guide us to and through your realms. It is a swift and silent hunter. As we add this sacred blood to the cauldron, we want to empower you! Unmask those who would deceive us!"

More powder. More smoke.

There was a pause for dancing and gyrations in honor of the Goddess.

Aslerai continued. "And finally, we add the head and tongue of the holy adder. Show us your strength and might, O rulers of the Great Darkness!"

As a finale to the sacrifice, the Bards added drumbeats to the music being played. The scantily clad dancers worked harder and faster, moving around the fire with spins and greater gyrations. For effect, Asarlai dropped two more pouches of cloud powder into the pot, effecting additional eruptions of great billows of green and yellow smoke.

Then, the wizard began to speak in a chanting rhythm, in an ancient tongue known only to those elevated to his levels in alchemy and magic. For some time, he chanted spells, and threw ingredients into the cauldron.

In all honesty, Asarlai had expected clouds to fill the sky at this point, and a lightning bolt to strike the objects of their cursing, wiping Joseph and the Culdees from the face of the earth.

As the Bards continued to play, and the Wikka continued to dance, he waited. When nothing happened, the wizard instructed his party to kneel, in a circle of thirteen, around the great pot.

They had missed something.

What was it, they wondered? Several of Asarlai's alchemy students made their way to the cauldron, drew out personal daggers. They cut themselves, adding their own blood to the spell's mix.

Nothing.

The sun was well above the horizon now, burning off the daily morning fog. Asarlai could sense an unseen window closing. There were only moments now. Surely, the Goddess Mother and her sons would respond to the sacrifices!

He had checked and double-checked the sacrifices required and their proper order. He was sure they had used the right combinations, and the words had been proper.

He had taken every precaution!

They had offered everything required!

He instructed his leaders and students to prostrate themselves. They began to chant in unison, begging their gods to respond with a show of power.

With lightning.

With wind.

With ..... anything.

Then, the Wikka dancer designated as the first month, the month of conception, drew a male from among the Druid students. She began to undress him in the middle of the circle. The couple engaged in sexual activity, complete with screams and ecstatic expressions, to win the favor of their Goddess.

Still nothing.

After two more hours of rituals, blood-lettings, spell readings, chants and offerings, screams and good ideas, Asarlai cried out in desperation.

"We need a human sacrifice! A boy!"

He looked into the cauldron to divine a confirmation of his conclusion.

In the anticipatory silence, all on the Tor's peak were surprised when a man's voice interrupted, speaking calmly.

"Let us see if Joseph's God has spoken before we kill another child."

Asarlai was instantly angry. Who would dare? He looked to find the source of the voice, and recognized King Arviragus. The Pendragon stood with the Culdees, some feet away on the peak of the Tor, next to Joseph of Arimathea.

"Fine!" the wizard pounded his hands against the top of the cauldron. His frustration evident, he looked at Joseph.

"What can your Jesus do?" he demanded.

He looked to the king. "Look at them! They have done nothing! *No-thing!* How can any of them expect their god to prove *anything!?*"

Arviragus lifted his eyebrows, and looked at Joseph, questioningly.

Joseph gazed at the ruler, and then at the Druid group, who were now on their feet, behind the wizard, waiting for an answer.

"I don't know whether He has answered yet or not," he told them. "You are welcome to come with me and see."

"Come *with* you!" Asarlai exclaimed. "You were supposed to provide proof on the top of the Tor!"

"I'm sorry," Joseph replied kindly. "I must have misunderstood. I thought we were to *meet* at the top of the Tor. My God instructed me to go to another location."

"Where?" The wizard had taken up his walking stick, or wand, and was striding towards Joseph. The rest of the Druids followed.

"The little hill where we arrived. I was there last night." Joseph met the wizard's gaze. "I did what the Holy Spirit commanded me to do. The rest is up to him, and He never fails."

"Show me where you arrived!" Asarlai demanded. "Did you bury an animal? Did you sacrifice someone last night?" He counted the Culdees, and realized all twelve were present. "All of your people are here. What did you do?"

"Come and see," Joseph replied. He moved through the group, and led them down the Tor, walking across the carved steppes of fertility ritual pathways. Offended by his path, the Druid party began to hurriedly run around the Tor, following the circular trails, fearful of breaking the power of Goddess energies. Arviragus, Joseph, the Culdees, and the rest of the crowd, waited for them, watching at the foot of the Tor.

The humor of the scene struck Mary, as she watched the group of twenty or so rushing along the ritual paths to meet them. She suppressed an inexplicable giggle as here and there; a few were bumping into each other, sending a domino effect through the line.

When everyone had arrived at the bottom, Joseph moved to the little ship, where he motioned for others to join him. Those in the crowd who had traveled to the Tor in the early morning also boarded their rafts. Then, following the Culdees, they all made their way to the little hill just a little over a mile away.

As they floated through the waterways, Simon Zealotes was watching for their destination to become clear. "Joseph," he asked, "was that tree always there?"

"What tree?"

Simon pointed to the hill. "That tree," he said. "I don't remember it being there before, do you?"

Joseph squinted in the morning sun. Then he smiled. "No, it *wasn't* there before." He looked at his friend, smiling. "Our God, ElShaddai, has done it again."

While Joseph steered the little ship to the bank, Martial jumped out with the rope, and tied the boat to one of the stakes already in the ground. Full of anticipation, the excited group of Culdees disembarked.

What had happened here?

Mary looked to her uncle. She waited for him to disembark. "What did He tell you to do?" she asked.

"Who?" Joseph asked quizzically, with a smile. "What do you mean?"

She smirked at him. "You know who," she answered. "What did the Holy Spirit tell you to do?"

He smiled at her, and put his arm around her shoulders, as they began to walk up the hill. "He told me to drive my walking stick into the ground. He said he would endorse us like he did Aaron, Moses' brother."

Mary stopped and looked to the top of the hill. "The tree!" she declared. "What kind is it?"

"My walking stick was made from a fig-tree burl. So, it's most probably a fig tree," he answered.

"No, Uncle Joseph," she told him. "It can't be!" She pointed. "Look at it. It's the wrong shape to be a fig tree, even a sycamore fig."

Noting she was right in her observation, Joseph quickened his steps. They made their way to the tree. The walking stick had enlarged overnight. No longer a staff, it was now a tree trunk; seven or eight inches across.

From the staff's top end, several branches had sprouted and grown. From the sides, branches had sprouted and grown on all sides. In fact, the branches had not only sprouted and grown; they had thickened into strong limbs. A casual observer would believe the limbs were part of a much older tree. Large white flowers grew in clusters on some of the branches; others were covered with clumps of ripe, red, haws (or berries).

Mary looked closely at the branches of the tree. They were covered with thorns. "Uncle," she said, "this is a haw-thorn tree! We have them back home in Judea!" Her mouth dropped open as she came to a point of discovery. "These were the type of thorns in the thorn helmet we took off Jesus' head."

"He made a hawthorn tree grow from a fig walking stick!" Joseph asked, astonished. "What does it mean?"

"You planted a tree, Joseph?" Arviragus asked, coming up behind him. Asarlai and the rest of the Druids were right behind him.

"No, not me," Joseph told him.

"Where did this tree come from?" the king asked. "I don't remember a tree being here before."

"There was no tree here before," the wizard remarked. "I was on this island yesterday, and it was free of trees!" He looked at Joseph suspiciously. "What spell did you cast? What sacrifice did you make?"

"I didn't do anything, except what the Holy Spirit told me to do," Joseph answered.

"What did he tell you to do?" Asarlai asked.

Joseph looked at the wizard. "When we arrived at the round-houses yesterday, after the meeting, I let everyone off near the well, so they could get some rest. The Holy Spirit told me to come here, and drive my walking stick into the ground, near the top. This was the first place we came to when we arrived. In fact," he said, "all the women, except little Mary, slept on into the later morning that day, so we let them rest."

Asarlai was frustrated. "Is that all you did?"

"Yes," Joseph answered. "That is all I did. Then I went back to the big round-house, and spent the night alone mostly praying, sometimes sleeping."

The Druid priest began to walk around the tree, inspecting its trunk, and the outgrowth of the branches.

"This happened overnight," he said. It was a statement, rather than a question. "And all you did was put your staff in the ground. You're sure you didn't plant this?"

The king reproached him. "Asarlai, the ground looks as it always has. There are no diggings, or loose soil. Think, man! This tree grew out of the ground overnight!"

The wizard looked at Joseph. "But you told me your staff was made of wood from a fig tree!"

Joseph nodded. "That's true, I did! And it is, or was!"

"These branches are not fig branches," Asarlai noted. "In fact, I worship trees! I am an authority on trees, and I've never seen branches like this before!" He bent down to inspect the trunk of the tree, looking it up and down. He looked at Joseph intently.

"The trunk of this tree seems to have the shape of your walking stick. I remember the knot that was right below the top. You wrapped your hand around it, and rubbed your thumb over it when you were thinking."

"Yes, I did do that," Joseph answered. "Quite often, in fact."

Asarlai pointed to the same knot, which was just much larger on the tree. "So you see how they are the same? This tree and your old staff?"

"Yes, I see it," Joseph replied. "This is an absolute miracle. Wouldn't you agree?"

The wizard nodded. "I've never seen anything like it," he declared. "Yes, I would say your God answered us, and mine didn't."

"WelJan." Joseph called the wizard by his family's name. "Are you ready to renounce your gods yet?"

Asarlai smiled. "I might be," he answered. "I just have a couple more questions. "What kind of tree do the branches come from?"

Mary spoke up. "It is called a *Crataegus*. It grows in our homeland. Some people call it a 'haw-thorn tree.' See the berries? Those are the 'haws.' They have great healing properties. We use them in salves and ointment for the skin, in tea, or as medicine. They helped a man I know who could feel his heart thumping in his throat all the time. He drank haw-tea every day, and even his head cleared. We make it into a tonic for stomach problems too.

"But the interesting thing are the thorns on the young branches. When Jesus was crucified, do you remember Joseph saying there were more than three varieties of thorns in the helmet they put on my son's head? This was one of the types of thorns."

Asarlai put his finger out to touch a thorn, and drew back in surprise. "They are stronger than they look, and sharp, too!" He put his finger into his mouth to stop the bleeding.

He directed his attention to Joseph. "What sacrifices do I need to make, in order to renounce the Druid gods?" he asked.

Joseph put his hand on the man's shoulder. "There are no more sacrifices to be made."

"How can that be?" the man inquired. "Nothing in life is free!"

Joseph smiled. "Jesus was ElShaddai, God the Creator. He came in human form to show us how to live; to show us the pathway back to relationship with

Abba Father. He died to be the last sacrifice for sin. All we have to do is to yield to Him and His Holy Spirit."

The candidate looked confused. "What is this relationship you have with your God? You say he is one God, but you refer to him as ElShaddai, Abba, Abba Father, Jesus, Holy Spirit..... Which one is it? Are they all different? Or, as you say, they are all the same?"

Joseph sensed it was time for a practical illustration.

Silently, he prayed. *Holy Spirit, please give me an answer to help them understand.*

Then, after a moment, he looked around for an implement to help him make an illustration in the earth. He crouched down to the ground and said, "Jesus told us we would be fishers of men."

Using the medium-sized stone, he broke the green surface of the mossy earth, etching a large sign of a fish in the black dirt beneath, with two semi-circles.

"Jesus said, 'I do only the things that please the Father, or Abba.' He told us 'he who has seen me has seen the Father.' That means that Jesus and Abba Father both represent the same God."

As he spoke, he drew once more in the earth, drawing a second fish, connecting the two fish at the tail.

"Then," Joseph paused, looking up from his crouched position, to meet eyes with the Asarloi, "Jesus taught us about the Holy Spirit. He told us the Spirit would lead us into all Truth, and teach us, showing us how to live. He told us we would be accompanied by, filled with, and led by the Holy Spirit. It is the Spirit of God who helps us to understand the Truth and the spiritual realm."

As he spoke, Joseph drew a third fish, joining the two fish at one end at the tail. At the end of the etching, the three fish were intertwined, and created something of a triangular knot.

Standing, he pointed to the shape he had made in the mossy earth on the island.

"This is a picture of our God. He is three-part but He is One. When I see one side of His nature, my heart becomes open to understand and more complete picture of who He is."

He pointed to the water around the island. "It is a little like the qualities of water. When it freezes, it becomes something I can touch, and hold, and taste. That is what happened when Jesus came. Our God became someone I could touch, talk to; a human being I could understand who I can relate with. But, when the water is in the form it is in now," he indicated with his hand, "it can have no limits. It fills all. It is in all. The islands exist in it. It has no limits."

Asarloi nodded. "What about the Holy Spirit?" he asked.

"He is like the mist which rises each morning, and sometimes fills the atmosphere here. That too is a form of water. I can sense Him, I can breathe Him in. He surrounds me, and infills me."

"So, like the water, the three are one, and the one is three," Asarlai pondered aloud.

Drawing once again, Joseph added a circle to run through the middle of each fish. "The three are fully connected. They are the same, and one is not elevated above each other. As such, they are a Trinity. They cannot, and will not, ever become separated from one another. The union is eternal, from eternity past through and beyond eternity future."

Joseph smiled at the wizard, waiting for the truth of the illustration to sink into the man's understanding.

Mary watched, amazed at the simplicity of the explanation provided through Joseph by the Holy Spirit. The symbol of the Trinity was there, plain and simple, for all to see, some three feet across.

"I want to know more," Asarlai answered.

King Arviragus spoke up. "Are you ready to yield?"

The wizard looked at the king. "I *am* ready to yield. But I am realizing there are so many things I don't understand. At first, I thought the stories Joseph and the Culdees shared were too good to believe. The more I listened, the angrier I became. It was like something was inside of me, stirring up my rage, preventing me from seeing the Truth.

"And then, we Druids offered sacrifices on the Tor. I put everything I knew into that confrontation. I used all of my resources. We did everything our gods required.

"Those spells and sacrifices had worked before. King Arviragus, you remember the days I called lightning down from the skies, and summoned clouds."

Arviragus nodded.

"Today, when nothing happened, I began to realize there was Greater Power; True Power in Joseph's God. Something or Someone greater than our gods had prevented the results we had seen happen in the past.

"Even on the way down to the bottom of the Tor, I saw the Culdees watching us. I wondered how those people were able to cross the Goddess' fertility lines without experiencing collapse. That got me thinking. The Goddess Mother and her sons were gods we trusted for centuries. And all these years, they have had us all chasing ourselves, walking in circles, like the paths on the Tor.

"But, those who were aligned with Joseph's God weren't afraid of punishment! They just cut through the energy fields, and treated the Tor as if it were just an ordinary hill.

"Then, we arrived here, to this little island where the Culdees first arrived. When I saw the Thorn tree, its overnight appearance was the closing of all my arguments. This God has power over the Earth, and its rulers; even over all of nature. This must mean then, that this God has power over the Goddess.

"He is the Great God. The Living God!

"Look at this! We are seeing something impossible with our own eyes. A thorn tree is growing from the trunk of a fig tree? Not only that, but it has taken root, expanded, bloomed and borne ripe fruit in one night! The Goddess Mother could never have done such a thing!"

Joseph put his hand on the wizard's chest. "But the true miracle is what happens inside of each of us when we yield."

"I do yield. Completely," the man replied humbly. He looked at the company from the little ship. "I can sense I need to do something here, but I'm not sure what it is."

Joseph took his arm. "Let's kneel right here," he said. "And let's not call you by your taken name as a wizard any more, WelJan. You're about to have an entirely new identity."

Immediately, the man fell to his knees. Joseph knelt beside him, as did the king. "Help me talk to him, Joseph," he said. "I don't know what to say."

The former priest put his arm around the former wizard. "Just talk to him like a friend, because He is a friend. He will stick closer than any brother to you."

WelJan, *the chosen*, began to speak with his Creator, for the first time in his life.

515

"Jesus, I don't know you very well yet. But I want to. I am sorry I fought against you."

"Now ask Him to make you His disciple," Joseph prodded.

His eyes closed, WelJan continued his prayer. "I want to become your disciple. Please teach me the right way to live. I give you my life, and ask you to give me Your life."

Then he remembered the illustration Joseph had drawn. "Abba Father, I open my heart to you. Jesus, I open my heart to you. Holy Spirit, I open my heart to you. Help me, please."

"And when we are finishing a prayer like this," Joseph told them, "it helps to signify it. We Culdees use the word 'amen,' which means 'so be it, and let it continue.' So, when I say that word, I am agreeing with what I just said, or with what I just heard someone else say. I am saying I want the desire in that commitment, or statement, to continue. Do you want to say 'amen'?"

"I felt something happen inside me," WelJan said, his eyes filled with tears. "It's good.... It's like when I was home.... and safe."

"You *are* home," Joseph told him. "You have traded your religion and its empty requirements for a relationship of substance with the Living God."

WelJan smiled. He closed his eyes and turned his head skyward, towards the sunlight. "Amen," he said softly. Then he said it again. And again.

Gradually, through his tears, he began to laugh.

Looking around, Joseph realized everyone around them was on their knees as well.

"Amen!" he sighed, in agreement and relief. "And thank you!"

"Amen!" WelJan repeated, a little more forcibly. "So be it, and let it continue!"

Unexpectedly, he continued to laugh, his tears flowing more freely. "I feel like I'm being washed on the inside!" he cried.

"Amen!" said Joseph.

"Amen!" said the king. "So be it, and let it continue!"

"So be it! Amen! Let it continue!" The crowd around them broke into joyful expressions, as they began to stand to their feet.

The Ecclesia at Glastonbury, England, was born.

Epilogue

In the years following the arrival of the Culdees to Briton, the church grew and multiplied exponentially. In fact, the Druid Schools were converted into seminaries. These became training centers for disciples, ministers and missionaries. Students came from all over the known world to learn from Joseph of Arimathea, Zebedee, Simon Zealotes and others who had come to live among the Britons.

From these seminaries, missionaries and teachers poured out into the civilized and uncivilized world alike. Simon Peter, Philip, Paul, Lazarus, Mary Magdalene, and others of the original company of Jesus, also visited Briton. These apostles further deepened the faith and confidence of the tribes in the reality of Jesus' identity as God.

During the Dark Ages, the Culdee church retreated to the island of Iona, Scotland, where the seminary continued for a thousand years. In fact, the Protestant Reformation began due to the teachings of a graduate from the Culdee School: John Wyckliff.

The round-house Jesus built became the gathering place for believers for many years. As the church in Glaston continued to grow, Joseph and his companions constructed a wattle-and-daub gathering place, in the dimensions of Moses' Wilderness Tabernacle, measuring 26'x 60.' Over time, it began to be referred to as a "church building."

In later years, St. Mary's Chapel was constructed by a man named David on the same site.

Mary, Jesus' mother, died in the winter of 48AD. She was buried in Briton, near her own little round-house, one of the twelve houses built after Jesus' round-house template. She was referred to by many as the "SanGraal," or "Prized Vessel." In fact, the Greek Orthodox Church still refers to her as the "Carrier of God," or the "Theotokos."

The church which began in Massillia, France, which is now Marseilles, was founded by Lazarus, Martha and Mary, and their small band of followers. The historical account of those adventures can be found in my next book; Journey - Book 3: Cephas.

For his part Pontius Pilate and his family evangelized much of northeastern Switzerland. There are many stories of their witness, in the oral traditions of the area. One which especially drew my interest was the account of Pontius Pilate

517

routinely making his way to a nearby mountain when he was on military tour of duty in the Alps. He would go there to pray.

When he died, the villagers named the mountain, Mount Pilatus. It still bears that name.

In their old age, Pontius and Claudia settled in the warmer climate of Vienne, France. Perhaps because his duties were completed, or because of the emerging of a new Caesar in Rome. Whatever the reason, both Pilate and his wife are buried in Vienne. After the crucifixion, in every location where Pontius and Claudia were known, they were regarded as kind, Christian, generous and caring members of Rome's ruling class.

In the summer of 82AD, Joseph of Arimathea died in Glastonbury. On his sarcophagus, these words were inscribed:

"To the Britons I came after I buried the Christ. I taught, and I have entered my rest."

The quiet trust and persistent humility of the man, Joseph of Arimathea, remains as an example of what Jesus will do with a yielded life. Holy Spirit, please help each of us to simply yield to Abba Father's purposes.

A Note to the Reader

(Why my research led me to write what I wrote)

In researching materials for this second book, I found myself adrift in manuscripts dating from 100AD forward. I also discovered a great deal of differences in accounts written by the early historians as to life-stories and timelines. In documents dated after 155AD, the diversities in accounts, and mysticism surrounding the people closest to the Person of Jesus also increased. As I studied, I came to understand there were viable reasons why this would be so.

During the life of Christ, the men and women who found themselves involved in His ministry, were common folk; fishermen, merchants, teachers, scholars, farmers. Once their lives were touched by Jesus Christ, they were never the same. They became filled with purpose and a sense of destiny and mission. The twelve who traveled with Jesus, and then the seventy, were men and women who gained an inner grasp on what was needed to bring hope and help to the world; they had come face-to-face with God. Because what they learned at the feet of Jesus was true and viable, upon His ascension, sharing it began to change their world; eventually causing even our calendar to put His earthly life at its center.

By 100AD, all of the twelve had died, passing on their experience and training to their students. Clement and Ignatius would be two of their students, who might have lived into the beginning of the second century. By 155AD, many of those students had died also, leaving a second century church in the hands of leaders, who, without a viable, personal encounter with the Living God; gradually became more concerned with tradition, form and practice, rather than experiential relationship. Such is human nature. We each have tendencies toward what is tried and true; places where we fear the unknown.

By 200AD, the early followers of Jesus had been elevated to the place of demi-gods; quoted and honored almost on the same level as Jesus Himself. Then, by the fourth century, during the rule of Constantine, Christianity became mixed with political power. The view of women within church government was Romanized, as were concepts of family structure and relationship. Roles of leadership became political rather than Holy Spirit led and apostolic. Miracles and the ministry of the Holy Spirit were brought under formalism. Pastors were no longer allowed to marry; rather they became the confessor, the intercessor, and final authority – for a time, even politically.

In the building of his cathedral and tomb in Constantinople, Constantine, the first Christian emperor sent word throughout the Roman Empire. He wanted to purchase viable artifacts; items belonging to the early followers of Christ; especially their bones. The design of his cathedral was to place his crypt in the central focus, surrounded by Christ's twelve apostles. His plan was to create an environment where a worshipper would sense himself or herself to be a part of the earthly life of Christ; a place where spiritual encounters would take place, with himself in the place of Christ.

Although parts of the emperor's original concept were somewhat admirable, his purpose became overshadowed by his practice. His search for what became known as "relics" developed into a catalyst for idolatry within the infant church. For, in searching for the bones of the apostles, Constantine had not anticipated the reaction of those unscrupulous individuals within his Empire. In an effort to preserve the purity of the relics, he gave an edict: all items had to be substantiated by proof; whether a miracle, a document, an oral testimony.

As a result, many false legends were generated in an effort to validate counterfeit relics, many of which were held to for centuries, creating confusion and division within the church at large at the time. Such legends have also clouded the true histories and miraculous accounts of the Holy Spirit's workings through his followers in the second and third centuries. It also made my own research, which was discovering the truth behind the legends, much more difficult.

Additionally, due to the fear of persecution during the first three hundred years of Christianity, many accounts had been handed down as oral tradition. We are fortunate, indeed, to have the Gospels recorded and circulated by the apostles in the days closer to the actual events. There are many manuscripts of such oral traditions. Sadly, though, as with any memorable story, the actual, cultural details considered common knowledge at the moment of writing can be lost and blurred over time. To equate in our day, compare the story of Pastor Nicholas of Myra, whose generous and unselfish nature evangelized much of Turkey in the fourth century. How did he become Santa Claus? To find the truth behind the myth, one must decipher historical truth.

Why?

Because, over time, embellishment and confusion cause fact to become legend. As more time passes, and persons who remember firsthand are no longer available, distancing causes legend to become myth, or fable.

TRUTH ⟶ LEGEND ⟶ MYTH/FABLE

Some stories are easily cast aside. Others have elements of truth which must be researched to the best of our abilities.

As I said before, during the investigation phase for this manuscript, I came upon varied accounts; even apocryphal documents said to have been written by the twelve. To help myself obtain a better picture of the early church, I realized I would need to construct a historical timeline, fitting in historical accounts. Even between the ancient historians, such as Eusebius and Clement, I found discrepancies in dating, so I decided to just do the best I could. After all, this is a novel, howbeit, hopefully a novel with substance.

So, in creating the timeline, I began with the first reliable history I had in hand, the New Testament. After putting the Scriptural accounts into chronological order, I created a chart and added dates. From that point onward, I added historical and archaeological findings to help myself obtain a better grasp of the world's history at that point. (The timeline became a book in itself, and an historical basis for future volumes.)

After the foundation was in place, I read Eusebius, Polycarp, and Clement. Then, I began to take apart the pertinent legends. Some have substance, such as the accounts regarding Joseph of Arimathea's arrest and subsequent experiences (taken from the oldest manuscripts available I could find of "The Gospel of Nicodemus" written by Nicodemus ben Gurion; an apocryphal work from the first century. Later, the original manuscript was merged with a medieval document known as "The Acts of Pilate." The manipulated text was altered significantly, rendering it useless).

Then, there were the difficulties presented in reconciling Orthodox views, and Roman Catholic views in regard to the structure of the family of Jesus. In the Roman Catholic view, Mary remained a virgin after the birth of Christ. According to mystical tradition, Mary's mother, Anne, conceived her as a virgin as well.

In 1611, when King James Stuart authorized an English translation of the original documents, it was not considered the viewpoint of most biblical scholars of the day had been deeply influenced by Roman Catholicism. For this reason, several key scriptures underwent a then traditional exegesis during that translation process; and unknowingly, under that influence.

The belief of Mary's perpetual virginity has created tremendous confusion as to the brothers of Jesus and his original, blended family structure.

For example, most biblical scholars agree Alphaeus, Cleophas and Clopas were differing names referring to the same individual; with Gospel writers' expressions being based upon their own cultural vernacular. Most also agree Mary, Jesus' mother, remarried her husband's brother, who was Cleophas, after Joseph's death, according to the Jewish custom of the day.

For historical purposes, the theological problem of belief in Mary's perpetual virginity destroys the ability to decipher the biblical record accurately. It also creates a plethora of women around the same age named "Mary;" too many for a realistic recounting (even with my own method, I counted four); or even a clear understanding of events told in the New Testament. (For a more thorough examination of this issue, please read my first novel, Journey -Book 1: The Magdalene.)

For instance, there is only one reference in the New Testament where "Mary of Cleophas" is mentioned: in John 19:25. The Greek word *ho,* translated "of" is an article, and not translated with a relational descriptive in any other translation. In 1611, under the remaining Roman Catholic influence, King James' translators added "the wife of" to explain the article. This came from the concept of Mary's perpetual virginity. It drew the reader to the conclusion this description referred to Jesus' mother.

However, the same Greek word is translated "son of" in Luke 6:16, in regard to Jude, the son of Zebedee's James.

To protect Mary's identity in days of persecution, the Gospel writers referred to her as "the mother of James and Joses and Judas," but not as "the mother of Jesus." These things being true, how could she be standing next to herself in John 19:25? The solution which presented itself to me is the one presented here; that Mary of Cleophas was Cleophas' *daughter*, and therefore a step-daughter to Christ's mother.

One more thing regarding this subject presented itself after construction of the novel began.

In 1596, Cardinal Baronius, appointed librarian of the Vatican, and noted historian for the Catholic Church, recorded his *Annales Ecclesiastica*, a work which took him more than thirty years to complete. Under the year AD35,

Baronius recorded Mary of Cleophas has having been exiled from Jerusalem by the Jewish religious leaders in the boat without rudder or sails.

And, while there are mystical *traditions* which support the life of Mary, the mother of Jesus, or "theotokos," (carrier of God; a term used through the centuries by the Greek Orthodox), as having lived and died in Ephesus and/or Jerusalem after the Christ's ascension, there are no historically confirmed *records* to substantiate those traditions. However, British historical records do substantiate Mary's life and death after the ascension as occurring in the presence of the tribes in the Tin Islands. This fact alone, would explain the confusion over the term "Holy Grail."

In Old and Middle English, the term "grail," was taken from the ancient word *sangraal*, which described "*a vessel made of earth or clay*," or "*a greatly prized vessel which can be filled.*" The words "San greal," meaning *kingly blood*, were not used until the Middle Ages, when it became the word "Grail," and attached to the Blood of Christ.

The Word of God refers to each of us as being seen by Abba as "vessels for the Master's use." So, it is a small step to make a correlation that the Holy Grail would have been a *person*, rather than a cup.

However, in recent years, confusion and cultish thinking has arisen around the idea that the "grail" term might refer to Mary Magdalene, as having been the earthly wife of Christ, with two sons emerging from the bloodline. However, if Mary of Nazareth was part of Joseph's company on the little boat, as historical records prove, then it would make more sense to associate the term "grail" with the concept of "theotokos," rather than fabricate an entirely new history for the Son of God.

When the historical accuracy of Mary's end of life emerged in my own understanding, it also raised then, the issue of the historicity of Jesus' early visit to Briton. Also, in my own heart; I have always hit a "speed bump" when I read Jesus' words in John 10:16:

> *"I have other sheep, too, that are not in this sheepfold. I must bring them also. They will listen to my voice, and there will be one flock with one shepherd."*

In studying for this volume, I came upon information regarding ethnic history of the first settlers in the British Isles. Most of the migratory peoples who eventually settled in Northern and Eastern Europe, ultimately made their way to Britain. The majority of these peoples could trace their lineage back to the scattered ten tribes of Israel. There are tremendous similarities between those Celtic peoples, and the nomadic Israelite tribes from which they evolved; language and religious beliefs being two areas confirming this research.

If this investigation represents truth, then it would stand to reason Jesus would have visited the mines with his great-uncle, Joseph of Arimathea, during either his childhood, or the silent years after his earthly step-father's death, before beginning of his ministry at thirty years of age. Because of the magnitude of Jesus' historical undertakings in Somerset, I placed his journey in his late teens/early twenties.

There are a great number of historical records which substantiate our Lord's schooling and works of craftsmanship in early Briton. I will share three of note here:

1. In a letter to Pope Gregory, regarding the history of the church in Britain, St. Augustine stated that there was a church building there "constructed by no human art, but divinely constructed (or by the hands of Christ Himself), for the salvation of His people."

2. The historian, Gildas, wrote in his annals that Jesus' "Light and precepts" were "afforded...to this island during the ...last years of the reign of Tiberius. Tiberius retired to Capri in A.D. 28.

3. Mining Ordinance maps for Old Cornwall present two fascinating names. "Corpus Christi" (Body of Christ), and "Wheel of Jesus" *("wheel" = Cornish name for mine)*. Added to these evidences is the peppering of the Cornwall mining region with "Tunic Crosses." The Tunic Cross is unique to Old Cornwall, found nowhere else on the planet. Marking landing sites, they are stone pillars, made up of a Christian cross with a young boy dressed in a short tunic; which certainly depicts Jesus in a different light than crucified or resurrected.

The mystical fables surrounding the Chalice Well indicate water sprung from the ground when Joseph of Arimathea tried to bury the "Cup of Christ." *(How would he have brought the Chalice to England if he had been surprised by a kidnapping in the middle of a day when persecution ruled the day? Would he have held it in a pocket?)* It made more sense to me that Jesus had dug the well when he built the original wooden house where he lived. This correlation alone would explain the mysticism which arose around the well and the island when Druid beliefs re-emerged in England in the area during the Dark Ages.

In regard to the Glastonbury Thorn tree. The tree which survived for more than a thousand years on Wearyall Hill in Glastonbury was known to bloom twice a year. Its beautiful white blossoms were seen at Christmastime, and in the Spring season, close to Easter. No other Hawthorn in the world blooms twice a year. Cuttings taken from the tree took root, but when planted, only bloomed once a year. (Incidentally, cuttings from its Christmas blooms have been taken to the king or queen of England each year, beginning with Queen Anne Boleyn.)

For this reason, it occurred to me that Joseph's staff might not have been made of hawthorn, as many have supposed. If, when the Aaronic-like miracle occurred, it had been the burgeoning of Hawthorn limbs from a Fig-wood source, the tree would have followed the Fig's pattern of fruition twice each year.

Additionally:

Regarding Judas Iscariot: I found it curious I Corinthians 15:4-8 clearly states that Jesus was seen by Peter, and then by "the twelve." This phrase, "the twelve," was used by the Gospel writers to refer to the twelve disciples. This discovery alone changes the timeline of Judas Iscariot's death, and raised questions in my own mind regarding Judas' motivations for betraying Christ in Gethsemane. I tried to present a plausible solution.

In researching for the past eight years, I came across many similar issues, seeking reconciling the biblical record, the traditional legends, and archeologically based historical findings.

Where my research provided, I have sought to remain true to the historical record. I am especially appreciative of McBirnie's information on the early apostles, written after the author's thirty years of hands-on research in various parts of the ancient world. The works by Professor Danin and Dr. Zugibe on the Shroud of Turin were invaluable, as were particle physicist Dame Isabel Piczek's lectures and papers regarding the Shroud. (See bibliography)

Where there were shadows in accounts, and "coincidences," I tried to give a workable/probable solution. Where legends and accounts had adverse disagreement, or have caused division in the Body of Christ at large, I sought to dig even deeper to find further archaeological and historical records, providing explanation for the reader.

At the end of the day, even though there has been extensive research, no one knows with viable accuracy (except for the canonized Biblical accounts) what happened completely, because none of us were eyewitnesses. I have however, sought to create a good read, promoting thought, to encourage you in your day-to-day relationship with the Living God and His Holy Spirit.

I am hopeful this humble offering will help you to identify your own personal growth struggles through bringing understanding of the growth struggles of early Christianity's believers. I hope you enjoy.

Debbye Graafsma
March, 2015

Journey- Book 2: Joseph of Arimathea
Bibliography

1. **New Testament Survey** by Merrill C Tenney, ©1961 Eerdmans Publishing, Grand Rapids, MI.

2**. Botany of the Shroud; The story of floral images on the Shroud of Turin** by Professor Avinoam Danin; Hebrew University of Jerusalem © 2010 Danin Publishing

3. **St. Joseph of Arimathea at Glastonbury (or the Apostolic Church at Britain)** by Lionel Smithett Lewis ©1922, 1955 Lutterworth Press

4. **The Orthodox Study Bible: Ancient Christianity Speaks to Today's World,** St. Athanasius Academy of Orthodox Theology

5. The Crucifixion of Jesus, completely revised and expanded: A Forensic Inquiry by Frederick T. Zugibe, M.D., Ph.D. ©2005 M. Evans and Company Publishers

6. **The Reese Chronological Bible,** edited by Edward Reese (dating system by Frank R. Klassen), © 1980 Bethany House Publishers

7. **The Search for the Twelve Apostles,** by William Stuart McBirnie, © 2008 Tyndale House Publishers.

8. **Relics of Repentance; The letters of Pontius and Claudia Procula** Issana Press (ISBN 0-9625158-2-5)

9. **The Shroud of Turin,** by Bernard Ruffin, © 1999 Bernard Ruffin.

10. Books by Alfred Edersheim: **Sketches of Jewish Social Life, Life and Times of Jesus the Messiah, The Temple; Its Ministry and Its Services**; various copyright dates, Hendrickson Publishers.

11. **The Hayford Bible Handbook**, Jack W. Hayford, editor, © 1999 Thomas Nelson Publishers.

12. **The Catholic Encyclopedia**

13. **The Church History,** by Eusebius

14. **The Archaelogical Study Bible,** Zondervan Publishers

15. **Holy Faces, Secret Places** by Ian Wilson, pg 162 and pg 88, pg 193

16. **James, the Brother of Jesus** by Robert Eisenman, © 1997 Viking Penguin Publishers. (in part a deconstruction of the legends surrounding the Shroud and King Abgar)

17. **On Illustrious Men,** by Jerome

18. **Early Church Writings,** Penguin Books

19. **The Jewish Encyclopedia,** various subjects

20. **Recognitions of Clement,** 1:65-66

21. **All the Apostles of the Bible,** by Herbert Lockyer, © 1972 Zondervan Publishers, Grand Rapids, MI.

22. **Eerdman's Handbook to the History of Christianity,** © 1977 Lion Publishing (Guideposts), Herts, England

23. **The Oxford Dictionary of the Christian Church**, edited by F.L.Cross, Revised © 1983, Oxford University Press.

24. **Rome Exposed, Roman Life** Sumair Mirza and Jason Tsang. © 1999 *Slavery*

25. *The People of the Palm Branch,* ©2003 That The World May Know Ministries, www.followtherabbi.com

26. Lev-Yadun, S and Holopainen, J. (2009). *New Phytologist* **Volume 183(3): 506-512. doi:**10.1111/j.1469-8137.2009.02904.x

27. http://carloz.newsvine.com/_news/2010/02/08/3870499 -- *"Asian skeleton found in ruins suggests Roman Empire larger than thought"*

28. **Galen on Food and Drink,** Mark Grant, London 2000

29. *Secrets of the Druids,* National Geographic, "The Truth Behind" series.

30. Assemani, "Bibl. Orient." ii. 156, iii. 522; Solomon of Bassora, "The Book of the Bee," ed. Budge, tr. p. 94 (Syriac manuscripts in British Museum. (Regarding Caiaphas' journey)

31. The Jewish Exploration Journal, Volume 61. *"The Ossuary of 'Miriam Daughter of Yeshua Son of Caiaphas, Priest of Maaziah from Beth Omri"* by Boaz Zissu and Yuval Goren. Page 74

32. **The Historia regum Brittaniae of Geoffey of Monmouth,** ed. Acton Griscom --London: 1929. *(Geoffey of Monmouth, **The History of the Kings of Britain,** trans. Lewis Thorpe-- London: 1966),* p. 121

33. *Disputes Among the Three Parties* Chart distillation by Professor Eliezer Segal, University of Calgary. http://people.ucalgary.ca/~elsegal/index.html

34. **The Shroud of Turin; Unraveling the Mystery,** Proceedings of the 1998 Dallas Symposium. Compiled by Michael Minor – Alexander Books 2002.   Highlights from specific lectures: *1. Radiation in the Formation of the Shroud Image (Alan D. Whanger, MD) 2. Nuclear Medicine and Its Relevance to the Shroud of Turin (August D. Accetta MC; Kenneth Lynons, MD, John Jackson PhD.) 3. Neutron Flux and the Resurrection (Isabel Piczek, Particle Physicist) 4. Non-Body Objects Imaged on the Shroud (Mary W. Whanger)*

35. **Annals Ecclesiasticus,** *Vatican Library, Cardinal Cesare Baronius, 1537* (records of ship "without oars" set upon Mediterranean by Jewish leaders in 35AD.)

36. **Memoirs,** by Hegesippus (2nd century historian). *References to James the Just as Jacob, half-brother of Jesus.*

37. **Genuissa, Arviragus, and Claudius**, *by J. C. Marler,* Associate Professor, Department of Philosophy and the Center for Medieval and Renaissance Studies, and Assistant Vatican Film Librarian, Saint Louis University

38. **Catalogue of Ancient Ports and Harbors** *by Arthur D. Graauw* (4th edition) © 2014

39. **Israel's Lost Ten Tribes (The Migration to Britain and the United States)** *by Vaughn E. Hansen* ©2011 (Cedar Fort, Inc. Publications)

40. **The Man in the Ice: The Discovery of a 5,000-Year-Old Body Reveals the Secrets of the Stone Age** *by Konrad Spindler* ©1995 (Three Rivers Press)

41. **The First Open Church, Followers of "The Way",** *by Jeffrey Crosby* © Clifton Emahiser (http://emahiser.christogenea.org)

42. **The Traditions of Glastonbury**, *by E. Raymond Capt.* ©2008 (Artisan Publishers)

43. **MAP - The Ancient Landscape Around Glastonbury: Energy Centres, Ancient Remains, Ley Alignments, Coasts and Islands** – *by Palden Jenkins*, ©2005, (Gothic Image Publications)